HAROLD ROBBINS

The Betsy
The Storyteller
The Pirate

CHANCELLOR
PRESS

The Betsy first published in Great Britain in 1971 by New English
Library

The Storyteller first published in Great Britain in 1985 by New English
Library

The Pirate first published in Great Britain in 1974 by New English
Library

This collected edition first published in Great Britain in 1994
by Chancellor Press
an imprint of Reed International Books Limited
Michelin House, 81 Fulham Road, London SW3 6RB
and Auckland, Melbourne, Singapore and Toronto

A CIP catalogue for this title is available from the
British Library

ISBN 1 85152 556 4

Printed and bound in Great Britain by The Bath Press, Avon

CONTENTS

The Betsy

THIS BOOK IS DEDICATED
with love to my wife, Grace, for
whom the name and the word were
created

Chapter One

I was sitting up in bed, sipping hot coffee, when the nurse came into the room. The English girl with the big tits. She got busy right away with the drapes at the window, pulling them back so that more daylight spilled into the room.

"Good morning, Mr. Perino," she said.

"Good morning, Sister," I answered.

"Today is the big day, isn't it?" she smiled.

"Yeah."

"Dr. Hans will be here any minute," she said.

Suddenly I had to pee. I swung my feet off the bed. She took the coffee cup from my hand. I went into the john. I didn't bother closing the door. After one month here nothing was private any more.

The water burst from me with a reassuring force. When I finished I turned to the sink to wash my hands. The white bandages covering my face stared back at me from the mirror. I wondered what I looked like beneath them. I would find out soon enough. Then a funny thought crossed my mind:

If my ass itched would I scratch my face?

She had a hypo waiting when I came back into the room. I stopped. "What's that for?"

"Dr. Hans ordered it. A mild tranquilizer. He likes his patients relaxed when the bandages come off."

"I'm calm."

"I know," she said. "But let's do it anyway. It will make him feel better. Give me your arm."

She was very good. There was only the faintest ping when she hit me. She led me to the chair near the window. "Now, sit down and let me make you nice and comfy."

I sat and she wrapped the light blanket around my legs and fluffed a pillow behind my head. "Now, rest a bit," she said, going to the door. "And we'll be back in a little while."

I nodded and she went out. I turned to the window. The sun poured down on the summer snow topping the Alps. A man walked by, dressed in Tyrolean shorts. A crazy thought jumped through my head.

"Do you yodel, Angelo?"

"Of course, I yodel, Angelo," I answered myself. "Don't all Italians yodel?' I dozed.

*

I was eight years old when I first met him. It was 1939 in a little park where my nurse often took me to play. I was pedaling the miniature racing car my grandfather had given me for my birthday. He had it especially made in Italy for me. With the leather straps over the hood, electric headlamps that worked, it was an exact replica of the Type 59 Bugatti that set the record at Brooklands in 1936, even down to the oval Bugatti insignia on the radiator.

I was pedaling madly down the path when I saw them in front of me. The tall nurse pushing the man in the wheelchair. I slowed down and honked my horn.

The nurse looked back over her shoulder and moved her chair slightly toward the right side of the path.

I swung left and began to pass her, but by then there was a slight incline and, pedal as hard as I could, all I could manage was to keep even with them.

The man in the wheelchair spoke first. "That's quite a machine you got there, son."

I looked over at him, still pedaling as hard as I could. I was told not to talk to strangers, but this one looked all right. "It's not a machine," I said, "It's a Bugatti."

"I can see that," the man said.

"The fastest car on the road," I said.

"No pickup," he said.

I was still pedaling with all my might but now I was beginning to run out of breath. "We're on a hill."

"That's what I mean," he said. "They're all right on the flat but give them a little hill and they have nothing in reserve."

I didn't answer. I had to save all my breath to keep pedaling.

"There's a bench just ahead of us," he said. "Pull off the road and let's have a look at your machine. Maybe there's something we can do about it."

I was only too glad to do what he told me. I was out of breath. I managed to pull up to the bench before him. The nurse turned the wheelchair alongside. I started to get out.

Gianno, who always came with us when the nurse and I went to the park, came running up, "You okay, Angelo?"

I nodded.

Gianno looked at the man in the wheelchair. They didn't speak but something seemed to pass between them and Gianno smiled. "Sure," he said.

The man leaned over the side of the wheelchair and looked into the car. He reached down and lifted the seat, exposing the gear and chain.

"Do you want to look under the hood?" I asked.

"I don't think so," he smiled, letting the seat drop back into place.

"Are you a mechanic?" I asked. There was a startled expression on his face when he looked at me. It was gone swiftly. "I guess you can call me that," he said. "Anyway that's what I used to be."

"Can you do something about it?" I asked.

"I think so." He looked up at his nurse. "Could I have my notebook Miss Hamilton?"

Silently she gave him a plain, hard-covered notebook much like the kind I carried to school. He took a pen from his pocket, and, looking down at the Bugatti, began to sketch swiftly.

I walked around the chair and looked at the pad. It looked like the strange combination of wheels and chains and lines. "What's that?" I asked.

"Variable gears." He saw the blank expression on my face and laughed. "It doesn't matter," he added. "It will work, you'll see."

He finished the drawing and gave the book back to his nurse. "What's your name?"

"Angelo."

"Well, Angelo," he smiled. "If you'll meet me here about this time the day after tomorrow, I'll have a surprise for you."

I looked over at Gianno. He nodded silently. "I can do that, sir," I said.

"Fine." He turned to his nurse. "Home now, Miss Hamilton. We have work to do."

I was early. But so was he. He smiled when he saw me. "Good morning, Angelo."

"Good morning, sir," I said. "Good morning, Miss. Hamilton."

She sniffed. "Good morning." I had the feeling she didn't like me.

I turned back to him. "You said you would have a surprise for me?"

He laughed. "Patience, young man. It's coming."

I followed his gaze. Two men dressed in white coveralls were carrying a large wooden crate up the path, followed by another man carrying a tool box.

"Over here," my friend in the wheelchair called. They put the crate down in front of him. "Everything ready?" he asked the man with the tool box.

"As you ordered, sir," the man replied. "I just took the liberty of allowing ten-millimeter leeway on the axle placement in case we had to make adjustments."

My friend laughed. "Still don't trust my eye, do you, Duncan?"

"No point taking chances, Mr. Hardeman," Duncan replied. "Now where is the car we're to work on?"

"Right here," I said, pushing it out in front of them.

Duncan looked down at it. "A fine lookin' automobile."

"It's a Bugatti," I said. "My grandfather had it made specially for me in Italy."

"Eyetalians do fine coachwork," Duncan said. "But they know nothin' about engineerin'." He turned to the other two men. "Okay, boys go to work."

For the first time I saw the lettering of the back of their coveralls. BETHLEHEM MOTORS. They worked swiftly with practised efficiency. Two bolts unfastened the sides and top of the crate from the bottom which then became a workbench as they placed my car on top of it.

The two mechanics got busy. I looked down at the ground where the opened crate revealed a rectangular steel frame filled with gears, chains, and wheels. "What's that?" I asked.

"A new chassis," my friend replied. "It was much simpler to build the whole thing in the shop with everything in it than to pull yours apart."

I didn't speak. By that time the two men had lifted the body of my car from its chassis and were going to work on the wheels. A few minutes later they had the new chassis on the crate and were mounting my wheels to it, and in less than ten minutes they had the body of the Bugatti mounted on the new chassis. They stepped back.

Mr. Duncan walked over to it and looked inside. He fiddled around a bit, pushing first one thing, then another. After a moment he stepped back. "Seems okay to me, sir," he said.

My friend grinned. "Did you need the ten millimeters?"

"No, sir," Duncan said. He nodded to the two men.

They lifted the car to the ground. I looked at it, then at my friend.

"Go ahead. Angelo, get in."

I climbed into the car as he wheeled his chair alongside me. "There are several new things I want to show you before you drive off," he said. "See that gear lever coming up near your right hand?"

"Yes, sir."

"Put your hand on it." I did as I was told. "It moves forward and back and when it's in the center it can move sideways and then forward again. Try it."

I moved it forward and back then to the center, and sideways forward. I looked up at the wheelchair. Something of what he had done suddenly began to make sense to me.

He picked it up from my eyes. "Do you know what that's for, Angelo?"

"Yes, sir," I said. "High, low and reverse."

He smiled. "Good boy. Now there's one thing I did. I put coaster brakes on your rear wheels. You slow down or stop merely by reversing the push on the pedals, just like you do on a bicycle. Understand?'

I nodded.

"All right," he said. "Try it. But be careful. 'It's going to be a lot faster than it was before."

"Yes sir," I said.

Cautiously I went down the hill, getting the feel of it and trying the brakes. Each time I came off the brakes it went a little faster, then I would hit the brakes again and slow down. At the bottom of the hill I turned around on the path by reversing, then going forward. I came up the hill almost as easily as going down. I stopped in front of them. "It's great!"

I got out of the car and walked up to my friend. "Thank you very much." I held out my hand.

He took it and we shook. "You're very welcome, Angelo." He smiled. "Just you be careful. You have a very fast car there."

"I'll be okay," I said. "I'm going to be a race-car driver when I grow up."

The men had been busy putting all the old bits and pieces into the crate. They started down the path and Mr. Duncan came over to us.

He held a sheet of paper toward my friend. "Sorry to bother you sir, but I'll need your signature on this."

My friend took it. "What is it?"

"A new system L.H. Two put in. It's a work order. He also wanted me to ask you what department to charge it to."

My friend grinned almost like I would. "Experimental car."

Duncan laughed. "Yes sir."

My friend signed the paper and Duncan turned away. I called him back. "Thank you, Mr. Duncan."

He looked down at me dourly. "Ye're welcome, lad. But don't ye forget, ye might be drivin' a Bugatti but ye're powered by Bethlehem Motors, thanks to Mr. Hardeman there."

"I won't forget," I said. I watched him hurry down the path toward the other men, then turned back to my friend. "Mr. Hardeman, is that your name?"

He nodded.

"You're very nice," I said.

He smiled. "Some people don't think so."

"I wouldn't pay any attention to them," I said. "Lots of people feel that way about my grandfather, but he's nice and I like him."

He was silent.

His nurse's voice came from behind me. "It's time for us to be going, Mr. Hardeman."

"In a moment, Miss Hamilton," he said. "How old are you, Angelo?"

"Eight."

"I have a grandson just two years older than you. He's ten."

"Maybe I can play with him sometime. I would let him drive my car."

" I don't think so," said Mr. Hardeman. "He's away at school."

I heard the nurse's voice again. "It's getting late, Mr. Hardeman?"

He made a face.

"Nurses are always like that, Mr. Hardeman," I said. "Mine is always after me for one thing or another."

He smiled. "I guess so."

"They tell me I won't have a nurse next year when I grow up. Why do you have one?"

"I can't walk," he said. "I need someone to help me get around."

"Did you have an accident?"

He shook his head. "I was sick."

"When will you be better?"

"I'll never walk again," he said.

I was silent for a moment. "How do you know? My daddy says that miracles happen every day. And my daddy should know. He's a doctor." I had an idea. "Maybe he could come and see you. He's a very good doctor."

"I'm sure he is, Angelo," Mr. Hardeman said gently. "But I've had enough of doctors for a while." He gestured to the nurse. "Besides, I'm leaving for Florida on the weekend and I won't be back for a long time." He held out his hand. "Good-bye Angelo."

I held onto his hand, not wanting to let go. Everybody I liked had to go away. First, Grandpa, now Mr. Hardeman. "Will I see you when you come back?"

He nodded.

I still held onto his hand. "I'll be in the park every Sunday at this time and I'll look for you."

"The first Sunday I'm back, I'll be here," he said.

I let go of his hand. "That's a promise."

I watched the nurse push him down the path until they were out of sight, then I got back into my car. It wasn't until almost twenty years later that I found out exactly how much trouble L.H. One had gone to in order to have the surprise for me.

I was in Duncan's office in Design Engineering getting a run-down on the car I was to be testing the next day when suddenly the old engineer turned to me.

"Remember that Bugatti L.H. One had us fix up for you when you were a kid?"

"How could I forget?" I replied.

It was true enough. From that moment on it was nothing but automobiles for me. Nothing else had a chance.

"Did you ever wonder how much it cost?"

"Not really."

"I have the original work order that he signed. I kept it as a souvenir." He unlocked the center drawer of his desk, took it out and gave it to me. "Do you know he pulled the whole office of Design Engineering and Fabrication off the line and had them working on your car for twenty-four straight hours?"

"I didn't know," I said. I looked down at the paper in my hand. "Experimental Chassis," read the charge slip. "Ordered by L.H.I. $11,347.51."

I felt a light touch on my shoulder and opened my eyes. It was the English nurse. "Dr. Hans is here."

I turned the chair around. He was standing there, his spectacles shining and, as usual, his six flunkies behind him.

"Good morning, Mr. Perino," he said. "How do you feel this morning? Any pain?"

"No, Doctor. It only hurts when I laugh."

He refused to smile. He gestured to the nurse and she pushed over a table on which there were shining steel instruments. "Now we shall see how good we were," he said in his usual half-whisper.

I stared down at the table in fascination. I felt half-hypnotized by the gleaming instruments. I watched him pick up a short-bladed curette. This was it.

How many men in their lifetimes have a chance to get a new face?

Chapter Two

It all began in May after the Indianapolis 500. My beast burned out on the forty-second lap and I pulled in. I didn't have to see the look on the pit boss's face to know I'd had it. I left the track without even waiting around for the finish.

It wasn't until I opened the door of my motel room that I realized that I had left Cindy back at the raceway. I had forgotten all about her.

I opened the small refrigerator and broke out some ice cubes and poured some Canadian whiskey over them. Sipping the drink slowly, I went into the bathroom and turned the hot water into the tub, then went back into the room and switched on the radio. I searched the dials for the race reports. TV was blacked out within a fifty-mile radius.

The announcer's voice came on. "It's Andretti and Gurney, one and two on the eighty-fourth lap. A real battle of the giants, folks—' I switched it off. It had been like that from the very start of the race.

I finished the drink, put the glass down on the refrigerator top and went back into the bathroom. I turned on the cold water and plugged in the portable jacuzzi whirlpool pump and watched the clouds of steam leap from the churning water while I stripped down. The bathroom was filled with steam by the time I eased myself into the hot water.

I leaned my head back against the tub and let the churning water push away at the aches and pains in my bones. I tightened up my gut and closed my eyes. It happened again. Like it always happened every time I closed my eyes for the past five years.

I saw the first lick of the flames coming up from the engine against the windshield. I down-shifted into the curve and fought the wheel. The high wall came up in front of my face and we hit at one hundred and thirty-seven miles per hour. The beast went up on its nose and hung there for a moment while I stared into the roaring stands, then the flames reached up and went over the wall into them. The sick sweet smell of my burning flesh and scorched hair came into my nostrils. In the distance I could hear myself screaming.

I opened my eyes and it was gone. I was back in the tub with the Jacuzzi singing its soothing song. Slowly I closed my eyes again.

This time it was all right. I floated in the water.

The telephone began to ring. Modern motels have everything. I reached across the john and took the telephone from the wall.

"Mr. Perino?" the long-lines operator singsonged.

"Yeah."

Mr. Loren Hardeman calling. Just one moment, please."

I heard the click and he came on. "Angelo, you all right?" There was a genuine concern in his voice.

"I'm okay, Number One. And you?"

"Good," he laughed. "I feel like a kid of eighty-five."

I laughed. He was ninety-one on his last birthday.

"What the hell is that noise?" he asked. "Sounds like you're going over Niagara Falls in a barrel. I can hardly hear you."

I reached over and cut the Jacuzzi. The roar faded. "That better?"

"Much," he said. "I've been watching television and saw you go into the pit. What happened?"

"Valves burned out."

"Where do you go next?"

"I don't know," I answered. "The only thing I've penciled in for sure is Watkins Glen. But that's not until the fall." I heard the outside door open and Cindy's footsteps come toward the bathroom. "I thought maybe I'd go over to Europe for the summer and try the action there."

Her face was expressionless. She turned back and went into the other room.

"Don't do it," he said. "It's not worth it. You'll get yourself killed."

I heard the refrigerator door slam and the clink of ice in the glasses. She came back with two Canadians on the rocks. I took one from her hand and she put the cover down on the john and sat there. She sipped her drink.

"I won't get killed," I said.

His voice was flat. "Quit now. You haven't got it any more."

"I've just had a run of bad luck."

"Don't give me that crap," he said. "I watched you on TV. I remember when you wouldn't give up a turn to God. On that last lap before you went in you left a hole big enough for Coxey's Army to drive through."

I was silent. I took a pull at my drink.

His voice softened. "Look, it's not so bad. You had some pretty good years. In '63 you were the number-two driver in the world. You would have been number one in '64 if you hadn't climbed that wall at Sebring and been laid up for a year."

I knew just what he was talking about. And I had the nightmares to prove it.

"I think five years is enough time for you to give yourself to find out you haven't got it any more."

"What do you think I should do?" I asked sarcastically. "Join the 'Wide World of Sports' as a commentator?"

A touch of asperity came into his voice. "Don't get fresh with me, young man. The trouble with you is that you never grew up. I should never have souped up that kiddie car for you. You won't stop playing with it."

"I'm sorry," I had no right to let out on him the frustration I felt toward myself.

"I'm in Palm Beach," he said. "I want you to come down here and spend a few days with me."

"What for?"

"I don't know." From the way he sounded I knew he was lying in his teeth. Or maybe they weren't his teeth at all. "We'll just talk."

I thought for a moment. "Okay."

"Good," he said. "You coming alone? I have to let the housekeeper know."

I looked across at Cindy. "I don't know yet."

He chuckled. "If she's pretty, bring her. There's little enough to look at down here besides the sea and the sand."

He clicked off and Cindy took the phone from my hand and put it back on the wall. I got up and she gave me a towel. She took my drink and walked into the other room.

I dried myself and, wrapping the towel around my waist followed her. My drink was on the table and she was on the floor doing things with her four-track tape recorder. I took another pull at the drink and watched.

She was placing the small reels in containers and marking the boxes. She was a motor-sound buff. Something about the roar of an engine turned her on. Some girls like vibrators, all she needed was noise. Put her in the car seat next to you, gun the motor and just wait for the action.

"Get any good sound?' I asked.

"Some." She didn't look back at me. "Is it over?"

"Why? Just because I forgot to pick you up?"

She turned around. "That's not what I'm asking," she said without expression. "Fearless says the talk around the track is that you're quitting."

Fearless Peerless was one of the backup drivers on J. C.'s team. He worked mostly on the dirt tracks trying to move his way into the big time. I tried to keep the edge of jealousy out of my voice. "Fearless bring you home?"

"Yes."

"You got eyes for him?"

"He's got eyes for me." It was fact. He wasn't the only one and I knew it. She was something special.

I felt the heat in my groin. "Set up the player."

She stared at me for a moment then silently put the player on a small table at the foot of my bed. Expertly she set up the four speakers, two on each side of the bed, and plugged in the lead wires. She glanced at me.

"Put on the big tape. The one you made at Daytona last year."

She took the reel from her case and threaded it into the machine. She turned to look at me.

By now my hard on had distended the towel around my waist into a tent. "Get out of your clothes."

She stripped and stretched out on the bed, her eyes watching me. She still hadn't said a word.

I reached over and switched on the player. The lead tape hissed and then the crowd noises filtered through. Suddenly there was an explosion of sound as the engines roared. The race had begun.

I stepped onto the bed and stood over her. Her lips were parted and she seemed to be scarcely breathing as the pink of her tongue parted her white teeth. She was all honey-brown and gold except for the narrow white band around her small full breasts and the triangle of her hips and legs. The coral pink of her nipples popped open and up at me and the soft down between her legs began to glisten with tiny diamonds.

I moved up on the bed and pushed my feet under her armpits until her shoulders rested on them. Then I pulled off the towel.

My hard slapped up against my belly. I stood there over her face and she stared up at me. I didn't move.

Suddenly she whimpered and reached up and grabbed me. She pulled me down making noises deep in her throat. I sank to my knees over her face moving with the writhing and thrusting of her hips behind me.

I felt her tongue licking at me, and all the while she held the knob of my cock in one hand, moving it like a gearshift to position me.

Her whisper was muffled. "Let me get on top of you."

I rolled over to my side, then on my back. Still holding me she clambered over me, then slowly lowered herself onto me. It was like dipping into a tub of boiling oil.

"Oh, God," she moaned, rocking herself slowly back and forth, rubbing her clitoris against my pubic ridge.

The roar of the racing engines began to travel from speaker to speaker around the bed, filling the room with an explosive violence of sound, and she moved with it, climaxing anew at each cycle around the track. I could feel the fuel of her excitement.

She began to half moan and scream with the frenzy of her passion. Wildly she shook her head from side to side, spilling her long hair into a constant fan. She began slamming into me, harder and harder. I smashed back against her.

"Good," she muttered. "That's so good."

I held my arms straight out from my sides, behind her. As she came back toward me I slapped her viciously, one hand on each buttock. She jammed into me and came back. I slapped her again and kept it up to the rhythm of her movements.

She began to climb the walls, her moans became half shrieks of pain and ecstasy. The roar of the engines as they came toward the finish line began to mount, almost drowning her out.

Suddenly Carl Yarborough crossed the finish line in his Sixty-eight merc at 143.251 miles per hour and she created her final orgasm, drowning me in the flood of her juices.

She hung there balanced on my cock for a moment, her eyes glazed and far away, then slowly, she crumpled and slid from me.

She lay quietly, her breathing slowing down to normal, her eyes open, looking into mine. "It was wild," she whispered.

I just looked at her.

She put her hand down on me. Her eyes opened slightly in surprise. She began to stroke me gently. "It's still hard," she whispered. "You're fantastic."

I still didn't speak. There was no point in telling her I hadn't made it.

She moved down and kissed me. After a moment she raised her head. "You're all covered with me."

I nodded.

She kissed me and turned her face and, holding my cock against her cheek, spoke softly. "Where will I ever find another man like you?"

I put my hand in her hair and turned her face up to me. "Are you going with Fearless?" I asked.

"Answer my question first," she said. "Are you quitting?"

I didn't hesitate. "Yes."

She did hesitate. I'll say that much for her. "Then I'm going with Fearless."

And it was over. Just like that.

Chapter Three

The soggy heat at the West Palm Beach airport came right through my shirt by the time I got to the Speed-Hire counter. I sprang my freebie card and pushed it at the girl.

She looked at the card before she looked at me. Then her expression changed. "The Angelo Perino?" she asked respectfully.

I nodded.

"I watched you on TV the other day. I'm sorry your car burned out."

"One of those things," I said.

"I was just a kid when my father took my brother and me to Sebring that time you went over the wall. I cried. I said prayers for you all week until I read that you would be okay."

She had that Speed-Hire look. All-American girl. "How old were you?" I asked.

"Sixteen."

I looked at her again. She was all orange-and-sun-country tan and over statutory age by now. "I owe you something for those prayers," I said. "Maybe we can make dinner."

"I have a date tonight," she said. "But I can break it."

"No, keep it," I said quickly. "I don't want to mess up your plans. We'll do it tomorrow night."

"Okay," she said. She wrote something on a slip of paper and pushed it at me. "That's my name and phone number. You can get me here before five and there after five."

I glanced at it. I might have guessed. Even her name was orange-and-sun country. "Okay, Melissa," I said. "I'll call you. Now what about a car?"

"We have a Shelby GT Mustang and a Mach One."

I laughed. "I'm not racing. Do you have something with the top down. I want the sun on my face."

She checked her list. "How about an LTD convertible?"

"Great."

She began to fill out the form. "Where are you staying?"

"The Hardeman place."

"How long will you need the car?"

"A few days. I don't know."

"I'll leave it open." She looked embarrassed. "Could I have your driver's licence? It's for the form."

I laughed and pushed it toward her. She copied down the number and gave it back to me. She picked up the phone and spoke into it. "LTD convertible, Jack," she said, "And give it super service. It's for VIP," She put down the phone. "Give us about ten minutes."

"Take your time, Melissa," I said.

Another customer came up and I walked over to the curb and lit a cigarette. I took off my jacket and threw it over my arm. It was hot.

I turned and looked back at the girl. I liked the way she moved. The way her breasts pushed against the tight-fitting uniform. There was more to look at down here than the old man thought. The trouble was that he couldn't get out to the right places.

After all, when you rent Speed-Hire, you don't just get a car. You get a company.

I pulled up in front of the electrified iron gates and pressed the signal button on the side of the driveway. While I waited for a voice to answer I read the signs on the gate.

PRIVATE PROPERTY.
NO TRESPASSING.

DANGER! GUARD DOGS PATROLLING!
SURVIVORS WILL BE PROSECUTED.

I laughed. Somehow it didn't seem very convincing. But I changed my mind real quick. By the time I had finished reading the signs, there were two giant Belgian shepherds standing just inside the gate, their tails wagging deceptively at me.

The voice came from the speaker box over the signal button. "Who's calling?"

"Mr. Perino."

There was a moment's pause. "You're expected, Mr. Perino. Drive through the gates. Do not get out of the car to close them, they shut automatically. Do not, I repeat, do not get out of the car until you reach the front of the house and do not let your arm hang out alongside the car door."

The voice clicked off and the gates began to roll back. The dogs stood just inside, waiting for me. I started the car slowly and they went to one side to let me pass and then began to run silently beside the car as I went up the driveway.

Every once in a while I would look out at them and they would look back at me and I just kept on driving. I went around a curve and, hidden behind the trees, was the front of the house. A man and a woman were standing on the steps. I stopped the car.

The man put a sonic whistle to his lips and blew it. I didn't hear a thing but the dogs did. they froze and watched me get out of the car.

"Please stand there a moment and let them sniff you, Mr. Perino," the man said. "They'll recognize you after that and won't bother you."

I stood still as he raised the sonic whistle to his lips again. The dogs came running over to me, their tails wagging. They sniffed around at my shoes and then at my hands. After a moment, they left me and went over to the car. In less than a minute they had squirted over every tire and had run happily off.

The man came toward me. "I'm Donald. Let me get your bags, sir."

"There's only one," I said. "In the back seat." I turned toward the house.

The woman smiled at me. She seemed in her fifties, her gray-black hair pulled severely back behind her face and very little makeup. She wore a simply-tailored black dress. "I'm Mrs. Craddock. Mr. Hardeman's secretary."

"How'd you do," I said.

"Mr. Hardeman apologizes for not greeting you but it's the hour for his afternoon nap. He asks if you will meet him in the library for a drink at five o'clock. Dinner is promptly at six thirty. We eat early here because Mr. Hardeman retires at nine."

"That's okay with me."

"Donald will show you to your room," she said, leading me into the house. "And you can freshen up. If you should care for a swim, there's a pool on the oceanside and a choice of swim trunks in the cabanas."

"Thank you. But I think I'll follow Number One's example. I'm a bit tired."

She nodded and moved off and I followed Donald up the staircase to my room. I went into the bathroom to wash my face and by the time I came out, my valise was unpacked, the bed turned down, the curtains drawn and a pair of my pajamas were laid out.

I took the hint and got out of my clothes. In ten minutes I was asleep.

*

He was waiting in the library when I came down the stairs. He held out his hand. "Angelo."

I took it. His grip was firm. "Number One."

He smiled. His voice was reproving. "I don't know whether I really like that. Makes me sound like an old Mafia chief."

"Nothing like it," I laughed. "If the stories I heard about my grandfather are half true, he was a Mafia chief and I never heard anyone call him Number One."

"Come over to the window and let me look at you."

I followed his wheelchair over to the large French windows that led onto the terrace overlooking the ocean and turned to face him. He peered up into my face. "You're not pretty, that's for sure."

"I didn't say I was," I answered.

"We're going to have to do something about those burn scars if you're coming to work for me," he said. "We can't have you going around frightening children."

"Wait a minute," I said. "Who said I was going to work for you?"

He peered up at me shrewdly. "You're here, aren't you? Or did you think I asked you down just to pass the time of day?"

I didn't answer.

"I'm too old," he continued. "I have plans. And I haven't that much time left to waste." He rolled his chair back into the room. "Fix yourself a drink and then sit down," he said. "I get a crick in my neck looking up at you."

I went to the sideboard and poured myself a Crown Royal on the rocks. He watched me hungrily as I sat down and tasted the drink.

"Damn!" he said. "I sure wish I could have one." Then he laughed. "I remember the time, back in 1903 or 1904, Charlie Sorensen had just given me a job over at the Ford Company building on the model K and Mr. Ford came around because he made it a point to interview each new man personally at that time.

" 'Do you drink?' he asked.

" 'Yes,' I answered.

" 'Do you smoke?'

" 'Yes.'

"Mr Ford was silent. He just stared at me. After a while I got to feeling uncomfortable and had to say something. 'But I don't run around with women, Mr. Ford,' I blurted out. 'I'm married.'

"He stared at me for another moment, then turned on his heel and walked away without saying a word. Ten minutes later Charlie came down and fired me. That same morning he had hired me.

"I guess he saw the expression on my face. I was stunned. With a wife and a kid on the way, I guess he felt sorry for me.

" 'Go over to the Dodge Brothers and tell them I sent you,' he said. 'They'll give you a job.' He started to turn away and then turned back. 'You know, Hardeman,' he said. 'Mr. Ford has no vices. Absolutely none.'

"But he was wrong. Mr. Ford had the one unforgivable vice. He was intolerant."

I took another pull at my drink. I didn't speak.

His eyes fixed on mine. "I want you to come to work for me."

"Doing what?" I asked. "I wouldn't be happy test-driving any more."

"I didn't say anything about that," he said. "I have other plans. Big plans." His voice dropped to a confidential whisper. "I want to build a new car!"

I think my mouth fell open. "You what?"

"You heard me!" he snapped. "A new car. Brand-new from top to bottom. Like nothing ever built before."

"Have you talked to anyone about this?" I asked. "To L. H. Three?"

"I don't have to talk to anyone about it," he said testily. "I still vote eighty percent of the company stock." He pushed his chair closer to me. "Especially not my own grandson."

"And what do you expect me to do?"

"Get me out of this goddamn chair," he said. "I expect you to be my legs!"

Chapter Four

He was still talking when we went in to dinner. We sat at a small table and the meal was simple. Salad, lamb chops and a vegetable, wine for me, a glass of milk for him. The wine was good, a '51 Mouton Rothschild, and so was the milk. Walker Gordon whole.

"The target date is the New York Automobile Show in the spring of '72. That gives us three years."

I looked at him.

He laughed. "I know what you're thinking. I'm ninety-one. Don't worry. I'm going to live to be a hundred."

"It's not going to be easy," I said.

"Nothing ever is," he said. "But I made it this far."

I laughed. "That's not what I'm talking about. I'm convinced you'll live to one hundred and fifty. I'm talking about a new car."

"I've been thinking about it for a long time," he said. "For thirty years I've let them pin me to this chair. And it's all wrong. I never should have let them do it.

"Before the war we had almost fifteen percent of the market. Now we have two percent. Even the lousy little Volkswagen sells more cars here than we do. And that's not all of it. The Japanese are coming. They'll wipe us all out. The little bastards are going to clean up the world. They'll underprice and outsell all the rest of us put together.

"This year and next, the American companies will be coming out with their subcompacts. It won't do them any good. Sure they'll sell cars. But they won't be stealing sales away from the foreigners, they'll be stealing sales away from themselves and reducing their overall price-per-unit volume.

"The only answer is a completely new car. Built in a new fashion. On a completely automated, electronic production line. I remember when Ford came out with his model T. It set the world on fire. For only one reason. Ford had a better idea. Since then they've been flying tail to General Motor's kite. And so has the rest of the industry. Even us."

"It's a pretty large order."

"It can be done," he said. "I don't like coming in out of the money. I'm a winner. I've always been a winner."

"I read the annual reports," I said. "Bethlehem makes money. They always make money."

"But not on automobiles," he retorted. "They account for only thirty percent of our gross. The appliance division supplies fifty-seven percent and the rest comes from manufacturing parts for the other companies. It's their way of making sure we stay in the business. They're afraid of antitrust and monopoly. Right now over seventy percent of our production space is used for that and not automobiles."

"I didn't know," I said.

"Very few people do. It all began during the war. Ford, GM, and Chrysler got all the big jobs. L. H. Two concentrated on the other areas. When the war was over, they were ready to go back into big production, we weren't. But we were equipped to go into the appliance field and, I must say, he did a fantastic job. It nets us better than forty million a year. But I don't give a damn. It's not automobiles."

I leaned back in my chair and looked at him. "What about Number Three?"

"He's a good boy," Number One answered. "But all he's interested in is profits. He doesn't care where it comes from, television sets, refrigerators or cars. It's all the same. Sometimes I think he would have taken us out of the auto business a long time ago, but he doesn't want to upset me."

"How are you going to tell him?"

"I'm not," he said. "Not until we're set up."

"You'll never keep it a secret," I said. "Not in our business. They'll pick it up the minute I go to work."

He smiled. "Not if we tell them something else."

"Like what?"

"Everybody knows what you are. A race-car driver. They don't know what I do. That you're a graduate of MIT in automotive engineering and design. Or that years ago John Duncan wanted to put you on to take over the department when he retired.

"We'll give you a title, vice-president, Special Projects, then we'll let on that we're going in for factory-sponsored race teams and cars. That should be enough smoke."

Donald came into the room. "It's time, Mr. Hardeman."

Number One looked at his watch, then back at me. "We'll talk some more at breakfast," he said.

I got to my feet. "Right, Number One."

"Good night," he said.

I watched Donald roll the chair out of the room, then sat down again. I lit a cigarette and looked at my watch. It was about eight thirty and I was wide awake. That afternoon nap blew it. On a hunch I called the girl from Speed-Hire.

A man's voice answered. "Is Melissa in?" I asked.

His voice had a father's defensive edge. "Who's calling?"

"Angelo Perino."

He sounded impressed. "I'll call her, Mr. Perino." He turned away from the phone and I heard him yell. "Melissa! Mr. Perino's on the phone!" His voice came back to me. "Melissa told me you were in town, Mr. Perino. I hope we get a chance to meet. I'm a real admiruh of yours."

"I hope so," I said. "Thank you."

I heard the telephone change hands. She had enough Southern tease in her voice to clog the lines. "Mr. Perino, this is a surprise."

"I had a hunch," I said. "What happened to your date?"

"I canceled him," she said. "He's really a bore."

"Want out?" I asked.

"That would be lovely," she said and I knew that her father was still somewhere nearby.

"Where can we meet?"

"Do you know Palm Beach?"

"Not really. I know how to get from the airport to here. But that's about all."

"Then maybe I'd better come over there and get you," she said.

"Good idea," I said. "How long will it take you?"

"About a half hour okay?"

"Good enough," I said.

When I put down the phone, Donald was standing a respectable distance away. "Is there anything I can get you, sir?"

"Do you have any brandy?"

"Of course, sir." There was reproach in his voice. "Will you have it in the library?"

I nodded and he followed me into the library. He poured the brandy into a snifter and, swirling it gently, gave it to me.

"Thank you, Donald." Then I remembered the dogs. "Someone's coming to pick me up in about half an hour; can you do something about the dogs?"

"I'll take care of it, sir. Will you be needing your car?"

"I don't think so."

He took a key from his pocket and held it toward me. "This will work the gate and the front door. Just leave it on the card table in the entrance foyer when you return."

"Thank you, Donald."

"Not at all, sir," he said and left the room.

I sank into one of the old-fashioned leather chairs and sipped at the brandy until I heard the roar of her car coming up the driveway. I went outside just as she came to a stop. Of course she had the Mach One.

I went down the steps and opened the car door. "That was quick."

"Super service." She smiled. "Want to drive?"

I shook my head and slid into the passenger seat. "No, I'm happy." I leaned across and kissed her cheek, then sat back and fastened my seat belt.

"Nervous?"

"Nope. Just habit."

"What would you like to do?"

I looked at her. "Let's go someplace and fuck."

Her voice was filled with honeysuckle reproach. "Why Mr. Perino!"

"All right, if you're going to be so formal about it, what would you like to do?"

"I know a lovely romantic place on the beach where we could drink and talk and dance."

"Good enough for me."

"That's better, Angelo," she smiled.

I smiled right back at her. "Then we'll go someplace and fuck."

She put the car into gear and we went down the driveway like we were going down the line at a Grand Prix. Why was it every time I got into a car someone had to prove to me how fast they could drive? I closed my eyes and prayed.

Chapter Five

I woke up to the ringing of the telephone. I groaned at the pounding in my head. That lovely romantic place she took me to last night wasn't exactly. The drinks were watered, you couldn't talk for the screaming acid rock and the dance floor was more crowded than the Edsel Ford freeway at rush hour.

"Mr Hardeman would like to speak with you, sir," Donald's voice came from the receiver.

"I'll be right down."

"The young Mr. Hardeman," he said quickly. "He's calling from Detroit."

Suddenly I was wide awake. And Number One thought there were secrets. I wondered who filed the report. Donald or the secretary. "Put him on."

"Mr. Perino?" It was a girl's voice.

"Yes."

"Just a moment for Mr. Hardeman."

I glanced at my watch. Eight thirty. Detroit was an hour earlier and he was already in the office.

"Angelo." His voice was friendly. "It's been a long time."

"It sure has," I said.

"I'm so pleased that you're down there visiting Grandfather. Number One was always very fond of you."

"I'm fond of him," I said.

"Sometimes I think he spends too much time alone down there." Concern came into his voice. "How does he look to you?"

"Feisty as ever," I said. "I don't think he's changed in the thirty years I've known him."

"Good. I'm glad to hear you say that. We get all sorts of wild stories back here."

"Like what?"

"You know. The usual things. Old-age things."

"You've got nothing to worry about," I said. "He's all there."

"I'm relieved," he said. "I've been meaning to get down there but you know how it is. The pressures never let up."

"I understand."

"There's talk about you retiring from racing," he said.

"That's what Number One is trying to talk me into."

"Listen to him," he said. "And if you should make up your mind, come up and talk to me. There's always a place here for you."

I smiled to myself. Very effectively, he let me know who was in charge. "Thank you," I said.

"Not at all. Mission accomplished. Good-bye."

"Good-bye." I put down the telephone and reached for a cigarette. There was a knock at the door. "Come in," I called.

The door opened and Number One came rolling in, followed by Donald bearing a tray. Donald set the tray on the bed and took the cover from it. There was orange juice, toast and coffee.

"How would you like your eggs, sir?' he asked.

"Nothing else, thank you," I said. "This will do just fine."

He left the room and Number One rolled his chair over to the bed. I picked up the coffee and took a swallow. It helped.

"Well?' he asked.

"Good coffee," I said.

"I know it's good coffee," he said irascibly. "What did my grandson have to say?"

I took another swallow of the coffee. "He said he was glad I was down here and he told me to come and see about a job if I were serious about giving up driving."

"What else did he say?"

"He said you were alone down here too much and wanted to know how you were."

"What did you tell him?"

"I told him you were nuts," I said. "You had some crazy idea about building a new car."

He started to get angry, then suddenly he began to laugh. I laughed with him and we were like two kids playing a joke on the teacher.

"I almost wish you had," he said. "I would have loved to see the expression on his face."

"He would have shit," I said.

Number One stopped smiling. "What do you think?"

"About what?"

"Me?" He spoke, cautiously, almost as if he were reluctant to get an answer. "Is what I want to do the crazy dream of an old man?"

I looked at him. "If it is, the whole world is crazy. And so is our business. A better car has to be everybody's dream."

"Last night I thought a great deal about what you said. It won't be easy."

I didn't answer. Just drank more of my coffee.

"It will take a lot of money. GM will have at least three hundred million dollars in their new sub-compact, Ford will be a lot less because they're just redesigning their British Car for the American market and will import the engines from Britain and Germany. And still it should cost them close to two hundred million." He looked at me. "I figure that's the least we would need."

"Has Bethlehem got that kind of money?" I asked.

"Even if they had," he answered. "I'd never be able to get my grandson to go along with me. And he has the board of directors in his pocket."

We were silent for a long time. I poured myself more coffee.

He sighed heavily. "Maybe we better just forget about it. Maybe it is just the dream of a crazy old man."

He seemed to be shrinking into himself before my eyes. I think it wasn't until that moment that I realized how committed I really had been.

"There is a way," I said.

He looked at me.

"It won't be pleasant and they'll fight you every step of the way."

"I've done that all my life," he said.

"It will mean getting out of Detroit."

"I don't understand," he said.

"Spinoff. Sell the appliance company. You said it nets forty million a year. You could get at least ten times earnings for that. Four hundred million. With your eighty percent of the stock alone, that's three hundred and twenty million."

"I vote eighty percent," he said. "But I own only forty-one percent, thirty-nine percent belongs to the Hardeman Foundation."

"Forty-one per cent is a hundred and sixty four million. It shouldn't be that hard to get the rest of it. Then you move the automobile division."

"Where?"

"California. Washington State. They're loaded with big aerospace assembly facilities that are going to turn to instant shit with the cutbacks that are coming in the next few years. It won't take much to make them into automobile assembly lines. They have the space and the trained labor pool right there."

He looked at me. "It might work."

"I know damned well it will," I said confidently.

"Who would buy the appliance company?"

"I know a lot of companies that would grab at it, but you'd wind up with very little money and a lot of paper," I said. "There's only one way to do it. Sell it to the public. And, maybe, at the same time, sell a little bit of the car company and get the rest of the money we need."

"That means going to Wall Street," he said.

I nodded.

"I never trusted them," he said suspiciously. "They want too much say in what you do."

"That's where the money is," I said.

"I don't know how to deal with them," he said. "We don't speak the same language."

"That's what you got me for. I'll translate for you."

He stared at me for a long moment. Then, slowly he began to smile. "I don't know what I'm so worried about," he said. "I started out poor. And no matter how it comes out, I had to be poor a lot longer at the beginning than I will at the end."

He turned his chair and rolled it toward the door. I got out of bed and opened it for him.

He looked up at me. "I wonder how my grandson knew you were here."

"I don't know," I answered. "You have a large staff."

"That girl you went out with last night. Where did she come from?"

"Speed-Hire-Rent-a-Girl."

"You're crazier than I am," he said and rolled his chair out into the hall.

Chapter Six

The plane put me down in Detroit at six o'clock in the evening and I was home by seven o'clock. Gianno opened the door and, in a moment, enfolded me in a bear hug.

"*Signora! Signora!*" he shouted, forgetting his English. "*Dottore!* Angelo is here!"

My mother came flying down the stairs. She was crying before she reached the halfway landing. I ran up the steps to her and put my arms around her. "Mamma."

"Angelo! Angelo! Are you all right?" Her voice was anxious.

"I'm fine, Mamma. Absolutely fine."

"I saw the smoke coming from your car," she said.

"It was nothing."

"You sure?"

"Sure." I kissed her. "You're as beautiful as ever."

"Angelo, you say such silly things. How can a woman of sixty be beautiful?" She was beginning to smile.

I laughed. "Sixty-one. And still beautiful. After all, I should know. A boy's best friend is his mother."

"Stop teasing, Angelo," she said. "Someday you will find a girl who is really beautiful."

"Never. They don't make girls like you no more."

"Angelo." My father's voice came from the doorway to the study off the foyer.

I turned to look at him. The gray hair over his slim patrician face was the only thing that had changed about him since I was a boy. I ran down the steps.

He stood there very quietly, his hand outstretched. I pushed it aside and hugged him. "Papa!"

He hugged me back and we kissed. There were tears in his eyes too. "How have you been, Angelo?"

"Fine, Papa, just fine." I looked into his eyes. He seemed tired. "You've been working too hard."

"Not really," he said. "I've been cutting down since my attack."

"You should," I said. "Who ever heard of a Grosse Point doctor going out all hours of the night?"

"I don't do that any more. I have a young assistant who makes my night calls."

We were silent for a moment. I knew what he was thinking.

I should have been that assistant. It had always been his dream that I would follow in his footsteps and come into his practice. But that was not the way it was. My head was someplace else. He never mentioned his disappointment, but I knew it was there.

"You should have let us know you were coming, Angelo," my mother said reproachfully. "We would have had a special dinner."

"You mean you have nothing to eat in the house?" I laughed.

"There's always something," she said.

At the dinner table I told them the news. Gianno had just put down the coffee. Espresso. Hot, thick, and heavy. I put two spoons of sugar into it and sipped. I looked at them.

"I'm giving up driving," I said.

There was complete silence for a moment, then my mother began to cry.

"What are you crying about?" I asked, "I thought you'd be happy about it. You always wanted me to give it up."

"That's why I'm crying."

My father was more practical. "What are you going to do?"

"I'm going to work for Bethlehem Motors. Number One wants me to be vice-president in charge of special projects."

"What does that mean?" my mother asked.

"You know," I said. "Handle problems. Things like that."

"Does that mean you'll stay here in Detroit?" she asked.

"Some of the time," I answered. "My job will keep me on the move."

"I'll have your room redecorated," she said.

"Not so fast, Mamma," my father cut in. "Maybe Angelo wants a place of his own. He's not a boy any more."

"Do you, Angelo?" my mother asked.

I couldn't stand the look in her eyes. "What do I need my own place for, when my home is here?"

"I'll get in touch with the painter tomorrow," she said. "You tell me what colors you like, Angelo."

"You pick the colors, Mamma." I turned to my father. "I want to get my face fixed. I'll be meeting a lot of people and I don't want to have to worry about it. I remember once you told me about a doctor who was the best in the world at it."

My father nodded. "Ernest Hans. He's in Switzerland."

"That's the one. Do you think he can do anything?"

My father looked at me. "It will not be easy. But if anyone can do it, he can."

I knew what he meant. It wasn't only the nose, which had been broken a few times, or even the left cheekbone, which had been flattened and crushed. It was the white patch of burn scars on my cheek and forehead. "Can you make the arrangements for me?"

"When do you want to go?" he asked.

"As soon as he will take me."

Two days later I was on the plane to Geneva.

Dr. Hans lifted the last gauze pack from my cheek and placed it on the tray. He leaned forward and peered closely at my face. "Turn your head from one side to the other."

I did as I was told. First to the right. Then left.

"Smile," he said.

I smiled. My face felt tight.

He nodded. "Not bad. We weren't too bad after all."

"Congratulations."

"Thank you," he said quite seriously. He rose from the chair opposite me in which he had been sitting. "You'll have to remain here about another week until the redness disappears. It's nothing to be disturbed about. Quite normal. I had to plane the old skin remaining on your face so that it would come in new with the grafted skin."

I nodded. After four operations in ten weeks another week more or less didn't matter.

He started to leave and then turned back. "By the way," he added, almost as an afterthought, "you can look at yourself in the mirror if you want to."

"I will," I said. "Thank you." But I didn't make a move to get out of my chair. Oddly enough, I wasn't in a hurry to look at myself.

He stood there for a moment and then, when he saw I was not getting out of the chair, he nodded and left the room followed by his six flunkies.

I sat there watching the English nurse cleaning the surgical tray and placing the bandages into a waste container. She didn't make a big thing out of looking at me, but I did notice that she kept glancing at me out of the corners of her eyes.

I caught her hand the next time she walked in front of me and turned her toward me. "What do you think, Sister?" I asked. "Is it that bad?"

"Not at all, Mr. Perino," she said quickly. "It's just that I never saw you before your accidents. I did see you when you came in. The transformation is quite remarkable. You have an interesting face, almost handsome I would say."

I laughed. "I was never handsome."

"See for yourself," she said.

I got out of the chair and went into the bathroom. There was a mirror over the sink. I looked into it.

In a moment I knew how it felt to be Dorian Gray and never grow old. It was almost the same face that I had at twenty-five. Almost. But there were subtle differences.

The nose was thinner, more aquiline. The doctor had taken the original Italian out of it. The cheekbones were slightly higher, making my face thinner and longer, my jaw more square. The ridges of proud flesh that had puffed up under my eyebrows after they had been split were gone, as were the white burn scars, and my skin was all pink and new and shining like a baby's. Only the eyes seemed wrong in that face.

They were old eyes. They were thirty-eight-year-old-eyes. They hadn't changed. They hadn't been made younger to match the rest of the face. They still held the pain and the glare of the sun and the lights of a thousand different roadways.

In the mirror I could see the nurse standing in the doorway behind me. I turned toward her and held out my hand. "Sister."

She came toward me quickly. There was concern in her voice. "Are you all right, Mr. Perino?"

"Would you be kind enough to kiss me?"

She looked into my eyes for a moment, then nodded. She came toward me and, taking my face in her hands, turned it down to her. She kissed me.

First, on the forehead, then on each cheekbone, then on each cheek, and finally, on the mouth. I felt the kindness and gentleness flowing from her. I lifted my face from her.

There were tears standing in the corners of her eyes and her lips were trembling. Did I make it better, Mr. Perino?" she asked gently.

"Yes, Sister," I said. "Thank you."

She really did make it better.

Chapter Seven

"It will be expensive," Loren Hardeman III said heavily.

I sat across the desk and looked at him. He was two years older than I, but he seemed much older. Maybe it was the office.

It was old-fashioned in heavy dark wood panelling, the chairs and couches were in black leather, the racing and automobile prints on the wall were ancient and faded. But it was THE OFFICE. It had been his grandfather's, then his father's and now it was his. It was the office of the man who ran Bethlehem Motors.

He had the look of a man who was running toward weight but was fighting it. He had the ponderousness of a young man on whose shoulders responsibility had climbed at a very early age. Neither his eyes nor his smile had any real fun in them. Maybe he never had a chance.

He had been twenty-one, elected executive vice-president of Bethlehem Motors, the year he had married the right girl, Alicia Grinwold, daughter of Mr. and Mrs. Randall Grinwold of Grosse Point, Southampton and Palm Beach. Mr. Grinwold was then vice-president of the Procurement Division of General Motors.

Everything followed in order. Alicia was delivered of their daughter, Number Two died, he was elected president in his father's place, Bethlehem Motors was awarded the largest parts contract ever given by GM to a competitive contractor, and he celebrated his twenty-third birthday.

That was seventeen years ago and the Detroit papers were proud of their third generation. Many articles were written about their two bright young men. Henry Ford II and Loren Hardeman III. They had come forth like knights in their shining automobile chromed steel to do battle for their four-wheeled liege.

"Very expensive," Loren added into the heavy silence of the office.

I didn't answer. I took a cigarette and lit it. The smoke curled upward in the still air.

He pressed a switch on his desk intercom. "Ask Bancroft and Weyman to come down if they're free," he said.

He wasn't about to make it easy for me. John Bancroft wouldn't be any problem. He was Sales and my plan could do him nothing but good. But Dan Weyman was another matter. He was Finances and anything that might cost money was anathema to him. It didn't matter whether there was any value in it or not. He would only part with the time under duress.

They came into the office and went through the usual Good-to-see-you-again bullshit. They they arranged themselves on chairs and looked expectantly at their master.

Loren didn't waste words. "Grandfather wants to put us into racing. He's suggested that Angelo spearhead the project."

They waited for a reading. Loren didn't disappoint them.

"I don't know whether the time for that hasn't really passed. With safety and ecology becoming an increasing pressure factor. I think the emphasis on power will diminish. And then there's the cost factor. It's way up there now. Ford has already announced their pullout. Chevy cut back. Dodge is still in but only until their contracted commitments are used up. I thought I'd get you fellows down and skull it around."

Bancroft was the first to speak. His booming salesman's voice echoed in the room. "Can't see where it would hurt. We could use some excitement. The dealers are all bitching that we haven't any glamour." His voice suddenly faded as he realized that he might be on the wrong track.

Dan Weyman took it up smoothly. "There are two sides to the problem. No doubt about it that a good effort on the raceway could help us. But we have to weigh its cost against its benefits." He looked at me. "What do you estimate?"

"The least we should field is three cars," I said: "Formula Three. We couldn't make it in One or Two. We haven't a standard car that could meet the competition, so we would have to go to prototype. I figure with personnel and design and engineering, about a hundred thousand a car. That would be for the first three, after that they would cost progressively less."

Weyman nodded. "Right now we're selling a little over two hundred thousand cars annually and we're losing about a hundred and forty dollars per unit. You would be adding about a dollar and a half per unit to that loss." He looked at Bancroft. "That means you would have to sell at least thirty thousand more cars just to keep the unit loss at present levels. Do you think you could do it?"

Bancroft was so hungry for the sales you could almost feel him taste it. "I think we have a chance." Then he added the qualifying Detroit constant. "Providing the economy doesn't go to hell."

I looked at Weyman. "How many units do you have to sell to break even?"

"Three hundred thousand," he said quickly. "That's a fifty percent increase over our present rate. Once past that, we break into the profit column."

"That should be easy," I said, slipping him the needle. "Volkswagen sells more than that."

"Volks doesn't field a full line," he said. "We have to cover the whole American market to meet the competition."

I didn't answer. We all knew that was a crock of shit. The only reason for a full line was to protect their own parts division.

Loren had been silent while we were talking. Now he spoke. From his tone I knew his mind had been made up. "I think we'll take a shot at it. I have a lot of respect for my grandfather. Besides it won't make a big difference whether we lose a dollar more per unit or not at this stage of the game. And, who knows, with Ford and GM out of it, we might even pick up a few trophies."

He got to his feet. "Dan, you take care of the details. Get Angelo set up in an office and see to it that he gets whatever assistance he needs." He looked at me. "Angelo, you report to Dan on costs, and to me everything else."

"Thank you Loren," I said and the meeting was over.

We walked down the corridor. "How's Number One?" Bancroft asked.

"Just fine," I answered.

"There's been a lot of talk around that he's slipping. Old-age things, you know."

"If he is, then we're all in trouble," I said. "He's as sharp as he ever was."

"I'm glad to hear that," Bancroft said. I could tell that he meant it. "He was a real automobile man."

"He still is."

"My office is right here," Dan said. "Come on in and we'll get the details over with."

I arranged to have lunch with Bancroft early in the following week and went into Dan's office. It was simple, efficient and modern, as befit the financial vice-president.

Dan walked around his desk and sat down. I seated myself opposite. "If my memory serves me right, you worked for us before," he said.

I nodded. He knew damn well that I did.

He picked up his phone and asked for my personnel file. He ran a tight ship. The file was on his desk within two minutes, even though the date of my last employment there was over eleven years ago. He opened it and looked at it. There was surprise in his voice. "Do you know that you still have a balance in our paid-up pension fund?"

I didn't know it but I nodded anyway. "I didn't exactly need the money," I said. "And it was as safe a place as any to leave it."

"Have you discussed your compensation?" he asked.

"We never got around to it."

"I'll take it up with Loren," he said. "Do you have any suggestions?"

"None at all. Whatever he says is okay with me."

"Have you discussed a title?"

"Number One suggested, 'Vice-President, Special Projects.' "

"I'll have to clear that with Loren," he said.

I nodded my understanding.

He stared down at my file for a few moments, then closed it and looked up at me. "I guess that's all I need." He got to his feet.

"Let's go over to Design and Engineering and see if we can find a nice office for you."

"Don't worry too much about it," I said. "I don't plan to be spending much time in it."

Chapter Eight

The frustrations began to pile up. I didn't need a Seeing Eye dog to sense that the word was out on me. I got all the cooperation I asked for, but everything took twice as long. Six weeks later I was still in my office trying to get Engineering to spring three Sundancer engines for me. The Sundancer was the top of their line.

Finally I picked up the phone and called Number One. "I'm boxed in," I said.

He chuckled. "You're in there with real pros, son. They make those kiddie-car drivers you've played around with look like rank amateurs."

I had to laugh. He was so right.

"What are you going to do?" he asked.

"I just wanted your permission to play it my way."

"Go right ahead. That's what I got you for."

My next call was to Weyman. "I'm leaving for the Coast tomorrow."

He sounded puzzled. "But the engines haven't come through yet."

"I can't wait for them. If I don't begin to set my pit crew and drivers now for next year, we may have cars but that's all."

"What about the modifications?" he asked.

"Carradine in Engineering has them all worked out. He'll begin the moment he gets the engines."

"And the shell?"

"Design is already working on it. I've approved the plans and they tell me that they're waiting approval from Cost." That was a shot at him.

"They haven't crossed my desk yet," he said defensively.

"They'll get there," I said.

"How long will you be gone?"

"Two, maybe three weeks," I said. "I'll check in with you the minute I get back."

I put down the telephone and waited. In exactly two minutes it rang. It was Loren III. It was also the first time I had spoken with him since the day I came in. He was always in meetings and too busy to call back.

"I've been meaning to call you," he said. "But I've been locked up. How's it going?"

"Can't complain. With a little luck we should field our first racer in the spring."

"That's good." There was a pause. "By the way, I'm having some people over for dinner tonight and Alicia thought it might be nice if you could join us."

"That would be lovely," I said. "What time?"

"Cocktails at seven, dinner at eight-thirty. Black tie."

"Haven't got one."

"Dark suit then. Alicia likes to dress up the table."

Carradine at Engineering was the next call. His voice was excited. "What did you do to them? I just got word that we'll have the engines tomorrow. They're pulling them off the line for us."

"When you get them, go to work," I said. "I'm leaving for California and I'll check in with you from there at the end of the week."

The next call was from Design. "We just got the approval back from Cost, but they cut us by twenty percent."

"Build them anyway."

Joe Huff's voice was puzzled. "You know better than that, Angelo. We can't build that design for twenty percent less."

"Did you ever hear of going over budget? You build it. I'll take the responsibility."

I left the office early, feeling better than I had in weeks. The smokescreen was up and working. Now I could get on with the real thing.

I was the first to arrive. The Hardeman house was only four blocks away. The butler ushered me into the living room and put a drink in my hand. I had just begun to sit down when a tall girl appeared in the doorway.

"Hullo," she said. "Am I early?"

I got back to my feet. "Not for me."

She laughed and came into the room. Her laugh had a warm, throaty undersound. She held out her hand. "I'm Roberta Ayres, Alicia's houseguest."

"Angelo Perino."

She let her hand rest in mine for a moment. "The racer?" Her voice was puzzled.

"Not any more," I said.

"But—" Then she remembered her hand and took it away.

I smiled. I was getting used to it. "I had my face put back together."

"Forgive me," she said quickly. "I hadn't meant to be rude. But I have seen you drive. Many times."

"That's all right," I said.

The butler came into the room. "And what will be your pleasure, Lady Ayres?"

The name rang bells. Her husband was a very good amateur driver who bought the farm coming out of an apex at Nurburgring a few years back.

"Very dry martini, straight up," she said.

"Forgive me," I said. "I should have recognized the name. Your husband was a very fine driver, Lady Ayres."

"It's kind of you to say so. But John's big trouble was that he was never as good a driver as he thought he was."

"Who is?" I asked.

She laughed and the butler placed the drink in her hand. She held it up. "To fast cars."

"Good enough," I said. We drank.

"What are you doing now?"

"Putting Bethlehem into racing."

"That should be interesting," she said politely.

"It is."

She looked at me curiously. "You don't talk very much, do you?"

I smiled. "It depends."

"See what I mean," she laughed. "You answer most of my questions with two words."

"I haven't noticed." Then I began to laugh. "That was three words."

Loren came in while we were still laughing. "I see you two have already met."

"We're old friends by now," she said.

A strange expression fleeted through his eyes. It was gone before I could record it. He bent over and kissed her cheek. "You look lovely tonight, Bobbie."

"Thank you, Loren." Her hand brushed his lightly. "I must say you look very mod."

"Like it?" He smiled with pleasure. "I had it made at that London tailor you told me about."

"Absolutely smashing," she said.

Then it all came together. Maybe there was hope for Loren yet. At least it proved there were other things on his mind beside business.

Alicia came down and I went over and kissed her cheek, "Hey, there," I said.

"Hey, there," she said and we both laughed.

Loren and Lady Ayres were looking at us.

"Private joke," I said.

"Angelo and I went to high school together," Alicia explained. "And that's how he used to call everybody. I told him that I wouldn't answer unless he called me by name."

"And then how did he call you?" Lady Ayres asked.

"Hey, Alicia," she replied. We all laughed. "It seems like such a long time ago now."

"You haven't changed that much, Alicia," I said.

She smiled. "You don't have to flatter me, Angelo. My daughter is seventeen."

The other guests began to arrive, and it turned into a typically intimate Grosse Point dinner for ten. Young-leaders-of-Detroit-society type.

The conversation was typical also. Taxes. Government interference in production. The new pressure of safety and ecology, and its apostle, Ralph Nader, came in for his share of damnation.

"We don't decry the need," Loren said. "But we do object to the way in which we are cast as villains. The public forgets very conveniently that they wanted greater horsepower and speed. We only responded to that demand. Even now, with all the hue and cry, give them the choice of a hot car and a slower, more ecologically considerate one in the same price range, they'll choose the hot one every time."

"What's going to happen?" someone asked.

"More government regulations," Loren answered. "More problems for us. The costs will be tremendous and if we can't pass them on to the consumer, we could be pushed out of the automobile business."

But he didn't seem very concerned about that, and the conversation turned to the generation gap and drug abuse in the schools. Then everyone had a chance to tell their favorite stories about their children.

I couldn't contribute much to that, so I spent most of my time nodding and listening. Once when I glanced down the table at Lady Ayres, I caught her watching, a glint of secret amusement in her eyes. She was a very aware lady.

I didn't realize just how aware she was until she stopped next to my seat on the plane the next day. I had requested the lounge so I could spread my papers out on the table and work on the way. I got to my feet. "Why, Lady Ayres, what a pleasant surprise!"

That same glint of amusement that I had seen in her eyes last night reappeared. "Is it really, Mr. Perino?" she asked, putting herself in the seat next to me. "Then why did you make such a point of telling me exactly what flight you would be on?"

I laughed. "Lady or no, I figured there's only so much of that anyone could take. You had to be human." I reached behind her seat and took the reserve card off and gave it to her.

She read her name on it and looked up at me. "You're pretty sure of yourself, aren't you, Mr. Perino?"

"It's time you called me Angelo."

"Angelo," she said softly, trying it on her tongue. "Angelo. It's a lovely name."

I reached for her hand. "Downhill all the way," I said.

The doors clanged shut and the plane began to roll away from the gate. A few minutes later we taxied down the runway and took off.

She looked out the window at Detroit for a moment, then back at me. "It's like getting out of jail," she said. "How can anyone live in that bloody boring city?"

Chapter Nine

There was a Telex waiting for me at the Fairmont Hotel when I stepped up to the registration desk. It was from Loren.

> Understand Lady Ayres on your flight to San Francisco. Would appreciate any courtesies and assistance you can extend to her. Regards. L.H. III.

I smiled wryly and gave it to her, then turned back to the desk and signed in.

The room clerk looked at the signature, then at the room chart. "We have your suite ready, Mr. Perino. It's in the new tower."

"Thank you," I said.

He signaled a bellboy. "Would you show Mr. and Mrs. Perino to 2112, please." He smiled at me. "Have a pleasant stay, Mr. Perino."

We followed the bellboy down the long corridor to the Towers elevators. She still held the Telex in her hand as we boarded. Silently she gave it back to me.

She didn't speak until we were alone in the room. "How do you think he knew?"

"The Detroit gestapo," I said. "Every motor company has one. They don't like secrets."

"I resent it," she said. "It's none of their affair where I go or what I do."

"You should be flattered. That sort of treatment is usually reserved only for people important to the business."

"What has that to do with me?"

"Come off it, Bobbie. I saw the way Loren looked at you. He's interested."

"All American men are interested. Young blonde widow and all that rot. Why should he be any different?"

"Because he's Loren Hardeman III, that's why. And kings are supposed to be above that sort of thing."

"Only American kings," she said. "We British know better."

I went over to the desk and pulled out a telegraph form. The bellboy came in with the luggage while I was writing. He put the valises in the bedroom. I signaled him to wait until I finished.

"Take a look at that," I said, handing the form to her.

She looked down at it.

Hardeman III, Bethmo, Detroit.
Instructions received. Everything under control. Regards, Perino.

She was smiling when she returned it to me. I gave it to the bellboy with his tip. He closed the door behind him.

The telephone rang just as he left. I picked it up. It was Arnold Zicker, otherwise known as the merger shark. He was responsible for more corporate mergers and acquisitions than perhaps any man in the United States.

"I've got Tony Rourke standing by for dinner," he said. "Eight thirty okay?"

"Eight thirty okay," I said. "Where?"

"Make it the hotel," he said. "It'll be easier." He was also one of the cheapest men in the world. If we ate at the hotel, it was only natural I should put it on my bill.

"Okay," I said. I put down the phone and looked up at her. "Dinner all right at eight thirty?"

She nodded. "Perfect. Do you have anything special to do until then?"

"No."

"Then let's go to bed and screw," she said. "You don't think I flew all the way out here just to have dinner?"

It was beautiful. Really beautiful. I think both of us were surprised, then a bit shaken by the deep emotional impact.

We clung together after the passion had been spent. I didn't want to leave her. I felt her trembling. Her flesh was my flesh.

"Hey, man," I said, still trying to understand it. "What happened?"

Her arms tightened around my neck, holding my cheek close to her. "The stars fell in," she whispered.

I was silent.

"I needed you," she said. "You don't know how much."

I put my finger to her lips. "You talk too much."

She nipped my finger. "Women always do," she said. "It's because they never know what to say afterwards."

I put my face down on her shoulder.

She turned her head to look at me. "Somehow I knew it would be like this with us."

"Don't get sloppy," I said. "It's not British."

"What do I have to say to make you realize that it isn't always like this?" she asked, almost angry.

I smiled at her. "What makes you think I don't know? I'm still inside you, aren't I? Usually, by now I'm out of bed, washing my cock."

"I'll take care of that," she said. "With my juices. I'll drown you."

Just then the telephone rang. I reached across her and picked it up. It was Loren. "I just got your wire," he said.

"Good."

"Everything okay? Where is she?"

"Right here. I'll let you speak with her." I put the phone in her hand.

"I'm fine, Loren," she said. "No, really, everything is all right. . . . It was lovely, but I'd imposed long enough. . . . Yes, thank you. . . . I'll stay on the Coast for a few weeks and then maybe I'll go over the pole back to London. . . . I'll call you before I do. . . . We're just about to leave for dinner. . . . Give my love to Alicia. . . . Good-bye."

She put the phone back on the cradle, then pushed me off her. I rolled over on my back and she sat up and looked down at me.

"You really are quite a bastard," she said.

Then we both began to laugh.

They were seated at the bar when we came into the cocktail lounge. Their eyes snapped open when they saw her. No one wears a micro-mini quite like an English girl. Her legs never stopped.

Arnold slid to his feet from the bar stool. "Tony Rourke, Angelo Perino."

Rourke was a big black Irishman with a squinting driver's face. I liked him right away. We shook hands.

I introduced her and they made room for her. All conversation halted for a moment as she climbed up on the bar stool. It was something to watch. Then we ordered drinks.

I allowed exactly five minutes for the usual pleasantries, then pushed right in. I looked at Rourke. "Arnold tells me that you might have the setup I'm interested in."

"We just might," he answered cautiously.

"It is right," Arnold came on enthusiastically. "Eighteen thousand acres of prime industrial site, two thousand of it with hangar construction that could fit right into your purposes, the rest can be developed as you need it. It also includes almost a mile of waterfront and railroad tracks coming right into it."

I ignored him. He was selling. "I don't understand," I said to Rourke. "Why are you looking for out?"

"Honest?"

I nodded.

"No tomorrows," he said.

I was silent.

"The handwriting is on the wall," he said. "With the cutbacks in defense coming up, we'll be the first to go."

"What makes you think that?" I asked. "They'll still need helicopters." That was their principal line.

"Nowhere near as many," he said. "We're fine as long as the big boys are busy with other projects. Boeing with their 747's, Lockheed's 10, 11, the SST which will never pass Congress. It will be easy enough to move it away from us and give it to them. And they'll have to do it, there's more to protect there than with us. More personnel, more capital."

"What about commercial application for your planes?"

"Forget it. That market's already sewn up. Besides our helicopter just isn't adaptable. It was designed as a fighting machine." He took another sip of his drink. "We're already on notice that we won't be renewed for next year."

"I appreciate that," I said, looking into his eyes. "You're being very honest."

He smiled. "That's what you asked for, that's what you got. Besides I didn't tell you anything you wouldn't find out for yourself when you checked around."

"Thanks anyway," I said. "You saved a lot of time and bullshit. Do you have all the plans and information with you?"

"Right here," he said, pointing to an attache case resting on the floor near his feet.

"Good," I said. "Let's go into dinner and then we can go upstairs and look them over."

It was after three o'clock in the morning when they finally left the suite. "I have a plane at the airport to bring you out to the plant whenever you're ready," Rourke said.

"Thank you. You'll hear from me tomorrow."

John Duncan was due in on a morning flight. He had retired from Bethlehem four years ago when he was sixty. He was the only other man that Number One took into his confidence.

"John Duncan is to me what Charlie Sorensen was to Henry Ford," he had said. "There's nothing he can't do in Production."

"But he's retired," I had said.

"He'll come back," Number One had said confidently. "If I know John he has to be bored out of his mind working alone on that gas turbine engine of his out in the garage back of his house."

And Number One had been right. All John Duncan wanted to know was when we were going to start.

The door closed behind them. I walked back into the room and fixed myself a drink. I pushed a pile of papers aside and sank onto the couch.

"They're gone?" Her voice came from the doorway to the bedroom.

I looked up. She was wearing a kaftan of polished cotton that clung to all the promises beneath. I nodded.

"I fell asleep," she said. "But I kept hearing the drone of your voice. What time is it?"

I looked at my watch. "Three twenty."

"You must be fagged."

"Not too bad," I said. "It's only one twenty in Detroit."

She made herself a gin and tonic and sat in the lounge chair opposite me. She tasted the drink. "It doesn't make sense," she said. "You don't need all that just to build racing cars, do you?"

I shook my head.

"You're onto something else, aren't you?"

I nodded.

She hesitated. "Does Loren know what you're about?"

"No."

She was silent for a moment while she sipped at her drink. "Aren't you worried?" she asked finally.

"About what?"

"About me," she said. "That I might say something to him?"

"No."

"Why not? You don't know anything about me."

"I know enough," I said. I got to my feet and added some Canadian to my drink, then turned back to her. "Besides happening to be one of the great lays of the world, I also happen to think that you're a very honorable lady."

She was very still, then she moistened her lips with her tongue. "I love you," she said.

"I know that too," I said. And grinned.

She threw her drink at me and we went to bed. It was still beautiful.

Chapter Ten

She came up behind me while I was shaving. I heard her over the hum of the electric razor. "You screamed in your sleep last night," she said. "You sat up in bed and covered your face with your hands and screamed."

I looked into the mirror at her. "I'm sorry."

"At first I didn't know what to do," she said. "Then I took you in my arms and you went back to sleep."

"I don't remember," I said, putting down the razor. But that wasn't true. The dream never left me. Asleep or awake. I splashed some aftershave on my face.

"What is it, Angelo?" she asked. "Is that why your eyes don't smile?"

"I died," I said. "The lucky ones stay dead when they've bought it. I didn't."

Abruptly her face disappeared from the mirror. Too late, I remembered about her husband. I followed her into the bedroom. She was standing at the window looking out at San Francisco. I put my arms around her and turned her toward me.

"I didn't mean that the way it sounded," I said.

She placed her head against my chest. I could feel the moistness of her cheek against me. "Yes you did," she said in a soft voice. "You meant exactly what you said. And the terrible thing is that I understand it and can do nothing about it."

"You're doing fine," I said. "You're beautiful."

Suddenly she was angry. She pulled away from me. "What's the matter with you people?" she cried. "John was the same way. Can't anyone, anything ever reach you? Don't you have room for anything else inside you beside that crazy wish to destroy yourselves against some stupid wall?"

"Okay," I said.

"Okay, what?" she snapped.

"I've already done that," I said. "So what else is new?"

She stared at me for a moment, then, her anger dissolving, came back into my arms. I could feel her body trembling against me. "I'm sorry, Angelo," she whispered. "I had no right to—"

I put a finger over her lips. "You have every right," I said. "As long as you care enough."

The Fan jet Falcon sat out on the airstrip among the 747's and 707's awaiting takeoff clearance like a sparrow among a covey of eagles. The pilot turned his head back to us. "We won't be long. We're number four on the line."

I looked across the seat at John Duncan. His face was grim and tight. He didn't like flying at all and when he saw this plane, he almost called a taxi.

I looked across him and smiled at Bobbie. "Comfortable, John?"

He didn't smile. Small talk wasn't going to make him like it any better. He didn't say anything until we were positioned on the runway awaiting takeoff, then he looked over at me. "If it's all right with you, Angelo," he said, "I'll come back by train."

I laughed aloud. The years hadn't changed him. Maybe his hair had gone a little thinner, but his hands and eyes were still quick and sure. He still looked the same man to me that fixed my car in the park over thirty years ago.

The plane set down on the factory airstrip. Tony Rourke was waiting for us. I introduced them.

He looked at us. "I've taken the liberty of booking you into a hotel near here," he said. "I figure you'll need at least two days to go over the plant completely."

Two days turned out to be an understatement. We were there almost a week. And without John Duncan I would have been completely over my head. I began to understand why Number One had such faith in him. There wasn't anything that escaped his attention. Even to the depth of the channel in the river leading to our docks in case we should ever want to bring in bigger freighters.

At the end of the week I sat with him in the hotel room with the plant blueprints in front of us. Bobbie put our drinks in front of us and went back into the bedroom. "What do you think?" I asked.

"It could do," he said. "The main assembly plant would have to be enlarged considerably for maximum production-line-efficiency, but there's no reason why that can't be done. There's space enough. The pre-assembly buildings are positioned well and we wouldn't have to build more than eighty thousand square feet more and it would be perfect. There's only one thing bothering me."

"What's that?"

"Steel," he said. "I don't know the West Coast mills. They might not have the capacity to supply us, and if it had to be shipped from the East we'd be broke before we started. I'd be happier if we had our own mill. That was where GM and Ford consistently wiped us out. They were turning out cars while we waited for steel."

"We'll look into it," I said. "Anything else?"

He shook his head. "Nothing I can think of at the moment."

"Do you have any idea of what it would cost to convert the plant?"

"Without any idea of the kind of car we're going to be building? No."

"I understand Ford put up a new plant to build their new compact. Do you know how much they're putting into it?"

"I hear a hundred million dollars."

"Would we need that much?"

"Maybe," he said. "I would like to put a cost engineering team on it. I don't like guesswork."

"How long would that take?"

"Three, four months."

"Too long," I said. "If we decide to go for this plant we have to make up our minds now. I can't keep them on the string that long."

"That's up to you," he said. He began to smile. "You remind me of Number One. He never could wait for the figures either."

"Do you think it's worth the six million Rourke's asking for it?"

"Did you have it appraised?"

"Yes," I answered. "Twice. One appraisal says ten million, the other, nine million six."

"What's Rourke planning to do with it when his contract is completed?"

"Sell it."

"He'll never find a buyer for the whole thing. He'll have to parcel it out. It will take him forever." He thought for a moment. "Depends on how hungry he is."

"I don't know," I said. "He should be in good shape."

"I've been wandering around the plant," he said. "I've developed a lot of respect for him. He'd make a hell of a production man in the auto business if he were interested."

"What are you saying?" I asked.

"Why don't you try him that way?" he suggested shrewdly. "Two years with me and he'd be the best man in the business. And I'm not getting any younger."

My appointment was for three o'clock. I walked into his office. I liked its look. No frills. It was a working office. From its windows he could see out on the plant.

He waved me to a chair. "Would you like a drink?"

"No thanks," I said.

He lit a cigarette. "What do you think?"

"I think I could give a long list of reasons why I'm not going to buy your plant," I said. "But I don't think it's important, do you?"

He was silent for a moment. Then he nodded. "I agree with you. The reasons aren't important." He dragged on his cigarette. "In a way I'm kind of relieved. I practically built this place with my own two hands. It's only right I should stick with it. A captain should go down with his own ship."

"No," I said. "That's a romantic crock. Any smart captain finds himself another ship."

"Where do I go?" he asked "Back to work for Bell? Sikorsky? Forget it. I've been on my own too long. Besides the helicopter's going nowhere. It's too specialized."

"Ever think about automobiles?" I asked. "They're all over the place."

"You got to be joking!" he said "What the hell do I know about automobiles?"

"There's not that much difference between building cars and planes," I said. "Only with cars, you build a lot more of them."

He fell silent.

"John Duncan says that in two years he can make you into the best man in the business," I said. "And if you know that canny Scot the way I do, you wouldn't take him lightly. If he thinks you can cut it, you can. That's all there is to it."

"But what do I do with this?" he asked, waving a hand at the windows.

"Sell it."

"Who to? It would take me five years to get rid of this in bits and pieces."

"I don't mean the plant," I said. "Sell your company."

"Who'd buy it? A company that's ready to go out of business?" By the time the assets were liquidated, they'd be lucky if there was a million dollars left."

"That's exactly the figure I had in mind," I said. "Providing you agree to come to work for us on a seven-year contract."

He began to laugh and stuck out his hand "You know I think I'm going to enjoy working with you."

I took his hand. "What makes you think that?"

"Because you're such a prick," he said.

"What are you complaining about?" I laughed. "I just made a millionaire out of you."

"Who's complaining?" he asked. He took a bottle from his lower drawer. "What's the next step?"

I watched him pour the drinks. "John Duncan is already on his way back to Detroit to put together a survey cost engineering team. He'll be back here within a week."

"Fair enough," he said, passing me a drink. "Now that you own the company, how about some operating cash? You have about two hundred thousand due the banks at the end of the month."

"I've already sent your balance sheets to our accountants with instructions to move in and get things organized."

"You seem to have thought of everything except one," he said. "What do you want me to do while all this is going on?"

"You're going out to buy us a steel mill," I said. "One big enough to give us enough steel for at least two hundred and fifty thousand cars our first production year and close enough so that it doesn't bankrupt us getting the steel here." I tasted the drink. "And one other thing. Better lay in a stock of Canadian whiskey. You're in the automobile business now."

Chapter Eleven

Arnold came storming into my suite at the Fairmont with blood in his eyes. "You screwed me out of a nine-hundred-thousand-dollar commission," he screamed. "You went behind my back and made your own deal!"

I smiled at him. "Cool it or you'll wind up with a coronary."

"I'll take you into court!" he shouted. "I'll sue you for every penny you've got!"

"Why don't you do just that," I said. "I'd love to get you on the witness stand and have you tell the world in your own words how you tried to stiff me for six million dollars when you knew the company was practically bankrupt."

He stared at me. "You wouldn't do that?" His voice was shocked.

"Why not? You've been getting away with murder so long you think it's your own special privilege. I don't think it would be too difficult to get the SEC and Congress to launch an investigation into how much money you fleeced out of publicly held corporations and their stockholders."

He was silent for a moment. His voice came down two octaves. "What do you expect me to do? Settle for a lousy fifteen percent commission on a million dollars?"

"Nope."

"I knew you'd see it my way. It just wouldn't be fair."

"Right," I said.

"What do you think is fair?" he asked.

"Five percent," I said.

He went purple and speechless. After a while he found his voice. "That's chicken-shit. I don't cross the street for that kind of money. I might as well take nothing."

"That's even better," I said.

"I don't do business like that," he said. "I have a reputation to consider."

I laughed. "That's okay with me too. But I was only beginning. There were other things I thought we might work together on, but if that's the way you want it—"

He didn't give me a chance to finish. "I didn't say I wouldn't take it. After all, there are more important things than money. Like relationships, for one."

"You're absolutely right, Arnold."

"I'm glad that's settled," he said. "Do I send the statement to Weyman at Bethlehem for payment?"

"No," I said. "Send it to me, care of Detroit National Bank."

"Why you?" he asked. "Aren't you acting for Bethlehem?"

I shook my head. "Whatever gave you that idea? I'm on my own in this one. The only thing I have to do for Bethlehem is field a race team."

He thought that over. I could see that he didn't believe me. "Okay," he said. "I'll go along with the game. Now what else did you have in mind?"

"I want a West Coast steel mill," I said. "Get in touch with Tony Rourke. He's coming to work for me and he'll fill you in on the requirements."

I put in a call to Number One the moment Arnold left. "Where've you been?" his voice came over the long distance line with a faint wheeze. "I haven't heard from you all week."

I brought him up to date.

"You move fast," he said finally when I had finished.

"I picked up a tow," I said.

"Have you heard anything from Detroit yet?" he asked.

"Not a word," I said. "But I don't expect that to last very long. Arnold Zicker just left here. He seemed to think I was acting for Bethlehem. I straightened him out. I told him I was acting on my own."

"Do you think he believed you?"

"No. That's why I expect some flap. He's going to do a little checking around in Detroit for himself. He can't stand not being on the inside."

"How are you handling the finances?" Number One asked.

"Out of my own trust account," I said. "You weren't the only rich grandfather in Grosse Point."

He laughed. "That's not very good business on your part. What if I don't come up with the money?"

"I'll take my chances. My grandfather said you were the best credit risk in Detroit. You were the only man who paid his bootlegger as if he were legitimate."

"You shamed me into it," he laughed. "How much are you in for?"

"About two million so far," I answered. "A million for the acquisition and about a million for operating expenses over the next few months."

"Will you take a million in cash and a million in BMC steak warrants?"

"Done," I said.

"It will be in your bank in the morning," he said. "Where do you go next?"

"Riverside, California," I answered. "To line up some drivers, then to New York. I have a date there with Len Forman about underwriting."

He was silent for a moment, "Forget Riverside. I think we've gone too far now to worry about a cover. Better get on to New York directly. I want to have as much preparation as possible before they catch up to us."

"Okay," I said "But I think I ought to call Loren then and let him know that I'm quitting. I don't mind playing games, but I don't like outright cheating. I did say I would field a racing team."

"You'll do nothing of the kind!" His voice was sharp. "Leave Loren to me. Besides, you don't think he believed your story even for a minute, do you?"

I didn't answer.

"You keep your mouth shut and go to New York," he said.

"Okay. He may be your grandson, but I still don't like it."

"I'm not looking for your approval," he snapped. "Just do your job!"

The telephone went dead in my hand and I put it down. I made myself a drink and went into the bedroom.

She was lying on the bed, leafing through a magazine. She looked up. "Meeting over?"

I nodded.

"Everything all right?"

"Yeah." I took a sip. The whiskey tasted good. "There's been a change of plans."

"Oh?"

"We're not going to Riverside."

"I'm not sorry," she said. "I couldn't care less if I never saw another raceway."

"We're going to New York."

"When?"

"If we pack now, we can make the redeye leaving at ten forty-five and we'll be in New York in the morning."

"And if we don't make the redeye?"

"We leave in the morning. But then I lose a whole day."

"Is that important?"

"Could be."

"Then we'll make it," she said, getting out of bed.

I watched her slip out of her robe and walk nude to the closet and reach for a dress. "Aah, the hell with it," I said. "Get back into bed."

I couldn't think of anything more stupid than spending the night on a plane.

Chapter Twelve

I had to say one thing for her. Lady or no, she ate like a stevedore. I watched her demolish her breakfast: juice, dollar-size pancakes with eggs and sausages, toast, marmalade and tea. And all the time I kept pouring coffee into myself to bring myself up to the day.

"You Americans eat such enormous breakfasts," she said between mouthfuls. "Lovely."

I nodded. We certainly did, I thought as I poured myself a fourth cup of coffee. The phone rang and I picked it up.

"Mr. Carroll at the front desk," the voice identified itself. "Sorry to disturb you, Mr. Perino."

"Quite all right, Mr. Carroll."

His voice lowered. "I have a long distance call for Lady Ayres. It's from Detroit and I thought perhaps it might be wise if I got your permission before we put it through."

I covered the mouthpiece with my hand. "Who in Detroit knows you're staying here?"

"The only one I told was Loren," she answered.

Since her name hadn't appeared on the hotel register, it meant that security was on the ball. I spoke into the phone. "Mr. Carroll, you're a gentleman of intelligence and discretion. Put the call through."

"Thank you, Mr. Perino." I could tell he was pleased because his voice held that man-to-man feeling. "If you'll hang up, I'll instruct the operator."

I put down the telephone and pushed it toward her. A moment later it rang.

"Hello," she said. There was a faint crackle in the receiver. "Why, Loren, how nice of you to call. . . . No, it's not too early, I was just having breakfast."

His voice echoed faintly on the phone. She listened for a moment, then covering the mouthpiece, whispered to me. "He said he was coming out to Palm Springs for a long weekend of sun and golf and wants me to join him."

I smiled. Loren had balls after all. I wondered if he just discovered them. "Tell him you were leaving for Hawaii today."

She nodded. "What rotten luck, Loren. I would have loved to see you but I've made plans to leave for Hawaii. I've never been there, you know, and I've always been so curious about the place."

His voice echoed again in the phone. Again she covered the mouthpiece. "He said that's even better. He knows some marvellous places on the outer islands. What do I do now?"

I thought for a moment. It wasn't the worst thing in the world. At least it would keep him out of Detroit, and the longer he stayed away, the better our chances were to get set. I grinned at her. "I guess you're going to Hawaii."

She spoke a few moments more into the phone, then put it down. She reached for a cigarette silently. I held the light for her. She dragged the smoke deeply into her, her eyes never leaving mine. Finally she let the smoke out. "I don't know whether I like it."

"Why not?" I asked. "It's not every day a girl gets a chance to go to Hawaii."

"That's not what I'm talking about and you know it." she snapped. "It's your attitude. You dispose of me as if I were some whore you picked up."

I smiled at her. "It seems to me that I read somewhere of an Englishman who once said that's the only way to treat a lady."

She didn't smile. "You really don't care anything at all about me."

"Don't say that. I would not love thee half as much, my darling, if I did not love honor more."

"Stop quoting at me," she said, annoyed. "What has honor got to do with it?"

"It seems a very honorable thing for me to do," I said. "To sacrifice myself for a friend. Noblesse oblige. After all, I do owe him something. If it weren't for him we would never have met."

She met my eyes levelly. "You want him out of the way, don't you?"

"Yes," I said simply.

"What if he falls in love with me?"

"That's his problem."

"What if I fall in love with him?"

"Then it's your problem."

"You're a real shit," she said. I started to get up. "Wait a minute. Where are you going?" she asked.

"Get dressed," I answered. "I have a plane to catch at ten o'clock."

"You're not going anywhere just yet," she said firmly. "I'm not meeting him at the airport until seven this evening. Now that you know he'll be out of the way, you can afford another day."

"What for?" I asked.

She looked up at me. "Because I'm going to fuck you into the ground. Fuck you until there's no juice left in your balls, no marrow in your bones. So much that you'll be lucky if you can raise a hard for a month."

I laughed and sank back into the chair. I reached for the phone.

"Who are you calling?" she asked suspiciously.

"Room service," I said. I had the sudden feeling I would need a large breakfast.

I went out to the airport with her even though my plane did not leave until two hours later. I checked my bags onto my flight, then went with her to the waiting area for the United flight from Detroit. We got there about fifteen minutes before the flight was due.

"We've got time for a quick drink," I said, and led her to the nearest bar.

The waitress put our drinks in front of us and walked away. I raised my glass. "Cheers."

She barely tasted her martini.

I looked at her. She had been silent all the way out. "Chin up," I said. "It's not so bad."

In the dim lights I could barely see her eyes under the wide brim of her soft felt hat. "I'm worried about you," she said.

"I'll be okay."

"You sure?"

"Sure."

She raised the glass to her lips, then put it down without tasting it. "Will I see you again?"

I nodded.

"When?"

"When you get back."

"Where will I find you?"

"I'll be around. I'll find you."

The mechanical voice came from the speakers built into the ceiling. "United Airlines, Flight 271 from Detroit, now arriving at Gate 72."

"That's you," I said. I finished my drink and we got to our feet. She hadn't touched hers.

We left the dark and walked into the million-watt fluorescents of the terminal. I stood there. "Have a fun vacation," I said.

She looked up into my face. Her voice was soft. "Don't get caught up in the dicing, there are other ways to get yourself killed besides climbing the wall."

"I won't," I said. I bent and kissed her lightly on the lips. "Good-bye."

I barely felt her lips move beneath mine. "Good-bye."

She made it as far as three steps away, then abruptly flung herself back into my arms. Her mouth crushed hungrily against mine. "Don't let me go, Angelo!" she cried. "I love you."

For a moment I almost heard the music, but the roll of drums was louder. "I'm not letting go," I said and gently took her arms from around my neck and placed them at her side.

She didn't say another word. This time she made it all the way. I stood there looking after her until she reached the gate.

The passengers were already coming through. He was among the first off the plane. He was a big man and he towered above the others with his gray Detroit felt snap brim.

A smile split his face when he saw her. He hurried toward her, removing his hat with one hand and holding out the other. Almost formally they shook hands, then awkwardly he bent and kissed her cheek.

I turned and got onto the electric walkway leading to the main terminal section and my flight. I looked back only once.

They were on the way into the bar we had just left. He had one hand on her arm as if he were supporting a basket of eggs, looking down into her face and talking.

The million fluorescent watts began to burn my eyes and I stopped looking. I couldn't wait until I reached the end of the walkway, then I headed for the nearest bar.

I had two hours before my flight and by the time I boarded, I was smashed. Not smashed outside, rolling and drunk, but smashed inside, bleak and empty.

I sank into my seat and fastened the belt. I leaned back and closed my eyes.

"Are you comfortable, sir?" the stewardess asked. "Is there anything I can do for you?"

I opened my eyes and looked into her professionally smiling face. "Yes," I said. "Give me a double Canadian on the rocks as soon as we take off and a pair of eye shades. Then don't disturb me for anything. No hors d'oeuvres, no dinner, no movie, no nothing. I want to sleep all the way to New York."

"Yes, sir," she said.

But it didn't work. Neither the whiskey nor the eye shades. Though I kept them on and my eyes closed for the whole of the flight, I didn't sleep.

All I could hear was the sound of her voice in my ear, all I could see was the expression on her face when she left me.

I was glad when the plane finally touched down in New York and I could open my eyes. The whole damn thing was too heavy.

Chapter Thirteen

It was three days later; we sat on the lawn overlooking the swimming pool and the private beach with its white sand going down to the water. A faint early September wind rustled in the palm fronds over our head. I closed my eyes and turned my face to the sun.

"Winter is coming," Number One said.

"It's still warm," I said.

"Not to me. Each year I've been thinking of going farther and farther south. Maybe to Nassau or the Virgins. As I grow older my bones seem to signal the oncoming cold.

I turned my head to look at him. He was sitting in his chair, his legs wrapped in the perennial blanket, his eyes looking out toward the sea. "What is it like to grow old, Number One?" I asked.

He didn't take his eyes from the white-capped water. "I hate it," he said, without giving his words any special emphasis. "Mostly because it's such a bore. Everything seems to be passing you by, you find out that you're not as important as you thought you were. The world moves on and after a while you become absorbed in the only game left to play. One stupid ambition: 12.01 A.M."

"12.01 A.M.?" I asked. "What's that?"

"Tomorrow morning," he said, turning to look at me. "The survival game. Only you don't know why you're playing it. Tomorrow is nothing but today all over again. Only more so."

"If that's it, why are you starting all this?"

"Because just once again before I die, I want something to matter more to me than 12.01 A.M." He turned to look again at the ocean. "I suppose I didn't think much about what was happening to me until last year when Elizabeth came down and spent a few days. Do you know her?"

Elizabeth was Loren's daughter. "We've never met."

"She was sixteen then," he said "And, suddenly she turned back the clock for me. Betsy, last summer, was the exact age that her great-grandmother was when we met. Time plays funny tricks on people, it jumps generations to recreate itself. For those few days I was young."

I didn't speak.

"I would get up early in the morning and look out from my window at her swimming in the pool. One morning, it was so beautiful that she dropped her swimsuit at the side of the pool and dove into the water. I watched her until the sheer youth and exuberance of her brought tears to my eyes. And then I realized what had happened to me. Too many years had gone by and I had not cared enough about anything to cry for it.

"My world had become my body. My body, my shell, my prison in which I served out my time. And that was very wrong. Because a prison is something you should try to get out of. I was doing exactly the opposite. My only concern was to find ways and means to spend more and more time in it. At exactly that moment I knew what I had to do.

"Take off my clothes and jump once more into the pool. For over thirty years I sat in this chair thinking I was alive when I was really dead. But I wasn't about to stay dead. There was still something for me to do, something I could do. Build a car for Betsy as I had built a car for her great-grandmother.

"When she came up from the pool and we sat at the breakfast table, I told her what I would do. She jumped up and threw her arms around me. And do you know what she said?"

I shook my head.

" 'Great-Grandfather, that would be the grooviest thing that anyone could ever do for me.' "

He was silent. "After she had gone, I called Loren. He thought it was a beautiful sentiment. But not very practical. Economically, our profit structure had stabilized, building a new car could possibly disturb that. Physically, we didn't have the space, over seventy per cent was committed to other forms of manufacture. But I did get him to promise to look into it."

"Did he?"

"I don't know. If he did, I never heard from him. After a while I realized that if I wanted it done I would have to find someone else to do it for me. That's how I came to you."

"Why me?"

"Because automobiles are your life as much as they are mine. I knew that ever since that day in the park and I knew it would be just a matter of time before you stopped playing with toys and got to the core of what you're about. I knew I was right the moment I heard your voice on the phone after the Indy."

"Okay, you got me," I smiled. "But there's still Loren."

A puzzled look came over his face. "I don't understand that at all. I know Loren's not stupid. He should have found out what we're up to, long before now. But not a word from him."

"Loren has other things on his mind," I said.

"Like what? One thing Loren never does is take his eyes off the business."

"This time he did."

"Don't be so damned mysterious," he snapped. "If you know something I don't, tell me."

"Loren has romance on his mind," I said. "Right now he's in Hawaii."

"How do you know that?" he asked sharply. "I've called his home and the office. Nobody knows where he is."

I laughed. "I practically did everything but put the girl on the plane with him." Briefly I told him the story and at its finish he began to smile.

"Good," he said. "I was beginning to wonder if he were human. Maybe there's some hope for him yet."

I got to my feet. "I think I'll take a look inside and see how the boys are coming along with their figures."

I left him sitting there, looking out at the ocean, and walked back up to the house and into the library. Despite the opened windows there were layers of blue cigarette smoke hanging in the air over the table around which the accountants were gathered. At one end of the table sat Len Forman a senior partner of Danville, Reynolds, and Firestone, representing the combined underwriters, and at the other end of the table, Arthur Roberts, a prominent New York Corporate Attorney, who had been retained as our counsel. The thing I liked about Artie is that he wasn't afraid of a fight and we all knew, going in, that this wasn't going to be a waltz.

"Where are we?" I asked.

"Almost finished," Artie said. "I think we can begin talking now."

"I'll get Number One," I said.

"Don't do that," Artie said quickly. "We'll come with you. After three days locked up in this room a little fresh air can't hurt."

"I still have a few things to clean up," Len said. "You go ahead, I'll catch up."

We went back down to the pool. Number One was still looking out at the ocean. He turned his head when he heard our footsteps. He came right to the point. "What do you think, Mr. Roberts? Can we do it?"

"It can be done, Mr. Hardeman," Artie said. "But I think we should examine the various ways to accomplish our ends."

"Explain," Number One said succinctly. "But remember to keep it simple. I'm a mechanic, not a lawyer or an accountant."

"I'll try," Artie said with a smile. He knew as well as I that Number One had thought it all out long before any of us got into the act. "There are several ways to go. One, take the whole company public. I believe this can be accomplished without serious tax disadvantages. Two, splitting the appliance and manufacturing division away from the main body of the corporation and either selling them or going public with them. Three, the reverse of two, splitting away the automobile division and going public with it. Because of its profitless structure, I think this would be the least attractive."

"Do you think we could raise the kind of capital we require?" Number One asked.

"I see no reason why we can't," Artie said. "Regardless of the plan we adopt." He turned to Forman, who had come up just as the question had been asked. "What do you think, Len?"

Forman nodded. "No problem. It should be the most marketable issue to hit the street since Ford went public."

"Which plan do you recommend?"

"The first plan," Artie said quickly. "Take the whole company public."

"Do you agree?" Number One turned to Forman.

"Absolutely," he nodded. "That would be the most attractive."

"Is that your reason also?" Number One asked Artie.

"Not really," Artie said. "I just can't see why you have to relinquish your equity in the more profitable areas of your company in order to do what you want. I think if we follow the Ford formula, you can have your cake and eat it too."

Number One turned away and looked out at the sea again. He was silent for a long while, then he took a deep breath and turned back to me. "When do you think my grandson will be back in Detroit?"

"Sometime during the coming week."

"I think we should go up there and see him," he said. "Maybe I've been wrong about him all along. I think he should have a chance to make up his own mind."

"That's fair enough," I said.

"I'll have Mrs. Craddock call his office and arrange a meeting at my home in Grosse Point, Wednesday evening." He began to move his chair toward the house. Donald appeared mysteriously and began to push him. Number One looked at us. "Come, gentlemen, let me buy you a drink."

We fell into step alongside the chair. Forman asked, "Have you thought of the kind of car you're planning to build, Mr. Hardeman?"

Number One laughed. "One that will run, I hope."

Danville was polite. "I mean its design."

"We're just beginning now," said Number One. "Automobile design is a very complicated art. An art. That's exactly what it is. Modern, functional art. A primary collage of our technocratic society. That's what it is, gentlemen. The Model T of Henry Ford does not belong in the Smithsonian. A more proper place for it would be in the Metropolitan Museum of Art."

"Have you selected a name for the car as yet, Mr. Hardeman?" Artie asked. "I understand that names are very important."

"They are. And I have." He looked at me and smiled a private smile. "The Betsy. That's what we'll call it. The Betsy."

Chapter Fourteen

I dropped Artie and Len at the airport so they could make the late afternoon plane to New York and when I came out of the terminal, Speed-Hire-Rent-A-Girl was standing next to my car. "I'm shuah disappointed in you, Angelo," she said in her honey-and-orange voice. "Heah you've been in town foh three days now and you haven't called me."

"Sorry, Melissa. But I've been busy."

She pouted. "And I thought you were interested."

"I am, Melissa," I said. "I am."

"Then how about tonight? That is, if youah not busy."

"Tonight is fine," I said. "But no more places like the last time. It took me three days to get my hearing back. Don't you know a nice quiet motel where we could just be together."

She came on with the "Mr. Perino," shit again. "Mr. Perino, this is a small town and a girl has to be careful of her reputation. Maybe we could just go for a long, quiet drive."

I remembered the way she drove and shook my head. "No thanks. Besides I'm too old for backseat screwing." I walked around the convertible and slid in behind the wheel. I turned the key in the starter. "Be seeing you, Melissa."

"No, Angelo," she said. "Wait a minute." Her voice lowered as she leaned across the car door, giving me a good look at the two ripe Sunkists pushing against her blouse. "I'll have to make arrangements," she whispered. "I'll tell my folks I'm going to spend the night with a girl friend who has a small cottage just north of town. She's away and she left the key with me."

"Now you're making sense."

She had the Mach One again when she came to pick me up. She got out of the car when I came down the steps. "You drive."

"Okay." I got behind the wheel. I clipped my seat belt and looked at her. She fastened her belt. We went down the drive-way.

"Turn right," she said. "There's a package store about a half mile up."

I swung the car into the road and keeping it in low gear, revved the motor to an almost roaring red line on the tach. I hit the brake hard and slammed to a stop in front of the package store. I looked over at her.

Her eyes were half closed and her mouth open as she sucked in air. Her legs were open too. I reached over and put my hand under her dress. Her pantyhose was soaked. She was a born bit popsie. She shivered.

"What are you drinking?" I asked.

She closed her knees on my hand. "Champagne," she said. French champagne. Make sure it's good and cold."

"Okay. Give me back my hand and I'll go get it."

I came back with three bottles of Cordon Rouge. I showed them to her. "This okay?"

She nodded. I got into the car and we pulled out onto the road. "You do drive a car, don't you," she said in a hushed voice.

"I do." I put my foot down on the accelerator. I knew just what she wanted. Lucky for me, there weren't any cops on the road. I think we made the seven miles to the cottage in under six minutes.

The cottage was one of the many exactly like it on a small road a half mile off the highway. I pulled into the driveway she pointed out to me and stopped under the carport. I switched off the motor and looked at her.

Her eyes were shining. "You blew my mind."

I didn't speak.

"Remember that time you were passing three cars and that car came up the road at us?"

I nodded.

"I looked at the speedometer. You were doing one-twenty. When you cut back into the lane I came so hard I half peed. After that I couldn't stop coming for almost a minute."

"I hope you have some left," I said.

She laughed. "Never dry," she said, and got out of the car. She reached behind her seat and lifted out a small flight bag. I grabbed the champagne and followed her into the house.

She went through the whole house closing the blinds and pulling the drapes before she would let me turn on a light. "My girl friend is always complaining about nosy neighbours," she explained.

"It's nice to know somebody cares," I said.

She opened the flight bag. "I have to hang up my dress for tomorrow so it won't be wrinkled." She put the dress in the closet and came back. "Do you smoke?"

"Sometimes."

"Good," she said. "I've got some great grass." She took out a small cellophane bag and a package of Zig Zag papers and put them on the table. "Do you like poppers?"

"They're fun."

"A wholesale drug salesman gives me a can of them every time he comes through. These are fresh, I just got them today."

"How lucky can I get?" I reached for her but she slipped away from me.

"Don't be in such a rush," she said. "You open a bottle of champagne while I grab a quick shower. I feel all icky."

I looked at her. If she came just half as much as she said she did, she had to be solid glue by now. "Okay," I said.

She took a paper bag out of the flight bag and gave it to me. It was ice cold. I looked at her questioningly. "Steaks," she explained. 'If we get hungry later."

I laughed and patted her on the ass. "Go take your shower."

She thought of everything.

Speed-Hire-Rent-A-Girl was climbing up the wall. Two sticks and a popper as she hit her first orgasm and she was on a trip that had no return. She was right about one thing. She was never dry.

Suddenly she pushed me away. "You won't think I'm awful?" she asked.

I shook my head.

"I want you to come in my mouth," she said.

'Do I get a fuck first?"

"Yes," she said, "but I still want you to come in my mouth." I rolled her over and went into her cunt from behind. She reached underneath her and grabbed my balls and squeezed. "Oh, God!" she said. "They're so full and heavy."

I felt it starting to come up. So did she. She got away from me and spun around grabbing me in her mouth. The sperm started spilling and she sucked until I lay there spent and exhausted.

"That was great," she said. "You taste like heavy sweet cream."

She was still holding me, playing with me. "Do you have to take a pee?" she asked.

"Now that you mention it, I do." I started out of the bed.

She followed me into the bathroom. "Let me hold it for you."

I looked at her. "Be my guest."

She stood behind me and aimed at the bowl, but it was awkward and splashed over the seat.

"Just what I thought,' I said. "Women don't know anything about taking a piss."

"Let me try," she said and climbed into the bathtub next to the toilet bowl. Then she held it. This time her aim was true.

I looked at her face. There was an expression of rapt concentration there that I had never seen before. A fascination that was almost childish. She turned her face up to me. Almost as if she were in a spell she put her free hand in the path of the stream. Abruptly she turned it to her.

I stopped in surprise.

She pulled angrily at my cock. "Don't stop!" she cried. "It's beautiful. Bathe me in it."

"Different strokes for different folks," I said. If that was what she wanted, who was I to say no?

It was a wild, crazy night. On top of everything else she turned out to be a screamer. Which only made a liar out of her girl friend. If the neighbors really had been nosy, they would have called the cops.

It was seven in the morning when she dropped me in front of the house. She put out her hand almost formally. "Thank you, Angelo," she said. "It was the most beautiful and romantic evening of my life."

I couldn't help but agree with her. She drove off. I went up the steps and into the house. Donald met me at the door.

"A Lady Ayres tried to reach you several times last evening," he said. "She left a call-back number. She says it's very important."

"Where's she calling from?" I said.

"New York," he answered. "Shall I try to get her for you?"

"Please," I said. I followed him into the library. There was a pot of coffee on the table. I filled a cup while I waited. A moment later, he signaled. I picked up the telephone near me. "Hello."

"Angelo." Her voice was very tight. "I've got to see you. Right away."

"What are you doing in New York?" I asked. "I thought—"

"Alicia knows about Loren and me going away," she said. "The office was trying to find him and they made the mistake of telling her."

"Why did the office want him?"

"It has something to do with you. He didn't say very much. But he was very angry and he said you might wind up in jail. Then Alicia called and he told her everything."

"The damn fool."

"He's not very sophisticated," she said. "It's a matter of honor with him. Now he wants to marry me."

"Where is he?"

"In Detroit. I must see you. Can I come down there?"

"No. I'll come up to New York. Where are you staying?"

"The Waldorf," she said.

"I'll be up this afternoon."

Her voice sounded relieved. "I love you, Angelo."

"Bye, darling," I said. Number One was in the doorway.

"Who was that?" he asked.

"The girl I told you about," I said. "The shit hit the fan. Loren is on to us."

"I know that," Number One said testily. "I've already spoken to him. But something else happened."

"Yes," I said. "Alicia nailed him with the girl. He wants a divorce."

"Oh, Jesus!" Number One said. "That boy will never grow up."

Chapter Fifteen

"I don't know what the hell I'm doing here," she said, pacing up and down the large living room of the Bethlehem Motors suite in the Waldorf Towers. "Everything happened so fast."

I sat in the chair looking up at her. I took a sip of my drink without speaking.

" 'Go to the company suite in the Waldorf,' " he said. "And wait there until you hear from me. Just don't worry." She stopped pacing and looked down at me. "It wasn't until I got on the plane to New York that I thought about what he said.

There was nothing to worry about. Nothing had happened between us."

I still didn't speak.

"You don't believe me, do you?" she demanded.

"Of course I believe you."

"You don't sound as if you do."

"Come over here," I said.

She crossed the room and stood in front of me. I leaned forward in the chair and kissed her right on the crotch, then looked up at her. "Now do you believe that I believe you?"

A half smile came to her mouth. "That's a very complicated question. You're crazy."

"Uh-huh," I said. "Now calm down and tell me exactly what happened. What might be nothing to you, might be something very different to him. Remember, we're talking about a very square guy."

"That's true," she said. "There is a boyish naivete about him which, at first, I thought was a put-on. But it wasn't. That's the way he really is."

"Did you share the same suite?"

"No," she said. "Our suites were next to each other."

"Connecting door?"

"Yes. But he never came through the door without knocking first, even if it was always open. He never kissed me good night without first asking my permission. And he never once mentioned that he was in love with me until after he had spoken to Alicia."

"He must have shown something."

"Of course he did," she said. "There were all the signs. The fresh flowers every day, the way he looked at me with big round eyes, the constant accidental touching of my hand, you know what I mean. I thought it was charming, but I didn't take it seriously. Who could? It was all so Victorian."

"If everything was so proper, how did Alicia get on to you?"

"Because everything was so damn proper," she said. "That's what was so stupid about the whole thing. Alicia's call came through while we were having a drink in my suite. If we had been sharing the same suite, I never would have picked up the phone. This way I thought nothing of it. She recognized my voice instantly."

"Was this before or after she spoke to his office?"

"Before. Actually that's what she was calling him about. To find out whether he wanted her to let the office know where to reach him."

"Oh, baby," I said. "That isn't being square, that's being stupid. It takes a special talent for a man to let his wife know where he's going to be, especially if he's going away with another woman. He was looking to get caught."

"Do you really think that?"

"What else is there to think?" I looked at her. "I knew he was interested in you that first night we met at dinner at their house. Alicia isn't blind. I'm sure she saw it too."

She thought for a moment. "Of course. That had to be it. How could I be so stupid?"

I smiled at her. "You just take it for granted that men fall at your feet."

"But why didn't he say something to me?"

"Maybe he was afraid that you would reject him," I said. "Who the hell knows?"

"What should I do?" she asked. "I don't need all this *merde*."

A signal bell began to ring in the back of my head. Why the sudden change in language? She hadn't hesitated using the English before. "What shit?" I asked.

"You know," she said. For the first time she was vague. "All this. His divorce next year."

"Next year?"

"Yes. He didn't want to get a divorce before Elizabeth's debut next September. He doesn't want to spoil it for her."

"He seems to have thought it all out very thoroughly," I said. "And he wants you to wait?"

She nodded.

I felt the gears begin to mesh. Slowly I let the clutch out. "Okay, Bobbie, playtime is over," I said. "Let's get down to the nitty gritty. How long have you been after him?"

She stared at me for a moment. "You have a nasty mind."

"It takes practice," I said. "Truth time. How long?"

She hesitated. "Two years."

"What took you so long? Why didn't you just grab him by the cock?"

"It would have frightened him off," she said. "I had to do the lady bit."

"You're probably right."

"You're not angry with me?"

"Why should I be? I've only known you a few weeks." I reached for a cigarette. "I can't see where you have a problem. You got what you went after."

She looked into my eyes. "I didn't figure on falling in love with you."

"What difference should that make?"

"I don't want to lose you?"

"You won't," I smiled. "I don't mind a little bit of adultery. It even adds some fun."

"You could ask me to marry you, you bastard," she said. "Just to be polite."

"No way," I grinned. "You just might take me up on it. And then where would we both be? No place either of us wanted."

"Then what do I do? Wait here for him?"

"No, that would be a mistake," I said. "You have to keep him coming after you. Don't give him the feeling he has you locked away for his own convenience. You get on the plane to London tonight."

"You're probably right," she said thoughtfully. "What do I tell him?"

"Be noble. Tell him you're leaving the country because you don't want to cause embarrassment for him, you respect him too much to allow that to happen. That should instil the proper guilt feelings in him."

She stared at me. "Last chance," she said. "Since you won't ask me, I'll ask you. Will you marry me?"

"No."

The tears suddenly came to her eyes. I held out my arms to her and she came into them. "I knew this would happen," she wept. "I tried to tell you in the San Francisco airport. Why did you let me go?"

"I had no choice. We both had already made our commitments."

Her voice was muffled against my chest. "Take me to bed. Please."

None of it made any sense at all. Everything had changed but nothing had changed. It was still beautiful.

We went directly from bed to the airport. I put her on her plane to London, then caught the last flight of the evening to Detroit.

We sat in the study of the Hardeman mansion in Grosse Point around a small, oddly-shaped, ancient wooden table whose surface bore the burns of many meetings like this. There were four of us: Loren, Dan Weyman, Number One, and myself.

They had been silent while Number One carefully explained to them his plans. Now he had finished and we waited for their response. It was not long in coming.

"I'm sorry, Grandfather," Loren said. "We just can't permit it. The risk is too great. We can't afford to gamble the future of our company on just one car."

Number One snorted. "How do you think this company was built? Just on that idea. The future of one car."

"Times are different now," Loren said. "The economy is different. Diversification has proven the savior of our company."

"I'm not doubting the value of the other divisions," Number One said. "But I don't agree that it is the savior of our company. I believe it has almost cost us our company. Our automobile business is almost gone. The tail is now wagging the dog."

"Conditions have changed in the thirty years since you were running the company," Loren said stubbornly. "The last new American cars on the market were the Henry J. and the Edsel. And look what happened to them. Kaiser went out of the business and the Edsel almost broke Ford."

"Kaiser would have made it had he kept on, but he wasn't an automobile man," Number One said. "The Edsel didn't stop Ford. They're bigger than they ever were. Next year they're all coming out with sub-compacts. Do you think they would do that if they thought they were going to lose money?"

"They have to," Loren said. "They have to meet the foreign competition. We don't have to. We're satisfied where we are."

"You may be, but I'm not," said Number One. "I don't like being second cousin in a business where we used to be part of the main family." He looked at me, then back at Loren. "If that's your attitude, I can't see any reason we stay in the automobile business."

"It may very well be that next year we won't be in it," Loren said flatly. "We can't afford it any more."

"We'll go out of the auto business over my dead body," Number One said in a cold voice.

Loren was silent. He didn't look well. There were blue circles under his eyes and his face was pouchy and drawn from lack of rest. For a moment I felt sorry for him. He had to be catching hell from all sides. At home as well as at the office. His next words dispelled my pity.

He stared right at his grandfather and spoke in an equally cold voice. It was almost as if they were the only two in the room. "At a special meeting of the board of directors held yesterday, three motions were passed.

"One, the immediate dismissal of Angelo Perino as vice-president of the company.

"Two, the institution of criminal proceedings against Mr. Perino for committing the corporation to certain expenditures without due and proper authorization.

"Three, to petition the courts of the State of Michigan to appoint a receiver for your stock in the corporation until such time as it could be determined that you are fully capable and responsible for your actions."

Number One was silent. His eyes never left Loren's face. He sighed. "Is that the way you want to play it?"

Loren nodded. He got to his feet. "Come, Dan. The meeting is over."

"Not quite." Number One's voice was calm. He pushed a sheet of paper across the table at Loren. "Read that."

Loren glanced at it. His face went pale and even more drawn than it had been. "You can't do that!"

"I've already done it," Number One said. "All proper and legal. You can even see the seal of the Corporation Counsel of that State of Michigan, attesting to it. Acting as major stockholder and voting trustee of eighty percent of the company, I have the right to dismiss any or all of the directors of the corporation with or without cause. And that's what I did. That board meeting you had yesterday did you no good. They've all been fired since Monday."

Loren stood there.

"You better sit down son," Number One said gently.

Loren didn't move.

Number One's voice was still gentle. "You have two choices. You can quit or you can stay. Your father and I didn't always see eye to eye with each other, but we stayed together."

Slowly Loren sat down. He still didn't speak.

Number One nodded "That's better," he said. "Now we can get down to the real business of this meeting. Building a new car. I promised your daughter I would build her a new car and by God, I'm going to keep that promise!"

I looked across the table at Loren. I would have felt better had he walked. Then I met his eyes and I knew I had been right.

Whatever else Number One thought, the war had just begun.

BOOK TWO

1970

Chapter One

He awoke, as usual, a few minutes before the alarm went off. He lay there motionless in bed, his eyes watching the softly illuminated numbers on the digital radio clock creep inexorably toward the time it would turn on the music. As usual, he pressed the cut-off button just before the sound switched on: 6 A.M.

Silently he swung out of bed, his feet finding the slippers on the floor; picking up his robe he made his way, silent still, to the bathroom. He closed the door behind him before turning on the light so that he would not awaken his wife. He reached for the cigarettes on the shelf under the mirror, lit one and sat down on the toilet seat. Three cigarettes later nothing had happened and he was debating lighting a fourth when he heard his wife's voice through the door.

"Dan?"

"Yes," he answered.

"How is it?"

"Nothing," he grumbled, getting to his feet and tying his pajama pants back around him. He opened the door. "That doctor doesn't know what the hell he's talking about."

"He does," she replied, reaching for the phone and pressing the intercom button. "Mamie, we're awake." She turned to him. "You're too tense. You have to relax."

"I'm relaxed," he said. "My own tensions have nothing to do with it. I'm just constipated, that's all. I've always been constipated. Ever since I was a kid. But then they didn't have fancy doctors who treated you with psycho-analysis, they gave you a laxative and pointed you at the nearest toilet."

"Don't get vulgar," she said.

"I'm not vulgar. All I want to do is move my bowels. Where's the Ex-Lax?"

"I threw it out. Eating Ex-Lax every day is the worst thing you could do. It prevents you from functioning naturally."

"Get some," he snapped. "I don't function naturally and after twenty-one years of marriage you might as well recognize that fact." He went back into the bathroom, slamming the door behind him.

Mamie came into the bedroom carrying the breakfast tray. She placed it carefully on the bed across Jane Weyman's legs. "Good mornin', Miz Weyman," she said, a bright smile on her dark face. She glanced toward the closed bathroom door. "How's Mistuh Weyman this morning'?"

Jane shrugged her shoulders. She uncovered the napkin over the toast. "The same."

"That po' man," Mamie said sympathetically. "I do wish he would let me fix him some grits in the mornin'. They's nothin' like grits to get the machinery workin'."

"You know him," Jane said, spreading jam lavishly on her toast. "All he'll do is drink coffee."

"That does nothin' but make his stomach sour," Mamie said. She stared for the door. "You-all tell him, I said grits'll straighten him out."

She closed the door as the telephone began to ring. Jane picked it up. "Hello," she said, annoyed. It changed quickly. "No, Loren, it's quite all right. I'm awake and having breakfast. I'll call Dan."

She didn't have to, he had opened the door and looked out at her with a face half-lathered. "Who is it?"

"Loren," she said, her hand over the mouthpiece. "Why is he calling so early?"

He didn't answer. He crossed the room and took the phone from her hand. The lather came off on the earpiece as he held it up. "Good morning, Loren." He wiped the phone with his free hand. "How was your flight in?"

Loren's voice was quiet. "Good. But I got in three hours late. I was wondering if you could come over for breakfast and fill me in before the meeting this morning?"

"Be there in twenty minutes," Dan said. He put down the telephone. "Loren wants me to join him for breakfast," he said to Jane. "There's a board meeting this morning and he wants me to bring him up to date."

"If he stayed home and paid attention to business instead of running around Europe after his English whore," Jane said, "maybe he wouldn't have to bother you at six o'clock in the morning."

"You better stop talking like that," Dan said. "Someday you're going to have to accept her as Mrs. Hardeman. Then what are you going to do?"

"Exactly what I'm doing now," Jane said. "I'll ignore her. Poor Alicia. After all she's been through."

"Poor Alicia," Dan mimicked. "Poor Alicia is going to get a six-million-dollar settlement for her pains. I don't feel sorry for her."

"I do," Jane said. "There isn't enough money in the world to compensate her for what she's going through."

"At least I won't have to show up in a tuxedo for dinner any more," he said, going back to the bathroom. He finished his shave quickly, came out and began to dress. "Turn on the radio and get the morning traffic report."

Jane reached over and pressed the button. Heavy rock music flooded the room. She lowered the volume. "Sometimes I think you never should have left Ford when Mac went to Washington. At least nobody bothered you early in the morning and your constipation wasn't as bad."

He didn't answer. He was busy tucking his shirt into his trousers. The zipper caught on his shirttail. "Damn!" he muttered, struggling to loosen it.

"Who knows?" she asked. "You might have been president there by now."

"Not a chance. I was never a favorite of Arjay's. He kept me too far down on the pecking order. Besides he didn't make it. Ford goes for automobile men. That's why Knudsen's there now."

"You'll never be president here either," she said. "Despite Loren's promise. Especially now that the Mafia has moved in."

"Jane, you have a big mouth," he said. "How many times do I have to tell you that Perino has no connection with the Mafia?"

"It's common knowledge that his grandfather was tied up with them," she said. "My grandfather used to sell him the trucks that brought the whiskey down from Canada."

"Your grandfather was also one of his best customers too," Dan said. "The way he used to drink I'm willing to bet that old Perino never had to pay a nickel in cash for those trucks. Besides, that has nothing to do with Angelo."

"You're defending him," she said accusingly. "And he's the man who became executive vice-president instead of you."

"I'm not defending him, Jane," he said wearily. "And he's exec VP of the auto division only, not the whole company. I'm still the senior vice-president."

"He doesn't report to you like all the others, does he?"

"No. He's responsible directly to the board of directors. He doesn't even report to Loren."

"That horrid old man," she said. "It's all his fault. Why didn't he stay in Florida like he was supposed to?"

He began to reply but held his tongue as the traffic report came on the radio. "This is WJR and the six-thirty traffic report."

The disc jockey's voice was as staccato and harsh as the music had been. "Traffic on all expressways running light to moderate in all directions except for a slight tieup on the Industrial Expressway around River Rouge where the normal shift traffic is slowing things up. US Ten, Woodward Avenue, clear into downtown Detroit, no traffic."

"Turn it off," he said.

She pressed the button and the voice dropped out of the room. "What's going to happen?" she asked. "There's rumors all over town that the old man's going to make Perino president of the company."

"That's possible. But not likely just yet. Perino still has to prove himself. Especially now that there are plans to go public. Even the old man knows that. Meanwhile Loren and I still run the only end of the business that's making a profit and we're doing better all the time."

He finished knotting his tie and slipped into his jacket. "I'll be leaving. See you tonight." He bent over the bed and kissed her cheek.

"Try to be home before eight o'clock," she said. "We have roast beef and I don't like it burned to a cinder."

He nodded and went to the door. Before he went out, he looked back at her. "Don't forget to get some Ex-Lax," he said. "I think three days is long enough to wait for psychology to work."

She waited until she heard his car leave the driveway, then she took the tray from the bed and placed it on the floor. She picked up the telephone and pressed the intercom.

Mamie answered. "Yes'm."

"I'm going back to sleep for a little bit," she said. "Wake me at nine. I don't want to be late for my tennis lesson."

She put down the telephone and turned off the light. She smiled slightly as she leaned back on the pillow. The new tennis pro down at the club was delicious. The way his lean body pressed against her from behind as he held her arm to straighten her forehand gave her the shivers.

*

The quiet hum of the 275-horsepower engine under the hood of the conservative all-black Sundancer reassured him as he turned out of his driveway onto the small road leading him to US 10. He looked both ways as he approached the highway. No traffic. He swung onto the road heading for downtown Detroit. He would follow Woodward Avenue to the Edsel Ford Expressway, then to Grosse Point. With a bit of luck the whole trip shouldn't take more than twenty minutes. The Sundancer responded to his pressure on the accelerator with a satisfying surge of power.

Loren was waiting for him in the breakfast room. "Sorry to be late," he apologized.

"That's all right," Loren said. "Gave me a chance to catch up on what's been happening around town." He gestured to a pile of back copies of the *Automotive News* on the floor next to him.

"Nothing much," Dan said. "Everything's pointing to the sub-compacts coming out in the fall. They're watching the Gremlin but they don't really expect any action until the Pinto and the Vega are available."

He studied Loren. Loren looked well. There had been a time a few short months ago when Loren had looked as if he were going through a wringer. But apparently that had passed. Now he seemed to be a man who was waiting patiently for the things he knew would happen. He sat down.

"I have some good news," Loren said "I've closed the deal in West Germany."

"Congratulations," Dan smiled.

"They'll be ready to begin manufacturing immediately. The whole line. Refrigerators, ranges, television. It opens the whole common market for us on a competitive basis."

"That would mean an additional net profit to us of better than two million dollars this year," Dan said enthusiastically. 'In three years we should be able to bring that up to fifteen million."

Loren nodded. "It means you will have to go over there next month to fine-print it. I also promised them a complete engineering team to train their own personnel."

"No problem," Dan said. He rubbed his hands together. "That will make good news for the board meeting this afternoon. So far, all they've been getting is approvals for appropriations. The money is beginning to fly out like a moon probe."

"The board doesn't seem to be concerned about it," Loren said.

Dan nodded. He knew what Loren meant. The new directors representing the banking and underwriting houses who had given them the advance funding went along with every suggestion Number One made.

"Strange," Loren continued in an almost puzzled voice. "Here we make the money but all they care about is a new car, which at best is a risky gamble. Do you know, even in Europe, that was what most of them wanted to talk about. The new car. It seems they all want to get into that."

"What do you say to them?" Dan asked.

"I look mysterious and tell them I will talk to them at the right time. It would look damn silly if I were to tell them the truth. That I really don't know any more than they do." He paused for a moment. "By the way, what is happening?"

"He's completed the modifications on the three racing cars," Dan said. "But that was weeks ago. I haven't heard anything since."

"And the new car?"

"Not a word," Dan said. "Maybe we'll hear something at today's meeting. We're being asked to approve the removal of the auto design and engineering department to the Coast."

"When does he want to do that?"

"Next month. He says the new plant will be ready for them at that time."

"Will my grandfather be at the meeting?"

"He's expected. He always shows up when there's something on the new car."

A voice from the doorway interrupted them. "May I come in Daddy?"

Loren looked up. His face, which had been serious, relaxed. "Of course, Betsy."

She came into the room and leaned over her father's chair and kissed his cheek. "Did you have a good trip?"

Loren nodded. She turned to Dan. "Good morning, Mr. Weyman."

She turned back to her father without waiting for Dan's reply. There was a curiously reproachful tone in her voice. "You didn't tell me we're coming out with a Sundancer Super Sport?"

Loren was puzzled. "A what?"

"A supercar. You know, a hot one."

Loren looked at Dan. They didn't speak.

"You don't have to go all mysterious on me," she said. "After all, I'm in the family. I never would have said anything to anyone."

The two men still didn't speak.

Betsy reached across the table and poured a cup of coffee. She started back for the door, the cup in her hand. "Okay, don't say anything if you don't want to. But I saw one on Woodward Avenue last night. And you know what, Daddy?'

Loren shook his head.

She smiled proudly. "It ran the wheels off everything in sight!"

Chapter Two

Loren looked down at the report. "Are you sure about these figures?"

Bancroft nodded his head vigorously. "Cost accounting checked them out. Dan says we can't miss. I have firm orders for three thousand cars. That's two million net profit for us first crack out of the box. The dealers are panting for it."

"Word gets around quickly in this business." Loren said.

"The car's been on Woodward Avenue every night for the past three weeks. By now every dragger in the country is anxious to get his hands on one."

"What does Angelo say?"

"He says he didn't build them for the market. They're test cars. Nothing else." Bancroft took a deep breath. "But Jesus it's the first time in ten years that the dealers are calling us instead of me begging them. Even Mr. Inside at Grand

Spaulding in Chicago called me. He's willing to put them on the lot with ninety miles run on them so he doesn't blow his Dodge franchise. That's how hot the car is."

"I'd like to see one," Loren said. "All I've seen is the designs so far."

"That's easy," Bancroft said. "One's at the test track right now on its way to fifty thousand miles."

Loren got to his feet. "Let's go." He pressed the button down on his intercom. "Call Dan Weyman," he told his secretary, "and have him meet us out at the test track."

It was a gray day with high clouds and occasional gusty bursts of wind and rain. The test track was out past the Willow Run Airport, southwest of the city, and it took them forty-five minutes to get there on the Industrial Expressway. They came off the highway and drove five minutes up a winding back road, finally coming to a stop in front of a wire cyclone fence behind which a tightly cropped cypress hedge obscured everything beyond it.

The security guard came out of his little booth in front of the gate. Another security guard watched them curiously from his booth inside.

Loren looked at him as he approached the car. He wasn't wearing the conventional gray uniform of their security force. Instead he wore the dark blue and Sam Browne belt of the Burns agency. "Gentlemen?" he asked in a pleasant voice.

Bancroft rolled down his window and leaned out from the driver's seat. "I'm Mr. Bancroft. This is Mr. Hardeman and Mr. Weyman."

The guard nodded politely. "How do you do, gentlemen?" He didn't move.

Bancroft looked at him irritably. "Well, don't just stand there man. Let us in."

The guard stared back at him unperturbed. "Do you have a pass?"

Bancroft jumped over his usually low boiling point. "What the hell do we need a pass for?" he shouted. "Mr. Hardeman is the president of the company and we're vice-presidents!"

"I'm sorry, gentlemen," the guard said in an unruffled voice. "I don't care if you're God, Jesus Christ and Moses, you don't get in here without a pass signed by either Mr. Perino or Mr. Duncan. That's my orders." He started back toward his booth.

Loren got out of the car. "Guard," he called.

The guard turned back to him. "Yes, sir?"

"Are either Mr. Perino or Mr. Duncan here?"

The guard nodded. "Mr. Duncan is."

"Would you be kind enough to call him and tell him that we're out here and would like to come in?" Loren's voice was pleasant but in the tone of command.

The guard studied him for a moment, then nodded. Without speaking he went back into the booth and picked up a phone. He spoke into it and then put it down. He didn't come out of the booth again, just stood there watching them through the glass window.

Loren reached for a cigarette and lit it. Bancroft and Dan came out of the car and stood there with him. "How come we're using Burns out here instead of our own security people?" he asked Dan.

"Angelo doesn't trust them," Dan replied. "He said he remembered when he was testing the air-cooled six-cylinder for us that Chevy had the plans almost before we did."

"Angelo doesn't trust anybody outside of engineers, mechanics and drivers," Bancroft added. He looked up. "Where the hell is Duncan?"

He walked over to the booth. "Did you speak to him?" he asked the guard.

"No, sir," the guard replied. "He was in the car with the driver. But they said they would get the message to him."

"Oh, Jesus!" Bancroft pulled a cigar from his pocket, stuck it in his mouth and, chewing it without lighting it, walked back to them.

It began to drizzle and they got into the car and sat there silently. Ten minutes passed before a car came down the road inside the gate and John Duncan got out. He signaled to the inside guard and the gate swung open. He walked over to their car.

"I'm sorry about the delay," he apologized. "But we didn't expect you."

"Quite all right, John," Loren said. "I've heard so much about the car, I decided at the last minute to run out and see it."

Duncan smiled. "I'm glad you could come. Follow me."

They followed him down to the road to the driving grounds. He pulled his car into a parking slot and they stopped beside him. They got out.

"We'll go down to the garage," he said. "We can keep dry there."

They followed him through the slight drizzle to the garage, located just inside the driving oval. A few men were sitting at a table, playing cards, and a girl was curled up on a couch reading a paperback book.

"The men are mechanics," Duncan explained. "The girl is one of our test drivers."

Bancroft eyed the girl appreciatively. "I knew Angelo would find a better way to do things."

Duncan's voice was flat. "Women do fifty percent of the driving and very few cars are bought without their approval. Angelo's idea is to get their point of view."

"That girl makes points of her own," Bancroft said.

"She's a first-rate driver," Duncan replied.

"Where's the car?" Loren asked.

Duncan walked over to the electronic tracker and pressed a button. The tape activated lights flashed on. "Just going through checkpoint three at the far end of the test track." He pressed another button. Numbers began to flash on the reading screen. "It's going through the tight turn at seventy-one point six two seven mph." The numbers began to drop rapidly. "It's down to fifty-two, now forty-seven point two three eight going into the corkscrew."

He turned to them. "Watch the screen. When it comes out of there into the straight, it should get up to one sixty by the time it passes here."

They watched the reading screen in fascination. Suddenly the numbers began to jump up rapidly. In a matter of seconds it seemed that they had gone over 140 and were still climbing. In the distance they could begin to hear the faint roar of the engine.

The engine roar grew louder and they moved toward the garage door to better see outside. In the distance the white headlight beams sparkled through the drizzle. Almost before they realized it, the beams turned into white blinding glare and the car flew by them, trailing the light like a wraithlike gray shadow, and disappeared down the track.

"A hundred and sixty-eight point seven one five," Duncan's voice came from the tracker.

"How fast will it go?" Loren asked, walking back to him.

"We've had it up to one-ninety-one," Duncan said. "But the track is wet and I told them not to take it over one sixty-five."

"How many miles have you logged?"

"Thirty-eight thousand. At forty we pull it in, service it and send it out again."

"Is the engine holding up?" Loren asked.

"Real good. Only normal changes despite the fact we have souped it up. Better than I thought. All the sensor readings are solid."

"I'd like to see the car," said Loren.

"I'll call it in," Duncan said. He pressed another button on the panel. A yellow light on a turret outside the garage glowed into life and began to whirl, throwing golden shadows into the windows. He leaned over the microphone built into the panel. "Duncan to Peerless, Duncan to Peerless. Over."

There was a slight rasp of static. "Peerless to Duncan. I read you. Over."

"Cool her off and bring her in. Over."

"Anything wrong?" The driver's voice seemed annoyed. "It looks good out here. Over."

"Nothing wrong," Duncan said. "Just bring her in. Over and out."

"Roger. Over and out." There was a click and the speaker went off.

Duncan hit another button and the tracking screen went to black. He walked toward the garage door. They followed him just as the car went by. It was already slowing down. "He'll come in on the next lap," Duncan explained.

Loren gestured to the tracking console. "I didn't know we had one of those."

"It's Angelo's idea," Duncan said. "He got it from watching the space launch and had it built for us by Rourke's people on the Coast. It turned out to be so good that we're building them now for GM, Ford and Chrysler, and we have orders coming in from all over the world."

The car pulled in just as the rain stopped. They walked out toward it.

Loren studied the car. It was the standard two-door Sundancer hardtop. There was no doubt about that. But there were subtle differences. The hood sloped slightly down toward the headlights and the almost square rear window had been softened and rounded, molding gently down to the spoiler mounted over the trunk, giving the car a definite European look.

The driver got out. He moved stiffly in his fireproof coveralls, flipping the chinstrap of his crash helmet open as he came toward them. "Okay," he said belligerently. "What did I do wrong?"

"Nothing," Duncan said. "Mr. Hardeman here just wanted to have a look at it." The driver let out a sigh of relief. He pulled a pack of cigarettes from his pocket. "Mind if I grab a cup of coffee then?"

Duncan shook his head. The driver walked into the garage.

Loren looked into the car. The dash was cluttered with all kinds of instrumentation. He looked back at Duncan. "What did you do to the car?"

Duncan moved up next to him. "The special instruments you see here all have built-in sensors which transmit readings to our control panel. We've put two four-barreled wide-scoop Webers, a new manifold and opened up the bore on the cylinders which gives us an eleven to one compression ratio and puts out up to three hundred and forty horse. The body is fiber glass draped on a steel wire net suspended from front and rear roll bars to a tubular chassis on an impact-absorbing suspension principle."

"Exactly what does that mean?" Loren asked.

"The harder you hit, the more it resists the impact," Duncan replied. "The same principle as the suspension bridge, the more weight, the stronger it holds. Combines safety with lightness and economy. This car weights six hundred and seventy pounds less than the standard Sundancer with the same equipment, and the body shell costs forty percent less to fabricate." Duncan took out a cigarette and lit it. "Of course the car would be lighter still but we had to beef up the axle and the driveshaft to take the power."

"How does it ride?" Loren asked.

Duncan looked at him. "Why don't you take a spin around the track and see for yourself?"

Loren looked around the table. The board meeting was almost over and it had gone quietly, in almost routine fashion. There had been a great deal of satisfaction expressed over the West German deal and he felt bathed in a glow of commendation. Even Number One, sitting in his wheelchair at the foot of the table, had been thoroughly impressed.

The last item on the agenda was now before the board. Approval to move Design and Engineering to the Coast. Loren turned the page.

"Gentlemen," he said. "You all have item number twenty-one on the table before you, and before we move on that item, I would like to say a few words."

He waited for their silent assent before continuing. "First, I think the directors should commend Mr. Perino for a fantastic job done with the experimental cars. As you already know, he has converted three standard Sundancer hardtops into high-performance machines. What you may not know, because he has not mentioned it, perhaps due to his own modesty, is that he has come up with one of the most exciting cars Bethlehem has ever had the good fortune to produce. And I know whereof I speak, gentlemen, for this morning I had the pleasure to ride in one. My congratulations to Mr. Perino."

"Thank you, Mr. Hardeman," Angelo's voice was polite but noncommittal.

Loren waited for the murmur that spread around the table to die down. "Perhaps none of us present realized the potential of this car. Oddly enough it came to my attention this morning through my young daughter, who saw one of the cars dragging on Woodward Avenue the other night and in her words, it 'ran the wheels off everything in sight!' "

He waited again for the pleased murmur to die away. "The other bit of interesting news comes from Mr. Bancroft. He informs me that he is besieged by dealers who want to take immediate shipment on the car, that he already has firm orders for three thousand, which incidentally brings us two million dollars in additional net profits, and he feels that he can without effort sell ten thousand of this particular model in the current model year."

There was a general smiling air around the table. Loren followed through. "Therefore I propose that we add to the agenda, together with the item on the table, approval from this board to begin immediate production on the Sundancer SS and take advantage of this particularly high interest."

There was almost immediate nodding of heads. "Just a minute, gentlemen." Angelo's voice was still noncommittal. "I do not think we should market these cars."

The directors looked puzzled. One of them, president of a Detroit bank, questioned him. "Why not, Mr. Perino? I know that the supercar market has been a very lucrative one for Dodge, Chevy and American Motors."

Angelo looked at him without expression. "There are several reasons. One, the test car, as is, cannot be marketed because it exceeds emission levels. Conforming to these levels would result in a considerable loss of power so that performance would not reach the heights of the test car."

Weyman spoke up. "Would the car fall below what we commonly understand are supercar standards?"

"There are no standards for supercars, Mr. Weyman," Angelo said drily. "In answer to your question, I say yes and no. Yes, it will have higher performance than the standard Sundancer, no, it will not match the performance of the Hemi and the Mopar." He looked down the table at Loren. "But even that is not the important consideration. We are about to undertake to build a new car. A car that will put us back solidly into the automobile industry. A specialized car, a supercar, no matter how attractive it may be, is not the answer to the main issue. The market is a limited one and my own personal feeling is that it will shrink rapidly due to the solid restraints of ecological measures being brought into law. For the sake of a few dollars in profit, gentlemen, I do not think we ought to risk the goodwill of an aware future market that we are targeting.

"I, perhaps, more than anyone here, enjoy a hot car. But that's not the business we're in. We're about to build a car for the masses, not for the speed afficionados. I think at the present time, seeking a hot-car image is wrong. That is something that should have been done seven years ago. Today it is out of date."

The banker spoke up again. He looked over at Number One. "Could you give us your opinion on the matter, Mr. Hardeman?"

Number One's face was unreadable. He had been doodling on a pad while Loren and Angelo were speaking. Now he looked up. "I think we should build the car," he said quietly.

The vote of the board of directors was sixteen for the proposal one against. The meeting was concluded several minutes after that, and they began to leave the room in groups.

Angelo had just finished returning his papers to the file when Number One called him. He looked up. "Yes, sir?"

"Wait a moment," the old man said.

Angelo nodded silently.

At last they were alone in the room. Number One pushed his chair toward Angelo. "You know that I agreed with you, don't you?"

"That's what I thought," Angelo said.

"I owe you an explanation why I voted against you," the old man said.

"You don't owe me anything. You're the boss."

"There was a time," the old man's voice was almost reflective, "that people used to say I had destroyed Loren's father by countermanding every decision he made. That eventually I was the cause of his death."

Angelo was silent. He had heard the stories.

The old man looked up into Angelo's face. "I couldn't let that story begin all over again, could I?"

Angelo let out a deep breath. "I guess you couldn't."

But later, when he got back to his office, he wondered whether Number One had been telling him the truth.

Chapter Three

He woke with a start. The faint sounds of the orchestra playing in the grand ballroom downstairs floated in through the open windows on the warm June night wind. He sat up in bed, grunting involuntarily as a sudden sharp pain stabbed through his temples. "Jesus!" he exclaimed, almost aloud to himself. "It can't be the booze. I didn't drink that much. Besides Perino told me it was the real stuff."

He got off the bed and padded in his bare feet into the bathroom. The marble of the floor was cold and he went back for his slippers. He turned on the water and splashed it on his face. The headache began to ease and he stared at himself in the mirror. Bit by bit the day came back to him.

It had begun with the wedding at St. Stephens at noon and then moved to the lawn reception at Hardeman Manor from two o'clock until five. Then everyone began to leave. But it wasn't over yet. They were merely going home to rest and change their clothes. The grand wedding ball was to begin at eight o'clock that evening.

He remembered going upstairs and taking off his jacket. But that was all. He did not remember undressing, but apparently he had, for he was in his pajamas and an entirely new wardrobe was laid out for him. He rubbed his chin reflectively. Another shave couldn't hurt.

He took the shaving mug with the engraved golden picture of the first Sundancer automobile he had built back in 1911 and began to stir the shaving brush in the cup, bringing up a full white lather. Slowly he applied the lather to his face and then massaged it into his skin with strong, firm fingers. Afterwards another layer of hot lather over the first and then he took the ivory-handled straight razor from its case and began to strop it gently against the leather strap hanging from the wall beside the mirror. A few moments later he was ready for his shave.

He began under his chin. Short, gentle strokes up from the neck. He smiled to himself. The razor was perfect. Carefully then he came down from his sideburns toward the chin, then sideways across his upper lip toward his cheek. He ran his fingers over his face. Smooth.

As carefully as he had stropped his razor, he rinsed it and dried it and placed it back in its case. Then he stepped into the shower and turned the water on full force. First hot, then cold, until he was completely awake and tingling. He stepped out of the shower and pulled a rough towel around him and began to rub vigorously. The tingling of his flesh warmed him.

He began to think of Loren Junior and his new bride. Now he remembered that they, too, had gone upstairs to change and he began to wonder if they had waited. Then he thought of his son, the studious, quite, gentle boy so unlike himself that at times he wondered how he could have a son like that. Of course Junior would wait. But his bride. That was another matter.

She was a Mormon. And he knew about the Mormons. They thought nothing of sharing a husband with several other women and the only times they quarreled was when one of them missed their turn in bed. They didn't like to be done out of their share.

Not that he blamed them. He didn't like being done out of his either. Especially since Elizabeth had always been such a delicate woman, and even more so after Loren's birth. He knew he was a big man and he tried to be gentle with her, but she was so small that he knew he hurt her, even if she bit her lips to keep from crying out when he entered her. He could see the pain in her eyes.

Good thing in a way that Junior wasn't as large as he was, though he didn't think it would matter with Junior's wife, Sally. She was a solidly built girl even if she was skinny in the modern flapper sense. She still had a big bust and wide hips no matter how much she dieted to get into size. She probably could take all Junior had to give her and then some. He hoped that Junior would be enough of a man for her. Then he felt the heat swelling into his loins and he laughed aloud. He had to be a dirty old man thinking thoughts like that about his son's wife. But then, he wasn't that old. He was forty-seven this twentieth day of June, 1925.

He threw the towel carelessly on the floor and walked into the bedroom. He pulled a union suit from a drawer and stepped into it, his fingers buttoning up the front as soon as his arms went through the sleeves. A pair of black silk sox were folded neatly over the tops of his black patent-leather shoes. He slipped into them and locked the garters tight and reached for the freshly starched dress shirt resting across one of the two wooden valets next to his closet.

The linen rustled sharply as he put on the shirt. He walked over to the dresser and picked up the diamond studs and began to fasten them into the shirt front. He slipped the matching cufflinks into the sleeves and picked up the gold collar stud. This was not easy. In less than a moment, he was red in the face and the collar was crushed. Angrily he threw it away and took another from the drawer. Holding it in his hand, he walked into Elizabeth's room.

He stopped in the doorway. His wife was not there. Only the young dressmaker who had come from Paris to make the gowns for this occasion.

She was kneeling, her back to him, on the floor in front of the dressmaker's form and placing some pins in the fold of a skirt. She had been humming quietly to herself as she worked. Suddenly she became aware of him and the humming stopped. She looked back without getting to her feet, then rose swiftly, raising her eyes to his face.

Her eyes were dark blue, almost purple in tone against her white skin surrounded by heavy black hair drawn tightly in a chignon behind her head. He stared at her as if it were the first time he saw her. They were deep limpid eyes and a hidden light seemed to be lurking in their depths.

After a moment, he found his voice. It sounded harsh and strange to his own ears. "Where's Mrs. Hardeman?"

Her eyes dropped. "Downstairs, Monsieur." Her voice was low and with the faintest hint of accent. "She is greeting the guests."

"What time is it?"

"Almost nine o'clock, Monsieur."

"Damn!" he swore. "Why didn't someone wake me?"

"I think Madame tried," she said, raising her eyes again. "But you would not, how you say it, awaken up?"

He started back to his room, his fingers fumbling with the collar stud. Suddenly he turned back to her. "I can't fasten this damn thing."

"Perhaps I can be of help, Monsieur," she said, coming toward him.

He placed the studs in her outstretched palm. She reached up toward his collar. "You are tall, Monsieur. You will have to bend a little."

He leaned toward her. For a moment her eyes looked into his, then turned away. Her fingers were light and sure as she pressed the stud into the back of the collar. She then tried to match the front of the collar to the shirt. It didn't work.

She looked closely at the collar and then laughed. "No wonder you could not place the stud," she said. "You have made the buttons in the wrong buttonhole."

He felt the shirt. She was right. He had matched the buttons and the studs one buttonhole short. "I'm sorry," he muttered, his fingers clumsily trying to unfasten them.

"Let me, Monsieur," she said. The faint scent of her perfume came to him as her fingers flew down his shirt front rearranging the buttons.

He felt the sudden strong surge of heat in his loins as her fingers came down to the bottom buttons. He felt his face begin to redden. He could tell that she was aware of what was happening to him, though she gave no sign. He felt he had to say something. "What's your name?" he asked awkwardly.

"Roxanne, Monsieur," she answered, not looking up. She was at the third button from the bottom of the shirt and moving down to the second.

He felt the pressure growing stronger against his union suit. A quick downward glance revealed his deepest fears. The swelling against his underwear was unmistakable. He bent his hips back away from her hand, trying to keep himself away from her. The position was awkward and also hopeless. By the time her fingers reached the last button, his phallus was swollen and beating against his shirt.

She stopped suddenly and looked up into his face. She did not raise her hands, her eyes were very wide. Her mouth opened slightly as if she caught her breath, but she did not speak.

He stared down into her eyes. After a moment, he spoke. "How much?"

Her eyes did not waver. "I would like to stay here and open a small shop, Monsieur. There is nothing for me in Paris."

"You've got it," he said in a harsh voice.

She seemed to nod slightly and slowly sank to her knees before him. Gently her fingers opened his union suit and he sprang out at her like an angry lion from its cage. Carefully she took him in both hands, one behind the other as if she were grasping a baseball bat. She stared at it in wonder. "*C'est formidable. Un vrai canon.*"

He laughed deep in his chest. He did not know the meaning of her words, but he did recognize the tone. It was not the only time he had heard it in a woman's voice when she first saw him. "You're French, aren't you?" he asked.

She nodded.

"Well, then, French it."

She opened her mouth wide and placed it on him. He felt the tiny sharpness of her teeth on his raw glans and in his excitement dug his hands deep into the chignon in her hair and jammed himself into her mouth.

She began to choke and cough. He held her for a moment and then let her pull away. She looked up at him, no longer quite sure of herself, her breath rasping in her throat.

"Take off your dress," he said.

Her eyes fell from his face and fixed on his thrusting phallus. She did not move.

"Take off your dress!" he said harshly. "Or I'll tear it off!"

She moved slowly, almost as if hypnotized without taking her eyes from his phallus. The dress fell from her shoulders revealing round, heavy breasts with bursting plum-colored nipples. Almost sluggishly she began to rise from it.

He tugged angrily at his shirt. The studs and buttons tore, flying wildly around the room. He threw the shirt away and pulled off his union suit. Naked, he looked even more like an animal than before. Shoulders, chest and belly covered with hair out of which sprang the massive erection.

She felt a weakness in her knees as she poised to take off her stockings, and she would have fallen if he suddenly had not put out a hand to steady her. His touch was hot against her arm and she felt the fire running into her and the wetness begin to pour from her.

He placed his hands under her armpits and raised her naked out of her shoes and held her high in the air over him. He laughed, the exultation deep inside him.

She almost fainted looking down at him. Slowly he began to lower her on him. Her legs came up, circling his waist, as he began to enter her. Her breath caught in her throat. It was as if a giant shaft of white-hot steel were penetrating her vitals. She began to moan as it opened her and climbed higher into her body, past her womb, past her stomach, under her heart, up into her throat. She was panting now, like a bitch in heat. But there was no other way she could breathe. She clung to him in sudden weakness.

As if she were weightless, he crossed the room with her wrapped around him. He stopped at the side of his wife's bed and with one hand flung the satin covers to the floor. He stood there for a moment, then suddenly threw her from him onto the bed.

She stared up at him in shock, her legs still open and drawn back, her knees almost at her belly. She felt empty, almost hollow, as if he had withdrawn all her insides with himself.

Then he was poised over her, like a giant animal blocking out the light until all she could see was him. His hands reached and grasped each of her heavy breasts as if he wanted to tear them from her body. She moaned in pain and writhed, her pelvis suddenly arching and thrusting toward him. Then he entered her again.

"*Mon Dieu!*" she cried, the tears springing into her eyes. "*Mon Dieu!*" She began to climax almost before he was fully inside her. Then she couldn't stop them, one coming rapidly after the other as he slammed into her with the force of the giant body presses she had seen working in his factory on a tour just the day before. Somehow she became confused, the man and the machine they were one and the same and the strength was something she had never known before. And finally, when orgasm after orgasm had racked her body into a searing sheet of flame and she could bear no more, she cried out to him in French.

"Take your pleasure with me! Please! Take your pleasure with me! Quick, before I die!"

A roar came from deep inside his throat and his hands tightened on her breasts. She half screamed and her hands grabbed into the hair on his chest. Then all his weight seemed to fall in on her, crushing the breath from her body, and she felt the hot onrushing gusher of his semen turning her insides into viscous, flowing lava. She discovered herself climaxing again.

"*C'est pas possible!*" she murmured against his ear as he lay quietly now across her. She closed her eyes as she felt him growing soft and smaller. She began to smile inside herself. The woman always was the victor. The man was only the stronger for the moment.

He got to his feet. "I've got to dress," he said. "Before someone downstairs comes looking for me."

"Yes," she said. "I will help you."

But what neither of them knew was that they had been seen. By the newly wedded bride who had thought it would be great fun if she were to be the one who could awaken her father-in-law and get him to come downstairs to his own party.

Chapter Four

Sally Hardeman shut the door quietly behind her and stepped out into the hallway. Suddenly her legs were too weak to support her and she leaned back against the door, trying to control their trembling. She took a deep breath, fumbling in her tiny evening purse for a cigarette. She lit it and sucked the smoke deeply into her lungs. It didn't matter now whether anyone saw her smoking. Somehow that wasn't very important any more. Not after what she had seen.

It was true. The stories she had heard. They were all true. Now she believed them all. Even the one her closest girl friend had told her about how at a very formal dinner in Hardeman Manor one night, she had felt a hand sliding up her back beneath her loose evening blouse. Almost before she had become aware of the touch, her brassiere had been unfastened and the hand came around, fondling and cupping her naked breast.

She almost shrieked aloud and turned angrily toward the man sitting next to her before she remembered who he was. Loren Hardeman. He wasn't even looking at her, his face turned away, talking to the woman on his left.

Only his right arm was there, behind her chair and under her blouse. She looked around the table. Everyone seemed engrossed in his own conversation. Even Mrs. Hardeman almost diagonally across the table from her was talking to her neighbor. It was with a feeling of shock that she realized no one seemed to notice the slightly billowing movement of her blouse as his hand circled and fondled the breast beneath.

"What did you do?" Sally had asked.

Her girl friend had looked at her with a curiously wise expression. "Nothing," she had answered flatly. "If no one saw what was happening or, at least, pretended not to, who was I to make a fuss? After all, it was Loren Hardeman." And then she giggled. "Then when I looked around the table and thought how stupid they all were not see what was happening, I began to enjoy it."

"You didn't!" Sally breathed.

"Yes," the girl answered. "There was something about his touch that was very exciting."

"Then what did you do?" Sally had asked.

Her girl friend had smiled. "After dinner was over I went to the bathroom and hooked up my brassiere."

That was all there was to that story, but there were others. Now Sally could believe them all. She dragged again on the cigarette but her legs still refused to stop trembling. She hoped no one would come into the hallway and see her like this.

She had knocked softly on the door when she had come upstairs. "Daddy Hardeman," she called softly.

There was no answer.

She knocked and called again, then thinking he was still asleep, she tried the door. It swung open silently and she went inside. "Daddy Hardeman," she called softly again before she saw that the bed was empty and noticed the light coming through the bathroom door.

She had turned to leave when a reflection in the large mirror over the bureau on the far wall transfixed her. In the mirror she could see through the open door into her mother-in-law's bedroom and silhouetted in it were two naked figures.

Her father-in-law was holding a naked girl in the air above him. He began to laugh and the sound seemed to rumble in the room as he lowered the girl onto him. The girl cried once and began to moan as he disappeared into her.

It wasn't until he began to walk across the room, the girl still with her legs wrapped around his waist, and disappeared from the mirror that Sally found herself able to move. There was a creak from the protesting bed-springs, then a cry almost of pain, and the mirror was empty. Quickly Sally slipped out of the bedroom.

The cigarette was half finished and she felt self-control coming back. She began to feel anger rising inside her. Almost as if she had suffered a strange kind of personal violation an ache began to spread through her loins with a warm, pulsing pain. He wasn't like a man at all, he was an animal not only in the way he looked all covered with hair with swollen giant parts but also in his brutal manner, careless of all sensitivities.

She began to feel better. Her anger had helped. How fortunate she was that Loren was nothing like his father. Kind, considerate, and gentle. Even today, when they had gone upstairs to their first bedroom together to rest for the ball this evening.

She had not known what to expect. But all he did was to kiss her softly and tell her to lie down on the bed and rest until it would be time to get ready. Then he lay down beside her and closed his eyes. In a moment, the soft sound of his breathing told her he was asleep. She could not fall asleep at once; she lay there watching his quiet face and after a while she, too, slept.

She dropped the cigarette into a tall urn standing in the hall and started for the staircase, when the door to her father-in-law's bedroom opened and he stood there.

"Sally," he said, his voice calm as if nothing had happened. "Why aren't you at the party? After all, it is in your honor."

She felt her face beginning to flush. "Actually," she said, "I was just on my way to get you. The guests were beginning to wonder where you were."

He looked at her silently for a moment, then he smiled. "How thoughtful of you," he said, taking her arm. "Then let's not disappoint them, shall we?"

Her legs began to tremble again at his touch and she stumbled slightly as they turned toward the steps. He paused and looked at her. "You're shaking. Are you all right?"

Again that curious, warm, pulsing pain inside her. Somehow she couldn't bring herself to meet his direct gaze. "I'm okay." She managed to laugh. "After all, it's not every day that is a girl's wedding day."

Elizabeth, looking up, saw them coming down the grand stairway. Loren's red hair was just beginning to pepper with gray but his face was as strong and as young as the day they had met. She felt a twinge inside as she saw Sally's blond head turn toward Loren. Loren and she used to be like that. At first it seemed as if they were always laughing.

But that changed as soon as they had arrived in Detroit. Back in Bethlehem Loren had always been fun, never serious, had a joke and a good word for everyone. Then he got into the automobile business and everything changed.

There were the early jobs at Peerless and Maxwell, then Ford, which was over almost before it had begun, and finally with the Dodge Brothers, where Junior had been born in 1901, Loren's first year there. He had remained with the Dodges for almost nine years until they had a falling-out. The trouble was that Loren wanted to build a better car which would sell for slightly more than the standard medium-priced car of the time and the Dodge Brothers, weren't at all interested. They were still angry at Ford and all they wanted to do was to compete with him.

In vain Loren had argued with them. The Model T was unassailable. There was nothing that could be built that could compete with it in its time. He correctly predicted that the Model T, which first came on the market in 1908, would sweep the country. And he had been right. In less than two years Ford was producing almost fifty percent of the cars in America, and Loren left the Dodge Brothers.

There was a market for a good medium-priced car, however, and Loren drew a tight bead on it. In 1911 the first Sundancer appeared on the streets of Detroit. And from that point on, none of the medium-priced cars could come anywhere near it in popularity. Not the Buick, nor the Leland, nor the Oldsmobile. They weren't even in the same league, and almost overnight, it seemed, Bethlehem Motors had become a big business and Loren had lost the gift of laughter.

But tonight he was smiling and there was something in his face that made him seem young again. The orchestra broke into a waltz and Loren held out his arm. Sally swept into it and they began to dance.

Tears filled Elizabeth's eyes. He looked so young, so strong, so vital that if one did not know, they could think that he, not his son, was the bridegroom. Junior came up to the couple on the floor and with a bow, Loren relinquished Sally to her husband. He turned and came toward her.

He kissed her cheek. "It's a beautiful party, Mother."

She looked into his face. "How do you feel, Father?"

He smiled ruefully. "A little bit hung over, I think. I'll have to learn to handle bootleg a little better."

The butler came up to them. His voice lowered discreetly. "Everything is ready, sir."

Loren nodded. He turned to Elizabeth. "Is it all right to do it now, Mother?"

She nodded and he took her arm and led her out into the middle of the ballroom floor. He held up both hands and the music came to a stop.

"Ladies and gentlemen." His voice boomed into every corner of the large ballroom. "As you all know, this is a very special occasion for Mother and myself. It isn't every day that our son finds himself a bride, especially such a beautiful one."

A ripple of laughter and a scattering of applause went through the room. "Loren and Sally," he called. "Come out here on the floor where the folks can get a good look at you."

Junior was smiling and she was blushing as they took up their places beside his parents. Junior stood next to his father, slim and straight and as tall, but without the bigness of the older man.

"This is Detroit," Loren said in his large voice. "And what better gift to give a newly wed couple than a brand-new car? That's the Detroit way of doing things, isn't it?"

An answering roar of approval came from the guests. Loren smiled and held up his hand for silence. He turned to his son. "So, Loren, here is the surprise we have for you and your bride—a brand-new car. New from front bumper to rear, from top to the very bottom of the tires. Your very own car. We're calling it the Loren II and next year it will be on sale in every Bethlehem dealer's across the country."

The orchestra broke into a popular Sousa march as the French doors to the garden opened. There was the quiet sound of a powerful motor and the automobile came into the ballroom. The crowd parted and the chauffeur carefully drove it to the center of the ballroom floor and came to a halt in front of the Hardemans.

A murmur of approval came from the crowd and they began to press forward to get a closer look at the new car. They were Detroiters and to them there was nothing more important. And this car was important. There was no doubt about that. The burgundy-red and black sedan was easily one of the most important cars ever to be seen in this automobile-conscious city.

They stopped, suddenly aware that the rear passenger compartment behind the chauffeur was completely filled with what seemed like thousands of sheets of green-and-gold-colored paper. Loren held up his hand and they all looked at him.

"I suppose you're all wondering what that is in the back of the car?" He didn't wait for their reply. Instead he walked over to the door of the car and opened it. The sheets of paper spilled out as if propelled. He picked up one sheet and held it over his head toward the crowd. His voice boomed over the sudden silence.

"Each one of these pieces of paper represents one share of stock in the Bethlehem Motor Company and there are a hundred thousand of them in this car. Each one of them made out to my son, Loren Hardeman, Jr. That hundred thousand shares is equal to ten percent of my company and my accountants tell me that they are worth somewhere between twenty-five and thirty million dollars."

He turned to his son. "And that, Loren, is just a small token of the love and affection your mother and I have for you."

Junior stood there for a moment, his face pale. He tried to speak but no words came. Silently he gripped his father's hand, then turned his mother's and kissed her.

At the same moment, Loren bent and kissed his daughter-in-law. A startled look came into her eyes and she felt the trembling suddenly return to her legs. She put a hand on his arm to steady herself, then turned to kiss her mother-in-law.

The guests went wild with approval and began to surround them with congratulations and good wishes. It was pandemonium.

At the back of the ballroom a reporter for the *Detroit Free Press* was busy scribbling his notes. The headline the next day was both a question and a statement. AND WHEN HENRY GAVE EDSEL A MILLION IN GOLD FOR A WEDDING PRESENT, HE THOUGHT THAT WAS SOMETHING?

Chapter Five

The faint sounds of "Three O'Clock in the Morning" came from the ballroom into the library of the Hardeman Manor where a bar had been set up for the men who wanted to have a real drink, away from the dance floor. Only champagne was served at the ball.

Loren was standing at the bar, one foot on the rail, the whiskey in his hand. His face was flushed and perspiring as he stood in the small circle of men. "The sedan is the car of the future," he said. "You mark my words. In the next ten or fifteen years the open touring car as we know it will be gone. People have got to be tired of freezing in the winter, getting soaked in the rain, and cooking in the sun. Someday they'll even have air-conditioners in cars the same way they're beginning to have heaters now."

"It won't seem like driving then," one of the men said.

"So what?" Loren retorted. "The idea is to get there in comfort. That's what it's going to be all about. The smoother the ride, the more customers for the car. Wait until the Loren II gets on the market next year, you'll see I know what I'm talking about."

The same man said doubtfully, "Seventeen hundred dollars is a lot of money."

"They'll pay it," Loren said confidently. "The American public knows what it wants. They'll pay a little more for quality anytime."

"Did you make a bid for the Dodge Brothers?" another man asked.

Loren shook his head. "It's not for me. I'm not about to go up against Ford and Chevy. I'm strictly middle range."

"I hear GM offered a hundred and forty-six million," the first man said.

"They're damn fools," said Loren.

"You mean the offer is too much?"

Loren shook his head. "Too little. They won't get it. I know a Wall Street house has come up with a higher bid." He turned around to the two men standing behind him. "Hey, Walter," he said to the taller man. "You're the one that ought to buy the Dodges. It could fill a hole in your line and then you could give GM a real run for their money."

Walter Chrysler smiled. "I looked into it. But I'm not ready yet. I've still got my hands filled with the Maxwell. Maybe in a few years."

"Once Wall Street gets their hands into something, it'll be too late. You know how those boys operate."

Chrysler smiled again. "I can wait, Loren. Wall Street may be able to sell stocks and bonds, but running an automobile company is another game altogether. They'll find that out. By then, I might be ready."

A butler threw open the two massive doors of the library which had insulated them against the rest of the house, and the sounds of the affair ending came into the room. Quickly the men finished their drinks and left to claim their wives and make their departures, and soon Loren was standing alone in the room except for the bartender. He had just poured himself another drink when Junior and Sally entered.

He held up his glass. "To the bride and groom." He swallowed the whiskey neat. "It was a great party," he said. "A great party."

Junior laughed. "That it was, Father."

Loren looked at him. "Where's your mother?"

"She went upstairs," Junior said quickly. "She asked us to find you and tell you. She was very tired."

Loren didn't speak. He signaled for another drink. The bartender refilled his glass. "Join me in a drink" he said.

"No, thank you, Father," said Junior. "I think we'll be going up too. It's been a long day."

Loren chuckled knowingly. "You kids can't wait, eh? I would've thought you'd already grabbed one during the matinee this afternoon."

A quick vision of the naked, hairy body she had seen in the mirror flashed through Sally's mind. Her voice was indignant. "Daddy Hardeman! How can you say something like that?"

Loren laughed genially. "I'm not that old that I don't know what's on the minds of you youngsters." He put his hands on her shoulders and spun around and sent her toward the door with a slap on the behind. "You go upstairs and get ready for your husband. I want to talk with him for a minute. I promise I won't keep him long."

She left the library, her nose in the air. Loren looked after her appreciatively, then turned to his son. "That's a fine hunk of woman you got there, Junior," he said. "I hope you know it."

"I know it, Father," Junior said quietly.

Loren clapped him on the shoulder. "C'mon, have a drink."

Junior hesitated a moment. "I'll have a brandy," he said to the bartender.

"Brandy!" Loren roared. "What kind of a sissy drink is that? Have a real drink. Bartender, give him a whiskey."

The drink was placed in front of Junior. "What did you want to talk to me about, Father?"

"Mother tells me you and Sally are thinking of buying a house out in Ann Arbor," Loren said.

Junior nodded. "We like it out there."

"What wrong with Grosse Point?" Loren asked. "I can get the Sanders' place. Or if you don't like that, any place else you choose."

"Sally and I like the country, Father," Junior replied. "We thought we'd get a place with some room and land for a few horses, things like that."

"Horses!" Loren exploded. "What the hell do you want with horses? We're in the automobile business!"

"Sally and I like to ride." Junior's voice became slightly defensive. "I don't think anyone can criticize us for that."

"No one is," Loren said quickly. "But Ann Arbor, that's way the hell out. You'll have nobody to talk to on the weekends. There's no automobile people out there. How about Bloomfield Hills? At least there are people there that you know."

"That's just it, Father," Junior explained stubbornly. "We want to be by ourselves."

Loren drank his whiskey and got another. "Listen to me, son," he said heavily. "Beginning the first of the year, you're the executive vice-president of this company, in a couple of years, you'll be president. I don't want to be working forever and I think your mother and I are entitled to some time off. When you have that kind of responsibility you got to be where people can get to you real quick. You can't live off somewhere in the wilderness where people can't find you."

"Ann Arbor isn't the wilderness," Junior answered. "It's only a little more than an hour away."

Loren was silent for a moment. He looked around the room. "You know, son, if it weren't for your mother, I wouldn't even live here. Maybe someday, I'll build an office building out at the plant and the top floor of it will be an apartment."

Junior smiled. "That's one way of keeping on top of things."

Loren looked at him and then laughed. "Okay, son, you do what you want. But mark my words, in a little while you'll be looking for a place back here."

"Maybe, Father. We'll see."

His father shoved him on the shoulder. "Okay, Loren, get on upstairs. It's not a good thing to keep a bride waiting on her wedding night."

Junior nodded and started to turn away, then he stopped and turned back. "Father."

"Yes, Loren?"

The young man smiled. Loren felt something tug inside him, he saw his wife in that smile. Almost the same gentleness. "Thank you, Father, thank you. For everything."

"Go on, go on," Loren said gruffly. "Your bride is waiting." Then he turned to the bar so that his son would not see the sudden wetness in his eyes.

"Good night, Father."

"Good night, son.' He listened to the footsteps recede and when they were gone he finished his drink. Junior's was still on the bar, untouched. He looked at it for a moment, then took out his massive gold pocket watch and opened it. The picture of Elizabeth and Junior taken so many years ago looked back up at him. It was 4 A.M. He sighed.

He closed the watch and put it back in his pocket. He left the library slowly and wandered through the house to the ballroom. It seemed strangely silent and empty now that all the people had gone and there were only a few scattered servants tending to the final chores of the night.

He went to the French doors leading to the garden. The Loren II was standing out there on the terrace, dark and beautiful in the pale moonlight. Slowly he walked over to it and around it.

It was sheer beauty, no matter from what angle you looked at it.

He opened the driver's door and got in. He sank comfortably into the cushions and put his hands on the steering wheel. Even without the motor running, it felt alive and strong to him. He wondered whether Junior felt the same things about the car that he did.

But even as he wondered, he already knew the answer. Junior did not. For Junior it was not the car itself, it was merely the business he happened to be born into. Maybe someday Junior would feel as he did. Junior had never built a car with his own hands. That could be the reason.

He leaned forward and rested his head on his arms on the steering wheel and closed his eyes. A peculiar weariness came over him.

"Loren," he whispered half to himself. "Couldn't you see? It wasn't the stock certificates, it wasn't the money. It was the car. That's what I wanted to give you. That's why I called it the Loren II."

He fell asleep.

Sally was naked beneath the sheets in the dark bedroom when he came back from the bathroom. He stood next to the bed, looking down at her while he buttoned the top button of his pajamas.

"Sally," he whispered.

"Yes, Loren."

He knelt beside the bed, his face level with her own. "I love you, Sally."

She turned and put her arms around his neck. "I love you."

He kissed her gently. "I will always love you."

She closed her eyes, her arms tightening around him, drawing him up to her. They kissed again.

He raised his head. "I know you must be very tired—"

She placed a finger over his lips, then drew his head down to her breast, letting him feel the nakedness of her. His breath drew in sharply and his mouth closed on her nipple. She felt the heat begin to run through her and closed her eyes.

A vision of a naked, giant hairy body jumped onto the screen of her lids and she climaxed even before her husband was inside her.

It was at that moment that she knew her father-in-law had taken possession of her body and had come between them on their wedding night.

Chapter Six

She fought her way up through the field of pain and opened her eyes. Her vision blurred, then cleared as she focused on the face of the doctor, leaning over her. As he straightened up, she saw the nurse behind him, and Loren.

Loren looked tired, as if he had been awake all night. The doctor stepped back and Loren came forward. He seemed so tall standing there beside the bed. So tall and so strong.

She tried to smile. "Loren."

His voice was gentle. "Yes, Elizabeth."

"It didn't turn out to be much of a vacation, did it?" she whispered.

He reached for her hand. "We can always have a vacation. When you're well again."

She made no reply. There would be no more vacations. Not for her. But she didn't have to say it. He knew that as well as she.

"Have you heard from the children?" she asked.

"I spoke to Junior on the telephone. He wanted to come down here. But I told him not to. Sally's due any day now."

"Good," she whispered. "He should be with his wife. Especially after they waited so long for the first baby."

"They didn't wait so long."

"They've been married almost four years," she said. "I was beginning to feel I would never be a grandmother."

"What's so important about being a grandparent?" he asked. "I don't feel like a grandfather."

She smiled. He didn't look like a grandfather. At fifty-one he was still a young man. Big and broad and virile. Bursting with the forces of life.

She turned her eyes toward the window. Outside the bright Florida sunshine fell from a clear blue sky and the breeze ruffled through the gently swaying palm trees. "It is beautiful outside?" she asked.

"Yes," he answered. "It's a lovely day."

Her eyes were still on the window. "I love it here. I don't want to go back to Detroit, Loren."

"There's no hurry," he said. "First, you get well—"

She turned to look up at him, her eyes were steady on him. "You know what I mean, Loren. Afterwards. I want to stay here."

He was silent.

She pressed his hand. "I'm sorry, Loren."

His voice was husky. "There's nothing to be sorry about."

"Yes, there is," she said quickly. There was so much she had to say that she could never tell him now. But now it was all clear. The triumphs, the failures, the laughter, the pain. There was so much they had shared together and so much more they might have shared that they had not. Now she could see it all. "I was never enough of a woman for you," she whispered. "Not that I didn't want to be. But I couldn't. You knew that, didn't you? That I wanted to be."

"You're talking like a ninny," he said gruffly. "You've always been a good wife, the only wife I ever wanted."

"Loren, I know I've been a good wife," she smiled, almost reprovingly. "But that's not what I was talking about."

He was silent.

"I wanted you to know I never blamed you for the others. I knew what it was that you needed and in a curious sort of way was glad for you that you could have it. My only regret was that I who wanted to give you everything, couldn't find it in myself to give you that."

"You gave me more than any woman ever gave a man, more than any woman ever gave me," he said earnestly. "You never failed me. Maybe it was I who failed you. But I love you. I have always loved you. You believe that, don't you, Elizabeth?"

She looked into his eyes for a long moment, then she nodded slightly. "And I have always loved you, Loren," she whispered. "From the moment I walked into your little bicycle shop in Bethlehem all that time ago."

Their hands tightened and memory flowed alive and present between them.

It had been a warm summer Sunday in Bethlehem; the great steel mills had banked their furnaces on Saturday night and only the faintest wisps of gray smoke came from the chimneys. The sun shone bright and high as Elizabeth walked her bicycle out the side door of her house to meet her girl friend.

The basket attached to the handlebars was filled with goodies for the picnic they had planned. She hadn't told her mother but there were also going to be two young men. Her mother was very strict about those things. Before she would let Elizabeth see any man, he had to come to the house first for an inspection, and by the time that was over, he had been made to feel so uncomfortable that she rarely ever saw him again. Now she knew better. The young men were to meet them at the edge of town where there would be no chance of her parents seeing them.

Her girl friend had been waiting, the basket on the handlebars of her bicycle also packed tightly. They started off, the wide brims of their hats flapping in the breeze, pulling against the ribbons tied under their chins.

They chattered as they rode along the quiet streets. It was early in the morning and there wasn't much traffic about. The carriages would be out later when it was time for church services. Then the streets would be filled and difficult to pass as each driver would try to urge his horse to step smartly.

The trouble came two blocks from her house when they turned off the cobble-stoned street onto a dirt road. Elizabeth didn't see the deep wagon rut on the side of the street and over she went, the picnic goodies spilling over the ground beside her.

"Are you hurt?" her girl friend asked, coming to a stop.

Elizabeth shook her head. "No." She got to her feet and began to brush off her dress. It wasn't too bad. "Help me pick up."

She began to place the food back into the wire basket when she saw the front wheel of the bicycle. "Oh no!" she groaned in dismay.

The wheel was bent out of shape. There was no way the bike could move. "What do we do now?" she asked. It was Sunday and all the repair shops would be closed. "That's the end of the picnic for me," she said. "I might as well go home."

Her girl friend said quickly. "I know where you can get it fixed." She picked up the last of the wrapped sandwiches. "My cousin just rented an old barn back of his house to a young man who repairs bicycles. He's there all the time. Even on Sundays. He's working on some kind of an invention."

Twenty minutes later they were at the barn back of the house. The door was open as they came up. Inside they heard a man singing in a loud, untuneful voice. The song was mixed with the clanging of a hammer against metal. They knocked on the open barn door. Apparently they weren't heard because of the singing and the banging went on uninterrupted.

"Hello," Elizabeth called. "Is there anyone in there?"

The singing stopped and so did the hammering. After a moment a voice came out of the dark interior. "Nope. Only some field mice."

"Do the field mice know how to fix a bicycle?" Elizabeth called back.

There was a silence, then a young man appeared out of the darkness. He was tall and broad and covered with a light red-gold hair down to his waist which was bare. He stood there squinting at them in the bright sunlight. Then he smiled. It was a warm smile filled with a very masculine knowledge. "What can I do for you, ladies?"

"First you can put on a shirt," Elizabeth said. "Then when you're properly dressed you can fix my wheel."

Loren looked down at the bicycle for a moment, then back up at her. He stood there silently, just staring at her.

Elizabeth felt the colour begin to flow into her face. "Don't be all day about it!" she said sharply. "Can't you see we're going on a picnic?"

He nodded, almost as if to himself, and disappeared into the barn. A moment later the tuneless singing and hammering began again.

Five minutes later after waiting in vain for the young man to reappear, she went to the barn door and peered in. At the back of the barn there was a forge with an open fire and the young man stood in front of it, swinging a hammer against a piece of metal on an anvil. "Young man!" she called.

The hammer stopped in mid-air. He turned. "Yes, ma'am?"

"Are you going to fix my bicycle?" she asked.

The answer came promptly. "No, ma'am."

"Why not?"

"Because you haven't told me who you're going to picnic with."

"You have a nerve!" she snapped. "What business is it of yours who I picnic with?"

He put the hammer carefully down on a bench and walked toward her. "I think the man you're going to marry has every right to know who you're going to picnic with."

She looked up into his face and there was something in his expression that turned her legs to water. She put a hand on the door to steady herself. "You?" she said breathlessly. "That's silly, I don't even know your name."

"Loren Hardeman, ma'am," he smiled. "What's yours?"

"Elizabeth Frazer," she said. Somehow the saying of her name seemed to strengthen her. "Now, will you fix my bicycle?"

"No, Elizabeth," he said quietly. "What kind of man would I be if I fixed your bicycle so that my girl could go off and picnic with another man?"

"But I'm not your girl!" she protested.

"Then you soon will be," he said calmly. He reached out and took her hand.

She felt the weakness come back into her. "But, my parents," she said in a confused voice. "You don't—they don't—know you."

He didn't answer. Just held onto her hand and looked down at her.

Her eyes fell. "Mr. Hardeman," she said in a small voice, looking down at the floor. "Now will you please fix my bike?"

He still didn't answer.

She didn't look up. Her voice grew even smaller. "I apologize for being rude to you when you came out, Mr. Hardeman."

"Loren," he said. "You might as well get used to the name. I'm not the old-fashioned kind who holds to the idea of wives calling their husbands 'mister'."

She looked up at him. Suddenly she smiled. "Loren," she said tentatively as if trying its sound on her tongue.

"That's better," he smiled back. He let go of her hand. "Now you wait right there."

He started toward the rear of the barn. "Where are you going?" she called after him.

"To wash up and put on a clean shirt," he said. "After all, a man should look his best when he goes to meet his future in-laws."

"Now?" she asked in an incredulous voice. "Right now?"

"Of course," he called back over his shoulder. "I'm not the type of man who believes in long engagements."

But he still had to wait almost two years before they were married. That wasn't until May of 1900 because her parents wouldn't let her marry before she was eighteen years old. And during the time they waited he built his first automobile.

It wasn't really an automobile. It was more of a quadricycle, with its strange bicycle wheels and tires and spindly frame. It ran well enough to get itself banned from the main streets in Bethlehem for causing a disturbance, but not well enough to satisfy him.

There was more he had to learn and he knew it. And only one place to get the knowledge. Detroit. There were more automobile builders there than anywhere else in the United States. Henry Ford. Ransom E. Olds. Billy Durant. Charles Nash. Walter Chrysler. Henry Leland. The Dodge Brothers. These men were his heroes and his gods. And it was to sit at their feet and to learn, that one week after their marriage, he and his already pregnant but unknowing bride moved to Detroit.

The memory was still warm within him. He glanced out the window at the sun and the swaying palms. "It was a day like this," he said. "It was a beautiful Sunday."

"Yes," she whispered. "I'm grateful for that. It was the first of many beautiful Sundays we had together."

"We haven't seen the last of them," he said, turning to look down at her. "Just you get well and—" His voice suddenly broke. "Elizabeth!"

There were to be no more beautiful Sundays for her.

Chapter Seven

Junior's voice was unemotional, the figures rattling from his tongue as if he were a tabulating machine. "The 1928 report looks good," he said. "The Sundancer passenger cars, all models, went over four hundred and twenty thousand units, eighty percent top of the line, mostly sedans. Accessories and extras were sold for over sixty percent of the units. The truck division also had a substantial increase, up twenty-one percent over the previous year, accounting for forty-one thousand units. The only line which did not show an increase was the Loren II. There we had trouble holding our own and if it weren't for the liberalization of the consumer credit terms and our own guarantee to the dealers we would have fallen back. As it is, we held even with thirty-four thousand units. It's the only division in which we're losing money. By the time the car is passed on to the consumer, we're dropping almost four hundred and ten dollars per unit."

Loren picked up a heavy Havana cigar from his desk and toyed with it. Slowly he clipped the end from it, then sniffed it gently. It smelled good. He lit a match and toasted the end of it carefully, then put it in his mouth and held the fire to it. After a moment, he blew out a gust of blue smoke which curled like a cloud over his head as it rose to the ceiling.

He pushed the box toward his son. "Have a cigar?"

Junior shook his head.

Loren took another deep puff and let the smoke out. "There are only two things that will ever get a man to wear perfume," he said. "One is if they make it smell like a fine Havana, the other is if they make it smell like pussy."

Junior didn't smile. "The dealers don't like the Loren II either. Their big complaint is that there's no service business on the car after they sell it."

Loren looked at him shrewdly. "You mean they're bitching because the car's too good."

"I didn't say that," Junior said. "But maybe that's it. Most cars require oil changes every thousand miles, the Loren II only once every four thousand miles. The same goes for brake adjustments. The Loren's the only car on the road right now with self-adjusting brakes."

"Are you suggesting we bring down the quality of the car?" his father asked.

"I'm not suggesting anything," Junior said. "I'm just calling it to your attention because I think we ought to do something about it. We're dropping almost fourteen million a year on it."

Loren studied the fine gray ash on the end of his Havana. "That's the best car I ever built," he said. "Pound for dollar it's the best car on the road today."

"Nobody is going to dispute that fact," Junior said calmly. "But what we're talking about is money. People shop price, not quality. Give them a big average quality car at an average price or a medium-size high-quality car at the same price and they'll pick the big one every time. Buicks, Olds, Chrysler, and Hudson are proving that every day. They're walking away from us."

Loren looked down at his cigar again. "What do you suggest?"

"The market in electrical refrigerators and ranges is growing every day," Junior said. "I have a chance to buy a small company that's turning out a very commercial line and is in trouble. They need capital for expansion and can't get it. I figured out that I can move them into the Loren plant and we'd wind up making a lot of money."

"Nothing will ever replace the icebox," Loren said. "Did you ever smell anything that comes out of those electric refrigerators?"

"That was years ago," Junior said. "Now it's different. General Electric, Nash, General Motors, even, they all are in it. It's the coming thing."

"And what about the Loren II?" his father asked.

Junior looked at him. "We'll drop it. We're licked and we might as well admit it."

Loren put his cigar carefully into a tray on the desk. He rose from the chair and walked over to the window of his office. Everywhere he looked there was activity.

Down at the far end of the plant, a train was beginning to move out slowly, trailing flatbed cars filled with automobiles. On the river side of the plant, a cargo ship was unloading coal to stoke the furnaces of the refining mill near the docks. The long, almost tunnel-like assembly plants were humming with activity as the raw materials went in one end and came out as automobiles at the other. And over it all hung the gray heavy pall of the smoke called industry.

"No," he said finally, without turning around. "We keep building the Loren II. We'll find a way to make it go. I can't believe that in the middle of the greatest prosperity this country has ever known a quality car won't sell. Remember what the President said—two cars in every garage, two chickens in every pot. And Mr. Hoover knows what he's talking about. It's up to us to make sure that in this year of our Lord, 1929, one of those two cars in every garage will be ours."

Junior was silent for a moment. "Then we'll have to do something about getting the cost down. At the present rate, the more we sell, the more we lose."

Loren turned from the window. "We'll get on that right away. You tell that young man, what's his name, in production-engineering, to come up and see me. I like his spirit."

"You mean John Duncan?"

"That's the one," Loren said. "I hired him away from Charley Sorenson at Ford. We'll turn him loose on the Loren production line. Let's see what he can come up with."

"Bannigan will be angry," Junior said.

Bannigan was the chief production engineer and head of the department. "Too bad," said Loren. "We pay off on work, not temper."

"He might quit," Junior said. "He's got that offer from Chrysler."

"Good," Loren said. "In that case don't give him a choice. Tell him to take the offer."

"What if he doesn't?"

"You're president of the company now, fire him anyway," Loren said. "I'm sick and tired of listening to him tell me why it can't be done. I want someone who will do it."

"Okay," Junior said. "Is that all?"

"Yes," Loren answered. The tone of his voice changed. "How's my grandson?"

Junior smiled his first smile of the meeting. "Growing. You ought to see him. He's almost eleven pounds now and only two and a half months old. We think he's going to be big like you."

Loren returned the smile. "Sounds great. Maybe I'll take a run out there one morning."

"You do that," Junior said. "Sally will be glad to see you too."

"How is she?"

"Fine. She's got her figure back but she keeps complaining she's too heavy."

"Don't give her a chance to get set," Loren laughed. "Have another real quick. And make it a girl this time. I think it would be nice to name her after your mother."

"I don't know. Sally had a pretty rough time with this one."

"She's all right, isn't she?" Loren asked quickly. "Nothing's wrong with her?"

"She's perfect," Junior replied.

"Then pay no attention to her, son. Women always have to have something to bitch about. You just do your job and you'll find soon enough that she'll have no complaints."

"We'll see," Junior was noncommittal. He started to leave. His father called him back. "Yes?"

"That icebox company your were talking about. You really think it's a good deal?"

"I do."

"Then buy it."

Junior looked at him. "But where will we put it? I was figuring on the Loren building."

"Come over here," Loren said. He walked to the window and opened it. The roar of the factory came flooding into the room. He leaned out of the window and pointed. "How about there?"

Junior stuck his head out the window and looked. "But that's the old warehouse."

Loren nodded. "It's also a hundred and ten thousand square feet of production space that ain't doing nothing but gathering dust and rust."

"It's also where we store parts and replacements," said Junior.

"Get rid of it," Loren said. "Why the hell did we establish regional parts depots all over the country if we're going to keep that junk in our own backyard?" He walked back to his desk and picked up his cigar. He smelled it with obvious satisfaction. "Ship it all out to the depots and tell them what a great favor we're doing them. Instead of the usual ten days or tenth of the month, they won't have to pay us for ninety days."

"That's not fair, Father, and you know it. They'll never sell at least fifty percent of that stuff."

Loren relit the cigar and puffed on it. "Who said anything about being fair? Shove it to them just like they shove it to us when they get the chance. One thing you better learn and learn real good. There's no such thing as an honest car-dealer. They're the direct descendants of the old horse-thieves. And they'll steal from anybody who gives them the opportunity. You, me, their customers, even their mothers. You didn't hear them weeping when they hit us for the extra two hundred dollars a car on the Loren II when they knew we were losing over two hundred a unit at that time. Oh, no, they promised to pass it on to the customer. But you and I know better. They kept it for themselves. So don't go feeling sorry for them. Save your sympathy for where it counts. For us."

Junior was quiet for a moment. "Somehow I can't believe that. Not all of them can be that bad."

Loren laughed. "Did you ever meet a poor automobile dealer?"

Junior didn't answer.

"Tell you what, I'll make you an offer," Loren said. "You take a lamp and go like Diogenes to look for one honest car dealer. Just one, no more. And when you find him, you bring him here to me and I will give you all the rest of my stock in this here company and quit the business!"

"Will there be anything else, Mr. Hardeman?" his secretary asked.

Junior shook his head wearily. "I think that should do it, Miss Fisher."

He watched her gather up the papers and leave the office. The door closed silently and respectfully behind her. He leaned back in his chair and closed his eyes. It seemed that the details never ended. It was always a surprise to him how much his father knew about what was taking place in the business without seeming to exert any effort. He had to exhaust himself just to keep up with the tiny day-to-day affairs, much less the overall management of the company.

Right now, he could use an administrative vice-president just to keep the organization moving smoothly. But his father was against it.

"The only way to run a business is to run it yourself," he had said when Junior asked for permission to hire an assistant. "That way everyone knows who is the boss. I did it that way all my life and it worked."

It didn't make any difference how much Junior explained that times were changing and the demands were greater. His father's final word on the subject was that he hadn't made him president of the company so that he could shirk his responsibilities. That he was not about to go off and leave his business in the hands of strangers. And that the only reason he felt secure in leaving for Europe in May for the first vacation he had ever taken in his life was because his son was in charge.

Junior had listened with a certain kind of inner skepticism. He had heard those tales before. He would believe them when his father got on the boat. He took out his watch and looked at it.

It was nine forty-five. He reached for the telephone. His secretary answered.

"Would you get Mrs. Hardeman for me?"

There was a buzz on the line and a moment later Sally answered. "Hello."

"Hello, darling," he said. "I'm sorry, I didn't realize it was so late. I hope you didn't wait dinner for me."

Her voice was cool. "When I didn't hear from you by eight, I figured you were tied up and had something."

"Good," he said. "How's the baby?"

"Fine."

"Look, it's late," he said. "And I don't feel up to that hour's drive home tonight. Especially when I have a seven o'clock appointment back here tomorrow morning. Do you mind if I stay down at the club?"

There was the barest hesitation in her voice. "No. Not if you're that tired."

"I'll make it home early tomorrow night," he promised.

"Okay," she said. "You get a good night's rest."

"You, too. Good night, darling.'

A click told him she had gone off the line. Slowly he put the telephone down. She was angry. He knew that. It was the second time this week he had stayed in town. His father had been right. It had been a mistake moving all the way out to Ann Arbor. This weekend he would have a long talk with Sally about moving to Grosse Point.

He picked up the phone again. "Call the club," he told his secretary. "Tell them I'll be in and to have Samuel wait for me. I'll want a massage before I turn in."

He began to feel better almost before putting down the phone. That was the ticket. A very light dinner, then a hot, relaxing bath. Afterwards he would climb into bed nude and Samuel would come in with his mixture of soothing oils and alcohol. The tensions would leave him almost at the first laying on of his hands and languor would overcome him. He would be fast asleep by the time the masseur left. A deep, safe, dreamless sleep.

Sally put down the telephone and walked back into the living room. Loren looked up at her from the couch. "Is there anything wrong?"

She shook her head. "That was Loren. He's staying at the club tonight. He's too tired for the drive home."

"Did you tell him I was here?"

"No,' she said. "It wouldn't have made any difference." She picked up another glass from the cocktail table in front of him. "Let me fix you a fresh drink."

"Fix one for yourself while you're at it," Loren said. "You look like you can use it."

"I can't have any," she said. "Not till I finish weaning the baby." She handed him a glass. "Now you just relax and make yourself comfortable while I give your grandson his ten o'clock feeding. I won't be long."

Loren got to his feet. "I'll come with you." ·

She gave him a curious look but didn't answer. He followed her up the steps to the nursery. A tiny night bulb glowed in a corner of the room, casting a faint yellow light behind the crib.

They walked silently and looked down at the baby. He was asleep, his eyes tightly shut. She reached in and picked him up. He began to cry almost immediately.

"He's hungry," she whispered, crossing swiftly to a chair and sitting in it. She was in the shadows, her back to the light. He heard the soft rustle of her clothing, then abruptly the cries ceased and instead there was a faint smacking sound as the baby fed.

She looked up at him. His eyes glowed like an animal's in the reflected yellow light. There was a strangely intense expression on his face. "I can't see," he said.

Slowly she turned in the chair until she and the baby were bathed in the soft glow. She heard his footsteps and when she looked up, he was standing over them.

"My God !" he said in a hushed voice "That's beautiful!"

A warm wetness rushed through her and she was suddenly angry. "You might try telling that to your son."

He didn't speak. Instead he placed his hand on her bare shoulder and pressed her reassuringly.

Startled, she looked up into his face for a moment, then turned and kissed his hand. The tears ran into her eyes and spilled down her cheeks onto his hand. She leaned her face against him. "I'm sorry, Daddy Hardeman," she whispered.

His free hand stroked her hair gently. "That's all right, child," he said softly. "I understand."

"Do you?" she whispered, almost savagely. "He's not like you. He's cold, he keeps everything inside himself, locked up where nobody can reach him." She looked up at him. "I'm not like that at all. I—"

He placed a silencing finger on her lips. "I said I understand."

She looked at him without speaking. She felt the strength of him flowing out and enveloping her and she knew he felt all the things that she did. "Is it so wrong?" she asked.

He shook his head.

"I saw you with that woman on my wedding night," she said.

"I know you did," he answered. "I saw it in your eyes."

"Then what makes that right and this wrong?"

Again he shook his head slowly. "The time. This is not the time." He looked down at the suckling child. "You've got more important things to do."

The old unreasoning anger came up in her. Why did he always have to be sure of himself, so right? "I'm a fool," she said bitterly. "A damned stupid fool."

"No, you're not," he said with a smile. "You're just a normal healthy young woman whose husband deserves a swift kick in the ass for neglecting his homework." He started for the door. "And maybe I'm just the man to do it."

"No," she said. "You keep out of it. There's only one thing I want from you."

"What is that?" he asked.

She rose from the chair and placed the baby back in the crib. Carefully she arranged the covers around the sleeping child and turned to him. She walked toward him, her fingers fastening the buttons on her blouse. She stopped in front of him and looked up. "You tell me when it is the time."

The muscles of his face seemed to reshape themselves into planed angular lines.

She could see a pulse beating in his temple. His hands shot out suddenly and took her breasts. She felt the milk from them seep through her blouse into his palms.

His voice was angry. "You bitch! You couldn't wait, could you?"

"No," she said almost calmly. She put her hands on him and felt his bursting strength. Her insides seemed to turn into a hot boiling liquid. Her legs gave way and she sagged against him. "My bedroom's through that other door," she managed to gasp.

He picked her up and carried her through into the other room. With one hand he closed the door silently behind him and carried her over to the bed. She tumbled into it and stared up at him as he began to undress. She reached across the bed and turned on the small night table lamp.

He was almost naked now. "What are you waiting for?" he asked savagely. "Take off your dress!"

She shook her head without speaking, never taking her eyes from him as his union suit dropped to the floor and he stepped toward her. Then she looked up into his face. "You tear it off me," she said. "The way you did that girl's."

In a moment the dress was torn into shreds and he was on his knees before her. He held her legs back and apart and lowered himself into her.

She shoved her half-clenched fist into her open mouth to keep herself from screaming. "Oh, God! Oh, God!" She was seized by paroxysm after paroxysm of climax and spending. She shut her eyes tightly and this time she was the girl she saw in the mirror.

Chapter Eight

She awoke a few minutes before the baby's two o'clock feeding. Loren was sleeping on his stomach, one arm thrown across the pillow, shielding his eyes from the night lamp, his long legs stretched down the length of the bed, his feet awkwardly reaching past the edge. This close he didn't seem to be as hairy as she had thought, his body covered instead with a fine, soft, red-gold fur through which the whiteness of his skin gleamed.

Carefully, so as not to awaken him, she moved from the bed. The moving made her suddenly aware of her own body. Every cell of her was filled to the bursting, alive, rich and completed. "So this is what it is like," she thought in wonder.

Silently, she slipped into a robe and went into the baby's room, shutting the door behind her. She stood over the crib, looking at the sleeping baby. For the first time it all made sense to her. He was not a baby any more. He was a man child and some day he would be large and strong and fill a woman just as she had been filled.

Her breasts began to ache and she touched them, then went to the dresser and took the already prepared warm bottle from its thermos container. She tested the temperature of the formula against the back of her hand. It was just right. She took the baby from the crib, sat in the chair, and gave him the rubber nipple.

He took one suck and spit it out. He cried protestingly. "Shhh," she whispered softly, pushing the nipple back into his mouth. "You have to get used to it sometime."

He seemed to understand because he began to suck hungrily at it. She bent and kissed his suddenly sweating face. "Man child," she whispered. She had never felt her love for him as strongly as she did at this moment.

She heard the door open behind her and when she looked up, Loren was standing over them. He was naked and tawny in the yellow light and the strong male smell of him was pungent in her nostrils.

"How come the bottle?" he asked after a moment.

"You left nothing for him," she replied simply.

He didn't answer.

"It's all right," she added. "He's in the middle of being weaned anyway."

He nodded without speaking and then went back into the other room. She looked down at the baby. The bottle was half empty, it was time to burp him.

When she came back into the bedroom, he was sitting on the edge of the bed smoking a cigarette. He looked at her inquiringly as she closed the door behind her. "He went right back to sleep," she said.

"It's a great life," he smiled. "Nothing to do but eat and sleep." He got to his feet. "Time for me to go."

"No."

He looked at her. "We've been crazy enough," he said after a moment. "The thing for me to do is get out of here and make sure it never happens again."

"I want you to stay."

"You're crazier than I am."

"No, I'm not," she said steadily. "Do you think I could let you go now that you taught me what it is like to really be a woman? What it is like to really be loved?"

"Fucked, you mean," he said flatly. "They're not the same things."

"Maybe to you they're not," she answered. "But they are to me. I love you."

"One good fuck and you're in love?" he asked sarcastically.

"Isn't that enough of a reason?" she returned. "I might have gone my whole life and never known how much I could feel."

He was silent.

"Look," she said quickly, the words tumbling from her lips almost one on top of the other. "I know that after tonight it will be over. That it will never happen again. But it's not tomorrow yet, it's still tonight and I don't want to lose a moment of it."

He felt the stirring in his loins and knew from the expression in her eyes that she was aware of it. He felt a sudden anger with his self-betrayal. "We can't stay in this room," he said harshly. "The servants—"

"You stay in Loren's room," she said. "Through the connecting door."

He began picking up his clothing. "What will you tell them?"

"The truth," she smiled. "That it was too late for you to drive home. After all, what can they say, you're still my father-in-law, aren't you?" She looked up at him. "One thing bothers me. I don't know what to call you. Daddy Hardeman seems ridiculous now."

"Try Loren," he suggested. "That shouldn't be too difficult." He followed her into the other room. "How long have you had separate bedrooms?" he asked.

"Always," she answered. She was reaching for the clothing over his arm. "Let me hang these for you, or they won't be fit to wear in the morning."

He watched her drape the suit neatly over the wooden valet. "I thought you had the same bedroom."

"Never," she replied. "Loren said that he was a poor sleeper. Besides, you and Mother had separate bedrooms."

"Only after she became sick," he said. "We slept in the same room for the first twenty years of our marriage."

"I didn't know that," she said, taking his shirt and placing it on a hanger.

"You're both too young to have separate rooms," he said. He looked at her shrewdly. "I know there's nothing the matter with you. What's wrong with Loren?"

"I don't know," she said, her eyes meeting his. "He's different. He's not like you."

"What do you mean, different?"

"He just doesn't seem to demand very much from me." She hesitated a moment. "Now that I think about it, the only time we ever make love is when I seem to suggest it. Even on our wedding night, I wanted him so badly that I lay naked in bed waiting for him, and he asked if I were too tired."

"He was never a very strong boy," he said awkwardly. "Sort of delicate. His mother used to worry a great deal about him. I thought she worried too much at times. But that was the way she was. He was her only child and she knew that she would never have another."

"I would like to give you a child," she said.

"You already did. A grandchild."

She shook her head. "More than that. One of your own. You're a man who should have had many children."

"It's too late for that now."

"Is it, Loren?" she asked, walking toward him. "Is it too late?"

He looked down into her face without answering.

"You never kissed me," she said.

He placed his hands under her shoulders and lifted her towards him. She felt his thumbs digging into her armpits, his strong fingers pressing into her back, crushing her breasts against him. His mouth came down hard against her lips. The hot liquid fire began to soak her loins.

She tore her mouth from him and laid her head on his chest. She closed her eyes and her lips brushed against his shoulder and he could hardly hear her soft whisper. "Oh God, I hope this night never ends."

He held her very still and very tightly. Because the one thing both of them knew was that morning was just a few hours away.

"More coffee, Mr. Hardeman?"

Loren nodded. He looked across the breakfast table at Sally and waited until the impassive butler had filled the cup and left the room. "You didn't eat your breakfast."

"I'm not really hungry," she said. "Besides I still have ten pounds to lose until I'm back to where I was before the baby was born."

He picked up his cup and sipped the strong black coffee. He thought of the way she looked at six o'clock that morning.

He awoke when she slipped from the bed to give the baby his morning feeding but he deliberately kept his eyes closed so that she would think he was still asleep. He felt her standing there at the side of the bed, looking down at him. After a moment, she moved away and he peeked at her through slitted lids.

She was nude and in the gray light of the early morning he could see the faint blue and purple bruises of his passion on her fair skin. She seemed to wander about the room almost aimlessly and without purpose. She paused before the dresser and suddenly there were two of her, back and front, one in the mirror. But she didn't look at herself. Instead she picked up his heavy pocket watch and looked at it for a moment, then put it down and took up the gold cufflinks made in the shape of the first Sundancer he had built. These she looked at for a long time. After she put them down, she turned and looked back at him in the bed. He shut his eyes quickly.

He heard her moving around the room again, then the closing of the door behind her and after a moment, the faint sound of running water coming through the walls from her bathroom. He rolled over on his back and opened his eyes.

He was in his son's bed, in his son's room, and the smell of his son's wife was still on the pillow beside him. His eyes wandered around the room. Everything in it reflected Junior's love of antique furniture. The dresser and mirror, the chairs, even the delicate Duncan Phyfe desk that sat in the bay of the window. All were his son's.

A peculiar sorrow seemed to weigh him down. Elizabeth had said so many times that his life had been a succession of failures when it came to his son. That he never really allowed for the differences between them and that try as he might, he could not reshape Junior in his own image.

He closed his eyes wearily. If those were failures, what was this? Another failure? Or betrayal? Or even worse, a final usurpation of his son's life and place? He drifted into a fitful sleep.

When he opened his eyes again it was after eight o'clock and she was standing next to the bed. She was wearing a simple dress and her face was scrubbed, without makeup, her eyes clear and her hair pulled back behind her head in a neat bun.

"Junior's calling you from the office." she said in a flat voice.

He swung his feet off the bed. "What time is it?"

"About eight forty."

"How did he know I was here?"

"When you weren't at the meeting this morning, they tried your house. They were told that you had mentioned you might come over here last night but they didn't think of calling until they tried several other places first."

"What did you say to him?" he asked.

"I told him that we were up late and that I thought you should stay over instead of driving back."

"Okay," he said, getting to his feet. A stab of pain shot through his temples. "Could you get me some aspirin?" he asked, walking to the small desk and picking up the telephone. "Hello."

"Father?" Junior's voice was thin and metallic in the phone. "I'm sorry I didn't know you were there, I would have come home."

"That's all right," Loren said. "I made up my mind at the last minute."

She came back into the room with two aspirins and a tumbler of water. He gulped them down.

"Duncan's completed the plans for the revised assembly line for the Loren II," Junior said. "We want to get your approval."

"How does it look?"

"It seems all right to me," Junior said. "We should be able to save about two hundred and ten dollars per unit by final assembly."

"Then okay it," he said abruptly.

"Without your seeing it?" There was surprise in Junior's voice.

"Yes. You might as well get used to taking the responsibility. You're the president of the company, you make the decisions."

"But—what are you going to do?" Junior was puzzled.

"I'm taking that vacation I promised myself," he heard himself saying. "I'm going to Europe for a year and I'm leaving tomorrow."

"I thought you weren't going until next month," Junior said.

Loren looked up at Sally. "I changed my mind,"

She looked into his eyes for a moment, then silently left the room. He turned back to the telephone. "I'll go home and change clothes," he said to his son. "I'll see you later this afternoon." He sat down wearily in the spindly Duncan Phyfe chair behind the desk and waited for the aspirin to take his morning headache away.

Now she looked across the table as he put his coffee cup back on it. Her voice was controlled. "You're running away."

"Yep," he nodded.

"Do you think it will make anything different?"

"Maybe it won't. But five thousand miles can keep us out of a lot of trouble."

She didn't speak.

He looked at her steadily. "I have no regrets about what happened. But we were lucky. No one got hurt. This time. But I know myself, If I were to stay, I wouldn't be able to keep away from you. And, eventually, that's got to destroy all the things and people we don't want to hurt."

She was motionless in her chair. "I love you."

He was silent for a long moment. "And I love you, I think." There was a note of pain in his voice. "But that doesn't matter now. It's much too late in the game. For both of us."

Chapter Nine

"You bitch! You low, whoring bitch!" Junior's voice rose to a shrill scream. "Who was it?"

She stared in amazement at the sudden transition in him. It was as if his body had been taken over by a virulent female spirit. For the first time, she noticed the subdued effeminate characteristics of him. With the knowledge, her fear seemed to vanish. "Lower your voice," she said quietly. "You'll disturb the baby."

His open hand slashed across her face and she went over with the chair in which she had been seated. The pain came like a red flash of fire a moment later as she stared up at him.

He stood over her, his hand outstretched, ready to strike again. "Who was it?"

She didn't move for a moment, then pushed the chair away from her with her legs. Slowly she rose, the white imprint of his palm clear on the redness of her cheeks. She backed away from him, until the dresser was against her. He followed her, threateningly.

She placed her hands on the dresser top behind her without taking her eyes from his face. His hand started down. She moved even more swiftly. He felt the sharp sting even through the heavy cloth of his vest. She spoke only one word. "Don't!"

His hand paused in mid-air as his eyes fell to his waist. The silver handle of the long nail file gleamed in her hand. His eyes went incredulously back to her face.

"You touch me again and I'll kill you," she said calmly.

He suddenly seemed to deflate, his hand fell to his side. The tears sprang to his eyes.

"You go back there and sit down," she said. "Then we'll talk."

As if in a daze he stumbled back to the armchair in the corner of the room and sat down. He put his hands over his face and began to cry.

The burst of anger that had engulfed her vanished as quickly as it had come. Nothing was left inside her except pity. He was not so much a man that he was not still a child.

She put the nail file back on the dresser and walked over to him. "I'll go away," she said. "You go get the divorce."

He looked up at her through the open fingers covering his face. "That's easy for you," he half sobbed, "but what about me? Everyone will know what happened and they'll all be laughing and talking behind my back."

"No one will ever know," she said. "I'll go so far away no word will ever come back to Detroit."

"I'm going to be sick!" he said suddenly. He got to his feet and ran to the bathroom.

Through the open door she heard him retching into the bowl. She followed him and saw him bent over the open toilet, heaving. His entire body shuddered and he seemed ready to fall. Quickly she moved in behind him and supported his forehead with her palm.

He sagged against her as he spasmodically heaved again. But he was already empty. Nothing came out. After a moment, he stopped shaking.

She reached across him and turned on the cold water in the sink. She took a washcloth and, after soaking it, applied it to his forehead. He began to straighten up. She rinsed the washcloth and wiped the traces of vomit from his mouth and chin.

"I made a mess," he said helplessly, looking down at the yellow and brown vomit splattered across the bottom of the upturned toilet seat and porcelain edges of the bowl.

"It's all right," she said soothingly. "I'll clean it up. You go inside and lie down."

He left the bathroom and she set about straightening up. When she came out a few minutes later, her room was empty, but the door leading to his bedroom was open.

He was lying on his back atop the covers of his bed, an arm thrown over his eyes. She walked over to him. "Are you all right?"

He didn't answer.

She turned and started back toward her room.

"Don't go," he said. "I feel faint. The room is spinning around."

She came back to the bed and looked down at him. His face beneath his arm was pale and sweating. "You need something in your stomach," she said. "I'll have them bring up some tea and milk for you."

She pulled the signal tassel on the wall. A moment later the butler was at the door. "Some weak tea and milk for Mr. Hardeman." she said.

"Yes ma'am."

She closed the door and went back to the bed. "Let me help you out of your things. You'll be more comfortable."

Like a child, he let her undress him and help him into his pajamas, then stood there patiently while she turned down the covers. He got back into the bed and pulled the sheets up around him.

The butler came back with the tea and placed the bed tray over his legs and left. Junior sat up, pulling another pillow behind him. She filled the cup with the tea and hot milk, half and half. "Drink that. You'll feel better."

He sipped slowly at the steaming cup and the colour began to return to his face. When the cup was empty, she refilled it.

She looked down at him. "Do you mind if I smoke?"

He shook his head silently and she went into her own room and returned with a cigarette. "Feeling better?"

He nodded.

She took a deep drag. The acrid smoke tingled through her mouth and nostrils. "I'm sorry," she said. "I didn't want to hurt you."

He didn't answer.

"Actually I was going to go away and leave a note for you. I never wanted you to know about it. The doctor promised he wouldn't say anything to anyone."

"You forgot to tell him that you included your husband in that," he said. "I didn't know what he was talking about when I ran into him at the club and he congratulated me."

"It's out now," she said. "And that doesn't matter any more. I'll leave tomorrow and you can handle the divorce any way you like. I don't want anything."

"No!"

She stared at him.

"You're not leaving."

"But—"

"You're going to stay and have the baby," he interrupted her. "Just as if nothing happened."

"A scandal right now would break the company," he said. "We're just completing bank loans for fifty million dollars to retool for the new 1930 cars. Do you think any bank would give us that money if this got out? Not one. On top of that, my father would kill me if I let anything happen that would keep us from getting that money."

They sat in heavy silence for what seemed a long while. She ground out one cigarette and lit another. He watched her.

"Why didn't you do something about it?" he finally asked. "What took you so long."

"I didn't find out about it until it was too late. Then no doctor would touch me. I was all mixed up with my periods after the baby was born."

"You won't tell me who the father is?"

She shook her head. "No."

"You don't have to tell me," he said. "I know who it is."

She didn't speak.

"It was him," he said.

He didn't have to mention his father by name for her to know who he meant. "You're crazy!" she said, hoping he wouldn't notice the sudden trembling of the hand that held the cigarette.

"I'm not so stupid as you seem to think," he said, a sudden effeminate craftiness appearing in his face. "He spent the night here and the next morning he suddenly decided to leave for Europe a month ahead of time."

She forced a laugh. "That doesn't mean anything."

"Maybe this does!" he said, getting out of bed. He crossed the room to the cabinet in which his sox and underwear were kept. He pulled open the bottom drawer and took something out and came back to her. He snapped his hand and the bedsheet billowed out on the floor in front of her. "Recognize this?"

She shook her head.

"You should," he said. "It was the sheet that was on my bed that night. The night he stayed here. Do you know what those yellowish ringed stains are?"

She was silent.

"Semen stains," he said. "Any boy could recognize them. And I don't think he's the type to have wet dreams."

"That still doesn't prove anything," she said.

"Then how about this?" With his other hand he flung something at her.

It fell to her lap and she picked it up. It was the nursing brassiere she had been wearing that night. Now the torn and ripped pieces of it hung from her fingers. She hadn't even missed it.

"Where did you get it?" she asked.

"In the hamper in my bathroom," he said. "I had dropped a shirt in it with my cufflinks still in the sleeves and when I opened the door to get it out, the sheet fell out and the brassiere was wrapped in it."

She was silent.

"He raped you, didn't he?" It was more a statement than a question the way he said it.

She didn't answer him.

"The sick, filthy old man!" he swore. "I don't know how my poor mother stood him all those years. He belongs in an institution. It's not the first time he's done something like this. He tore the clothes off you, didn't he?"

She looked down at the brassiere in her hand. "Yes," she half-whispered.

"Then why didn't you do something?" he asked. "Why didn't you scream?"

She took a long, deep breath and looked up at him. Her voice was clear and steady. "Because I wanted him to."

His shoulders suddenly slumped and he seemed to shrink inwardly; before her eyes he seemed to grow twenty years older. His face turned gray and pale. He put out a hand and sat on the edge of his bed.

"He's hated me," he whispered as if he were talking to himself. "He's always hated me. From the moment I was born. Because I came between my mother and him. Ever since I was a child, he always took things away from me. Once I had a doll. He took it away and gave me a toy car. Then when I wouldn't play with it, he took the car away too."

He stretched out on the bed on his stomach, burying his face in the crook of his elbow and began to cry again. Her face began to throb with the ache. Wearily she got to her feet and started back to her room.

"Sally!"

She turned and looked back at him. He sat up in the bed, the tears streaking his cheeks. "You're not going to let him take you away from me too, are you?"

She stood there without answering.

"We'll forget it ever happened," he said quickly. "I'll be good to you, you'll see. I'll never say anything about it again."

He got out of the bed and fell to his knees and clasped his arms around her legs, burying his face against her thighs. "Please, Sally," he begged. "Don't leave me. I couldn't bear it if you left me."

She let her hand fall on his head and rest there. For a moment, she felt as if he were her child. And maybe that was the way it was supposed to be.

"Get up and go back to bed, Junior," she said gently. "I won't leave you." Then she turned, closing the door behind her.

On a day that came to be known as Black Friday in the economic history of the world, the New York stock market plummetted from the heights, throwing the nation and the world into the depths of an economic depression never known before.

Four months later in the middle of January, 1930, the doorbell rang in the suite at the Hotel George V in Paris where Loren was staying.

"Roxanne," he called from his bath. "See who it is."

A few minutes later she came into the bathroom. "A cable from America for you."

"Open it and read it. My hands are wet."

She tore open the pale blue envelope. Her voice was expressionless as she struggled with the English words.

> *Loren Hardeman, Sr.*
> *Hotel George V*
> *Paris, France.*
>
> *Have ordered production stopped and discontinuance of Loren II at bank's insistence to reduce losses due to lack of sales. Stop. Other economies in work and will keep you informed as to decisions taken. Also wish to inform you that my wife gave birth to a girl, Anne Elizabeth, yesterday morning, at eight o'clock.*
>
> *Loren Hardeman II*

Chapter Ten

Angelo looked out the window as the plane settled into its final approach pattern in a wide banking turn over the Ford River Rouge Plant. The giant industrial complex sprawled like a hydra-headed monster beneath him, its clouded breath rising toward the skies, its liquid wastes pouring into the grayed cloudy waters of the Detroit river, the multipatterned colors of the tiny cars parked like clusters of ants in the lots between the buildings. The no-smoking signal snapped on just as the late afternoon sun brightened the glass windows and façade of the long Ford Central Administration building.

He snubbed his cigarette out in the tray and began to place the papers on the table back into his case. Finished, he pushed the table up to the seat and put the case on the floor.

The stewardess came down the aisle. She looked down at him. "Seat belt fastened?"

He nodded, holding up his hands so that she could see it. She smiled and went on to the next row. He looked at his wristwatch. Four thirty in the afternoon. Right on schedule. He turned to the window again.

River Rouge was now behind the plane. For the first time he began to feel a tinge of admiration for the men who had conceived it. It had to be an almost impossible task. He knew that now. In the year since he had been working on the West Coast plant, one problem after the other had arisen until there were times when he thought he was going out of his mind. And that plant wasn't even ten percent of River Rouge.

But there were two things that made it all work and both were people. The knowledge, experience, and wise counsel of John Duncan, and the driving, indefatigable energy and enthusiasm of Tony Rourke who became part of it all as if he were born into the automobile business. That, plus his inventive use and adaptation of the new technologies he had used in aerospace, brought them over the first and perhaps the most difficult hurdles.

The design and engineering division had been successfully transferred from Detroit and had been functional for over six months. The steel foundry they bought in Fontana was in the process of changeover to their production requirements, and the mill they had built at the plant would be ready for operation by the summer of next year. The casting division would be ready for work a few months later, and the final assembly line could be in operation as early as September, 1971, if need be. The labor pool was in the process of being analyzed, the requirement plans were being drawn and the thousand and one other details were being buttoned up. Now, all that was needed was a final decision on the kind of car to build. And that was the one problem on which no one seemed to be in agreement.

Perhaps it was because of the present state of the industry itself. Over the past few years a storm had been brewing, and now the eye of the hurricane was upon them and the whole industry was searching frantically for a place of safety with no clearly defined shelters in view. In response to pressure, local and federal governments were imposing stringent regulations that would affect the performance and production of automobiles. Ecological and environmental factors were subjected to new controls and stricter standards. There was a five-year plan to which the industry had to conform to reduce gasoline engine emissions to certain acceptable levels by 1975. Other safety factors were being regulated to protect the driver and the passenger, even against their own mistakes. All in all, it was a direct refutation of the policy that had been the industry's privilege all these years. No longer were these decisions that concerned the public's safety and welfare to be left to their own tender mercies. Despite their cries of economic ruin and that the costs would have to be passed along to the consumer, the standards would have to be met or the cars would not be allowed on the road.

There was another side to the problem. And that seemed to be the changing taste of the American car buyer. It seemed only a few years ago that the little Volkswagen Beetle had only been a subject of puns and jokes. But that was twenty years back. Suddenly Detroit turned around and found the little bug was the fourth largest selling car in America in 1969 and that for 1970 the industry had already conceded that it would knock Chrysler Motors' Plymouth out of third place in sales it had held for many years. Then, to add to their woes, in 1967 another invasion began to take place, this one from the opposite side of the world. Japan. In just four years the little men had captured another giant section of the American market with their products, until Datsun, Toyota and others were now a viable part of the American scene. Their rate of market growth and penetration was so rapid and so complete, and even more remarkable perhaps was that it showed no sign of slowing up. For the first time not only Detroit showed evidence of concern, but also the Volkswagen company, who saw its own eminent position in the American market being threatened. Now Volkswagen, like the Ford Motor's famous Model T of many years ago, felt itself in danger of being bypassed in styling and improvements, and was casting about for a new car that would eventually replace the Beetle. But that was still in the future.

For now, the American companies had come forth with their version of the economy compact: the Vega, Pinto and Gremlin. Chrysler was still holding back from domestic production but had two of its cars which had been manufactured abroad imported into the States and sold under their own names: Dodge's Colt and the Plymouth Cricket. But it was all stopgap and even Detroit was ready to admit that.

The first reports on the sales of the American sub-compacts indicated that their market was drawn from their own sales of larger cars and that the sales of the import cars were not affected at all but continued to show an appreciable rate of increase.

All of these factors, plus the additional investment and costs added to the sales and manufacturing burden by governmental edict, turned the industry's eyes inward upon itself. Trim, cut, pare, and prune as much as they would or could would not of itself supply the answer.

The answer itself would only come with a totally new car, one that was born of the technology of demand, a new car that would have built into it all the requirements of both the government and the consumer. And that was the one thing that Detroit was not yet ready to consider. For that meant calling the old ball-game and beginning a new one. And there were still too many fans in the old stadium.

The wheels of the plane touched the ground, jarring Angelo from his reverie. He sat there quietly while they taxied to the gate. They had to make the commitment. It was the only choice they could make. And at tomorrow's board meeting, he was going to put it on the line. The Sundancer was yesterday's automobile. It had to go. If they were going to build a new car, it would have to have the total commitment of the corporation behind it. Any continuation of the Sundancer would be taken as a hedge and would, in his opinion, lessen the chances of success of the new car.

The plane rolled to a stop and he picked up his attaché case and rose to his feet. But that was tomorrow and tonight there was another matter that was almost as important in the world of Detroit.

An event that had been heralded in the Detroit papers as the great social affair of the year, the preparations for which had been as religiously reported as the preparations for the inauguration of a President of the United States.

Elizabeth Hardeman's debut. She was eighteen years old. And ready to take her place in the world.

"You look very well, Grandfather," the Princess said.

Number One smiled. "I feel good, Anne. Better than I have in years."

"I'm glad," she said simply. She walked over to his wheelchair and kissed his cheek. "You know that, don't you."

The faint scent of her perfume came to his nostrils. He reached out and patted her hand. "I know it," he said. "And you? Are you happy?"

She nodded thoughtfully. "As happy as I could be, I guess. I've long ago given up the childish dreams of what happiness should be. Now, I'm content. Igor is very good to me. He looks after me. You know what I mean."

He nodded. He thought he understood but never would be quite sure. The problem of being an heiress had destroyed the lives of many others. Being a rich girl had its own peculiar hazards. But she seemed to be one of the fortunate ones. It was difficult for him to realize that she was now forty years old, she was still a child in his mind. "Where is Igor?" he asked. "I haven't seen him."

"In the library downstairs with Loren," she said. "You know Igor. He loves the chance to talk business, man to man. And if there's a bottle of good whiskey around that doesn't hurt either."

He smiled. "How is business in Europe?"

"Igor was concerned," she said. Igor had taken over the operation of Bethlehem Motors S.A., France, when they had been married, and much to the surprise of everyone had done a very creditable job of it. "You know how he loves cars. He hated it when auto sales fell off, even if the other divisions went well. Now he's all excited again. He couldn't wait to get to Loren and talk about the new car.

Number One said, "I'll have him invited to the board meeting tomorrow. I think he'll like that."

"Are you kidding?" Anne laughed. "He'll love it. That's what he always dreamed about. Being there when the big decisions are made. He'll be in paradise."

"Good."

"What time is it?" she asked.

He looked at his wristwatch. "Seven thirty."

"I'd better begin to dress."

"What's the rush? The party doesn't begin until ten."

"I'm not as young as I used to be," she smiled. "And looking like a princess takes a little longer."

"You always looked like a princess to me," he said.

"Do you remember, Grandfather? That's what you used to call me when I was a little girl. Princess. And Daddy used to get angry. He said it was un-American."

"Your father had some peculiar ideas," he said.

"Yes." She was thoughtful. "I always had the feeling that he didn't like either of us. I used to wonder about that."

"Does it matter?"

"Not now." She looked at him and smiled. "You know, I'm glad I came home. I'm glad you opened the Manor for this party. I've always heard how grand the parties were here."

"Some of them were pretty good."

"How long has it been, Grandfather?" she asked. "Since the last one?"

He thought for a moment. Time washed over him like the tide of the ocean. He closed his eyes and for a moment it was yesterday and then he opened them. "Forty-five years ago," he said slowly. "For your father and mother's wedding."

Chapter Eleven

It really was two parties not one. The main ballroom was the formal affair. In that room one of Meyer Davis's society orchestra's held forth with what Elizabeth's friends termed "music for the middle-aged."

The other party was in the giant game room of the pool house. This had been transformed into a discotheque, and music was electronically blasted forth by two alternating rock groups.

Both parties were jammed with people and even standing room was measured in centimeters. There had been nothing like it ever seen in Detroit. It was an Armageddon of sound and confusion.

The warm late September gardens were also thronged with people wandering back and forth between the two parties, anxious to see everything and be everywhere at the same time. It was almost midnight before the jam of automobiles that had backed all the way down the long driveway into the streets around the house was cleared and Angelo found himself entering the wide-flung great wooden doors.

The reception line had long since broken down; Loren, smashed even before the party began, was nowhere to be seen, and Betsy had adjourned to the discotheque with her friends. Only Alicia, slightly frazzled and the worse for wear, remained anywhere near the entrance.

For the third time, Angelo presented his invitation for inspection. The first two times had been at the driveway entrance and in front of the house. This time a butler in formal livery took it.

The gray-haired man turned to the room. "Mr. Angelo Perino," he announced in sepulchral tones that were completely lost in the clamor.

Angelo walked down the steps towards Alicia. He kissed her cheek. "You look lovely."

"I look terrible and you know it."

"Quite a party," he said, glancing around the room.

"Yes," she said. "But I wish we had never given it. Somehow it all seems such a waste. But Loren insisted."

"It looks like fun," Angelo said.

"I hope he's enjoying himself," she said sarcastically.

"Where's the deb?" he asked. "Shouldn't I congratulate her or something? I don't know exactly what you do at things like this."

For the first time that evening she laughed. "Angelo, you're marvellous. You have to be the only honest person left in Detroit." She glanced around. "I don't see her anywhere. She must be out in the game room with her friends."

"I'll catch up to her," he said.

"Come," she said, taking his arm. "I'll find some pretty young thing for you to dance with."

"What's wrong with you?"

"Me?" There was a note of surprise in her voice. She hesitated. "I don't know. I should remain here. Someone should."

"Why?"

She stared at him for a moment, then nodded. "You know something? You're absolutely right. There's no reason at all why I should stay here."

He led her out to the dance floor and she came into his arms. She was slightly stiff at first. He moved her closer to him. "Relax," he smiled. "You're allowed to have fun at your own party."

She laughed again and they moved off to the music. She rested her head against his shoulder and after a moment, she looked up at him. "Thank you, Angelo."

"For what?"

"For making me feel I'm really here. I've had the strangest feeling all night that I wasn't."

"I don't understand."

"You know what's happening," she said. "Everyone does. It's an open secret that Loren is keeping that girl in the apartment on top of the administration building out at the plant and that I'm leaving for Reno the day after tomorrow. People have been looking at me with that, 'the queen is dead, long live the queen,' sort of look. It's been very strange. They're just not quite sure how friendly they should be."

"You're imagining things," he said. "You grew up here. These people have always been your friends. Married to Loren or not won't make any difference."

A sad look came into her eyes. "At one time I thought so. Now I'm not that sure."

The song ended and they stopped on the floor. A woman's voice came from behind them. "Alicia, darling! Where have you been hiding this perfectly ravishing man?"

They turned and Angelo saw the beautifully tailored couple standing next to them. The woman's face had a vaguely familiar look.

Alicia smiled. "Angelo Perino, my sister-in-law and her husband, the Prince and Princess Alekhine."

The princess held out her hand. Angelo took it. 'Kiss it or shake it?' he smiled.

"You can do both," she laughed. "And the name is Anne. You went to school with my brother but we never met."

"My hard luck." He kissed her hand and turned to take the hand of her husband.

The prince was taller than Angelo, with thick gray-black hair and bright dark eyes set in a strong, tanned face. His grip was firm and direct, "You call me Igor," he said in a deep friendly voice. "And I have been looking forward to meeting you. There is much we have to talk about. I want you to tell me all about the new car."

"That can wait," Anne said. "Tomorrow is time enough for you men to talk business." The music began again. "Igor, you dance with Alicia," she commanded, taking Angelo's arm. "I want to learn all about the new man in Detroit."

She came into his arms with all the assurance of a woman who had been there many times before. He looked down at her. "You've been reading too many magazines," he said.

"Of course," she answered. "What else do you think Americans in Europe do with their time? They read magazines and that way they keep in touch. It makes them feel a part of things."

"They could come home," he said.

"Aren't you clever?" she smiled. "Changing the subject so quickly. But I won't be put off that easily. I saw the article in *Life*. The one about DeLorean at Chevy, Iacocca at Ford, and you. Is it true what they said about your grandfather? That he was the liquor dealer who supplied the liquor for my parents' wedding in this house?"

"Not true," he said. "He was never a liquor dealer, he was a bootlegger."

She began to laugh. "I think I'm going to like you. I'm beginning to understand what Grandfather sees in you."

At one o'clock in the morning the grand portieres were drawn back, revealing the sumptuous buffet and the gaily decorated dinner tables. Half an hour later, the dinner entertainment began.

The orchestra leader spoke into the microphone, but even with the amplification his words were lost in the greater bedlam coming from the tables. He turned and gestured to the wings of the small temporary stage. The girl who stepped in front of the microphone was recognized by everyone there. For years they had seen her face on television every week and for a long while she had even been the voice for one of the major automobiles. Now she opened her mouth to sing but no one could hear her or even cared to listen. They were too busy with their conversation and food.

Loren stood at the side of the stage, swaying slightly. He tried to hear her, but nothing. He moved closer to the stage until he was standing right beneath her. Still nothing. Suddenly he was angry.

He climbed up on the stage quickly and crossed to the microphone. The singer looked at him in bewilderment. He held up a hand and the orchestra stopped playing. He turned and looked out at his guests.

Not one had even noticed what was happening on the stage. He bent down and picked up a spoon from a table in front of the stage and banged it on the edge of the microphone until he had caught their attention. Bit by bit the room began to quiet down.

He stared out at them, his face flushed and angry, his collar wrinkled and soft with his perspiration. "Now, listen to me, you slobs!" he shouted into the microphone which carried his slurred words into exaggerations that filled every corner of the two giant rooms. "I paid fifteen thousand dollars to bring this little lady all the way here from Hollywood to sing for you and and you all better shut up and goddamn well listen!'

Suddenly, the room was silent, not even the sound of a fork or spoon could be heard. He turned to the singer and made an exaggerated courtly bow.

"It's all right, little lady," he said. "Now you can sing."

The orchestra began again, and as her soft voice began to fill the room, Loren turned and started from the stage. He stumbled slightly on the last step, but recovered his balance before he fell and weaved off toward the bar.

Angelo was standing at the bar as Loren came up to him. He put his hand out to steady him.

Loren shook his hand away. "I'm alri'." He turned to the bartender. "Scotch on the rocks." He looked at Angelo as if he had just seen him for the first time. "Ungrateful bastards!" he mumbled. "They don't appreciate anything you do for them."

Angelo didn't answer.

Loren picked up his drink and tasted it. "Good Scotch," he said. "You don't get the hangover you do from Canadian. You ought to try it sometime."

"I get hangovers from everything," Angelo smiled. "Even Coco-Cola."

"Ungrateful bastards!" Loren said again, looking out at the crowded rooms. He turned back to Angelo. "When did you get into town?"

"This afternoon."

"You didn't call me," he said.

"I did," Angelo replied. "But you had already left the office."

"I want to see you before the meeting tomorrow," said Loren. "We have some important things to talk about."

"I'm available."

"I'll call you," Loren said. He put his empty glass on the bar and started away. He turned back abruptly. "There won't be time tomorrow morning," he said. "You meet me here at the bar when the party is over. That'll be around three o'clock."

Angelo looked at him. "It's a pretty large evening. Sure it won't keep until the morning?"

"Think I do' know what I'm doing?" Loren asked belligerently.

Angelo smiled. "I know you don't," he said easily.

Loren's eyes narrowed and his face flushed even more. He stepped toward Angelo.

"Don't," Angelo said quietly. "It would be a shame to spoil your daughter's party."

Loren stood there for a moment, then he relaxed. He even smiled. "You're right," he admitted. "Thank you for keeping me from making a horse's ass of myself."

Angelo returned his smile. "That's what friends are for."

"Will you do me a favor?" Loren asked.

"Of course."

"Will you meet me at three fifteen and drive me back to the plant?" Loren asked. "I don't think I'm in any condition to drive myself."

"I'll be here," Angelo said.

He walked out through the giant French doors into the garden. The gaily-coloured lanterns hung along the paths swayed gently in the late night wind. He lit a cigarette and started down the path toward the pool house.

The heavy beat of the rock group grew louder as he approached the building. Through the large picture windows, he could see into the discotheque. It was filled with wall-to-wall dancers who seemed oddly frozen in flashes of coloured light.

He walked in through the open doorway and pushed his way to the bar. He ordered a drink and the bartender put it down in front of him. He picked it up and sipped it. His nostrils also picked up the acrid-sweet smell of marijuana. He looked around him. In the dark he could not tell who was smoking the grass or who was on tobacco. Cigarettes filled the room like fireflies.

"Do I know you?" The girl's voice came from behind him.

He turned around. She was young, there was no doubt about that, but then so were all the girls in this room. Her eyes were a pale blue and her long blonde hair fell straight along her face to her shoulders. There was an oddly familiar look about her mouth and chin.

"I don't think so," he smiled. "But then, I don't know you, so that makes us kind of even."

"I'm Elizabeth Hardeman," she said imperiously.

"Of course," he said.

"What do you mean?" she asked.

"Who else could you be?" he smiled. "Is it proper to congratulate you, Miss Elizabeth?"

She stared at him. "You're making fun of me."

"I'm not really," he said quickly. "I just don't know what's the right thing to do in these circumstances."

"You're not putting me on?"

"Honest injun," he said seriously.

She grinned suddenly. "Can I tell you the truth?"

He nodded.

"I really don't know what's proper either," she laughed.

"Then I'll let my congratulations stand," he said.

"Thank you." She snapped her fingers. "I never forget a face. You're the man who was driving the Sundancer SS the first time I saw it on Woodward Avenue one night last winter. You were with that girl with the big—. The one who looked like Miss Hurst Golden Shifter, I mean."

He laughed, "Guilty."

"Do you work for my father?" she asked. "Are you one of the test drivers?"

"In a kind of way," he admitted. "I guess you can put it like that."

A dismayed look suddenly crossed her face. "I know you," she said. "I saw your picture in *Life*. You're Angelo Perino."

"That's right," he smiled "But I'd rather be listed as your unknown admirer."

"I'm sorry, Mr. Perino. I didn't mean to put my foot in my mouth."

"I'll forgive you if you give me this dance," he said.

She looked at the dance floor, then back at him. "Here?" she asked doubtfully. "Or back at the main house?"

"Here," he said, laughing and leading her onto the floor. "I'm not really as old as I look."

Chapter Twelve

The Meyer Davis orchestra began playing. "Three O'Clock in the Morning," and the sound of it filtered through the half sleep into Number One's bed. A vague memory stirred and he pushed himself upright, pulling the pillow behind him. He sat there thoughtfully for a moment, then pressed the button on the night table beside him.

A moment later Donald came into the room. As usual, he was dressed as if he had never gone to bed.

"Tell Roxanne I want to see her," Number One said.

"Roxanne?" Donald's voice was puzzled.

Number One looked at him. Then he remembered. Roxanne was gone. Many years ago. That was the trouble with memory. You never outlived it, only people.

"Get me dressed," he said. "I want to go downstairs."

"But the party is almost over, sir." Donald said respectfully.

"I don't care," Number One said, annoyed. "Get me dressed."

Twenty minutes later, Donald pushed the wheelchair out of the room and down the long corridor. Number One held up his hand as they came to the balcony overlooking the grand staircase leading to the entrance hall. Donald paused and they looked down.

The guests were still thronged around the door as they waited for the parking attendants, to bring their cars. They were still talking brightly and seemed reluctant to leave.

"It must have been quite a party," Number One said.

"Yes, sir."

"About how many people do you think?"

"Between four-fifty and five hundred," Donald answered.

Number One looked down at the crowd silently. People never changed. They weren't very different than the people that came to his parties all that many years ago. He looked back at Donald. "I don't want to get caught in that crowd," he said. "Take me to the library elevator."

Donald nodded and turned the wheelchair around and they went back along the corridor. At the end of the corridor, they turned into another that led to the other wing of the house. They stopped in front of the elevator door and Donald pressed the call button. The clock on the wall next to the elevator door told them it was ten minutes to four.

The discotheque was silent, only the musicians were left, disconnecting their electronic amplifiers and gathering their instruments. Somehow, now that they were not playing, they seemed oddly awkward and their monosyllabic instructions to each other were strangely stilted and archaically formal.

Angelo put his drink on the bar and looked at Elizabeth. She seemed curiously pensive and into herself. "I guess we're the last," he said.

She glanced around the darkened room. "I guess so."

"You're down," he said shrewdly.

She thought for a moment, then nodded.

"It's always like that after a big one," he said. "Somehow you gear up for it and while it's happening, everything's a ball. But the moment it's over—boom! You crash."

"I could use a drink," she said.

He signaled the bartender.

"No," she said quickly. She looked at him. "What I mean is—I would like a drag. Liquor doesn't turn me on. I don't like the taste of it."

"All I have is cigarettes," he said.

"I'm cool," she said, opening her small evening purse, taking out what looked like a package of cigarettes. She opened the fliptop box and shook out a corktip filter cigarette. She placed the cigarette in her mouth.

He held the light for her. "That is cool,' he said. "I've never seen them like that."

"There's a dealer who brings them in from Canada. You can get your favorite brand. Kent, Winston, L & M's, Marlboro, you name them." She dragged deeply and then giggled. "Only you have to be careful sometimes you don't pass them out by mistake."

He smiled.

She looked at him. "Do you turn on?'

"Sometimes," he said. "But not when I'm drinking. They don't mix."

She dragged again on the cigarette. This time she held the smoke in her lungs for a long while before she let it out. She blew the smoke out toward the ceiling. "I'm beginning to feel better."

"Good."

She laughed. "Matter of fact, I'm a little high." She looked at him. "But then I figure that I'm entitled to it. I haven't had one drag all night, even though everyone else was turning on."

"So I noticed," he said dryly.

She took one more pull on the cigarette then ground it out in a tray on the bar and got to her feet. Her eyes were smiling again. "Okay, Mr. Perino," she said. "I'm ready to go back to the manor house and face my family." She laughed humorlessly. "What's left of it, that is."

He took her arm and they walked out into the garden. The hanging lanterns went out, plunging the paths into darkness. She stopped abruptly and faced him.

"It really was a farce, wasn't it?"

He didn't answer.

"You know my mother's leaving for Reno tomorrow to get a divorce, don't you?"

He nodded.

"Then why the hell did they have to put me through all this?" she exploded. Suddenly she began to cry. The hard, bitter sobs of a child.

He took a handkerchief from his pocket and gave it to her. She dabbed at her eyes and stepped toward him, burying her face against his chest. "What were they trying to prove?" she sniffled.

He held her lightly, almost impersonally. "Maybe they didn't want to cheat you out of anything."

"They could have asked me," she said.

"The one thing I've learned about parents, Miss Elizabeth," he said quietly, "is—that they always ask when they shouldn't and that they never ask when they should."

Her sniffling stopped. She looked up at him. "Why do you call me Miss Elizabeth?"

In the night, his teeth flashed whitely. "Because it's your name. And I like the sound of it."

"But almost everyone calls me Betsy."

"I know," he said.

She touched her eyes with the handkerchief. "Do I look all right?"

"You look all right to me."

"I hope my eye makeup didn't run. I don't want anyone to know I've been crying."

"It didn't," he said.

"Good." She returned the handkerchief. "Thank you."

"Not at all," he said, putting it back in his pocket.

They walked along silently for a moment, hand in hand. Suddenly she stopped and looked up at him. "Do you believe in astrology?"

"I haven't made up my mind," he answered.

"I do," she said firmly. "I've just had my chart made up. You're Taurus, aren't you?"

"How did you know?" he smiled. He really wasn't. He was a Leo.

"You had to be!" she said excitedly. "It was all in my chart. I was due to meet an older man and he would be a Taurus and I would dig him very much."

He laughed aloud. "And do you?"

A mischievous smile came to her lips. "You wouldn't want me to make a liar out of my chart now, would you?"

"Miss Elizabeth," he smiled. "That's the very last thing in the world I would want to do."

Abruptly she put her hands on his face and standing on her toes, kissed him. Then her mouth grew hot and opened and her body clung to him. His arms tightened around her, almost crushing the breath from her, then let her go as quickly as he had taken her.

He looked down, shocked at his own unexpected response to her. "Why did you do that?"

She smiled a secret smile and suddenly she was no longer a child. "Now you can stop calling me Miss Elizabeth," she said.

Number One came through the elevator doors into the library. A lonely barman was there cleaning away the remnants of the party. He looked up when he saw them.

"Don't put away the whiskey," Number One said.

"Yes, Mr. Hardeman." The barman picked up a bottle of Canadian and placed it on the bar.

Number One turned to Donald. "You find my grandchildren and bring them here. All of them. Betsy too."

Donald hesitated.

"Go on, do what I say!" Number One snapped.

Donald still hesitated. "You're not going to drink, are you, sir?"

"No goddamnit!" Number One roared. "What kind of a fool do you think I am? You fetch them here!"

"Yes, sir."

Alicia was the first to enter the library. "I didn't know you were still awake, Grandfather."

"I couldn't sleep," he said. "Besides, I thought at least one time this evening we should all be together. Where's Loren?"

"I don't know," she said. "I haven't seen him for several hours."

"Donald will find him."

Igor and Anne were the next to come in. "Grandfather," Anne said, crossing the room to him.

He held up an interrupting hand. "I know," he said. "You didn't know I was still awake."

"Are you all right?"

"I never felt better," the old man said. He looked up as Elizabeth and Angelo appeared in the doorway. He gestured to her.

"Come in, my child."

Betsy ran across the room to him. "Great-Grandfather! I didn't think we'd see you tonight!" There was a genuine pleasure in her voice.

He smiled at her. "I didn't want to miss seeing you, especially tonight."

"Great-Grandfather, you're lovely!" She kissed his cheek.

He saw Angelo begin to walk away. "Angelo!" he called after him. "Please join us."

Angelo hesitated.

"Please do, Angelo," Betsy said quickly. "I know Great-Grandfather feels as if you're one of the family."

Number One glanced at her, then at Angelo. He smiled. "That's an official invitation."

Angelo came into the room. Donald appeared in the doorway behind him. "I can't seem to find Mr. Loren anywhere, sir," he said.

"He should be around somewhere," Angelo said. "We arranged to meet here after the party. I'll help you look for him."

"No need to bother," Loren's voice came from the open terrace door. He came into the room. "You're a half an hour late, Angelo," he said. "I told you we'd meet at three fifteen."

"I'm sorry," Angelo said. "I'm afraid I lost track of the time."

Loren shot him a hard glance, then turned to his grandfather. "Now that we're all here, Grandfather, what did you have in mind?"

Number One looked up at him. "I thought since this may be the last time we are all in this house together, it might be nice if we shared a final drink."

Loren nodded. "That's a nice sentimental gesture." He turned to Alicia. "I'll bet you never thought my grandfather was so fond of you that he would offer a farewell toast."

Number One's voice was suddenly icy. "Being my grandson doesn't excuse bad manners. I think you owe Alicia an apology."

"I owe her nothing!" Loren flashed. "She's already gotten all she's going to get from me."

The old man's voice became even colder. "I won't allow Hardeman women to be spoken to like that."

"In a few weeks she won't be one," Loren retorted.

"But right now she is still your wife," Number One snapped. "And, by God, you will treat her with respect or—."

"Or what, Grandfather?" Loren asked sarcastically. "You'll cut me out of your will?"

"No," the old man said quietly. "I can do better than that. I'll cut you out of my life."

There was a long silence in the room as they stared into each other's eyes. Loren's eyes dropped. "I apologize," he mumbled in a low voice.

"Barman." Number One turned his chair. "Give everyone a drink."

They were silent while the servant filled glasses and handed them around. Then they turned to Number One.

He held up his glass. "First—to the debutante. May she have many happy years."

He touched the liquor to his lips while they all drank, then he raised his glass again. "There's one other thing I have to tell you," he said.

"This is the last party that will ever be held in Hardeman Manor. When your grandmother and I built this house we had dreams that it would be filled with the laughter and the sound of our family. But it didn't quite work out that way. I guess neither of us ever thought that our children would go their own way and make their own lives. Maybe it was foolish of us to even dream of it, but now that the dreams are gone, I have no use for it.

"Tomorrow, Hardeman Manor will be closed. In the course of the next few weeks, certain personal things will be removed to Palm Beach and at the beginning of next month the State of Michigan will take it over to do with it what they will. That's why I wanted this last party to be held here. To just once more feel this house alive with people."

Number One looked around him. He held up his glass. "To Hardeman Manor, to my wife, to all my children, and to you."

He touched the glass to his lips, hesitated a moment, then threw the liquor down his throat. He coughed once, the tears coming to his eyes, then smiled. "Don't look so sad, children," he said gruffly. "It just shows you how far an old man will go to find an excuse to drink a shot of whiskey!"

Chapter Thirteen

Dan Weyman's voice was dry and flat. "What you're doing, Angelo, is asking us to throw away our dirty water before we get clean. That doesn't seem good business to me."

"Then we go thirsty," Angelo said. "But I'm sure that we'll have what we need."

"Sure?" Weyman's voice was unchanged. "Between the new plant on the Coast and research, we have already invested over sixty million dollars and we haven't even got an idea of what our new car will be."

"Maybe," Angelo replied. "But we do know what it will not be. And that's a step in the right direction."

"It's a negative step," Dan said. "What we have to take before the board is something positive." He looked across the desk at Loren who had been silent. "I, for one, can't go along with Angelo's idea to scrap the Sundancer for a car that nobody knows and may never be built. Half a loaf is better than none and in one year without a new car we may never get back into the market."

"According to the figures you gave me," Angelo said, "that half a loaf cost us almost forty-one million last year. If that's true, dumping the car will in one year pay for the original capital investment in the new plant."

"I pointed out that was an extraordinary loss," Dan said. "Almost half of it was due to the failure of Sundancer Super Sport to sell."

Angelo refrained from mentioning that he was the only member of the board who had been against the hot car, that he had correctly predicted the turning of the market.

"Let me just recap your recommendations so that I clearly understand them," Loren said. He placed his palms together judicially on the desk in front of him and studied them. "It is your recommendation that the Sundancer line be converted to a production line for the engines and transmission of the new car so as to create greater space on the Coast for final assembly. Is that correct?"

Angelo nodded. "Have you taken into account the cost of shipment to the Coast of those items and then the reshipment of the same parts in completed cars back East to market? Wouldn't that be a wasteful additional cost?"

Angelo nodded again. "It might. Perhaps it would be better to ship shells for the eastern market back to Detroit for assembly here, if we can find room on the line for it. I don't know yet and I won't know until the car is designed and approved. Then we can refine manufacturing procedures."

"I fail to see the rush to disavow the Sundancer," Loren said.

Angelo looked at him. "Because it's yesterday's automobile and I want to establish a brand-new outlook. A point of view that reflects today's market in both attitudes and concerns."

"Have you spoken to Number One about this?" Loren asked.

"Not yet," Angelo said.

"Do you think he will like the idea of stopping production of the Sundancer?" Loren asked. "After all, it was the car that built this company."

"I don't think he will like it," Angelo answered.

"Then why don't you try to find a compromise, a middle ground, one that will be easier for him to accept?"

Angelo looked at him. "Because that's not what he asked me to do. He asked me to build a new car that would get this company back into its former position in this industry. That's what he asked me to do and that's what I'm going to try to do. He didn't ask me to make him like it."

"I know my grandfather," Loren said. "And I suggest you better talk it over with him before the board meeting."

"I intend to do that." Angelo rose to his feet. "Thank you, gentlemen. See you later this afternoon."

They watched the door close behind him, then looked at each other.

"What do you think?" Dan asked. "Is he holding something back on us? Like maybe the design plans for the new car?"

"I don't know," Loren said thoughtfully. "I really don't know."

"He's talking awfully positive for a man who doesn't know what he's doing."

Loren looked at his friend. "Don't you make the same mistake that I did once."

"What do you mean?" Dan huffed.

"Once I thought he didn't know what he was doing and you saw what happened. In his own quiet Machiavellian manner, he almost destroyed us." He picked up a cigarette and lit it. "I'm not in the mood to give him another shot at me."

"Then what do we do?" Dan asked.

"We sit tight and wait," Loren said. "He's the man in motion, he has to prove himself. We don't have anything to prove. Our end of the business is paying the freight for all of us."

There was a message to call John Duncan at the Coast lying on his desk when he returned to his office. He picked up the telephone and held on while the operator put the call through.

The old Scot's voice came burring through the lines. "How was the party, laddie?"

"Fine," Angelo replied shortly. "But that's not what you called me about."

Duncan laughed. "What's happened to your sense of humor, Angelo?"

"Gone," Angelo snapped. "Along with eight missing hours of sleep. What's up?"

"I want your okay to do some work on my gas turbine engine."

"You finish the tests on the Japanese Wankel?"

"Not yet. But we know already it's good. Very good."

"Then maybe we can make a deal."

"Not a chance, laddie. One, they're planning to come on strong in the States next year; two, Ford's already wheeling and dealing for a share of Toyo Kogyo and they have the inside track. And with GM making their own deal with the Germans, we might as well forget it. They'll royalty us right out of the market."

Angelo was silent.

"I've been going over the turbine with Rourke," Duncan said. "And we'd like to try some experiments with titanium and steel castings. We have a feeling that we can get it to take the heat and stress as well as the nickel and carbon alloys. If it can, we may have a way to bring down the cost."

"Okay," Angelo said. "Try it." He reached for a cigarette. "Do you have the aerodynamics report on the designs yet?"

"No," Duncan said. "We have the models sideways in the wind tunnel to see what will give first but nothing's come through from them."

"Keep me posted," Angelo said.

"I will, laddie." Duncan hesitated a moment. "Tell me, how does Number One look to you?"

"Good."

"Have you spoken to him about the Sundancer yet?"

'No," Angelo replied. "I'm going to try to get to him before the meeting."

"Good luck, Angelo," Duncan said.

"Thank you. You too." Angelo put down the telephone. It rang again. He picked it up.

"Lady Ayres on the line," his secretary said.

He switched over. "Hello, Bobbie."

"You could have called me, Angelo." Her voice was faintly reproachful.

He laughed. "Stop putting me on. Mere vice-presidents don't call the boss's intended."

She laughed. "Now, you're putting me on. I thought I might invite you to lunch."

"I'd love to," he said. "But I have a hectic afternoon coming up. I thought I'd grab a sandwich at my desk."

"That's funny," she said. "That's exactly what Loren told me. Is that common among American executives? A sign of diligence or something?"

"I don't really know," he answered.

"Then come upstairs," she said. "I promise not to eat you."

"Wrong promise," he laughed.

"You come upstairs," she said, "and I'll promise to give you my latest American discovery for lunch."

"What's that?"

"A hero sandwich," she answered.

He laughed aloud. "I'll be right up. You certainly know the way to an Italian boy's heart."

"Take the last elevator on the bank," she said. "I'll clear the switch so that it comes up to the penthouse."

She was waiting at the door when he came off the elevator. The doors closed behind him and they stood there silently for a moment, just looking at each other.

"I'm only a bird in a gilded cage," she sang in a cracked voice. She tried to smile but she couldn't make it. Then she came into his arms and they stood there very quietly for a long time.

After a while she stepped back and looked up at him. "You've lost weight."

"A little."

"I've missed you."

He didn't speak.

"I've really missed you," she said.

He remained silent.

"You don't know what it's like, staying up here. There were times I thought I would go crazy."

"You could have left any time," he said. "You weren't chained here." He turned and pressed the call button for the elevator to return.

"Where are you going?"

"Back downstairs," he answered. "I was stupid to come up in the first place." The doors opened and he stepped into the elevator.

She placed a hand on the door to keep it from closing. "Stay."

He shook his head. "If I do, I might blow it for you. Do you really want that?"

She stared at him.

"Do you?" he repeated.

She let her hand fall from the door. He saw her turn and walk away as the doors rushed shut. Slowly, the elevator began its descent.

Number One sat quietly at the foot of the long directors' table. "Then we're all agreed, gentlemen," he said. "We'll approve production of the Sundancer until April of '71 and if Mr. Perino has completed satisfactory plans for the new car by that time, we will entertain a motion to convert."

He looked at Angelo. "Is that acceptable to you?"

"No, sir," Angelo said steadily. "But do I have a choice?"

"You don't," Number One said.

"Then there is just one further item I would like to call to the attention of the board," Angelo said. "I had set as a target for production and sales of the new car, five hundred thousand units in the first year. What you are doing is making that goal impossible to achieve by half, simply because it will take that much time to break down the old assembly line."

"We'll make a note of that in the minutes," Number One said. "In that case, with no further business to come before the board, I declare the meeting adjourned."

The door chimes finally made their way into his sleep. He opened his eyes and it took him a few moments to realize that he was in his suite at the Pontchartrain. He got out of bed and staggered through the living room to the door and opened it.

Betsy stood there. He couldn't tell which of them was the more surprised. "I'm sorry," she said. "I didn't think you'd be asleep so early."

"I was wiped out," he said groggily. "I've only had about four hours sleep in the last three days."

"I'm sorry."

"Don't apologize any more. You'll make me feel guilty. Come on in."

He led the way into the living room. "What time is it?" he asked.

"About ten thirty."

He pointed to the bar. "Help yourself to a drink while I get my robe." He padded off into the bedroom, his pajama trousers flapping around his legs.

When he came back she was drinking a Coke in a tall glass choked with ice cubes. He crossed to the bar and made himself a Canadian and water. He turned to look at her, taking a long sip of his drink. "Now, Miss Elizabeth," he said heavily, "What can I do for you?"

She looked at him for a moment, then her eyes fell. "I need a favor," she said, "A very important favor."

He took another pull at his drink. "Like what?"

Her eyes came up and met his gaze. "You'll think I'm being silly, or stoned, or something."

"No, I won't."

"Angelo," she said in a small voice.

"Yes?" he said, beginning to feel annoyed.

She hesitated for a moment.

"Yes?" he repeated.

"My chart says it will work out okay."

"What will?"

"You know," she explained. "You, me. Taurus and Virgo."

"Oh, sure," he said, completely bewildered.

"Then it's all settled," she smiled. She put the glass down on the bar. "And we can go to bed." She placed her arms around his neck.

"Wait a minute!" he protested. "Don't I have anything to say about this?"

"Not really," she said. "It's all written in the stars."

"But I'm not a Taurus," he said. "I'm Leo!"

An expression of hurt came into her eyes. "What's the matter, Angelo?" she asked. "Don't you want to marry me?"

BOOK THREE

1971

Chapter One

A hush fell over the small hearing room in the old wooden building that served as the county courthouse in the little town midway between Seattle and Spokane. Quietly, the coroner's jury filed into the room and took their seats on the wooden chairs that were placed near the table that served as the coroner's bench. The coroner, a tall man with a weatherbeaten face, ambled to his chair and sat down. He nodded to the bailiff.

The bailiff turned to the room. "The coroner's court is now in session to hear evidence into the cause of death of one Sylvester Peerless while driving a test car in the employ of Bethlehem Motors Corporation." He glanced down at a sheet of paper he held in his hand. "The court calls Miss Cindy Morris as witness."

Cindy turned in her chair and looked at Angelo. "I'm nervous. What do I tell them?"

Angelo reassured her. "Tell them the truth. You can never go wrong that way."

She got to her feet. An appreciative murmur went through the little room as she made her way to the witness chair, the form-fitting jump suit with the words, "BETHLEHEM MOTORS," lettered across the back, left no one with the illusion that she wasn't a girl.

The bailiff administered the oath quickly and asked her name.

"Cindy Morris."

"Please sit down," he said and went back to his own chair.

She sat down as the county prosecutor got to his feet. Like all the men in this portion of the country, he was a tall man who gave the impression that he might have stepped out of a Marlboro Country advertisement. But the outdoors look did nothing to hide the keen intelligence of his gray eyes.

He stopped in front of her. His voice was soft with deceptively gentle western twang. "How old are you, Miss Morris?"

"Twenty-four," she answered.

"Twenty-four," he repeated, nodding.

"Yes."

"You are an employee of Bethlehem Motors?"

"Yes."

"In what capacity?"

"Test driver and design consultant."

"Please explain your duties."

"I drive the cars and report to the design and engineering chief as to a woman's point of view about the cars."

"How long have you been thus employed by Bethlehem Motors?"

"About a year and a half."

"How many cars have you driven and tested in this time?"

"Approximately nineteen."

"Do you regard your work as dangerous?"

"Not really."

The district attorney looked at her. "That's a curious answer. What do you mean by it?"

"I feel much safer driving a car on a test track where every possible safety precaution is taken than I do driving in ordinary every day traffic."

He was silent for a moment, then he nodded. "I see." He walked back to his table and picked up a sheet of paper. Holding it in his hand, he walked back to her. "Were you acquainted with the deceased driver, Sylvester Peerless?"

"Yes."

"In what manner?"

"We were good friends."

The attorney looked down at the paper. "I have here a copy of the registration card at the Starlight Motel. It reads and I quote, 'Mr. and Mrs. Sylvester Peerless, Tarzana, California.' In brackets after that, 'Cindy Morris'. Were you ever married to Mr. Peerless?"

"No."

"Then how do you explain the registration?"

"I said we were good friends. We shared the room. I wasn't aware of how Fearless registered us.

The attorney smiled. "You mean to say you were roommates and that's all?"

Cindy smiled back at him, her nervousness disappearing completely. This kind of talk she understood. "I didn't say that, you did. If you are interested in whether Fearless and I ever had sexual relations, why don't you ask?"

"Did you?" the attorney shot back.

"From time to time," she said calmly. "When we felt like it."

The attorney stood there silently. Then he shrugged his shoulders and went back to his table. He put the sheet of paper back on it and turned to her. "Were you present at the test track the day the deceased met his death?"

"Yes."

"Was there anything unusual about the circumstances of that day?"

"Yes."

"What were they?"

"Fearless got himself killed."

A small ripple of laughter ran through the room. The attorney made a face and waited for it to pass. "Was there anything else?"

She thought for a moment. "I don't think so. That was unusual enough."

Again the ripple of laughter. Again the attorney waited for it to pass. "I mean," he said, "was there anything unusual about the performance of the car he was testing?"

"I didn't think so," she answered. "I turned the car over to him after my two-hour trick and it was behaving perfectly."

"Did he say anything to you that might have indicated his concern over the performance of the automobile?"

"No."

"Did he say anything at all to you at that time?"

"Yes, he did."

"What did he say?"

"He made a remark. A joke. You know."

"I don't know," the attorney said.

"A private joke," she said uncomfortably. She glanced around the room. "The kind of thing you don't say in public."

"What did he say?" the attorney insisted.

Her face flushed and she looked down at the floor. She spoke in a low voice. "He said he felt so horny he hoped his cock wouldn't get caught in the steering wheel."

The lawyer's face reddened as a murmur ran through the room. "Did you say anything to him?"

"Only what I usually say."

"What was that?"

"Drive carefully."

The lawyer was silent. "What did you mean by that?"

"Nothing," she answered. "I always say that whenever someone gets behind the wheel of a car."

"You didn't mean that to indicate something special that might be wrong with the particular car you were driving?"

"No," she replied. "I always say that."

"Did you see the accident happen?"

"No, I did not," she said. "I went back to the motel and went to sleep."

The attorney looked at her for a moment, then walked back to his desk. "I have no further questions."

The coroner leaned across his table. "Do you have any ideas or opinions as to what might have caused the accident that resulted in Mr. Peerless's death?"

"No, sir, I do not," Cindy answered.

"I understand that the car was powered by a new kind of engine," the coroner said. "A gas turbine. I also understand that kind of engine could sometimes explode under certain conditions. Do you think something like that might have happened and caused the accident?"

Cindy looked at him thoughtfully. "It might have but I doubt it. That engine had over thirty thousand miles on it and if it was gong to blow up, it would have done so long before then."

"But it might have?" the coroner persisted.

Cindy's voice was level. "I don't know. But isn't that the purpose of this court? To determine what happened?"

The coroner looked at her. His voice was cool. "We expect to do just that, young lady." He glanced at the jury. "Do you have any further questions?"

A murmur of no's came from the jurors and he turned back to Cindy. "That will be all, Miss Morris. Thank you. You may step down now."

The room was silent as Cindy walked back to her seat. She looked at Angelo. "Was I all right?"

He patted her hand. "You were fine."

"The son of a bitch," she whispered. "He didn't have to ask me all those questions."

"You told the truth," Angelo said. "Don't worry."

The bailiff's voice came through the room. "Will Mr. John Duncan take the stand?"

The Scotsman got to his feet. He didn't look his sixty-five years as he walked firmly to the stand and took the oath.

"Your name, please?" the bailiff asked.

"John Angus Duncan," he replied and sat down.

The county prosecutor rose and walked toward him. "Would you please tell us your position with Bethlehem Motors?"

"Vice-president, engineering."

"How long have you held that position?"

"One and a half years."

"And before that?"

"I was for twenty years vice-president of automotive production at that company. At the age of sixty I retired. Two years later I rejoined the company in this present capacity."

"Would you please define your present responsibilities?"

"I am in charge of the engineering part of the Project Betsy."

"What is Project Betsy?"

"It is the building and development of a new car presently being considered by the company."

"Can you elaborate on that?"

"No." The Scotsman was terse. "It would be disclosing confidential information privileged to my employer."

The county prosecutor glanced at his notes. "I understand that you hold certain patents in connection with a turbine engine. Is that true?"

"Yes," Duncan nodded. "I might point out that they are held jointly with my employer."

"Is that the engine used in the vehicle in which Mr. Peerless met his death?"

"A variation of that engine was used."

"Can you elaborate on that?"

"No." Duncan was firm. "For the same reason mentioned by me before and also that certain patents are currently pending and disclosure would give information to our competitors."

The county prosecutor went back to his table. "Were you present at the scene at the time Mr. Peerless met his death?" he asked.

"Yes, I was."

"Could you tell us about it?"

"Mr. Peerless entered curve number four at a speed of one hundred and seventy-one miles per hour despite our warnings to him and went off the track into the wall."

"You say he was warned. How was this done?"

"We are in constant radio communication with the driver of the car."

"You were able to judge the speed of the vehicle?"

"Yes. Our test cars are equipped with radio sensor devices which constantly send information back to a control computer which records the performance of every part of the automobile."

"Would it be possible for us to see this record?"

"No," Duncan replied. "For all the reasons I mentioned before."

"But your sensor devices indicated there was nothing mechanically wrong with the car?"

"The car was operating perfectly."

"Do you have a record of your warning to Mr. Peerless?"

"Yes. There is a tape of that communication."

"Is it possible for us to hear that?"

Duncan looked across the room at Angelo. Angelo turned to Roberts, sitting next to him. The attorney nodded.

"Yes," Duncan said. "I have a tape playback unit in my attaché case which I left on my seat and can play it for you right now."

The coroner leaned forward. "Would the bailiff please fetch Mr. Duncan's case?"

The bailiff brought the case to Duncan. The Scotsman opened it and took out a cassette playback unit. He looked questioningly at the coroner.

"It's all right, Mr. Duncan. You can place it on the table in front of me."

Duncan got up and set the small machine on the table. He pressed the button. A faint hum filled the room. He turned up the volume control. The hum grew louder.

"I don't hear any engine sound," the coroner said.

"There is very little," said Duncan. "This is a turbine engine and the noise level is negligible compared with the normal I.C. engine. The only background sounds you might hear are the wind and the tires."

A man's voice broke into the tape. "I read one seventy-five on the speedometer. Verify. Over."

Duncan's voice came on the tape. "One seven four point nine nine seven, verified. Better start taking her down, you're coming up on number four. Over."

For a moment there was nothing but the background hum on the tape, then Duncan's voice came on again. "We read you at one seven three point one two five. Bring it down. You're running out of time. Over."

Silence again, then Duncan's voice. This time there was a note of urgency in it. "Duncan to Peerless. We read you at one seventy-one point zero five zero. Bring it down! This is an order! Over."

Silence. Duncan's voice harsh and angry. "Are you crazy, Peerless? Bring it down before you get yourself killed! Over."

Peerless's voice came on. He laughed. "Don't be such an old fuddy-duddy. I can take her through."

Duncan's voice overrode him. "You've only got a four percent grade, you'll never make it!"

"You got no faith in your own machine, old man," Peerless laughed. "Leave it to Fearless Peerless. I know what I'm doing. I drive with the angels."

For a moment there was nothing but the faint whine, then the sound of a faint pop, then nothing. Complete silence.

There was a complete silence in the room as Duncan reached out and turned the machine off. He looked at the coroner.

The coroner cleared his throat. "Were you able to hear that?" he asked the jury.

The foreman stood up. "Yes."

The coroner turned to Duncan. "You mentioned a four percent grade on that turn. What did you estimate a safe speed for it? Maximum?"

"One hundred ten."

"Were there any warning signs posted to that effect?"

"Yes, sir. Every two hundred yards beginning two miles before the turn."

"Then you estimate that Mr. Peerless entered that turn at sixty miles per hour in excess of the maximum safe speed?"

"Yes, sir."

"Could you tell me at what point then the engine exploded?"

"The engine did not explode," Duncan said.

The county prosecutor cut in. "But previous witnesses testified that there was an explosion followed by a fire. How do you explain that, Mr. Duncan?"

The Scotsman turned to him. "The explosion did not take place in the engine. It took place in the fuel tank ignited by an electrostatic spark as the tank cracked open."

"Then there could have possibly been a fault in the fuel tank?"

"There was no fault in the fuel tank. It was equipped and built with every safety precaution known to man. But there is nothing in our present technology that will enable us to build a tank that can resist an impact at one seventy miles an hour."

"How can you be sure that it was the fuel tank and not the engine?"

"Because we have the fuel tank. It is smashed beyond repair but the engine itself is mostly in one piece. If it had exploded, it would have been scattered all over the place."

The county prosecutor nodded and went back to his seat. The coroner looked at the jury. "Do you have any further questions?'

The foreman stood up hesitantly. "I drive a car, Mr. Duncan. And because of the high power performance of your engine, I suppose you have to use a very high octane gasoline. Is that what was used?"

"No, sir." Duncan said. "That is one of the advantages of a turbine engine. It does not require high octane or leaded gasoline to achieve maximum efficiency."

"What kind of gasoline did you use then?" the foreman asked.

"We did not use gasoline."

"What did you use then?"

"Kerosene," Duncan replied.

"Thank you," the foreman nodded and sat down.

The coroner leaned across his bench. "Do you think, Mr. Duncan, that had you used gasoline instead of kerosene the explosion and the fire that followed it might have been prevented?"

"Not under the circumstances." Duncan was very sure of himself. "As a matter of fact, it would have been more susceptible to explosion and fire. The octane rating in gasoline is a measure of its combustibility, thus the higher the rating, the more combustible."

The coroner glanced around the room, then back at the Scotsman. "It seems there are no further questions. Thank you, Mr. Duncan. You may step down."

The room was silent as the Scotsman returned to his chair. Angelo shook his hand and Cindy kissed the old man's cheek. "You were wonderful," she said.

The Scotsman flushed, pleased. "But I'm still angry," he whispered. "What I want to know is who put them up to this?"

"We'll find out," Angelo said calmly. "First let's see what happens next."

The coroner and the county prosecutor were conferring in whispers. After a moment the attorney returned to his seat and the coroner looked at the court.

"There will be no further witnesses called," he said. He turned to the jury. "You have heard the testimony of the doctors who performed the autopsy on the remains of Mr. Peerless as to the fact that his death was due directly to injuries received in the course of the collision and that the burns on his body were after his decease. You have also heard the testimony of other witnesses supplying information in connection with circumstances surrounding the death of Mr. Peerless. Do you have any further questions to ask pertaining to this matter?"

The foreman shook his head. "No."

The coroner nodded and continued. "You are then requested to reach a determination as to the cause and responsibility for Mr. Peerless's death. There are several such determinations available to you. Let me list some of them.

"One, in the event that you feel Mr. Peerless's death was the fault of anyone other than himself, you may so state. If you further feel that there was criminal negligence resulting in that fault, you may so state. You do not in either of above cases need to name the person or persons responsible, though you may if you should so desire.

"Two, in the event that you feel Mr. Peerless's death was his own fault, you may so state. In that case you may state simply that the cause of death was due to driver error."

He paused and looked at the jury. They were silent. "Do you wish now to retire and consider your verdict?"

The foreman of the jury leaned over to his confreres. For a moment there was a whispered conversation, then he rose to his feet. "No, sir."

The coroner looked at him. "Ladies and gentlemen of the jury, do you wish to render your determination?"

The foreman nodded, "Yes, sir."

"And that is?"

The small room was very silent as the foreman began to speak. "It is the unanimous conclusion of this jury that in the matter of the death of Mr. Sylvester Peerless, the cause of his death was his own fault, driver error and plain damn foolishness on his part."

A rustle of noise burst in the small room as reporters began to rush toward the door. The coroner's gavel banged on the table before him. His voice could hardly be heard over the bustle of sound.

"The determination of the jury has been heard and the coroner's inquest into the death of Sylvester Peerless is now closed."

Chapter Two

In the corner of the dimly lit cocktail bar of the Starlight Motel, a goateed black piano player made gentle drink-time noises which tinkled behind the hum of conversation in the crowded room. They sat jammed into a tiny booth against the far wall.

Artie Roberts looked across the table at Angelo. "What's my best connection to New York tomorrow morning? Spokane or Seattle?"

Angelo shrugged. "I think Seattle has more flights but Spokane is sixty miles nearer. Check it out with the front desk."

Artie got to his feet. "I'll do that now. Be right back."

Cindy picked up her drink and stared into it. "It's the death wish, that's what it is."

"What did you say?" Angelo asked.

She didn't look up from the glass. "I think that's what it is. You all really want to die, don't you?"

Angelo didn't answer.

"You know, I knew he was going to kill himself when he got in that car," she said, still staring into her glass. "That's why I went back to the motel instead of hanging around for him. I didn't want to be there when he did it."

"If that was the way you felt, why didn't you try to stop him?" Angelo asked.

"What for? If he wouldn't do it that day, he would another. I wasn't going to be around to stop him forever."

Angelo signaled for another round. She picked up her fresh drink and tasted it.

"I think I'll be moving on tomorrow," she said.

"What for? Got anything better to do?"

She shook her head. "No. But this isn't my bag. You know that. These cars don't make any noise."

"Someday all cars won't make noise," he said. "Then what'll you do?"

"By that time, I'll be too old to enjoy it anyway," she said.

"You're a good driver," said Angelo. "I know Duncan won't like to lose you. He says you have a good point of view."

"I like the old man. But I only took the job to go along with Fearless. He thought you were going into racing then."

"So did we," Angelo said. "But that's not where it's at any more. At least not in what we're trying to do."

"I know that," she said. She picked up her drink and looked at it. "When did you stop being crazy?"

"What do you mean?"

She looked at him. "You were like all the others once. Ready to buy it any time, any place, on any corner. Then, like all in one crazy day, it was over and you weren't the same man in the afternoon that you were in the morning. I knew that when I came and found you in the tub."

"We all have to grow up sometime," he said. "Maybe that was my time."

She was silent. She put her drink down with a kind of finality. "Maybe that's it.

I don't want to grow up. Grown-ups don't need me. They can manage very well by themselves. But guys like Fearless, like you used to be, need someone to hold them together when they're not behind a wheel. Someone who can make them feel a little bit alive when they're not doing what they're about."

She rose. "I had them move me to another room."

"That's a good idea," he said.

"I have some new tapes you haven't heard. Maybe after dinner you'll come over and we'll listen to them."

"We'll see. I'll give you a call about eight o'clock when we're ready for dinner."

"Better make it closer to seven if you figure on getting anything to eat," she said. "They roll it up early around here."

"Okay." He watched her thread her way through the crowded lounge and there was something very alone and young and wistful in the way she moved.

The waiter appeared at his elbow. "There's a long distance call for you, Mr. Perino."

He followed the waiter to a booth in the corner of the room. He closed the door and the sounds faded into the background.

"Mr. Perino?" the long lines operator singsonged.

"Speaking."

Number One's voice came on. "You're a hard man to find," he complained irascibly.

"No, I'm not," Angelo replied. "This is the only bar in town."

"I just heard over the radio about the coroner's finding. I thought you were going to call me."

"I figured it was too late back East by the time we got out of court. But it worked out all right."

"We were lucky. It could have turned up a real stink," the old man said.

"I would still like to find out who put the finger on us," Angelo said. "I'm sure the coroner and local county prosecutor didn't dream this up by themselves."

"You sound more like your grandfather every day," said Number One. "He was always convinced there was a plot behind everything. That nothing happened by itself."

"Maybe he was right," Angelo said. "But you know as well as I that had we been caught off base, the publicity could have wiped out the whole project before we even got started. Doesn't it seem a little strange to you that the news and wire services had the story on the inquest even before we were served?"

"We're building a new car," Number One said. "That's big news. You might as well get used to it. They'll be watching you every minute."

"I know that already," Angelo said. "The photographers have been all over the place trying to get pictures of the car. They've even come over the proving grounds in helicopters with telescopic cameras."

"They get anything?"

"Not of our design. But they have plenty of photos of Vegas, Pintos and Gremlins. Maybe even a Maverick or Nova or two."

Number One chuckled. "That should annoy them. How many cars do you have on the road?"

"Thirty-one on the roads all over the West and South-west. Eight on the proving grounds plus six without camouflage which we run only at night."

"You're doing all right. When do you think you'll be ready to freeze the design?"

"Seven, eight months. September or October," Angelo replied.

"We won't make the fall showings."

"That's right," Angelo said. "But I figure we can make the New York Automobile Show in the spring. It might even be to our advantage. All the other seventy-two's will be frozen, we can be the first out with a seventy-three."

"I like that," Number One said. His tone changed. "I have someone here who wants to talk to you."

Angelo heard the phone change hands. Betsy's voice came on the wire. It had a faint, breathless quality. "When are you going to let me come out and drive one of those cars?"

"When we're finished with our tests, Miss Elizabeth," he replied.

"You don't have to be so formal, Angelo," she said. "I told Number One about the night I came to your hotel room."

He laughed. "I hoped you also told him I drove you home."

"I told him that too and he wanted to know why?"

"Could be you just turned eighteen," Angelo said.

"That's how old great-grandmother was when he married her. You better think it over. Girls like me don't stay available too long."

Angelo laughed. "Maybe it's just that I'm not the marrying kind, Miss Elizabeth."

"I'm going to Europe to visit my aunt after Daddy's wedding," she said. "You know about the men over there."

"I know about them," he smiled. "I hope you do."

"You still think I'm a child. Just because you went to school with my mother doesn't mean that I'm not old enough for you."

"I don't doubt that for a minute," he said. "But I'm the old-fashioned type. I think the man should do the asking."

"Okay," she said. "Ask me."

"Not just now," he laughed. "I've got a car to build." There was a knock on the door of the phone booth. A sheriff's deputy stood there. "Hold on a moment," he told her and opened the door.

"Mr. Perino?" the deputy asked politely.

"Yes?"

"This is for you." He handed Angelo an official-looking document.

It seemed to be a standard warrant form. His name, Duncan and Bethlehem Motor Company were typed on the cover sheet. He opened the paper and looked at it. It was an injunction signed by a judge forbidding them to drive any of their test cars powered by a gas turbine engine on any road in the State of Washington. He looked up. The deputy was already halfway through the lounge. He turned back to the telephone. "Put Number One back on."

A note of concern came into her voice. "Is there anything wrong?"

"Plenty," he said sharply. "Put him on."

"What is it?" Number One's voice echoed in the phone.

"I was just served an injunction that orders us not to drive any of our cars on public roads in this state."

"What?" Number One was surprised. "How can they do such a thing?"

"I don't know how they can do it but they did," he said. He paused a moment while he fished for a cigarette with his free hand. "Now, tell me that no one's behind all this."

Number One was silent.

"Whoever it is has a lot of muscle going for him," Angelo said.

"What are you going to do?"

"Artie Roberts is still here," Angelo replied. "He was checking the next flight to New York. But he's not going to make it. He can fight this in the courts."

"That could take a lot of time," Number One said.

"If it was nothing but time I wouldn't be that worried," said Angelo. "If we don't get this injunction lifted, the Betsy may never get on the road."

Chapter Three

"Only thirty days more and the divorce will be final," Loren III said.

Bobbie put down the empty Martini glass. "By that time it won't matter. Another month here and I'll go out of my mind. I'm not used to being a prisoner."

"You're not a prisoner, darling," he said patiently. "You know the people here. Once we're married everything will change. We'll move out to the house and life will become normal."

"What makes you think that?" she asked sarcastically. "The few times we have gone out, Detroit has done a pretty good job of cutting me dead."

"Stupid women," he replied. "It will change. Believe me, I know it will."

"Fuck them!" she said angrily. "I don't need them or their bloody approval." She rose from the couch. "I just have to get away from here for a while."

He looked up at her. "Where do you want to go?"

"I don't know. Anywhere. Just as long as it's away from here." She walked to the bar and poured herself another martini from the pitcher. She looked back at him. "I swear to God I'm becoming an alcoholic."

"I can't get away just now," he said.

"I know that." She walked over to the window and looked out. The factory lights gleamed in the dull black night, the tips of the chimneys belching rose-colored flames into the sky. "Look at that view," she said bitterly. "You know for almost a year I've been looking out this window without ever seeing a tree or a bit of green. I think I've almost forgotten what they look like."

Loren got to his feet and came over to her. He put his arms around her and drew her to him. She rested her head on his shoulder. "I know it hasn't been easy," he said. "But we expected it."

"I'm sorry," she said. "I know it hasn't been any easier for you. But at least you have your work to keep you busy. I have nothing to do but go out of my mind."

"Look," he said. "Give me a few days to clear things up here and then maybe we'll go out West and take a look at how they're doing with the test cars. It's time I went out there anyway."

"I'd love that. I have a feeling the new car will be great."

"I hope so," he said without enthusiasm.

She looked at him. "You're worried about it, aren't you?"

He nodded.

"Why? When everybody in the business is so excited about it?"

"They can afford to be," he said dourly. "It's not their money. If the car misses, it can take the whole company down with it." He walked back to the bar and picked up his drink. "If it hits, we'll do all right, but within a couple of years, GM and Ford will step in and take over the market, so in reality all we're doing is risking our capital for them."

He walked back to her. "I remember the year I was made president of the company. 1953. The year the Kaiser-Frazer company finally gave up the ghost and went down the drain. They had a good car but they couldn't beat the system. Between the competition and the Korean War, which cut their sources of supply, they got wiped out. I made up my mind then I was not going to fight them. I would settle for whatever share of the automobile market we could squeeze out and concentrate on the other areas for profit. And I wasn't wrong. There hasn't been a year since in which the company netted less than six million after taxes. Now, a ghost from the past threatens to blow the whole company sky high."

It was the longest speech she ever heard him make. She stared at him thoughtfully. "Did you ever tell Number One that?"

His voice was bitter. "There's no one alive that my grandfather will listen to. Except maybe Angelo. And, even then, only if Angelo tells him what he wants to hear."

"But what about you?" she asked. "Wouldn't you like to build a new car? A car that everyone would want?"

He looked at her. "Of course I would. That's the dream of every man in this business. But when I was a boy I wanted to be the first man on the moon. That didn't happen either."

"Then why didn't you get out of the automobile business altogether?"

"I should have. I know that now." He looked down into the amber of his drink. "But I knew that if I did, my grandfather would die. That was the only reason for him to stay alive, that was all he cared about."

She was silent for a moment, then put her drink down and took his from his hand. She put it down beside her own. "Come to bed," she said.

"The big problem with the turbine engine has been acceleration response and lack of engine braking," Tony Rourke said. "We think we finally licked it." He gestured to the blueprints on Loren III's desk. "By adding a counter rotor to the drive rotor which would be activated by a stator vane deflecting the thrust pressure as the throttle is lessened, we create the artificial equal of normal I.C. engine braking. It also serves to hold the car from rolling when in gear and idling at normal speeds. And, conversely, it eliminates the response lag normally present in a turbine, so that speed for pickup and passing is always there."

Loren looked across the desk. "Has this been tested?"

"Thoroughly," Rourke said. "It's been in use on all the test cars since last December and so far has averaged approximately twenty thousand miles in use per car."

"It's expensive," Loren said. He looked at Weyman. "You have the figures?"

Weyman nodded. "It will add approximately one hundred and thirty-one dollars to the cost of each engine if we manufacture it here in quantities of two hundred thousand or more."

Rourke turned to him. "Does that include the savings resulting from the fact that we won't have to build an auxiliary power source to operate the accessories at idling speeds?"

Weyman nodded. "We took that into consideration," he answered in his precise accountant's voice. "The principal factor is labor costs here in Detroit. At the moment fine tolerances involved in manufacturing these rotors take the job out of the unskilled classification into that of skilled machinists."

"It can't be that bad," Rourke said. "Toyo Kogyo is building rotors and selling them in low-end cars."

"That's the edge the Japanese have on us," Weyman said. "Their labor is much more controlled."

"I could build them for less on the Coast," Rourke said. "I'm sure of that. But it doesn't make sense to build the rotors there, ship them here for incorporation into the engine, then ship them all back for final car assembly."

"By the time you get through with all that you wouldn't be saving very much." Weyman spoke positively. "It wouldn't be worth it."

"What does the car cost out at now?" Loren said.

"Nineteen hundred and fifty-one dollars before adding the new rotors. They put us up to almost twenty-one hundred."

"It doesn't make sense," Rourke said. "I'm sure that the Gremlin doesn't cost American Motors much over seventeen hundred to manufacture."

"It costs less," Weyman said. "That's what they average from the dealer, including federal taxes. But that's stripped. They don't have to include power accessories and air-conditioning to use up available engine power. There's almost seven hundred dollars of extras that we have to have on our car which have to be included in the cost."

"At that rate the Betsy would have to retail at about twenty-five hundred dollars," Rourke said.

"Twenty-four ninety-five is the figure Sales came up with," said Loren.

"Sounds high compared with the others. The Pinto at nineteen, the Vega at twenty-one, not to mention the imports. They'll kill us."

"Now you're getting an idea of what we're up against," Weyman said.

"It's not that bad," Loren put in. "With accessories and options you can add four hundred dollars to the average selling price of those cars. We're not far off on a net basis."

Rourke looked at him. "Then you think we have a chance?"

Loren's gaze was steady. "Not the chance of a snowball in hell. Not the way the costs on this are climbing. It will take a miracle car to convince the public that paying more in this case is actually paying less. We're going to price ourselves right out of the low-end market and we'll be right back where we are now. The only difference will be that we'll be out some three hundred million dollars." He reached for a cigarette and lit it. "I'm afraid my grandfather is still living in the past. When Henry Ford showed the world how the American production line could bring down the cost per item. But since then the world has caught up and in the case of Japan and Germany has even surpassed us in new equipment and automation. And they have a fantastic advantage that we don't. German labor costs are sixty percent of ours and the Japanese maybe forty percent."

He blew out a cloud of smoke and ground the cigarette into the tray on his desk. "The way I see it, Angelo made one big mistake. He should have built his plant in Japan instead of on the Coast. It was the only way he could be cost-competitive."

"Your grandfather wanted an American-built car," Rourke said.

"I know he did," Loren replied. "But that doesn't make it right. People don't care any more where the thing is built. Only if it is good and its price is right."

"I'd like a chance to go over those figures," said Rourke. "Maybe I could come up with something."

"I hope you can," Loren said. "We can use all the help we can get."

"I won't make any promises," Rourke said. "Your boys are pretty good."

"How are things going out there?" Loren asked.

"Okay, now," Rourke answered. "That injunction last week threw us. But after we showed them that Chrysler had car turbines on the road since '63 and Ford and GM are bringing it out in trucks, it was lifted. Angelo still thinks someone is trying to throw a monkey wrench into the works."

Loren smiled. "It doesn't make sense. The other companies know we're doing them a favor by going so far out on the limb. They're not risking a penny of their own money and while we're doing that, they're minding the store and taking it in as usual."

"You got to admit that it seems like more than a coincidence. The inquest and the injunction right on top of it."

"Probably some hot local crusader trying to make a name for himself," Weyman said.

"If so, why hasn't he come to the surface yet?" Rourke asked. "I've been out there ten years now and have a lot of friends but no one seems to know just where it came from."

"Will you be talking to Angelo later?" Loren asked.

"Yes."

"Would you ask him to reserve a suite plus two extra bedrooms for next Friday through Tuesday. I'm coming out there with my daughter and my fiancée."

Rourke looked at him curiously. He was about to mention that he had met the Lady Ayres but decided to keep his mouth shut. "I'll give him the message," he said. "But if you want to stay near the proving grounds, I don't think the Starlight Motel has any suites."

"We'll settle for three large rooms then," said Loren.

"I'll take care of it." Rourke got to his feet. He held out his hand. "Thank you for your time, Mr. Hardeman."

Loren took it. "You don't have to thank me. It may not seem like it at times but there is one thing I would like you to remember. We're all on the same team."

Rourke met his gaze. "I never doubted that for a moment, Mr. Hardeman." He looked down at Weyman. "I'll be over in Production Estimating when you want me, Dan."

"Right." Dan sat in his chair and when the door closed behind Rourke, he spoke again. "What do you think, Loren?"

"I think Angelo picked himself a winner. Rourke's a good man."

"What I want to know is do you think they'll come up with who is behind their troubles out there?"

Loren looked at him steadily. "It all depends on how clever your man was in covering his tracks."

"He's supposed to be very good," Dan said. "At least for the money he cost us, he should have been."

"Then stop worrying about it," Loren said. He got to his feet. "I guess there's nothing we can do now to stop it. Just watch the Betsy drive us down the merry road to bankruptcy."

"You're still president of the company," Dan said. "There's something you can do if you want to."

Loren's voice went cold. For a moment he sounded like his grandfather. "Leave it alone."

Weyman got to his feet. He made a gesture with his hands. "As you say. You're the boss. Just remember one thing. Time's running out. In less than sixty days from now we're going to have to decide if we turn over the Sundancer plant to Angelo or not."

Loren stared at him. "Aren't you getting things just a little mixed up, Dan? The question isn't whether we turn the Sundancer plant over to Angelo. The question is, do we drop the Sundancer and go with the Betsy."

"It's the same thing," Weyman said smoothly. "What I can't make you understand is that in the eyes of the industry and the public, the man who builds the car runs the company." He rose from his chair and walked toward the door. There he paused and looked back at Loren. "But the man they'll hold responsible for the losses will be the president of the company. And that's you."

Chapter Four

The interior of the giant hangarlike garage hummed with activity. Jump-suited mechanics in white with BETHLEMEM MOTORS lettered in red across their backs swarmed in bee-like clusters around various cars, each over a pit, the body shell raised on front jacks so that the engine and chassis of the car were completely exposed.

"Those are the chameleons," Angelo explained as he led them toward the rear of the garage.

"Chameleons?" Bobbie asked.

"Camouflaged cars," Angelo explained. "We use bodies of other companies' cars so that they can't get our design. It enables us to test the car on the road without attracting attention."

He paused in front of giant doors at the back of the hangar. A large sign was posted:

RESTRICTED PERSONNEL. ALL OTHERS KEEP OUT!

He unpinned the plastic I.D. card from his lapel and inserted it into the slot of an electric lock. The doors began to whir open. He withdrew the card and they walked through, the doors automatically closing behind them. Behind the doors there was a large screening wall, so that no one outside could see into the back when the doors were opened. Angelo led them around the wall.

They came into a large open area in the center of the garage. In this room there were no cars to be seen; instead they were each kept in large, closed-in stalls around the sides of the room. An occasional mechanic would come out of one stall and enter another. An armed security guard came toward them.

He recognized Angelo and nodded. "Good afternoon, Mr. Perino."

Angelo gave him the I.D. card. He turned to the others. "Give him your I.D. cards. He will return them when you leave."

Loren unpinned the card and gave it to the guard. He looked carefully at Loren's photo on it, then at Loren. He nodded and collected the cards from Bobbie and Elizabeth and walked away.

Angelo explained. "The reason for the extra security in this room is because in here we keep our production design prototypes."

John Duncan came out of one of the stalls. He came toward them a smile on his face. "Loren!" he said with obvious pleasure.

"John!" They shook hands. "You look fifteen years younger."

"I feel that way," the Scotsman said. "We're at it again. Doing what we should do."

"I'd like you to meet my fiancée, Roberta Ayres. Bobbie, this is John Duncan, whom I told you so much about."

The Scotsman's face gave no visible sign that they had met before as he took her hand. "A pleasure to meet you, Miss Ayres."

"My pleasure, Mr. Duncan," she said politely.

"And you know my daughter, Betsy?" Loren added.

Duncan smiled. "She's grown a little since I saw her last. How are you, Miss Hardeman?"

"Fine, thank you." She turned to Angelo. "Now can we see the car? I can't wait any longer."

Angelo looked at Duncan. "Can we get the Silver Sprite out here?"

The Scotsman nodded. "I think we might." He walked back toward one of the stalls.

"The Silver Sprite is a prototype high-performance sports car. We don't intend to put it on the market until after we establish our production line. We plan to use it for auto shows and maybe in a race or two if we can get it qualified." Angelo looked up. The doors to one of the stalls were opening.

The car appeared rolling toward them, being pushed by four men, while Duncan sat in the driver's seat, guiding the wheel. It came to a stop in the center of the hangar, the light from the bright fluorescents overhead shimmering on its aluminium body.

"It's beautiful!" Betsy caught her breath, the surprise echoing in her voice. "Oh, Angelo, it's just beautiful."

"What did you expect? A funny car?"

"I didn't know what I expected," she said. "I thought with all that talk about a popular car, it would turn out something like a Volks."

"With a name like Betsy? Do you think either your father or your great-grandfather would let me get away with that?"

She turned to her father. "Did you see it?"

Loren shook his head. "I saw the clays, mockups and drawings. This is the first time I've seen the car." He looked at Angelo. "It's a great design."

"Thank you, Loren. I hoped you would like it."

They walked around the front of the car. The sloping hood led down to a contoured oval air scoop, larger at the top than the bottom, looking very much like the jet engine scoop of the 707. An additional air scoop rose from the engine cover with still another air scoop mounted under the nose. The total overall effect was that the car seemed to be lunging toward you even when it was standing still.

"The scoops are all functional," Angelo explained. "The nose scoop directs all the air into the main combustion chamber, the hood scoop directs cool air between the heat wall and front interior panel, further insuring passenger compartment comfort from the very high combustion heat of the turbine."

Duncan got out of the car, leaving the door open. "Want to get behind the wheel?" he asked.

Elizabeth didn't wait for another invitation. She was in the car before the others had even walked around it. "When do I get to drive it?"

"Supposing I take you all out for a drive in it first?" Angelo said. "At the same time I can explain to you the few things you'll have to know in order to drive this baby. A turbine is a little different from a conventional I.C. engine."

"I'm ready," Betsy said.

"You'll have to wait until dark," said Angelo. "We don't take any of these models out during the day."

A public announcement system blared overhead. "Mr. Perino, telephone. Mr. Perino, telephone."

Angelo straightened. "You'll have to excuse me." He turned to Duncan. "Would you take over for me? I'll be back as soon as I can."

He heard the Scotsman's voice as he walked away. "The first thing ye have to learn, lassie, is that you just don't put the key in the switch in this car and start it. A turbine doesn't work like that. There are two igniter switches and a starter generator switch that are activated electronically when you turn the key to position one. You will note that when you do, a red light appears on the dash in front of you. After about ten seconds, the red turns off and a yellow light comes on, then you turn the key to position two. This fires the turbine. In about five seconds, the yellow light should be replaced by a green light. That means your engine has reached idling speed and you can go. Since the turbine heat is so great, sometimes in firing up they overheat. In that case the green won't come on and the red light will come back, only this time it will be blinking. In that case, switch off and start all over. Just one thing. Nothing will start unless the car is in parking gear and the parking brake is on. Now, for important lesson number two—"

By this time Angelo had gone into the small office and the Scotsman's voice disappeared as he closed the door. The guard looked up from his desk.

"May I use the phone?" Angelo said, picking it up. The guard nodded as the operator came on. "Mr. Perino here."

"Just a moment, Mr. Perino," the operator said quickly. "I have Mr. Rourke on your office line. I'll transfer him over."

"Is it worth a thousand dollars to find out the name of the man who put the county prosecutor up to getting an injunction against us? I have a friend in Olympia. He says he can get it for us."

"Pay it," Angelo said.

"Where will you be tonight?" Rourke asked. "I'll call you."

"I'll be at the Starlight." He put down the telephone and walked over to the observation window looking into the hangar.

Loren was behind the wheel now, Duncan was still talking and Bobbie and Elizabeth were standing next to him. From the window it almost seemed as if they were sisters.

The door opened. Cindy came in and stood at the window beside him. After a moment she reached over and took the cigarette from him and dragged on it, then passed it back.

"He's younger than I thought," she said. "His pictures make him look much older."

"Yeah."

"Which one is his daughter."

"The one on the right."

She took the cigarette from him again and pulled on it, watching them. "She likes cars. More than her father."

He looked at her curiously. "What makes you say that?"

"I saw her reaction while they were rolling the car out. She was the only one of them who was really excited."

Angelo gave up on the return of his cigarette and lit another. He turned back to the window without speaking. Duncan had raised the hood and was now explaining the engine to them.

"Going to marry the girl?" Cindy's question was unexpected.

"They're getting married next week I understand," he answered before he realized she wasn't asking about Loren and Bobbie. "You mean me?"

Cindy smiled. "There's been some talk."

"You ought to know better than that," he said. "I'm not the marrying kind."

"But she is," Cindy said. "And I can see enough of Number One in her to know that she generally gets what she wants."

"She's still a kid."

"She's as old as I was when I first went down to the track," Cindy said. "She's not as much of a kid as she plays at being."

Angelo didn't answer.

"What about the other one?" Cindy asked.

"What about her?"

"She's got an eye for you too. And I don't mean like a future mother-in-law."

"Forget it," Angelo said shortly. "She's a money-player and she just took the big one."

"It won't keep her from trying to pick up a side bet here and there. She never looked at the car even once. All she kept watching was you."

Angelo turned and looked out the window. Bobbie was standing almost alone now as Loren and Betsy bent over the open hood of the car. She seemed to be waiting patiently for them to finish.

A note of surprise came into Cindy's voice. "You fucked her, didn't you?" Without waiting for him to answer. "That's what it's all about. I should have guessed."

Angelo didn't look at her. "Now you've really topped off."

"I'm not crazy," she said. She looked at him. "Don't forget, I've been there too. And it takes one to know one."

Chapter Five

The white tensor lamp splashed down on the blueprint on the desk. Angelo stared at it. Space, the problem always was space. This time it was the trunk. Due to the oversize exhaust ducting necessary for the turbine, the trunk had less than half the space considered normal in the average American car and with the spare tire inside, there was practically no room for luggage.

He moved the template idly across the blueprint. If there were only some way he could take the space from the engine compartment and move it to the trunk he could solve the problem. Even with all the power equipment there was room to spare under the hood because of the smaller size of the turbine engine.

He picked up the wheel and tire template and looked at it. Too bad they couldn't mount it on the side of the car as they did many years ago. That would solve the problem. He remembered the '29 Olds Viking his father had when he was a child and the '31 Duesenberg of his grandfather. There was something to be said about the side-mounted wheels and tires. They did give the automobile a sporting flair. It was economics as much as design that probably finished it off. One spare wheel and tire cost less than two.

He placed the template on the drawing and moved it along the side drawing until he came to a stop alongside the front right fender under the hood. He stared at it. It could fit there with room to spare. But there were other problems.

Interstage heat in the turbine at normal operating driving temperatures averaged 800° centigrade. There wasn't a tire made that could withstand that temperature constantly. It needed insulation, venting and perhaps additional cooling. He made some notes on the comment sheet to have Design and Engineering look into it and come up with its practicality and costs.

The telephone rang. "Hello."

The familiar British voice was in his ear. "Angelo?"

"Yes, Bobbie?"

"What are you doing?"

"Working," he answered.

"Would you like to have a drink?"

He was surprised. "Where are you? I thought you went out to the test track with the others."

"I didn't feel up to it," she said.

"Anything wrong? You sound strange."

"No." She seemed vague. "I don't know. Anyway it's not important. I'm sorry I disturbed you."

The phone abruptly clicked off as she hung up. He stared at it a moment, then put it down. He thought about calling her back but decided against it and got up and made himself a drink instead.

The phone rang again as he was walking back to the desk, the ice tinkling in his glass. He picked it up. "Yes, Bob—"

Rourke's voice interrupted him. "Angelo, I have the name of the man. Mark Simpson. He's with an outfit called the Independent Automobile Safety Organization. IASO. They're out of Detroit. Know anything about them?"

"Not the outfit," Angelo answered. "But I heard something about the man—" The doorbell rang. "Hold on a minute, I have to get the door."

He put down the telephone and crossed the room. The doorbell rang again. He opened the door. Bobbie stood there.

She looked up at him. "Am I interrupting anything?"

"No." He shook his head. "Come in. I'm on the telephone."

He went back to the phone and picked it up while she closed the door behind her. "Help yourself to a drink."

"Tony," he said into the phone. "The guy's a hustler. He claims to be another Ralph Nader but that's a lot of crap. He publishes a weekly newsletter which supposedly gives out inside information on new cars. There's been talk around Detroit that he's on the take, but nobody seems to know from whom."

"Why would he go after us?" Tony asked.

"That's a good question," Angelo said. "As far as I know, he's never been near our place. Somebody there has got to be backing him."

"Well, I've done everything I could," Tony said. "Detroit's your town."

"I'll take care of it," Angelo said. "Thanks for the information."

He put down the telephone and looked across the room. Bobbie hadn't moved from the door. "You made it this far," he said. "You might as well come all the way in."

She walked toward him, her eyes taking in the piled-up papers on the desk and the file cabinets along the wall. "You really were working," she said.

"What did you think I was doing?"

She didn't answer. She crossed the room to the table on which the bottle of whiskey and ice rested. She poured some into a glass. "I didn't know you had one room fixed up as an office."

"I do a lot of work here," he said. "The days aren't always long enough."

"I don't want to disturb you."

"You said that before," he said pointedly.

"I know." She put her drink down on the table without touching it. "I'm sorry. I'll leave." She started back to the door.

"Why did you come down?" he asked.

She stopped and looked at him. "I was jealous. I thought you had a girl here. That was stupid of me, wasn't it?"

He didn't answer.

"I love you," she said. "I thought—"

His voice was harsh. "Don't think. We went all through that once before."

"I made a mistake," she said. "I thought I knew what I wanted. But it's not too late."

"It is too late. You're supposed to be married next week, remember?"

"I know that," she said. She walked back toward him slowly. She looked up into his eyes. "But there will be times. We can still see each other once in a while."

He didn't move. A pulse began to beat in his throat. "Now you're thinking with your cunt," he said. "I liked it better when you thought with your head."

She put her arms around his neck and pressed herself against him. "You tell me you don't want me," she whispered.

He stared into her eyes without moving.

"Tell me!" she repeated, a note of triumph in her voice. She dropped a hand to his trouser front. Quickly she zipped open his fly and searched him out. "Tell me if you can while I hold you, hard and hot in my hand."

She began to go down on him and was almost on her knees when a knock came on the door and it swung open.

"Angelo! The car is fantastic!" Betsy's voice trailed off as she saw them.

They stared at her. Bobbie almost stumbled and fell as she got back to her feet. Angelo turned away for a moment, adjusting his pants. By the time he turned back to her, she was inside the room, her face suddenly very pale and very young.

"I know it's hard to understand," he began.

"Don't say anything. Please," she said in a thin small voice. She looked at Bobbie. "Daddy's on his way to your room to get you," she said, almost calmly. "You better go to the bar and tell him you were there waiting for him. Because he was going to bring you down here to have a drink to the new car."

Bobbie looked at her for a moment, then at Angelo. He nodded. She went silently past Betsy and out of the room. Her footsteps echoed down the corridor outside.

They stared at each other silently until the sound of the footsteps vanished. He picked up his drink from the desk behind him.

"I guess the stories I've heard about you are all true," she said. "You're not a very nice man, Mr. Perino."

He held the glass without drinking, his eyes steady on her face. He didn't speak.

"Don't think I did it for either of you," she said. "I did it for Daddy. He's very much in love with her. And it would break his heart. You see, he's not like you. He's really a very naive man. Not hip at all."

Angelo still didn't say anything.

"You could have been honest with me," she began to sniffle. "You didn't have to go through that virtuous shit and how-important-it-was-that-we-get-to-know-each-other-first routine with me."

"It was the truth," he said.

"No it wasn't!" she cried bitterly. "And you'll never get me to believe you! Why didn't you just lay me when I wanted you to?"

He didn't answer.

"Was it because you thought I didn't have enough experience for the great Angelo Perino?"

"Now you are talking like a child," he said.

She came toward him, her clenched fists pummeling at his chest. "I hate you, Mr. Perino! I hate you!"

He caught her wrists and held her still. She looked up into his face. Suddenly she slumped against him, weeping.

"I'm sorry, Miss Elizabeth," he said quietly. "Truly sorry."

"I feel such a fool," she cried.

"Don't," he said.

"Leave me alone!" She pulled away from him. "You don't have to patronize me!"

"I'm not—"

"Good-bye, Mr. Perino," she said frostily.

He looked at her silently for a moment. "Good-bye, Miss Elizabeth."

She stared back at him, then began to cry again and, turning abruptly, ran out into the hall, almost stumbling over Number One's wheelchair in the corridor.

"Betsy!" Number One called.

She didn't turn back. "Not right now, Great-grandfather," she shouted over her shoulder as she ran down the steps.

Number One pushed the wheelchair into the open doorway and looked at Angelo. "What the hell is going on here?" he asked irascibly. "When I get on the elevator downstairs, Loren's girl comes off it looking all upset; when I get up here, Betsy comes storming out of your door, crying like a baby."

Angelo stared at him. "Oh, Jesus!"

Number One looked at him and then began to smile. He pushed the wheelchair through and the door shut behind him. "You look like a man who's just been caught with his cock out."

Angelo swallowed his drink in a single gulp. "Aah, shit!"

Number One laughed aloud. The more things changed, the more they were the same. He could still remember the last time it happened to him.

And that was over thirty years ago.

Chapter Six

The engine of the big black 1933 Sundancer sedan bearing the licence plates L H 1 purred quietly as the chauffeur turned the car off Woodward Avenue onto Factory Road, three and a half blocks before the plant gate. The sidewalks on both sides of the street were filled with men, standing patiently in the cold March drizzle.

"What's going on?" Loren asked from the back seat.

"I don't know, sir," the chauffer replied. "I never seen nothin' like this before." He began to slow the car down. As they came nearer the gate, the lines of men grew thicker, spilling over into the roadway.

"Turn on the radio," said Loren. "Maybe we'll get something on the news."

The familiar voice of H. V. Kaltenborn filled the car. "In closing, I would like to repeat to all Americans once again this morning the words President Roosevelt uttered in his Inaugural Address yesterday in Washington. 'The only thing we have to fear is fear itself'."

"They are well worth remembering. This is H. V. Kaltenborn signing off from New York."

Another voice came on. "This closes our morning newscast. The next news will be on at noon."

They were almost at the gate. "Turn it off," Loren said.

The car crawled up to the gate through the men thronged before it. The chauffeur blew the horn. The men looked back and slowly parted to let the car inch its way forward. Two men opened the gate so the car could go through, then closed it.

Loren rolled down his window. "What happened, Fred?"

The older guard looked at him. "We advertised in the papers for six machinists, Mr. Hardeman."

"Six machinists?" Loren looked back at the crowd. "But there must be at least a couple of hundred out there."

"More like a thousand by my reckoning, Mr. Hardeman."

"Did we hire them yet?"

"No, sir. The personnel office doesn't begin interviewing until nine o'clock."

Loren looked at his watch. It was a few minutes after seven. "That means they have to stand out there two more hours in this freezing rain."

"Yes, sir," the guard said. "A lot of them have been here all night since the evening papers came out yesterday."

Loren looked back at the crowd. Some of the men held their newspapers over their heads to keep off the rain, others had their coats pulled up over their necks across the brims of their hats. Their faces were all the same pale gray of the morning.

He turned back to the guard. "Call the canteen and have them send a truck down here with hot coffee and doughnuts for them."

"I can't do that, sir," the guard said uncomfortably. "It's against the rules."

"What rules?" Loren was too surprised for the moment to get angry.

"From the personnel office," the guard said in a nervous voice. "They said if we start that we'll have a lineup of men every morning whether we need help or not, just to get themselves a free breakfast."

Loren stared at him without speaking for a moment. "Who made that rule?" he asked finally.

"I was told that it came from the president's office," the guard answered. He was very careful not to mention Junior by name.

"I see." Loren drew back into the car. "Drive on," he said. The chauffeur drove the car behind the administration building into the parking place beside Loren's private entrance. Loren got out of the car without waiting for him to open the door. The small elevator was in use so he went up the stairs to the second floor, then down the long corridor. He pushed open the door and walked past the startled secretaries into Junior's office.

Junior was just putting down the telephone. His voice was excited. "I was just speaking to Washington. There's talk that the President's going to call a bank holiday right away!"

Loren stared down at him. "Did you have breakfast?"

Junior was bewildered. "Didn't you hear what I said? The President's going to close the banks! Do you know what that means?"

"Did you have breakfast?" Loren repeated.

"Of course I had breakfast," Junior answered, annoyed. "What's that got to do with what I just said. If he closes the banks we're on the verge of anarchy, a revolution can break out the next day and the Communists will take over the country!"

"Bullshit!" Loren exploded. "Come over here to the window."

Junior got out of his chair and walked over. Loren pointed to the crowd of men beyond the gate. "See them?"

Junior nodded.

"Did you sign an order that the canteen was not allowed to give them coffee and doughnuts?"

"No. That would come out of Warren's office."

"If it came out of Joe Warren's office that means you approved it. He's your man."

"Father," Junior's voice was placating. "How many times do I have to tell you that Joe has nothing but our own best interests at heart? If it weren't for him, those kidnappers might have got their filthy hands on Anne and Loren III. And you have to admit that there have been no problems with labor since he took over.

"Sure, I approved the order but we're not the only one that has that rule. Half the companies in Detroit have adopted it. Bennett over at Ford says if we don't keep a firm hand on things, they'll take over."

"Who'll take over?" Loren's voice was sarcastic. "And what makes Bennett such an expert? He's nothing but an ex-sailor."

"Joe says that Bennett's the number one man at Ford. He says that Mr. Ford trusts him implicitly and keeps Edsel in there only for window dressing."

"Then the old man has reached his dotage. Edsel's got more brains than all of them," Loren said. "I want those men to have coffee and doughnuts."

"No, Father," Junior said stubbornly. "I'm afraid I'm going to have to overrule you on this one. Believe me, I know what I'm doing."

"You stupid little shit!" Loren stared at him. "If you like being president of this company, you'll call that prick Warren in here and see to it that those men out there have coffee and doughnuts."

Junior's face was pale. "No, Father."

Loren's voice went hard and cold. "Then I'll expect your resignation on my desk in ten minutes." He turned and started from the office.

"Father," Junior's voice turned him around. "I won't give it to you."

"Then you're fired!" he snapped.

"You can't do that either, Father." Junior's voice held a thin edge of bitter triumph. "Along with those notes you signed for the bank loans, you escrowed your voting stock into a trust voted by them until such time as the loans are repaid. And the bank is very satisfied with my management of the company."

Loren stared at him speechlessly.

"Unless you have thirty million dollars in cash to repay their loans, Father, you might as well get used to the idea that I'm the chief operating officer of this company."

Loren was still silent.

"If the idea doesn't appeal to you," Junior continued, "I would like to suggest that you might find it much more pleasant if you were to go back to Europe with your French whore."

"Is that all you have to say?" Loren asked.

"Not quite," Junior answered. He was very sure of himself now. "I hadn't intended to raise the issue this soon but since we're speaking frankly, we may as well face it.

"We've managed quite well the past three years while you've been away. Now that you've returned with a wild idea to rejuvenate the automobile business with a new low-priced car, I might as well inform you that the matter has been completely gone into by both the board of directors and the banks. There is unanimous agreement among them to reject your plan. They have no intention of committing another twenty million dollars to experimentation in this kind of market with industry sales peaking at about a million and a half cars this year. Now that we have the automobile division under control we plan to eliminate further losses on that end by going into subcontracting bodies for Ford. Bennett was kind enough to give us a contract for one hundred thousand units since they've been having problems with Briggs. For the first time in two years we'll be in the black and everybody likes it."

"You haven't changed have you?" Loren said. "When you were a little boy you used to hide behind your mother's skirts, now you're hiding behind Harry Bennett."

"It's merely good business," said Junior. "We're guaranteed a profit without risking a penny of our own."

"You're also delivering your company into the hands of Bennett. Before long he will be able to dictate everything you want to do and all he will have to do to close you up is cut you off." Loren's voice was sober. "Even you have to see that. The only chance we have to stay alive is to stay independent."

Junior laughed. "I'm afraid you've lost touch with reality, Father. See those lines out there? I've been watching them grow for three years now. Do you think any of them can afford to buy our cars?"

Loren stared at him. "I'm sorry, Junior," he said reluctantly. He began to tug at his leather trouser belt. "I guess you're still a child and will have to be treated like one." The belt came free and, holding it in his hand, he started toward Junior.

Junior stared at him, horrified. "You wouldn't dare!"

Loren smiled. "Watch me." He raised his arm, the belt dangling from his hand.

"No!" It was almost a scream. Junior darted behind his desk, pressing a button on it. "You can't hit me! I'm president of the company!" He pushed the button frantically.

"You're still my son," Loren said coldly, moving behind the desk after him.

The door to the connecting office opened and Joe Warren came into the room. Yes, Jun—?"

Junior darted behind him, holding Warren between himself and his father. "Joe! Don't let him hit me, Joe!" he almost shrieked. "He's gone crazy!"

Warren turned to Loren. "Let's all calm down, Mr. Hardeman," he said. "I don't know what the trouble is but I'm sure we can settle it like reasonable men."

Something in his voice told Loren that he already knew exactly what the trouble was. He glanced down at Junior's desk. The intercom switch above Warren's name was open. He had been listening to every word said in the office. He looked back at Warren. His voice was ice cold. "Keep out of this, Warren. It's a family matter."

He started forward again, then stopped. A revolver suddenly appeared in Warren's hand. "Now, will you be reasonable?" Warren asked.

Loren looked into the man's eyes. They were glinting with a curious kind of triumph. He relaxed slightly. "You're not going to pull that trigger, Warren," he said quietly, moving toward him. "Or you'll spend the rest of your life regretting it."

Warren's eyes stared back at him balefully. "Don't push me, Mr. Hardeman. Just stop where you are!"

Loren's hand moved almost too quickly for the eye to follow. The looped belt caught Warren's wrist, pulling the gun from his hand, sending it clattering to the floor. Warren dove for the gun as Junior shrieked and ran into the other office.

Warren's fingers were just closing around the revolver when Loren's shoe came heavily down on his forearm. He screamed in sudden pain as the arm snapped like a matchstick. He stared up into Loren's face with a kind of frozen horror.

"This may teach you to keep out of family matters," Loren said calmly.

Warren saw Loren's shoe coming towards his head but there was nothing he could do to avoid it. The world exploded in a shattering fireworks of pain. Then blackness.

Loren looked down at the man lying at his feet. Warren's head was against the corner of Junior's desk, blood streaming from his nose and mouth. He turned and walked to the connecting door.

It was locked and bolted. He took half a step backward and kicked. The door flew open, half torn from its hinges, and he stepped through.

The other office was empty. The open door at the far end told Loren that Junior had fled. He went back into Junior's office.

Warren was moaning, trying to sit up. Loren crossed the room to the far door and opened it. The two secretaries, who had their ears pressed to the panel, almost fell into the room.

"Clean this mess up," Loren said emotionlessly and walked past them.

Chapter Seven

He walked up the flight of stairs to his third-floor office and let himself into it through his private entrance. The room was dark in the poor gray light of the morning. He pressed a wall switch and the lamps around the room went on. He went behind his desk and pressed the intercom switch down.

His secretary's voice came from it. "Yes, Mr. Hardeman?"

"I want two canteen trucks with coffee and doughnuts down at Gate Three right away."

"Yes, Mr. Hardeman."

"Then I want you to get Coburn and Edgerton up here."

"Yes, Mr. Hardeman."

He flicked up the switch and walked from the desk to the window. In the rain the men outside the gate were still huddled together like so many animals seeking shelter. He stood there for a moment watching them, then went back to his desk and sat down.

The pain began in his temples and started to throb. He groaned to himself. That was all he needed. Another migraine headache. Doctors were all stupid. There was nothing they could do about it he had been told. Avoid excitement and take aspirin. He pressed the intercom switch down again. "Get me three aspirin tablets and a cup of hot black coffee."

"Immediately, Mr. Hardeman."

He leaned back in his chair. The aspirin should help and the doctor in Switzerland had told him that the caffeine in coffee made the aspirin work faster.

The door opened and a girl came in. She carried the sterling silver tray with the cup and saucer and coffee pot to his desk. Cream and sugar were in small silver servers. Next to it was a bottle of aspirin and a glass of water. She shook three aspirin out into her hand.

He looked up at her as he took the aspirin. "You're new here, aren't you?"

"Yes, Mr. Hardeman," she answered, giving him the glass of water.

He swallowed the aspirin with a gulp of water. "What's your name?" he asked, giving her the glass.

"Melanie Walker," she said. She picked up the coffee pot. "Black?"

"Yes. No sugar, no cream." He took the coffee and tasted it.

"Is it all right?"

"Fine. What happened to the girl who was here all last week?"

"Miss Harriman?"

"I never did get her name."

"She went back to her regular job in personnel."

"I see," he said, taking another sip of coffee. "What department are you from?"

"Personnel," she said.

He was silent for a moment. "Do you have a regular job there?"

"Yes, Mr. Hardeman. In the steno pool. We fill in whenever a regular girl is absent."

"What do they pay you for that?" he asked curiously.

"Twenty-two fifty a week."

He gave her the empty coffee cup. "Thank you."

"You're welcome, Mr. Hardeman." She picked up the tray and started for the door.

"Would you also ask Mr. Duncan to come and see me?" he called after her.

"Yes, sir."

He watched the door close behind her. Warren had it all organized. The steno pool was a perfect nucleus for an espionage system to check on what everyone was doing.

Duncan was the first to arrive. "Sit down Scotty," Loren said. "I'm waiting for Coburn and Edgerton."

Duncan took a chair just as the other two men arrived. Loren waved them to their seats, then sat looking at them silently for a minute. He opened the cigarette box on his desk and took one out and lit it. The faint sound of an ambulance siren came from outside.

The silence grew uncomfortable. The three men glanced uneasily at one another, then back at him. Loren drew on his cigarette calmly.

The siren grew louder and then stopped abruptly. Loren walked over to the window. The ambulance was parked in front of the main building entrance and two white-coated men were hurrying inside with a stretcher.

He walked back to his desk and looked at them. "Okay," he said. "You tell me. What the hell is going on around here?"

"I don't know what you mean," Coburn said quickly.

"Don't give me any of your lawyer crap! You know damn well what I mean, Ted!"

They were silent.

"What the hell are you guys afraid of?" Loren asked. "You've all known me for years and you've never been afraid to open your mouths before. This isn't a prison."

"You don't understand, Mr. Hardeman," Edgerton said. He was a big man, almost as large as Loren, the last person in the world to look like the accountant he was.

"I know I don't Walt," said Loren. "That's why I asked you to come up here."

There was a moment's silence while they again exchanged uncomfortable looks. Finally Coburn got out of his chair. He walked around Loren's desk and bent over the intercom. His fingers checked all the switches, making sure they were down.

"What are you worried about?" Loren asked. "No one can listen in."

Coburn didn't answer. Instead he bent down beside the desk and pulled the cable plug connecting the intercom to its socket from the floor. "There's no point taking any chances," he said, straightening up. He turned to Loren. "Now send your secretary out of the office on an errand."

"Why?" Loren asked. "She seems like a nice girl."

"She is a nice girl. Too nice," Coburn said. "But she's one of Joe Warren's girls."

Loren looked at him for a moment. Without a word, he went to the secretary's door and opened it.

The girl looked up at him. "Yes, Mr. Hardeman?"

"Go down to the canteen and have some coffee. I'll call you there when I want you back."

She met his gaze. "I can't do that, Mr. Hardeman. The rules are that I can't leave the desk without relief."

"I just changed the rules," he said.

"But the phones? There will be no one to answer them."

"I'll answer them," he said.

She sat there silently, not moving. "I'll lose my job," she said finally.

"You've already lost it," he said. "You're only chance to get it back depends on how fast you can get your ass out of here!"

She started at him for a moment, then picked up her purse and went out the door.

Coburn's voice came from behind him. "Lock that door while I lock your private entrance."

Loren locked the outside door and walked back into his own office. He walked around his desk and sat down. "Now, I want some answers and I want them fast!"

"You want it fast, Mr. Hardeman?" Coburn said. "I'll give it to you in two words. Joe Warren. You can't get it any faster than that."

Loren got to his feet and walked to the window. Outside, the ambulance was still parked. The attendants came out of the building, carrying a man on the stretcher between them.

Loren gestured to the men in the room behind him. They came to the window. He pointed to the stretcher being loaded into the rear of the ambulance. "There goes your Joe Warren."

An attendant ran around the ambulance and got in behind the wheel. The siren began again as the ambulance started for the gate.

Loren walked back to his desk and sat down. "Now maybe we can get back to the business of building automobiles," he said.

"It's not going to be that easy," said Edgerton. "Between Warren and your son, they have the board of directors and the banks sewed up."

"Leave them to me," Loren said. "What we're here to talk about is building a low-priced car to compete with Ford and Chevy and Walter Chrysler's new Plymouth."

"We haven't got the money to retool," Edgerton said quickly. "That will take fifteen million dollars and the banks won't give it to us."

"How much have we got?"

"About one and a half million in cash and another three million in receivables."

"Could we discount the receivables?"

"For twenty percent."

Loren turned to Duncan who had been silent until now. "Can you get a new car on the line for four million dollars?"

Duncan shook his head. "Impossible."

"Nothing's impossible," Loren said. "Do we still have the jigs for the Loren II?"

Duncan nodded.

"Supposing we cut two feet out of the car by going from four doors to two? Would that be an expensive retooling job?"

Duncan was thoughtful. "It shouldn't be. But there is another problem. We'd have to design a whole new engine for it."

"Why?" Loren asked. "Couldn't we make the small Sundancer ninety-horsepower fit?"

Duncan smiled suddenly. "I think we could. It would also reduce our inventory. We overproduced that engine by almost fifty thousand units last year."

"That's more like it," Loren said. "You get down to your office and start on it right away. Check your costs out with Walt. I want figures in two days." He turned to the lawyer. "Now I want some answers from you, Ted. Is there anything in the book that can keep me from doing this?"

Coburn thought for a moment. "Not if you're not challenged."

"And if I am?"

"There are only two people who can do it. Your son and maybe, Warren. I'm not quite sure, but he is the executive vice-president and his powers might spill over into that area."

"What about the board and the bank?"

"They don't come into it until the next meeting. And that's almost a month away. Of course, your son can call a special meeting any time."

"I understand," Loren said.

"Just another word," Coburn said. "Make sure that you don't dictate any memos on your plans. All secretaries now have to make a blind copy of everything they type. It's Warren's way of knowing everything that goes on."

Loren looked at him. "Did my son know about that too?"

"I don't know," Coburn said carefully. "None of us can see him unless the appointment is arranged by Warren. I haven't seen him except at board meetings for more than a year now."

Loren turned to Edgerton. "How about you?"

"Much the same story."

He looked at the engineer. "How about you, Scotty?"

"The last time I spoke to him was the time he told me to stop production on the Loren II. That was three years ago." The Scotsman's voice was caustic.

Loren was silent for a moment, then he got to his feet. "Okay," he said. "Go to work."

They got to their feet and started for the door. Loren's voice stopped them. He was smiling. "Can one of you fellows reconnect this damn thing?" he asked, pointing to the intercom. "I might have to use it for something legitimate."

Chapter Eight

The telephone began to ring just as she came from the kitchen after talking to the cook about the children's lunch. She picked it up in the living room. "Hello."

A familiar voice echoed in her ear. "Sally?"

She sank into a nearby chair. "Yes."

"This is Loren."

"Yes, I know," she said. "How are you?"

"Fine," he answered. There was an awkward pause. "I wanted to come out and see you and the children but I've only been back a few days and I've been tied up."

"I understand," she said.

"Is Junior home?"

"No. Isn't he in the office?"

"No," he answered.

"He left early as usual," she said. "Maybe the car broke down on the road."

"No. He was in the office." There was the barest hesitation in his voice. "We had an argument and he left. I want to reach him. Do you have any idea where I might find him?"

"Sometimes he goes to the Athletic Club for a steam and rub-down."

"Thanks," he said. "I'll try there. Good-bye."

"Loren!" she said quickly.

"Yes?"

"Aren't we going to see you?" she asked. "Loren III is a big boy already and you've never even seen your granddaughter." She had just caught her tongue in time to keep herself from saying daughter.

"I'll be out later this week," he said. He hesitated a moment. "Are you all right?"

"Yes," she said.

"If Junior should come in, tell him to call me."

"I will," she said.

"Good-bye."

"Loren, I still love you," she said quickly. But the click in the telephone told her he was off the line and hadn't heard her. Slowly she put the phone down and sat there. She could still feel the pounding in her heart and wondered if she would ever get over the way she felt about him.

The front door burst open and Junior came rushing in. Through the archway he saw her seated in the living room and came toward her.

Still filled with her own thoughts, she spoke to him. "Your father just called. He wants you to call him."

"He's crazy!"

For the first time she saw how distraught he was, his face pale and ashen. "What happened?"

"He tried to kill me! Joe Warren's in the hospital with a broken arm and possible skull fractures! He's crazy, I tell you!"

"Why?" she asked.

"All I told him was that he couldn't build a new car and he went crazy. He came after me. If it weren't for poor Joe, I might have been the one in the hospital, not him."

"It doesn't make sense," she said, bewildered. "There has to be a reason. He sounded perfectly calm on the phone just now."

He stared at her. His voice changed. "Go upstairs and pack. We're taking the children and going away for a while."

"Calm down," she said, rising. "Let me fix you a drink."

"I don't want a drink," he said sharply. "Just do as I tell you. We're going over the border to the summer cottage in Ontario."

She looked at him. "I'm not dragging the children anywhere," she said stubbornly. "Not until I know what we're running away from."

"You're on his side!" he shot accusingly.

"I'm on no one's side," she replied. "I've just got two small children that I'm not going to drag around like so many pieces of baggage, that's all."

"I've turned it all over to my attorneys," he said. "They told me to go away for a while. He can't take the company away from me."

"But how could he?" she asked. "It's not your company, it's his."

"Don't tell me whose company it is!" he almost shrieked. "I'm its chief executive officer."

She didn't speak.

"He's going to jail!" Junior snapped. "Joe signed an assault and battery complaint and right now the police are on their way out there to pick him up. I signed a deposition."

"Joe had to do something to get himself hurt," she said. "I don't believe your father would—"

"You don't believe!" he almost screamed. "You're in love with him!"

She didn't answer.

"Listen," he said earnestly. "All Joe did when Father came after me was to get between us. Even the gun Joe had didn't stop him!"

"Joe had a gun?" The amazement showed in her voice.

He was suddenly silent. Then he looked at her shrewdly. "What if he did?" he asked defensively. "He was only trying to protect me."

"Did you say that in your deposition?" she asked.

He didn't answer.

"Is that why your attorneys want you to go away? So that you don't have to answer questions?"

"What difference does it make?" he asked. "It's about time someone showed my father that he can't run the world."

"You were willing to let that cheap thug pull a gun on your father?" Her voice filled with a strange loathing. "You're really sick."

"You're jealous!" He screamed suddenly. "You were jealous of my friendship with Joe from the moment I first met him! Because he's a real man, that's why."

"He's a cheap gangster who does nothing but terrorize and threaten people weaker than he is. And if you were a real man, you wouldn't need friends like that!"

He started toward her, raising his hand.

"Don't!" she said sharply, picking up the telephone. "If you're going anywhere, you better go upstairs and pack because I'm going to call your father right now and tell him you're here."

He stood there for a moment as she began to dial. Then he started for the door; suddenly, he stopped, bending almost in two, clutching at his stomach. "I'm going to be sick!" he said in a small, frightened voice.

She put down the telephone and went toward him. He began to retch, dry, hard, gasping breaths. She put an arm around his shoulders and he leaned weakly against her as she steered him into the guest washroom off the foyer. He began to vomit into the toilet bowl.

"You've got to help me," he said weakly, between gasps.

"I am helping you," she said quietly. "Can't you see that if I let you destroy your father you're destroying yourself? If you weren't his son, who do you think would even give a damn whether you lived or died?"

"I've got to get away," he said. He began to wring his hands. "I don't know how I'll manage if anything happens to Joe."

"You can go if you want to," she said calmly. "But if you do, you'll do it without me and the children. And when you come back, we won't be here."

Hardeman Manor seemed strangely dark and deserted as she drove up the long winding driveway to the front door. Even the light in the entranceway was off as she stopped the car under the stone-pillared car portals. She turned off the engine and got out.

The moonlight cast a pale shadow as she walked up the steps to the doorway. She pressed the bell. From deep within the house, she heard an answering sound. It echoed in the still night.

She waited quietly. After a moment when there was no answer, she pressed the doorbell again. Still no answer.

She pulled a cigarette from her purse and lit it. The match flared briefly in the dark, illuminating her face in the curtained glass window of the door. Then it went out, leaving only the glowing tip of the cigarette shining back at her.

She went down the steps again and looked up at the house. It was dark and quiet, not a light behind any of the front windows. Slowly she began to walk around to the side of the house, her high heels crunching and sinking into the gravel of the driveway. It was the only sound in the night.

She turned the corner of the building and saw the light glowing from a room on the second floor. She knew the room. The small sitting room next to Loren's bedroom where he would have his morning coffee while he read the papers and the mail.

She hesitated a moment, looking up at it. The light meant that he was home, but now that she knew it there was a peculiar reluctance to see him. Then she bent down quickly, scooped up a small handful of gravel and threw it up against the window. It rattled strangely in the night and fell with scraping sounds down the sides.

A moment later, the French windows opened and he stood there, silhouetted, the light of the room against his back. He stood there silently, looking down into the night.

From her angle he looked even taller and larger than she remembered and it was a moment before she realized that he could not see her because she was standing in the shadows. She felt her heart begin to pound inside her. "Oh, God!" she thought wildly, suddenly wanting to run and hide. "What will I ever say to him?"

His voice echoed in the night. "Who is it?"

Somehow the strength in the sound of him moved her out, where the pale moonlight shone on her face. Suddenly she giggled, a feeling of light-headed ridiculousness overcame her. "Romeo, Oh, Romeo," she called. "Wherefore art thou, Romeo?"

He was silent for a moment, looking at her, then he laughed. "Wait there, I'll be right down." He took a half step back, then vaulted over the low windowsill.

"Loren!" she screamed, as he hurtled down. He hit the ground and sank half to his knees, his hands breaking his fall. He was straightening up by the time she got to him.

He grinned at her, brushing his hands off against his trousers like a small boy. "How's that for a Douglas Fairbanks?"

She stood very still, looking up into his face. "You're crazy! You might have been killed!"

His eyes went from her up to the window and then back to her. A rueful tone came into his voice. "You know, you're right." Then he laughed again. "But it was something I wanted to do ever since I built the house and I never had the excuse." He began to rub his hands together.

"Here, let me see." She took his hands and looked at them. They were scratched and dirty. "You're hurt," she said.

"It's nothing." He took her by the arm and began to walk her around to the front of the house. "Come on let's go inside."

"How?" she asked. "I rang the bell twice. No one answered."

"The servants aren't all back yet," he said. "And the butler left after dinner."

They walked up the steps to the front door. "Then how are we going to get in?" she asked.

"Easy," he said. He turned the knob and the door swung open. "It isn't locked." He switched on the lights as they went into the house.

"Let me see your hands again," she said.

He held them out toward her, palms up. Traces of blood seeped through the scratches.

"You better wash them right away. And put something on them so you don't get infected."

"Okay," he said. "I have some peroxide in my bathroom."

She followed him up the staircase into the bathroom. She turned the faucet on in the sink and took the soap from the tray. "Let me do that for you," she said.

He held his hands under the water and she washed them gently. After a moment, she looked at them and, still not satisfied, cleaned them again with a washcloth. "Where's the peroxide?"

He gestured to the medicine cabinet. She opened it and took out the bottle. "Hold your hands over the sink."

He held out his hands and she poured the peroxide over them. He winced and pulled them away. "That burns."

"Don't be a baby," she commanded. "Hold still." She emptied the bottle and the liquid bubbled and sizzled over his hands. She took a clean hand towel from the rack and patted his hands gently dry. "Now, isn't that better?"

He looked at her. "Yes."

She felt the color rising in her cheeks. Her eyes fell. "I had to see you," she said. "Come," he said, "let's get a drink."

She followed him downstairs into the library. He opened a cabinet and took out a bottle of Canadian whiskey and two glasses. "I can get ice if you like."

She shook her head.

He poured the liquor into two small tumblers and gave one to her. "Cheers."

She tasted her drink and the whiskey burned its way down her throat. He swallowed his and refilled his glass. "Sit down," he said.

She sat down on the leather couch and awkwardly straightened her skirt over her knees as he pulled a chair opposite her. She looked at him. "Junior went to the cottage in Ontario," she said.

He didn't speak.

"I refused to go with him," she said.

He was still silent.

"I'm leaving him," she said.

He hesitated a moment. "What about the children?"

"I'm taking them with me."

"Where are you going?"

She stared at him. "I never thought about that." There was a note of surprise in her voice. "I'll think of someplace."

He emptied his glass and got up, walked back to the bar and refilled it. He turned and looked back at her. "I'm sorry," he said.

"It would have happened sooner or later."

He hesitated a moment. "I suppose so," he said, walking back toward her. "I just didn't want it to happen because of me."

"I know," she said. "But it wasn't that reason. I think I had that straightened out in my mind. But from the moment he met Joe Warren, it began to go from bad to worse."

He stared at her. "Joe Warren," he said bitterly. "Everywhere I turn I hear that name."

"Junior told me that Warren signed an assault complaint against you and the sheriff's office was going to pick you up."

"I know about that," he said. "But I have some pretty good friends downtown. They sat on it."

"I'm glad," she said. "But don't think that it's over. Joe is a real bastard and he won't give up. He's got Junior under his thumb."

He stared at her. "That's the one thing I don't understand. What the hell power has he got over Junior that makes him jump when he pulls the strings?"

"Don't you know?" she asked, her eyes meeting his steadily.

"No."

"Joe Warren is Junior's boy friend," she said in a matter-of-fact voice.

A puzzled look crossed Loren's face. "His boy friend?"

Suddenly the naivete of this giant of a man, his blindness about his son, reached out and touched her. Her voice grew very gentle. "I thought you knew," she said.

"It seems as if everyone else, in Detroit knows it. Ever since the day they met in the steam room at the Athletic Club."

She could see the shock well up into his eyes and he looked at her. His hand began to tremble, spilling the whiskey over the sides of the glass. Slowly he put the glass down on a table next to him. She could see the gray winter of age etch its way into his face. Suddenly, he put his hands up to his face and hard, wracking sobs shook his body.

She was very still for a moment, then went over to him and knelt in front of his chair. She pulled his head down to her shoulder and held him tightly against her.

"I'm sorry," she said softly. "I'm so sorry."

Chapter Nine

It was a few minutes after seven o'clock in the evening when Melanie Walker got off the streetcar and started the four-block walk to her house. It had turned cold during the day after the rain of the morning had stopped and now the night winds blew strongly through her thin coat. She pulled it tightly around her as she turned the corner and started down the street.

"You're late," her mother said as she came in the door. "We already ate. You'll have to make do with the leftovers."

"I don't care," Melanie said. "I'm not really hungry."

"We thought—" her mother began to say.

"Shut up!" her father yelled from his seat in front of the radio set in the corner of the kitchen. "Can't you see I'm listening to 'Amos and Andy'?"

She took off her coat and walked into the room. She hung it carefully on a hanger on the back of her door. Then she got out of her dress and slip and laid them neatly on the bed. She would iron out the wrinkles after dinner so that it would be crisp and neat for the morning. She slipped into a cotton housedress and, tying the sash around her waist, went back into the kitchen.

Her mother had laid out some cold cuts on a plate on the table together with some already browning lettuce and squashy sliced tomatoes next to a plate of bread and butter.

She looked at it. "Not liverwurst and bologna again?"

Her mother shook her head. "What did you expect? You should have been home in time for dinner."

"I had to work late," she said. "I was in Mr. Hardeman's office today."

"You should have called," her mother said.

"I didn't have time. Besides you know Mr. McManus doesn't like us to bother him too much."

McManus was their neighbor on the floor below. He was the only tenant in the house who had a telephone. He was a cop on the city police force. "We don't bother them that much," her mother said.

Her father erupted in a shout of laughter. Still chuckling he got out of his chair and walked over to the icebox and took out a bottle of home brew. With a practiced motion of his hand, he swept off the stopper and got the bottle in his mouth before the foam had a chance to spill over. He took a long pull, then held it down in front of his large stomach. "Those niggers are the funniest," he belched. "Especially that Kingfish. He talked Amos into buying a new car and now Amos can't make the first payment and he wants the dealer to take the car back and give him back his old flivver." He began to laugh again thinking about it. "Andy got into the act to straighten it all out and now the dealer has both cars and they have nothing."

Neither of the women laughed. He stared at them for a moment. "It's funny, see," he explained. "Amos bought a new car and—"

"If you think niggers are so funny then why are you so mad because they're moving in a few blocks from us?" her mother asked.

"That's different," he said. "Amos and Andy are good niggers. They know their place. They ain't trying to move into white neighborhoods. They stick with their own kind like they should."

The women didn't answer him; he looked over at Melanie who had just begun to butter a slice of bread.

"How come you're so late?"

"I had to work late in Mr. Hardeman's office today," she said. She picked at a piece of liverwurst.

Her father grinned. "At least you don't have to worry about him trying to grab a feel of you when you walk past his desk."

"It wasn't that one, it was his father," she said. She chewed at the liverwurst. It tasted mealy and flavorless.

"You mean Number One?" her father asked, curiosity in his voice. "He's back?" She nodded.

"Your boyfriend ain't going to like that."

She stared at him. "How many times do I have to tell you that Mr. Warren isn't my boyfriend? Just because I have dinner with him once in a while don't mean anything."

"Okay, okay," her father said placatingly. "So he ain't your boyfriend. He still ain't going to like it. He's got Number Two under his thumb. The old man is another story. Nobody pushes him around."

Melanie tried the bologna. It was no better. She pushed the plate away from her. "I'm not hungry," she told her mother. "Do you have a cup of coffee?"

"How about some eggs?" her mother asked.

She shook her head. "No. Just coffee." She looked at her father. "Did you go out for a job today?"

"What for?" her father answered. "There ain't nothin' around."

"There were openings for six machinists at our place today. Over eight hundred men showed up."

"You don't expect me to get on line with all them rednecks, Polacks and niggers, do you? Don't forget I was a foreman out at Chrysler."

"Right now, you ain't nothin'," her mother said. "You been out of work for almost three years. If it wasn't for Melanie's workin' we'd all been on the streets."

"You stay out of this!" her father snapped angrily. He turned back to Melanie. "Besides didn't your boyfriend promise me the first openin' that came along?"

Melanie nodded.

"But that was for a foreman's job," her mother said. "None of the plants are hiring foremen. What are you going to do, wait around forever for one to come along?"

"I told you to stay out of it!" her father roared. "What do you want me to do? Come down in the world?"

"I just want you to get a job," her mother said stubbornly.

"I'll get a job," her father muttered. "Just as soon as we can get rid of all those foreigners and niggers that came pilin' up here after the war to grab the easy money."

"They ain't goin' away," her mother said. "The war's over fifteen years now an' they're still here."

"We'll get rid of them," her father said. "You wait and see. We'll show them that nobody can push real Americans around." A blast of music from the radio caught his ear. "That's the Fleischman Comedy Hour," he said, starting back to the radio. "Now you women talk real quiet. I don't want to miss any of it."

"Is there enough hot water for a bath?" Melanie asked. "I'm so tired, I think I could use one."

"Wait a minute, I'll see." Her mother walked to the corner of the kitchen and put her palm on the outside of the water tank. "No."

She knelt beside the water tank and turned on the gas heater at the same time, Striking a match. Nothing happened. "The meter must have gone off again," she said. "Do you have a quarter?"

"I'll get one," Melanie said. She went into the bedroom and opened her purse. She took a coin from the small pile of change she kept in it and went back into the kitchen. "Here."

Her mother took the quarter and pulled a chair over to the sink, then climbed on it. She reached up and placed the coin in the slot in the meter and hit the meter two resounding slaps as the coin tinkled its way into it.

"You always do that," Melanie said.

"Makes the meter give you two extra hours of gas that way," her mother said smugly, getting down. She went back to the water heater. This time the gas went on.

She was just about to step into the tub when her mother knocked at the bathroom door. "There's a telephone call for you from Mr. Warren on McManus's phone downstairs."

"I'll be right there," she said, reaching for her housedress. She went down the flight of steps. The McManus door was ajar. She knocked on it before she went in. Mr. McManus was in front of the radio in much the same position as her father upstairs. Mrs. McManus came to the door.

"I'm sorry to bother you," Melanie said.

"That's all right," the woman answered.

Melanie went into the tiny hallway between the kitchen and the bedrooms. The phone was on a small table. She picked it up. "Hello."

"Melanie?" asked the familiar voice.

"Yes."

"I want to see you right away. I'm in St. Joseph's Hospital."

"I know," she said. The stories and rumors were all over the plant. "Are you all right?"

"I'm fine," he said. "But the stupid doctors won't let me out. They want to keep me in for observation."

"Maybe you'd better rest," she said.

"I want to see you."

"I was just going to take a bath," she said. "Besides it will take me almost two hours to get there by trolley."

"I'll send a car for you," he said flatly. "You be downstairs in front of your door in half an hour." The phone went dead in her hand and she put it down.

She went back into the kitchen. "Thank you," she said to the little Irishwoman.

McManus turned from his radio and looked at her. Something in his policeman's eyes told her that he knew she was naked under the housedress. Unconsciously her hand pulled it closer over her chest. "Is your father workin' yet?" he asked.

"Not yet, Mr. McManus," she answered politely, moving toward the door.

"Times are bad," he said heavily. "No tellin' now what's goin' to happen."

She was almost out of the door. "Thank you for letting me use the phone, Mr. McManus."

"That's okay," he said. "As long as you don't abuse it like some people I know."

"Good night," she said, closing the door behind her. Half an hour later she came out of her room fully dressed.

Her mother looked at her in surprise. "Where are you going this time of the night? It's almost nine o'clock."

"I'm going to see Mr. Warren," she said. "He's in St. Joseph's Hospital."

Her father turned from the radio. "What happened to him?"

"He had an accident. He says it's nothing serious."

"It'll take you almost two hours to get there this time of the night," her mother said. "It's not safe for a girl to be out alone in this neighborhood now that the niggers are only a few blocks away."

"He's sending a car for me."

Her father got to his feet. "He must want to see you real bad. What for?"

"I don't know. But he is my boss. It's probably business."

Her father leered. "Monkey business, you mean." He turned to her mother. "I think maybe Mr. Warren has got something on for our little girl."

Her mother made a face. "Stop thinking with your dirty cracker mind. I know my Melanie. She's a good girl."

"I'll be back as soon as I can," Melanie said, slipping out the door.

Her father called after her as she went down the stairs. "Don't forget to remind him of the promise he made to your daddy!"

He was sitting up in bed, his right arm held out in front of him on a pulley sling, his head bandaged, and several large square patches on his right cheek. He didn't wait for her to speak as she came into the room.

"Personnel told me over the phone that they didn't receive the usual nightly batch of blind carbons from your office today."

"There weren't any," she replied. "Mr. Hardeman didn't dictate a single note."

"That's strange," he said. "He was in three days last week and spent all day writing memos."

"There were none today," she said. "There are stories all over the plant that Mr. Hardeman beat you up. What happened?"

"I tripped on a rug in the office and hit my head against the corner of a desk, that's all."

She looked at him without speaking. If it had happened in Number Two's office like they said, he should know better than to tell a story like that. Mr. Hardeman, Jr. did not have any rugs in his office.

"They didn't get your telephone call sheet either," he said.

"Mr. Hardeman came out at the end of the day and took it away from me. Besides he made all his outside calls on his private line. That doesn't cross my desk."

"What about his meetings? Who came to see him?"

"First thing in the morning, he called Mr. Coburn, Mr. Edgerton and Mr. Duncan."

"What did they talk about?"

"I don't know," she answered. "He sent me down to the canteen. When he called me back, they were gone."

"Who else came to see him?"

She thought for a moment. "In the morning, Mr. Williams of Sales and Mr. Conrad of Purchasing."

"What did they talk about?"

"I don't know."

"You were told to keep your intercom switch open whenever there was a meeting in his office so you could make notes!"

"I did," she said. "But nothing came through. He pulled the plug every time someone came into his office."

Warren was silent for a moment. "Anybody else come?"

"In the afternoon, no one from the plant."

"Anyone from outside?"

"Yes," she said. "A Mr. Frank Perino."

"I know what they talked about," Warren said. "Perino's his bootlegger. And Number One likes his whiskey."

"That wasn't it," she said. "Mr Perino's son is a doctor and he wanted Mr. Hardeman to get him into a Detroit hospital. It seemed he was having trouble because of his background. Mr. Hardeman fixed it."

He was surprised. "How do you know about that?"

"Mr. Hardeman called me into his office for coffee and aspirin. I was there all the time with Mr. Perino." She hesitated a moment. "Mr Hardeman takes a lot of aspirin. He must have had at least twelve tablets during the day."

"Okay,"he said. "Just keep your eyes and ears open. Find out as much as you can and call me every night."

"I'll do that," she said. "How long do you expect to stay here?"

"The doctors say they'll let me out in a couple of days."

"I'm sorry you were hurt," she said.

He looked at her. "Do you know why I picked you to go into Number One's office?"

She shook her head.

"Because you're a big girl and he likes big women."

"I don't understand," she said.

"Don't be stupid," he snapped. "You know his reputation. Sooner or later, he'll make a pass at you."

"Then what do I do?"

"You pretend to go along with him," he said. "Gain his confidence. Then we'll have him."

"What if I don't go along with him?"

He stared at her. "There are other girls who would like that job."

Her eyes fell. She was silent.

He laughed. The tone in his voice changed. "You said you were going to take a bath. Did you have anything on when we talked on the phone?"

She didn't look up. The look on McManus's face flashed through her mind. "A housedress."

"Anything under it?" His voice was getting husky.

"No."

"Come closer to the bed."

She raised her head, looked at him, then at the man who had driven her here. He was standing, his back against the door, watching them impassively.

Warren caught her glance. "Don't mind Mike, He's my bodyguard. He really doesn't see anything."

She didn't move.

"I said come over here!"

Reluctantly she moved to the bed. He took her hand and put it on the sheet between his legs. "I got a hard-on just thinking about it," he said.

She was silent.

"Pull the sheet down."

She started to move the sheet. He winced in sudden pain. "Carefully, damn it!"

She moved the sheet down slowly until the bottom of his hospital gown revealed skinny, hairy legs. The front of the gown hung like a small tent over his erect phallus. "Push the gown up and jack me off," he said. "But be careful, don't shake the bed because that hurts my arm."

She raised the gown gently. His organ was full and erect. Slowly she freed it and began to massage him.

"Oh, Jesus, that's good," he said, leaning his head back against the pillows, his eyes closed. "Put your other hand under my balls."

His testicles felt like small rocks in her hand. "Faster, faster!"

She began to pump him rapidly; his mouth opened and his breathing seemed to keep time with her motion. "Now, you really got it," he groaned.

A moment passed. "Take me in your mouth!" he said suddenly. "I'm going to come!"

She hesitated, glancing at the man standing against the door. His eyes looked blankly back at her. Then she felt Warren's hand in her hair, pulling her face down to him. Her mouth opened automatically.

She swallowed quickly to keep from choking and after a moment it was over.

He leaned back against the pillow, his eyes closed. "You're almost as good a cocksucker as some of the little pansies I know."

She didn't answer.

He opened his eyes and looked at her, then at his bodyguard. "What do you think, Mike? Is she as good as our little friend?"

"It don't look like it, Boss," the bodyguard replied. "He seems to like it more,"

Warren laughed. "Maybe when we get out of here, I'll have you give her some lessons."

For the first time the bodyguard's voice was shocked. "You know I don't like girls!"

Warren laughed again. "I don't mean that. I mean show her how to really do it." He turned back to her, his voice going cold. "Get a washcloth and a towel and wipe me off."

She went into the small bathroom. In the mirror her cheeks were shining and wet. She wiped her face and then went back into the room.

A few moments later, the sheets were straightened over him once again. "That's better. No point having the nurse know what's going on."

She didn't speak. This was what happened every time she went with him. Not once had they ever had sex together nor had he ever wanted it. Had she been a virgin, her hymen would have been intact if it were up to him.

"Give her five dollars and send her home in a cab," he said to the bodyguard.

Mike came toward her, a five-dollar bill in his hand. She took it from him and he walked back to the door. She turned to the bed.

"You call me here right after work tomorrow," he said.

"I will," she said. "Good night."

"Good night," he answered.

Mike stepped aside and opened the door to let her out. She heard the door close behind her as she walked down the long hospital corridor.

Once outside, she looked down at her hand. The five-dollar bill was still clutched in it. The clang of a streetcar approaching came to her ears. She looked at the bill again, then at the taxi line. Suddenly she began to run toward the corner to the trolley stop.

It might take her more than two hours to get home. But five dollars was more than a whole day's pay.

Chapter Ten

Edgerton walked across the office. "I'm, worried, Mr. Hardeman," he said. "This is the second pay day the banks have been closed and we're getting a lot of complaints from the employees. The stores won't accept our checks."

"We're good for it," Loren said.

"It's not only us," Edgerton said. "It's the bank. Too many have already closed down for good. Now I hear talk that the men won't show up for work unless they get paid in cash."

"Pay them in cash then," said Loren.

"We haven't got it," Edgerton said flatly. "Our weekly payroll is over a hundred and forty thousand. Nobody keeps that much cash on hand."

"Get it then."

"Where? The banks are closed to us as well as to them."

Loren was thoughtful for a moment. "What does personnel have to say about this?"

"Warren bucked it to me. He says it's the treasurer's job to provide money for the payroll."

"Has he explained the situation to the employees?"

"He says he has."

"That's not what I asked. Has he?"

"I don't know. I heard that a group of men came in to talk to him about it and that he fired the whole bunch of them."

"Why?"

"He says they were troublemakers. All Wobblies trying to unionize the plant and that they were just using this as an excuse."

"What do you think?"

"I know some of those men. They're old-line employees. I don't think they are Wobblies."

"If they were would it make any difference? Wouldn't they still be entitled to their pay?"

"Yes," said Edgerton.

Loren flipped the switch on his intercom. Melanie's voice answered. "Yes, Mr. Hardeman."

"Ask Mr. Warren to come up here right away," he said, flipping off the switch.

A few minutes later, Joe Warren came into the office. His arm was still in a sling, his eyes wary.

"Warren, I hear we're having problems over the fact that employees can't cash their pay checks."

Warren began smoothly. "You have to recognize that fact, Mr. Hardeman, that during the past few years we have been infiltrated by the I.W.W., Communists and union organizers. It isn't our men stirring up the trouble. It's them."

"You mean to say our men can cash their checks?"

"No," Warren said. "But our men aren't complaining."

"How do you know?"

"I know the good ones and the bad ones," Warren said.

"And only the bad ones are complaining, is that it?" Loren asked sarcastically.

"Yes, Mr. Hardeman."

"Did you explain the situation to them?" Loren asked.

"There's nothing to explain," Warren answered. "Every other company in town is in the same boat. They all know that."

"But if they can't cash their checks and they can't get credit at the stores, how are they going to eat?" Loren asked.

"That's not our problem," Warren said. "We can't be expected to manage our employee's money. If they can't establish their own credit, it's unfortunate."

"If the stores won't accept our checks," Loren asked, "don't you think it's our credit that's being questioned, not theirs?"

Warren didn't answer.

"Have you taken any steps to assure the local merchants that Bethlehem Motors will back up their checks regardless of the bank upon which they were issued?"

"I didn't see where it was necessary," Warren answered.

Loren was silent. He studied the man sitting in front of him. Warren had a feral quality, even while sitting still. There was an air of cold ruthlessness about him that no amount of surface amenities could dispel.

"I don't see why you should concern yourself with such petty details, Mr. Hardeman," Warren said. "I can control the situation. Meanwhile we can use the circumstance to smoke out the bad employees in our plant and get rid of them."

Loren didn't speak.

"We've already rid ourselves of more than twenty troublemakers," Warren said. "And we have our eyes on more of them."

Loren was still silent.

Warren rose to his feet. "Just leave everything to me, Mr. Hardeman. I'll work it out, you'll see." He started for the door.

"Sit down, Warren!" Loren snapped. "I didn't give you permission to leave!"

Warren hesitated a moment, then returned to his seat. Carefully he rested his sling on the arm of the chair.

"I want you to send a letter out to every merchant and store in the area that Bethlehem Motors will guarantee every pay check issued by them regardless of the bank concerned."

Warren shook his head. "Can't do that, Mr. Hardeman. Such a letter has to be approved either by the president of the company or the board of directors."

"Then get the president to sign it," Loren said.

"I don't know where he is," Warren said blandly. "I haven't seen him for over two weeks. Have you?"

Loren stared at him. Warren knew damn well he hadn't seen his son since that day in the office. "Then prepare the letter, I'll sign it."

"You haven't the authority," Warren said calmly. "You cannot commit the company to that kind of loss in case the bank should fail."

"There's nothing in the company bylaws to prevent me from guaranteeing those checks personally, is there?"

"What you do personally is none of our concern," Warren said.

"Then prepare the letter that way for my signature," said Loren.

"If you like," Warren said. "Is there anything else?"

"Yes," Loren said. "Also inform the employees that the next payroll will be cash."

"I'll do that," Warren said. "But all hell will break loose if the money isn't there on payday."

"That will be my problem," Loren said. "You can go now."

They were silent until the door closed behind Warren, then Edgerton turned to Loren. "Where are you going to get the money?"

"I'll get it from someplace," Loren said. He looked at the closed door. "What's the latest report from Duncan?"

"Everything will be set in a week. The new cars should be rolling off the line within the month."

"Good." Loren smiled with satisfaction. "That cuts Charlie Sorensen's new model changeover time at Ford exactly in half. Six weeks instead of ninety days." He took a cigarette from the box on his desk. "Do you think he knows anything about it?"

"With his spy system?" Edgerton asked, then answered his own question. "I'm sure that he does."

"But they've done nothing about it." Loren asked, "What do you think they're waiting for?"

"Actually, there's very little they can do at the moment. The bank closing played right into our hands in this case. The bankers are too busy with their own problems to pay attention to us. And the board meeting is still more than a week away."

Loren thought for a moment. "Get after Duncan and tell him I want the production line rolling within a week and I don't care how he does it. I want that car coming off the line before the board meeting."

"That means dumping the contract with Ford for car bodies," said Edgerton.

"Dump it then."

"Bennett will be sore. He'll sue."

"No, he won't," Loren said. "I'll straighten it out with Edsel and Charlie Sorensen." He was silent for a moment. "I wonder if there's any tieup between Bennett and Warren?"

"I know they're good friends," Edgerton said. "Warren just built a house on Grosse Point Isles next to Bennett."

Loren looked at him. "I understand all purchasing has been consolidated into Warren's department."

"It's not a bad idea," Edgerton said. "Central control. We get better prices than purchasing department by department."

"I'm not saying it's not," Loren said quickly. "I'm just wondering if a close look into purchasing won't be useful."

Edgerton smiled. "It can't hurt."

"Can you do it without him becoming aware of what's happening?"

"I think so," Edgerton said. "It's near the time for our annual audit. I'll just have the boys take an extra hard look at the purchasing contracts."

"You do that and keep me posted." Loren got to his feet.

Edgerton rose also. He looked at Loren. "Mr. Hardeman," he said tentatively.

"Yes, Walt?"

"I'm glad you're back," he said.

"Grandpa! Grandpa!" The children's voices greeted him at the door. He opened his arms and swept them up to him. He kissed Anne's cheek first, then Loren III.

"Were you a good boy today?" he asked his grandson.

"He was a very good boy," Anne said in her three-year-old voice. "He only hit me once today."

"Only once?" Loren pretended shock. He looked at the boy. "Why did you do that?"

"I deserved it," Anne said. "I hit him first."

"Remember the rules," he said sternly. "I said no more fights."

"We're trying to remember, Grandpa," the little boy said. "But sometimes we forget."

"Don't forget," he said.

"Piggyback! Piggyback!" Anne cried.

"Yes! Piggyback!" her brother echoed.

Loren put them down and got on his hands and knees. The children climbed on his back, Anne in front, her little hands digging into his hair, Loren III in the back, clutching his grandfather's belt.

"Pony Express!" the boy yelled, slapping Loren's behind with his hand.

"Faster! Faster!" Anne yelled happily.

Loren crawled rapidly into the library with them bouncing up and down on his back. He came to a stop in front of silk-clad legs in high-heeled shoes and looked up.

"Exactly what do you think you're doing down there?" Sally asked, trying to keep her voice stern.

"Look out," Loren said. "We're the Wells Fargo Pony Express." He set out at a rapid gallop around the room. He came to a stop again in front of Sally.

"All right, children," Sally said firmly. "That's enough annoying your grandfather. It's time for your dinner."

"We want to play!" Loren III yelled.

"Your grandfather is tired. He had to work hard all day," Sally said, lifting him from Loren's back. Anne slid to the floor. "Now give Grandfather a kiss and go into dinner."

"Can we play some more after dinner?" Anne asked.

"No. After dinner, you're both going to bed, but if you both eat all your dinner, Grandfather will come upstairs and tell you a bedtime story."

"Will you, Grandpa?" Loren III asked.

"You bet your sweet patootie," Loren said, getting to his feet.

The children picked it up. "You bet your sweet patootie!" they shouted, running from the room, their voices echoing back from the hall. "You bet your sweet patootie!"

Sally frowned. "That's a fine thing to teach the children," she said, trying to keep a straight face. "You're more a child than they are."

He laughed. "It won't hurt them."

"I have ice and whiskey on the bar," she said. "Want me to fix you a drink?"

He nodded, watching her go to the bar. She came back to him the whiskey amber and the ice tinkling in the glass. He took the drink from her. His eyes were on her face. "I always said a house needs a woman's touch."

She looked at him for a moment without speaking, then turned and went to the bar and made herself a drink. She came back to him. "I spoke to Junior today," she said without sitting down.

"Yes," he said in an expressionless voice.

"He wanted me to return home. He said he would come back if I did."

He sipped at his drink without speaking.

"I told him I was never coming back," she said.

"Then what did he say?"

"He got nasty and said all sorts of things."

"What sort of things?"

"That he knew what we were doing and we didn't fool him or anyone else. That he had the evidence that we were sleeping together and he wouldn't hesitate to use it in court to take the children away from me."

Loren shook his head sadly.

"It's more than that," she said. "He hates so much he's blind."

Loren looked up at her. "What are you going to do?"

"I can't stay here," she said. "There's no point in dragging you into this mess. I was thinking of moving to England."

"Would you get a divorce first?"

"Yes," she said. "If he would agree I could go to Reno."

"Then what would you do?"

"Go to England with the children. The schools are very good there. And at least they speak the same language."

After a moment, he put his glass down. "When did Junior say he would return?"

"Next week. He said something about having to be here for a board meeting."

That added up. It also provided the reason why Warren was lying low. They were going to let him dig his own grave. He got to his feet. "You don't have to go anywhere, you know that," he said. "You can stay right here in Hardeman Manor. The children are happy and I don't give a damn what he does."

She looked into his eyes. "The children have never been happier. You've played with them more in these two weeks than their father has since they were born. But it's not fair to you. You have enough problems as it is."

"Think about it," he said. "Don't make up your mind yet."

She nodded.

"I'm going upstairs to lie down a bit before dinner. Call me when it's ready."

"Headache again?"

He nodded.

"Want me to get you some aspirin?"

"No. I had enough of those today. I'll try to do without it. Maybe I'll feel better after a little rest."

She watched him leave the room and heard his footsteps on the staircase, then sank into a chair. She could feel the tears just behind her eyes. It wasn't fair. It just wasn't fair.

A thought suddenly came to her. She ran up the steps and into his room without knocking at the door.

He was just coming from the bathroom, his shirt already unbuttoned. He looked at her.

"I never thought of you," she said quickly. "Or of what you want."

He didn't speak.

"I'll go back with him if it will make things easier for you."

He took a deep breath, then held his arms open toward her. She came into them and laid her cheek against his broad chest.

"I don't want you to go anywhere but here," he said.

Chapter Eleven

Melanie's voice through the intercom was hushed and impressed. "The White House calling, Mr. Hardeman."

Loren flipped the switch and picked up the telephone. "Hello."

A man's voice spoke. "Mr. Hardeman?"

"Speaking."

"Just a moment for the President of the United States." There was a click.

"Mr. Hardeman?" There was no mistaking that voice. He had heard it too many times on the radio.

"Yes, Mr. President."

"I regret very much that we have never met but I want you to know that I am personally very grateful for your contribution to the Democratic campaign fund."

"Thank you for being so kind, Mr. President."

"Now I have an important favor to ask of you, Mr. Hardeman, and I beg of you to consider it." The President came right to the point. "As you know, I consider the most important problem facing this country to be the depression and the unemployment resulting from it, so I have placed before Congress a bill which I have entitled the National Recovery Act. Contained within this bill is the framework to rebuild and rehabilitate our industries through an adoption of mutual practices to be effected by self-help and government regulations."

"I've read about it, Mr. President," Loren said. The Detroit newspapers were already filled with it, denouncing it for the most part as an attempt to socialize and bring the automobile industry under government control.

"I'm sure you have, Mr. Hardeman." The President paused for a moment. "And I'm equally sure that you've read nothing good about it."

"I wouldn't say that, Mr. President. There are some practical proposals in it that merit further consideration."

"That brings us to my favor," the President said. "I would like you to come to Washington to help develop that section of the NRA that pertains to your industry. You, of course will be working directly under General Hugh Johnson who has accepted the position of overall responsibility. Since we regard the automobile industry as the keystone of our economy, you can see how important a contribution you can make to your country."

"I'm most flattered and honored, Mr. President," Loren said. "But I am certain there are others more worthy and more capable for that position."

"You're being modest, Mr. Hardeman," the President chuckled. "And that's not in keeping with what I've heard about you. But you are our first choice and I do hope you will give it every consideration."

"I will, Mr. President," said Loren. "But my own company is in serious trouble and I don't really know if I could leave it at this time."

"Mr. Hardeman," the President said. "The entire country is in serious trouble. I am sure that as a responsible citizen you cannot fail to see that unless the country recovers from its malaise, neither will your company." He paused for a moment. "I would appreciate your decision within the week, Mr. Hardeman, and I do hope that it will be favorable."

"I will let you know, Mr. President," said Loren.

"Good-bye, Mr. Hardeman."

"Good-bye, Mr. President." Loren put down the telephone. He reached for a cigarette and lit it. President Roosevelt didn't waste time. He promised to stir up some excitement and that was exactly what was happening.

The intercom buzzed again. He flipped the switch. "Yes, Miss Walker?"

"It's almost time for the board meeting, Mr. Hardeman."

"Thank you, Miss Walker. Will you bring in my folder?"

"Right away, sir."

A moment later she came into his office and placed the folder on his desk. Instead of leaving, as she usually did, she hesitated.

He looked up at her. "Yes, Miss Walker?"

She blushed. "Was that really President Roosevelt on the telephone?"

"It was." He nodded. He opened the folder and looked at it, then looked up. She was still standing there. "Yes, Miss Walker?"

"I voted for him," she said. "It was the very first time I voted."

"So did I," he smiled.

She smiled suddenly. "I like the sound of his voice on the radio. It's so warm and friendly. It seems like he's really talking to you."

It was the first time he had seen her smile. He looked at her. "You know, you're a very pretty girl, Miss Walker," he said. "You should smile more often."

She blushed, again. "Thank you, Mr. Hardeman."

He watched her walk to the door. Odd that he had never really looked at her before. She was an attractive girl. The door closed behind her and he looked down at the file folder.

He deliberately arrived a few minutes late. The other board members were already in the room, clustered in small groups, deep in conversation. They fell silent as he entered. He wasted no time on the usual greetings. Instead he rapped his knuckles on the table.

"Will the board members kindly take their seats?" he asked.

Silently they took up their positions around the long rectangular table. Junior sat facing him at the foot of the table, Warren sat at Junior's right. There were eleven others at the table as it came toward him. Coburn and Edgerton were the only other company employees on the board. The rest consisted of representatives of the banks and insurance companies to whom they were in debt and several token members, officials of other non-competitive corporations.

"The chair calls this meeting to order and will entertain a motion to suspend the reading of the minutes of the previous meeting, a copy of which is in the folder in front of you."

He waited. Coburn made the motion, Edgerton seconded it, and it was carried, unanimously and quickly by the rest of the board. That done, he awaited a motion to place the current agenda before the board.

"Mr. Chairman!" Junior said.

"Yes, Mr. President," he said formally.

"I would like to place a motion to delay the consideration of the agenda in favor of other and more important business."

"The chair has no objections, Mr. President," he said. "Do I hear the motion seconded?"

"Second the motion," said Warren "The chair will abstain from the vote," he said. "The board will now vote on the motion placed before it by the president. All in favor say 'Aye'."

There were eleven Ayes, the two Nays came from Edgerton and Coburn. He smiled. "The motion is carried." He took a cigarette from the box on the table before him, lit it and leaned back in his chair.

Junior was on his feet almost before Loren could let out his first breath of smoke. "I accuse the chairman of the board of overstepping his authority in the exercise of his duties and of other gross improprieties detrimental to the welfare of the company and I demand his resignation!"

There was a stony silence in the room. Loren smiled again. He put down the cigarette carefully. "The chair will be pleased to consider Mr. President's request if he puts it before the board properly as a motion." He paused for a moment but not long enough to give Junior a chance to speak again. "The chair will also be pleased to entertain a motion for the board to visit Assembly Plant Number Three before any other business."

Coburn came through on cue, Edgerton seconded. Curiosity swung the board in their favor. The only two votes against were Junior and Warren.

"The motion is carried." Loren got to his feet. "The meeting is adjourned to Assembly Plant Number Three. Follow me, gentlemen."

Duncan fell in step beside him as they came out of the administration building. "Walk slow," the Scotsman whispered out of the corner of his mouth. "The first car isn't due to reach the end of the assembly line for another ten minutes."

Loren nodded. Deliberately he led them the long way round. It was exactly nine minutes until they arrived at the end of the production line in Assembly Plant Number Three.

Loren turned to the board members. "I assume all you gentlemen know how to drive a car?"

They nodded.

"Good," Loren smiled. He looked down the production line. A car was coming toward them. "In case you gentlemen are wondering why I asked you to come down here, I want to show you the reason."

The car came through the final inspection shed and arrived, dark blue and shining before them. "Here is the first Baby Sundancer off the line. It will sell for under five hundred dollars and put us firmly in the low-car market with Ford, Chrysler, Plymouth and Chevrolet!"

He paused a moment. "Mr. John Duncan, our chief engineer and designer, will drive off in the first car to the freight yard where the car will be loaded on a train and begin its journey to the dealer. If each one of you will take a car as it comes off the line and follow Mr. Duncan, you will have an opportunity to judge for yourself how well the car performs and handles. A bus will be waiting there to bring you back to the Administration Building at the end of your drive."

Duncan got into the car and started the engine. He moved off slowly just as the second car arrived. This was a dark burgundy color.

Loren took one of the directors by the arm. "Go ahead, drive it."

The man got into the car and started it. After that there was no problem. The men couldn't wait their turn. They were like children with a new toy. One car after another took off until only Loren, Junior and Warren were left.

"You can't get away with this!" Junior snarled.

Loren smiled. "I already did, son." He took a pack of cigarettes from his pocket. "Let's face it. You already lost the fight. The minute those men got into the automobile."

Loren lit his cigarette. "My advice is that you jump into the next car off the line and drive down to the freight yard to accept the congratulations of the board. There's no one here will say anything to the contrary."

Junior hesitated. He looked at Warren.

"Better make up your mind," Loren said. "Here comes the next car. If you don't get into it, I will."

The car, a bright yellow, came to a stop. Without a word, Junior got into it and drove off.

The next car arrived, carbon black and shining. Warren looked questioningly at Loren. Loren hesitated a moment. "That's car number thirteen off the line," he finally said.

"I'm not superstitious," answered Warren.

Loren shrugged his shoulders. He watched Warren jump into the car and drive away eagerly. The car was about five hundred yards down the road when the explosion came.

The roar echoed around the plant, bringing men and women from their offices and production lines. A pall of dust hung in the air and when it settled, there was nothing to be seen of the automobile but twisted and tortured pieces of metal.

Loren turned and began walking toward the administration building as people ran past him. There were three white-suited jumped-clad mechanics, the blue letters B.M.C. across their backs, walking toward the gate in front of him.

The smallest of the three fell back and into step with Loren. They walked silently until they reached the door of the administration building. Then Loren turned and looked down at him. "I told him it was car number thirteen," he said. "But he said he wasn't superstitious."

The small man's dark brown eyes peered up at him from under heavy black brows. "A man without superstition is a man without a soul," he said.

Loren didn't speak for a moment. "I wonder what would have happened if I got into that car," he said finally.

There was a note of injury in the small man's voice. "My boys are very professional," he said. "You never would have been allowed to start that car."

Loren nodded. A flicker of a smile came into his eyes. "I apologize for even having the thought," he said. "Good-bye, Mr. Perino."

"Good-bye, Mr. Hardeman."

Loren stood there looking after the little man as he hurried after his two companions. He saw the security guard at the gate carefully turn his back so that he would not see the three men walking through.

The receptionist at the entrance desk to the administration building was just putting down the telephone as he came into the building. "Mr. Hardeman!" she exclaimed in an excited voice. "A car just blew up outside of Assembly Three!"

"I know," he said, walking to the elevator and pressing the button.

"I wonder who was in it," she said, as the elevator doors opened.

He walked into the elevator and pressed the button. "Some unlucky bastard."

Chapter Twelve

The snow falling in soft white flakes partly laced the brightly lit great dome of the Capitol as she looked out of the window of the small house in Washington in which they had spent the last year and a half. It was after nine o'clock. Another late night.

She went back to the sofa in front of the blazing hearth. The leaping flames threw their warmth at her, lending a familiar, odd comfort. So many nights had she waited for him in this chair, in front of this fire. Somehow there always was an emergency in Washington.

"Government by crisis," he had said one night when he had come in particularly late. "It can't be much fun for you."

"I'm not complaining," she had said. And she had meant it. Detroit seemed far away and another world. A completely self-centered world whose horizons began with a front bumper and ended with the rear bumper. "I don't ever want to go back," she had added.

He had given her a curious look but didn't speak.

"The children like it too," she said. "Every day their nanny takes them to someplace new, someplace exciting and filled with history. Imagine how much they've learned since they've been here. It's like growing up with everything in the world happening in front of your eyes."

"It hasn't been lonely for you?" he asked. "Away from your friends?"

"What friends? Back in Detroit the friends I had were the wives of men who either worked for Bethlehem or wanted to. I was more alone there than here. At least here when we go to a party we have more things to talk about than just automobiles."

The sound of the front door interrupted her thoughts. She rose from the sofa and walked toward the foyer. The butler had already taken Loren's snow-covered hat and coat and was hanging them in the closet when she reached him.

"I'm sorry I'm late," he said, kissing her cheek.

His lips were cold. "That's all right," she said quickly. "Come inside in front of the fire where you can warm up."

He sank wearily onto the sofa, stretching his hands out towards the fire. She looked down at him with concern. She had never seen him so tired before, his brows knitted with the headache he seemed to have constantly now. "Let me fix you a drink."

She went to the sideboard and made his drink quickly. When she came back, he had leaned his head against the sofa and closed his eyes. He felt her next to him. Silently he took the drink and sipped it. She sat down beside him without speaking.

He turned to her. "Well, it's over," he said in a tired voice.

She looked at him in bewilderment. "What do you mean?"

"You didn't near the news?"

She shook her head. "I was reading a book. I didn't listen to the radio this evening."

"The Supreme Court ruled today that the NRA was unconstitutional."

"What does that mean?" she asked.

A half smile came to his lips. "For one thing it means I'm unemployed. Out of a job like a lot of other people." He sipped at his drink and smiled again. "I wonder how much severance pay a dollar-a-year man is entitled to."

"Maybe two dollars a year?" she suggested.

He laughed. "Anyhow, the President never did promise me that the job would be a steady one."

"Did you see him?"

"No. But I did see Hugh Johnson. The General was in rare form, swearing a blue streak, convinced the country would go to rack and ruin without him at the helm."

"What happens now?" she asked.

"I don't know," he said, shrugging his shoulders. "As near as I can make out, in the world of politics when you lose, you fold your tent and silently steal away in the night."

"It's so sudden, I still can't believe it," she said.

"You'd believe it if you saw clerks and secretaries loading up their briefcases with supplies and paper clips," he said.

"When did you find out?"

"This morning when the Supreme Court convened. It was instant pandemonium. Everybody running around in circles doing nothing except adding to the general confusion." He was suddenly angry. "Worst of all was the news from Detroit. They went crazy out there. They did everything except declare a holiday. The damn fools!"

He took a swallow of his drink. "What no one seemed to realize was that without the NRA they might as well turn around and hand the entire industry over to the Big Three. Nash, Studebaker, Willys, Hudson, Packard, they're all doomed. It will only be a matter of time before every independent auto manufacturer will be out of business."

"Surely they can see that," she said.

"They can't see their noses," he said sarcastically. "They think they can compete with Ford, GM and Chrysler now that controls are off. They don't stand a chance. The big companies will make it cheaper and sell it cheaper."

"Does that go for Bethlehem too?" she asked.

He looked at her. "Yes."

"Can anything be done about it?"

He nodded. "Concentrate on the low end of the medium priced range. A car priced between the Chevy and the Pontiac. That should be the Sundancer market for at least the next ten years."

"What about the Baby Sundancer?" she asked.

"It served its purpose," he said. "It kept us going when the only market was the low-price end. But now the costs are climbing and we can't compete against the others. I figure that by next year, times should improve enough to let us discontinue it."

She thought for a moment. "I'll be sorry to see it go. I liked that little car."

"It was a little bastard," he said affectionately. "Made out of leftovers of other cars, but it did have something going for it."

The butler knocked discreetly before he entered the room. "Dinner is served, Madam."

It was after midnight when he looked up from his desk in the small study, his work finished. He began gathering the papers and placing them in his briefcase. He stared down at the briefcase a moment. Then he snapped it shut. There was a finality to the gesture. It was done. A part of the past. There was nothing more to keep him here tomorrow after he returned the papers to the office.

He got to his feet and, turning off the light, left the room. He went silently up the darkened staircase and down the corridor to his room.

He was just about to switch on the light when her voice came from his bed. "Loren! Don't turn on the light!"

He stood there a moment, then closed the door softly. "Why?"

"I've been crying," she said. "And I know I look awful."

He crossed the room to her, his eyes getting accustomed to the dark. She was sitting up, the pillows behind her back. "Crying won't help," he said. "It never does."

"I know. But we've been happy here."

He dragged on a cigarette. She held out her hand. "May I?" Silently he gave it to her. The tip glowed red, casting a faint light on her face. Her eyes were almost luminous. "Loren?"

"Yes?"

"I'm not going back." Her voice was gentle. "You knew that, didn't you?"

"Yes," he said.

"But I want to be with you."

"Then come back," he said quickly. "Hardeman Manor is big enough. We can—"

"No, Loren," she interrupted. "It won't be the same. Detroit isn't Washington. Here I'm accepted. I'm your daughter-in-law acting as hostess for her widowed father-in-law. There I'm still your son's wife, living with you while her husband lives a few miles down the road. It won't work."

"Then divorce him," he said harshly. "And we can get married."

"No. The one thing I learned about Detroit is that you can get away with murder but not divorce. You still owe the banks twenty million dollars. One open scandal and you lose everything you've spent your whole life in building."

He was silent.

"You know I'm right, Loren," she said. "I would ask you to come with me but I know you must do what you have to do. You build automobiles, Loren. You can't stop or you'll die."

He walked over to the window. The snow had stopped and the night was clear, the stars sparkling in the dark blue sky. "What are you going to do?"

"Stay here for a while," she said. "Then, maybe move up to New York. Soon the children will be starting school. There are good schools there for them."

"I will miss them," he said.

"They will miss you even more. They've grown to love you very much."

He felt the tears come to his eyes and blinked to hold them back. But now even the stars were blurred. "May I come to visit them?"

"I hope you do. Very often."

Slowly he began to undress. He placed his clothing on a chair and started for the bathroom. She called him and he paused.

"Loren, no pajamas tonight, please. I want to sleep naked with you."

"Can I brush my teeth?" he smiled.

"Yes," she said. "But hurry. I want you inside me."

"Then why wait?" he asked, coming to the bed.

Her legs rose up to enfold him, his large, strong hands gripped her buttocks as he entered her. "Oh, God!" she cried, a sudden despair in her voice. "How will I ever live without you?"

Chapter Thirteen

Melanie was sitting at the kitchen table reading the evening paper when her father came home. He looked over her shoulder at the headlines.

SHOWDOWN DUE AT FORD TODAY
Dearborn Gives UAW Right to
Distribute Handbills Outside
River Rouge

He began to unbutton the gray blouse of his Ford Security Police uniform, walking to the icebox. He took out a bottle of beer and opened it. Holding the bottle to his mouth he drank until it was half empty, then put it down on the table and belched.

Melanie didn't look up. She began turning the pages to the women's section.

"You can tell your Commie-loving boss to watch tomorrow and see how a real company handles the union," her father said, taking off his blouse. He pulled open his tie and picked up the beer again.

"What do you mean?" She looked up at him.

"You'll find out tomorrow." He smiled secretively. "All I can tell you is that we're ready for those Commie bastards. They're going to wish they never got that okay from the City of Dearborn."

"There's nothing you can do," she said, her eyes going back to the newspaper. "They have the law on their side."

"Ford's got a right to protect its property," he said. He looked at her. "Just because your boss folded up and gave in to the union don't mean that we have to lay down and take it."

"Mr. Hardeman says it's only a question of time before the whole industry is union."

"That's what he thinks," her father answered. "Tomorrow he'll find out different." He finished the beer. "How come you're still dressed?"

"I'm working tonight," she said. "Mr. Hardeman has an executive committee meeting over at the house after dinner. I'm going out there to take notes."

He leered at her. "No wonder he lets you use a company car. You've been doin' a lot of night work lately."

She didn't answer.

"Where's your mother?" he asked suddenly.

"She'll be up in a few minutes," she said. "She's downstairs with Mrs. McManus."

He took another bottle of beer and dropped into the chair opposite her. His voice took on a confidential tone. "You can tell your old man. He knows about those things. What's goin' on between you an' Number One?"

"Nothing," she said.

He opened the bottle. "Nothing? You're too smart a girl to expect your old daddy to believe that?" He took a pull at the beer. His voice turned sly. "Like nothing went on between you an' Joe Warren either."

She didn't answer.

"I know all about that," he said. "And I don't blame you for doin' it. If you didn't, there would be a hundred girls jumpin' at the chance."

She felt her face begin to flush. She got out of her chair. "You got nothing but a dirty mind."

He smiled up at her. "There's a guy workin' at Ford with me. He used to be Warren's bodyguard. His name is Mike. Remember him?"

Her face was burning, she didn't move.

"He doesn't know you're my daughter. The names don't mean nothin' to him, there were so many of them. But he remembers picking up a girl one night an' bringing' her to Joe Warren in the hospital. He also remembers what she did." He took some more beer from the bottle. "So don't try playin' Miss Innocent with me an' expect me to believe you ain't doin' at least as much for Number One and maybe more. Girls like you don't get cars and fifty bucks a week just for typin'."

She tried to speak but the words stuck in her throat.

He began to laugh. "I just think you're givin' it away too cheap. Number One's used to shellin' out big dough for his girls. Mike says he was banging his own daughter-in-law an' that he gave her a cool million bucks to get a quiet divorce last year so the shit wouldn't hit the fan."

Abruptly she turned and ran down the hall to her room. She slammed the door shut behind her and began to cry. Through the thin walls she could still hear the sound of his obscenely derisive laughter.

The letter was lying on the library desk when Loren came home. He recognized the handwriting on the envelope, the peculiar wavering underlining of the word "Personal." He picked it up. It was postmarked New York, May 23 P.M.

He picked up the silver letter opener and carefully slit the envelope. It had been more than a year since he had heard from her. Since the time that they had agreed not to see each other again. He had the strange presentiment that he already knew the contents of the letter. He wasn't wrong.

> *Dear Loren,*
>
> *A long time ago when you told me that I was not the kind of woman who could live alone and that someday I would find a man I could love, I did not believe you. If you will remember, I said to you at that time, it was easy for you to talk. You were a man and you have known many women, and perhaps even loved some of them in your own particular fashion. I also said that it would not be so with me, that I did not think I could ever love another man.*
>
> *I was wrong, as you always knew I would be. On Tuesday next I will be married to Capt. Hugh Scott USN. He commands an aircraft carrier based in Pensacola, Fla., where we will live. The only reason I have for writing this letter is that I wanted you to hear about this from me rather than the newspapers. The children are well and happy and so am I. If you have anything to wish me—wish me—*
>
> > *Love,*
> > *Sally*

He folded the letter carefully and placed it back in the envelope. For a moment, he thought of picking up the telephone and calling her in New York. But it would not change anything. It was over and done. Slowly he tore the letter into tiny pieces and dropped them one by one into the wastebasket.

Melanie arrived just as he was finishing dinner. He looked up as the butler showed her into the dining room. "Have you had your dinner yet?"

"Yes," she answered. "I came from home."

"Sit down then and have some coffee with me."

The butler held a chair for her and then placed a cup of coffee in front of her. He left the room and she sipped at her coffee silently.

After a while Loren smiled at her. "You're very silent and solemn tonight, Melanie."

"I think my father knows about us."

Loren looked at her. "Knows or suspects? There's a big difference."

"Not to my father," she said. "It's the same thing."

"What if he does?" Loren asked. "There's nothing he can do about it."

"To you maybe," she said. "But he can make my life miserable at home."

"Then why don't you move out and get your own place? He's working now, it's time you used some of the money for yourself."

"I couldn't do that to my mother. You don't know my father. All he cares about is himself. If I weren't there he would drive her crazy."

"I'll give you a raise," he said. "That way you can still give them the same money."

"It's not just the money," she said. "It's him. He's plain mean. And it shows even more since he's gone to work for Bennett at Ford."

"What's that got to do with it?" he asked.

She looked at him. "You know what's going on over there. The whole River Rouge plant is terrorized by Bennett and his gang and my father loves being part of Bennett's storm troopers as they're being called."

"I don't understand it," he said. "Edsel isn't that kind of a man. He wouldn't tolerate it."

"Edsel has nothing to do with it," she said. "My father told me that Bennett has the old man's ear and Edsel Ford is simply ignored."

"The old man will live to regret it," he said. "Someday that whole place will blow up."

"It might come tomorrow," she said. He looked at her. "What do you mean?"

"You saw this evening's papers?"

He nodded.

"My father says that Bennett is readying a surprise for the union. All of Bennett's goons will be waiting when the union organizers show up."

"There's nothing they can do about it," Loren said. "As long as the union keeps off Ford property."

"What if they go up on the overpass over Miller Road in front of Gate Four?"

"What if they do?" he replied. "It's a public pedestrian bridge. It's always crowded with peddler and ice cream vendors doing business when the shifts change."

"My father told me that Bennett says it's Ford property because they built it."

He thought for a moment, then nodded. "That could mean trouble." He looked up at her. "Get Richard Frankensteen or one of the Reuther brothers on the phone for me. I don't want to see anyone hurt. It will be a black eye for the whole industry. I'll warn them to keep off the bridge."

She went to the telephone on the sideboard and called a number. After a brief conversation, she put a hand over the mouthpiece and spoke to him. "They're all out at meetings," she said. "And no one knows just what time they will be back."

"Tell them that the first one to come back should call me immediately. It's very important."

She relayed the message and came to the table. She was about to sit down when she changed her mind. Instead she walked to his chair and kissed him.

"That's not very secretary like," he said with a smile.

"I don't care," she said. "I like you."

He reached up and put a finger on the tip of her nose. "I'll give you a chance to prove how much as soon as the meeting is over."

She took his hand and kissed it, letting her tongue lick the center of his palm. "I can't wait."

"Junior, you sit next to me," said Loren. "Wait, you, Ted and Scotty sit opposite us."

Silently they took their seats, Melanie took her place at the foot of the rectangular library table and opened her notebook.

Loren looked at her. "You don't have to take notes, Miss Walker. This is an unofficial meeting."

She closed the book. "Do you wish me to remain, Mr. Hardeman?"

"Please do."

She sank back into her chair as he turned to the others. "You fellows don't have to look so solemn. Nothing terrible is going to happen."

The tension in the room eased slightly. They leaned forward attentively.

"I'll make it simple and brief," Loren said. "What I have to say to you concerns the future management and operations of the company."

He paused for a moment. "I will begin by telling you something I have no doubt that all of you already know. With the repayment of the final installment amounting to two million one hundred thousand dollars of our bank loans today, I have received in return all rights to the stock I own in the company."

"Hear, hear!" Duncan said softly.

Loren smiled at him. "I echo your sentiments. I don't like bankers any more than you do. At the same time I received the resignation of the four directors they had on the board provisionally until the next board meeting."

"Again, hear, hear!" This time the Scotsman couldn't contain himself. He began to clap his hands silently.

A moment later the others joined in.

Loren gestured and they stopped. "Now for my plan."

There was a slight rustling in the chairs. The men settled back, waiting.

"I own ninety percent of the company," Loren said. "My son, ten percent. I am also fifty-nine years old and next year, when I am sixty, I intend to retire from active participation in the affairs of the company."

He paused and the silence around the table deepened. "And so, accordingly, I have made the following disposition of my stock.

"To my grandchildren, Loren III and Anne Elizabeth, five percent each, a total of ten percent for the two. This stock will be held and voted for them by their father as trustee until such time as they come to maturity. Further provisions have been made in the event of the decease of any of the parties interested in order to protect both the survivors and the company."

He paused and looked at Melanie. "May I have a glass of water and two aspirin, Miss Walker?"

Silently she went to the bar and returned with the water and aspirin. The men did not speak while he took the pills. They were used to seeing him eat aspirin.

He put down the glass of water. "At the same time I have endowed a charitable foundation to be known as the Hardeman Foundation with thirty-nine percent of the stock. It will be the purpose of this foundation to use the funds they so acquire for the good benefit of the public. The voting rights to the stock held by the corporation are held by me in trust for the remainder of my lifetime. Upon my decease, the voting rights will be held by the trustees of the foundation who will be selected from the foremost educators and public-spirited citizens in the country. My son and I will automatically be lifetime trustees of the foundation."

A curious surprise came into Junior's face. "I do not—"

Loren held up a hand. "Let me finish before you say anything," he said pleasantly. Junior nodded. He sat back in his chair, the surprise still etched on his face.

"I will still own personally forty-one percent of the stock," Loren continued. "Which will be disposed according to my will after my decease among members of my family, the foundation and certain other people and charitable projects as I may elect."

He picked up the glass of water and sipped from it. "Beginning with the next meeting of the board of directors I shall place a proposal before the board which will, in effect, pass the control of the company from one man, myself or my son, at the moment, into the hands of the five-man executive committee, presently headed by myself and upon my retirement by my son. The head of the committee will have no vote on policy unless there is a tie vote between its members, in which case he will have the right to cast the deciding vote."

He took another sip of the water. "Until my retirement I will remain as a director and chairman of the board of the company, while my son will continue as president and chief operating officer, bound to carry out the policies of the executive committee and the board of directors. Upon my retirement, my son will assume the chairman's duties in addition to carrying on with his own."

He fell silent for a moment, looking down at his hands. Then he looked up again. "There is more, gentlemen, much more to my proposal, but there is no point in my going into it at the present time. Other points cover such items as pension plans and profit-sharing for executives, special insurance and similar side benefits for the employees of the company. Before you leave, Miss Walker will give each of you a folder containing all the details of these proposals as well as those I have spoken about."

He rose to his feet. "I guess that about covers all I have to say at the moment. Thank you, gentlemen."

They rose with him. Quickly Melanie distributed the folders. Within a few minutes, all of them had gone except Junior. He sat in the chair looking at his father.

"May I have a word with you?" he asked.

Discreetly Melanie disappeared from the room.

"Come, have a drink," Loren said.

Junior followed him to the bar. Loren poured himself a Canadian; he looked at his son: "Still drinking cognac?"

"I'll take whiskey," Junior said.

Loren nodded. He poured a good shot into Junior's glass.

"Ice?"

Junior nodded.

Loren walked behind the bar and took some ice from the bucket on the shelf. The ice tinkled in the glass he gave Junior. He stayed behind the bar and picked up his own drink. "Cheers," he said. He threw the whiskey down his throat and was reaching for the bottle while Junior was still sipping at his.

Silently he refilled his shot glass. This time he sipped at it slowly while looking at his son. Junior's face was thin and pale and there were blue circles under his eyes from lack of sleep. He waited for his son to speak.

After a moment, Junior reached into his pocket, took out an envelope and placed it on the bar, without speaking.

Loren looked at it. "What's that?"

"Open it and see," Junior said. "The envelope's not sealed."

Quickly Loren took the paper from the envelope. It was neatly typed on Junior's personal stationery.

> To the Chairman of the Board
> and
> the Board of Directors of
> Bethlehem Motors Company, Inc.
>
> Gentlemen:
> I hereby tender my resignation as president and chief operating officer of Bethlehem Motors Company, Inc. I also tender my resignation as a member of the board of directors of that company as well as officer and/or director of any of its subsidiary companies. All such resignations to be effective immediately.
>
> Very truly yours,
> Loren Hardeman II

Loren looked at his son. "What do you want to do a thing like that for?

"You know, Father, when you called this meeting tonight," Junior replied, "I thought it was for the purpose of firing me."

Loren looked at him steadily. "What made you think that?"

"Two things," Junior answered. "One, you got your stock back and, with it, complete control of the company. Two, I deserved it. I gave you enough reasons. I wouldn't have blamed you if you did."

"It makes sense except for one thing," Loren said slowly. "You tell me. It seems easy enough for a man to fire an employee, but how does a man go about firing his son from being his son?"

Junior looked at him steadily. "I made war on you where no war existed."

"We did enough damage to each other," Loren said quietly. He began to tear the letter in half. "Long ago when I said all this would someday be yours, I meant it. I haven't changed my mind. You're still my son." He placed the torn halves of the letter back in the envelope and gave it to Junior.

Junior took the envelope, looked at it silently for a moment, then put it in his jacket. He looked up at Loren. He blinked back his tears. "Thank you, Father," he said huskily.

Loren nodded. He didn't speak, for he didn't trust his own voice.

"I'll try not to let you down again," Junior said. "I'll do the best I can."

"That's all anyone can do," Loren said.

They were silent for a moment, then Loren came around the bar and embraced him. They were very still, then Loren stepped back. "You go home and get some sleep, son. You look like you can use it."

Junior nodded and started for the door. He turned and looked back. "It will be just like old times, won't it, Father?"

Loren smiled. "Just like old times."

Junior returned his smile. "Good night, Father."

"Good night, son." Loren waited until the door closed before he turned back to the bar and poured himself another drink.

Melanie came into the room. "Let me do that for you," she said taking the glass from his hand. She went behind the bar and put ice cubes in his glass and then gave it back to him. "Everything all right?"

He nodded wearily, tasting his drink. He looked at her. "It's been a long day."

"I'll go upstairs and draw you a hot bath," she said. "It will make you feel better."

She came around the bar and started for the door.

"And don't go putting all those damn perfumes in it," he called after her. "You make me smell like a French whore."

She smiled back at him from the doorway. "Stop complaining," she said. "You know you love it."

He came out of the bathroom; the towel draped around his middle, his hairy chest and shoulders shining blackly in contrast with the white towel.

"I'm relaxed."

"Do what I tell you," she said. "I know how hard you worked today."

Obediently he crossed to the bed and stretched out on his stomach. Her fingers were strong as they dug into his neck, bit by bit they moved over his shoulders and down onto his back. Slowly the muscles loosened under her hand.

"How does that feel?" she asked.

"Fine," he said. He rolled over on his side. "But I'm getting a hard-on."

"I know," she said looking at him. "You always do."

"What are you going to do about that?" he laughed.

"It's a muscle just like any other," she grinned mischievously. "It can be handled." She took his penis in her hands. At her touch, his erection came to full stand. Holding his phallus in one hand she gently stroked his testicles with the other, then slowly began to move her hand up and down.

"You have a beautiful cock," she said, fascinated by the giant strength of him. She bent toward him, her mouth opening slowly.

He sank his fingers into her hair and turned her face up to him. "I want to fuck," he said.

"Yes, yes." She got to her feet and began to undress. Her breasts tumbled free from her brassiere and she pulled off her girdle, revealing her lush, full hips and the heavy black triangle beneath her belly.

He pulled her down on the bed and began to roll over on her.

"No," she said quickly. "You relax. Let me do it for you."

He fell back and she got to her knees over him. Holding his penis in one hand her other hand balancing herself against his chest, she lowered herself on to him slowly, guiding him into her.

Impatiently he grabbed her buttocks and pulled her toward him. The air spilled from her lungs in a gasp. "Christ! You fill me up!"

Slowly at first, then more rapidly, she began to grind herself against him. His hands reached and he squeezed her breasts and pulled them toward his face. He took her nipples in his mouth and sucked until they were bright red and swollen.

She pulled back from him and reached down behind her back until she found his testicles with her hand. They were hard and tightly knotted at the base of his shaft. She felt her orgasms approaching and began to shudder as they wracked her body. She felt his testicles swell in her fingers and begin their discharge. A fiery liquid heat began to sear her loins.

"Loren! Loren!" she cried, falling against him in the throes of their mutual orgasm. She clung to him until she stopped the aching shudder.

Slowly she felt him relax inside her, then she rolled off him suddenly. Holding her cupped hand over herself so that she would not spill on the rug, she started for the bathroom. "You wait there," she said. "I'll come back and wash you off. I want you to rest."

"Bring some aspirin with you. My head feels like it's in a vice."

"Okay," she said.

A few minutes later, when she came out, he seemed to be sleeping peacefully, his face turned away from her on the pillow. Silently she knelt on the floor beside the bed and washed him with the warm washcloth, then gently patted him dry.

His hand moved toward her as she started to get to her feet. "You sleep," she said softly. "You need it." She walked back to the chair and picked up her brassiere.

"Melanie!" His voice was hoarse and strange.

"Try to sleep, Loren," she said gently, fastening the brassiere and picking up her girdle.

"No, Melanie!"

Something in his voice made her look at him as she was poised, one foot through her girdle. He was turning toward her. But there was something wrong in the way he was moving. It was almost as if she were watching a slow motion film and everything he was doing took just too much effort. Finally, he made it almost to a sitting-up position in the bed, his wide, agonized eyes staring at her. The words seemed to come thickly from his lips. "Melanie! I'm sick. Call the doctor!"

Then slowly, as if the words had taken all the strength he had, he began to tumble forward. She leaped to catch him, but his weight proved too much for her and he slipped from her arms and rolled heavily to the floor.

"Loren!" she screamed.

The Detroit evening papers the next day carried banner headlines and pictures of what came to be known as the Battle of River Rouge. Bennett's flying squad descended upon the unsuspecting union organizers in force. Frankensteen and Walter Reuther were in the hospital, the latter with a back broken in three places after being dragged down a flight of thirty-six steps. Several others were also hospitalized, among them a pregnant woman who had been kicked in the stomach. But perhaps what incensed the press even more was that after Bennett's boys had finished with the union people they turned on the reporters and photographers, working them over and breaking cameras. It was reported by them as one of the most disgraceful episodes in the history of American labor relations.

Because of the tremendous news impact of the River Rouge story across the nation, the story about Loren Hardeman was relegated to the inside pages. There was a small headline in column four of page two of *The New York Times* of May 27th, 1937.

LOREN HARDEMAN ILL

Detroit, May 26 — Loren Hardeman I, chairman of the board and founder of Bethlehem Motors, is resting comfortably in a Detroit hospital, doctors report, after an operation for the removal of a benign brain tumor which had been troubling Mr. Hardeman for some years.

Chapter Fourteen

John Bancroft, vice-president of sales, Bethlehem Motors, swiveled around in his chair as Angelo came into his office. He rose, the salesman's smile broad on his face, his hand outstretched. "Angelo! It's good to see you."

His grip was a salesman's grip. Firm, hearty, impersonally friendly. Angelo returned his smile. "Good to see you, John."

"Sit down," Bancroft said, returning to his seat behind his desk.

Angelo sat down silently and lit a cigarette. He came right to the point. "I got your message. I'm here."

Bancroft looked uncomfortable. "I'm glad you came. We have problems."

"I know that," Angelo said. "What's so special about yours?"

"I'm starting to lose dealers."

"Why?" The surprise was evident in Angelo's voice. "I thought we had more requests for new dealerships than we ever had before."

"We have," Bancroft admitted. "But they're all fringe dealerships. Used-car men trying to up-grade, foreign car dealers who are not making out too well with their own lines trying to get in on something new. The big problem is that ninety percent of them haven't enough money to back up their sales with an adequate service department. The other ten percent check out all right, but most of those are in areas where we are already well represented."

"That still doesn't add up to losing dealers," Angelo said.

A worried look knitted the salesman's brow. "In the last two months I've been getting letters from our established dealers. Some of them with us ever since the company started. They're beginning to worry about discontinuing the Sundancer. They're afraid the Betsy won't hold their place in the market for them. I've got almost four hundred letters like that." He paused for a deep breath. "But what's even worse we've gotten cancellation notices from about ninety dealers. Chrysler, Dodge and Plymouth got about half of them, Pontiac and Buick about thirty,

American Motors about ten, Mercury four, and Olds one." Despite the air-conditioning, he mopped his brow. "They were all good producers. God only knows if the new ones can match them."

Angelo dragged on the cigarette. After a moment, he spoke. "I don't get it. The Mazda Rotary with the Wankel engine has dealers begging for it from coast to coast and we have trouble. What is it?"

"Most of them are probably the same fringe dealers who are coming to us. They'll take a shot at anything new. Besides Mazda is trying to crack the American market. They're supplying financing for the service departments." He looked across the desk at Angelo. "If we had to do that we'd need another fifty million dollars to spread across the country. That's why Mazda is concentrating only in California in Florida. If they can take off in those markets and build up a demand, they hope they won't have to finance the rest of the country."

Angelo nodded. "And we're locked in. We've got to go across the country in one shot because we're already there."

"Now you're getting it," Bancroft said.

Angelo put out his cigarette. "What do we do?"

"I can give you my answer from a sales point of view. I can't answer for your production problems."

"Go ahead," said Angelo.

Bancroft's voice was deliberate. "One, don't discontinue the Sundancer. That will keep the dealers from worrying too much. Two, follow the Japanese plan for infiltrating the market by concentrating on limited testing areas and building up demand. If it takes off, we can expand slowly and in two or three years, when we're in solid, drop the Sundancer."

"And if we drop the Sundancer now?"

"My best guess is that we'll lose a net of six hundred more dealers after picking up the new ones."

Angelo got out of his chair and walked thoughtfully to the window. "I need the Sundancer plant to build the Betsy engines."

"I know that," Bancroft said. "But with only about seven hundred dealers left throughout the country we're out of business even before the car is on the market."

Angelo knew what he meant. They had averaged out the dealerships at four new cars a week, counting on at least fifteen hundred dealerships. That was six thousand cars a week, three hundred thousand a year. They broke even at two hundred and twenty thousand units. Seven hundred dealers would only add up to one hundred and forty thousand units and that would be disaster. A one-hundred-and-sixty-million-dollar loss the first year.

He walked back to Bancroft's desk. "Who else have you told about this?"

Bancroft returned his gaze steadily. "Nobody. I just put the figures together and you're the first one I've talked to about it. But Loren III returns from his honeymoon tomorrow and I have to alert him before the board meeting on Friday."

Angelo nodded. The Friday board meeting was for the express purpose of reaching a decision about the Sundancer. "I appreciate your telling me, John."

The salesman smiled. "Look, Angelo, you know I believe in the Betsy as much as you do. But I can't make the arithmetic work."

"I understand," Angelo said. "Let me give it some thought. Thank you, John."

He was half way down the corridor to his own office when the thought struck him. He turned and went back to the sales manager.

Bancroft was on the telephone. He looked up in surprise at Angelo's return. He finished his call and put down the phone.

Angelo said, "Doesn't it seem strange to you that suddenly, in the last two months, you begin to get dealer letters all bearing the same message?"

"I don't know," Bancroft answered. "I never really thought about it. We usually go through something like this at the end of every car year."

"As many letters?"

Bancroft shook his head. "No. Normally we get like twenty to forty or fifty. Usually from dealers who blew their quotas and are looking to squeeze us. All companies go through the same thing."

"Have you read all the letters?"

Bancroft nodded his head. "I have to. That's my job."

"Is there any one particular item or thought that seems to be almost the same language common to the letters?"

Bancroft looked thoughtful for a moment. He pressed the intercom on his telephone. "Bring in the file on the last batch of dealer letters."

A moment later his secretary came in with several folders in her hand. She placed them on his desk and left the office. John opened the folders and began glancing through them.

Angelo waited silently as the sales manager skimmed through letter after letter. Almost ten minutes passed before Bancroft looked up, a strange look on his face. He looked down at the letters again, this time picking up a pencil and circling lines in several of the letters in red. A moment later, he handed some of them to Angelo. "Just read those lines."

The language was different in each of the letters but the thought was basically the same. They were all concerned that the turbine engine could prove dangerous and might explode at high speeds.

John was still marking letters when Angelo spoke. "It's beginning to make sense."

Bancroft put down his pencil and looked up at him. "What do you mean?"

"Did you ever hear of an outfit called the Independent Automobile Safety Organization?"

"Yeah. It's run by a slimy bastard by the name of Mark Simpson. I threw him out of my office a half a dozen times but he keeps coming back every year."

"What's he looking for?"

"Basically it's a shakedown, I guess." Bancroft reached for a cigarette and lit it. He pushed the pack toward Angelo. "But he's clever about it. He runs this rag which is sent out to a national mailing list; it gives a phony evaluation of cars and makes a great point of its honesty because it doesn't accept advertising."

"What does he do?"

"I'm not quite clear," Bancroft said. "I never got that far into it with him. As near as I can make out, however, he either owns or has interests in some used-car lots across the country. You know the kind. Dealer dumps. Really new cars but with fifty to a hundred miles on them to qualify as used. He intimated that if a hundred Sundancers were made available to him, the car would get a good rating. That's when I threw him out of the office."

"Do you know if any of the companies do business with him?"

"None of them. They don't like him any better than we do."

"Then how does he stay in business?"

"Dealer pressure on the local level," Bancroft answered. "Dealers are always running scared. They figure giving him a few cars won't hurt and besides it helps them make their quota."

"I have a feeling he's the man behind this," said Angelo. "We found out he was the man behind our trouble out West."

"That doesn't make sense," Bancroft said. "Simpson doesn't do anything unless there's something in it for him. What the hell can he gain by keeping the Betsy off the market?"

"That's what I'd like to find out," Angelo answered. "The kind of campaign he's running has got to cost a lot of money. From the looks of it he's getting all around the country."

"Where do you think he's getting it?" Bancroft asked. "He's not the kind of man who puts out on spec."

Angelo looked at him. "I don't know. But whoever he's getting it from doesn't want us to get the Betsy on the road."

"It's not the other companies," Bancroft said. "I know that. They're happy to let us do the pioneering. Do you think it might be the gasoline outfits?"

Angelo shook his head. "No. We've already got arrangements made with all the national gasoline chains. They've agreed to have kerosene pumps at all their stations when we come out on the market."

They both fell silent. Angelo walked to the window. A freight train was pulling out from the yards, filled with automobiles, their colors shining brightly in the sun. He watched the train move slowly out of the yard and then went back to Bancroft's desk.

"You get on the phone and talk to every one of those dealers," he said. "Find out if Simpson or anyone connected with him actually spoke to them."

"What good will that do?"

"There has to be something illegal about what he's doing and maybe we can prove it. Slander. Libel. I don't know. I'm going to turn that over to the lawyers and let them figure it out." He took a cigarette from the package on Bancroft's desk. "Meanwhile you reassure them that there's absolutely nothing wrong with the car. Tell them about our tests."

"They'll think I'm bullshitting them," John said. "Simpson's line seems to back up the trouble we had when Peerless killed himself; and they read all about that in the papers."

"Then you invite every one of them to come out to our testing grounds at our expense and actually see how the car performs," said Angelo. "That ought to convince them."

"I don't know whether it will convince them," Bancroft said. "But they sure as hell will come. I've never known a dealer yet who turned down an all-expense-paid trip to anywhere, even if it was only across town."

Angelo laughed. "I'll leave that to you. Meanwhile I'll see what I can learn on my end. We're not dead yet."

"I'm beginning to feel better," Bancroft said. "At least we're doing something instead of just being sitting ducks." He rose to his feet. "We still can't afford to ignore any of this."

"I don't intend to," Angelo said. He looked at the sales manager. "I didn't take on this job to destroy this company and I intend to do what's best for it, whether or not it fits into my personal preferences."

Chapter Fifteen

Prince Igor Alekhine awoke with the sunlight flooding into the windows of his room overlooking the blue waters of the Mediterranean. He leaped from his bed, smiling, went over to the windows, throwing them wide, and breathed deeply of the sweet morning air. He tugged at the pull cord for the butler to bring his coffee and began to do his morning situps.

Religiously, in front of the window, every morning. Inhale, two, three, four. Exhale, two, three, four. Each time swinging his arms wide. Twenty times. Then the pushups. Up, two, three, four. Down, two, three four. Also twenty times.

By then the butler appeared with the coffee and the morning newspapers. The local *Nice Matin* and the *Paris Herald Tribune*. The butler placed the tray on the small table near the window. "Will there be anything else this morning, sir?" he asked as he had a thousand times before.

"Twenty," Igor looked up. He got to his feet, breathing slightly from the exertion. He looked down at his stomach. Flat and hard. Not bad for a man of fifty. He smiled at the butler. 'I don't think so, James."

It didn't matter that the butler's name was Francois. Once they were employed by the prince, they all became James. "Thank you, sir," he said, his face expressionless. He turned to go.

Igor called him back. "Is the Princess awake yet?"

"I don't think so, Master," the butler answered. "We haven't received her signal in the kitchen as yet."

"Let me know as soon as you hear from her," he said.

"Yes, Master," The butler left the room.

Igor walked to the table, and still standing, poured a cup of coffee. He raised the coffee to his lips at the same time flipping open the *Herald Tribune* to the stock market report. His experienced eye glanced down the columns quickly. Automotives, steady. Metals, steady. AT&T, Eastman Kodak, relatively unchanged. Dow Jones Index up, .09. He put the paper back on the table and took his coffee cup to the window and looked out. All was well with the world.

A yacht was heading toward Monte Carlo, the white sails billowing in wind as it skimmed the calm blue waters. Another power yacht was going by, heading for its berth in Beaulieu sur Mer. It looked like a good day to be out on the water. He would ask Anne when she awakened whether she would like to have lunch aboard the yacht. Until then, he might as well have a swim and work on his tan. She rarely awoke before eleven thirty.

He took the elevator all the way down to the private beach. He came out of the building, his eyes blinking in the sun. He looked back up at the villa.

It loomed five stories tall. It was built of native Pyreneean stone in a group of turretlike buildings into the side of the cliff that descended from the Bas Corniche to the water's edge. Inside the house, the rooms were on different levels, each turret connected to the other by an interior archway. It was a crazy house but he loved it. It was the nearest thing to a castle that he could build on this property.

He walked out on the edge of a small dock and knifed his way into the water. The cold caught his breath deep inside him. He came up sputtering. Damn, it was June and the water was still freezing. He began to swim vigorously and by the time he was back on the dock twenty minutes later, he felt warm and glowing.

He climbed the short stairway to the pool terrace and took a towel from the Cabana. Rubbing himself vigorously, he went behind the bar and pressed the intercom switch to the kitchen.

"Yes, Master?" The butler's voice echoed hollowly from the box.

"Bring some coffee to the pool, James," he ordered. He flipped off the switch and came out from behind the bar. He went around the side of the small building to the pool. It wasn't until then that he saw her.

A broad smile came to his lips. He liked his niece. "Good morning, Betsy," he said heartily. "You're up early."

Betsy sat up on the *matelas*, her hands holding the straps of the brassiere to her breasts. "Good morning, Uncle Igor," she said.

He laughed. "For all the cover you get from that bikini, you don't have to be so nervous."

She didn't smile, instead she fastened the strap.

He turned and looked out at the water. "Another beautiful day on the Riviera." He waved his arms. He turned back to her. "It is hard to believe sometimes with all the trouble there is in the world that here the sun is shining."

She was silent.

He looked at her. It was not like her to be so quiet. "Are you all right?" he asked. Then he remembered. "Weren't you supposed to go sailing this morning?"

"I didn't feel like it," she said shortly.

"Why not?"

She looked at him, her eyes squinting in the sun. "Because I felt sick and nauseous all morning."

"You better let me call Dr. Guillmin," he said with quick concern. "I thought that bouillabaisse was a little too spicy last night."

"It's not the bouillabaisse."

"What is it then?" He was puzzled.

"I think I'm pregnant," she said in a matter-of-fact voice.

He stared at her, his dismay showing on his tanned open face. "How could that be?"

She laughed. "Uncle Igor, for a man who used to be one of the top playboys in the world, you're remarkably naive. It's really very simple. I brought everything to the Riviera with me except my B.C. pills. I forgot them."

"France is a civilized country," he said stiffly. "You could have gotten them here."

"I didn't," she said. "So forget it."

"Are you sure you're pregnant?"

"I missed two periods," she said plainly. "And I never did that before."

"We better make sure," he said. "I will arrange an appointment with Pierre Guillmin in Cannes this afternoon."

"Don't bother," she said. "I'm leaving for the States this afternoon. Abortions are legal in New York and Max has made all the arrangements. He says I will have the best doctors."

"Max Van Ludwige?" he asked in an incredulous voice. "Was it him? But he is supposed to be so happily married. He has a daughter almost your age."

"He is happily married," she said. "But sometimes things like this happen. We were alone on the boat three days while we were sailing to pick up his family."

"What happens if the doctors think it's too late to have an abortion?"

"Then Max will get a divorce and marry me," she said. "After I have the baby, I will give him a divorce and he will remarry his wife."

"You sound very sure of yourself."

"I am sure," she said calmly. "The three of us have it all worked out."

"Three of you?" His voice rose. "Who else is in on this?"

"Rita," she said. Rita was Max's wife. "The only sensible thing to do was tell her about it. Neither of us wanted to hurt her. She was very nice. She understands it was nothing but an accident. That Max really and truly loves her."

The butler appeared with the tray and silver coffee service. "Where will you take your coffee, sir?"

Igor stared at him speechlessly. He pointed to a small table nearby. The butler placed the tray down carefully. Igor finally found his voice. "Get me a cognac, James," he said, and then, as the butler turned away. "Better make it a large one!"

Loren III looked at the tall, good-looking Dutchman. Max Van Ludwige seemed to be about his own age, but his blond hair and the blues eyes in the deeply tanned face made him look much younger.

"These things are always embarrassing," the Dutchman said in his precise English. "One never knows quite what to say."

"I don't know," Loren said stiffly. "I've never been in a situation like this before."

"We both regret it very much," Van Ludwige said.

Loren was silent. "Where's Betsy now?"

"She'll be down in a moment," Max said. He looked up as the butler came into the living room of the Sutton Place brownstone that his family had owned in New York for many years. "What would you like to drink?" he asked politely.

"Scotch and water," Loren said automatically.

"I'll have a dry martini, straight up," Bobbie said.

Van Ludwige looked at the butler. "My usual Scotch."

The butler nodded and left the room. An awkward silence fell over them. Van Ludwige tried to break it. He looked at Bobbie. "How long is it since I've seen you, Bobbie? Was it at Le Mans in '67?"

She nodded. "I think so. You had two Porsches entered if I remember correctly."

"That's right," he laughed. "But I had bad luck. Neither of them finished." The butler returned with the drinks. After he had gone, Max held his drink in his hand. "I was sorry to hear about Lord Ayres but I am very glad that you are happy once again." He held up his drink. "I hope it is not too late to offer my congratulations?"

"Thank you," Bobbie said. She looked at Loren. "Today is our anniversary."

Loren was surprised. "It is?"

"We're married three months today," she said.

"Let's drink to that," Max said. "To many more happy anniversaries."

They sipped their drinks and the awkward silence returned. Again Max tried to make conversation. "There is a great deal of interest in Europe in your new car. It's a turbine engine, isn't it?"

"Yes," Loren answered.

"Do you expect to have it on the market for the coming year?"

"I don't know," Loren said. "We've been on our honeymoon the past two months. Actually I was supposed to be in Detroit yesterday for a board meeting this week to make some final decisions. But this came along and I put it off."

Max got to his feet as Betsy came through the door. She hesitated a moment, then came toward them. "Hello, Bobbie," she said.

Bobbie looked at her. There were circles of sleeplessness under the young girl's eyes. Impulsively, she got to her feet and kissed Betsy's cheek. "Hello, Betsy."

Betsy smiled a quick smile, then turned to her father, who was standing, watching them. She didn't move. "Hello, Daddy."

He made an awkward gesture with his hand. Then she ran into his arms. "Oh, Daddy, Daddy! I hope you're not angry with me."

He shook his head, kissing her. "I'm not angry with you, baby."

"I really made a mess of things, didn't I?"

"It will be all right," he said. "We'll get everything straightened out."

She took a deep breath, regaining her self-control. "At first I was angry with him. But now I'm glad that Uncle Igor telephoned you."

"He did right. He was concerned."

"I know," she said. She turned to Max. "See, I told you my father would understand."

The Dutchman bowed stiffly. "I am most happy for your sake."

Loren turned to face him. "Now that my daughter is here, I assume we can discuss the plans."

"Of course," Max said. He went to the door and closed it. "The servants have long ears."

Loren nodded. He sat down again, Betsy next to him on the large couch. Loren picked up his drink and looked at Max expectantly.

"I've made arrangements to fly to Nassau with Betsy next week. Preparations have been arranged for the granting of an immediate divorce and we will be married. It's as simple as that."

Loren turned to his daughter. "Is that what you want?"

Betsy looked at him, then at Max, then back to her father again. "No," she said in a firm voice.

For a moment there was a stunned silence, then they all began talking at once. "I thought—" Max said.

"What do you mean?" Loren asked.

Betsy glanced at Bobbie. A look of understanding flashed between them. She turned back to the men. "It's a farce," she said. "I don't see why we have to go through with it. Max doesn't want to marry me any more than I want to marry him. He's just being a gentleman. I don't see why we have to put Rita and him through all this just because I've been stupid enough to get pregnant."

"What do you want to do then?" Loren asked.

"What's wrong with just having the baby?"

Loren was suddenly angry. "I won't have any bastards in my family!"

Betsy stared at him. "Don't be so old-fashioned, Daddy. There are plenty of people who are having children who don't want to be married. But this is stupid. Getting married just to have the baby and then getting divorced. Why can't I just go away somewhere quietly and have the baby?"

"Because there have been enough rumors and gossip about your being pregnant in the papers already," Loren said. "There is no quiet place for you to hide."

"Then let the papers have it!" Betsy said. "I don't care."

"Betsy, listen to me," Max said.

She turned to him. "No. I'm not going to put you through all that hassle."

"Betsy, I want to marry you!" Max said.

Betsy stared at him. "What for? You're not in love with me."

"Betsy, suppose you have a son," Max said.

"Suppose I do?" she retorted.

"Don't you see what that would mean to my family?" he asked. "I have three daughters and no son to carry on the name. My father would be in seventh heaven."

"That's a great reason," Betsy said sarcastically. "And in case I have a girl or a miscarriage, I suppose I'll get a second chance."

"Betsy, you're being foolish!" Max said.

"No, she's not being foolish," Bobbie said suddenly. They all looked at her in surprise. She ignored the men and addressed herself to Betsy. "You're right, and ordinarily I would agree with you and even help you do what you want. But this time you're not being fair."

"I am being fair," Betsy said heatedly. "To Max and Rita. To myself."

"But not to your child," Bobbie said. "I don't have to tell you that Max is a fine man, you already know that. You owe it to your child to know his father. You also owe it to your child not to deny him his heritage."

Betsy was silent. After a moment, she spoke. "At least you're honest," she said. "You put it exactly where it's at, don't you?"

"I try," Bobbie said. "You made a mistake."

Betsy suddenly understood that Bobbie had known all along why she had acted as she did. Angelo. To show him that she could do as he did; she realized now she had been stupid.

"Don't make another mistake," Bobbie said quietly.

"Okay, I'll go through with it," Betsy said quickly. Then the tears came to her eyes.

Nothing ever worked out the way you wanted it.

Chapter Sixteen

"We're in trouble," Angelo said. "Big trouble."

"So what else is new?" Rourke asked.

Duncan smiled grimly. "I've spent forty-five years of my life in this business and I've always been in trouble."

"Not like this time," Angelo said seriously. He got to his feet and paced the long length of the living room. He stopped and looked out the windows of the Portchartrain. Across the street the marque of Cob Hall advertised the coming events. The next big attraction was a convention of brassiere manufacturers. He half smiled to himself at the ridiculousness of it. Those men had to have a ball. All they had to think about was tits.

He came back to them. "I wouldn't have brought you both in from the Coast if I weren't concerned."

They nodded attentively without speaking.

"Last week Bancroft told me that we were losing dealers and that we stood a good chance of blowing the dealer network if we dropped the Sundancer." They started to break in but he held up a restraining hand. "We checked it out. It's our friend Simpson again and the IASO. There's been a whole campaign mounted against us, and right now they are so far in front of us, there's nothing we can do to catch up to them."

"What's that guy got against us?" Duncan asked. "We've never done anything to him."

"I don't know," Angelo said. "But I'm trying to find out. His money has to come from somewhere. He hasn't the resources to pull off a thing as large as this on his own."

He was silent as he walked to the bar and refilled his drink. He looked at them. They nodded and he made fresh drinks for them. He brought the drinks over and dropped into a chair opposite.

"What's going to happen?" Tony asked.

"It's anybody's guess," Angelo replied. "My own feeling is that the board will cut back the Betsy program at next Friday's meeting and vote to keep the Sundancer."

"But I'm committed to seventy million dollars worth of materials," Rourke said.

"I know that," Angelo looked at him. "But a lot of that would be absorbed if they continue with the Sundancer. That's not the point, however. You have to measure the material loss against the loss of the entire company."

"You sound as if we're already dead," the Scotsman said dourly.

"Not yet," Angelo answered. "I have several ideas. But I don't know how practical they are."

"Try them on us," Rourke said.

Angelo looked at him. "What are the chances of building the Big Betsy engine in our Coast plant instead of the Betsy Mini's?"

"No chance." Rourke said flatly. "It would take us another year to retool and even then we would only have the capacity for about fifty thousand units a year at the max."

"How many Mini's were you planning on?"

"A hundred thousand."

Angelo thought carefully. The Betsy Mini was their answer to the sub-compacts. The Volks, Pinto, Vega, Gremlin. It was styled simply, much like the British minis, which were successfully copied by the Japanese Honda, but it gave greater power and better performance and was priced competitively at $1,899.

"And how many Silver Sprites?"

"Seven to ten thousand," Rourke answered.

The Betsy Silver Sprite was the sports car of the line, much the same as the Corvette was to the Chevrolet. It was the only car of the line in which all the performance wraps were off. Everything about it was high performance. Axle, heavy-duty suspension, steering, reinforced chassis. The speedometer stopped at 220 miles per hour but in straight-away tests they had the car up to 270.

Angelo reached for a cigarette. "How soon can you get into production?"

Rourke and Duncan looked at each other. Duncan supplied the answer. "If we get the okay now, we could have cars coming off the line in November."

Angelo looked at him. This was the beginning of July. November was five months away. "No sooner?"

Duncan shook his head. "That's pushing it, laddie. We'll be lucky to make it."

Angelo was silent. That left the Betsy JetStar, the mainstay of the entire line. There were two basic models, the smaller of which corresponded to the Nova and Maverick, the other, slightly larger than the Chevelle and Torino, yet priced within the same range. It was for this car the Sundancer factory was needed. It was the only plant with the capability of turning out two hundred thousand units per year or better.

He put down his drink. "That leaves us with only one choice. To go abroad to build our engines."

"Number One isn't going to like it," Duncan said. "He wanted this to be an all-American car."

"He won't have any choice if he wants to get the car on the market," Angelo said. "Even he has to realize you can't market a volume car if your dealer network falls apart."

"It's late in the game to set up a plant somewhere else that would have the capacity we need," Rourke said.

"We have two shots," said Angelo. "Matsuoka in Japan and Waggoner Fabrik in West Germany. Both of them have the industrial capacity and both have expressed interest in licensing the engine from us for their own use."

"If we give them a license," Duncan said, "we're only building our own competition."

"If we're successful we won't be able to hold it back," Angelo said. "Look at what happened with the Wankel. GM here has the rights to it and Tokyo Kogyo already has its version on the market." He stubbed his cigarette out in an ashtray and lit another. "It might even work out to our advantage. If they're eager enough we can set up joint venture companies with them."

Rourke nodded. "That could mean a lot of money for us."

"Forget the money part of it," Angelo said. "The important part of the deal is that they must guarantee to deliver a minimum of at least one hundred and fifty thousand engines to us in the next year."

"It's not going to be easy," Rourke said. "Those babies are sharp traders. They'll smell we're in trouble."

"It's up to you to convince them that we're not," Angelo said. He got to his feet. "Tony, you take Japan. Duncan, you have the Germans."

"Okay," Rourke said. "When do we leave?"

"Right now," Angelo answered.

Duncan got to his feet. "I'm getting too old to be running around like that," he grumbled.

Angelo grinned at him. "You know you love it. All those big blonde frauleins."

"Laddie, at my age all I can do is look," the Scotsman said. "And if I haven't got my glasses on, even that doesn't help much."

Angelo laughed. "You'll make out all right."

Duncan looked at him. "What about the Mini and the Silver Sprite? Do you want us to put them in the works?"

"Not yet," Angelo said. "That will have to hold until after the board meeting on Friday. The decision has to come from them."

The board room was filled with smoke and tension. John Bancroft had made his report simply without dramatics. But the eventual result was clear to all of them. Without the full dealer network, the Betsy didn't stand a chance.

Angelo cut into the welter of futile conversation. "We'll deal with the problem of Simpson at a later date. That's not the issue before us at the moment. Our problem is how do we do both, get the Betsy on the market, and, at the same time, deliver the Sundancer to the dealers so that we keep them satisfied?"

Silence fell around the table as they turned to look at him. He continued. "We all recognize that if we do not have the Sundancer plant available to us, there's no way we can produce the Betsy JetStar in enough quantities to make the entire venture profitable as well as practical. However there are certain solutions available to us. They are being explored at this very moment.

"Tony Rourke is in Japan talking to the Matsuoka Heavy Industries and John Duncan is in West Germany speaking to Waggoner Fabrick about manufacturing JetStar engines for us. If a satisfactory agreement can be reached with them, it will be possible to produce the JetStar on the third and fourth assembly lines of the Sundancer plant. It would mean an additional investment to get these lines in operative condition again because they have not been in use for many years, but I think the investment will be reasonable in view of our overall program."

He was silent for a moment, then while a murmur of approval rose around the table, he spoke again. "Of course, you realize, gentlemen, we have no choice, I think, but to delay and reevaluate the Betsy project."

"No, goddamn it!" Number One's fist slammed into the table. "I won't have any part of it! The Betsy is an American car and it will be built right here. All of it. I don't intend to go crawling to no goddamn foreigners to help us do what we taught them!"

In contrast with Number One's vehemence, Loren III's voice was calm, almost cool. "You're being most unreasonable, Grandfather. I think Angelo has stated our position very clearly and fairly. We have no choice but to follow that path."

"No fucking foreigners will have anything to do with this car as long as I'm alive!" Number One snapped. "It's my company and my money and I will say what's going to be done with it!"

Loren stared at his grandfather steadily. "You can't do that any more," he said quietly, almost patiently. "The time when a company could be run at the whim of one man who could dictate its life or death policy is over. Men like you, Henry Ford and Walter Chrysler belong to another time. You cannot make decisions based solely on your own equity and selfish vanity. There are thirty thousand employees of this company, many of them who have devoted their lives to it, and you have no right to play Russian roulette with their welfare and their future. They have earned as much right to this company as you have and deserve to get every consideration that you expect. We have no choice but to continue with the Sundancer."

"Goddamn it! No!" Number One roared. He held his arms out in front of him. Quickly he undid the buttons of his jacket sleeves, revealing the shirt cuffs beneath. With a pull he tore the cuff links from them and held them out toward them in his hand. They were gold and shining in his palm.

"Look at these cuff links!" he ordered in an angry voice. "They are models of the first Sundancer I ever built. That was fifty years ago. You talk of living in the past when all you want to do is cling to it!"

He snapped his arm violently, throwing the cuff links away from him. The heavy links crashed into the casement windows. The fragile glass gave way with a tinkling sound and the cuff links disappeared outside.

He turned back to the silent room. His voice was calm and quiet now. "The Sundancer is dead, gentlemen. This meeting is over."

Silently they filed from the room until only Angelo, Loren III and Number One were left. After a moment Loren III got to his feet.

He looked down at Number One. "You know I don't intend to let you get away with this. You can ride roughshod over all the others, but not me. I'm going to fight you on this with everything I have in me."

Number One replied. "You do just that," he said in almost pleasant voice. "But don't come cryin' to me when you get the shit kicked out of you."

"I don't intend to lose," Loren III said. Now he sounded exactly like his grandfather. "Someone has to care about the responsibilities this company has assumed towards its employees over the years. And there's one thing you seem to forget."

Number One didn't speak.

"Under the law, minority stockholders have some privileges. My sister and I own twenty percent of this company. And Anne has given me her proxy. Neither of us intend to allow you to destroy this company."

"And I own eighty per cent," Number One said.

"No," Loren answered calmly. "You vote eighty percent. You only own forty-one percent. There's a big difference." He turned and walked from the room.

Number One watched the door close behind his grandson then turned to Angelo. "The kid's developing some gumption," he said almost respectfully.

Angelo studied him silently for a moment before he spoke. "He's not entirely wrong. You're going into an S curve at three hundred miles an hour."

Number One stared at him. "Who the hell's side are you on anyway?"

Angelo didn't answer. The telephone on the table in front of him began to ring. He picked it up.

"I have a call for you from the Bahamas, Mr. Perino," the operator said.

He was puzzled. "Who's calling me?"

There was a click on the line, a moment's silence, then the operator came back on. "Miss Elizabeth Hardeman."

He shot a look at Number One. "Put her on," he told the operator.

"Angelo?" Betsy's voice came on the line.

"Yes." There was a faint hum in the wires like the sound of the surf breaking behind her.

"Angelo." Her voice was strained and tense as if she had been crying. "This is the last time I'm going to ask you. Will you marry me?"

He tried to make a joke of it. "When?"

"No funnies, Angelo," she said sharply. "I mean it. Right now. Right this minute. This is the last time."

He still tried to keep it light. "I told you Miss Elizabeth. I'm not the marrying kind."

Abruptly the telephone went dead in his hand. Slowly he put it down. She sounded wild, almost as if she were stoned out of her mind. He looked across the table at Number One.

"That was Betsy," he said, in a wondering voice. "I thought she was in France. What the hell is she doing in the Bahamas?"

Number One shot a strange look at him. "Didn't you know?" he asked. "It was in all the papers."

"I haven't looked at a newspaper in weeks," Angelo said, still bewildered.

"Too bad," Number One said slowly, a note of sadness coming into his voice. "My great-granddaughter is getting married there tonight."

Number One rolled his chair to the door. He opened it and looked back at Angelo still sitting at the table. "I'll see you in the morning."

Angelo lit a cigarette as the door closed and sat there in the empty room. It wasn't until the cigarette almost burned to his fingertips that he dropped it into the tray and left.

He came out of the building into the red-gold rays of the sun setting through the Detroit smog. He looked up at the building behind him. The cracked windowpane of the board room looked down at him with its single eye.

Impulsively, he turned off the path onto the lawn beneath the window, his eyes searching the ground beneath him. He found the first cuff link almost immediately, directly under the window among some pieces of glass. The second took almost fifteen minutes to find. It was lying hidden beneath a privet hedge. He picked it up and stepped over back on the cement walk.

He looked down at the cuff links in his palm. The red-gold sun brought out every exquisite detail of the artist's design. The tiny rendition of the Sundancer was so real that it would take only a breath of imagination to give it life and have it go roaring into the evening.

His hand tightened so hard around the small gold cuff link that they were almost cutting into his palm. Slowly he walked down the path to his car.

BOOK FOUR

1972

Chapter One

The white January sun beat down on the salt flats, turning the miles in front of us into sparkling diamonds, that would have blinded us if it weren't for the shadowed glass of our crash helmet visors. The only sounds were the whine of the turbine, the shriek of the wind and the rumble of the giant oversize tires biting into the earth between us. I held the wheel steadily in my hand, aiming the car at the horizon where the white sand met the winter blue sky.

Cindy's voice came into my earphones as calm and as quiet as if we were cruising gently down some country lane. "Red line, sixty-eight thousand rpm; speed, three hundred eleven mph; turbine reactor temperature steady at twelve hundred degrees centigrade."

Radio-control broke in over her voice. Duncan's voice through the earphones had even more of a burr, than usual. "Ye're redlining at sixty-eight thousand, laddie."

"We already have it," I said.

"All systems read normal," he said "Bring it up to seventy thousand and hold it there for one minute. I'll give you the time. Cindy you set your clock to check me if radio is lost."

"Wilco," Cindy said. Her hand, holding the chronometer, came into view in front of me.

I opened the throttle. A fraction of a moment later, Duncan came back on. "Start minute. Red line seventy thousand."

Cindy's thumb pressed the button. I caught a brief glimpse of the second sweep hand begin its trip around the clock. Then her hand disappeared as she drew it back. Her voice was matter of fact.

"Red line, seventy; speed, three twenty-five; temp, twelve hundred; time, fifteen seconds." There was a pause, then she began again. "Red line, seventy; speed, forty-five; temp, twelve hundred; time, forty-five seconds." A moment later. "Sixty seconds."

Again the radio overrode her. "Sixty seconds! Bring it down, laddie. Slowly now."

I was already easing off on the throttle. "Wilco," I said. It wasn't until we were down to under seventy miles an hour and coasting that I dared turn to look at her.

Despite the air-conditioned cockpit, her face was flushed and there was a fine patina of moisture over her upper lip. Her voice was breathless. "Do you know how fast we were going?"

I shook my head. "No."

"Three ninety-one," she said. "I came twice."

I grinned. "I would have come too but I was too busy."

Duncan's voice came dryly through the earphones. "Remember you're on radio. Stop talking dirty."

We laughed. Her hand found mine on the steering wheel. "Hey, baby," she said. "What a car!"

I looked at her. "Imagine what we could do with this at Indy if it were eligible?"

End of track came up about a mile in front of us. I touched the brake pedal. That was all I had to do. The electronic brake pumping system did all the rest.

By the time I got out of the shower and dressed, they were already rolling the Betsy Formula One prototype up the track into its air-conditioned van, ready for its trip back to our own testing grounds.

Duncan turned toward me as I came out of the building, his eyes squinting through the sunlight. "It was a good drive, laddie."

"Thank you," I said. "Everything go all right?"

"Perfectly," he said. "The director told me the helicopter shots should be clear as a bell and all the other cameras were working perfectly."

"Good," I said. "We were lucky with the weather."

He nodded. "Well the TV commercial people should have no complaints. We've given them everything they asked for."

I looked at him. "Was it any easier in the days before television?" I asked. "When all you had to do to introduce a new car was put it in the showrooms?"

He smiled. "At least we didn't have to waste all our time doing things like this. Imagine the nerve of that director? Saying he wanted more dramatics in my voice while I was talking to you on the radio."

I laughed. "No wonder I thought you were a little hammy."

Cindy came out of the building. She walked toward us, her hair loose and shining in the sun. "Number One's calling you from Palm Beach."

I went back into the building and picked up the telephone. "I was just going to call you," I said. "The Formula One did three ninety-one breezing."

"Who was driving?" His voice was irritated.

"I was."

He was silent. I could feel the explosion building. I held the phone away from my ear. "You stupid son of a bitch!" he shouted. "Vice-presidents don't go around driving test cars. When are you going to give up playing with toys?"

"I'm entitled to a little fun out of the job," I said.

"Not with my money," he snapped. "Why the hell do you think I gave you options on two hundred thousand shares of my stock? Not in order for you to kill yourself and put us out of business."

I didn't answer. The only reason he gave me those options was because he didn't want to return the million dollars I advanced for the deposit on the Washington plant a few years ago.

"You keep out of those fucking cars, do you hear?"

"Yes, sir," I said. "But I have the feeling you'll be happy with the commercials. I'll arrange to have them flown down to you as soon as they're completed."

"I can wait until I see them on television," he said. "We have other problems."

That was the understatement of the year. So far. The year was practically brand-new. "Which one are you talking about?"

"My grandson," he said shortly. "We finally heard from him."

"Oh?" Loren III had been peculiarly quiet the last few months. I was wondering when it would break.

"I don't want to talk about it on the phone," Number One said. "You get down here right away."

"But I'm due back in Detroit to give final approval of the new assembly lines."

"Leave that to Duncan," he snapped. "You get your ass down here!"

The phone blacked out in my hand and I put it down. Duncan and Cindy came into the room. "Number One happy with everything?" Duncan asked.

"Not everything. He wants me down there as soon as possible."

Duncan looked at me. "What's wrong?"

"I don't know," I answered. "He didn't want to talk on the phone."

The Scotsman was silent for a moment. "Do you think he found out?"

"Found out?" My head was some other place. "What?"

"The Sundancer project?"

"No, I don't think so," I said. "At least he didn't mention it. Something to do with Loren III." I looked at Cindy. "Get on the phone and call the airlines. Get me on the quickest connection to Palm Beach." She nodded and went to the telephone as I turned back to Duncan. "You go into Detroit and okay the assembly lines for me. I want everything ready to start on the twentieth."

Cindy covered the phone with her hand. "You're too late for direct flights. The best connection leaves Salt Lake at six tonight; change planes at Chicago to Fort Lauderdale and drive up from there."

"Okay. Confirm it."

"No change in plans?" Duncan asked me. "Lines one and two, Sundancer standard, three and four, JetStar?"

"That's the way they go," I said. "You check with Tony and make sure he has everything ready out there. I want everything to go like clockwork."

"It will," the Scotsman said. "But—"

"But what?" I asked.

"Number One is not going to be happy when he finds out what you've done."

I looked at him. "By the time he presses the starting button, it will be too late for him to do anything about it."

It had all been worked out: 11 A.M. in Florida was ten o'clock in Detroit and eight o'clock in Washington. The gold telegraph key was already installed in the library of the Palm Beach house. The cameraman and photographers and news media were all alerted and ready to cover the ceremony. At exactly eleven o'clock, Number One would press the gold key on his desk, starting the assembly lines in Detroit and Washington at exactly the same moment. Fifty-five minutes later the first car should roll off each of the assembly lines and after that, a car every three minutes. On Lincoln's Birthday, less than one month later, every Bethlehem dealer in America would present the new cars.

Cindy put down the phone. "You're confirmed on the flights all the way through."

"Good," I said. "Thanks."

She looked at me. "What do you want me to do? Go back to the test track?"

I shook my head. "No. You go into Detroit. You'll be heading up the test group running checks on production-line cars."

"What about Stanforth?" she asked.

Stanforth was the chief test driver. "He'll stay on the Coast and run the group out there," I said.

"Do I get a raise?" she asked, with a smile.

"What does Stanforth get?"

"Thirty thousand," she said.

"That's what you get," I said.

"He's not going to like it. A woman getting the same salary as him."

"Tough shit," I grinned. "Didn't he ever hear of Women's Lib?"

She was fooling around with her stereo tape player when I came out of the bedroom. "I'm packed," I said.

She looked up at me. "Would you like a farewell fuck before you go to the airport? It'll help you sleep on the plane."

I laughed. "Since when are you worried about my sleeping on planes?"

"Listen to this," she said, turning the "play" switch on the machine.

The roaring sound of a whoosh of air mixed with the peculiar high whine of a turbine came from the far speaker and raced across the room toward me as it traveled through the different speakers. Suddenly her voice came from the center speakers. "Turbine, reactor temperature eight hundred degrees centigrade."

Duncan's voice came thin and reedy from the far speakers. "Start on signal. Ten seconds . . . nine . . . eight."

She turned the player off. "How do you like that?"

I stared at her. She never ceased to amaze me. I would have sworn she didn't have the time. "How did you get it?"

She smiled a secret smile. "I had them make duplicates of the computer tape and the camera tapes. All I had to do was mix them."

I was silent.

"Well?" she asked.

I grinned. "Okay. Come on back into the bedroom."

"No, there isn't time," she said. "If I have to set up in there, you'll miss your plane. Let's do it here on the floor."

She hit the switch again. The sound came on and she started across the floor toward me on her knees. The whine of the turbine and Duncan's voice came from the speakers.

" 'ven . . . six . . . five . . . four . . .' "

By the time he reached "One and start," she had my fly open and her mouth working.

Chapter Two

The giant shepherd guard dogs knew me but not the car, so they followed the car suspiciously up the driveway until I got out and then came running over, tails wagging and breaking themselves in half to be petted. I scratched their heads before they could knock me down. "Hello, Donner, hello, Blitzen."

The silent call from the sonic whistle pulled them away from me. Number One's man stood on the steps of the house. "Good morning, Mr. Perino."

"Good morning, Donald," I said.

"May I get the luggage from the car?"

"There isn't any," I said. "Just the small bag I have here."

He took it from me and I followed him into the house. "Is Mr. Hardeman awake yet?"

"He's in the breakfast room with Mr. Roberts," he answered.

I continued on through the foyer to the back of the house where the breakfast terrace looked out over the beach and the sea. Number One and Artie were seated at the table. They looked up as I came through the doors.

"Good morning, Number One," I said. "Good morning, Artie."

Artie rose and gave me his reassuring lawyer's handshake. The don't-worry,-I'll-take-care-of-everything grip. "Good morning, Angelo."

Number One grumbled. "It took you long enough to get here."

"I was in Fort Lauderdale at one thirty this morning but somehow I had the idea you wouldn't like me to wake the house up." I pulled out a chair, sat down and poured myself a cup of coffee. "It's a lovely morning."

"You won't think it's so lovely after you read this," Number One said, throwing a copy of the morning *Miami Herald* over to me.

I picked it up. It was folded to page two. A small banner headline over two columns, circled in heavy red crayon, down in the corner of the page, caught my eye.

LOREN HARDEMAN I SUED FOR CONTROL OF FOUNDATION BY GRANDCHILDREN

Loren Hardeman III and his sister, the Princess Anne Elizabeth Alekhine, trustees of the Hardeman Foundation, petitioned the courts of Michigan to set aside and revoke the trust agreement by which the Foundation gave to their grandfather the voting rights to the stock in Bethlehem Motors Corporation for his lifetime. Arguing that such an agreement was illegal and invalid and contrary to the public interest which is the principal purpose of the Foundation, they further stated that such voting rights gave Mr. Hardeman control of Bethlehem Motors, which constitutes the only asset of the Foundation, and that his control thereof endangers these assets and as such, imperils the work, welfare and purpose of the Foundation. They were joined in their petition by the Attorney General of the State of Michigan as amicus curiae on behalf of the people of the State of Michigan, who further said that in his opinion the loss of and/or the devaluation of the assets of the Foundation would negatively affect those projects for the benefit of the people of the State of Michigan in which the Foundation and the State had joined together. Chief Justice Paul Gitlin took the matter under advisement and set the date of January 17th for a hearing; he gave the Foundation and Mr. Hardeman I until that date to reply to the charges.

I put the paper down and looked at Number One. "Now tell me what it means."

He stared balefully at me. "It means we're fucked!"

"I don't get it," I said. "I thought you told me there were were five trustees. That means there are two more besides your grandchildren and yourself."

"So what?" he snapped. "I haven't been near there for years. For that matter neither has Anne. But Loren has always worked closely with the other two and he has them in his hip pocket."

"Did you talk to them?" I asked.

"I can't get them on the phone' he said sarcastically. "They've mysteriously disappeared. Loren's done his job well."

I turned to Artie. "What are our chances?"

"Do you want a long legal opinion or do you want it short and sweet?"

"Short and sweet," I said.

"We lose." He looked at me. "I can't say it any shorter than that."

Why?" I asked.

"It's a conditional gift. When Mr. Hardeman gave the Foundation the stock, he either withheld or demanded the voting rights to that stock as a condition of his giving it to them. The court would have to rule that it was an incomplete gift and, since the validity of the Foundation is not at question here, order Mr. Hardeman to surrender those voting rights to the Foundation."

"What if the validity of the Foundation is questioned?" I asked.

"Then the stock would retroactively become once again the property of Mr. Hardeman. And, of course, he would then become liable for the income received by the Foundation due to dividends from the stock. A rough calculation by me determined that approximately one hundred million dollars was received in that manner since 1937 to date. Assuming federal and state income taxes averaging sixty-five percent, that gives us a tax liability to Mr. Hardeman personally of sixty-five million dollars together with interest thereon at six percent from the year of earned income, which can very well put his tax liability at over double the base tax or one hundred thirty million dollars."

I turned back to Number One. "You're right. You are fucked."

The old man nodded glumly. "That's what I said."

We were silent for a moment. I sipped the coffee. It didn't taste so good right now. Somehow the sparkle had gone out of the morning. I looked down at the newspaper. Something in the story caught my eye. I put my finger on the line and read it aloud.

"—such voting rights gave Mr. Hardeman control of Bethlehem Motors which constitutes the only asset of the Foundation, and that his control thereof endangers these assets." I looked up at Artie. "Don't they have to prove that in order to win?"

"Not really," he said. "Merely the showing of the fact that the entire capital of the company is risked to manufacture and sell a new car would be sufficient for the court. Generally, prudent business sense doesn't permit commitments like that. Part of the capital, yes. All of it, no."

"But if the car is a success, the company will make more money than it ever made in its history," I said.

Artie looked interested. "When will you know that?"

"Six months to a year after the car is on the market."

"Too late to do us any good." He shook his head. "I can't hold them off that long."

"If Loren gets control of the company, the Betsy is dead," I said. "And the company blows a hundred million dollars just like that."

"But they don't lose it all," Artie said. "That's less than half of what I understand you might lose if you can't sell at least two hundred thousand of the new cars."

"I'd feel more positive about selling enough Betsys if we weren't having all that trouble with the dealers," I said.

"That's it!" For the first time Number One's voice had an edge in it.

We stared at him.

"That prick Simpson," he said. "We all knew he didn't have the money to pull of a campaign like that on his own. Someone had to be backing him."

"We checked around," I said. "Nothing turned up."

"Who was doing the checking?" asked Number One.

"Dan Weyman, of course," I said. "That comes under his department."

"Dan Weyman." Number One's voice was sarcastic. "And you took his word for it?"

I didn't speak.

"Weyman is Loren's boy," Number One said.

"You're implying that your grandson is behind that campaign?" Artie asked incredulously. "I can't believe that. Why would he want to destroy the company of which he is president?"

"I'm not saying he is and I'm not saying he's not," Number One answered slyly. "But my grandson's getting more like me every day. And if I were him and I wanted to throw a scare into management, I would do a thing like that. The only thing wrong with it was that we didn't scare."

"If we tie Simpson in to Loren, will that help us in the court?" I asked Artie.

He thought for a moment. "I don't think so. I think that the court would remove Loren as a trustee for violation of his fiduciary responsibilities, but it won't alter their right to vote the stock."

"But if we catch Loren with his pants down, surely they'll switch their votes to Number One," I said.

"If we catch Loren," Number One said, "We won't need the Foundation's votes."

"You got me," I said puzzled.

"I have forty-one percent right?" he asked.

"Forty," I said. "I just decided to exercise my warrants."

He grinned. "Why now?"

I grinned back at him. "I figured you might need another million in cash with all your problems."

He laughed. "Okay. Forty percent. You got one percent. My granddaughter Anne has ten percent. That's fifty-one percent. I don't need any more than that."

"But how do you know she'll go along with you?" I asked.

"I know my granddaughter," he said. "If she loses her faith in her brother, she'll turn to me. Her husband will see to that. He goes where the money is."

"Then we have only one problem left," I said. "That's to tie Simpson and Loren together."

"That's your problem," Number One said. "You do it and you only have eight days left to do it in."

"How the hell do I go about doing a thing like that?" I asked.

"I don't give a damn!" the old man snapped. "Do anything you have to. It was money that got to Simpson. Money will buy him back."

"What if that doesn't work?" I asked. "What if Loren is really clean?"

The old man stared balefully at me. "Frame him then! This is no child's game that we're playing!"

Chapter Three

There was a telephone message in my box at the Ponch when I returned to Detroit that evening. I read it in the elevator going up to my apartment.

"PLEASE CALL MRS. HARDEMAN."

There was a New York operator and a telephone number. I looked at the time at the top of the message. 7.10 p.m. I checked my watch, wondering what Bobbie was doing in New York. It was close to nine o'clock.

The faint sound of the music from the cabaret on the floor above my apartment filtered down through the ceiling as I let myself in. I picked up the telephone at the far end of the living room and looked out the window down at Cobo Hall while I waited for my call to go through.

This week's convention was the morticians. That had to be a fun thing. The operator came back on. "I have Mrs. Hardeman on the line for you."

"Hello, Angelo?" It was not Bobbie's voice. It was Alicia.

I hid my surprise. "Hey there."

She laughed. "Hey, there," she said. She hesitated a moment. "I suppose you're wondering why I called?"

"Yes," I said frankly.

"I know you're busy so I won't take up too much of your time."

"Don't go formal with me, Alicia," I said. "We've known each other too long for that."

She laughed again. This time her voice was relaxed. "Sorry," she said. "But since the divorce I'm never quite sure where I stand with people I knew when I was married."

"I knew you before you got married."

"Okay," she said. "I'll still keep it simple. As part of my divorce settlement I received half of Loren's stock in Bethlehem."

"I didn't know that."

"Very few people do," she said. "Loren didn't want to give it any publicity. That's why he has my voting proxy."

"I see." That meant that Loren owned only five percent of the company stock, not ten as we thought.

"I read in the papers about the lawsuit," she said. "I heard Loren and Dan Weyman talk about it many times but I never thought he would really do it." Then her voice went hard. "I don't want them to have control of the company."

"That makes two of us."

"I spoke to my attorney and had him draw a new proxy in favor of Grandfather," she said. "I want you to tell him that for me."

"Why don't you call him? I'm sure that he'll appreciate it."

"No," she said. "His secretary-housekeeper, Mrs. Craddock, reports back to Loren. I don't want him to know anything about it."

I was right and I was wrong. I had figured Number One's man to be the leak. "I'll make sure Number One hears about it."

"I'm sending the proxy to you at the hotel," she said. "Tell Grandfather to vote it any way he sees fit."

"I will," I said. I was curious. "You say Loren and Dan spoke about this many times?"

"Yes. It was nothing new. Every time Loren was angry at Grandfather it would come up. Especially after they learned about the Betsy."

I tried a wild shot. "Did you ever hear them talk about a man named Simpson?"

"Mark Simpson?"

"That's the man," I said.

"He's a friend of Dan Weyman's," she said. "Dan brought him over to the house to talk to Loren several times. They were working on something together. It had to do with automobile safety, I gathered."

Jackpot! I deliberately kept the excitement from my voice. "Would you do me a favor and write a note to me just mentioning the times you recalled they met at your house?"

"Of course," she said. There was a curiosity in her voice. "Will that help?"

"It might," I answered cautiously. I looked down at the message slip in my hand. "If I have to reach you again, will you be at this number?"

"No," she answered. "I'm leaving tomorrow night for Gstaad."

"I didn't know you skied."

She laughed. "I'm not going there for the skiing. Betsy's due to have her baby any day now and I want to be with her."

"How is she?"

She laughed again. "She's very calm about the whole thing. Her husband Max, is more excited about it than she is, but I still can't believe it. I'm going to be a grandmother."

"Grandmothers are getting younger every year. You can thank the younger generation for that. Give Betsy my best."

"I will," she said. "Good-bye, Angelo."

"Good-bye, Alicia." I put down the telephone and walked over to the bar. I broke out a tray of ice cubes, opened a new bottle of Crown Royal and made myself a stiff drink. I needed it.

Number One had been right in his thought that Weyman was covering up. But I wondered whether he really thought that Weyman and Loren were involved with Simpson. It just didn't make sense. Until now.

The music from the cabaret was growing louder. I was annoyed. I went back to the phone and called the assistant manager. "You have to do something about those amplifiers in the cabaret upstairs," I complained. "They're driving me out of my mind."

"You must be mistaken, Mr. Perino," the A.M. said smoothly. "The cabaret is closed tonight. Perhaps one of our guests has the radio on too loud. We'll check into it."

"Please do," I said shortly. I put down the phone and started for the bedroom, the music growing louder. I had enough troubles to manufacture my own headaches without outside help. I opened the bedroom door. The blast of music from the eight speakers almost knocked me down.

Cindy was sitting up in bed, her long hair falling across her naked shoulders and breasts to the sheet over her legs, stoned out of her mind on the sound. She turned to look at me, her head until nodding to the beat. A slow, happy smile came to her lips. "Welcome home, Angelo. Isn't it beautiful?"

"Turn it down!" I shouted above the noise. "What are you trying to do? Break my lease?"

She picked up a remote control device and aimed at the tape player across the room. The volume went down to a respectable level. "The latest thing," she said. "I couldn't resist it."

I stared at her. "How did you get in here?"

Her eyes went big and round. "Would you believe there wasn't a vacant hotel in this whole town when I came in yesterday?"

"That's not answering my question."

She got to her knees on the edge of the bed. "Come over here," she said.

I walked over to her and she put her arms around my neck and pulled herself up against me. Her lips were warm and soft.

I pulled my mouth away. "That's still not answering my question."

"It wasn't too difficult, darling," she said, her eyes smiling into mine. "I merely told them that I was installing the new sound system you had ordered."

"But that was yesterday," I said. "How come they let you stay all this while?"

"Everybody knows you can't do installations like this in one day," she said innocently. "Besides I was very quiet. Until just now when I heard you come in and go right to the telephone to call another woman." She stuck her hand under the pillow and came up with a telephone message which she thrust into my hand. "Especially her!"

I looked down at it. It was the door copy of the message I had picked up downstairs. When I looked up again, her face was so angry I had to laugh. "You're jealous," I said. "That's not like you. I thought you were too cool for that sort of thing."

"I'm not jealous!" she said heatedly. "But how would you like it if you spent two days in bed waiting for me to come home and when I did, I went right to the phone to call another guy?"

"But I didn't know you were waiting," I laughed.

"That doesn't matter!" she snapped. "I didn't think that was very nice. You could have at least looked in the bedroom first!"

"It was business," I said.

"Oh, sure," she said sarcastically.

"It was," I said. "You got the wrong Mrs. Hardeman. This was the first one."

"My God!" she said in a shocked voice. "Don't tell me you've been there too?"

Duncan was waiting in my office when I got to the plant in the morning. Carradine of Engineering and Joe Huff of Design were with him.

I didn't need a second look to know they weren't there to bring glad tidings. I walked around behind my desk. "Okay, gentlemen," I said. "Hit me with it."

"How do you want it, laddie?" Duncan said. "One at a time or all at once?"

"One at a time," I said. "This is Monday morning and I'm not in very good shape."

"Okay," he said. "On Friday all work on the production line was stopped. Orders from the president."

"He can't do that. He hasn't the authority. Number One is still chairman of the board and chief operating officer."

"He did it," Duncan said flatly.

"Well go in there and start it again," I said.

"We can't," Duncan said. "We've been barred from the plant. We can't even get into our own offices. This is the only place we could come."

I was silent. Loren wasn't waiting. Maybe he was even a little ahead of himself. "That's one," I said. "What's next?"

"Union troubles," Duncan said. "The U.A.W. said they won't let the assembly line start until all the reclassifications are agreed on. They claim too many jobs are being downgraded."

"I thought we approved a schedule that was satisfactory to them."

"You mean you approved it," Duncan said. "Weyman never passed it on."

Weyman again. He wasn't being very helpful. I was starting to really dislike him. "He's supposed to negotiate only on the basis we give him," I said. "He has no right to alter or withhold our proposals."

"He did," Duncan said. "Of course, he had direct orders from the president."

I looked at him. "Is that all?"

"No," he said. "Did you read the *Wall Street Journal* this morning?"

I shook my head.

"Here, read it," he said, giving me the newspaper.

It was a front-page story. Banner headline across the first two columns.

HUNDRED-FIFTY-MILLION-DOLLAR NEW CAR OF BETHLEHEM MOTORS ALREADY A DISASTER?

I read on. The story was out of Detroit, dated Friday.

Special to the Wall Street Journal — Informed company sources inside Bethlehem Motors today indicated serious doubts over possible success of their new car, the Betsy, due to be introduced later in this year. These doubts came to the surface with the filing of a lawsuit by Loren Hardeman III and his sister, Princess Alekhine, against their grandfather, Loren Hardeman I, and the Hardeman Foundation for what basically amounts to control of the giant motor company.

Company sources further revealed that Mr. Hardeman III began to feel concern over the mounting costs on the project together with progressive reports as to the safety of the car itself, and that he initiated this suit reluctantly after endeavoring to persuade his grandfather to abandon the project in the interest of the public.

There was more but I had read enough. I put the paper down. There was no doubt in my mind as to who the "informed company sources" were. Weyman. As executive vice-president, he had a pipeline right into the paper. I had the feeling this was only the beginning, there would be more stories like it going to newspapers around the country. If they wanted to kill the Betsy before it reached the market, they couldn't find a better way. A few more stories like this and the public wouldn't buy the car if it were given to them on a silver platter.

"Wait here," I said. Then I went down the hall to Loren's office.

Chapter Four

"Mr. Hardeman's in a meeting," his secretary said, holding up a restraining hand as I went to his door.

"Beautiful," I said, brushing past her.

Loren III was behind his desk, Weyman and a man I didn't know were sitting opposite him when I entered.

Loren was the only one who didn't seem surprised. "I've been expecting you," he said.

"I don't doubt that," I said.

The other man and Weyman got to their feet quickly. "We'll be in my office when you're free," Weyman said. They started out.

"You wait," I said to Weyman. "What I have to say concerns you too."

Weyman shot a questioning glance at Loren. Loren nodded and sank back into his chair. "Wait in my office, Mark," he told the other man.

The man nodded and left. I didn't wait for the door to close behind him. "Is that Mark Simpson?" I asked.

Weyman hesitated. Again Loren nodded, "Yes," Weyman answered.

"I thought so," I said. "The scum's beginning to come to the surface."

They didn't answer.

"I'll get to him later," I said. I moved to the side of Loren's desk where I could look at both of them. "You saw the story in the *Wall Street Journal* this morning?"

"Yes," Loren answered.

"Don't you think you've overreached with that one?" I asked.

"No," he said. "I think it reflects the truth."

"As you see it," I said.

"As I see it," he echoed.

"Have you thought what might happen to the company if you should lose?"

"I won't lose," he said confidently.

"Even if you win," I said, "you lose. A few more stories like that and you'll control a bankrupt company. There won't be a single person left in the world who will buy any car that this company produces."

"What happens to this company won't be any of your concern," said Loren.

"That's where you're wrong," I said. "I am concerned. I happen to be the owner of two hundred thousand shares of stock in this company which I purchased from your grandfather for two million dollars cash."

For the first time surprise showed on Loren's face. "I don't believe it. Grandfather would never sell a share of his stock to an outsider."

"It's easy enough to check," I said. "Why not pick up the telephone and ask him?"

Loren didn't move.

"As a stockholder I have certain rights. If you read the bylaws of the company as carefully as I have you will know what I'm talking about. I have the right to ask indemnification and damages against any officer of the company who interferes with work currently in progress, if that interference leads to losses directly attributable to it."

Loren reached for the telephone. He spoke quickly to Jim Ellison, the company's general counsel. He put down the telephone and looked at me. "You would have to prove it first," he said.

I smiled. "I'm no lawyer, but that should be a cinch. You halt production on the Betsy now and a hundred and fifty million dollars goes down the drain."

He was silent.

"I'll make it easy for you," I said. "I'll give you the time it takes for me to go from here back to my office. And when I get back there if I don't hear from you that work on the production line has started again and my boys can go about doing their normal jobs without interference, I'm going to hit you and your little prick friend here with a lawsuit requiring you both to come up with the biggest indemnification bond any of you ever heard of. One hundred and fifty million dollars worth."

I started from the office. Halfway to the door I turned back. I looked at Weyman. "And you have exactly one hour to be in my office with the U.A.W. people to straighten out our contract."

I almost smiled at the expression on his face. His devotion to Ex-Lax was a running gag around the plant. He didn't look as if he would need any today.

I turned to Loren. "If I were you," I said almost mildly, "I would go about finding a way to deny or counteract that story in today's paper before it has a chance to catch up to you."

I went back to my office the long way round just in case they needed time to think about it. I passed Weyman's office. On an impulse I went in.

"Is Mr. Simpson here?" I asked the secretary.

"He's just left, Mr. Perino," she said brightly. "He told me to tell Mr. Weyman that he had an important appointment and that he would call him later in the day."

I nodded and went out. The man had all the good instincts of a jackal. He smelled trouble and he was going to be nowhere around when it was happening. I made up my mind to get to him later in the afternoon if things here were under control.

I leaned against the outside door to my office and smoked a whole cigarette before I went inside. I wasn't taking any chances. I wanted them to have all the time they needed.

My secretary looked up at me as I came in the door. "Mr. Perino."

I stopped at her desk. "Yes?"

"I just received a peculiar message for you from Mr. Hardeman's office," she said, a puzzled expression on her face. "I didn't understand it, but he said you would."

"Read it to me," I said.

She looked down at her shorthand notebook. "He said to tell you that everything was arranged the way you wanted it but that he, personally, would come down to say good-bye to you next week."

I smiled. I knew just what he meant. I went into my own office. "Okay, fellows, get back to work. We've already blown four days on this shit."

Duncan looked at me. "How did you get them to back down so easily?"

I grinned. "I used my Italian charm," I said. "I threatened to sing 'O Sole Mio' for them."

We didn't finish the meeting with the U.A.W. representatives until after nine o'clock that night and by then it was too late to go chasing after Simpson. There was a lot more to building a car than just getting it from the drawing board to the assembly line.

It was the first time I had ever been closehand to a union negotiation and as far as I was concerned, I was willing for it to be the last. But, as little as I liked the son of a bitch, I had to admit that Dan Weyman was good at it.

He was professional and precise. I hadn't realized up to now the number of different classifications that existed within the same assembly-line framework. He did. And knew the exact definition of work responsibilities for each class. Once he got down to it, I was fascinated at the efficiency and subtlety he brought to his work. I only wished that he were on our side, not Loren's, but that did not keep him from doing a good job for the company.

At one point when things got a little sticky, he dug right in and explained it to them in basic terms. "We'll give a little, but so will you have to bend a little." His voice was calm as if he were lecturing a class at college, which I understand he had done before he went to Ford with the whiz kids. "We're all breaking our asses to keep the Japanese and Germans from walking away with our market. Not only in sales but in manufacturing. It would have been comparatively easy for Bethlehem management to decide to build this car abroad and it would have cost less. You know it and I know it. Last year our average hourly rate of pay was $6.66, substantially higher than most other companies in the industry. And we lost twenty million dollars on our automotive division. We had every justification in the world to go abroad and build the new car. But we didn't. Because we have a respect for and obligation to our employees, and to do so would cause a great deal of hardship among them. Now all we ask is their cooperation. To increase their productivity together with our own. You give a little, we give a little. Maybe between us, we can bring some of the business back home where it belongs."

I watched the faces of the union representatives while he made his little speech. I couldn't read much in them, but they, too, were professional and experienced in their jobs. From that point on, it took hours. But eventually it was all done.

After they had gone I looked at Dan Weyman who was gathering up his papers. "You did well," I said.

He didn't answer.

"You could have saved all of us a lot of trouble if you had done it when you were asked in the first place," I said.

He snapped his attaché case shut. He stared at me for a moment as if he were about to say something, but then he turned abruptly and walked out of the office without speaking.

Cindy met me at the door of my apartment when I let myself in after ten o'clock. She handed me a message slip. "Try to tell me that this is business too," she said sarcastically.

I looked down at it. "Am in the piano bar downstairs, Must see you right away." It was initialled B.H.

I looked up at Cindy. "It probably is."

"Sure," she said. "She called before the message came up. I would recognize that British accent anywhere. But she hung up before I could ask who was calling, then the message came up."

"How long ago was that?" I asked.

"Maybe a half an hour ago."

I thought for a moment. The bar was no place to meet. Bobbie had to be looking for trouble. "Go down there and tell her to come up," I said. "Then get lost for an hour."

"What do you expect me to do?" she asked.

"Go to a movie, sit in the bar. I don't know," I answered.

A bitchy smile came to her lips as she moved obediently to the door. "Can't I come back upstairs?" she asked. "I'll stay in the bedroom, out of the way. You won't even know I'm around."

"Uh-huh." I shook my head.

"At least then, let me set up a mike," she said. "Maybe that way I can learn something. I was always curious how the British ladies did it."

"I've had a rough day, Cindy," I said wearily. "Now do as I say or I'll belt yuh."

She looked at me for a moment. "Not now," she said. "When I come back." The door closed behind her.

Chapter Five

I had the martini, very dry and very cold, in a glass clouded with frost beads waiting on the bar for her when she came in. Silently I put it in her hand.

"You didn't forget, did you, Angelo?" she asked.

I raised my glass to her. "Angelos like elephants, never forget."

We drank silently. She finished her drink in what seemed like one swallow. I remembered that too. I refilled her glass from the martini pitcher. I still didn't speak.

She crossed the room and looked out at the sparkling lights of Ontario. The blinking sign on the side of the river went on-off: COME ON OVER!

She turned to me. "You have a good view from here at night."

"When it's clear," I said. "Not so good on smoggy days."

She sipped her drink and turned back to the window. "I'm leaving him," she said. "I made a mistake. I know it now."

I didn't say anything.

She turned to look at me. "Did you hear what I said?"

I nodded. "Yes."

"Don't you have any comment to make?" Her voice was brittle and thin.

"No."

"Nothing?" She laughed. "Not even, I told you so?"

"Nothing."

She turned away again and looked out the window. "The girl that came downstairs. Is she—?" She didn't finish the question.

"We're old friends."

We were silent again. She emptied her glass and held it out to me. I refilled it and gave it back to her.

"Thank you," she said.

I nodded.

"Still don't talk very much, do you?"

"Only when I have something to say."

"Then say something," she said sharply.

I looked at her. "Why?"

She didn't look at me. "Because it's not the way I thought it would be. All he cares about is the company. That's all he lives for. That and the determination he has to avenge his father's death."

"Avenge his father's death?"

"Yes," she answered. "He's a man split in two between his respect for his grandfather because of the old man's accomplishments and his hatred of him for hounding his father to suicide."

"He blames Number One for that?"

She nodded. "He said the old man never got off his father's back, just as he won't get off his."

"I can't believe that."

She turned to me. "I didn't either until one night he showed me a letter which he keeps in the wall safe in the house. It was the first time he ever showed it to anyone. Even Alicia never saw it."

"What letter?"

"The letter his father left him when he committed suicide," she answered.

"But there was no letter," I said. I remembered the newspaper stories. "The police never found one."

"Loren did," she said. "He was the one who discovered his father's body. He found the letter too. And hid it. Even then he was afraid that if the contents of the letter were revealed the company would be finished."

"What did it say?"

"I only saw it once but I won't forget it," she said. "It was not addressed to anyone. It was just a note scrawled in his father's handwriting.

" 'I cannot go on any longer. He will not leave me alone. I do not have one day's peace and there is not a day that passes that he does not make impossible demands on me. I have tried for years to get him to leave me alone but now I see that he never will. And I no longer have the strength to fight him. This is the only way out. Believe me. Forgive me.' "

"It was signed simply, L.H. II."

I didn't speak.

She looked at me. "Loren said it was exactly the way his grandfather treated him. But that he was stronger than his father. He could fight back and would."

I turned away silently to refill my own glass. I took a sip of my drink. "Why didn't he do something about it then?"

"The reason he gave me, and for one other," she said. "He was afraid that his grandfather would not make him president of the company if he did." She took a sip of her drink and held out her empty glass again.

I refilled it and gave it back to her.

"I'm getting smashed," she said. "I've probably been smashed since I came up here. I had two doubles while I was waiting downstairs."

She held her liquor well, her eyes were clear. "You look all right to me."

"I feel it," she said. "I know myself."

I didn't speak.

"You see, even way back then, all he cared about was the company. And nothing's changed. He really doesn't need a wife or even a woman. He doesn't need anyone."

"Then why did he marry you? He could have had you and kept Alicia. It would have saved him a fortune."

She laughed. "But he didn't know that, did he? You knew it and I knew it. But he didn't. I remember you said once he was square." She laughed again. "You don't know how square he really is."

I pulled at my drink silently.

"Do you know every time we make love he asks if I made it before he has his orgasm?" She giggled. "Sometimes I drive him crazy and say no just to make him wait. He goes out of his mind."

"I think you are smashed," I said.

"What's the matter, Angelo?" she asked. "Don't you like to hear me talk about my sex life?"

I looked at her. "If you want the truth: No."

"You're getting very proper, aren't you, Angelo? Like that time out at the test track in Washington and now you won't even talk about it."

I was silent.

"I remember the way it was in San Francisco between us. Do you remember, Angelo? It was beautiful."

"I remember." I also remembered the pain when she left me in the airport. Strange, but there was no hurt now.

She came close to me, so close I could taste the smell of her in my mouth. "It could be like that again."

"No."

She put her drink down and her arms around my neck. Her open mouth seized hungrily on mine, her tongue ravishing my mouth. Nothing.

I held her away from me, my hands gripping her arms. "No."

"Give it a chance, Angelo," she said, her eyes searching mine. "It could be like that again!"

"It won't be, Bobbie. Ever again."

"Why do you keep saying that, Angelo?" she cried. "I love you! I've always loved you!"

This time I brought her to me and kissed her. For a long time, until her arms fell to her side and she stepped back, looking up at me, a strangely lonely look in her eyes.

"You were only making another mistake," I said. "Running from him to me isn't the answer."

Her voice was clear now, she wasn't the least bit smashed. "How did you know?"

I took her hand. "I didn't hear the music," I said.

She was silent for a moment, looking down at our hands, then she drew her hand away. "Do you have another martini left in that pitcher?"

I refilled her glass. I watched her drink half of it before she stopped.

"I'll miss you. You do make a good martini."

"I'll give you the recipe," I said. "Straight gin. Lots of ice. No vermouth."

She smiled. "That's a dirty trick."

"It's also a great martini."

"My bags are downstairs. I'm going out to the airport. I'm not going back to him."

I didn't say anything.

"I can make a late plane to Chicago. And leave from there for London in the morning."

"Does he know you're gone?" I asked.

She shook her head. "I'll call him from the airport just before I get on the plane."

"Won't he miss you before then?"

She laughed. "He was locked up in a meeting with Dan, a fellow named Mark Simpson, and a few other gentlemen I never saw before when I left. Rough-looking characters they were too. Not the usual kind of men that have come to the house before. Chances are that he won't go up to bed until the wee small hours." A curious expression came into her eyes. "Now that I think about it, I remember they were talking about you when I passed the doorway."

"Really? Something good I hope?"

"Nothing good," she said seriously. "Apparently you did something today that's gotten Loren very incensed. Did you?"

"I might have," I admitted. "But I work for his grandfather and we don't exactly see eye to eye these days."

"I heard Loren's voice as I went down the hall," she said. " 'I'll play as tough and dirty as the old man anytime and Angelo might as well find that out right now,' he said."

"What else did he say?"

"I didn't hear anything else. By that time I was down the hall and out of earshot." Her eyes were troubled. "I don't like it."

"It's probably just some words out of context that sound much worse than they really are."

She finished her drink and gave it to me. I placed the empty glass on the bar. "You'll be careful?"

I nodded and we started for the door. "You have a coat?" I asked.

"I checked it downstairs."

I held the door open for her. She stepped through and turned to faced me. I bent and kissed her cheek. "Good-bye, Bobbie. Good luck."

I could see the hint of tears in her eyes. "Apparently we're always saying good-bye, aren't we, Angelo?"

"Seems like it," I said.

She held back her tears. Her chin came up proudly. "Well, at least we don't have to go through that again, do we?"

"No."

She caught at my lapels and pulled me down to her. Her lips were gentle on mine. "Good-bye, Angelo. Don't think badly of me. Just remember that we did love each other. Once."

I looked into her eyes. The tears were there now. "I'll remember," I said gently.

Then she turned abruptly and walked to the elevator, her back straight and stiff. I stood there until the elevator doors closed behind her. She never looked back. Not even once.

Chapter Six

When I came out of the bathroom after my shower, the waiter had left the breakfast table rolled up against the bed and Cindy was sitting up, eating a Danish, getting crumbs all over the sheet, the stereo blasting.

"Oh, Jesus!" I said, tightening the towel around my waist and pouring myself a cup of coffee. "This early in the morning?"

"It's the Pocono Inaugural Five Hundred last July," she said. "I just got the tapes yesterday."

I swallowed some of the coffee. It was black and hot and tasteless, like all hotel coffee. "You couldn't wait?" I asked sarcastically.

She paid no attention to me, intently following the roar of the motors racing from speaker to speaker. "That's Mark Donohue," she said excitedly. "Hear that other car moving up on him?"

I lit a cigarette without answering. I listened. She was right. There were two roaring engines chasing from speaker to speaker. Now it seemed almost as if they were in the same speaker.

"That's Joe Leonard!" Now he's passing him. He's passed him! Mark chickened out on the oil slick on the second curve of lap two and Joe sneaked by him. Listen! That's A. J. and Mario right behind them!"

The telephone rang. I picked it up. "Hello," I shouted over the sound of the speakers.

"What's that damn noise?" Number One demanded. "Where the hell are you?"

"Cindy, turn that damn thing off!" I yelled. She picked up the remote. The tape whirred to a stop. I turned back to the phone. "That better?"

"Who is with you?" the old man asked.

"Cindy. My test driver."

"What the hell is she doing?" he asked. "Driving a Formula One around your bedroom?"

I laughed. "Practically."

"It's three days," he said, "I didn't hear from you."

I remembered what Alicia told me about Mrs. Craddock. "I had nothing to report," I said.

"Then what the hell have you been doing?" he snapped. "Driving your test driver around the bed?"

"Why don't you call me later from outside?" I suggested, cautiously.

"What for?" he retorted. "You know how I hate to go out in this town."

"Security," I said.

He was silent for a moment. I could hear the sound of his breathing in the phone. "Are you talking about Craddock?" he asked.

"Yes."

"I know all about her," he said shortly. "Besides she's out of the house right now doing the marketing. You can talk."

"If you know about her, why do you keep her?"

"She's the best damn secretary and housekeeper I ever had. And, believe me, good housekeepers aren't easy to come by these days." He chuckled. "The way I figure it, the money my grandson pays her makes her job the best in the world and keeps her from blowing it."

"But what good is it if Loren knows everything you're doing?"

He chuckled again. "He only knows what I want him to know. That way everybody's happy. She's not in the house now. See what I mean?"

"Okay," I said. I wondered if any one of us would ever catch up to him. There had to be something to being ninety-four. If there was anything to the old saying that practice makes perfect, being ninety-four was a lot of practice.

He listened quietly while I covered the last two days. When I finished, he was still silent. The line echoed emptily. "Are you there?" I asked.

"I'm here," he said. I heard a deep sigh. "My grandson wants to beat me so bad he can't wait."

It was my turn to be silent.

For the first time I heard resignation in his voice. "When you're young, you're always in a hurry. He should take his time. Monday will come soon enough."

"A lot can happen in six days."

"I told Roberts to turn back the voting trust to the Foundation," he said. "I'm not even coming in for the court hearing."

"Why?" I asked. "Because you know you're going to lose?"

"Don't get impertinent, young man," he snapped, fire coming back into his voice. "No, not because I'm going to lose but because it's the right thing to do. The Foundation is too important to become a football."

I said nothing.

"Besides, that's just the skirmish. The real battle comes at the stockholders' meeting on Tuesday morning. That's where you win or lose. I'll be there for that one." He chuckled ironically. "Of course, my grandson figures that he's got it won or he wouldn't have called the meeting for the day after the hearing."

"He's lost Alicia's votes," I said. "Maybe we can change some others."

"They don't have the same reason that she has. The only chance I see is if we can tie him into Simpson. Even the trustees of the Foundation won't go along with a president who tried to sabotage his own company."

"We've got a beginning," I said. "We already know that he has more than a passing acquaintance with him."

"That's up to you. There's nothing I can do about that down here."

"I'll try," I said. "I remember what you told me before I left."

"Forget that! I was only talking because I was angry. I don't want him framed if he had nothing to do with it."

"Why the sudden change of heart?" I asked. "You develop a conscience in your old age?"

"No, goddamn it!" he roared. "Just don't forget that he is my grandson and I'm not going to hang him for something he didn't do."

"Then get ready to lose if I can't tie it together," I snapped back at him.

"I won't lose!" he said sharply. "Remember what I said when we started this thing. We would build a new car and by God, that's exactly what we did!"

"Mr. Hardeman's waiting in your office," my secretary told me when I came in.

"Fine. Bring in two cups of coffee."

I opened the door and went into my office. Loren was standing at the window. He turned to me. "Good morning, Loren. You're a week early, aren't you?"

"This isn't a business visit," he said heavily. He walked slowly from the window toward my desk. He looked like a man who hadn't slept all night, weary lines tracing their gray way into his face, his eyes red and pouchy. "My wife left me last night."

My secretary came in with the coffee. We were silent while she placed the cups on the desk and left. I pushed a cup toward him. "You better drink that. You look like you could use it."

He sank into the chair opposite me and reached for the coffee cup. But his hands were shaking so much that some of the coffee spilled over the rim and he returned the cup to its saucer without tasting it. "You're not surprised," he said.

I looked at him. "Should I be? Were you?"

His eyes fell for a moment. "I suppose not," he said in a low voice, almost as if to himself. I could see it coming for a long time. But there was nothing I could do about it. Detroit wasn't her idea of the world."

I sipped my coffee without speaking. Office coffee was just as bad as hotel coffee, only instant.

He raised his eyes. "You saw her last night?"

"Yes."

"Did she say anything to you?"

"No more than you told me," I answered.

"Damn!" he exploded. He got to his feet and went back to the window and pounded his fist into his open palm. "Damn!"

I watched him silently, sipping my coffee.

After a moment he regained his self-control. He turned to me. "Why did she go to you?" he asked in an almost normal voice.

I looked into his eyes. "Because we were friends, I guess. And there was no one else here for her to turn to. I think you put your finger on it. Detroit wasn't her idea of the world. But then, Detroit never tried very hard to make her welcome."

He turned back to the window. "I don't know what to think." After a moment he came back to the desk. "I was jealous of you," he said. "I know she was out in San Francisco almost all the time you were there."

"But that was two years ago. Long before you decided to get married."

"I know," he said. "But when I was told that she stopped off at the Ponch to see you on her way to the airport, I began to think. After all, you're much more her type than I am. I was never very much of a ladies' man."

In spite of myself, I had to smile. "And I am?"

At least he had the grace to look embarrassed. "Come on now, Angelo," he said. "You know what I'm talking about. Stories about you and women have come back here from all over the world."

I laughed. "You have to tell me them sometime. I might discover something about myself."

"Angelo, would you give me a straight answer if I gave you a direct question?" He was in deadly earnest.

"Try me."

"Did you have an affair with my wife?"

"No." I looked right into his eyes, secure in the knowledge I was telling him the truth. Bobbie and I never had an affair after she married him.

He took a deep breath and nodded his head. "Thank you," he said. "Now I can put that away and forget I ever thought about it."

"Okay," I said.

He turned and started out of the office. I called him back. He stopped in the middle of the room. "Yes, Angelo?"

"Would you give me a straight answer if I asked you a direct question?"

He came back to the desk. "Try me," he said.

"If I could work out a compromise between you and your grandfather, will you give up this stupid fight between you in which one of you will get hurt but only the company will suffer?"

His face settled into grim lines. It was amazing how much he looked like his grandfather. "No."

"Why?"

"Because he's a despot. And I'm not going to let him destroy me as he did my father."

"But that was a long time ago," I said. "He's an old man now and in a wheel-chair—"

"He was old then and in a wheelchair!" he interrupted me. "But it didn't stop him then and it won't stop him now!" His eyes grew cold. "Besides you never had to walk into a room and find your father with the top of his head blown off!"

I stared at him. "And you're absolutely sure that your grandfather was to blame?"

"As sure as I'm standing here," he said.

I got to my feet. "I apologize for asking," I said. "Your grandfather would have canned me if he knew I even brought it up. But I had the wrong impression."

"What was that?"

"For a moment there," I said, "I thought you were almost human."

Chapter Seven

Marion Stevenson, head of Bethlehem Security, had the faceless look of the FBI agent he used to be. His dark gray suit and characterless tie did nothing to dispel the illusion. He was the kind of man you could overlook in a crowd. He was a medium man in every way except one. He had the palest eyes I ever saw. You could almost see through them to the back of his head.

"You wanted to see me, Mr. Perino?" His voice was as expressionless as the rest of him.

"Yes. Mr. Stevenson. Thank you for coming by." I usually wasn't this formal but I remembered his resentment when I first put the Burns people out at the test track. He had enough J. Edgar left in him to take it as a personal affront. "Please sit down."

"Thank you," he said, equally formal.

The telephone rang. I picked it up. It was Max Evans of the purchasing department. He had a problem.

I covered the mouthpiece while I listened. "Excuse me," I said to Stevenson. "I'll only be a moment." Stevenson nodded and I went back to the phone.

"We've just received a revised estimate from the contractor for the electrostatic connectors for the driver's seat belts. Up three dollars and forty cents."

"Why?" I asked.

"Additional insulation for lead wires and grounding wires to come up to Underwriters' fire and safety standards."

"Wasn't that covered in our specs?" I asked.

"Yes," he answered. "But Underwriters changed their requirements on us two weeks ago."

There was nothing we could do about it. The driver's seat belt was one of our featured, standard, no-extra-cost safety items. It was connected electrically to a governor on the engine. All belts unfastened, the car would go no more than ten miles per hour. Seat belts fastened, the speed went up to twenty-five miles per hour. Shoulder harness fastened released the governor completely. But still it was a lot of money. Over a million dollars on three hundred thousand cars.

"Have you checked with other contractors?" I asked.

"Yes," he said. "When we sent out for the original bids. But it's too late now. It would take any one of them at least eight months to get set up for us."

"Then we have no choice," I said.

"Yes, sir," he answered.

"Wait a minute," I said. "This comes under Cost Control. Don't you usually get approvals on things like this from Weyman's office?"

"That's right," he said apologetically. "But as of this morning we were told to secure all approvals on the new cars from you."

"I see." I saw more than that. There were hundreds of items like this every week. If Weyman could unload them on me, I would be so busy shovelling shit that I would have time for nothing else.

"Is it okay to go ahead, Mr. Perino?"

"It's okay, Max," I said. "Send up a purchase order and I'll approve it."

I put down the telephone and turned to my visitor. I took a cigarette and held the pack out to him.

"Gave them up, thank you," he said.

I lit up and leaned back in my chair. I let the smoke drift idly from my mouth while I sat there watching him. After a few moments I noticed he was getting slightly restless.

The telephone rang. I picked it up. "Hold all calls, please." Then I put it down and continued smoking silently.

After about a minute, he made a point of looking at his wristwatch. I ignored it until I had finished the cigarette and ground it thoroughly into the ashtray. "I know you're a busy man, Mr. Stevenson," I said, "but you'll have to bear with me if I seem slow to you this morning. I have a great many things on my mind."

"I understand, Mr. Perino," he said smoothly.

"I have been reading the Table of Organization," I said. "And if I read it correctly, you are responsible directly to the president and executive vice-president."

"That's correct."

"And your responsibilities are all security matters pertaining to the company's business from employee malfeasance to protection of corporate records and industrial secrets."

He nodded. "Yes, sir."

"Let me pose a hypothetical question," I said. "Should you discover a security leak in my office, would you report that to the president?"

"No, sir," he said. "First to the executive vice-president."

"And if you discovered a leak in either of their offices?"

"To the president, if the leak was in the executive vice-president's office, and vice versa."

"And if the leak came from both offices?"

He thought for a moment. "I would then have to assume that the leak was a matter of company policy and approved by them."

I pushed the copy of the *Wall Street Journal* story to him. "Have you seen that story?"

He nodded.

"Would you say that the information contained in that story resulted from a breach of company security?"

"I wouldn't know, sir."

"I call your attention to the phrase, 'informed company sources.' I also call your attention to certain figures quoted in that story. They happen to correspond exactly to the figures in our secret company cost records. There are no more than a dozen executives in the company who are privy to those figures. Suddenly that information appears in a national newspaper and in such a manner as to be potentially.harmful to the company. Wouldn't you say that was a serious breach of company security?"

He was getting uncomfortable. "I couldn't say, sir."

"Might I assume then that you feel this matter comes under your classification of approved company policy?"

He was genuinely uncomfortable now. Lawyers and policemen make the worst witnesses. They hate to be questioned. "I can't answer that question, Mr. Perino."

I nodded. "That article happens to be unsigned. Would you know the name of the writer by any chance?"

"Yes, sir," he said.

"Could you tell me?"

"I'm sorry, Mr. Perino," he said. "I've already given my report on that subject to Mr. Weyman."

I paused for a moment. "Do you know of a man named Mark Simpson?"

"Yes, sir."

"What do you know about him?"

"He's head of an outfit called the IASO and publishes a weekly newsletter concerning the automobile industry."

"What else do you know about him?"

"Mr. Weyman has my report on that gentleman," he said. "I'm not allowed to distribute copies of it."

"I see. Is it also against regulations to supply me with a list of the times Mr. Simpson visited this plant and whom he saw on each visit over the past two years?"

"No, sir," he said. I could see he was pleased to find there was something I asked that he could do. "I will have it in your office this afternoon."

"Thank you," I said. "You've been very helpful."

His face flushed. He knew exactly how helpful he had been. Zilch. He got to his feet.

I looked at him. "You have my permission to report this conversation to your superiors if you wish."

"Mr. Perino, if I thought this conversation should be reported to my superiors I would do so with or without your permission," he said stiffly. "I would like to point out that I am in charge of plant security, not plant politics."

I rose to my feet. "Mr. Stevenson, I apologize." I held out my hand.

He hesitated a moment, then took it. "Thank you, Mr. Perino."

I called Weyman the moment he left the office. His voice was almost pleasant when he came on the phone. I think he was expecting a bitch from me about unloading the cost approvals on my office. He didn't get it.

"Number One is bugging me for the report we asked for on Mark Simpson some time ago," I said. "I just spoke to Stevenson in Security and he tells me that he left it with you."

He flustered easily. "I remember seeing it. I'll look around for it and shoot it right over to you."

I put the telephone down knowing damn well I would never see that report but, at least, I was on record as knowing that he had it.

Early in the afternoon, I received Stevenson's report on Simpson's visits to the plant. There were quite a few of them in the past few years and with the exception of one visit to Bancroft of Sales, all the rest were with Weyman.

I made up my mind to get out of the office and pay Mr. Simpson a visit, but one thing led to another and it was four o'clock before I could leave. I called Cindy at the apartment.

"How would you like to have dinner at the Dearborn Inn?" I asked.

"Fantastic," she said. "I've never been there but I've heard about it. It's right in the middle of Ford country, isn't it?"

"Smack dab in the middle," I laughed. "But don't hold that against it. It's really quite good. I have one stop to make on the way out there, but that shouldn't take long. Be downstairs at the auto entrance in fifteen minutes. I'll pick you up."

"Fifteen minutes on the dot," she said. "I'll be there."

And she was. Even wore a dress for the occasion. I stared as the doorman held the door of the Maserati for her. It was the first time in almost two years that I'd seen her wearing anything but slacks.

"Hey! You're a girl," I said, putting the car into first.

She turned to me with a smile as she finished buckling up. "Man, you're awfully slow. I thought you'd never find out."

The IASO offices were located on Michigan Avenue outside the high-rent district on the way to Dearborn. It was a nondescript two-story building next to a used-car lot. Downstairs was occupied by job printers, with large blacked-out painted windows in what in better days had to be a new-car showroom. Upstairs, over them, the small windows bore the letters IASO in faded blue paint.

I pulled the car into the small off-street parking place in front of the job printers and reserved for their clients and got out. "I won't be long."

She nodded, opening her purse and taking out a cassette. "Mind if I use your tape player?"

By the time I walked away from the car, she had Creedence Clearwater blasting from all four speakers and was leaning back, bathing in the sound, a beatific expression on her face.

There was no separate entrance to the upper story that I could see, so I went into the print shop. The sound of a rolling press hit my ears as I opened the door. There was a beat-up old wooden counter separating the entrance from the rest of the shop. A rusted punch bell sat on top with a sign next to it: RING BELL FOR SERVICE.

I hit the bell but its sound was lost in the roar of the presses. I hit it again.

Several workmen stuck their heads out from behind the machinery to see who was there.

"IASO?" I shouted above the noise, pointing with my hand at the ceiling.

A big man with black hair, his face and hairy arms covered with printer's ink stepped out from behind the press. He made a sweeping gesture with his arm. "Around the building," he shouted. "There's a staircase in the back alley."

"Thank you," I shouted. I went outside, glad to get away from the hammer of the presses. Cindy saw me and smiled, beginning to roll down the window.

I shook my head and pointed around the building. She nodded and rolled the window back up, leaning into the sound again.

There was a black rusted-steel staircase on the outside of the building off the alley. On the building there was a small sign with an arrow pointing to the steps. IASO. I climbed the steps and went into the building through the faded gray, painted steel door.

I entered a deserted reception room. The walls were painted a dull green and were covered with posters: BUCKLE UP FOR SAFETY! SPEED KILLS! And others like it. From somewhere in the back I heard the sound of a bell announcing my arrival.

A moment later a heavy blonde girl in a shapeless black sweater and miniskirt appeared. "What can I do for you?" she asked in a voice equally as bored as the expression on her face.

"Is Mr. Simpson in?"

"Do you have an appointment?"

"No." I shook my head.

"Your name please?"

I told her. There was no change in the bored expression of either her voice or face. "Please have a seat. I'll see if he is available."

She left the reception room and I heard the door lock behind her. I sat down on a wooden bench next to a table, the top of which was covered with the latest issue of the IASO weekly newsletter.

I lit a cigarette and idly glanced through a copy. *En passant*, I learned all about the improvements that GM had built into the new 72 Vega that could not be seen on the outside and the additional performance that could be gotten from the Pinto with the new Boss package, all of which could also be learned from the printed ads and TV commercials of the companies concerned. I got to the last page without having once come across an item that dealt with automobile safety.

I looked for an ashtray in which to stub out my cigarette. There wasn't any, so I got to my feet, opened the door and snapped it out into the alley. Through the thin walls behind me, I could hear the sound of the bell. At the same time, the faint vibration in the door and the muffled roar of the presses downstairs suddenly stopped. I looked at my watch. Four forty-five. I had been there more than ten minutes.

The blonde girl reappeared in the doorway. A surprised expression chased the bored look from her face as she saw me. She looked over my shoulder. "Did anyone just come in?"

"No," I answered. "I just threw out a cigarette."

She looked at me. "Are you waiting for someone else?"

"No," I said. "Still waiting for Mr. Simpson."

"Wasn't his secretary out to see you?"

"No."

"Damn!" she said, a hopeless look coming into her face. "This is the most disorganized place I ever worked in. She was supposed to come out and tell you he was out of town."

I looked at her. "Is he?"

"Mister," she said in a disgusted voice, "the way things are run around here, he might be the next man on the moon for all I know."

She slammed her way back into the inner office and I left. The daylight had almost gone while I was waiting and I stopped to light another cigarette on the steel landing before starting down the steps. I supposed that it had been naive to expect that Simpson would have seen me under any circumstances. Not after the way he took off from Weyman's office the other day. From beneath the steps I heard the voices of the pressmen leaving their work as I walked down.

The voice came from behind me as I reached the bottom step. "Hey, buddy, got a match?"

"Sure," I said, turning around. From the corner of my eye I caught a glimpse of a large hamlike fist coming at my face.

Instinctively I started to duck. But not fast enough. The fist exploded into my face with all the force of a trip-hammer. I felt myself begin to fall backward, a shower of sparkling lights dancing before my eyes. I shook my head groggily, trying to clear my vision.

Hands grabbed me by the shoulders and began to drag me back into the alley. Even then I didn't suspect that it was anything more than a mugging. I tried to tell them that my wallet was in my back pocket but my lips felt paralyzed and couldn't move.

I felt myself being propped against the building wall. I managed to squint at them through half-shut eyes. There were three of them but I couldn't see their faces. It was too dark.

Then the pain began. Slow. Deliberate. Methodical. And professional. In my ribs, my stomach, my guts, my balls. I slid down the wall slowly and the pain began again on my face. I felt it bursting against my ears, nose and mouth, and I could taste the warm blood pouring back into my mouth as I sank to the ground.

And still I didn't lose consciousness while they put the boot to me. There was a distant nagging thought dragging in the back of my head.

Someone had warned me to be careful. But I couldn't remember who. Somebody had said I would learn they could play rough and dirty. But I couldn't remember who.

I started to pick myself up. I got as far as my knees and was beginning to straighten up when I saw the heavy boot.

There was nothing I could do about it. It caught me under the chin and I felt myself lift into the air and somersault backward into the wall.

I was almost happy to find that night finally had come.

Chapter Eight

In the distance I heard the girl crying. "Angelo! Angelo!" I felt her warm tears spilling on my face. Slowly I fought my way up to her.

In the night her white, frightened face was very close but her features seemed blurred through my puffed and swollen eyes. I felt her arm go under my head and draw me close to her breasts. The tears kept spilling on my face as she held me there, rocking back and forth as she knelt.

"Cindy." My voice was an alien croaking sound that came from my throat. "Help me up."

"Don't move," she whispered. "You're hurt. Let me call an ambulance."

I tried to shake my head but there was too much pain. "No!" I tried to push myself up. "Take me home. My father is a doctor."

"Angelo, please."

"Help me up!"

She responded to the urgency in my voice and put an arm under my shoulders. I almost screamed when I felt the pressure against my sides as she pulled at me. It seemed like hours but she finally had me on my feet, my back supported by the building.

"Don't walk," she said. "Let me bring the car back here."

I nodded.

"Can you stand?" she asked anxiously.

"Yes," I rasped.

She looked into my face for a moment. I don't know what she saw there but a moment later she turned and I could hear her footsteps running down the alley. I didn't look after her because it hurt too much to turn.

Again time seemed to drag and there was the vacuum of space churning around in my head. Then I heard the heavy throat of the Maserati coming toward me, its bright white headlights cutting up the dark. I blinked with the pain of it.

She was a shadow coming around the car and opening the door. She came toward me. "Can you put an arm around my shoulder?" she asked.

I raised my arm and she slipped under it. I let my weight rest on her and we made the half mile to the door. She turned me around and let me slip to the seat back first, then she picked up my feet and put them in the car. Quickly she buckled the seat belt around me and let the seat back down gently until I was almost stretched out. "You all right?" she asked.

"Yes," I grunted. In the reflected light I could see bloodstains all over the front of her dress.

She closed the door and came round to the driver's side and got in. She leaned across me to press down the door lock.

"I'm sorry," I mumbled. "I ruined your dress."

She didn't answer. Instead she reversed the car out of the alley and turned back toward Michigan Avenue. "Now, where do we go?"

Very carefully and very explicitly I gave the directions to my parents' house. I felt a hole in my mouth with my tongue where some teeth used to be. I hoped at least they were caps and not some of the few I had left.

She moved onto the avenue. "Now you rest," she said.

I closed my eyes, then opened them. "How did you find me?"

Her eyes stayed on the road. "By five thirty, when you hadn't come back, I got curious. The building was completely dark and I had seen everyone go home. So I went around the back, up the stairs and tried the door. It was locked. I knocked. No answer. Then I heard you moan. I ran down the steps and found you behind the corner of the building." She stopped for a light and looked down at me. "Now, no more talking until I get you home. Rest."

I closed my eyes and sank back into the dark. I opened them again as the car came to a stop in the driveway of the house.

"I'll help you out," she said, opening my door and reaching in for me.

We managed to get my feet out of the car but I couldn't make it any further. Even with her help, the pain wouldn't let me walk. I clung to the door. "Ring the bell," I said. "Gianno will help me."

She ran up the steps and pressed the doorbell. A moment later the entrance lights came on and Gianno opened the door. All she could manage to say was my name then he was down the steps and picked me up in his arms as if I were still the baby he used to carry around.

"*DOTTORE! DOTTORE!*" he shouted at the top of his lungs as we entered the house. "Angelo, he is hurt."

My mother was the first one there. She took one look at me and clutched a fist to her mouth. "*Figlio mio!*" she cried. "What have they done to you?"

My father was right behind her. He took one look at me. "Carry him into my office," he said, his face settling into grim lines.

Gianno carried me through the house to the wing that Father used as his office when he saw patients at home. We went into the examination room and Gianno put me gently on the white table.

My father opened a cabinet and took out a syrette and hypodermic. "Call the hospital and have them send an ambulance right away," he told Gianno.

"No hospital," I said.

Gianno hesitated but my father shot a glance at him and he went right to the telephone.

"What happened?" my father asked quietly as he prepared the hypo.

"Three men worked me over," I said, watching him.

I heard my mother gasp. My father turned to her. "Mamma!" he said sternly, "you wait outside."

"But Angelo—" Her voice faltered.

"Angelo will be all right," he said firmly. "I promise you. Now wait outside." He looked past her at Cindy who was standing right behind my mother. "You too, young lady."

My mother took Cindy's arm. "You tell me everything that happened," she said as they left the room.

I looked at the needle in my father's hand. "What's that for?"

"Pain," he said. "I'm going to start cleaning you up and it's going to hurt a lot more than it does now."

"I don't want to go to sleep," I said. "I have to make some calls."

"Who do you want to call?" he asked casually looking down at me. "Maybe I can help you."

I scarcely felt the prick of the needle in my hip as my father deftly slid down my slacks and hit me with the hypo all in one practiced motion. "First I want to talk to Uncle Jake," I said.

"Uncle Jake?" he asked. I just managed to catch the note of surprise in his voice as the hypo knocked me back into dreamland.

Gianno and I were playing cowboys and Indians in the shrubbery at the side of the house. Right now I was Tom Mix and he was my faithful horse, Tony, and I was firing my six-shooter after the Indians we were chasing through the brush, just as we had seen them in *Riders of the Purple Sage* yesterday at the Saturday children's matinee.

"Whoa, Tony!" I yelled, pulling at his shirt collar as we got to the edge of the driveway. "I think I hear a covered wagon."

I jumped off his back and crouched down in the shrubs. My grandfather's giant black and tan Duesenberg came up the driveway. I waited until it had passed us, then I jumped on Gianno's shoulders. "After them!" I shouted. "We have to warn them about the Indians!"

Gianno galloped wildly up the driveway at the side of the car, holding on to my legs so that I would not fall off.

I fired my six-shooter into the air, the caps exploding and making a racket. "Look out, Grandpa!" I yelled. "The Indians are coming!"

Through the windows of the closed tonneau behind the chauffeur, I could see my grandfather. He was sitting on the back seat between two men. Another man was seated on the jump seat in front of them.

The automobile stopped in front of the house. Gianno and I waited for them on the steps as they got out. The two men who were on the back seat with my grandfather waited, leaning against the car as he and the other man came up the steps toward us.

I brandished my six-shooter in the air. "There's Indians in the hills!"

Grandfather stopped in front of us. He was not a tall man, slight, almost small; in fact Gianno, who was five foot eight, towered over him. But it made no difference. No matter who was around my grandfather, he was the big man.

He held out his hand to me. "Give me the gun, Angelo."

I looked in his eyes for signs of displeasure but I could read nothing there. They were dark brown, almost black like his hair, and unfathomable. Silently I handed down my six-shooter.

He took it in his hand and looked at it with distaste. He turned his gaze back to Gianno. "Who gave him this?"

"*Padrone*, it's only a toy." Gianno almost bowed but couldn't manage it with me on his shoulders.

"I don't care," my grandfather said in a flat voice. "I thought I said no guns. Not even toy guns. They are a bad thing for children."

This time Gianno managed to bow even with me on him. "*Si, Padrone.*"

Grandfather gave him the six-shooter. "Get rid of it," he said, then held his arms up for me. "Come, Angelo."

I slid from Gianno's shoulders into Grandfather's arms, glad that he wasn't angry with me. Grandfather kissed me as he carried me up the steps into the house. "Guns are dangerous for children to play with," he explained. "Even toy guns."

We walked into the living room where my mother and father were waiting. The moment my mother saw him, she began to cry. Awkwardly, Grandfather shifted me to one arm and put the other around Mother.

"Now, now, Jenny," he said gently. "Don't cry. Sicily is not the end of the world."

"But you're going to be so far from us," she wept.

I began to cry also. "I don't want you to go away, Grandpa!"

"Now, Jenny, you see what you did?" my Grandfather said reproachfully. "You made him cry." He turned to my father. "*Dottore*, tell your wife to stop. It's not good for Angelo to be upset like that."

My father's eyes weren't exactly clear either, so I took advantage of his momentary hesitation to let out an even greater yell.

"I don't want you to leave me, Grandpa!" I clung to him sobbing fiercely.

This one was so loud that even my mother stopped crying and looked at me. "He's getting hysterical!" she said, reaching for me.

My grandfather brushed her arms away. "I told you," he said triumphantly. "Let his grandpa handle him."

My mother fell silent as my grandfather swung me around in his arms so that he could look into my face. "I'm not leaving you, *Angelo mio*," he said. "I'm going to Sicily, to Marsala and Trapani where I was born."

I was losing ground but at least he had forgotten about the six-shooter. I tried one more yell. "I'll never see you again!"

Now the tears filled his eyes. He hugged me very tightly. I could hardly breathe. "Of course you will," he said in a choked voice. "In the summer you can come to visit me with your mamma and papa and I will show you the vineyards and the olive groves on the side of Mount Erice where your grandpa grew up."

"Can we play cowboys and Indians there?" I asked, my eyes round.

"No, that's a bad game," he said. "All games are bad where you play at killing people. You be like your father, a doctor, where you can save people, not kill them." He looked at me, not quite sure that I understood him. "Besides there are no Indians in Sicily," he added.

"Only good guys?" I asked.

He knew when he was licked. "There are only good guys in Sicily," he said, giving up and resorting to his ultimate weapon. Bribery. "Besides Grandpa is going to send you a very special present when he gets there."

"What kind of present?" I wanted to know.

"Anything you want. Just tell your grandpa."

I thought for a moment. I remembered the movie Gianno and I had seen the week before. It was with Monte Blue and he played a daredevil race car driver. "A real race car that I can drive?" I asked tentatively.

"If that's what my Angelo wants, that's what he'll get. I'll have a special Bugatti race built for you!"

I squeezed my arms around his neck. "Thank you, Grandpa." I kissed him.

He turned to my parents. "See," he said triumphantly. "I told you. He's perfectly all right now."

All the while this was going on, the man who had come in with us was watching and kind of smiling to himself. Now my grandfather waved him forward. "Jake, come here."

"This is my son, Dr. John Perino," my grandfather said proudly. "And his wife, Jenny. This is Judge Jacob Weinstein who I told you about."

Judge Weinstein, a brown-haired man about my father's height and age, shook hands with my parents.

"Don't forget me," I said, holding out my hand.

He turned, smiling, and took my hand. "I don't think I can," he said.

"I made a lifetime contract with Jake to look after family business affairs while I'm away," Grandfather said. He put me down. "Now you go and play while your father and the Judge and me talk a little business."

"Come with me to the kitchen," my mother said quickly. "I just baked some cookies. You can have them with a glass of milk."

She took my hand and began to lead me to the door. I pulled her to a stop and looked back. "Will I see you again before you go away, Grandpa?"

Grandfather caught his breath and I saw his eyes go misty again. He nodded. "Before I go," he managed to say.

About an hour later, we stood on the steps in front of the house and waved good-bye to my grandfather as the big Duesenberg started down the driveway. I saw him looking back at me through the rear window and I waved again to him. He raised his hand and then the car turned out of sight at the end of the driveway.

We stood there a moment, then I looked up at my parents. "Those men waiting for Grandpa were wearing guns under their coats," I said. "I wonder if they know Grandpa doesn't like guns."

My mother and father stared at each other for a long moment then my mother's eyes filled with tears again. My father picked me up with one arm and put the other around her. We stood there silently like that on the steps in front of the house for a long time while my mother hid her face against my father's chest. I looked at my father. There were unshed tears in his eyes too. I felt a strange lump come up in my throat. There were so many things I did not understand.

But in the time to come I would learn many of them. Like those two men that waited for Grandfather were federal agents who were to escort him to New York where he would board a ship for Italy.

Like Judge Weinstein, or Uncle Jake as I came to know him, wasn't really a judge at all but an attorney in charge of all his business affairs.

For many years thereafter, almost until the time I left for college, Uncle Jake was a once-monthly visitor at our house for Sunday dinners.

Then shortly after I was twenty-one and I was down from MIT early in January 1952, I found out how rich a man my grandfather had really been. By that time, my share of his estate had grown under Uncle Jake's prudent management to more than twenty-five million dollars and my parents' share was twice that.

I remember looking at my father and Uncle Jake in complete bewilderment. I knew we were well off. I didn't know we were rich. "What do I do with all that money?" I asked.

"You'd better learn," my father said seriously. "Because some day you're going to have all of it."

"I'd suggest you go to Harvard Business School when you graduate," said Uncle Jake.

"But I'm not interested in business," I said. "I'm interested in automobiles."

"Automobiles are a business too," Uncle Jake said.

"Not my kind," I said. "All they do is cost money."

"Well, at least you can afford that," Uncle Jake smiled.

"I don't need all that," I said.

"Then I suggest you set up an investment trust at the bank and let them manage it," Uncle Jake said.

I looked at him. "Why can't you just keep on with it the way you have?" I asked. "I remember Grandfather said he gave you a lifetime contract. If it's good enough for him, it's good enough for me."

He glanced at my father. "I'm sorry," he said, turning to me. "I can't do it."

"Why?"

He cleared his throat. "Because of certain other business activities of mine which the government says are allied with organized crime, I feel it's wiser to cut you loose rather than chance the possibility of having you and your parents involved in something none of you have anything to do with."

I knew what he was talking about. I read the newspapers too. His name had come up very often in connection with investigations into organized crime. "But can we still call on you if we ever have a problem?" I asked. "A real problem, I mean."

He nodded. "Of course you can. After all, your grandfather did give me a lifetime contract." He got to his feet. "Everything's pretty much set up at the bank, John," he said to my father, "perhaps you and Angelo can come downtown tomorrow. We can have lunch, then go over to the bank, sign a few papers and make it official."

We did that and when I went back to school I got a subscription to the *Wall Street Journal* and for a while religiously checked the market every day against the list of stocks and securities that the bank held for me. But then it got to be a bore and I stopped looking at it entirely, just depending on the bank's quarterly statements to keep me up to date. And most of the time, they wound up in my drawer unopened. After all, how wrong could I go when I started with twenty-five million dollars in blue chips?

Uncle Jake didn't entirely lose his fight with the government, but the following year he gave up his practice and moved to Las Vegas where he had interests in several hotels. We exchanged Christmas cards and once in a while when he came East my parents would see him, but I was always somewhere else. Then just a few years ago I read in the papers that he had sold his interests in Las Vegas and had moved near Phoenix, Arizona, where he embarked on a large program of land development tied to a sport and spa hotel and country club complex called Paradise Springs. I remembered receiving an invitation from him to attend the grand opening of the resort, but as that was about the time I had begun working for Number One I couldn't attend. Mother and Father, however, did go and carried with them my explanation and regrets and good wishes. Mother loved it, and my parents had returned there several times a year since. Father told me that Uncle Jake looked relaxed and content for the first time since he had known him and had gone brown-as-berry native, even to the extent of wearing a white ten-gallon Stetson out on the links for his morning round of golf.

In the time that passed I had learned many things, but of all of them perhaps the greatest regret was that I never got to see my grandfather again. It took him almost two years to get me the Bugatti that he had promised, but it finally came. And a year later so did the war in Europe and he wrote my parents not to come to visit as he did not want them to take any chances with me. Then we were in the war and for almost two years we heard nothing until the American troops landed in Italy.

But then, it was too late. My grandfather had died of cancer the year before.

Chapter Nine

I opened my eyes to the sunlight streaming into a room filled with flowers. I moved my head slightly. No pain. I grew bold. It hurt like hell. "Damn!" I said.

The nurse who had been sitting in the corner of the room got to her feet. Her uniform rustled as she came to the bed and looked down at me. "You're awake," she said.

I already knew that. "What day is this?"

"Thursday."

"What happened to Wednesday?" I asked.

"You slept," she answered, reaching for the telephone. She dialed a number. I heard the faint crackle of an answering voice. "Will you please page Dr. Perino and tell him that 503 is awake. Thank you.

"Your father is on his rounds but he wanted to be notified the moment you awoke," she explained.

"What time is it?"

"Ten o'clock," she said. "How do you feel?"

"I don't know," I answered. "And I'm afraid to find out."

The door opened and my father came into the room. No Anglo-Saxon bullshit with us, we were Italian. Doctor he might be but he was my father first. We kissed on the lips. "Mother and Cindy are on the way up from the coffee shop," he said.

"Before they get here, how bad is it?"

"You've had worse," he said. "A couple of broken ribs, numerous and heavy body bruises and contusions, but no internal injuries as far as we can determine, mild concussion, you'll have headaches for a while." He paused. "They did make a mess of your face though. Undid all the work you had done in Switzerland. Broken nose in two places, there's a slight crack in your jawbone, not too serious— it will heal practically by itself. I figure you lost about five teeth, mostly caps, and it looks like they shifted your right cheekbone a little, but we can't tell until the swelling goes down. Cuts over the eyes and around the mouth. All in all, not too bad."

"Thank you, Doctor, I said. I reached for his hand and kissed it. Like I said, we were Italian. When I looked up at him there were tears in his eyes.

Then the door opened and Mother and Cindy came in and my father had his hands full for the next ten minutes trying to keep Mother from crying all over me.

Cindy stood there at the foot of the bed, almost shyly watching us. I think it was the first time she had ever seen an Italian family in action. It really was something to see.

Finally when Mother had kissed practically every part of me, including my feet, she straightened up. "Cindy, come here," she said. "Angelo wants to thank you."

My mother turned back to me. "She's a good girl, your friend. She saved your life and brought you home to us. I thanked her a thousand times. Now, you thank her."

Cindy leaned over me and kissed my cheek chastely. I returned her kiss, equally chaste on her cheek. "Thank you," I said gravely.

"You're very welcome," she said formally.

"Now, that's a good boy, Angelo," my mother said proudly.

Cindy and I had all we could do to keep from breaking up. We didn't dare look at each other.

"Who sent all the flowers?" I asked.

"The story about your mugging was in all the papers," Cindy said. "They started arriving yesterday. Number One, Duncan, Rourke, Bancroft. Even Number Three and Weyman sent flowers."

"Angelo has good friends," my mother said proudly.

"Yeah," I said dryly, looking at Cindy.

"Number One called you from Palm Beach," Cindy said. "He said not to worry. He would see you on Monday when he came up here."

Suddenly it all came back to me. Monday was only five days away. I had lost one precious day of time sleeping. I looked up at my father. "How long do I stay in here?"

"I figure over the weekend," he answered. "If everything checks out all right we could let you go Monday or Tuesday."

"If I left the hospital for one day and then came back would I do any damage?" My father studied me. "Is it that important?"

"Yes. This was no mugging and you know it. Nobody took my watch or wallet."

He also knew a professional beating when he saw one. You didn't practice in Detroit hospitals for over forty years without learning about that. He was silent.

"There's something I must do," I said. "It's the only chance I have to keep them from taking the company away from Number One."

A strange expression came to my father's face. "You mean old Mr. Hardeman?" I nodded.

He thought for a moment. "You'll come back within one day?"

"Yes."

"You'll be in agony every minute," he said.

"Give me some pills."

"All right." He took a deep breath. "I'll give you one day. I have your word. You'll be back."

"No!" Mother cried "You mustn't let him! He'll hurt himself!" She started for me, crying. "My baby!"

My father held out his arm to stop her. "Jenny!" he said sternly.

Mother looked at him in surprise. It was a tone that I doubt she had ever heard from him.

"Leave men's work to men!" Father said.

Sicilian women know where it's at. "Yes, John," my mother said meekly. She looked at me but spoke to him. "He'll be careful?"

"He'll be careful," my father said.

I woke up the next time in the cabin of the big, chartered DC–9. The stewardess was looking at me, Gianno standing next to her.

"We'll be landing in Phoenix in fifteen minutes, Mr. Perino," she said.

"Raise me up," I told Gianno.

He bent down beside the stretcher bed and turned the crank, raising the back of the bed until I was in a half-reclining position. "That okay, Angelo?"

"Fine," I said. The afternoon sun was brighter at thirty thousand feet here than it was in Detroit. The seat belt sign went on with a pinging sound.

Gianno bent over me to tighten the straps. That done he checked the floor locks on the bed. Satisfied, he returned to his seat and fastened his belt. The stewardess went forward to the pilot's cabin.

I leaned back with a good feeling. Father really had it all arranged. It had begun that morning when I asked Cindy to check the flights to Phoenix while I put in a call to Uncle Jake.

"Forget it," Father said. "I'll take care of everything."

"But I have to get to Phoenix today."

"You will. You just rest. I'll call Jake and get you to Phoenix today."

"But how are you going to do it?"

"Stop worrying," he smiled. "It's time you learned there are some advantages to being rich."

After he had gone, Cindy came over to the bed. She stood next to Mother who was seated in a chair watching my every motion with an eagle eye. "I think I'll go back to the hotel and get some sleep," she said. "I'm beat."

"I don't want you to go back to the hotel. They know you were with me and I don't want anything to happen to you."

"Nothing will happen to me," she said.

"That's what I thought."

"Cindy can stay at our house," Mother said quickly. "She can have the guest room she had last night."

I looked at Cindy. She nodded. "I don't want anyone to know where you are."

"Okay," she said. "I'll tell Duncan to keep it quiet."

"No, you'll tell him nothing. You won't even call him or anybody else for that matter. I don't trust any of the telephones in the plant."

"But I promised to let him know how you are," she said.

"The hospital will give him the information. You just keep out of sight until I give you the word."

"She'll do what you say, Angelo," Mother said. "Won't you, Cindy?"

"Yes," Cindy answered.

"See?" Mother said triumphantly. "I told you she was a good girl. Now don't worry about her. I'll take care of her every minute. Nobody will know where she is."

I could see the beginning of a smile come to Cindy's lips. But it wasn't a funny ha-ha smile. It was the kind of smile you have when you find a friend.

I nodded my head. "Thank you, Mamma."

My father came back into the room. "Well, it's all arranged," he said obviously pleased with himself. "I spoke to Jake and he'll meet you in his office at five o'clock."

He really did have it arranged. A private ambulance took me from the hospital to the airport where it rolled right onto the field up to the chartered jet. Gianno rode with me and in the plane made sure that the stretcher bed was securely locked into place. Five minutes after we were airborne, he came over to me, a hypo in his hand.

"What's that?" I asked.

"Sleep shot," he said. "The *Dottore* wants you to rest until you get to Phoenix."

"I'll rest," I said.

"The *Dottore* said if you give me trouble I turn the plane back to Detroit."

"Okay," I said wearily. "Hit me."

Father taught him well. I think I was asleep before he got the needle out of my ass.

There was an ambulance waiting on the tarmac when the big plane rolled to a stop. Thirty-five minutes later we pulled into Paradise Springs. I had to say one thing for it. It was a hell of a way to beat the traffic problem.

We were directed to the private entrance to Uncle Jake's office. It was through a screened-in garden facing the golf course.

Uncle Jake was behind his desk in the large, wood-paneled room. Logs crackled in the fireplace, fighting a losing battle against the air-conditioning.

Uncle Jake saw me looking at it, as Gianno cranked up the bed. He got out of his chair and walked toward me, his snow-white Stetson startling against the dark wood walls. "This air-conditioning is so goddamn efficient in here that sometimes I find myself freezing," he said. "And I'm still enough of an Easterner to like a log fire at which to warm my hands."

I smiled at him. "Hello, Uncle Jake." I held out my hand.

He took it. His grip was as strong and friendly as it had always been. "Hello, Angelo." He turned to Gianno. "Good to see you again, Gianno."

Gianno bowed. "Good to see you, *Eccellenza*." He moved to the door and left the office.

Uncle Jake turned back to me when the door had closed. He pulled a chair from in front of the desk and sat down, looking at me. "Do you always travel like this?" he smiled.

"No." I laughed. "Only when I'm too tired to get out of bed."

"Your father told me you really caught it," he said, still smiling. "You should have learned to duck."

"I did," I said. "Right into a kick in the teeth."

The smile left his face. The drooping, heavy lids over his large eyes, the large, curved, roman nose almost reaching the center of his upper lip above his wide, thin-lipped mouth and pointed, dimpled chin, all combined to give him the dangerous, hooded look of a hunting falcon. "Who did it?" he asked.

"I don't know," I said, deliberately pausing for a moment. "But I can guess."

"Tell me."

I went through the whole story from the beginning. From the very first call I got from Number One almost three years before. I left nothing out, business or personal, because that's the way I knew he would want it and that's the way it had to be. An hour and a half later I came to the end of my story with the conversation I had with my father that morning.

He was a good listener, interrupting me only a few times to clarify a hazy point. Now he got to his feet and stretched. He was in fantastic shape for a man in his late sixties; physically he looked more like a man in his fifties, and not late fifties at that. "I could use a drink," he said.

"So could I."

"What will be your pleasure?"

"Canadian on the rocks."

He laughed. "Your father said you would ask for that, but all I'm allowed to give you is two ounces of cognac neat."

"Father knows best."

There was a bar hidden in the wall which came out at the touch of a button. He poured cognac into two snifters and gave me one.

"Cheers," I said. The cognac burned its way down my throat. I coughed and winced as the pain ran through my side.

"You're supposed to sip it, not gulp it," he said. He sipped his drink. After a moment he looked down at me. "Okay, now that I've heard your story, exactly what do you want from me?"

"Help," I said simply.

"In what way?"

"There are two things I want you to do. If you can. One is to find out where Simpson got the money to push his campaign against us. If he got it legitimately, good and well, I'll forget about it. But if it came in any way from someone in our company, I want to know it.

"Two, I want that suicide note that Loren III has in his home safe."

"What good do you expect that to do you?"

"I don't know," I said. "I just have a hunch it may be the key to all of this if I can get it out into the open."

"You're not asking for very much, are you?" Without waiting for me to reply. "A little bit of detective work and a little bit of safecracking, that's all."

I didn't say anything.

"How much time do we have?" he asked.

"Until Monday night," I answered. "I need the information for the stockholders' meeting on Tuesday morning. That's our last chance."

"You know you're asking me to participate in an illegal act with full, prior knowledge," he said. "That's something I've never done. I've been a lawyer all my life and the only thing I've ever done was defend my clients to the best of my ability after they committed the act."

"I know that," I said.

"And you still ask me to do what you want?"

"Yes."

"Why?"

"You're a lawyer, you shouldn't have to ask that question," I said, looking steadily at him. "You made a lifetime contract with my grandfather to handle my business affairs. And this is my business."

He thought for a moment, then he nodded. "You're right. I'll see what can be done. But I'm not promising anything. My contacts in Detroit may not be as good as they used to be."

"That's good enough for me, Uncle Jake," I said. "Thank you."

He looked at his watch. "Time I got you back on the plane. It's after seven and I promised your father you would be on your way by then."

"I'll be all right," I said. But I wasn't. The pain was beginning to dance around inside me.

"Where will you be nine o'clock Monday night?" Uncle Jake asked.

"Either the hospital or home," I answered. "Depends on what Papa will let me do."

"Okay," he said. "At nine o'clock, Monday night, wherever you are, someone will contact you. They will either have what you want or tell you they haven't."

"Good enough."

He walked to the door and opened it. Gianno was standing just outside. "Okay, Gianno," he said. "Take him back."

"*Si, Eccelenza.*" Gianno took a small metal box from his breast pocket. He tore the wrapper from the disposable syringe and began filling it from a small vial.

"I can understand why your father let you come to see me while you're like this," Uncle Jake said. "But I don't see why you're doing it, what you're getting out of it."

"Money for one thing. That stock could be worth ten million dollars someday."

"That's not it," he said. "You have five times that by now and you never paid attention to it. There has to be another reason."

"Maybe it's because I gave my word to the old man that we would build a new car. And I don't consider the job done until that car comes off the assembly line."

He looked at me. There was approval in his voice. "That's more like it."

Then I had a question to ask him. Something that had been puzzling me. "You said you knew why Papa let me come down here. Why did he?"

"I thought you knew," he said. "It was old Mr. Hardeman who got your father into the hospital as a resident after every one of them had turned him down because he was your grandfather's son."

"Turn on your side a little bit," Gianno said.

Automatically I did as he asked, still looking up at Uncle Jake. I felt the faint jab in my buttock.

Uncle Jake began to smile. "The wheel never stops turning, does it?" Then right in front of my eyes he began to disappear.

That had to be one of the world's greatest shots. I slept all the way from Uncle Jake's office in Phoenix until nine o'clock the next morning when I awoke in my hospital bed in Detroit.

Chapter Ten

By Saturday afternoon in the hospital, I was going coo-coo. The aches and pains had subsided enough so that I could handle them with an abundance of aspirin, and I paced up and down my room like a caged animal. I flipped channels on television and spun the radio dial until it came off in my hand. Finally the nurse fled the room and came back ten minutes later with my father.

He looked at me calmly. "What's the matter?"

"I want out!"

"Okay," he said.

"You can't keep me in here any more," I said, not listening to him. "I've had it!"

"If you'd pay attention instead of running off at the mouth," my father said, "you'd know I said 'okay.' "

I stared at him. "You mean it?"

"Get dressed," he said. "I'll be back to pick you up in about fifteen minutes. As soon as I finish my rounds."

"What about my bandages?"

"You'll have to keep your ribs taped for a few more weeks, but I'll be able to replace your head and face bandages with a couple of Band-Aids." He smiled. "I'm really very pleased. I just saw your X-rays and lab reports of this morning. You're fine. Now we'll give Mamma's miracle drug, pasta, a chance to do a little work on you."

Of course Mamma cried when I came home. And so did Gianno and my father. I looked over my mother's head at Cindy. Even she stood there, tears welling in her eyes.

I grinned at her. "I see Mamma's been giving you instructions on how to become Italian."

She made a face and turned away. When she turned back, she was fine. "Also spaghetti sauce," she said. "We've been in the kitchen ever since this morning when your father told us he was bringing you home."

I looked at him. "At least you could have told me, Papa."

He smiled. "I wanted to check the reports first just to be sure."

"Gianno, you help him upstairs," my mother said.

"*Si, Signora.*"

"Undress him and get him right into bed," she continued. "I want him to rest until it's time for dinner."

"Mamma I'm not a baby," I protested. "I can manage myself."

My mother ignored me. "Gianno, don't pay any attention to him," she said firmly. "Go with him."

I started up the steps, Gianno following me.

"And don't let him smoke in bed," my mother added. "He'll set himself on fire."

By the time I got to bed, I knew I wasn't as strong as I thought I was. I was grateful for Gianno's help. I fell right asleep.

Cindy came by before dinner just in time to catch Mother forcing a shot glass full of Fernet Branca down my throat.

I swallowed about half of it, almost gagging at the lousy taste it left in my mouth. I made a face. "That's enough!"

"You'll drink it all," she insisted. "It will do you more good than all those little pills."

I stood there stubbornly, the shot glass in my hand. My mother turned to Cindy. "You make him finish it," she said. "I have to go down to the kitchen and start the water for the pasta." She went to the door and stopped there. "You make sure that he finishes it before he comes down for dinner."

"Yes, Mrs. Perino," Cindy said obediently. My mother went down the hall and Cindy turned back to me. "You heard your mother," she said with a smile. "Finish it."

"She's something, isn't she? Her trouble is that she really believes it when I tell her that a boy's best friend is his mother."

"I've never met anyone like her," Cindy said with a sound of envy in her voice. "Or like your father either. The money they have doesn't affect them at all. All they care about is each other. And you. They're real people."

"I still won't drink this shit."

"You'll drink it," she said, looking into my eyes. "Just to make her happy."

I swallowed the rest of the Fernet Branca in one gulp. I grimaced, giving her the glass. "Oh, God. It's really awful."

She didn't say anything, still looking into my eyes.

I shook my head in wonder. "My mother's really done a number on you, hasn't she?"

"You don't know how lucky you are," she said seriously. "My family's got more money than yours. Much more. And my mother and father never even seemed to know I was alive."

I looked, surprised. She had never talked about her family before.

"Did you ever hear of Morris Mining?" she asked suddenly.

I nodded. Of course I had. Now I knew why money never seemed to matter to her. It was one of the blue chips. Right up there with Kennecott Copper, Anaconda and the Three M Company. I even owned a thousand shares.

"My father's chairman of the board. My brother's president. He's fifteen years older than me. I was a change-of-life baby and I always had the feeling that they were embarrassed by my arrival. Anyway, they shipped me off to all the best schools as soon as they could. Once I was five years old I wasn't around the house very much."

I thought of my own childhood and how different it had been from hers. She was right. I was lucky. I held up my hands in surrender. "Okay, baby, I'll confess. I love them very much."

"You don't have to tell me," she said. "I know you do. You came right home when you were hurt. All my life I kept running away when I was hurt."

There was a knock on the open door. Gianno came into the room. "*La Signora* sent me to help you dress and bring you downstairs."

I straightened up in bed, smoothing the covers over my legs and smiling up at Cindy.

She knew what I was thinking. Mother had really done her number.

Dinner was more than an hour away. There was no rush to dress. But good girls don't spend too much time in Italian boys' bedrooms. It's not proper.

At dinner, I found out much to my surprise I was ravenous. Mother had really turned it on for me. The pasta was just the way I like it. Al dente. Cooked firm and not soft and mushy. And the sauce had everything in it. Hot sausage, sweet sausage, green peppers browned slightly first in oil, tiny meatballs blended delicately with finely chopped pork, quartered Italian tomatoes cooked into a rich red sauce with just the right touch of oregano and garlic. There was only one fault. As usual it was too sweet. It is very Sicilian to add a lot of sugar.

But I put it away like food was going out of style. I was too hungry to get finicky.

Mother looked at me proudly. "You like the sauce?"

I nodded, my mouth full. "Great!"

"She made it," my mother said. "All by herself."

I looked at Cindy wondering if I could tell her that if Mother gave her another shot at it to go easy on the sugar. Cindy's own words blew that thought to hell.

"Your mother is just being kind," she said. "All I did was to put what she handed me into the pot and stir once in a while."

I should have guessed that. "It's very good anyway," I said.

"A few weeks with me," Mother said, "and I'll make a real Sicilian cook out of her."

The pasta was better than sleeping pills. I found my eyes closing a half hour after dinner, right in the middle of my mother's favourite television show. I went to sleep.

The next morning was Sunday and the usual routine was that the whole family, including Gianno, went to ten o'clock mass. This Sunday the routine was changed because my mother didn't want to leave me alone in the house.

Gianno went to nine o'clock mass and when he returned, my parents went to the ten o'clock. Much to my surprise when I went looking for Cindy, Gianno told me with a secret, knowing smile lurking in his eyes that she had gone to mass with them.

I went back to my room, mumbling to myself. It was then I knew I was really getting better. I was horny as hell. But Mother was operating in really top form.

I must have dozed off again, for when I opened my eyes, my father was standing over the bed, looking down at me.

He bent and kissed my forehead. "I thought if you were feeling up to it, we'd go down to my office and I'd take the bandages off."

"I'm ready," I said.

I sat, my legs dangling from the examination table, while he snipped carefully at the bandages around my head. Then, as gently as he could, he peeled the adhesive that held my nose bandage and lifted it off. He was just as cautious with the adhesive and bandage on my cheek-bone, the side of my chin, and over my left ear.

He picked up a bottle and poured some of the liquid over a wad of cotton. "This is going to sting a bit," he said, "but I want to clean you up."

It was the usual professional understatement. It stung like hell. But he was quick about it. When he finished he peered at me critically.

"It's not too bad," he said judiciously. "When you have some time, you can jump over to Switzerland. Dr. Hans can make it right again without too much trouble."

I got off the table and looked at myself in the mirror over the sink on the wall. A very familiar face looked back at me.

Suddenly I felt good. I was myself again. All the time I had the other face I had been someone else. Now my eyes didn't look old any more. They belonged to the rest of my face.

"Hello, Angelo," I whispered.

My face whispered back at me. "Hello, Angelo."

"What did you say?" my father asked.

I turned to look at him. "I'm not going back to Dr. Hans," I said. "I think I'll keep this face. It's mine."

I woke up jumpy as a cat Monday morning. And it didn't get any better. Especially after I read the morning newspapers.

It was a page one story and picture. The photo showed a gutted mass of what used to be a building. The headline above it was simple.

MYSTERIOUS EXPLOSION AND FIRE DESTROYS
MICHIGAN AVENUE PRINT SHOP AND BUILDING

I almost didn't have to read the rest of the story to know what had happened. Shortly after midnight, last night, two violent explosions that shattered windows as far as three blocks away, followed by a flash fire of intense heat, took the Mark S. Printing Company, the IASO, and forty late-model used cars on Simp's used car lot next door out of circulation permanently. When attempts were made to reach Mr. Mark Simpson, the proprietor of all three businesses at home, they were informed that Mr. Simpson was away and could not be reached. Police and the fire department arson squads were conducting an investigation into the circumstances surrounding the occurrence. Fortunately there was no one on the premises and no injuries were reported.

That news didn't exactly add to my comfort. I wondered whether Uncle Jake's contacts hadn't gone a little overboard in their enthusiasm. Then I pushed the thought from my mind. If Uncle Jake didn't know what he was doing, then nobody did.

Still the jumpiness didn't leave me. It got worse and worse as the day seemed to drag on. I went upstairs and tried to sleep but my eyes wouldn't stay shut. So I went downstairs again.

I turned to a pro football game on the tube. But my head wasn't into it. I sat there staring at it blindly, smoking cigarette after cigarette. Finally I turned it off in disgust and went back upstairs and stretched out on my bed, my arms on the pillow behind my head, and stared up at the ceiling.

I heard my door open. I didn't look around. My father stood over me. I didn't speak.

"You're in no condition to get yourself all worked up like that," he said.

"I can't help it."

"Let me give you a shot so you can get some sleep," he suggested.

"No."

"Then let me give you a couple of tranquilizers. They'll calm you down."

"Leave me alone, Papa."

Silently he turned and started from the room. I sat up in the bed, swinging my feet to the floor. "Papa!"

He turned, his hand on the door.

"I'm sorry, Papa."

He nodded. "That's all right, Angelo," he said and left the room.

I had no appetite for dinner and picked my way through the meal where no one talked. After dinner I went back to my room. At eight thirty I went downstairs and sat alone in the living room. From the den I could hear the sounds coming from the television set. At eight forty-five, the telephone rang. I dove for it.

It was Donald, Number One's man. "Mr. Perino?"

"Yes," I answered, disappointed that it was not the call I expected.

"Mr. Hardeman asked me to find out if you'll be able to attend the stockholders' and board meetings tomorrow," he said.

"I'll be there," I answered.

"Thank you, I'll inform him," he said. "Good night."

"Wait a minute!" I said quickly. "Can I speak to Mr. Hardeman?"

"I'm sorry, sir," he said, "but Mr. Hardeman is already asleep. We had to make a special stop in Pensacola and have just arrived. Mr. Hardeman was very tired and went right to bed."

"All right, Donald. Thank you," I said, putting down the telephone. I didn't know how the old man did it. He had to be made of ice to be able to sleep at a time like this.

But then what was it that I had read once. General U.S. Grant used to take a nap just before every big battle. He claimed that and whiskey freshened him up for the fight.

Maybe I couldn't sleep but the whiskey didn't seem like a bad idea. I looked at my watch. Five minutes to nine. I started for the bar.

I was on my second shot at exactly nine o'clock when the front doorbell rang. I heard Gianno start for it but I beat him to the door and opened it.

A man stood there in the shadows, his hat pulled down and his coat collar up. I couldn't see his face. "Mr. Angelo Perino?"

"Yes," I answered.

"This is for you," he said thrusting a large red manila envelope into my hand. "Compliments of the Judge!"

"Thank you," I said. But he had already gone down the steps and into a car which sped down the driveway.

I closed the door and walked slowly back into the living room, untying the flat ribbon that closed the envelope. Inside were two file folders.

I sank into the couch and opened them. The first was the letter I had asked him to get from Loren's safe. I read it quickly. It was almost word for word what Bobbie had told me. I put it back into the file and opened the other one.

This was everything I wanted and more. Names, dates, places, everything. Even photostats of the checks he received as well as his disbursements. Simpson had to be a nut for keeping records. It was either that or he had plans for blackmail at some future date. And from what I knew about him so far, it had to be the latter.

Suddenly I looked up. They were all standing there, watching me anxiously. My father, mother and Cindy. Even Gianno was in the doorway looking on.

"Was it what you wanted?" my father asked.

I broke into a smile. Suddenly the heaviness that was in the air all day was gone. I jumped up, kissed my father, kissed Cindy and began to dance my mother around. "Hey, Papa!" I said, looking over my shoulder at him. "Who says Grandfather isn't watching over us?"

My mother stopped dancing and crossed herself. "He's up there in heaven with the angels," she said solemnly. "Looking after his children."

Chapter Eleven

It was impossible for me to drive with my ribs still taped, so Cindy dropped me at the administration building at eight thirty in the morning. "Shall I come back for you?" she asked.

I caught my breath. It wasn't that easy getting out of a Maserati with a couple of broken ribs. "No," I said. "You go back to the hotel. I'll grab a cab and pick you up for dinner when I get through."

"Good enough," she smiled. She held out her fist in a thumbs-up gesture.

I grinned and gave it back to her and she spun off down the road. I went into the building and directly to my office. My secretary wasn't in yet, which was just as well. I sat down at her desk, put a sheet of paper in her typewriter and began knocking out a few notes.

I had just finished when she came in at ten to nine. I pulled the last note out of the machine, signed it and stuck it in my inside pocket.

"How are you feeling, Mr. Perino?" she asked. "Better?"

"Much better."

"We were all so shocked when we heard what happened," she said.

"No more than I was," I picked up my attaché case and started for the door. "I'm going to Number One's office."

"Don't forget you have the stockholders' meeting at nine o'clock."

"I won't," I said, as if I needed the reminder.

Number One had not arrived as yet. "He'll be a little late," his secretary said. "He had to make one stop before he came in."

I went back to my office, had a cup of coffee and, exactly at nine o'clock, went down to the board room for the meeting. The room was crowded, they were all there. Except Number One.

Loren III rapped a gavel on the table. The conversation in the room stopped. "I have just been informed that my grandfather will be a few minutes late," he said. "While we are waiting for him, I will explain briefly a few procedural changes that have been instituted solely for the meetings today of the stockholders and the directors. These changes have been explained to my grandfather and he is in accord with them."

He paused for a moment, his eyes glancing around the table. I didn't think he recognized me at first glance because his eyes came back for a flash second look, then went on, but I couldn't be sure.

"Both stockholders and directors have been invited to attend both meetings," he said. "At the stockholders' meeting, those directors who are not stockholders will retire from the table to the seats provided for them around the room. Seated at the table with the direct stockholders will also be those trustees of the Hardeman Foundation who will today vote the stock in the company held by the Foundation. I would like to introduce to the general company those trustees of the Foundation present other than myself."

He paused for a moment. "My sister, the Princess Anne Elizabeth Alekhine."

Anne, looking every bit the princess in a chic, tailored Parisian suit, nodded regally, then sat back in her place at her brother's right hand.

"I might also add," Loren said "that my sister will also vote the stock she holds in the company in her own name."

He gestured with his hand. "Seated on her right is Dr. James Randolph, executive director of the Foundation, and on his right, Professor William Mueller, administrative director of the Foundation. Stockholders will also be entitled to have legal counsel seated next to them at the table if they should so desire."

He paused again for a moment. "For the board of directors' meeting, the exact opposite will hold. That is, those stockholders who are not directors of the company will retire from the table so that the directors may proceed without delay and interference to the business of the company for which the meeting has been called.

"If the nonstockholding directors will now retire from the table, we will be able to proceed with the stockholders' meeting as soon as my grandfather arrives."

A shuffling sound rose in the room as the crowd rearranged themselves. When it died down, there were only five of us left at the table: Loren III, Anne, the two Foundation trustees and myself.

I sat alone at the opposite end of the table from them. Loren looked at me but didn't speak. There was a thousand yards of open battlefield between us. A low hum rose from the other seats around the room. I couldn't help but feel that we were like gladiators in an ancient Roman arena.

Silence fell abruptly across the room as the door began to open. Number One came through first, his arms pushing the wheelchair over the threshold vigorously. Behind him came Alicia, a tall, gray-haired, striking woman whom I did not know, and Artie Roberts.

Number One paused for a second, looking around the room then propelled his chair to the table. Artie pulled a chair away so that the wheelchair would have a place. Number One gestured to the women and they took seats at the table next to him. Artie sat down in the chair directly behind Number One.

Loren III's face was pale as he stared angrily at his grandfather. Anne got to her feet quickly and came down the table toward Number One. Reluctantly, Loren followed her.

Anne stopped at the gray-haired woman and kissed her warmly on the cheek. The surprise was clear in her voice. "Mother! I didn't expect to see you. You should have let us know you were coming!"

Now I knew who the striking lady was. Admiral Hugh Scott's wife. No wonder Loren III was so angry at his grandfather. Bringing to the meeting both his mother and his ex-wife.

Anne greeted Alicia with a peck on the cheek and a "Nice to see you again," pecked Number One on the cheek silently, then made her way back to her seat.

Loren was much more reserved. He kissed his mother's cheek politely, nodded silently to Alicia, ignored his grandfather and went back to his seat.

He picked up the gavel and rapped smartly on the table. "The meeting of the stockholders of the Bethlehem Motors Company, Inc., is hereby called to order." He glanced down at his grandfather. "Before we commence the business before this meeting, the chair questions the right and propriety of the seating of Mrs. Scott and the former Mrs. Hardeman at this meeting. It is the contention of the chair that they have no interest, proprietary or otherwise, in this company that would permit their seating, since the chair already holds the proxy of Mrs. Hardeman to vote at its discretion and Mrs. Scott has no interest whatsoever in this company that the chair is aware of."

Artie leaned forward, putting a paper in Alicia's hand and whispering in her ear. She nodded and rose to her feet. "Mr. Chairman!"

"Yes, Mrs. Hardeman," Loren answered formally.

With Artie whispering behind her, Alicia spoke in a thin, clear voice. "I beg to submit, for the consideration of the chair, this notice of revocation by me of the proxy previously given it and the return to me of the voting privileges contained therein." She placed the paper on the table pushing it toward her former husband, and sat down.

Loren picked up the paper and looked at it. He turned and handed it to Dan Weyman, sitting behind him, who passed it on in turn to the company counsel. Loren began to speak without waiting. "It seems to me that this revocation is illegal and contrary to a contracted agreement and is therefore invalid at this meeting."

Artie leaned forward and whispered rapidly into Alicia's ear. Alicia leaned forward; this time she did not get up. "This stockholder is willing to agree to an adjournment of this meeting until the question is settled in court. It would seem to me that the rights of this stockholder to vote her own stock are no less valid than the right claimed by the chair for the Foundation under similar circumstances on which a judgement has already been rendered and accepted by all parties concerned."

Loren turned in his chair and whispered to the company counsel. After a moment, he turned back. He shrugged his shoulders contemptuously. It was only five per cent. He still held a clear majority, with the inclusion of the Foundation stock. Fifty-four percent. "The chair will concede the revocation," he said. "But the chair still objects to the presence of Mrs. Scott."

This time Number One threw a sheet of paper on the table. "In accordance with the right given to me in the articles of incorporation of the Hardeman Foundation whereby I have the right to designate my successor as trustee of the Foundation should I retire from that position, I now do so. You will find on that sheet of paper my formal resignation as trustee of the Foundation and my designation of Mrs. Sally Scott as my successor trustee."

Loren picked up the paper and handed it to the executive director of the Foundation. The man read it quickly and nodded. Loren turned back to the table. "The Foundation recognizes Mrs. Scott as trustee and the chair welcomes her personally to this table."

Mrs. Scott smiled. "Thank you, Loren."

He nodded. After all, it was no skin off his teeth. He still held four of the five trustee votes. "Now, can we proceed to the business at hand?" he asked sarcastically.

Number One nodded pleasantly. "I guess we can do that, son."

Loren glanced around the table to a chorus of nods until he came to me. I shook my head. He stopped.

"Mr. Chairman," I said.

"Yes. Mr. Perino," he replied.

"Before we come to the proper business of this meeting, would it be at all possible to have a private meeting of only those stockholders who have personal equities in the company, and members, past or present, of the Hardeman family?"

Even Number One looked at me curiously now.

Loren was puzzled. "That's a very strange request, Mr. Perino."

"In view of certain information I have available, Mr. Chairman," I said calmly, "I think it is a reasonable one. Since the information I have concerns members of the Hardeman family personally, I see no point in airing it publicly."

"Would it be possible for the chair to see this so-called information you have so it may better evaluate the propriety of your request?"

"I have no objections," I said, opening my attaché case. I took out the two file folders and separated the originals from the Xerox copies I had made early that morning. I gave them to him.

He looked down at them for several seconds, his face running the gamut of colors from angry red to deathly pale. Finally, he looked up at me with stricken eyes. "I won't be blackmailed!" he said hoarsely. "What I did was for the good of the company!"

"Let me see them," Number One said.

Angrily Loren flung them on the table in front of his grandfather. Number One picked them up and read them. After a few minutes, he looked at me. I saw a tremendous hurting pain in his eyes and I felt sorry for him. It was still his own flesh and blood.

Slowly he looked around the room. "I think we'd better talk this over privately in my office," he said in a weary voice.

And that was the end of the Stockholders' meeting.

Chapter Twelve

"I think we're entitled to know how you came by this information," Number One asked me in a level voice from behind his desk.

"Last night at nine o'clock, a man came to my door and asked if I was Angelo Perino. I answered in the affirmative. 'This is for you,' he said, putting the papers in my hand, and he disappeared." It was the truth, not all of it but enough to answer his question.

"Did you know the man, ever see him before?" he asked.

I shook my head. "No."

"You say this letter is supposedly a suicide note left by my late son?" His voice held a faint tremor.

"Goddamnit, Grandfather!" Loren III suddenly exploded. "You know damn well it is. You recognize his handwriting. Or maybe because he was writing about you, you don't want to recognize it?" He took a deep breath. "How Angelo got that letter I don't know, but for all the years since my father died I kept that copy locked away in my safe! So that the world would never find out that you were a son of a bitch enough to drive your son to suicide!"

He began to cry. "Oh, God, how I hated you for it! Every time I thought of my father lying there on the cold library floor, his head blown off, his brains staining the carpet, I hated you more. But even then I couldn't believe it. I also remembered when I was little how you used to play with us. But then when you started with the Betsy, it all came back. You were acting to me exactly as you had acted toward my father. But I made up my mind. You weren't going to do to me what you did to him. I would destroy you first!" He sank into a chair and covered his face with his hands.

"Is that what you believe I did to your father?" Number One asked in a quiet voice.

Loren III had regained control of himself. He looked at his grandfather. "What else is there for me to believe? I know what happened to him. I read the letter in which he accused you in everything but name. And I know how you acted toward me."

Number One's voice was still quiet. "Did you ever stop to think that your father might have meant someone else?"

"Who else could it be but you?" Loren charged.

Number One looked across the room at Mrs. Scott. "Truth will out," he said heavily. "If you live long enough it all catches up with you."

She looked at him, then at her son, the same warm compassion in her eyes for the two of them. Finally she spoke. "Your grandfather is telling the truth, Loren," she said. "Your father wasn't writing about him in that note."

"You're only saying that to defend him!" Loren accused. "I've heard the stories about you and him, Mother. And I know how you felt about him. I remember that too when I was a little boy."

"Loren," Mrs. Scott said. "Your—"

"Sally!" Number One said sharply. "Let me tell him!"

Mrs. Scott ignored him. "Loren, your father was a homosexual. For several years he had an affair with a man who worked for him, Joe Warren. Joe Warren was a sick terrible perverted man and after his death we thought it was all buried with him. But it wasn't.

"It seemed that Warren had made a careful pictorial record of their relationship and it fell into the hands of an equally unscrupulous man. For years this man bled your father until he could no longer stand it. We were as shocked as you were at the news of his suicide and at a loss to understand it.

"But your father's death did not end the man's greed. He then came to your grandfather. I remember talking to your grandfather at that time. The only good thing about it, he told me, was that the blackmailer came to him and not to you. This way you would never have to learn about your father.

"Your grandfather saw that the blackmailer went to jail and that all the pictures were destroyed. It cost your grandfather a fortune to keep it quiet. And he did it not so much for himself, but to keep you and your sister from hurt. Despite everything that had happened, you see, he still loved his son and wanted to protect your father's memory."

Loren III looked at her, then at his grandfather. "Is that true?"

Number One nodded slowly.

Loren III put his head in his hands. I looked around the room. I was the only outsider. They were all Hardemans, past or present.

The telephone began to ring. Number One ignored it. It continued to ring with demanding persistence. Finally, he picked it up. "Yes?" he snapped impatiently. He listened a moment, then beckoned to Alicia. "It's for you."

Alicia, still dabbing the tears with a handkerchief, crossed the room. Standing next to Loren III's chair, she took the phone from Number One. "Yes," she said into it. "This is Mrs. Alicia Hardeman."

An excited voice crackled into the room from the receiver. "Yes," she said. "Yes, yes. Give them both my love." Slowly she put down the telephone.

She turned to Loren III. "Loren," she said.

He looked up at her with a drawn face. "Yes, Alicia," he said in a dead voice. "I really made a mess of it. In every way I could."

"No, Loren," she said. "That's not what I'm talking about. That was Max on the telephone."

"Max?" he repeated dully.

"Yes!" she said, suddenly excited. "Max. Our daughter's husband. He called from Switzerland. Betsy just had a baby boy! They're both fine." A sudden awe came into her voice. "My God, Loren, think of it! We're grandparents!"

And suddenly too, they were a family again. All kissing and crying and laughing.

I walked out and down the hall to my office. For a moment there, I was becoming convinced the whole world was Italian.

Half an hour later, my office door opened and Number One rolled his chair inside. He pushed the door shut and sat there looking at me.

I watched him.

After a moment he spoke. "You fucked up," he said. "You're fired!"

"I know," I said. "I knew that coming in this morning." I took my resignation from my inside pocket and got out of my chair. I walked over and gave it to him.

He opened and read it quickly, then glanced shrewdly at me. "By God, you did know!"

I nodded.

"Do you know why?" he asked.

"I know that too," I said.

"Tell me."

"I wasn't supposed to win," I said. "I was supposed to lose."

"That's right," he said in grim agreement. "But if you knew you were supposed to let him win, why didn't you let him?"

"Because there was no way I could do it," I said. "Even if I tried, I couldn't give it to him. It was my track all the way."

"No hard feelings?"

"No hard feelings."

Again he peered up at me. "You didn't do so bad. That stock you own will be worth twelve million dollars when we go public next year."

"Sure," I said. I stuck my hand in my pocket. "I have something of yours." I put the gold Sundancer cuff links in his hand.

He looked down at them. "You fucked me on the Sundancer too," he said. "Why did you change the name of the Betsy JetStar back to Sundancer?"

"Because it was too good a car for too many years to let it go like that."

He thought for a moment. Then he nodded. "Maybe you're right." Carefully he took the cuff links from his shirt and replaced them with the Sundancers. He dropped the others into his jacket. Then he looked up at me again. "Maybe you're right," he repeated.

I held the door for him while he pushed his chair through, then I let it shut and went back and began to clean out my desk.

Cindy was at the door when I let myself into the apartment. "I plugged in your portable Jacuzzi and filled the tub with your favorite bubble bath."

I kissed the tip of her nose. "I can use it."

She followed me through the apartment into the bathroom and stood there taking my clothes from me while I undressed. "It was on the radio beginning with the noontime news," she said.

"This is the place. Automobile news travels fast."

I put my hands on the wall to brace myself. Getting down in the tub wasn't going to be easy with my ribs all taped up. "You better help me," I said.

She put an arm under my shoulders and I started to ease myself down into the water.

"You got some calls," she said.

"Anything important?" I asked, my ass just about touching the surface of the water.

"Nope," she said nonchalantly. "Just Iacocca of Ford, Cole of General Motors—"

"You're full of shit," I said, looking up at her.

"I am not!" she said indignantly. She pulled her arm out from behind my shoulders.

I went the rest of the way with a jarring thump. "Oh, Christ!" I yelled.

She was out of the bathroom and back in a moment with a batch of telephone messages for me. "See! I was telling the truth. Also Chrysler, also American Motors. Even one from Fiat in Italy!"

I switched on the Jacuzzi. The water began to churn and sing its soothing song. I leaned my head back against the wall behind the tub and sighed. It felt good.

"What do you want me to do with these?" she asked, waving the fistful of messages at me.

"Leave them on the table. I'm not that crazy about going back to work in a hurry. It interferes with my being rich."

The doorbell rang.

"Go see who's there," I said.

She left tossing her head and was back in a moment, slightly subdued. "It's Number One to see you."

I looked at her. "Send him in."

"Here?" she asked.

"Where else?" I retorted. "You don't think I can make it out of this tub in less than a half hour, do you?"

She left the bathroom and came back, pushing him through the door. Then she walked away again.

"Jesus, it's hot in here," he said, looking after her. "Who's the doxie?"

"Cindy." I saw the blank expression on his face. "You know, the test drive."

"I didn't recognize her," he said. "She looks different somehow."

"I think she just discovered dresses," I said.

"For Christ's sake, do you have to keep that damn thing on?" he shouted. "I'm busting my lungs yelling over it."

I flicked off the switch. The sound faded. "That better?"

"Much better." He peered at me. "You look different too."

I smiled. "I got my own face back."

"I was on my way to the airport when I remembered I had something of yours," he said. "So I stopped off to give it to you."

"Yeah?" I couldn't think of anything of mine that he might possibly have.

He stuck his hand in his pocket and came out with a small jewelry box. He opened it and gave it to me.

They were platinum cuff links. The Betsy Silver Sprite. I stared at them. Whoever had made them hadn't missed a single detail of the car. They were beautiful. And I never wear cuff links. I pushed them back toward him. "They're not mine, they're yours."

He didn't take them. "They're ours," he said. "But they're more yours than mine. You keep them!"

He pulled the chair back through the doorway and turned it around. "Young lady!" he yelled. "Help me get out of here!"

Still looking at the tiny Silver Sprites I turned the Jacuzzi back on. They were beautiful. Now I would have to buy some shirts with French cuffs to go with them.

I came out of the tub, wrapping the towel around my waist, still looking at the Silver Sprite cuff links. "Cindy look at these."

"They're beautiful," she said. She looked at me. "You're beautiful too. You know, I never really liked your other face."

"I didn't either," I said.

"How are you feeling?" She had that familiar, lovely look in her eyes.

"Horny as hell," I said, taking her hand. "Come on into the bedroom and let's fuck."

"Okay," she said.

We walked into the bedroom. I looked around. "Something's different," I said, as she wiggled out of her dress. Then I had it. "Where'd you hide the stereo, under the bed?"

"I threw it out," she said walking naked into my arms. "Everybody, even a girl, has to grow up sometime."

"Isn't it kind of sudden?" I asked, chewing on the lobe of her ear.

"Not really," she answered. "I'm twenty-four."

"That's pretty old," I said, beginning to work on her neck.

"That's just right," she said. Abruptly she turned her head and looked into my eyes. "Besides you don't really need stereo."

"Sure?" I asked kissing her lightly on the lips.

She caught my face in her hands. Her eyes were large and dark. "Absolutely sure," she said. "I love you."

I was very still for a moment, then I knew it too. "And I love you."

Then we kissed. She was absolutely right. We didn't need the stereo.

We both heard the music.

The Storyteller

For Grace

Prologue

Fear is the surrogate for pain. It comes first. You look in the rear window, then the side window. You're traveling at thirty miles an hour, in the correct lane, heading for the Wilshire turnoff on the San Diego Freeway. Everything is in order. Then you see the big trailer truck barreling you, cutting in front of you from the left lane, racing you to the turnoff.

"Stupid!" I said, hitting my brakes to allow the truck to move in. It was then the fear began. The truck was still beside me. I hit the brakes even harder. The fear began clutching into my gut and throat. The trailer was tilting toward me, looming above me like a gray prehistoric monster. I turned the wheel away from it.

It appeared as if in slow motion that it was falling toward me. I think I screamed in fear. "You're going to kill me, you son of a bitch!"

The truck jackknifed, turning its six headlights, glaring and blinding. Then the fear was gone, replaced by an agony of pain and I screamed again as a million pounds of steel tumbled down, pushing me into the dark.

I opened my eyes to the fluorescent ceiling lights of the intensive care unit. A nurse was staring at me. "How did I get here?" I asked.

"The paramedics," she said shortly. "Your personal doctor was also here." She turned again and called to one of the doctors, "He's awake."

There were two doctors on duty, one man and one woman. The man glanced at me, then turned away, leaving the woman to stand next to me. "What did the goddam truck do to me?" I asked.

"You have a hip fracture, but it could have been worse," she said consolingly. "It shouldn't keep you from working, it's not your writing arm."

She was a young doctor, very pretty, pretty enough to be starred in the television medical soap programmes. I looked at her. "Okay. So I can write," I said. "But what about fucking?"

Her face expressed her shock, then she answered quite seriously, "That will be a problem. You see, the fractures are located so that you cannot move your hips for that form of activity."

I smiled at her. "Then oral sex?"

She looked down at me. "You're sick."

"I know that," I said. "But that has nothing to do with the broken hip."

She placed a reassuring hand on my arm. "You're going to be all right. We're getting ready to transfer you to a private room."

I was curious. I felt that I had been there only a short time. "What time is it?"

"Almost ten in the morning," she said. "You were brought in here about eleven last night."

"I was out that much?" I asked.

"Just as well," she answered. "You were in a lot of pain. We shot you up with enough dope so that you could get through the examinations and the X rays, then brought you back down here and put on the life systems and monitors."

"It was that bad?" I asked.

"Not really," she said. "But we have a reputation to protect. We don't want a patient with even a minor problem to sneak up and die on us."

"That's reassuring," I said sarcastically.

"You were really in no danger," she said.

She blushed. I looked up at her. "What made you so sure of that?"

"The moment we shot you with some Demerol, you got an erection and began talking dirty."

"Like how dirty?"

Now she was laughing. "Pretty dirty." She looked around to see if anyone was close. "Like in your books. You wanted me to play with you, suck you, fuck you and a lot of other things I don't care to say."

"Really," I said. "And what did you do about it?"

"Nothing. Just worked together with the orthopedist to rig up your leg traction. By then you were asleep and it was over."

"Don't feel bad," I said. "I'll give you another chance when I have my private room."

"I'm in IC," she said. "I never go up to the private rooms."

"Ever?" I asked.

"Only sometimes," she said. She looked down at me. "I have several copies of your books at home. Would you mind signing them for me?"

"Of course," I said. "But only if you bring them up to my room."

She didn't answer. I watched her turn as two attendants rolled a gurney over to my bed and stopped beside me. She turned back to me. "We're going to transfer."

I pointed at the traction hanging over my right knee and under the ankle. "How do you manage it with that?"

"We know how," she said. "Just relax and let us do the work. We'll try not to hurt you too much."

"You don't have to be so honest," I said. "I'd rather you lied a little and give me another shot of dope."

"Don't be a baby," she said, the attendants helping me across to the gurney with the sheet under me.

I felt the stab of pain racing through and caught my breath. "Shit!"

"It's over," she said. "It wasn't that bad."

"Promises, promises," I said.

She bent over me, wiping a cool washrag across my face. "You're okay," she said.

"You're okay, too," I said as the attendants began to wheel the gurney away.

I felt stupid as they pushed me through the corridors, lying flat on the gurney looking at my leg hanging on the traction over me and beyond that the ceiling. Out of the corner of my eye I saw people moving aside to allow me to pass; I felt embarrassed even though I realized that most people paid no attention to me. This was normal living in the hospital. I closed my eyes. I didn't feel like looking at any people looking at me. I had had enough.

Strangely that clicking of the wheels of the gurney crossing the stone floors of the corridors brought memories of the subway wheels on the tracks many years ago. I didn't know. Maybe I dozed. I always dozed standing up on the subway, my back to the door, the crowd pushing against me holding me up. Then I woke up as the crowd moved off at Forty-second Street, and I would follow them to the station and up to the street toward the office where I worked.

July and August were always a bitch in the subway. The heat and sweat mixed, swirling the peculiar air down from the fans. I would always travel in my shirt-sleeves, my jacket and tie folded across my arm. I was seventeen at the time and had a summertime job as a copy boy on the *Daily News*. The day I met her it was extraordinarily hot.

The crowd behind her pushed more tightly against me. She looked up at my face. "If you could turn your arm off your chest to the side, I would have a little more room."

Silently, I nodded, moving my arm carefully against the post so that I didn't lose my jacket and tie. She smiled her thanks to me, then turned around, her back pushing against me. The train began moving out of the station and the normal swaying of the cars began speeding up. I think it took less than thirty seconds and I was raising a hard.

I felt the sweat beginning from my face down to my shirt collar. I glanced down. She had her buttocks jammed into my groin. I began trying to think of other things but nothing worked. My hard kept getting more confined in my shorts. Trying not to allow her to learn of my predicament, I managed to slip my hand into my pants pocket and carefully moved my prick into a more comfortable position straight up behind my fly. I glanced down at her again. I began to feel better. I guessed she hadn't noticed anything.

The train came to a stop in the tunnel between the stations and the regular lights went out and the emergency lights pushed out a dim yellow flicker. The girl looked back over her shoulder up at me. "Are you comfortable?" she asked.

I nodded. I had to concentrate. I couldn't talk too much. "Fine," I said.

She smiled up at me in the flickering lights. "I can feel you against me."

I looked at her. She didn't seem angry. "I'm sorry," I said.

"That's all right," she said. "You wouldn't believe how many men do that on the subway." She waited for me to answer her but I didn't know what to say. She nodded. "You're the fourth man this week. I don't like most of them though, they're pigs. But I don't mind you, you seem nice and clean."

"Thank you," I said.

She looked at me. "Did you come yet?"

I shook my head, no.

"Would you like to?" she asked.

I stared at her, but before I could answer I felt her hand reach behind her back and cup my testicles through my pants crotch. That did it all.

At the same time, the train lurched into motion, the regular lights came on as it moved into the station. My knees seemed to turn into jelly as my orgasm kept my prick slamming against my belly. I hung on to the post to keep from falling as I felt the hot viscous ejaculation spreading over my underwear.

Then the train doors opened on the opposite side and she turned to me and looked up smiling. "That was fun," she said and walked through the open doors.

I watched her, still hanging on to the post, as she went out with the crowd on to the station. I would have followed her to call and try to make a date but I couldn't walk. Then I felt the damp soaking through my pants with my jacket in front of my arms.

I tried to catch her eye as she walked along the platform as the train began to move again. But she was gone as the windows moved quickly away from her.

"Shit!" I thought. I was really stupid. I had it all in my hand and I blew it. All I had to do was talk a little bit more instead of being a dummy. I blinked my eyes to look back at the station but when I opened them, I looked up at my leg hanging over me in the traction.

I looked around the room. It was the private room. Washed-out blue walls and ceiling. I heard shoes on the floor and turned to see a nurse coming to me with a wet washrag.

She was comfortable lady in her forties. She held out the washrag toward me. "Wash your private parts."

"What for?" I asked, taking the washrag.

"You had a dream while you were sleeping," she said. "But don't worry about it. It's quite normal when you have a few shots of pain killers."

"I only remember being put into the gurney downstairs."

"You were asleep when they transferred you here."

"I remember the gurney reminded me of the subway," I said. "That's strange."

"Clean yourself up and forget it," she said. "You have been sleeping over three hours and your doctor should be coming in almost any minute now."

Less than five minutes later, Ed came into the room. Looked around at my traction device and then pulled a chair next to me in the bed. "You're pretty lucky, sport," he said.

"Glad you think so," I said sarcastically. "It hurts like a bitch."

"It could have been worse. Your fractures will heal in time, but I've known of some others that would have put you into a wheelchair for life."

I looked at him. For the first time I saw his weariness in his watery blue eyes lined with red from lack of sleep. "I'm sorry," I said. "I guess I screwed up your dinner date."

"That's okay," he said. "You're going to be out of action for a while so you can send over some of your reserve stock."

"How long will it take me to heal?"

"It's not easy to say. It all works in steps. First step, you stay in this traction in the hospital for about a week until we make sure that the various bones are lined up in place. Then you can go home. You start very slow. Walk carefully, with a walker, later with crutches, always slow and a little bit at a time, get a lot of rest and bed time. After a month of that we shoot a few more X rays. If that goes well then we can let you move around a little more but still on the crutches. A month after that, more X rays, and the fractures should be healed. Then working with one crutch or cane you walk slowly for another few months until we're sure that your cartilage and the articulation in your hip socket are cool. Then you can get into your usual routine."

I added up the time. "Six months?"

"About," he said.

"Can I work?" I asked.

"I suppose," he said. "But you'll be in constant pain so you'll have to go slow."

"How much time will it take for the pain to go?"

"At the scale of ten being now, three months will bring you down maybe to five, and when you're completely healed you'll go down to two or one, but that is something that you will learn to live with. It won't interfere with any of your activities."

I looked at him. That was one thing I respected about him—he told the truth. No pie in the sky. "Really fucks up my schedule," I said. "This weekend I was supposed to turn in the bible for a television series. A week after than an article for a British newspaper. Then I was supposed to begin my new book and have the first part of it in three months."

"I don't think you can make that schedule," he said seriously. "But what do you have to worry about? Your last book is still on the best-seller-list and it's been there more than a year."

"It's also about more than that year that I spent the money I received for it. I have a big machine to keep running."

He was silent for a moment, then he nodded. "I guess that's true. Life in the fast lane is not cheap. Just with homes here in Beverly Hills, on the Riviera in France, a villa and a yacht, and a winter place in Acapulco, how do you manage?"

'The same way you do," I said. "I keep working."

"You also piss out a lot of money on booze, parties, dope and girls. Cut out some of that and you'd save a lot of money."

"You're beginning to sound like Paul, my lawyer. What neither of you understands is that it's the icing on the cake that binds it all together and makes it worthwhile. Just putting money in the bank doesn't bring you any fun. At least I spend my money on a lifestyle that brings me pleasure and enjoyment."

"But you still have to work," he said.

"So? Don't you?"

"Yes," he said. "But people don't think like that about you."

I laughed. "They think about my books and it makes them think of me that the books and I are the same thing."

"Do you mean you always worked like that? Even when you were beginning?"

"Always," I said. "Maybe even more so."

Part One

1942

Chapter One

"Joe!" His mother's voice echoed faintly through the closed bedroom door. He rolled over slowly and peered at the alarm clock next to the bed. It was eleven in the morning. He turned back and covered his head with a pillow.

This time his mother's voice sounded louder. He peeked out under the pillow. The bedroom door was open and his cousin, Motty, was standing outside in the hall. He stared at her. "What the hell are you doing here?"

"Your mother wants you," she said.

"I heard her," he said truculently. "I'm still tired."

"You better get up," Motty said. "It's important."

"It can wait another half an hour," he said, ducking back under the pillow.

A moment later, he felt the blanket pull away from him. "What the hell are you doing?" he said, covering his genitals with his hands.

Motty laughed at him. "You've been jerking off again."

"I was not," he said angrily, sitting up.

"Bullshit," she said. "I see the come stains on your sheet."

He looked down at the sheet. "I was sleeping."

"Yeah," Motty said sarcastically. "You always say that. I know better. I've known you since you've been a kid."

"What makes you such an expert?" he asked. "You're only a little older than me."

"I'm twenty five," she said defensively. "That's old enough. I remember when I used to give you baths when you were practically a baby."

"And you were playing with my prick most of the time," he replied.

"I was not!" she said emphatically.

He took his hands away from his genitals. "I got a hard on now," he said. "Would you like to give me a bath again?"

"Pig!" she snapped. "You have a perverted mind. I read all the stories you write for those magazines. Spicy love stories, spicy detective stories, spicy adventures."

He looked up at her. "You don't have to read them."

"I was curious what you were doing," she said.

"Did they turn you on?" he asked.

"They disgust me," she said. "If you want to call a writer, why don't you write for some decent magazines? *Saturday Evening Post, Collier's, Ladies Home Journal.*"

"I tried," he said. "I can't write their kind of stories." He sat silent for a moment. "But it's not too bad. I'm averaging about fifteen dollars a week from them."

"That's not much," she said. "I get thirty-five a week writing ad copy for A and S."

"I don't call that writing," he said. "Besides, you also work at the sales counter in the store."

She ignored his remark as she walked to the door. "You better get downstairs," she said. "Your mother is upset."

He waited until he could hear her footsteps going down the staircase to the entrance hall before he got out of bed. He stretched and breathed deeply in front of the wide-open window. It was October, but the air was still warm and humid. It seemed as if the summer never wanted to let go. He leaned against the windowsill and looked down at the small driveway that separated their house and the house next door. He saw Motty coming out the side door.

"You're going to be late to work," he called.

"It's Thursday. The store opens late on Thursday."

"Oh."

She looked up at him. "Are you working late tonight?"

"No," he said.

"Maybe you'll come by the store and pick me up. I don't like the idea of coming home alone by myself. That's a scary area at night."

"I'll call you," he said. "I'll try."

"Okay," she said, and walked along the driveway to the street.

He turned back into his room. Motty was all right even though sometimes she was a pain in the ass. She had been living with them since she was ten years old. Her mother and father had been killed in an automobile accident, and since his mother was the only relative she had, it was only right that his mother would take in her sister's child.

He turned back to the room. His brother's bed was still on the other side of the room as if he was expected home every night. Steven was his older brother, seven years older, and was in his third year in medical school in Oklahoma, and he made it home only about two weeks a year around the holidays. Sometimes he wondered if Steven was really his brother. Steven was always very serious, always studying, and ever since he had been a child he knew he wanted to be a doctor. He used to tease Steven that the reason he wanted to be a doctor was so that he could talk Motty into taking her clothes off and examine her. But Steven had no sense of humour. He never laughed.

Joe took a cigarette from a package on the dresser, lit it, and took a drag. The taste wasn't that great. He really preferred Luckies but even though Luckies Green had gone to war—as the slogan put it—they still cost more than Twenty Grands, so that was what he smoked. He put on his bathrobe and went out into the hallway, past his parent's room next to the bathroom.

His mother had her back to him as he came into the kitchen. She didn't turn to him. Still paring and scraping carrots over the sink, she spoke over her shoulder. "Would you like some breakfast?"

"No, thanks, Mama," he said. "Just a cup of coffee, please."

She still hadn't turned to face him. "Coffee on an empty stomach is not good for you."

"I'm not hungry," he said, sitting at the kitchen table. He sat there holding and rolling the clincher between his fingers until the burnt end of the cigarette had tapped off.

His mother stared at the cigarette as she brought him a cup of coffee. "Cigarettes are the worst thing for you," she said. "It will stunt your growth."

He laughed. "Mama, I'm already five ten. I don't think I'll be growing anymore."

"Did you see your letter?" she said suddenly.

He put down his cup of coffee before he tasted it. "What letter?"

It was on the kitchen table. She pushed it toward him. It looked like an official envelope. It had also been opened. He picked up the letter. It was official. It was from his draft board. Quickly he took the letter out. All he had to see was the first line: "Greetings."

"Shit!" he said, then looked at his mother.

She was already crying.

"Cut it out, Mama," he said. "It's not the end of the world."

"One-A," she said. "In three weeks they want you to report to Grand Central for your physical."

"That doesn't mean anything," he said. "I've been One-A for over a year. And, besides I saw in the papers that only forty percent of the draftees pass their physicals. I may not even pass."

"You should be so lucky," she said snuffling.

He laughed again. "I'm sure we can do something. Papa's a very close friend of Abe Stark. And there's some others too we can talk with." He didn't want to tell her that Papa was very big with the Brownsville boys. She knew it but never wanted to mention it. She wouldn't even acknowledge that her husband was loan-sharking as well as running his chicken market off Pitkin avenue.

"With the draft board nobody has any influence," she said. "You really have to have something wrong with you."

"Maybe they'll find out I have the clap," he said.

She peered at him. "You have it?" She didn't know whether she should be happy or angry.

"No," he said.

"What happened with your job at the *Daily News*?" she asked. "They don't draft newspaper people. You shouldn't have quit it."

"I didn't quit it," he said. "I told you many times, they fired me. They didn't want anyone working for them in One-A because they couldn't depend on it that he could keep the job."

"Your girlfriend, the big writer on the paper—she could have done something about it."

He was silent for a moment. There was no way he could tell her that it was because he was fucking Kitty that he got fired. He lit the clincher and blew out some smoke, then lifted his coffee to his lips. "At least you don't have to worry about Steven, Mama," he said. "He has to be safe for another four years."

"You would have been safe too," she said, "if you had taken the job at your Uncle Izzy's machine shop."

"We weren't in the war then," he said. "Besides, you know I couldn't do that kind of work. I'm a writer."

"You should have gone to City College," she said. "Maybe that would have gotten you a deferment."

"Maybe," he answered. "But I didn't pass the tests."

"The trouble was, you were never serious," she said. "You were always running around with those little whores."

"Come on, Mama," he said. "The next thing you'll tell me, that I should have gotten married."

"For a deferment," his mother said, "I wouldn't have complained even if you married one of those whores."

"What would that have gained me?"

"Three-A," she said. "And if you had a baby, maybe more."

He shook his head. "But that's all over. I never did any of those things so let's forget about it."

She looked at him and the tears began to come again. "I spoke to your father. He wants you to go down to his place and talk to him."

"Okay," he said. Then he smiled. "Maybe I'll sleep at the chicken market for three or four nights before I go to Grand Central. Maybe I'll be so covered with chicken lice that they'll throw me out."

"Don't make fun of your father," she said.

He was silent. She had had a special shower built in the garage so that his father could leave his clothes there and wash up before he came into the house after work.

She went back to the sink. "Go upstairs and get dressed," she said. "I'll get you some breakfast before you go out."

He walked slowly through the lunch-hour crowd on Pitkin Avenue. Looking through the windows of the Little Oriental restaurant, he could see every table already filled and a line of customers waiting for their turn to eat. Across the street, Loew's Pitkin theater was taking down the sign advertising the early-bird matinee; now until six o'clock admission would be twenty-five cents. He wasn't interested in the double feature they displayed. He liked it more when they used to have a stage show and a movie rather than the double features. They used to have great masters of ceremonies then—Dick Powell, Ozzie Nelson, all were wonderful. There were others too, but now all of them had gone to Hollywood to get into the movies.

He had walked four more blocks. Now there were no more expensive shops; the stores were plain and less decorated. Even Rosencrantz's Five-and-Dime didn't have the pizazz that Woolworth's, just five streets before, had. He turned to the corner near the street where his father's chicken market was located.

It was near the middle of the side street, in a large lot with a wire fence that completely enclosed it. In the corner of the lot was a small building about twenty feet square, then, next to the building, the wire fence continued, and in the middle two long wire gates that allowed the farm trucks to enter and bring the fowl from the country. Through the gate at the far end of the lot there was a long shed where the chickens and other fowl ran back and forth in narrow pens, adding to the noise of the street with their cackling and honking. He stood across the street and looked up at the painted sign across the whole front of the wire fence.

PHIL KRONOWITZ—ALBERT PAVONE
LIVE CHICKENS   GALLINE VIVE
KOSHER KILLED   RESTAURANTS SERVED
RABBINICAL SUPERVISION
WHOLESALE and RETAIL

The sign was painted with bold white lettering on a shining Italian green background. He stood there on the sidewalk while he finished his cigarette. His father didn't like him to smoke.

He dropped the cigarette into the street and crossed to the small building. He turned the door knob. The door was locked. "Damn," he said to himself. He hated to walk into the market through the open area. He disliked the smell and the noise and the blood of the fowl screaming their disaster.

Behind the building, he walked past the long shed. The first half of the shed was devoted to the kosher fowl. In front of it were a dozen triangular iron scoops, the bottom of each attached to a pipe that went into a pail. This was where the *sochet* slit a chicken's throat and then thrust its head down into the scoop until the blood had been drained from its body. Then the *shochet* muttered a prayer and gave the chicken to the customer—or, for an extra nickel or dime, handed the chicken to a "chicken-flicker" who plucked the feathers from its body, then passed it quickly over a fire to get rid of the lice and quill ends of the feathers. This was his father's part of the market.

Al, his father's partner, was a fat, smiling Italian. He sold many more fowl than Phil Kronowitz—not only because they were sold for less, but because there was no ritual to slow down the work. His workers just slit the fowls' throats, then let them run crazy, splattering blood around the pen; and when they were dead, they were thrown into a vat of boiling water so that the feathers could be taken off with the large wire brush.

There were no customers in front of his father's side. Two chicken-flickers and the *shochet* were sitting against the wall of the office building. The *shochet* was smoking a cigarette. He was a tall man with a long black beard and *payess* covering his cavernous face.

Joe spoke in English. "How are you, Rabbi?"

"How should I be?" the *shochet* answered. "*Ich mach a leben*," he said in Yiddish, even though Joe knew he spoke English as well as he did.

Joe nodded. "Where is my father?"

"Where should he be?" the *shochet* replied.

"There's nobody in the office," Joe said. "What about Josie?"

Josie was the big lady who was the cashier and the bookkeeper. "She went out to lunch," the *shochet* said.

"With my father?" he asked. He always had a feeling that his father was screwing Josie. She was a busty, big-assed lady—the kind his father liked.

The *shochet* seemed to think the same thing. "I mind my own business. I don't know what anybody does on their own lunchtime."

"Shithead," Joe said to himself and walked across to where Al was standing near the boiling vats. "*Buon giorno*, Tio Alberto," he said, smiling.

"*Vass machst du*, Yussele?" Al laughed. "Not bad for a *luksh*?"

Joe laughed too. "You speak better Yiddish than I do, Uncle Al."

Al didn't have to be asked. "Your father is having lunch at the Little Oriental. He told me you should go over there right away."

"Little Oriental?" Joe asked. "I thought that Jake wouldn't let him in the restaurant because he was afraid my father would bring some chicken lice into the place."

"Your father took a bath and has a real suit on," Al said. "And besides, even if he didn't, Jake would let him in. Your father is having lunch with Mr Buchalter."

"Gurrah?" Joe asked. Al didn't have to answer. Joe knew who they were. Lepke and Gurrah owned Brownsville and East New York. Even the Mafia wouldn't fuck with them.

"Okay, Uncle Al, I'll get right over there. Thanks."

"I'm sorry about the One-A," Al said. "I hope everything will be all right."

"Thank you, Uncle Al," he said. "It'll be okay, whichever way it goes."

Chapter Two

Louis Buchalter was about five feet seven, with a pudgy face and expressionless eyes hidden by the broad-brimmed fedora that sat squarely on his head. There were two other men seated beside him at the round table as Joe sat down next to his father.

"So you're the writer?" he said to Joe in a surprisingly thin voice.

"Yes, sir," Joe said.

Buchalter looked at Joe's father. "He's a good-looking boy, Phil. So what's the problem?"

"He's One-A and his mother is going crazy."

"He's being called up for his examination already?"

"Yes," Phil said. "In three weeks."

Buchalter was silent for a moment. "Grand Central?" he finally said. "That's going to make it expensive. It would have been easier if we had heard about him at the local draft board."

"But you could do it?" Phil asked anxiously.

"Everything can be done," Buchalter answered. "But like I said, it'll be expensive."

"How expensive?" Phil asked.

Buchalter's eyes were inscrutable. "Two grand cash and twenty-five percent of the bank profits instead of ten."

Joe looked at his father. "It's not worth it, Papa. I have a forty percent chance that I can get a Four-F."

"*Grosser k'nocker*?" his father said angrily. "What makes you such an expert?"

Joe was silent as Phil turned to Buchalter. "There's no other way, Louis?" he asked.

Buchalter shook his head, then paused a moment. He looked at Joe but spoke to Phil. "Does he have a job?"

"No," Phil said. "He works at home. He has a typewriter up in his room."

"Could he work in a store?" Buchalter asked.

"What kind of a store?" Phil asked.

"It's clean," Buchalter said. "All he has to do is answer telephone messages, and once in a while deliver some packages."

Phil was silent.

"And it will make it easier for us to change his classification. The store is in Manhattan, and if he gets a room near there, we would lose his draft papers and give him a whole new set under another name." Buchalter looked at Joe. "Do you mind if you work with a shvartzer?"

Joe shook his head. "I don't mind."

"You'll get twenty-five a week."

"That makes it even better," Joe said. "But will I have time to write?"

"You'll have all the time you want," Buchalter said. "No customers come into the store."

"I don't want my kid to wind up in the clink," Phil said.

"Phil, would I do a thing like that to you?" Buchalter said.

"I know you wouldn't," Phil said. "But sometimes things go wrong."

"I'll guarantee it," Buchalter said. "And if you do that for me, you can forget about the twenty-five percent of the bank and we'll go back to the old figures."

"And the two grand?" Phil pressed.

"That you have to pay," Buchalter said. "The money is not for me. It's for the guys who have to handle the paperwork."

Phil thought for a moment, then held out his hand. "It's a deal."

Buchalter shook his hand, then turned to Joe. "Do you have your draft card and notice with you?"

"Yes, sir," Joe said.

"Give them to me."

Joe took them out of his pocket and handed them across the table. Buchalter looked at the papers for a moment and handed them to one of the men sitting next to him, who put them in his jacket pocket.

"Kronowitz," Buchalter said. "We have to change that name. Do you have any ideas?"

"Joseph Crown is the name I write under," Joe said.

"That's good enough," Buchalter said. He turned to the man next to him. "Make a note of that."

The man nodded.

Buchalter turned again to Joe. "Write down this name and address. Tomorrow morning at ten o'clock, you go there." He waited until Joe took out a pen and a small notebook. "Caribbean Imports, Fifty-third Street and Tenth Avenue. The man's name is Jamaica. You can get the telephone number in the book."

"Yes, sir," Joe said.

"Anything else, Phil?" Buchalter asked.

"Nothing, thank you, Louis," Phil said. "I'm really grateful to you."

"That's what friends are for," Buchalter said. He rose to his feet, the two men with him. "I'll go out through the kitchen," he said, then looked down at Joe. "Good luck, kid."

"Thank you, Mr Buchalter," Joe said.

His father waited until Buchalter and his friends had gone, then looked at his son. "If it weren't for your mother," he said bitterly, "I would have let you go in the army and get yourself killed."

Joe was silent.

Phil looked at him and shook his head sadly. "You want some lunch?"

"No, thanks, Papa," Joe said. "Mama made me have breakfast just before I came down here."

His father rose to his feet. He was a big man, almost six feet tall. "Let's go then," he said. "This is Thursday afternoon and we'll be very busy."

Jake came running from the front of the restaurant to the table. "What is this, a meeting hall?" he complained. "Nobody ate."

Phil looked at him contemptuously. He threw a ten-dollar bill on the table. "This should take care of it," he said and walked out.

Joe stopped outside the restaurant with his father. "I have an appointment at the magazine."

His father looked at him. "You have nothing else to say?"

Joe looked up at his father, then reached up and kissed him on the lips. "Thank you, Papa."

There was a glint of tears in Phil's eyes. "I'll see you tonight, *tateleh*."

He came out of the IRT subway station at Canal Street. The clatter of the trucks coming and going from the Holland Tunnel was deafening. He stood on the corner waiting for the traffic lights to change so that he could cross to the opposite corner to the building where the magazine offices were located.

It was a renovated loft building, and the old freight elevator was used for passengers as well. The elevator operator pulled up the wire grill to let him on. He got out on the fifth floor and walked through the opaque glass doors to the magazine. The simple black paint lettering read: "Searchlight Comics."

He walked down the long corridor. Alongside the windows was the art department. There the illustrators and artists were working on their drawing boards and easels. Along the corridor on the inside wall were the offices that held the editorial staff and the business department. The cubelike offices without doors were lined up like glass-walled prison cells. He paused and entered one of the open offices.

Mr. Hazle, the editor of the magazine group, was almost hidden behind a pile of manuscripts and artwork on his desk. He looked up over them and gestured for Joe to come in.

"Come in, Joe," he said. "I was just thinking about you."

Joe smiled. "Hello, Mr. Hazle. I hope you have a check for me."

"In another day or so," Mr. Hazle said, his owl-like eyes peering behind his round glasses under his bald head. "The reason I wanted to talk to you, was that we liked your story for *Spicy Adventure* very much."

"That's good," Joe said, still standing. There was no room for another chair in the tiny office.

"I was talking to the boss," Hazle said. "He liked it too, but he said that twenty-five hundred words is too much for the story. Without illustrations it would take up ten pages, and we haven't enough space for it. Five pages a story is our limit."

"So what do we do?" Joe asked.

"The boss said he liked it so much he wants you to turn it into a serial, maybe twenty chapters, one in each issue."

Joe looked at him. "Five hundred words a chapter at a penny a word, that's only five dollars a story. I know the illustrators are getting more than that. They're getting twenty-five dollars a page."

"That's the kind of a magazine it is," Hazle said. "Our customers don't read, they want to look at drawings of tits and ass."

"Still, I should get more money," Joe said.

Hazle stared at him. "I have an idea. The boss liked the story, especially the character of the girl, Honey Darling. Maybe I can talk him into you turning it into a feature every month, a different adventure with Honey Darling in it. That way he will pay two cents a word, and feature stories run seven hundred fifty words. That will give you fifteen dollars a month and wouldn't stop you from writing other stories for us."

"Do you think he'll buy it?"

"I'll go right in there and ask him,' Hazle said. "Just give me the word."

"You got the word," Joe said.

"Grab one of those chairs in the corridor," Hazle said. "I'll be back to you in a few minutes."

Joe sat down in the corridor as Hazle walked to its end and entered the only closed office on the floor. Joe reached for his pack of cigarettes and lit one up. He took a deep drag and looked across the corridor to a girl sitting at a typewriter. She glanced at him for a moment and then turned back to her typewriter. He kept watching her type as he dragged at his cigarette.

After a moment she turned toward him and called out, "Are you Joe Crown?"

He nodded.

"I thought so," she said. "I've read most of the stuff that you sent in. You're good, maybe the best writer that comes in here. Hazle himself said that."

"That's good," he said.

"You're too good for them," she said. "Maybe you should try some better magazines."

"I haven't got the contacts," he said. "You need contacts; otherwise they don't even read your stories."

"You should have an agent then."

"I need a contact for that too. Agents don't want to waste their time with beginners."

She looked at him. "I'll give you the name of an agent that I know," she said. "But don't let Mr. Hazle know that I told you."

"I won't, I promise," he said.

She looked over her shoulder to make sure that Hazle wasn't returning. Then she quickly typed the name on a sheet of paper, and handed it across the corridor to him. "Put that in your pocket—quickly," she said nervously.

"What's your name?" he asked, doing as she said.

"I put my name and telephone number on the paper too," she said. "But you can only call me on Sundays. That's the only day I have off."

"Okay," he said. "I'll call you. Thanks a lot."

She nodded and turned back to her typewriter as Hazle came down the corridor. Joe looked up at the bald man.

"Mr. Kahn wants to see you," Hazle said.

Joe followed the editor to the closed office. It wasn't large, but one corner had four windows. The walls were mahogany veneer and there was a fake mahogany desk. On the wall were paintings of various magazine covers.

Mr. Kahn was a big, jovial man with a bushy head of hair and large tortoiseshell eyeglasses. He came from behind his desk and held out his hand. "Joe," he said in a deep baritone voice, "I like to meet writers of talent, and I consider that you are one of our best."

"Thank you, Mr. Kahn," Joe said.

"I told Hazle that we'll make that deal. You get the two cents a word. Like I said, we like to reward talent."

"Thank you, Mr. Khan."

"Nothing at all, Joe," the publisher said. "You just come in anytime you want to see me. We're all one family here." He went back behind his desk. "Too bad we can't talk some more but there's so much work to do."

"I understand, Mr. Kahn. Thank you again," Joe said, and followed Hazle out of the office.

Hazle walked into his small cell-like office. "I knew he would go for it," he smiled.

"What made you so sure?" Joe asked.

"You remember that last scene in your story where the Arab cuts open Honey Darling's brassiere with his scimitar and her jutting breasts burst out?"

"I remember," Joe said.

"Mr. Kahn said the imagery from that scene gave him the biggest hard on he had since he read Pierre Louÿs's *Aphrodite*."

"Maybe you should have asked him for three cents a word then," Joe laughed.

"Just give him time," Hazle said. "Now you have to get to work. First, you have to edit the twenty-five hundred words into three seven-hundred-and-fifty-word stories."

Chapter Three

He waited until he was in the street outside the office building before looking down at the sheet of paper the typist had given him:

Laura Shelton
Piersall and Marshall Agency

34 East 39th Street
Tele: Lexington 2200

Underneath was the typist's name. Kathy Shelton. Tele: YOrkville 9831. P.S. Don't call my sister until tomorrow so that I can tell her about you tonight. K.S.

He felt good. That was a stroke of luck. He had heard about that agency. It was one of the best literary agencies in the city. Several times he had tried to make an appointment with them but the operator or the receptionist would never let him through.

He walked along Canal Street. Traffic was building up as rush hour began. He checked his watch; it was almost five o'clock. He went into a candy store on the next corner and ordered an egg cream. The counterman looked at him. "Small or large?"

He still felt lucky. "Large," he said.

"Seven cents," the counterman said, placing a large glass of the white-topped chocolate drink in front of him.

He left a dime on the counter and took his drink over to the pay phone opposite the counter. He heard his nickel tinkle down the box, then dialed the number. It was one of the new pay telephones, and it seemed strange not to hear the operator's voice answer. He sipped his drink as the ringing of the telephone sounded in his ear. A voice answered, "Hello."

"Lutetia?" he asked. "Joe."

Her voice was thin and tinny through the receiver. "How are you, Joe?" She sounded as if she was stoned.

"Is Kitty home?" he asked.

"Yes. But she's asleep."

"Smashed?" he asked.

"Out of her mind," Lutetia answered.

"Shit," he said. "She told me that she'd give me the five bucks for the work I did. She said she'd have it for me today."

"If she said she had it for you, she probably had it," Lutetia said. Then she laughed. "But you'd have to wake her up first."

"I was counting on that money," he said.

"Come up anyway," she said. "Maybe you'll get lucky and she'll wake up."

He thought for a moment. There wasn't anything else he had to do. "Okay," he said. "I'll be over there in about a half-hour."

Lutetia stood in the open doorway as he came from the staircase. The light in the entrance hall behind shone through the sheer chiffon dressing gown, revealing her naked body beneath.

"She's still out," she said as he walked through the door.

He turned to her as she closed the door. he saw the glass of red wine in her hand. She seemed to be moving in slow motion, her long sandy brown hair falling to her shoulders, the large black pupils vague in her soft blue eyes. The scent of marijuana hung in the apartment. "You seem pretty gone yourself," he said.

"Not like her," she said. "Vodka and tea don't mix."

He followed her into the combination living-and-dining room. She sprawled onto the couch, the dressing-gown falling from her legs up to her waist where the gown was fastened by a soft belt. She looked up at him. "There's a bottle of wine and some glasses on the cocktail table," she said.

"Not for me," he said. "I walked up from Canal Street. The heat and the humidity got to me. I'd like a cold drink."

"We've got Canada Dry and Coca-Cola in the icebox," she said. "You know where to get it."

When he returned from the kitchen with a glass of ginger ale, she was lighting another joint. The acrid scent of the marijuana wafted into the room. Her hair fell forward as she bent over the cocktail cabinet. Now the upper part of her gown opened, revealing her breasts. She held up the joint toward him. "Want a drag?"

"Not right now," he said, sitting in the easy chair opposite her and sipping his drink.

She took two more drags on the joint, then put it in an ashtray and lifted her wineglass. She leaned back against the couch. "I'm bored," she said.

He smiled. "What else is new?"

"I'm horny," she said.

"You can take care of that," he said.

"I've been masturbating all afternoon," she said. "But it's not that much fun alone."

"Masturbation is a solo sport," he said.

"Doesn't have to be," she said.

He sipped his ginger ale without answering.

Still leaning against the couch, she spread her knees wide apart and, turning her index and middle fingers into an inverted "V for Victory," opened her blond-haired pussy until the pink, moist lips seemed to be shining at him. She watched him looking at her. "Getting a hard on?" she teased.

"I'm not dead," he said, feeling the throbbing in his phallus.

"How'd you like to eat that hot juicy pussy?" she asked.

"Wouldn't mind," he answered rubbing himself through his pants. "But what's in it for me?"

"I'll jerk you off," she said.

"I can do that better myself," he laughed. "Suck it or fuck it, either will be okay with me."

"You know I'm not into cock," she said. "They're all ugly."

He unbuttoned his trousers and took out his penis. He could feel the juice already dripping. He looked at her. "It's right here," he said. "Just sacrifice yourself a little."

"Prick!" she said.

"That's where it's at," he laughed. "No suckee, no eatee."

She stared at him for a moment, then she nodded "Okay, come over here."

He stood up and let his trousers fall off, then went over to her. He held her head between his hands and pulled her face to his phallus. She kept her lips clenched. "Open your fucking mouth, you bitch!" he said angrily.

Stubbornly she was turning away from him, moving her face from one side to the other. Finally, he was able to hold her face still, but by then it was too late. His orgasm swept through him, spurting his semen wildly over her. He stared down at her.

She lay still, looking at him. "It's disgusting," she said trying to control her voice. "Disgusting."

"Dyke bitch!" he said, wiping himself with the corner of her dressing gown. He put on his pants, then turned to her.

"Where are you going?" she asked.

"Leaving," he said.

"You can't go now," she said. "You said you'd give me some head."

"That was only if you gave it to me," She said.

"I was going to," she said. "It's not my fault that you couldn't hold it long enough until I was ready."

He stared at her for a moment and then began to laugh. "Okay, you bitch," he said. "Wipe off my come and get out of that stupid kimono. I'll eat your cunt until your ass falls off."

Two hours later, Kitty was still asleep. He looked at Lutetia. "It's almost eight o'clock," he said. "I guess there's no chance that she'll get up now."

"That's right," Lutetia said. She smiled. "You know, you don't give such bad head for a man."

"Thanks," he said dryly. "Can I use your phone?"

She nodded. She watched him call his cousin and arrange for her to meet him at the main entrance of the store on Fulton Street. He put down the phone. "I have to get going now," he said.

"Okay," she said. "What do you want me to tell Kitty?"

"I'll check her tomorrow."

"Okay," she said, picking up her wineglass. "You're not angry with me, are you?"

He smiled. "No. But next time I'd like equal time."

As he waited in front of the main entrance of Abraham and Straus, the hands of the big clock on the iron post in front showed five minutes to nine. A special policeman took his place at the inside doors; in a few moments a second policeman came to guard the outside doors. First to come out were the customers; by the time the closing bells began to ring at nine o'clock, most of them had gone and the policeman locked all the doors except the single double door in the center. The last customers straggled out and the first of the employees began leaving the store.

Motty was late; she didn't come out until it was almost nine-thirty. She smiled as she saw Joe. "I'm sorry I took so long," she said. "But the ad manager wanted some changes in Sunday's ads at the last minute."

"It's okay," he said. He took her arm and they walked across the corner and passed Gage & Tollner's restaurant. The restaurant was busy.

"A lot of our executives have dinner there on Thursday nights," she said.

"Are they good?" he asked.

"They're expensive," she answered.

He took her through the side streets to the Atlantic Avenue subway station. It was a shortcut, almost three blocks shorter than staying on Fulton. The streets were dark and gloomy, lined with old tenements filled with colored and Puerto Ricans, all on relief. The people they saw didn't seem friendly. Hurrying past them, Motty held onto his arm unconsciously. He heard her sigh of relief as she saw the lights shining brightly on Atlantic Avenue. The subway entrance was on the corner.

He had the nickels ready and they went through the turnstiles. They walked quickly to the head of the platform. The first car was usually less crowded; it also was just opposite the exit at the New Lots Station where they would get off.

They were lucky. The first train rumbling into the station was an almost empty New Lots Avenue express. They sat down on the long, hard straw bench. He looked at her. "Okay?"

She nodded. "Thank you for picking me up. Last week one of the girls from the store was raped on the side street."

"She probably wanted it," he said.

"That's not true," she said angrily. "I know her. She's a nice girl. Why do you guys always think that a girl wants to get raped?"

"They do," he said. "Just look at the way they dress, even the way you do. Your dress is so low-cut that your tits are sticking out and so tight across your ass that every wiggle seems like an invitation."

"You really have a dirty mind," she said.

"It's normal," he laughed. "Tits and ass. Every guy gets a hard on."

"You have a hard on all the time," she said. "Even when you were a kid."

He didn't answer.

"Did you meet with your father?" she asked.

"Yes."

"What happened?"

"Nothing," he answered. "Everything's okay."

"Was your father angry?"

"You know Papa," he said. "But everything worked out. I wound up getting a job at an importing company in New York."

"What about the draft?" she asked.

He was annoyed. "I said everything was taken care of."

She was silent for a moment; then, looking down at her handbag on her lap, "I got a letter from Stevie," she said in a low voice. "He wants me to marry him when he comes home for the holidays."

Surprise sounded in his voice. "My brother?"

Now *she* was annoyed. "You know any other Stevie?"

"I don't understand it," he said. "How did you get the letter before my mother?" His mother opened everybody's mail before she passed it on.

"He didn't mail it to the house," she said. "I got it at the store when I came in this morning."

"He's been writing to you?"

"Now and then," she answered.

"Ever said anything about it before?"

"No."

"Sneaky bastard," he said. He looked at her. "What are you going to do?"

"I don't know," she said. "I'm afraid of what your mother will think of it. After all, we are first cousins."

"That don't mean shit," he said. "That's very normal in Jewish families. You know the saying, the family that marries together stays together."

"It's no joke," she said.

He looked at her. "How do you feel about it? Do you want to marry Stevie?"

"I like him," she said. "But I never thought about marrying him. In his letter he said that he had always thought about me. And if we could get married we would have a good life. First of all, this next year would be his last year in medical school and if we were married he wouldn't go right into the army, he would take his residency in a regular hospital for three years instead of the medical corps. He already had been offered positions from eight hospitals across the country. We could live wherever we wanted. There's a big shortage of doctors."

He stared at her. "That sounds good. Even Mama wouldn't argue about that. I don't think you have to worry about her."

She was silent.

"What's bothering you?" he asked.

"I don't know," she said huskily, her voice close to tears. "You know, it seems so cut-and-dried. I used to dream of love and romance. Maybe I'm being stupid. I'm twenty-five already. There's a war on and there are no men around. Another couple of years and I'll be an old maid."

He reached for her hand and held it gently. "Don't feel like that," he said. "You're a wonderful girl."

There were tears in the corners of her eyes. "But he never said in the letter that he loved me."

"Not at all?" he asked.

"Maybe at the end of the letter. He signed it, "Love Stevie.""

"Then what are you complaining about? He said it." He smiled. "That's Stevie, my brother. He's a doctor, not a writer."

In spite of herself, she began to laugh. "Then you think it's all right?"

"Great!" he answered. "And just remember, if he doesn't give you enough, you can always call on me. That's what brothers-in-law can be counted on for."

Chapter Four

The pushcarts were stretched out along the sidewalks between Fifty-second Street and Fifty-fourth Street on the west side of Tenth Avenue. The vendors were mainly Italian, and that was the language Joe heard as he walked along the sidewalks. He looked at the carts piled high with fruits and vegetables; others had Italian cheeses wrapped in gauze or shaped in a ball and hanging in thin ropes. There were pushcarts that displayed cheap housedresses and underwear, and others that sold housewares, knives and forks, plates and sundries. The sidewalks were crowded as women and men argued and bargained with each other as the shopping day began in earnest. It was almost ten o'clock when Joe crossed between two of the pushcarts to the other side of the street to the small store window that was lettered, "Caribbean Imports."

The window was dusty and probably had not been washed in months. There was no way he could have seen into the store. He opened the door, which was as dusty as the windows. If it had not been for the small card that read "Open," the store would have seemed closed.

Inside there was a counter, and a single light burning dimly over it. He looked around. There were some shelves on which were displayed an assortment of knives and forks of various sizes held by wooden and steel holders. On the counters were several costumes. On the walls behind were paintings, square, oblong and rectangular, in bright colors and representing scenes of people and villages indigenous to the Caribbean Islands.

He stood there for a moment. The store seemed empty—no one there and no sound. He knocked on the counter and waited. There was no answer. Then he glanced to the back of the store where there was a door in the rear wall behind the counter. In amateurish lettering was painted "Private." He hesitated a moment, then knocked on the door softly.

A few seconds later a faintly British-accented black voice came through the closed door. "That the new boy?"

"Yes," he called. "Joe Crown."

"Mon!" the voice called. "Ten o'clock already?"

"Yes, sir," Joe answered.

The sound of chain locks rattled and a tall black man peered out through the crack of the door. "Anyone else here with you?"

"No," Joe answered. "I'm alone."

"Lock the front door and turn the sign. Then come back in here." The man watched through the crack of the door as Joe locked the store and returned to him. Then the big man opened his door. He stood in the doorway completely naked and held out his hand. "I'm Jamaica," he said in a resonant Island voice.

Joe shook his hand. "Joe Crown."

"Come in," Jamaica said. "I'll jump into a pair of pants."

Joe followed him into the back room. There was a dim lamp resting on an old-fashioned roll-top desk. A faint scent of marijuana hung in the air. Jamaica pulled a pair of shorts and his pants from behind the desk chair and climbed into them. There was a sound against the far wall. Joe turned toward it.

A three-quarter sofa bed stood in the middle of the room. His mouth fell open in surprise. Three very pretty black girls, also naked, were on the bed.

Jamaica glanced at him and smiled, his teeth white and large. "Don't pay no attention to them," he said. "They all wifes."

"Your wives?" Joe felt stupid.

"Sort of," Jamaica said. "They my girls. They work for me. I have six more of them. I'm their sweet man."

Joe stared at him. "How can you take care of all of them?"

Jamaica laughed. "It's easy. I never take on more than three of them at the same time."

"How do you remember their names?" Joe asked.

"That's easy too," Jamaica answered. "They all have the same name. Lolita." He turned to the girls on the bed. "Now git your asses dressed an' ready for work," he said. "I got big business with this man."

He pulled his shirt from the chair and began to slip into the sleeves, then looked at Joe. "I'm forgetting my manners," he said. "Would you like a fuck off'n one of them before'n they get dressed?"

"No, thanks," Joe said, staring at them.

"Well, any time," Jamaica said. "They available. An' that's free for you. Jes' one of the extras on this job."

Joe nodded.

"Then let's go out into the store," Jamaica said. He looked back at the girls. "One of you Lolitas get your ass out to the coffee shop down the corner an' get us some coffee an' sweet rolls.'

Jamaica followed Joe into the store and sat behind the counter opposite him. He looked at Joe. "They told me that you a writer."

"That's right," Joe answered.

"What do you write?"

"Stories. For magazines—you know," Joe said.

"I don't read much," Jamaica said. "But I have respect for writing."

"That's okay," Joe said.

Jamaica looked at him. "You know them girls are not part of your job," he said. "They a sideline of mine."

"Not bad." Joe smiled.

"Keeps me a little busy but it's okay," he said.

Joe nodded.

"Your job is mostly to stay in the store an' answer the telephone because I'm mostly outside. Sometimes you have to make some deliveries after the store closes. You'll get extra for that." Jamaica looked at him. "That okay?"

"It's fine," Joe said. "But I still don't know what I'm doing or what we're selling here. I don't know anything about these things I see on the shelves and walls here."

Jamaica shook his head. "Mr. B. never told you?"

Joe shook his head.

Jamaica met his eyes. "Gumballs, ganch an' happy dust."

Opium, marijuana and cocaine. "Mr. B. never told me," Joe said.

"There's nothing to worry about," Jamaica said. "I have a very high-class clientele. All musicians and high-society people. An' Mr. B. has an agreement with the syndicate. They have a big blanket on us so there's never any trouble."

Joe was silent.

"It's a good job," Jamaica said. "Most of the time you don't do nothin' here an' you can write all you want. And along with twenty-five dollars, you'll probably pick up twenty or thirty a week extra on deliveries."

"That's fine," Joe said.

Jamaica looked at him shrewdly. "You scared?"

Joe nodded.

"Look at it like this," Jamaica said. "Jes figger you're better off bein' scared here than being scared shitless with your head bein' shot off in the army."

Joe was silent. That was one way of looking at it. The rear door opened and one of the girls came out. She was dressed in a cheap print housedress wrapped tightly over her big breasts and her big muscular buttocks. She looked at him curiously with her dark eyes, then, tossing her black hair ironed into soft curls around her face, turned to Jamaica. 'Kin we get coffee an' danish for us too?"

He looked at her. "The work tables set up?"

"Almos' finished," she answered.

He peeled a five-dollar bill from a roll in his pocket. "Okay," he said. "But make it fast, we have a lot of work to do."

She took the money and looked at Joe. "Cream an' sugar in your coffee?"

"Just black, thank you," Joe said.

She smiled. "If'n you like black, you jes my kin' of man."

"Get goin'," Jamaica said sharply. "Save your cock-teasin' for after we finish working." He watched her as she left the store and then turned back to Joe. "Gals are a pain in the ass," he said. "Have to keep showin' them all the time that you in charge."

Joe was silent.

"Your hours will be noon to seven," Jamaica said. "I'll be out from one to six."

Joe nodded.

"Come on," Jamaica said. "Let's see how the gals are doin'."

Joe followed him into the back room. It had suddenly been changed into a workroom. Two fluorescent ceiling fixtures gave a harsh blue light. The sofa bed had been made up and turned into an imitation-leather couch. Two tables, each covered tightly with a black oilcloth cover, were placed together to form a T-square. The two girls still in the room were also wearing cheap print housedresses.

Jamaica pulled a key chain from one of his pockets. For the first time Joe realized that one of the walls was covered with tall, locked metal closets, and at the far end were two new electric refrigerators. The refrigerator doors were also fitted with locks. Quickly Jamaica began to unlock the closets and the refrigerators.

Quickly and expertly he and the girls began to remove the equipment from the closet and set up their sections on the table. The T end of the tables held a hand-operated mill grinder and a large electric flour mixer with two rotating blades that fit into a mixing-bowl, and next to it was a large sifter that emptied into another bow. In the center of the table was a balance scale, the small weights against it measuring from a half gram up to two ounces. At the other end of the T-square were small leaves of paper, one side waxed, the other side either pink or blue; beyond that were brown glass bottles already labeled. Joe looked at one. "Merck," then "COCAINE. Flaked Crystalline Snow. Seven (7) Grams."

The long rectangular table was divided into one small section and one longer section. The small section held a small hand press that made ten pills at a time. The larger one, another kind of a roller for marijuana, with small teeth like spikes, was used to strip leaves from the branches, which then were placed into another sifter that allowed the leaves to fall into a tray without the seeds. Next to that was a large, hand-operated cigarette roller.

Jamaica took several boxes from the refrigerators. Two gray boxes were placed on the T tables. He opened the boxes, which held ten brown bottles each. This was the real thing, original bottles of prescription cocaine. Next to the bottles he placed a large round tin labeled "Lactose" and a small bottle labeled "Strychnine." He looked at Joe. "Prescription coke is seventy percent pure. It could blow your head off," he said. "We cut into equal parts of coke and lactose, then a pinch of strych to give it the bitter taste that hides the sweetness of the lactose. That way everyone is happy."

Joe didn't answer. That it made a better profit was not even mentioned. He continued to watch while Jamaica placed a large square brownish-black block of pressed gum of opium in front of one girl, and then a large box filled with stems of marijuana before another.

Jamaica looked over at him. "Do you use any of this stuff?"

Joe shook his head. "A joint now and then. But I'm really not into it, gets me crazy."

Jamaica smiled. "Just as well. If you can't handle it, you're better off leaving it alone."

There was a knock at the door and the girl he'd sent out for coffee stuck her head into the room. "Coffee's on the counter out here," she said.

Jamaica smiled. "Okay," he said. He looked at the girls. "Let's go."

The girl standing behind the T-square tables spoke to Jamaica. "Kin we all have a toot?" she asked. "We have to get ourselves up. Don' forget we didn' git much sleep last night. It was seven in the morning by the time we got in here."

Jamaica stared at her for a moment, then nodded. He took out a small vial and a tiny silver spoon. "Okay. But on'y one toot each," he answered. "Don' forget we got a lot of work to do this morning. This is the weekend coming up."

The girls clustered around him like a little flock of sparrows begging for bread crumbs. Jamaica looked at them and then at Joe. "They all Lolitas." He smiled again. "All cunts."

Jamaica rose from his chair behind the counter. He placed his empty coffee container down and looked at the girls. "Party time's over," he said. "Let's get back to work."

He watched the girls as they went to the back room, then turned to Joe. "Kin you start tomorrow at noon?"

"I'll be here," Joe said.

"I'll have more time to explain what you have to do," he said. "Right now, I have to keep my eye on those girls. If I'm not there, they'll steal my ass off."

"Okay," Joe said.

The telephone rang and Jamaica picked it up from under the counter. "Caribbean Imports," he answered in a guarded voice. He listened for a moment. "Need it right away?" he asked. Another moment passed before he answered. "I'll take care of it."

He put down the telephone and looked at Joe. "Can you do me a favor?"

Joe nodded.

Jamaica gestured for Joe to follow him into the back room. The girls were already working. He took out two brown paper bags, putting one into the other, then very quickly filled them and closed them. His movements were so fast that Joe couldn't even figure out what had been put into the bags.

Jamaica tied the bags with a brown cord and handed them to him. He scrawled an address on a piece of paper.

Joe looked down at it. "25 C.P.W. Penthouse C$1000.00."

"Got it?" Jamaica asked.

He nodded.

Jamaica gave him a five-dollar bill from his roll. "Give this to the doorman," he said. "He'll let you in." He walked into the store with Joe. "This is a big customer," he said. "He's a big Broadway composer, so make it fast. He said he's making the Twentieth Century to California at two o'clock."

"COD?" Joe asked.

"That's the only way we do business," Jamaica said.

It took less that ten minutes for Joe to reach the apartment house. The doorman peered at him, then pocketed the five-dollar bill and took Joe to a closed elevator and up to the apartment. He waited in the open elevator door and watched Joe deliver his package and receive an envelope. Joe checked the envelope and before he could nod his thanks the apartment door had closed. He returned to the elevator.

It took approximately ten minutes for Joe to return to the store. It was empty. Joe knocked at the rear door. Jamaica came out into the store.

Joe gave him the envelope and Jamaica went behind the counter and counted the bills, then stuck them into his pocket. His came up with a ten-dollar bill in his hand and held it out to Joe. "The customer just called me and told me that he was in such a hurry he didn't have time to give you a tip."

"It's okay," Joe said. "I can wait for it."

Jamaica smiled. "Keep it," he said. "I'll see you tomorrow."

"Thanks," Joe said. It was not until he was outside in the street that he realized that he had just passed the first test.

Chapter Five

He closed the door of the telephone booth that shut the outside noise away. "Miss Shelton? I'm Joe Crown," he said into the phone. "I'm the writer that your sister asked to call you."

Miss Shelton's voice was educated, self-important and cool. "Yes, Mr. Crown." She seemed to offer no encouragement.

"Can I have a moment of your time for an appointment?"

She answered, still cool. "You're the writer?"

"Yes, Miss Shelton."

"What have you had published?" she asked. "Beside the stories in the magazines I already know about."

"None," he said. "But I have written a number of short stories and novellas."

"You have submitted them to magazines?" she asked. "What has been their reaction?"

"Only rejections from those who read them," he answered. "Usually they came back unopened with a note that they do not read a manuscript unless submitted by an agent."

"Kathy thinks you could be a good writer," she said.

"Your sister is very encouraging."

"Can you send me several of those stories so that I can appraise your work? Try to select some of those you think are among the best."

"I'll do that, Miss Shelton," he said. "Shall I mail them or deliver them to your office?"

"Mail will be all right," she said. "I'll contact you as soon as I have time to read them."

"Thank you very much, Miss Shelton," he said.

"Not at all, Mr. Crown," she said formally. "I have a great deal of respect for my sister's opinion and will look forward to seeing your work. Goodbye, Mr. Crown."

"Goodbye, Miss Shelton," he said. There was a click in the receiver against his ear. The nickel tinkled down into the box as he hung up the phone. Automatically he put his finger into the return slot. This was his lucky day. He looked down at his palm. There were four nickels in his hand.

He invested one of the coins to call his cousin. Motty came on the phone. "What did my mother say?" he asked.

"I didn't talk to her," she said. "She left the house before I woke up."

He nodded. He had forgotten Friday morning was the busy time at the chicken market and his mother helped his father out on Fridays. That was the only day they needed two cashiers to handle the rush. "When are you going to tell her?"

"I think Sunday would be the best. Saturday is too hectic. With the morning at the *shul*, then rushing home to make dinner."

"Okay," he said. "If you need any help with her, call me."

He put down the telephone and placed another coin in the slot and dialed. Lutetia answered the ring. "Kitty there?" he asked.

"Wait a minute, I'll put her on the line."

A moment later Kitty came on the phone. "Joe?"

"Yes," he answered. "I stopped by yesterday afternoon but you were sleeping."

"I know," she said. "I really tied one on."

"You okay now?"

"Perfect," she said. "I have your money for you if you want to stop over now."

"I'll be right there," he said. He waited until the coins had tumbled down. But this time there was no jackpot.

Marta turned from the cashier's window that looked out over the chicken market. Phil was turning the lock in the deep drawer of his desk. She saw him strap on the shoulder holster, then check his Colt Police Positive .38-caliber revolver and slip it on. She looked at her husband. As she said every Friday that he strapped on the gun, "Why is it so important that you have to carry a gun just to collect lousy five-dollar bills?"

"That's not just five dollars," he answered as he usually did. "It comes to one thousand or two thousand dollars in the afternoon. There's a lot of *meshuggeners* that try to grab it."

"And you're going to kill them?" she asked.

"And you want them to get away with it?"

"What if they kill you first? You're such a sharpshooter, you'll be faster?" she retorted.

"You don't understand it," he said. "I don't wear a gun because I expect to use it. It's because if they know that I wear a gun, they won't bother me."

She dropped the subject as she collected a bill from a customer in front of the window. Then she watched him stuff his billfold with five-dollar bills. "Where's the *shiksa*?" she asked. "She's always late after her lunchtime."

"It's only twelve-thirty," Phil said. "That's only a half-hour since she's gone. She's allowed an hour for lunch."

"She knows that Friday is our busiest day. She should have more consideration and take only half an hour. But what do you expect from a *shiksha*?" Marta said sourly.

"She has to make lunch for her two kids when they come home from school," he said.

"She should make an arrangement," she said.

Phil didn't answer her. Josie already had an arrangement. He started to leave. "I'll be back by four o'clock."

"So be careful," Marta called after him as he walked out the door. She turned back to the window where several customers began lining up before her.

Josie's apartment was only two blocks from the market. The door was open. He walked into the living room. Josie came in from the kitchen. "What took you so long?"

"We got busy," he said, taking off his jacket and placing it over the back of a chair.

"You mean your wife was yakking about me," she said, annoyed.

He didn't answer her as he slipped off his gun and shoulder holster. He began unbuttoning his shirt, then realized that she was still completely dressed. "What's bothering you?"

"Your wife doesn't like me," she said.

"So?"

"She knows," she said.

"She knows shit," he said. He dropped his pants to the floor and opened the fly of his BVDs. He took out his already erect phallus and held it toward her. "Feel these fucking balls," he said. "They feel like fucking rocks."

"We've only got twenty minutes," Josie said. "I'll be late. You know that your wife will be pissed off at me and give me a hard time the rest of the afternoon."

"The only hard time you're goin' to get this afternoon is my prick in your hot wet pussy," Phil said angrily.

"By the time I get undressed and out of my girdle and then dressed again, it will take over an hour," Josie said.

"Then don't get undressed," Phil said. "Bend your ass over the side of the couch and I'll shove it into you from the rear."

She stared at him for a moment. "You got your rubber ready?"

"What the fuck are you doing to me?" Phil said half shouting at her. "You trying to make me crazy?"

Silently she turned away from him and bent herself over the arm of the couch as he had told her. She slipped the back of her skirt up and flipped it over her back. Then she pulled up the bottom of her girdle to the top of her buttocks. He didn't give her the time to drop her panties, just enough to allow them to drop down against her garters to her stockings. She felt his strong hands gripping her by her hips as he slammed himself inside her. "Oh, Jesus!" she half-screamed. "You're sticking that fucking thing all the way up to my goddam throat!" He felt like a triphammer slamming into her. A groaning animal sound came from her. She turned her face to look at him. His face was contorted purple with the blood rushing into his veins.

She reached underneath herself with one hand and cupped his testicles, squeezing them gently. "I love your balls, Phil," she said, catching her breath. "You got the biggest balls I ever saw on a man." She began squeezing them hard. "Oh God, Phil!" she said. "Why do we always have to make it so fast? Why can't we spend more time together?"

"Fuck, don't talk, you cunt!" he said harshly. Then he caught his breath. "Oh, shit," he yelled. "I'm coming!"

She reached for his phallus. "You got the rubber on?" she asked in a frightened voice.

"Fuck the fucking rubber!" he yelled.

Angrily she pushed him off her with her elbow and turned around to look at him. "My God!" she said. "You son of a bitch. You're still shooting your jism all over my damn couch."

He stared at her silently until he could recover his breath. "Get me a washrag for my dripping cock," he finally said.

"Fuck your cock," she snapped. "Look what you did to my couch! You ruined it!"

Suddenly he felt drained. "I'll get you another fuckin' couch," he said. "Just get me a washrag and get yourself dressed. You're already late for work."

She looked at him, then smiled. "Come to the bathroom with me," she said. "I'll clean you up. It won't take long to get to work."

He followed her into the bathroom and stood there as she knelt cleaning him. She looked up at him. "Can't you come over tonight instead of going to *shul*?" she asked.

"I wish I could," he said seriously. "But tonight I'm one of the *minyan*. That's one of the ten men needed to begin the service. Maybe next Friday night."

She stood and watched as he began to put on his clothes. "Okay," she said.

He was ready to leave. "I have to go," he said.

"I know," she said sadly. She lifted her face to his and kissed him. "You know, Phil, I really love you."

There was a strange sadness in his voice. "I know, Josie," he said. "I know."

It was almost five o'clock when he returned to his office at the market. From the window outside he could see the market was already cleaned and closed. "How did it go?" Marta asked.

"How should it go?" he said. "It goes." He didn't look at Josie as she sat counting the cash at her window. Neither did she turn to look at him.

"Josie will have the night deposit finished in a few minutes," Marta said.

Still not looking at Josie. Phil called to her. "How much?" he asked.

"A hundred and fifteen dollars, Mr. Kronowitz," she answered.

Marta looked over at Josie. "Try to hurry," she said softly. "Mr Kronowitz might be late for *shul*."

"I'll better go and get the car," Phil said. "I have to hide it two blocks away from the *shul* or the rabbi will see it."

Josie looked at him as he went out. "Have a nice weekend, Mr. Kronowitz," she said.

"You too, Josie," Phil said, looking back at her. "Have a nice weekend."

Marta got into the car beside him. "She doesn't work on the weekends?" she asked.

"She works on Saturday. Al pays her extra to help him," he said.

"Then she doesn't work on Sunday?" she asked. "Why not?"

"*Goyim* are entitled to a *Shabbes* too," he said.

Chapter Six

Kitty Branch was seated behind the typewriter with her usual coffee mug on one side and the deep ashtray filled with cigarette butts on the other. Her short curled pepper-and-salt hair style was attractive with her black-rimmed eyeglasses. Despite the warmth of the apartment she wore a gray linen skirt and a soft long-sleeved shirt. She looked up from the desk as Joe entered the room. Her voice was raspy from whiskey and weariness. "Want a coffee or a cold drink, Joe?"

"Coca-Cola is fine," he answered. He looked down at her. "You look tired."

Despite her ladylike appearance she spoke like a truck-driver. "I'm fucked. I have to dry out. Too damn much booze. It's going to kill me."

Joe dropped into a chair opposite her. "You know what's best for you."

"I know," she said. "But I never do it."

Joe didn't answer.

She called to the other room. "Lutetia, bring Joe a Coca-Cola." She turned to Joe, taking five singles from her desk, and handed them to him. "You were very helpful, thank you," she said.

"Thank you," Joe said. "I was glad to do it."

Lutetia brought the bottle of Coca-Cola and a glass with ice cubes. "Anything else you want?" she asked Kitty sulkily.

Kitty stared at her. Lutetia was wearing the same sheer chiffon dressing gown that she had worn yesterday. "For Christ's sake!" Kitty snapped. "Don't you ever put on clothes?"

"What the hell for?" Lutetia retorted. "We don't go out anymore. For the last week all you've done is drink and pass out, drink and pass out. I'm getting tired of it."

"Why don't you get a fucking job?" Kitty snapped.

"Doin' what?" Lutetia asked angrily. "The only job I can make money at is modeling over at the New School, and you don't like me doing nude modeling."

"You used to be a good secretary," Kitty said.

"Sure. For twenty a week. Modeling I could make fifteen dollars a day, twenty-five a day for private sessions. And at least I'd get to talk to some people." She glanced at Joe and then back to Kitty. "The only one I saw yesterday was that asshole friend of yours who thinks that the sun shines out of his prick!" Angrily she stalked out of the room.

"What's getting into her?" Joe asked.

Kitty looked at him. "I think she's getting ready to leave me."

He filled his glass. "Don't worry about it. Let her go."

"You don't understand," Kitty said, a hint of tears in her voice. "I love her."

Joe sipped at his glass without speaking.

Kitty looked across at him. "She told me that you tried to rape her."

He met her eyes. "Do you believe that?"

Kitty hesitated, then shook her head. "No. I know her. She gets pissed off even if I want to get a stiff cock inside of me once in a while."

Joe was silent.

"What did happen yesterday?" Kitty asked.

"She wanted me to french her," he answered.

Kitty looked at him. "And did you?"

"Yes," he said.

"What did she do for you?" she asked.

"Bullshit me," he replied. "She promised to suck me but she faked it until I came off in her hand."

Kitty began to laugh. "She's a real bitch."

"Yeah," he said sarcastically.

"But she's got the sweetest pussy I ever tasted," Kitty said.

"Sweet pussy is not enough," he said. "That's not the only thing in life."

"She's still a kid," Kitty said. "She doesn't know any better."

"Okay," he said. "But she's goin' to screw up, I'll bet on that."

Kitty looked at him for a moment, then reached for a cigarette. "I know that," she said sadly. "But what can I do about it? I love her."

"I'm sorry," Joe said.

She shrugged her shoulders. "I'll manage," she said. "I've been though it before." She looked up at him. "I heard that the front desk wants a five-part story on the Gould family. You know, they built the New York Central with the Astors. If it comes through I'll have about twenty hours of work for you."

"That's okay," he said. "I have an afternoon job in a store meanwhile and I have a deal for several stories for the magazine."

She smiled. "I wish you could connect with one of the decent magazines."

"Maybe I'll get lucky," he said. "Meanwhile I'm not complaining. It may not be much money but I'm being paid for writing."

"That's right," she said. "That's the name of the game." She squashed out her cigarette. "You'll keep in touch? Maybe we'll have dinner one night?"

"Right," he said rising to leave. "I hope things work out okay for you."

She took him to the door. "So do I," she said.

Motty walked through the driveway between the houses. The garage door was open. Uncle Phil's car was not there. She opened the side door of the house and entered the kitchen. The house seemed empty. The wall clock in the kitchen read six o'clock. That was normal for Fridays. She left work early and her aunt and uncle spent the evening at the synagogue. Usually they didn't get home until ten or eleven at night.

She walked to the two pots standing on the stove's gas burners and looked. Pot roast and small round potatoes in the large pot and *tsimmes*—carrots and peas cooked with either honey or brown sugar—in the smaller pot. All she had to do was heat them slowly. She hesitated for a moment. She really was hungry so she decided to go up to her room and have a shower before dinner.

The tap, tap sound of the typewriter came from Joe's room as she started up the staircase. She stopped in front of his door. The typewriter was really rattling; he was speeding along. She knocked on the door. "It's me," she called.

"I'm working," he shouted through the door.

"I know," she said. "I'm taking a shower before dinner. Call me when you're ready and I'll heat the dinner for us."

"Okay," he called back.

The sound of the typewriter began again and she walked into her room. Slowly she closed the door. Suddenly she felt tired. She took off her dress and stretched out on the bed in her slip. She closed her eyes and began to doze. Half asleep, she began to dream.

It wasn't a dream, it was a nightmare. Her aunt Marta was screaming at her. "No, over my dead body you'll marry my Stevie! You have to be crazy! What money have you got to help him! So could he open an office? Get an apartment and furniture to live in? My Stevie is going to be a doctor, a professional man. He has to marry a girl from a family with money. Not a girl we had to bring up, who we had to take care of so that she wouldn't grow up in the street!"

She felt the tears running down her cheeks. "But, Tante, we love each other. We always loved each other, even when we were kids."

"Love, shmove!" Aunt Marta shouted at her. "Out! Out of my house, you whore, you Jezebel! Out!"

Motty turned to Stevie, still crying. "Stevie, tell your mother! We love each other. Tell her!"

Stevie stared at her through his horn-rimmed glasses with the solemn look he always had. "We have to think about it," he said nervously. "Maybe we're acting too hastily. Mama is only trying to do the right thing for us."

Then all she could do was cry until the tears blurred her eyes and she could barely see. Still crying, she felt strong hands gripping her arms. "Stevie!" she cried. the tears still rolling down her cheeks, she looked up. "Joe."

"You were crying out loud," he said. "I could hear you from my room."

She sat up in bed. "I'm sorry."

"Don't be," he said. "Everyone has bad dreams sometimes."

"This was stupid," she said. She looked up at him. "I guess I'm really afraid of your mother. You know how she feels about Stevie."

Joe laughed. "I know. She thinks that there's no girl good enough for him. Her son the doctor."

"She doesn't feel that way about you," she said.

"I'm a nogoodnik," he said. "What's a writer who doesn't work?"

"It's a different kind of work," she said.

"I know it. You know it. But she doesn't," he said wryly.

"Let me change," she said. "I'll heat up dinner."

"No rush," he said. "I'll be working. Just call me when you're ready."

She sat on the edge of her bed until she heard the sound of his typewriter. Slowly she took off her slip and looked at herself in the mirror over the dresser. There were dark circles under her eyes. She turned the light on in the room. Daylight was fading quickly. She switched on the bedside lamp and turned back to the mirror. The circles under her eyes seemed even darker. Slowly she unfastened her brassiere and her girdle. In the mirror she could see the red lines on her flesh where her undergarments had compressed it. She rubbed the marks on her thighs and hips, then cupped her breasts. They felt heavy in her hands and she wondered whether they were becoming bigger and softer. She hoped not. A 36 C cup was big enough. She always felt embarrassed about the size of her breasts. At work, the men were always looking at them, trying to grab a feel of them or talking about them. She felt an aching in them.

Quickly she checked the date. She was only a few days away from her period. Maybe that was why she felt so heavy. She tended to gain a few pounds before her period, and maybe that was also why she now felt so blue and down. Automatically she touched her pubis. It, too, felt heavy and swollen. Quickly she fingered her clitoris, but the moment she felt the pleasure and excitement she stopped. She always felt very horny just before her period, but nice girls didn't do the things she wanted to do. She turned to the bathroom. A quick shower would make her feel better.

Joe's door was standing open as she walked past it in the hallway on her way to the staircase. The sound of the typewriter went clackety-clackety, faster and faster. "I'm going down to the kitchen," she called in to him.

The typewriter kept clacking; he seemed not to have heard her. She hesitated a moment, then went into his room and stood behind him looking down at the page in the typewriter.

The razorlike scimitar slit her brassiere and suddenly her naked breasts leapt forward.

Motty read the words on the page.

Quickly, she tried to hide her beautiful globules with her hands but without avail. Her breasts were too big to hide, and they overflowed her small graceful fingers. Then she felt the Arab's hot lips and breath moving down her throat and neck, down and down, the heat growing more intensely as he moved toward her breasts. Honey wanted to scream for help but there was none available. She was completely in the savage's power and no one to save her. With one hand she tried to push away but he only laughed and slipped the scimitar under the belly band of her harem pants and slowly began to cut them away from her beautifully rounded curvy hips and legs. "No!" Honey cried. "Please, no. I'm a virgin!"

Haroun Raschid smiled, leering. "Of course," he said in his fascinating sexy voice. "Only a virgin's blood is pure enough to mix with a sheik's love."

The scimitar flashed. She moved quickly, running toward the entrance of the tent before she ever realized she was completely nude. The tent flaps opened and two giant Nubian slave warriors pinned her arms.

"Bring her here," the sheik ordered.

They brought her to the center of the tent, still squirming and trying to escape. "Bind her wrists and her ankles to the two center poles."

Instantly, they obeyed, and turned silently from the tent. Honey tried to move but it was impossible. They had tied her securely. She shook the blond hair around her face. She stared at him as he slowly moved around examining every tiny secret corner of her nude body. Now she couldn't see him because he was completely behind her. She felt his hands touching her back, the soft curves of her buttocks. "What are you going to do to me?" she cried.

"You will see," he said softly and came out from behind her and stood unmoving. Then raising his right hand he uncovered the soft silk strands of a cat-o'-nine-tails whip.

Her eyes were wide and frightened. "You're going to hurt me and beat me!" she cried.

"No, my love," he said softly. "Believe me, you will never feel any pain, only pleasure. The pleasure that will bring a passionate excitement into your body that only the magic of our love can satisfy."

As if hypnotized, Honey stared as the whip in his hand raised up and up, before her. She held her breath as it began falling toward her . . .

The typewriter was suddenly still. Joe looked up at her beside him, his eyes glazed, as if he had been far away.

She felt a strange heat inside her as she looked down at him, then, "Jesus!" she exclaimed, suddenly realizing that he had been seated in nothing but his undershorts. "You've got a hard on!"

He blinked down at himself, then up at her. "That's right."

"How can you write with a hard on?" she asked.

"When I write like that, I have a hard on," he said. "I feel everything I write. When I write tears, I cry, when I write fear, I'm frightened. Whatever I write I feel. I even feel what other people feel when I write about them."

"Even real people?" she asked.

"Even about you or Mama and Papa. Stevie, everyone."

"Does your feeling come from writing or do you feel and then write?"

"I don't know," he said. "Sometimes one comes first, sometimes the other."

She looked down at him. "You still have your hard on."

He opened his fly and held his penis in his hand. "Yes."

"What do you do about it?"

"You know, jerk off or take a shower—and there's always the real thing. I could get laid." He looked up at her. "You read it over my shoulder. Didn't it get you horny?"

She didn't answer. The truth was, it had. The heat in her loins felt like fire. "No," she answered huskily.

"Touch it a little," he urged. He remembered a phrase from his childhood. "Kiss it and make it better."

She was shocked. "I'm going to marry your brother."

"You're not married yet," he said.

She let out a deep breath. "You are a shit!"

"That's right," he said.

She stood next to him for a moment, then smiled. "I think that you're not as bad as you like people to believe you to be."

"I still have a hard on," he said.

"That's your problem," she said. "I'm going downstairs to get supper ready."

Chapter Seven

The bell over the store door rang for the first time in the two weeks he had been working there. He rose from behind the narrow counter aisle in which he had jammed the typewriter table where he worked. A flashily dressed, pretty black girl walked toward him. "Hello, Joe," she said in a soft southern voice.

He looked at her blankly.

She smiled. "You don't remember me, do you? I'm Lolita."

He still drew a blank. But he did remember there had been three girls the first day he had come to the store. "I remember," he said. "But which Lolita were you?"

She laughed. "I was the one who went out for the coffee."

He nodded, but really did not recognize her. "Lolita?" he said questioningly.

"My name is not really Lolita," she said. "But that's what Jamaica calls all of us. My name's Charlotte. Charlie for short."

"Nice to meet you, Charlie," he said, holding out his hand. Her hand was small and warm in his palm. "What can I do for you?"

"I was just in the neighborhood," she said. Her hand still rested warmly in his clasp. "What are you doin'?"

"Working," he said, gesturing to the typewriter behind the counter.

She glanced at it. "Writin'?"

"I'm trying."

She withdrew her hand. "Jamaica around?"

"Not until six o'clock," he said. He glanced at his wristwatch. It was only a quarter to four.

"I was hopin' I'd find him here," she said. "I wanted to make a little contact."

"Sorry," he answered. "He doesn't leave me with any. That's his department. All I do is take telephone messages."

"I can always find up some scrapins in the back room," she said.

"The back room's locked," he replied. "And he keeps the key on him."

"Shit!" she said. "I'm really feelin' down." She looked up at him. "You don' know how bad it is out there on the street. I must have been up and down Broadway from Columbus Circle to Times Square three times and never scored."

He felt disappointed for her. Then he remembered. "I have a small clincher of a joint. I don't know how good it is because I have had it a long time."

"Anything will be a help," she said.

He took out his pack of Twenty Grands and tapped out the small piece of cigarette. She took it in her fingers and held it under her nostrils.

"It's not bad," she said. She opened her purse and took out a bobby pin. Carefully she clipped the joint in the pin, then lit a match. She inhaled slowly and deeply. She looked at him through the curl of smoke. "This is a godsaver!"

He lit a Twenty Grand for himself and stood there without speaking. The pungent smell of the marijuana was overriding the tobacco in the cigarette. He began to feel it in his head. He stared down at her breasts swelling over the square-cut decolletage of her blouse.

She smiled at him. "Like them black beauties?"

"Unbelievable!" he said.

With her finger she pulled down her blouse. "Ever see such purple nipples?" she asked. "They stick up like little black pricks."

He stared silently. He could feel the surging in his penis. Still smiling, she placed her hand on his fly. She laughed. "You have a real friend there."

"We better cut it out," he said. "The front door is open."

"It don't mean a shit," she said. "Nobody ever comes in here. Like french?"

"I'm not crazy," he said.

"I give the best french in the world," she said. "Let's get in the back corner behind the counter. Nobody can see us back there."

She followed him behind the corner. Carefully she pinched out the joint and knelt in front of him and opened his fly. Expertly she cupped his testicles with her hand, and resting the shaft of his penis on her palm, gently began to lick her tongue in a slow circle around his glans as her teeth sharply touched him in unexpected tiny bites.

He felt his legs becoming weak, the sensation running through himself under his groin into his anus. Suddenly the telephone began ringing. "Jesus H. Christ!" he exclaimed. Picking up the receiver he spoke into it. "Caribbean Imports."

A very formal woman's voice came to him. "Mr. Crown?"

He could barely answer. "Yes." He looked down at the black girl. She was really into her work, her eyes smiling at him, her large white teeth nipping at him.

"Laura Shelton," the voice came into his ear. "I have good news for you."

He leaned on one arm so that he would not fall from the counter. "Yes, Miss Shelton," he managed to say.

"I'm sorry I haven't called you before, but I have been very busy. But despite that I have been working for you. You know that story you sent to me, "The Shoplifter and the Store Detective?"

"Yes," he gasped.

"I just sold it to *Collier's* magazine for one hundred and fifty dollars," she said.

"Oh, my God!" he shouted, no longer able to control himself. His orgasm was tearing throughout the whole of his body. He looked down at the black girl; his semen was overflowing from the corners of her mouth to her chin and onto her cheeks. "Oh, my God!" he yelled.

She must have sensed a strangeness in his voice. "Mr. Crown?" she asked quickly. "Mr. Crown, are you all right?"

"Yes," he gasped. "I was just overwhelmed."

"You must be very excited," she said with self-satisfaction in her voice. "Especially since we've never even seen each other face to face."

He looked down at Charlie, still kneeling before him, her hand holding his erection tightly, her tongue still licking him as if he was a popsicle. "Yes," he said more calmly. "I never felt anything quite like it."

"We have some details to work out," she said. "Could you come into the agency tomorrow morning? I'll have the agency contract ready for you, and the magazine check."

"Ten-thirty okay?" he asked.

"That will be fine," she said.

"Thank you very much, Miss Shelton," he said. "And also pass along my thanks to your sister for bringing us together."

"I will do that, Mr. Crown," she said. "I'm looking forward to meeting you at last. Goodbye, Mr. Crown."

"Goodbye, Miss Shelton," he replied and placed the telephone on the counter. He looked down at the black girl, whose fist still held him tightly. "What the hell are you trying to do?" he asked. "Break it off?"

She wiped the semen from her cheek and chin with the back of her other hand and licked it off. "One good come deserves another," she smiled. "There's still a lot of juice in your balls."

He stared at her as she brought him into her mouth again. Her cheeks went concave as she drew him in tightly. Then a sharp knifelike pain tore into his anus as she forced two long-nailed fingers inside him. He almost fell as the pain richocheted through his groin. He yelled in agony and almost automatically hit her across the face with his open hand, knocking her to the floor. "Bitch!" he snapped angrily.

She held her hand against her cheek, a peculiar expression on her face as she looked at him. "I was jus' tryin' to pleasure you," she said.

The back-room door opened behind her. Joe had forgotten the secret alley door that Jamaica used to the back room. Jamaica glanced at him, then down at the girl. His voice was cold. "You tryin' to put a hurtin' on that boy, Lolita?"

The sound of fear echoed in her voice as she tried to grovel toward him. "No, sweet man. I was jus' foolin' with him."

"Bitch!" he snarled. With his heavy boot, he kicked her in the ribs and she rolled sidewise across the store. "How many times done I tol' you never to come into the store less'n I ask?"

She curled herself into a ball, crying. "I didn' mean nuthin'," she said. "I jus' was so horny for to see you."

"Lyin' bitch!" he said coldly, drawing his belt from his trousers. "You were lookin' for some dope." He slashed the belt across her back and buttocks until she slumped half-unconscious on the floor. Then he picked her up with one hand under her armpit, and half-dragging her across the floor threw her into the back room and closed the door behind her. He turned to Joe, the leather belt sliding back into the loops of his trousers.

"I'm sorry, Jamaica," Joe said.

"It's not your fault," Jamaica said. "She a schemin' bitch. She know the rules."

"I didn't mean for her to get beat up like that," Joe said.

Jamaica looked at him as if he were stupid. "You hit her, didn't you?"

Joe didn't answer.

"Don' you know that was what she wanted?" Jamaica smiled. "That's the way she gets her kicks. She's happy now. Now she knows she's really loved."

"I don't get it," Joe said.

"You're young yet," Jamaica smiled. "You'll learn." He glanced at the telephone still on the counter. Usually it was on the shelf underneath. "Who was on the phone?"

"It was my agent," Joe said. Then it suddenly dawned on him. He was now a real honest-to-God writer. "*Collier's* magazine just bought a story of mine!"

"First time?" Jamaica asked curiously.

"With a real classy magazine," Joe said.

"That's great," Jamaica said. "Congratulations."

"Thanks," Joe said. "I still can't believe it. I bet she thought I was crazy. Lolita was still frenchin' me while I was on the telephone."

Jamaica laughed. "Not too bad," he said. "You were gettin' it both ways."

Joe shook his head. "I still don't get it."

Jamaica sniffed. "Thought I caught a smell of ganch when I came in."

"Yes," Joe said. "I had half a joint. I gave it to her."

"No, shit for any of those girls unless I okay it. *Capish*?" Jamaica's voice was emphatic.

"*Capish*," Joe said. "I'm sorry."

"Now you know, forget it." Jamaica opened a small notebook. "I have several extra deliveries. Have the time for them?"

"That's my job," Joe said.

Chapter Eight

The Piersall and Marshall Agency was located in a renovated brownstone house in the middle of the street between Fifth and Madison Avenue. A square plaque attached to the iron-spike railing indicated that the offices were on the fourth floor. He entered down the steps to the basement entrance and into a small hallway with an old-fashioned grilled elevator. The elevator was empty and he went into it, closed the gate and pressed the button. The elevator screeched and ground to the fourth floor.

He left the elevator and walked into a small reception area where the receptionist sat behind a desk and a telephone switchboard. She looked at him.

"Miss Shelton," he said.

"Your name?" she asked officiously.

"Joe Crown."

"Do you have an appointment?"

"Yes." He nodded.

She pressed two keys on the switchboard. "Mr. Crown is here for Miss Shelton," she said. She listened for a moment, then put down the telephone. "Take a chair," she said. "Miss Shelton is in a meeting but she will be with you in a few minutes."

There were a two-cushion couch and two chairs, all in old, worn leather, gathered around a small coffee table covered with magazines. He looked around. The walls were covered with tired, peeling tan paint and several ancient equally tired framed prints. He glanced at the receptionist. She ignored him, her eyes staring into space.

The telephone switchboard buzzed. "Piersall and Marshall Agency," she sing-songed. A sound of excitement came into her voice. "Yes, Mr. Steinbeck, I'll put you right through to Mr. Marshall." She turned to the switchboard keys, then turned to Joe. "That was John Steinbeck, the author," she announced importantly.

Joe nodded.

"I'm sure you've heard of him," she said. "He's one of our clients."

He resented her snobbery. "I'm one of your clients too," he said.

Her nose turned up. "I never heard of you."

"You will," he said, getting up from his chair. "Which way is the men's room?"

"It's downstairs on the main floor behind the elevator," she said. "But Miss Shelton should be ready to see you any minute now."

"Then she'll have to wait," he said walking to the elevator. "Unless you want me to take a piss in the pot holding that rubber plant in the corner." Then before she could reply, he pressed the button for the main floor and the elevator went down.

"The second office on the left beyond the glass doors," the receptionist said grudgingly as Joe came from the elevator.

"Thank you," he said and walked through the glass door. Miss Shelton had her name on the office door. Joe knocked.

"Come in," she said through the door.

He went inside. It was a small office, the desk covered with manuscripts, yet everything was neatly in place. She was a tall girl in her middle twenties, her sandy hair wrapped tightly in a bun, her fair skin faintly shining with the warmth of the office, her blue eyes clear behind her eyeglasses. She rose and held out her hand. "Mr. Crown," she said pleasantly.

"My pleasure, Miss Shelton," he said.

She gestured to the chair opposite her. "You were surprised at my call?" she said, smiling.

"More than that," he replied. "I couldn't believe it."

"I could tell that from your voice," she said. She met his eyes. "I have some papers for you to sign."

"I understand," he said.

"Only three things," she said. "First, an agency contract that will give us authorization to represent you for a period of one year from each sale we make for you. The period is not cumulative—the period is only from the last sale."

He nodded.

"The second is that we would develop a small bio about you so that we can help with publicity and supply information to publishers and reviewers who might be interested in you and your work. And several snapshots would also be helpful for that purpose."

"What kind of bio?" he asked.

"Age, where you were born, education, hobbies. Things like that."

"That's easy," he laughed. "I never did very much. Born in Brooklyn, age twenty-five [a lie—he was twenty-two]. CCNY, majored in literature and journalism but did not graduate because I left in the third year in order to help out with family finances." Lies, all lies.

She looked at him. "Any hobbies? Sports, games, chess?"

"None like that," he answered.

"But you do have other interests?" she asked.

"Yes," he said. "But I don't think they're relevant."

"Let me be the judge of that," she said.

He hesitated, then shrugged. "Sex," he said.

She laughed, faintly blushing. "You have a delicious sense of humor, Mr. Crown."

"Call me Joe," he smiled. "You said there was a third item."

She was slightly flustered. "Oh, yes. I have the acceptance agreement and the check from *Collier's*. You will notice that the agreement is for one hundred fifty dollars. From that we deduct our normal ten percent and expenses, phones and mail, etcetera. The net check will be for one hundred and twenty-eight dollars."

Joe looked down at the check, then at her. "Miss Shelton. I could kiss you," he said.

She laughed. "Not yet," she said. "Let's wait until we have a few more contracts under our belts. Now, I want you to make sure you send as much material to me as you can, so that we can begin mining the market. You are a good writer, Mr. Crown. I feel you will do very well."

Jamaica was standing behind the counter as he came into the store. "I have good news for you." He smiled.

Joe was puzzled. "Good news?"

Jamaica nodded. "You're movin' uptown to a better job."

"I don't get it," Joe said. "I'm happy with this one."

Jamaica looked at him. "You don't have any choice," he said flatly. "Neither do I. This is from Mr. B."

Joe was silent for a moment. "What is it?"

"I'll explain it to you in the car," Jamaica said.

Joe followed him into the back room. It was empty. The work tables had been put away, the girls already gone. Quickly Jamaica locked the cabinets and the refrigerator. "Lock the outside door," he said. "And meet me in the alley."

A moment later, Jamaica pulled up behind the driver's wheel of his black shiny 1940 Packard 12. He gestured and Joe climbed into the seat behind him.

"Who is going to look after the store?" Joe asked.

"It'll keep," Jamaica said. "This is more important." He turned the car up Eighth Avenue, then around Columbus Circle and uptown along Central Park West before he spoke. After a moment, he glanced at Joe. "You know about the Lolitas I take care of?"

"Yes."

"I have another group of Lolitas," he said. "These are high-class girls. Okay girls, real society types. It's a big operation and Mr. B. and the Italians have a fifty percent cut."

Joe watched him as he moved the big Packard expertly through the traffic. "What's that got to do with me?" he asked.

"I own four brownstones on Ninety-second Street off Central Park West that I joined together and turned into a furnished apartment house. It comes to about seventy apartments, and almost half of them are rented by the girls. We supply maid service and a janitor and handyman to take care of repairs. The girls pay us between two hundred and four hundred a week depending on their business. Our former resident manager cut himself a piece of our action."

"You fired him?" Joe asked.

"In a kind of way," Jamaica said. "But that wasn't my department and I don't ask my partners what they did. This morning Mr. B. called me and told me to send you up there."

"What if I don't want the job?" Joe asked.

Jamaica glanced at him. "That wouldn't be smart. Mr. B. is doing a big one for you and your father. He does one for you, you do one for him."

Joe was silent.

"It won't be permanent," Jamaica said gently. "Two or three months, just until they can move in a professional. They know you're a writer and you got no stomach for that kind of thing. But Mr. B. said you could take care of this for a while, and he'll consider your marker paid off."

Jamaica slowed the car and then cut into Ninety-second Street between ongoing traffic. He pulled to the curb in front of a yellow-canopied entrance. He turned off the ignition.

Joe looked at the entrance. The white lettering on the sides of the canopy, spelled out UPTOWN HOUSE. FURN. APTS. The entrance was a wide glass double door. "Is there an office for me here?" he asked.

"You could kind of call it that," Jamaica said. "But actually it will be your apartment."

"Why an apartment?"

"You'll be living here," Jamaica said. "That's part of the deal. Mr. B. already told that to your father. He said you have to stay away from your house. Something about the neighbors might squeal to the draft board if they see you around."

"They haven't anything to squeal about yet. I haven't got a new draft card."

Jamaica took a small envelope from his pocket and handed it to him. He watched Joe open the envelope and read the card. JOE CROWN. Classification: 4F. Dated Oct. 22, 1942. "Now you do," he said without expression.

Joe stared at him.

Jamaica smiled. "It's really not the end of the world. Actually, if you really love pussy like you say you do, you might even think you're in heaven."

Chapter Nine

His mother looked suspiciously at him. "What kind of a janitor's job pays one hundred dollars a week? With a three-room apartment also? Janitors are lucky if they get a room in the cellar of an apartment house for free, not also with getting money. It's something wrong, you'll probably wind up in jail or worse."

"Jesus! Mother," he said. "First, I'm not a janitor. I'm a resident manager. I manage seventy apartments that make maybe seven, ten thousand dollars a week. And I have enough time to write. That's the most important thing. This first check for a hundred and fifty dollars for the story from *Collier's* magazine is only the beginning."

"First of all, you didn't get a hundred and fifty, you got a hundred and twenty-eight, second of all, how do you know you can sell any more stories? You got guarantees?"

"Shit!" Joe said. He rose from the table and looked down at his father, who had been unusually quiet. "Papa, would you explain to her why I have to take that job?"

He stared at Joe for a moment, then turned to his wife. "It's a good job, Marta," he said softly. "Believe me, my friend wouldn't do anything to get him into any trouble."

"Your friend's a lowlife gangster!" Marta snapped.

Phil's face turned purple with anger. "Gangster!" he shouted. "It was you who wanted her baby to get out of the draft, not my friend. But it's my friend that did what you wanted. Now, Joe has a Four-F draft card. And he's got to pay for it, and I have to pay for it whether you like it or not!"

"So my son has to go to jail or get killed or something even worse!" she yelled at him.

"Your little baby boy will go to fucking jail if they ever find out about his goddamn draft card!" Phil was almost out of breath. "So shut up already or I'll have another fucking heart attack!"

Marta felt frightened. "Phil, calm down. Quiet, I'll get you a pill." She looked up at Joe. "See! See what you made your father do?"

"I'm all right already," Phil said. "Just let's have some peace and quiet."

"I would still like to look at the apartment before he moves in. You know how dirty people are, the place might be covered with cockroaches and mice. How do I even know the sheets are clean?"

Phil spoke calmly. "Okay. You can see it. But not right now. Wait until he gets settled down. Then nobody will bother him."

"Okay," Marta said finally. "But what do I tell the neighbors when they don't see him around here?"

Phil shook his head in amazement. "The whole neighborhood knows he was going for his physical. Tell them he went into the service. That's why we had to get him away from here."

"And what about Stevie and Motty's wedding? What will the neighborhood say when he doesn't come home for his brother's wedding?"

Joe looked down at Motty, still seated at the table. She had never let him know she had told his parents about her and Steven. Motty didn't meet his eyes. He turned to his mother. "Maybe by the time that happens, I'll be able to come home for it."

"No," Phil said emphatically. "You're supposed to be in basic training by the time they get married around the holidays, and everybody knows they don't give leaves during basic training."

"I'd better get up to my room and begin packing," Joe said.

Phil rose from the table. "I have to go out for a couple of hours," he said. "I'll be home by ten-thirty."

"Every Monday and Wednesday night you go out for a couple of hours to make some collections," Marta complained. "Why don't they pay on Friday afternoon like they used to all the time?"

"We're doing more business," Phil answered. "If I don't chase after them, we'll never get our money back." He walked toward the door. "I'll be back by ten-thirty," he repeated.

"Don't forget to keep your pills in your pocket," Marta said.

Phil held up a small bottle. "I have them, I have them," he said.

Joe had just finished his packing and closed his valise when he heard his father's car come up through the alley between the houses. Then he heard the side door open, and his father walked heavily up the staircase and into his parents' bedroom. A moment later he heard sounds from their bathroom; finally, the noises subsided and Joe noticed the light had gone out from under their door to the hallway.

Joe pushed some of his manuscripts off the bed. Then one of the stories caught his eye and he sat down on the side of the bed to reread it. It was a story he had written in pencil on a lined yellow paper pad about five years ago. He had written it to impress his high school English teacher, who was the first person ever to tell him he had talent and should become a writer.

The fact that the square-cut decolletage of her dress gave him a completely exciting view of her exquisite full breasts and pink nipples had nothing to do with his decision to become a writer. But it had helped. That was basically what this story had been about. A young high school student had fallen in love with his English teacher because he thought that the view she had afforded him of her decolletage was especially for him. His dreams had been shattered when he took her a bouquet of flowers, and her door was opened by her husband. Almost a full year she had been in his thoughts and dreams, almost ten jars of Vaseline had been wasted on his sore, irritated penis and stained bedsheets. Now, as he reread the story, he realized that the last year of his frustration should have been the story—not the one he had written. He threw the manuscript on the floor and undressed and got into bed. For a moment, he thought about brushing his teeth but he was too bored with it and turned off the bed lamps. He looked into the dark and the faint light from the streetlight at the end of the alley made patterns on the ceiling. The shadows were beginning to blur when a soft tapping sound came into the room.

He sat up in bed. The sound was strange. It was not coming from the door or from the hallway. The soft tapping sound echoed again. Motty's voice whispered from the wall against Stevie's bed on the far side of the room.

Kneeling on the bed, he pressed his ear to the wall. "Motty?"

"Yes," she whispered. "Pull out the bolts of the old sliding doors between our rooms."

Then he remembered—the sliding doors between the two rooms had been closed when Motty had been given Stevie's room. He pulled the bed slightly away from the doors, then opened the bolts. It was difficult. The bolts had been closed for many years. Finally, with a small scraping sound, they gave. He managed to open the doors slightly.

She held her face between the open doors. "Are you awake?" she asked.

"Of course not," he answered sarcastically. "I always do things like this in my sleep."

"Don't be shitty," she said. "I want to talk to you."

He was still kneeling on the bed, and his face was even with her own. "Then why didn't you come through the regular door?"

"I didn't want your parents to see me in the hall," she said. "You know how they are. Especially your mother."

He nodded. "I know. Come in then." He began to move off the bed.

"You'd better come in here," she said. "Your room is right next to theirs."

Silently he moved across the bed and then squeezed himself through the narrow opening into her room. He found himself against the back of a chest of drawers. As he slipped out from behind it, he scraped his shoulder. "Shit!" he exclaimed, rubbing his shoulder.

"Did you hurt yourself?" she asked.

"It's nothing," he said, looking at her. "Now what was so important?"

She stared at him. "You're naked!"

"I was fucking asleep," he said shortly. "I wasn't planning to go visiting."

"I'll get you a towel," she said.

He watched her walk across the room and get a towel from the closet. She was wearing a cotton nightgown under her bathrobe. She held the towel to him, her eyes averted. He wrapped it around himself. "Okay," he said.

She looked up at him. "I didn't congratulate you for selling a story to *Collier's*."

"Thank you," he said. He smiled. "I should really congratulate you. Remember that story you told me about the store detective who caught that girl shoplifting and took her into a dressing room to take her clothes off and raped her?"

"That's the story that *Collier's* bought?" Her eyes were wide.

"I changed it a little," he said. "I turned it into a love story. That he tried to protect her and wound up losing his own job."

"That's beautiful," she whispered. "Really beautiful." She was silent for a moment; then her eyes began to overflow.

"Now, what the hell's the matter?" he asked.

"I'm frightened," she whispered.

"What about?" he said. "Everything's okay. You and Stevie are getting married. Mama's happy for you and she's happy that I got a Four-F. What's there to be frightened about?"

"Everything's changed," she said. "You're moving out. You won't be in the next room anymore."

"It don't mean a shit," he said. "You'll be able to meet me in New York. It's only across the river, not across the world."

"But I have no one to talk with here at home."

He put his arm around her and brought her head to his shoulder. "Don't be a crybaby," he said softly. "We can talk all the time on the phone."

"It's not the same," she whispered.

"Soon you'll get married and it'll be better," he said. He stroked her hair softly, he felt her shivering against him. "It will be better, you'll see."

"No," she cried, turning her face to him. "It won't be the same."

He looked down at her face, his eyes searching deep into hers. Slowly he moved his lips to her forehead, then to her cheek, finally to her mouth. He felt the heat from her body pressing, heavily against him. His phallus sprang wildly toward her. He tried to push her away from himself. "This is crazy," he said hoarsely.

She didn't move, just falling even more heavily against him, her groin moving toward his searching need. Silently they moved to the bed, the towel falling from him to the floor. Quickly he moved her robe, then the nightgown, and bent over her. "Motty!" he said.

"Don't talk!" she said. "Just tear me apart and fuck me!"

Chapter Ten

The sound of the engine came up from the alley as Uncle Phil's car backed into the street. Quickly she moved from her bed to the window. In the faint gray of morning she saw the car turning and moving away. Quietly she went back to the bed.

Joe was fast asleep, lying naked on top of the blankets. She stared at him. It was strange. It was as if he had always been there in her bed with her. She had always thought that if they ever did it she would feel upset and guilty. But it was not like that. Instead she felt annoyed at her stupidity. Why had she denied herself her desires for so many years? She touched him lightly on the shoulder.

He turned on his side slowly, still asleep. She felt the excitement beginning to move inside her as she saw his erection, full and strong in the morning. Gently she held his phallus in her hand. His eyes opened, sleep disappearing from his dark pupils. He looked down at her hand holding him, then up at her face. He was still silent.

A soft, quiet smile came to her face. "It's beautiful," she said.

He didn't answer.

"Why did we wait so long?" she whispered.

He shook his head. "I wanted to but you—"

"I was stupid," she interrupted him. "But I was afraid."

"But now that we did it, we'll find a way to manage it," he said.

She shook her head slowly. "No," she said softly. "It was beautiful, and I want to keep it that way. If we try to make it any more than it has been, we'll turn it into something sordid and it will destroy all of us. All of us in the family."

He felt the beating in his pulse. "I'm beginning to juice."

"I'm soaking wet too," she said and looked down at him. "Damn!" she said in surprise. "The sheets are covered with blood!"

"What happened?" he asked nervously. "Beginning your period?"

She stepped from the bed. "No, you stupid jerk, I was a virgin."

He stared at her, his mouth agape.

"Now I have to strip the sheets from the bed," she said quickly. "If your mother finds out, she'll know what happened and she'll kill me!"

Despite himself he felt a sense of pride. Even in high school he had never copped a cherry. "Mother doesn't have to know. Just tell her you were surprised with the period."

'Not your mother," she whispered. "She watches my cycles better than I do."

Jamaica had already brought his typewriter and the boxes of manuscripts and typing paper from the store before Joe had arrived at the apartment. Quickly Joe began to unpack.

The apartment was not bad. The furniture was slightly tacky but serviceable. The living room contained an imitation-leather three-seater couch with a matching easy chair placed in front of a coffee table and lamps placed on end tables on each side of the couch. In one corner of the room was a small dining table with two chairs placed in front of one of the windows that faced the street. The kitchenette was a closet angled from the table. The bedroom was painted dark green; a three-quarter wooden bed in a lighter shade of green matched the dresser and a chest of drawers. A yellow imitation-satin bedspread covered the sheets and pillows. The bathroom was American Standard white fixtures, with a yellow curtain hanging from the shower rod and a matching curtain covering the small window. There were two lights in the bathroom, one on the ceiling, the other attached to the medicine cabinet over the sink.

In less than two hours, Joe had put away his clothing and placed the two valises on a shelf over the bedroom closet. He carefully placed the typewriter on the dining table so that the light from the window shone over his shoulders onto the typewriter, and placed paper and manuscripts on either side of it. He was still looking down at it when he heard a knock at the door. He crossed the room and opened it.

Jamaica was smiling. "How is it?"

"I'm unpacked," he answered.

Jamaica came into the apartment. "I have a few more things for you. Fred's bringing them up."

Fred was one of the two handymen that worked in the apartment house. "What?" Joe asked.

"We're bringing in a new combination electric refrigerator and tabletop stove. The one here is fucked. The telephone will be installed this afternoon. We have our own switchboard downstairs. All calls go through it."

"Including the girls?" Joe asked.

"Especially the girls," Jamaica answered. "The switchboard monitors them, and each morning will give you a list of their bookings."

Joe nodded. "I understand that. Now who collects the money?"

Jamaica answered. "The girls have to turn in the money to you each morning. The switchboard service will let you know how much money each of the girls owes us."

"Complicated," Joe said.

"Not really," Jamaica said. "The girls average about five hundred a night, that's five tricks a night at one hundred a pop. Special services like group parties, shows and S and M are at the girls' discretion for extra charges."

Joe looked at him. "What are the girls like?"

Jamaica laughed. "The best-lookin' chicks in the world. You'd think that each one of them came right out of Billy Rose's Diamond Horseshoe. These kids are not Lolitas. Real okay society class. You'll probably fuck yourself to death in less than a week."

"Not me," Joe smiled. "I have to work. Writing and fucking don't mix. Each takes too much time."

"That may be." Jamaica smiled. "But that's your problem, not mine." Another knock came from the door. "That's probably Fred with the furniture," he said.

But Jamaica was wrong. A young girl stood in the open door. Long straight brown hair, horn-rimmed glasses, loose tan sweater over a brown skirt. She seemed more like a college student than a hooker. She looked at Jamaica. Her voice was soft and cultured. "I thought I'd drop downstairs and meet your new man and see if there's anything I could do to help him."

Jamaica nodded and gestured. "Joe Crown, Allison Falwell."

Allison held out her hand. "Nice to meet you, Joe."

Jamaica stopped Joe's hand. "Mr. Crown," he said disapprovingly to the girl.

Allison stared at Jamaica. "But he seems so young."

Jamaica's voice went cold. "Mr. Crown," he repeated.

Allison turned to Joe. "Nice to meet you, Mr. Crown. Is there anything I can do for you?"

"No, thank you," Joe said coolly but politely, taking his cue from Jamaica. 'But if there is anything, I will call you."

Jamaica closed the door behind her "Bitch!" he said. "You'll see more of them soon. All trying to get an edge."

"So?" Joe asked.

"You can't let them," Jamaica said. "If you want to be a good pimp you treat all of them the same way. You don't like what they're doin', just belt them."

"I don't know if I can do that," Joe said.

Jamaica stared at him. "Jes' think that everyone of them wants to tear your ass out with their fuckin' fingernails like Lolita did. Then you'll fin' it easier to belt them." He paused a moment before adding, "Jes' remember, no matter how great they look, they nuthin' but whores."

His mother answered the telephone. "It's already eight o'clock," she said as she recognized his voice. "Have you had dinner?"

"Not yet, Mama," he said. "I've just been straightening up. And I had to learn all the details about the job."

"You have a kosher restaurant near you?"

"There's two good delis within blocks of here," he answered.

"The apartment is clean? Is the bed good?"

"Everything's okay, Mama," he said reassuringly. "Don't worry, I'm a big boy." He changed the subject. "Papa home yet?"

"No," Marta answered. "This is one of his nights he has to make collections."

"Motty there?"

"Yes," she said. "You want I should call her to the phone?"

"Please, Mama."

His cousin's voice came through the receiver. "Joe?"

"You okay?" he asked.

"I'm okay," she said. She lowered her voice almost to a whisper. "The house seems empty."

"I know what you mean," he said.

"How's the job?" she asked.

"It's a job," he said noncommittally. "It'll be okay. Jamaica told me it's only temporary. I should be out of this in about three months."

"And then what do you do?"

"I don't know. But this takes off my marker and I'm a free agent. I'll keep on writing and looking around."

"Your mother seems down. I think she misses you."

He didn't answer.

"I miss you too,' she said.

"Maybe we can meet one night," he said. "I'll take you to some chinks."

"I don't think so," she answered. "I don't think I can handle it if we spend some time together. Believe me, it will be better if you just stay away."

He was silent for a moment, then sighed. "I guess you're right."

"But you will call me, won't you?"

"Of course," he said. "Take care of yourself."

"You, too," she said and hung up the phone.

He stared down at the telephone. He hadn't said it, but he, too, felt lonely. This was really the first time he had ever lived away from home. There was a knock at the door and he rose to open it.

Allison was standing outside the door. "I tried to get you on the phone," she said. "But the switchboard said that your line was busy."

He nodded. "It was."

She held out a bottle of champagne. "One of my johns gave me this. I thought it would be fun if we shared it. Sort of like a welcome home party for you."

He looked at her. "But I haven't had time yet to get glasses."

She smiled and with her other hand held out two champagne glasses. "I thought of that too."

He hesitated a moment, then stepped back. "Come in." He closed the door as she walked to the table.

"You open the champagne," she said. "I'll go into the bedroom and make myself comfortable."

It was the first time he had ever opened a champagne bottle and finally the cork popped out and he quickly caught the champagne in the glasses.

"Bring the champagne in here," she called from the bedroom.

He walked into the open doorway. One small light shone from the bed table. She was stretched out nude over the bed cover. She held her hand out for a champagne glass. She saw him staring at her. "Like what you see?"

He laughed. "What am I supposed to say? That you're ugly?"

She sipped from the glass and then smiled. "Then why don't you get out of your clothes?" He stood there silently. Quickly she reached and opened his fly. "What's taking you so much time?" she asked. "You're ready."

"I'm always ready," he said.

"So am I," she laughed, then guided his erection to her mouth.

Chapter Eleven

Thanksgiving Eve and the first snowfall of the season. Joe stood at the window looking down at the street. The snow was swirling down but the gutters were already muddy and brown from the traffic. He lit a cigarette and checked his Ingersoll—three-thirty in the afternoon. He knew the offices would be closing earlier. The holiday and the snowstorm would be an unbearable combination. By nightfall the streets would be deserted.

The telephone next to his typewriter rang. He picked it up. "Crown."

He recognized the voice. "Happy Thanksgiving," Laura Shelton said.

"Happy Thanksgiving, Miss Shelton," he replied. Then he asked curiously. "Are you still in the office?"

She laughed. "I've been working and I wanted to pass along some good news to make your holiday a really happy Thanksgiving."

"You sold another story?" he asked excitedly.

"That, too," she said. "But also something even more exciting."

"Don't make me crazy." He laughed.

"*Collier's* bought your story 'Coney Island Holiday' for two hundred and fifty dollars."

"That's great," he said. "What could be better than that?"

"Universal Pictures read 'The Shoplifter and the Store Detective' and want to make it into a movie. They want to make it with Margaret Sullavan and James Stewart. You remember, they were a big success in *The Little Shop Around the Corner*."

"I don't believe it!"

"It's for real," she said. "They offered twenty-five hundred for the movie rights and they want to give you five thousand to go to Hollywood for twenty weeks to co-write the screenplay and pay all your expenses to go out there."

"I don't know anything about screenplays," he said. "Do they know that?"

"They know it," she said. "But they do it all the time. That's why they put a screenwriter to work with you. But that's only the first offer they made. I'm sure I can bring it up a little. Thirty-five hundred for the rights and seventy-five hundred for the screenplay."

"Don't scare them off," he said nervously. "Maybe they won't think it's worth it."

"I won't scare them off," she said reassuringly. "I've been through this before. We can always grab their offer and run."

"You're the expert," he said. "I'm with you."

"Thank you," she said. "I appreciate your confidence."

"No, Miss Shelton," he said. "I thank you."

"Don't worry about it," she said. "We'll have this sewed up over the weekend. I'll talk to you on Monday for sure."

He looked down at the telephone, and the news finally seeped in. "Hot damn!" he shouted into the empty room. He picked up the phone and called home. Maybe now they would believe that he really was a writer. But there was no answer at home.

He felt himself exploding with the news. He had to talk to someone. He called his cousin at work. "I'm just going into a meeting," Motty said hurriedly.

"I won't take a minute," he said. "I have news for you. I just sold another story to *Collier's* and Universal wants to make a movie out of the 'The Shoplifter and the Store Detective.' "

"Congratulations," she said, but she didn't sound excited. "I have news for you too."

"What news?" he asked.

"I think I'm pregnant," she whispered into the phone. "I'm three weeks late."

"Shit!" he exclaimed. "Are you sure?"

"I'm afraid to check with the doctor," she said. "Stevie is coming in next week. What can I tell him?"

"Tell him nothing," he said. "The marriage is scheduled for the weekend. Five weeks means nothing. Many first babies are born early."

"You're a shit," she said angrily. "Stevie is your brother. Doesn't that mean anything to you?"

"Sure it does," he said. "That's why I'm telling you to sit tight. Open your mouth and everybody gets hurt. The whole fucking family."

She was silent for a moment. "Do you think it will work?"

"Sure it will," he said positively. "You won't even be showing until three months."

"My breasts feel heavy," she said.

"That could be premenstrual too," he said. "You told me many times that your tits swell before your period."

"I'm nervous," she said. "Stevie is a doctor. What if he figures it out?"

"Doctor or not," he said, "Stevie is still an asshole. You just do as I tell you."

"I have to run," she said. "I'm late for the meeting."

"We'll talk later," he said. "Just stay calm." He heard the click of the phone as she put it down. He stared at the telephone still in his hand. "Balls!" he said to himself. "Who the hell was it that said a virgin never gets knocked up on the first time?"

Phil cut a big slice of the *brust flanken* on his plate and smothered it with red horseradish. He looked across the table at Marta and Motty, speaking through his full mouth. "We sold a hundred and twenty-one turkeys today."

"That was good," Marta said approvingly.

"The *luksh* sold over four hundred," he grumbled.

"Don't complain," his wife said. "I remember five years ago we were lucky to sell twenty or thirty. Who knew about turkeys in those days? Chickens or capons we knew, but turkeys were for *goyim*."

He wiped his sour rye bread in the gravy on his plate. "It's good, Mama," he said, tasting it.

"You're lucky you're in the business," she said. "Or maybe you'd be eating turkey instead of *brust flanken* with the way meat stamps are given out. And with capon and chicken so high and hard to get, that's why our people are buying turkeys."

"I'd starve first," Phil said. "Turkey meat is dry with no *shmaltz*, and without no *schmaltz* there's no flavor."

"Stop complaining," Marta said. "You make more money with turkeys than anything else."

"You're such a *k'nocker*," he said. "Why don't you go into the market like you used to? You have nothing to do all day in the house."

"Al's wife doesn't come to the market," she said.

"She never did," Phil said. "She never had the time, she was too busy having another baby every year."

"It doesn't matter," she retorted. "How would it look if I stayed in the market and she didn't? Everybody would think that you were not doing as well as he did."

"It's nobody's business what I do," he said. He cut another slice of meat on his plate. "Jews get in trouble if people think they are doing too well. How do you think those nazis started on them? Because they were too jealous of us."

"This is America, not Europe," she said.

"Don't be stupid," he retorted. "We have plenty of Nazis right here, so we should be smart and quiet. Don't give any of them a reason to be envious of us."

"Maybe Uncle Phil is right," Motty said suddenly.

"What do you mean?" Marta asked, looking at her.

"A big wedding at the Twin Cantors might not be the right thing to do just now. There is a war on and everyone knows how expensive the Twin Cantors are."

"You mean you don't want a wedding at the Twin Cantors?" Marta asked in surprise. "Every girl in the world should be so lucky to get married at the Twin Cantors."

"Wait a minute," Phil said. "The girl might be right. Not only because of the money, but remember that we have two sons and none of them are in the service. There would be many people that won't like that."

"Stevie is a doctor and everyone knows that married doctors don't have to go into the service," Marta said.

"Sure they know, but everyone will think that's why he's getting married," he said. "And there are those who think that Joe is a draft dodger. Why give them a chance to prove it?"

Marta was silent for a moment, then turned to Motty. "Then what kind of a wedding would you have?"

Motty looked at her aunt. "Just us, the family. At Borough Hall where no one would know us."

"Without a rabbi?" Marta was shocked.

"They don't have rabbis at Borough Hall," Motty said. "But it's just as legal."

"Maybe just us here at home with a rabbi?" Marta asked. "Somehow without a rabbi and a *chupa* it doesn't seem like you're married."

Motty nodded. "We could do it here, but remember then that Joe couldn't come. We can't take the chance that someone would see him and ask questions. At Borough Hall nobody would know who he is."

Phil looked at his wife. "The girl has *saichel*. Smart and quiet. That's the way to do it."

Marta's eyes began to fill with tears. "All I want for my children is *naches*, not problems."

Motty went quickly to her aunt's side and put her arms around her. "Please, Tante Marta," she said softly, her own eyes beginning to tear. "Please."

"Why, God?" Marta cried, "did it have to happen at a time like this?"

"Don't blame God," he said rising from the table. "Fuck Adolf Hitler!"

Marta's tears turned to anger. "Then I don't give a damn. No rabbi, no wedding. I will not allow my children to live in sin!"

The telephone rang and Phil picked it up. "Hello." He listened for a moment then called to them over his shoulder, "It's Joe." Then, back into the receiver, "Yes, Joe?"

Joe's excited voice crackled through the phone. "I sold another story to *Collier's* and Universal Pictures wants to buy my first story for a movie in Hollywood. They want to pay me seventy-five hundred dollars!"

"Seven thousand five hundred dollars?" Phil asked incredulously. "What's the catch?"

"No catch, Papa," Joe answered. "It's on the up and up. They want me to go to Hollywood to write the screenplay."

"When?" Phil asked.

"Right away, probably next week."

"So soon?"

"It doesn't matter, Papa," Joe said. "This is an opportunity of a lifetime!"

Phil turned from the telephone to his wife. "Marta," he said proudly, "our Yussele is a real writer. He's going to Hollywood to make a movie. I guess that means you can have a wedding with a rabbi after all.

Chapter Twelve

Jamaica sat down and put his long legs up on the table. He looked at Joe, who was staring down at his typewriter. "You don' look happy?" he asked.

"I'm fucked," Joe said morosely.

"I don't get you," Jamaica said.

"I have this job to write a movie in Hollywood," Joe said.

"That sounds good," Jamaica smiled. "For good money?"

"Yeah," Joe said. "But there's a problem. They want me in Hollywood next week and Mr. B. wanted me for three months. I still have six weeks to go."

"Tell Mr. B.,' Jamaica said. "He's not an unreasonable man."

Joe looked skeptically at Jamaica. According to the newspapers, Mr. B. was accused of at least half the murders in Brooklyn and was head of all the rackets. He remained silent.

Jamaica read his mind. "You kin' talk to him. He's not as bad as all that."

"Could you talk to him for me?" Joe asked.

Jamaica shook his head. "I didn't make this deal, an' something I learned about is not to butt into somebody else's business. That's how you get hurt."

"You can tell him that I'm really no good at this job," Joe said.

"Even though that's the truth," Jamaica said, "he the boss. I don't say nuthin'."

Joe met his eyes. "You're afraid of him?" he accused.

"You betcha' yo' white ass," Jamaica answered honestly. "I'm jes' a little nigger baby tryin' to make out in a cruel cold world." Then he laughed. "But you have nuthin' to worry about. Only thing he kin' say to you is that you have to stay on the job. An' then, he might say okay. But if you don't ask, you don't get."

Joe stared at him for a moment—then his ego began to bother him. "Am I really as bad as that on this job?"

Jamaica smiled. "The worst," he said, without rancor. "But that's not your first love. You a writer, not a pimp. A good pimp has to be born, not taught."

"Writers have to be born, too," Joe said defensively.

"I don't know about writers," Jamaica said. "But the fac' is that business here has gone down more'n twenty percent since you came in. The girls have been layin' on their ass on the job, not trickin'. Not once even have you beaten up on one of them. An' remember I tol' you about that. That's how to get respect."

"I also said I didn't think I could handle it," Joe said.

"That's right," Jamaica said easily. "That's why I'm not complainin'." He paused for a moment, then got to his feet. "I really like you, kid," he said. "That's why I hope Mr. B. lets you out. That way everybody'll be happy. You'll get what you want an' we'll get back to makin' real money."

Joe looked up at the black man. "Jamaica, you're something else," he said, respect in his voice. "Thank you."

Jamaica nodded. "Then you're goin' to ask him?"

"Yes," Joe said. "I'll have to see my father before I meet with Mr. B. It was my father who made the introduction."

It was slightly less than an hour since Joe had taken the subway from the station at Ninety-sixth Street and Broadway to the end of the New Lots line and walked across Pitkin Avenue to the market. The lights were bright at the stores on the avenue but the market lights were dark.

Only one lamp was shining through the locked door on the street. Joe walked to open the gate to the pens. His father's car was still there. It was a little after seven-thirty, but he knew that his father stayed after the market closed at seven o'clock to check the day's receipts. He turned the knob on the car rear door. It, too, was locked.

He was about to knock at the door when a woman's scream sounded from inside. Automatically he slammed his shoulder against the door and the flimsy lock tore from the rotted wooden doorjamb.

He was just inside the door when he heard the second scream. It came from his father's small office. It was unlocked, and it opened at his touch. Then he froze in the doorway, his eyes blinking in surprise.

Josie's eyes were staring in fear as she turned to him. "Your father!" she cried. "Your father—"

Phil was lying lengthwise across her on the small couch, his pants down to his knees, his hips still embraced by Josie's fat legs, her dress high above her breasts. Phil's eyes were almost shut in pain as he gasped for breath. Slowly he began sliding to the floor.

Joe grabbed his father's coat from the chair behind the desk and pulled out the bottle of pills that were always in the breast pocket. He knelt on the floor and raised his father's head against his knees. "Get some water!" he shouted at Josie.

Shaking, she grabbed the glass of water that was always on the desk. Quickly Joe forced the pills into his father's mouth, and involuntarily his father's throat shuddered and he swallowed the pills. He looked up at Josie, who was still shaking. "Call Dr. Gitlin. Tell him it's an emergency! Ask him to call an ambulance!"

His father was gasping and spitting with difficulty. When he turned his father's face to the side, the spittle dripped from his mouth. Then he turned his head and vomited.

Josie called from the telephone. "Dr. Gitlin said he'll be here in a few minutes."

"Get me a wet towel to wipe Papa's face!" Joe said. She handed it to him. He began mopping the perspiration from his father's forehead.

"I'm sorry, Joe," Josie said, crying. "It's not my fault. I always told him to be careful. Screwing's too much for you, Phil,' I used to say. 'Frenchin' is easier and better for you." But he's an old-fashioned man and he likes only the old-fashioned way."

"It's not your fault, Josie," Joe said. He looked down at his father's face. The strain was disappearing and his color began returning to normal as his breathing came more easily. "Get another towel to wipe his cock," he said. "Then help me pull up his pants. We don't want anyone to see him here like this."

She was still crying as she did everything he asked. "I'm sorry, Joe, I'm sorry," she repeated. "I'll never let him do it again."

"Okay. Don't worry. He's going to be all right," he said. "Now, you get out of here and go home. And say nothing about it to anyone. Just come in to work tomorrow like nothing ever happened."

"Thanks, Joe," she said gratefully as she ran to the door. "Thanks."

His father's head moved. Then he opened his eyes and saw Joe bending over him. "What—what happened?" he asked weakly.

"Nothing, Papa. You're okay. Rest."

"But what happened?" Phil insisted hoarsely.

"You almost fucked your brains out!" he said, his fear turning into anger. "Now lie down and rest. Gitlin will be here in a minute."

Phil took a deep breath. "And Josie?"

"She's a good girl, Papa," he said. "She was never here."

Phil looked into his son's face. "I feel ashamed," he said, staring into his eyes. "I was pretty stupid. Milton warned me, but I didn't listen to him."

"You're not stupid, Papa," he said. "You're human."

"But I love your mama, I shouldn't have done it."

"It's over now, so forget it." He heard an automobile in front. A moment later, Dr. Milton Gitlin came in, his small doctor's satchel in his hand.

He looked down at them. "What happened?"

"I came in here," Joe said, "and saw my father gasping on the floor. I shoved two of those pills you gave him into his throat."

Dr. Gitlin wasn't stupid. He saw the disarray of Phil's clothing but said nothing. He opened his satchel, and took out a stethoscope and listened for a moment while he took Phil's pulse. Quickly he checked the blood pressure, and peered with an ocuscope light into the corners of Phil's eyes. He nodded slightly, fixed a quick hypo of adrenaline and shot it into Phil's arm. "You'll be okay," he said. "The ambulance will have a tank of oxygen for you on the way to the hospital."

"I'm not going to the hospital," Phil said stubbornly.

"You're going to the hospital," Dr. Gitlin said firmly. "You have had a big strain on your heart, and don't think an angina won't put you away. If everything's okay in the morning I'll let you out."

Marta was angry when she came into the waiting room at the hospital as Joe rose to meet her. He saw Motty just behind her. He kissed his mother on the cheek. "Hello, Mama."

She glared at him. "Why did they call you and not me? I'm his wife ain't I? It's only right that I should be the one they call first."

"That's right, Mama," he said. "But I was right there in the market when it happened. I gave him his pills and called Dr. Gitlin."

"I still don't know what happened," she said. "The operators at the hospital tell you nothing."

"He strained his heart."

"How could he do a thing like that?" she asked suspiciously.

"Lifting twenty crates of chickens would kill a bull," Joe lied, thinking quickly.

"Stupid," she snapped. "He knew he wasn't to do things like that. But your father always thought he was Samson."

"How is he now?" Motty asked.

Joe kissed her cheek. "Better, much better."

"Let's go up to his room," his mother said.

"Wait a minute, Mama," Joe said. "Dr. Gitlin said he'll let us in when they have finished all the tests."

"Your father is a shmuck," Marta said. "Sometimes I feel I could kill him, he's so stupid."

Joe looked at her reprovingly. "He almost saved you the trouble," he said.

Marta stared wide-eyed at him, then suddenly began to cry. "My Phil, my Phil!"

Joe put his arms around her. "He'll be okay. Calm down now."

"It's lucky that Joe was there with him, Tante," Motty said.

"Yes, yes," Marta said. Then she looked up at him. "Why were you there? I thought you were to stay out of Brooklyn?"

"I had to ask Papa a question," he said.

"What question?" she insisted.

"If he could ask Mr. B. to let me out of the job so I can take the job in Hollywood."

Marta looked at him. Suddenly she was stronger. About this, she was in charge. "Don't you worry. That lowlife will do anything you want or I'll make him wish he was never born!"

Dr. Gitlin came into the waiting room. He was smiling as he came toward them. "Everything's all right. The electro-cardiogram shows normal, no more damage, blood pressure one thirty-five over eighty-five, no fever. A good night's rest, and he can go home in the morning."

"Thank you, Doctor," said Marta gratefully. "Can I see him now?"

"You can," he said. "But remember to be very calm, don't get him excited, and stay only ten minutes. I want to make sure that he sleeps."

"We'll wait here, Mama," Joe said. He watched his mother follow Dr. Gitlin into the elevator and then turned to Motty. 'You look all right," he said.

"I'm almost five weeks late," she said sarcastically. "Isn't that the time when pregnant women are supposed to look their best?"

He tried to make her smile. "That should make Stevie very happy."

She didn't smile; instead she frowned. "Stevie will be here the day after tomorrow. That's Wednesday. The wedding's set for Sunday afternoon. That is, if he doesn't suspect anything before."

"He won't," he said confidently.

"I'm not that sure," she said. She looked at him. "When are you supposed to go?"

"My agent said Saturday on the Twentieth Century from Grand Central."

"I guess that's it," she said. "But I don't feel good about it."

"You'll feel better when you've gotten married," he said.

"I don't know," she said. "I'm confused. I'm worried. Maybe the marriage will be delayed because your father is sick."

"My father will be home in the morning. Everything will go according to schedule. Now, you stop worrying."

"I can't stop."

He smiled. "Normal bride's jitters."

Chapter Thirteen

Miss Shelton handed two envelopes to Joe across her desk. "The first envelope holds your train tickets, first class, of course. The second is a letter of introduction to Mr. Ray Crossett who is in charge of the story department at the studio and your immediate superior. The second envelope holds your checks, one for the story rights, twenty-five hundred less our ten percent commission, twenty-two hundred fifty net, also one hundred dollars in cash for expenses. Your weekly salary check will be sent to us here and we will forward it to you after we deduct our usual commission and expenses."

"I can't thank you enough," Joe said, glancing through the envelopes. "I've never had this much money in my life."

"Don't thank us," she said. "You wrote it, you've earned it."

"I still think I should do something special for you," he said. He looked at her. "How about we go out on the town?"

"I don't think that's such a good idea," she said. "This agency his strict rules. They don't allow personal relationships with their clients."

"What's so personal about going to dinner and a show?"

She watched him for a moment. "You asked my sister Kathy, before."

"She never called me back," he said. "I figured she wasn't interested."

"She was interested," Laura said. "But she moved to L.A. She found a better job out there—actually she is working at the same studio as you. You should give her a call when you get there; maybe she'll be able to help you."

"I appreciate that," he said. "But what about us? Nobody in the agency will know what we do on our own time."

"I'd like to go out with you but I would always worry that someone at the office would see us. And that would be a real problem for me. I don't plan to spend my whole life as an agent. I'm working to get into editing for one of the big publishers."

"That sounds pretty good," he said. "But I hear that editors need to bring along some writers."

She stared at him. "Write a novel. You're really good and that could help me."

"I've thought several times about writing a novel, but I don't know anything about it," he said.

"I can help you," she said. "Fifty percent of my work here is working with novelists. You do it—and we'll both get what we want."

"I want money," he said.

"Come up with a good novel, and the money you would get for that makes this amount look like peanuts."

"Then what happens with the agency?"

"I really don't give a damn," she said. "All I get here is thirty-five a week, while a decent editor commands a hundred to a hundred twenty-five just for starters."

"And what does a novel get?"

"A best-seller can make twenty-five thousand and more."

He rose to his chair. "I'm beginning to like you more and more."

She came around from behind her desk, holding out her hand. "I like you too."

He held her hand in his own. "And then we can have dinner?"

She laughed. "Anything you want."

He smiled. "I'm getting horny already."

She dropped his hand and went back to her desk. "You have a good trip to the Coast and keep in touch with me."

"I'll do that," he said, walking to the door. "Just remember your promise. We'll be in touch. 'Bye, now."

It was the middle of the lunch hour when he pushed his way into the Stage Delicatessen. He looked down at the tables. Stevie was already seated and waved to Joe.

Joe sat down at the table opposite him. He smiled. "I was beginning to think we'd never meet."

"I've been busy," Stevie said. "I had seven interviews with various hospitals. They all offered me residencies."

"That's good," Joe said.

The waiter came up. He placed a bowl of pickles and green tomatoes and sauerkraut next to another basket of rolls. "So?" he asked.

"Corn beef on club and a celery tonic," Joe said.

"I'll have the same," Stevie said. He smiled at Joe. "Deli is one thing you don't get in Oklahoma."

Joe laughed. "Excited about the wedding?"

"Mama's making a big deal about it and probably Motty is too. The girls at the department store are giving her a luncheon shower today. I guess that weddings are more important to women than men."

"You're not excited?" Joe asked curiously.

The waiter placed their sandwiches before them and walked away. Stevie picked up his sandwich and bit into it. "This is good," he announced with a full mouth.

Joe took a bite of his sandwich. "How's things at home?"

"Papa's okay. He's back to work already. Mama's running around for the wedding. Everything's okay."

"Motty too?" Joe asked. "I thought she looked great."

"She's fine," Stevie said. "I think she's a little too heavy but that's normal. Jewish girls are usually a little heavier than *shiksas*."

Joe was silent as he took another bite of his sandwich. He wondered if Stevie suspected anything.

Stevie looked at him. "So you really did it," he said.

"Did what?" Joe asked.

"You said you'd be a writer and you did it. Now you are on your way to Hollywood. Papa said you're getting seventy-five hundred dollars for the job."

"That's right," Joe answered.

"That's a lot of money," Stevie said, a tinge of envy in his voice. "All the hospitals offer me is thirty-five hundred a year for a residency. And that's in New York. Out of town they offer less."

"You knew that before," Joe said.

"Yes," Stevie answered. "After one year I can get on staff; then I'll get between fifteen and twenty."

"That's not bad," Joe said. "I don't know whether I'll get another job. There are no guarantees in my work."

Stevie looked at his watch. "Damn it!" he exclaimed. "It's one o'clock already and I have an interview at NYU hospital at one-thirty." He finished his sandwich and stood up. "I have to run."

Joe said, "I'm sorry."

"I'm sorry too," Stevie said. "Too bad you can't join us at the wedding."

But Joe realized that his brother had other things on his mind. He shook his brother's hand. "Good luck," he said.

"Thanks," Stevie said.

"And give the bride a kiss for me." Joe smiled.

"Sure," Stevie said absent-mindedly and rushed for the door.

Joe sat down, slowly finished his sandwich and called the waiter for the check. Then he smiled to himself. Stevie never picked up a check. He had always been cheap.

Joe climbed up the stairs to Kitty's apartment. Lutetia opened the door. "She's expecting you," she said.

He walked into Kitty's small library-den. Kitty rose from her typewriter and hugged and kissed him. "So you made it!" she said excitedly.

"I guess so."

"I'm proud of you," Kitty said sincerely. She took out a sheet of paper. "I have a list here of a number of friends I know out there. Give them a call. They'll all be happy to meet you."

"Thank you," he said.

"Have time for a drink?" she asked.

"A quick one," he said. "I still have a lot of packing to do."

"Lutetia!" Kitty called.

Lutetia came into the room with a bottle of champagne and three glasses. Quickly she opened the bottle and filled the glasses. Kitty held up her glass. "Congratulations and bon voyage."

"And good luck," Lutetia added.

"Thank you," Joe said, strangely touched. "Thank you very much."

It was eleven o'clock at night when Jamaica came into his apartment. He glanced at the packed valises. "All packed?"

"About," Joe answered.

"I have something for you," Jamaica said, handing him a small cardboard box.

Joe opened the box. The small brown vials shone up at him. "What's this for?" he asked.

"Insurance," Jamaica said.

"But you know I don't use the stuff," Joe said.

"I know," Jamaica said. "But there's fifty grams in there, and they'll get you from twenty-five to fifty dollars a gram out there. And you'll never be sure that you might not get the shorts. That's why I call it insurance. It's better than money."

Joe laughed. "Thanks. I'll remember that."

"What time are you leaving here in the morning?"

"About ten o'clock," Joe said.

"Then I won't see you before you go?" Jamaica said.

"I guess not," Joe said.

"Nervous?" Jamaica observed.

Joe nodded. "A little. I hope I can cut the mustard."

"You'll cut it," Jamaica said reassuringly. "All the stars are out in Hollywood, aren't they?"

"That's right," Joe answered.

"Then you'll do okay," Jamaica said. "Just remember. You doin' the right thing—you can touch the stars."

He called home in the morning just before he left for the station. Stevie answered. "Is Mama or Papa home?" Joe asked.

"They're at *shul*," Stevie answered.

"How about Motty?" he asked. "I'd like to say goodbye to her."

"She just left for work," Stevie said.

Joe hesitated a moment. "Then give them all my love and tell them I'll call them from California."

"I'll give them your message," Stevie said. "Good luck again."

"You, too," Joe said and put down the telephone. He checked around the apartment to make sure that he hadn't forgotten anything, then picked up his valises and caught a taxi to Grand Central.

A redcap grabbed his valises at the Forty-second Street entrance. "Where to, suh?" the redcap asked. "Have yo' ticket handy?"

"Right with me," Joe said, following him. The big clock on the wall read a quarter after eleven. The gateway to the Twentieth Century was just to the left side of it. He was checking his ticket when he felt someone touch his arm.

"Remember me?" Motty said.

He stared in surprise. "Stevie told me you had gone to work."

"That's what he thought," she said. She met his eyes. "I'm not going anywhere except with you."

"You're nuts!" he exclaimed.

"I'm not," she said. "I don't love him. Now I know I never loved him. And he doesn't love me either. I'm just a convenience for him. He never once even kissed me, not even when I met him here at the station. He just shook my hand."

"Stevie never was emotional," he said.

"He doesn't think about anyone except himself. He thinks he's better than everyone, even his parents."

"But the wedding's tomorrow!" he said.

"Fuck it!" she said vehemently.

"They'll all go crazy," he said.

"They'll get over it," she said. he turned to face him squarely. "I love you. I've always loved you. And you knew that, didn't you?"

He took a deep breath, then nodded slowly.

"Then are you taking me with you, or aren't you?" she asked in a trembling voice.

He saw the tears struggling behind her eyes. Suddenly he took her in his arms and kissed her. She clung to him tightly.

"We better make it fast, sir," the redcap said. "We have only fifteen minutes till check in time."

"Then take us to the ticket counter, we have to pick up another ticket in a hurry," Joe said. "This is heavy romance!"

Part Two

1946–1947

Chapter Fourteen

He lay back on the bed, propped up by the pillows behind him. He watched her standing naked as she put on her makeup in the mirror. Carefully, expertly, she penciled in her eyebrows. "You've got a great ass," he said admiringly.

She watched him in the mirror continuing her work with the eyebrow pencil. "You say that to all the girls," she said without inflection.

"Not all the girls," he said, smiling. "Only those who have them."

"You're terrible," she said. "Aren't you going to work this morning?"

"Today I'm due at the unemployment line."

"You're off the payroll again?"

"Temporarily," he said. "A.J. said he'll have a project for me in a week or two."

"The last time he told that to you," she said sarcastically, "you waited two and a half months."

"This time he means for sure," Joe said. He changed the subject. "Where's the baby?"

"Caroline's downstairs in the kitchen with the Mexican. She's having *huevos racheros* for breakfast."

Joe shook his head. "What kind of a breakfast is that for a Jewish baby? Bagels, lox and cream cheese would be more like it."

"For thirty dollars a month you get Mexican help," Motty said. Her makeup finished, she turned to Joe. "My makeup okay?"

"Fine," Joe said. "And so are your thirty-four Bs and juicy pussy."

"It's the exercise," she said. "I owe that to the nurse at the obstetrician's office. She said if I didn't diet and exercise after the baby, everything would droop."

"I'll send her a thank-you letter," Joe said. He threw off the covers. "Look at this," he added, feigning surprise. "I've got a hard on."

"So what else is new?" she laughed, walking to the closet.

"Time for a quickie?"

She laughed again. "And ruin my makeup? Not a chance. I have an important meeting this morning."

"What could be more important than a morning fuck?"

"A new job," she said. 'Mr. Marks, the executive vice president of the Beverly Hills branch of the store, wants me to be the buyer of the high-fashion department."

"I thought you were happy in the advertising department?" he asked.

"I was. But this is twice the money, and besides, with the veterans coming back from service, I don't know how long I can hang on in that department. Before the war, most of the department staff were men."

"How much will you get?" he asked.

"Could be a thousand a month but more probably eight hundred. But that's okay. There's a lot of extras with the job."

He was silent; then he looked at her. "What's the extras? You get to fuck him?"

"You've got a dirty mind," she said, annoyed. "That's all you think about. Mr. Marks is a very conservative man. Wears a striped tie and a boutonnière all the time. Besides, he's at least fifty."

He watched her fasten her brassiere and step into her panties. "The studio is loaded with fifty-year old fuckers."

She slipped into a white silk long-sleeved shirt and began buttoning it. "It's a different kind of business. The studio is loaded with a bunch of whores who want to be actresses."

"You're beginning to sound more and more like my mother," he said.

"It's the truth," Motty said flatly. "And I've seen lipstick stains on your shorts to prove it."

He sat silently as she wrapped her skirt around her waist and then straightened the seams of her stockings. "I thought Rosa did the laundry."

She didn't answer.

"Don't you want me to explain?" he asked.

"No," she said flatly. "There's nothing to explain. It isn't as if I hadn't known you before. I've known you all your life."

He stared at her. "And you're not angry?"

She looked into his eyes for a long moment, then turned away. "I have to get started," she said. She paused at the door and looked back at him. "If all you have to do is go to the unemployment office, why don't you get back to work on your book? You can put in a lot of work in two weeks."

He didn't answer.

"Your agent, Laura, said if you could send in edited changes of the finished manuscript she could get you a good deal!"

"Yeah," he said unenthusiastically. "Sure, and she becomes an editor, which is what she really wants."

"Wish me luck," she said.

He got out of bed and walked to her. "Good luck," he said, kissing her. He stood there as she walked out on the balcony that led to the stairway down to the living room, then closed the bedroom door behind him. He sat on the side of the bed and took a cigarette from the night table and lit it. "Shit," he said.

He heard the front door slam shut, then, still dragging on the cigarette, he walked out to the balcony. "Rosa," he called to the Mexican girl downstairs in the kitchen.

She came from the kitchen into the living room and looked up at him on the balcony. "*Sí, señor?*"

"Can you bring me some coffee?"

"*Horita, señor.*" She giggled, still looking up at him.

"What are you laughing about?" he asked, irritated. She was always giggling.

"*Nada, señor,*" she replied.

"*Nada,* shit," he said. "You're laughing about something."

She giggled again, looking boldly up at him. "*Los pantalomes de sus pijamas están abietos.*"

He glanced down. The fly of his pajama pants was indeed open. He closed the button. "Don't look at it," he said. "You're too young for things like that."

"*Sí, señor,*" she said, ignoring his comment. "*Toma usted el café en la cámara?*"

"No," he said. "I'll be in the study." He watched her as she walked slowly back to the kitchen. Cock-teasing bitch, he thought as she tossed her shinning long black hair that hung just above her swaying hips as she walked. She paused in the kitchen doorway and looked back, smiling at him over her shoulder.

He turned and walked along the balcony. He passed the baby's bedroom, which Rosa shared, sleeping on a narrow bed, to the small room that was intended to be a servant's room, into which he had managed to cram a small desk for his type-writer, a typist's chair, prefabricated bookshelves and a second hand leather easy chair.

He sat down at the desk and looked at the typewriter. There was a blank sheet of paper in it. He tried to remember what he had been working on when he placed it there. He couldn't remember. Angrily he pulled the sheet out of the typewriter, crumpled it into a ball and threw it in the wastebasket. He leaned forward without getting out of the chair and picked up the stationery box that held the manuscript of his novel. He opened the box and stared at the title page.

Nor Any Star Pursue
a novel by
Joseph Crown

Quickly he riffled the pages. There were forty-five pages of notes, but only ten pages of the beginning of the novel itself. He looked at them with disgust. Only ten pages, and he was still jerking off with the first chapter, in the chicken market. It had been more than eight months since he had written it. Since then he had been working on two screenplays. He stared at it again. It was shit. At least screenplays were more fun. You could work with other people and meet new people and bullshit your way around. Writing a novel was a lonely job. No one could help you there. Just you and the typewriter. And the only fucking you got was off the pages you wrote. It was another form of masturbation, and without the pleasure. Laura was nothing but another pain in the ass with her ideas for changes.

"*Señor?*" Rosa's voice came from the door.

He turned to look at her. She held a tray with a pot of coffee, a cup and saucer, a sweet roll on a plate, sugar and a spoon. He gestured to the desk. "Okay."

She bent over the desk and placed the tray in front of him. The scoop neckline of her soft cotton dress fell forward, and he could look down into her small apple breasts almost completely past her little belly to her pussy hairs. She didn't straighten up until she had filled his coffee cup, then she looked at him. "*Eastá bien?*"

He sipped the coffee. "Good," he said. She turned to leave, but he called her back. An idea came to him. "Did you show the *señora* the lipstick on my shorts?"

He knew she knew what he was talking about. "No, *señor.*"

"How did she find it then?" he asked.

"Each day the *señora* checks the *ropa lavada.*"

"All the time?"

"*Todo,*" she said.

Silently he sipped at his coffee. He lit another cigarette and let the smoke curl from his nostrils while he watched her sourly.

"You are angry with me, *señor*?" she asked.

He shook his head. "Not with you. With myself." He stared down at the typewriter. Nothing was working. He knew the book was in there, but he couldn't get himself to bring it out. Maybe it was too easy here in Hollywood. In the three and a half years they had been here, he had made more money doing less work than he had dreamed in New York. Everything was easier. The girls were prettier and more available. Sex was a way of life for them. No hassle. Fucking for writers, producers and directors was a path to getting a job in a movie. A big part or a small, it didn't matter—the important thing was to get on the screen. Even the weather was easier. Sometimes it rained, but it was never really cold—never the bitter cold that he had been used to in New York.

Even Motty said that it was easier here. The only trouble was, there wasn't anything to do. That was why she went to work six months after the baby was born. In just a few months she had been promoted to assistant to the department's head of advertising. She had told him, laughing, that California girls could never make it in New York stores because the only thing they majored in at school was tennis.

He looked up from the typewriter. Rosa was still standing in the doorway. He was vaguely surprised. He had forgotten she was there. Her body was silhouetted through the thin cotton dress from the light behind her. He felt himself getting hard. "Why don't you wear underwear?" he asked angrily.

"I have only one pair," she said. "During the day no one is home so I wear only when I go out with child. Each night I must wash it."

"How much does underwear cost?" he asked.

"Brassiere, panties and slip, *dos dolares*," she answered.

He pulled open the desk drawer, where he always left some money. There were several bills—three singles and a five. He took them out and held them out to her. "Here," he said. "Buy some."

Slowly she came over to him. and took the money from his hand. "*Muchas gracias, señor.*"

"*Por nada,*" he said.

Her eyes fell away from him. "You are sad, *señor*," she said in a low voice. "Can Rosa help you?"

For a moment he didn't understand what she meant, then he realized that she had been looking at the bulging fly of his pajamas. "How do you know about such things?" he asked.

"I have five brothers and my father," she answered. "In my *casa* I have to help all of them."

He stared at her. "How old are you, Rosa?"

She still didn't meet his eyes. "*Tengo* sixteen, *señor.*"

"Shit," he said. "You fuck all of them?"

"No, *señor*," she said. "*Solamente*—" she made a fist and moved it up and down in front of her.

He smiled. "It's not necessary, Rosa," he said gently. "But thank you anyway."

She nodded seriously and left the room. He watched her go, her hips swaying. It meant nothing to her, he thought. That was the way she lived.

He ground out his cigarette in the ashtray and took a bite of the sweet roll. It was really sweet, not at all like the danishes in New York. Here they were coated with sugar icing. He washed it down with more coffee.

He stared down at the typewriter again. "How about it?" he asked. "Do you feel like writing a novel?"

The empty white page stared back at him blankly. The telephone began to ring and he picked it up. "Hello."

"Good morning," Kathy said. As her sister had told him, Kathy was working in the studio as one of A.J.'s secretaries. "What are you doing today?"

"I was pink-slipped," he said. "Today I'm registering at unemployment."

"Do it in the morning," she said. "A.J. wants to see you at three o'clock."

"He has a job for me?" he asked.

"I don't know," she answered. "He just told me to call you in. Maybe you'll get lucky."

"I'll be there," he said. "What are you doing this evening?"

"Nothing special."

"How about a happy hour?" he asked.

"At my apartment or at a bar?"

"Your apartment."

She hesitated for a moment. "My apartment," she said. "But you bring a bottle. Six o'clock okay?"

"Okay," he said.

"And bring rubbers too. I'm too close to my time," she added.

"I'll take care of it," he said. "See you at the office at three."

He put down the telephone and picked up his coffee. "You have another day off," he said to the typewriter. The typewriter didn't answer.

He sipped the last of his coffee. Thirty thousand dollars in the bank, a good apartment, two cars, a three-year-old daughter and a wife who paid her own way—what more could he ask?

He didn't have any answers. Nothing had changed. All he ever thought about was new pussy and new money.

Chapter Fifteen

"We need a new look for the main floor of the Beverly Hills store," Mr. Marks said to her as he sat behind his large, oak executive desk. "A more sophisticated look, more New York. We have to attract the new younger marrieds now that the war is over."

Motty nodded seriously. "I agree."

"You've worked in the New York stores, you know what I mean," he said.

"Exactly," she said. "More like Saks Fifth Avenue."

"Like that," he replied. "But also like Macy's. We have to realize that our clientele is not quite ready to jump into the high price range. We have to give them the illusion that we're a classy store, but cheaper."

"Bloomingdale's," she said.

"Right on the nose." He smiled. He looked down at several blueprints spread across his desk. "We have some preliminary drawings of the main floor. Would you like to see them?"

"Very much," she said.

At his gesture she came around the desk, looking down at the blueprints as she stood beside him. The blueprints were a jumble of white lines. They were not easy to follow.

"This is the main entrance," he pointed with his finger. "Off to the right side we plan the book department. That shows class. Off to the left side we plan a great-looking fur salon, then right in front and through to the back of the store is all the better line of coats and dresses. All real class."

He looked up at her for comment. She was silent. "What do you think?" he asked.

"I don't know," she said honestly. "You have more experience than I do, so I have to assume that you are right."

He swiveled his chair toward her; his shoulder brushed her breast and the faint aroma of her scent came to him. 'I'm not the kind of an executive that needs yes men. The reason I wanted you for this job is because you express your own opinions."

She looked at him. He was not looking at her face; his eyes were traveling down her decolletage. She felt her nipples hardening, and she flushed, embarrassed. Now she was angry with herself for wearing a silk blouse instead of a less clinging one. She knew her nipples were pressing against it.

He looked up at her face, a faint smile on his lips. "What do you think?" he asked.

She took a deep breath. The right answer might blow the job, but she didn't know what else to say. "It really shows class," she answered, "if that's what we want. But I thought we wanted to bring in a new young clientele. One that buys rather than just looks."

Now she had his attention on business. "What do you mean?"

"You gave me the idea," she said tactfully. "You mentioned Macy's. I had a letter from a friend of mine who works for them. They're moving the book department from the main floor to the seventh floor because it doesn't bring in traffic."

"What are they replacing it with?" he asked.

"She didn't tell me," she answered. "I don't know if they have decided yet."

"What would you do then?"

She met his eyes steadily. "Cosmetics. Perfumes. Beauty accessories. On half the main floor, as soon as the customer comes in."

"That's Woolworth's," he protested.

"It's also almost twenty percent of the sales," she said. "And there's nothing wrong with that."

"But they sell cheap lines."

"We go up a step. Now that the war is over, all the French companies are coming into the country. They will have cachet and are not much more expensive. We can set up a separate counter for every line. That would make it really important. And it will bring in the kind of clientele that we want."

"It could be expensive," he said.

"They want to get into the market," she said. "I'm ready to bet they will share the costs with you."

He stared at her. "You really are bright."

"Thank you," she answered.

"Do you have any other suggestions?"

"That's just off the top of my head. I haven't really thought it out," she answered. "I know what I bought the first moment they came back on the market: small appliances. Electric iron, toaster, fry pan. New dishware, pots and pans. Silk stockings, lingerie. I'd really have to study it."

"I guess we'll all have to study it more." He turned from her and looked down at the floor plan. "There's thirty thousand square feet on the main floor. We have to make each foot pay off."

She walked around the desk and faced him. "Yes, Mr. Marks."

"We can't afford any mistakes," he said.

"I realize that," she said.

"I want the Beverly Hills store to become our flagship," he said. "We'll either make our reputation or fall with it." He looked at her across the desk. "Perhaps we should take a trip to New York to see what they are up to. Their marketing techniques are years ahead of us."

She met his eyes squarely. "You want me to go to New York with you?"

"That's part of your job," he said smoothly. "You'll probably have to make at least one trip a year to Paris as well."

"I've never been to Europe," she said.

"I've been many times, before the war," he said. "It's very exciting. I could show you things you would never imagine."

"But I'm a married woman with a child, Mr. Marks," she said lamely.

"I'm a married man, Mrs. Crown," he said smoothly. "But we're talking business. Nothing more."

She wished she could believe that, but even her nipples didn't. They were tingling as his eyes caressed them. She avoided his gaze. "I'll have to talk to my husband about it."

"You do that, Mrs. Crown," he said unctuously. "You can explain to him that's why your base salary is eight hundred and fifty a month and with bonuses you can make up to fifteen hundred to two thousand a month. And that's a very important salary."

"I realize that, Mr. Marks," she said. She held her hand out to him, hoping that her palm didn't feel sweaty. "Thank you very much."

"Daddy going to work?" Caroline lisped from her high chair as he came into the kitchen.

He bent to the child and kissed her. "That's right, darling."

"Bring me some candy?" She smiled, her soft brown ringlets shining in the light.
"Of course."

"Now," she said imperiously.

He glanced at Rosa, then gestured in surrender. He took two penny Tootsie Rolls
from his jacket pocket and gave them to the child. "What does Caroline say?"

"Thank you." She smiled, already tearing the candy wrapping. She was concentrating on the candy, no longer interested in him.

The doorbell rang. He left the kitchen, crossed the living room and opened the
door. The mailman looked at him. "Parcel post, Mr. Crown."

Joe took the rectangular box. The words, "Returned Manuscript" were penciled
several times in red crayon on the box. Silently Joe signed the receipt book for the
mailman.

"I'm sorry, Mr. Crown," the mailman said. "Tough luck. This is the second one
you got this month."

Joe looked at him. The mailman nodded sympathetically. "That's the way it
goes," Joe said.

"Maybe next time it'll be better," the mailman said. "Good day to you."

"You, too," Joe said, closing the door. He stared at the wrapped package. He'd
never thought the postman was that interested in what he delivered. Quickly he
broke the string and tore the wrapping from the package. He looked down at the
opened box. It was not a manuscript. Instead there were forty carefully folded
paper envelopes, each holding a quarter-gram of cocaine. At twenty-five dollars per,
that was a thousand dollars for him. He sent Jamaica only two hundred fifty for
it. He closed the box. This time, he made up his mind—he was going to rent a
post-office box. He was in luck that A.J. had called him into the studio. All it
would take him was an hour on the music-recording stages and he would get rid
of all the envelopes. Musicians were the best customers for any kind of dope. If
only he could make a connection with ganch, he would become a millionaire.

He walked back to the kitchen doorway. Caroline's face was already smeared
with chocolate. Rosa was doing laundry in the deep wash basin. She looked back
at him.

"Tell the *señora* that I will be at the studio this afternoon," he said.

"*Sí, señor*," she said.

It was about ten o'clock when he parked his pre-war Chrysler Airflow on the street
across from the California Employment Office building in downtown Hollywood.
The parking lot was already full, automobiles waiting in line at the entrance. The
moment a car moved out another moved in. He glanced down the street. He parked
the car a few blocks from Fountain; there were limousines with chauffeurs nearby
as though hiding from the common people. He smiled to himself. The California
Club, it had been called at the studios. Sometimes there were so many movie stars
in the lines inside waiting for their weekly unemployment check that this had
become a popular stop for the tour buses.

He walked past the public entrance to the rear of the building to the employees'
entrance and went in, waving to the old man in his guard's uniform. The black
lettering on the frosted glass window down the corridor read simply, "Mr. Ross."
He knocked lightly and opened the door.

Jack Ross, a heavyset man with thinning hair, looked up from his desk. He smiled and gestured for Joe to come in. "How are you doin', Joe?"

Joe shook his head. "The usual, Jack," he said. "I was pink-slipped."

Ross took a printed form from a pile next to him. "Okay," he said. "We'll get right on it."

Joe nodded. "Just one problem. Christmas is coming up next month. It takes six weeks for the first check."

Ross looked at him quizzically. "That's the rules."

"Maybe we can bend them a little," Joe said.

"We're really jammed," Ross said. "It's always like that near the holidays."

"I know," Joe said. "I saw the limos hiding around the corner."

Ross smiled. "Even the stars are showing up. Ilona Massey. Richard Arlen."

"'Tis the season to be jolly," Joe said.

Ross looked down at the printed forms. "I can backdate seven weeks for you but it'll cost. Twenty-five dollars up front and ten percent of each check you collect."

"That'll be fine," Joe said. He laid twenty-five dollars on the desk in front of him.

The money disappeared in Ross's pocket. Quickly he filled out the form and pushed it over to Joe. "Sign this in the three places marked."

Joe signed it and pushed the form back to him. "When do I get the check?"

"I'll have it here tomorrow morning at nine-thirty," he said. "You'll have two weeks' checks."

"Thanks, Jack," Joe said. "I'll see you tomorrow then."

Ross smiled. "I'll be waiting for you. You take care, hear?"

"I will," Joe said. "We better make lunch sometime soon."

"After the holidays," Ross said. "Too busy right now."

"Okay," Joe said, heading for the door. "You name the day. Thanks again."

Chapter Sixteen

Triple S Studios were located in the valley. Although smaller in size and acreage than Universal and Warner Brothers, they were complete with four good-sized film stages and three smaller stages that doubled for filming and music recording. A three-story brick building painted a boring gray contained the executive offices just inside the studio gates. Beyond that were two two-story wooden buildings, also painted the same gray. One building housed the producers' offices. The other slightly shabbier building held the restaurant commissary on the ground level, and the upper story was crowded with cubbyholes that served as offices for writers and the script department. A number of rickety bungalows were scattered around the studio lot for directors and their staff, and wartime Quonset huts at the far end housed the music department. Large barnlike buildings took care of the sets and the costume department. Without enough acreage to film exterior shots, the studios had an arrangement to use the Warner Brothers facilities adjacent to them.

The gray-shirted, bored studio guard leaned against the small wooden shack at the gate entrance as Joe stopped his car beside him. The guard looked at him strangely. "I thought you were pink-slipped yesterday," he said hoarsely.

"That's right." Joe smiled. "But A.J. called me in for a meeting."

The guard stepped into his shack and checked the visitors' list. He called to Joe. "That's for three o'clock," he grumbled. "It's only one o'clock."

"I like to be early," Joe said. "Where do you want me to park the car?"

"Use your usual place. We haven't reassigned it yet."

"Thanks," Joe said. He looked up at the guard. "Maxi Keyho around?"

"Gotta hot tip?" the guard asked curiously. Maxie Keyho was a music contractor; he was also the unofficial studio bookie.

"Not today," Joe said. "He's got a five-dollar marker of mine."

"I just saw him walking over to the commissary," the guard said.

Joe waved his hand at him and drove his car around to the parking lot in front of the writers' building. He locked the car and went into the commissary. The restaurant was a long room, its walls covered with pictures of stars and featured actors that had been in the studios' movies. It was divided into two sections: the rear section was for executives and important actors and producers, complete with tables and waitresses; the main section, the biggest part of the room, had a long counter spread with an assortment of foods, and the service was cafeteria style— you picked up your food and found a place to sit at any table that happened to be vacant. Usually the first customers entering tried to hold chairs at their table for friends. This didn't often work, especially when the commissary was busy. But no one ever bothered Maxie Keyho, who had had the same table every day for years. It was in a corner near the entrance where he could see everyone entering.

Keyho, as usual, was dressed in a black suit, shirt and tie, and sat alone. No one sat at his table unless invited. He looked up at Joe, his watery, pale blue eyes curious. "I thought you were pink-slipped yesterday," he said without greeting.

"A.J. called me in this afternoon," Joe said. The studio grapevine always worked overtime.

"Sit down," Keyho invited. "What's goin' on?"

"I don't know what A.J. wants," Joe answered, slipping into a chair. "I thought maybe you did."

Keyho shrugged his shoulder. "The only thing I heard is that he's meeting with a new banker from New York."

"I don't know what that means to me," Joe said. He lowered his voice. "Talking about New York, I just received a fresh package and thought maybe you could use it."

Keyho stared at him for a moment. "Money is tight. Everybody is getting laid off."

Joe didn't answer.

"How much?" Keyho asked.

"Forty packages," Joe said. "Usually it's a grand but I don't know whether I'll be on the lot. I'll turn it over to you for eight-fifty."

"Seven hundred," Keyho offered.

"Seven-fifty and you have a deal," Joe said.

"It's a deal," Keyho answered. "Do you have it with you?"

"In the trunk of my car."

Keyho nodded. "After lunch, at two-thirty. I'll be outside recording stage C."

Joe rose from his chair. "I'll see you there."

He walked to the counter and picked up a tray. He felt good. Seven-fifty was a good deal. A quick five hundred profit, and he didn't have to hang around a week buttonholing customers. He moved down the self-service line and looked over at the girl standing behind the hot-food table. "Salisbury steak and mashed potatoes with gravy," he said, then looked over his shoulder to see if any of the writers he knew were there.

He opened the door and looked at Kathy sitting at her desk. "Am I too early?" he called.

She waved to him to enter while she spoke into the telephone. He closed the door behind him and crossed to her desk as she put down the telephone. "Where's Joanie?" he asked.

Joan was the number one secretary. "She called in sick," Kathy answered. The telephone rang again. "Everything's jammed up," she added as she picked up the phone again. She transferred the call to A.J. and turned back to him. "We'll have to cancel our happy hour," she said. "With Joanie out, I'll have to work late."

"Okay," he said.

She stared at him. "You're really a prick. You don't even seem disappointed."

"What am I supposed to do?" he asked. "I know when you have to work, you have to work."

"A.J. called Laura. He wanted to know if you would be okay for a project he had in mind."

"What did she say?" Joe asked.

"She said you would be good." She looked at him. "Then she took off on me. She said you were a hustler and I should stay away from you."

Joe was curious. "Why would she say that?"

"I have my own idea," Kathy said. "I think Laura has a yen for you."

"She never let me see that," he said.

"That's Laura," she said. "She covers her feelings. It's her business camouflage."

"I don't get it," he said. "Maybe she knows about us?"

"It's not that," Kathy said. Suddenly she seemed cold. "When A.J. gets off the phone, I'll let him know that you're here," she said.

"I'm sorry," he said. "I'll leave the bottle of vodka in your car when I go out."

"You don't have to," she said.

"I'm just as disappointed as you are. It's not your fault."

She didn't answer.

"How about tomorrow?" he asked.

"Maybe," she answered. The white light next to the telephone on her desk flashed on. She picked up the phone. "Joe Crown is here for you, Mr. Rosen." She listened for a moment then nodded and gestured to Joe. "He's on the way in, sir."

"Thanks," Joe said to her as he walked to the door of A.J.'s office.

She looked up at him. "Good luck," she said sincerely.

A.J. sat behind his desk like a fat, bald Napoleon. His chair was raised beneath him so that he could look down on the visitors sitting across his desk. His fat cheeks creased in a smile. "Thanks for coming in on such short notice, Joe," he said.

"It's my pleasure, Mr. Rosen."

"I might have a project for you," A.J. said importantly. "You're a New Yorker, aren't you?"

"Born and bred," Joe answered.

"Movies about New York do pretty good at the box office," A.J. said. "*The Dead End Kids* from Universal, then *The East Side Kids* from Monogram after Universal dropped it and it became a series."

Joe nodded seriously. He still didn't understand what A.J. was talking about.

"I'm thinking about a picture more important than those. More like the movie *Dead End* that Sam Goldwyn made."

"Fine film," Joe said.

"One of my New York bankers gave me the idea for it," A.J. said. "It's really not a bad idea at all. A New York gangster falls in love with a gorgeous showgirl and decides to take her to Hollywood to become a movie star."

Joe expressed the proper enthusiasm. "That's really a great idea, Mr. Rosen."

A.J. smiled. "I thought you might like it."

"I do, Mr. Rosen," Joe nodded. "Knowing you, you already have the leads in mind."

"I have the girl already," A.J. answered. "But I have been trying to decide on the leading man. It's a toss-up between Bogart, Eddie Robinson or Cagney."

Joe nodded seriously. He knew as well as A.J. that there was no chance of any of those actors doing the part. "You said you have the girl," he said tactfully.

"I have," A.J. said, picking up a publicity still photograph and pushing it across the desk to Joe. "Judi Antoine."

Joe looked down at the provocative picture of the girl in a skintight silver gown that out-Betty'd Betty Grable and put Lana Turner away. "I know her," he said.

"The whole world knows her," A.J. said enthusiastically. "She's been under contract for three months and though she's never even been in a picture we get a thousand requests a week for photographs of her. She's in every magazine and newspaper in the country."

"She's hot," Joe agreed. He didn't want to tell A.J. that on the lot she was nicknamed "The Screamer," because she shouted so loudly while fucking. She even traded him a quickie to introduce her to the director doing the movie he had been working on.

"Even my banker thinks she'd be perfect for the part." A.J. nodded, then said as if he had just thought of it, "My wife and I are taking the banker for dinner at Perino's. Why don't you pick up Judi and join us?"

Joe rubbed his chin to feel if his beard was growing. "Tonight?"

"Tonight," A.J. nodded.

"Maybe she's not available," Joe suggested.

"She's available," A.J. said firmly. "I arranged that."

"I'll have to explain it to my wife," Joe said.

"She'll understand," A.J. returned. "It's business."

Joe thought for a moment. "Okay. Now when do you want me to start working?"

"Right away. You'll get twenty-five hundred for the treatment; if we go to script, you get another twelve thousand five."

Joe nodded. "Good enough."

"Dinner will be at seven-thirty. It should be over between nine-thirty and ten."

"What do I do after that?" Joe asked.

"Drop her off at the banker's hotel and wait for her to call you at the cocktail lounge. Then you can drop her home. You should be finished by midnight."

Joe nodded silently.

A.J. looked shrewdly at him. He was in touch with the studio grapevine after all. "Just tell her not to holler too loud. Bankers are nervous by nature. He might lose his hard."

Joe closed the door behind A.J.'s office and looked at Kathy. "You knew?"

She nodded. "But not until Joanie called in sick. Usually that's her department."

"It's shit," he said.

"It's a shitty business," she replied. "But what the hell, you got a job out of it. Now you better call Laura and tell her you got the job."

Chapter Seventeen

He walked to the writers' building and up the rickety stairway outside the restaurant. The door opened into the steno pool, where the small desks were crowded close to each other. The head steno sat at the desk against the far wall, much like a teacher at her desk at the head of a classroom. Only two girls were typing at their desks; the head steno was proof-reading a script. She looked up as he entered. "I heard you were coming back." She smiled. "I didn't even take your name off the office door."

"Thanks, Shirley," he said.

She opened a desk drawer and took out a room key. He took it from her. "Everything's in there," she said. "Pads, paper, pencils, even a typewriter."

"You're okay," he said.

"What's the new project?" she asked.

"A New York story," he answered. 'I don't know too much about it yet."

"It must be a hot one," she said. "It's not often that A.J. is in that much of a hurry."

"I guess so," he said. "I just have a few calls to make. I'll be in in the morning."

"Anything I can do, let me know," she said. "Good luck, Joe."

"Thanks, Shirley," he answered and walked down the corridor to the small cubbyhole that served as his office. He opened the door with his key. The office was just big enough to hold a small desk and two chairs, one behind it and one in front of it. Any more than two people in there would have to stand in the doorway or in the corridor. He shut the door and sat down behind the desk. He stared at the telephone for a moment and just as he reached it, it rang. He picked it up. "Joe Crown," he said into it.

"Judi Antoine," a girl's voice whispered into his ear. "I hear you're my date for tonight."

"That's what I hear," he answered.

"You got two Cs?"

"What are you talking about?" he asked.

"The two hundred bucks I get for the night," she said.

"Wait a minute," he said. "Nobody told me about that. I'm just the beard for A.J. and his banker at dinner. I thought publicity arranged it."

"Publicity told me you would take care of it," she said. "I have expenses," she added. "How do you expect me to make out on the one twenty-five a week they pay? My apartment at the Sunset Towers costs three hundred a week alone."

"Didn't they tell you that you're getting the lead on the picture I'm writing?"

"All the time," she said. "I must have heard that at least a thousand times."

"That comes from A.J. himself," he said. "His banker who's financing the picture has the hots for you. I was supposed to drop you off at his hotel room after dinner and wait for you at the cocktail lounge. I thought it was all set up."

"Nighttime fucking is on my own time," she said flatly. "It don't say nothing in my contract about that."

"So what do you expect me to do?" he asked.

"Get me the money," she said. "Otherwise I don't show up. Let me know what's happening, I'll be at home until five-thirty."

"Come on, Judi," he cajoled. "Didn't I introduce you to Ray Stern, the director, when you wanted to meet him?"

"I don't remember," she said.

"We had a quickie leaning against the wall in my office because there wasn't enough room for a couch," he said, trying to jog her memory.

"I don't remember," she repeated. "All johns are the same to me. Just get me the money." She hung the phone up.

He stared at the silent telephone for a moment, then called A.J.'s office. Kathy answered. "I have to speak to A.J.," he said.

"He's gone for the day," she said.

"I have to talk to him."

"Sorry, Joe," she said. "I can't help you. He's on his way home."

"Can we get him there?"

"Not until six-thirty," Kathy said. "Is it really important?"

"Important enough," he said. "His leading lady is an overtime hooker. She won't show up without two hundred in advance."

"Damn!" Kathy said. "I would help you but the cashier's office closes at three."

Joe thought for a moment. "Okay, honey," he said. "Don't worry about it. I'll figure a way out."

He put down the telephone and stared down at it. He pulled his wallet out of his jacket pocket. The seven hundred fifty dollars that Keyho had given him made it heavy. Slowly he took out four fifty-dollar bills and put them in his pocket. Paying money to hookers was against his religion—even more so when it was not for himself. He was boxed in. But a job was a job, and he *was* getting something out of it. He picked up the telephone again and called Judi at her Sunset Towers apartment.

Motty came into the bedroom while he was knotting his tie. "Rosa told me this afternoon that you were going to the studio."

He nodded, staring at the tie in the mirror, then untied it and began to do it over. "A.J. called me. I've got a job. A new picture."

"A good one?" she asked.

"They're all good ones starting out," he said, finishing the knot on his tie. He turned to her. "Do you like it?"

She looked at it critically. "It looks kind of big."

"That's the way it's supposed to be," he said. "It's called the Windsor knot. Sinatra uses it all the time." He reached for the dark blue jacket.

"What's with the bar mitzvah suit?" she asked curiously.

"A.J.'s invited me to dinner at Perino's with his banker."

"That's a switch," she said. "Never happened before. Just the three of you?"

"A.J.s wife and a starlet the banker has the hots for," he answered.

She met his eyes. "Where do you fit in?"

He smiled. "I'm the beard."

"You know the girl?"

"Not really," he answered. "But it's a New York story and I'm a New York writer so I got the job. The banker wants her to play the lead so I have to pick her up and deliver her."

"What's her name?" Motty asked.

"Judi Antoine."

"Never heard of her," she said. "What movies has she been in?"

"She's never been in one yet," he replied. "But she's been under a starlet's contract for the last three months. She's the number one studio pinup photo."

"A hooker," Motty said flatly.

He laughed. "For once you're right. She's the worst." He knew the moment the words passed his lips he should have kept his mouth shut.

"Did A.J. give you the job because of your experience as a pimp or a writer?" she said cynically.

"Hey, that's not fair," he protested.

"You could have turned him down," she said. "We don't need the job that bad. You can always work on your book."

"That will take a lot of time," he said. "Maybe more than a year. We don't have that much money to carry us."

"We could manage," she said. "Mr. Marks offered me the promotion. I'd get eight-fifty a month and with bonuses it can amount to fifteen hundred to two thousand."

"There has to be a kicker in it for that kind of money," he said.

"Of course, I'll have to go on a couple of buying trips during the fashion seasons."

"Where to?" he asked.

"New York. Maybe Paris," she answered.

"Alone?" he asked skeptically. "Without him?"

"You have a dirty mind," she snapped.

"How do you know that he doesn't?" he replied. He took the money from the dresser and put it in his pocket then turned back to her. "If I have to pimp for a living, I'd rather pimp for strangers than my own wife."

He sat at the bar in the dimly lit cocktail lounge outside the entrance to the Coconut Grove. The faint music of the big band echoed from the show room. The bartender walked toward him as he nursed his second drink. "The show's goin' on in a few minutes downstairs," he said. "Want me to get a table for you?"

"No, thanks," Joe answered.

The bartender gestured to the drink. "Fill it up?"

Joe shook his head. "Two's my limit." He picked up a cigarette.

The bartender flashed his lighter. In its flickering flame, Joe saw the time on his watch. Ten minutes to eleven. The bartender noticed the glance. "Your date running late?"

"No." Joe smiled. "I came early."

The bartender gestured toward a table at the end of the lounge. "If she doesn't show up," he said, "there's two pretty ladies over there. I can introduce you."

Joe laughed. "You're okay," he said, placing a five-dollar bill on the counter for him.

The money disappeared. "Just tryin' to help, sir." The telephone rang on the back bar. The bartender picked it up. "Mr. Crown?" he asked, looking at Joe. Joe nodded. The bartender shook his head and put down the phone. "Your date said she will meet you in the lobby."

He made it to the hotel lobby just as she came from the elevator. "Okay?" he asked.

"Okay," she said. Silently they went outside and waited for the parking attendant to bring his car.

He gave the attendant a dollar bill and moved the car out of the driveway into the street. "Take you home?" he asked, glancing at her.

"Mind dropping me at Dave's Blue Room?" she replied.

"Whatever you say," he answered.

Judi looked at him. "Is that guy for real?"

Joe stopped the car for a traffic light. "Mr. Metaxa?"

"Yeah," she said. "He really owns all those banks?"

"I don't know," Joe answered, starting the car again. "All I know is A.J. said the loan agreements for two million dollars will be signed in the morning."

"He said that he was putting up the money for my picture and that I'd get a new contract starting at five hundred a week instead of the hundred twenty-five I was getting. He also wants to set me up in a new apartment so that I'll be available when he comes out here every other week."

Joe glanced at her. "You must have given him the greatest fuck of all time."

"That's what I don't understand," she said puzzled. "We didn't do anything."

"Nothing?" Joe was surprised.

"Not even cop his joint," she said. "I stood there naked in front of him and he just kept talking to me as if my dress was still on. I don't think he even noticed when I put it on again."

"I don't understand it," Joe said.

She looked out the car window for a moment, then back at Joe. "Do you know Mickey Cohen?"

"The gangster?"

"Who else?" she answered.

"Only from the papers," he said.

"Would you like to meet him?"

He looked at her. "Tonight?"

"Yes. That's who I'm meeting."

"I'd like to meet him," he said. "But I have to get home. My wife is pissed off enough over tonight."

"I bet Mickey will know something about Mr. Metaxa," she said thoughtfully.

A light dawned in Joe's head. "You know Mickey a long time?"

"Long enough," she said. "He was the guy who told me when I was in New York to go to Hollywood. That I had everything I needed to become a movie star."

Joe stopped the car again for a traffic light and stared at her. "Is it Mickey who staked you out here?"

She nodded. "We've been real good friends."

He had to force his attention on the traffic. It was for real. That was exactly the story that A.J. had told him. He pulled the car in front of Dave's Blue Room. For a moment he was tempted to go in with her, then changed his mind. This wasn't the time. He had to have a little more information about the banker.

The doorman opened the door to let her out. She turned to Joe. "Thank you," she said politely.

"My pleasure," he said, equally polite. "Call me at the studio tomorrow. And tell Mr. Cohen that I'd like to meet him at his own convenience whenever he wants."

He watched her walk into the entrance of the restaurant, then he moved the car into traffic and started for home.

Chapter Eighteen

"A great script," A.J. said into the telephone. "But we have problems."

"I don't understand," Joe replied.

"Did you ever see any of her tests?" A.J. asked.

"No," Joe answered. "Nobody ever asked me."

"Meet me in projection room B," A.J. said. "You'll see what I mean."

Joe looked down at his desk at the white-bound script. He had felt good about it until just this minute. In three months he had come up with a treatment that worked and a completed script that he knew was good, maybe the best script he had ever written. For a moment he thought of bringing the script to the projection room, but it would mean nothing. He left it on the desk as he walked over to the projection room.

A.J. wasn't alone. Mr. Metaxa, the banker, Ray Stern, the director, and another man Joe didn't know were there. A.J. nodded to him. "You know Mr. Metaxa and Ray. Say hello to Mickey Cohen."

Joe looked at the small heavyset man. He held out his hand. "Happy to meet you, Mr. Cohen."

The little man smiled as they shook hands. "Good to meet you finally, Joe," he said, in a deep voice. "I have heard about you many times. Good things."

"Thank you, Mr. Cohen," Joe said.

"Call me Mickey," Cohen said.

A.J. gestured and Joe slipped into a seat as the room lights were turned down. For the next fifteen minutes they watched Judi's tests. One of them was even in color. She sang, she danced, she read lines—all badly. Only the color test was good. She was wearing a one-piece bathing suit and running on a beach. She ran toward the camera, then into the surf. She turned from the water back to the camera. The camera showed every secret of her body, the jutting nipples of her firm breasts, even the curly pubic hair straggling out of the silken swim suit. It was not a sound test and it finished on a closeup of her face. She was breathing heavily after running. The expression of her face gave the impression that she was having an orgasm. Then the screen went black and the room lights were turned up.

Joe kept silent. So did the others. They all waited for A.J.'s comment.

Finally A.J. sighed audibly. "We fucked ourselves."

"Maybe she needs more coaching," Mr. Metaxa said.

"We've given her three months with the best teachers," A.J. said. "They've all quit on her. Now we're really fucked. I signed Steve Cochran for fifteen grand as the lead and I borrowed Pat O'Brien from Warner for ten grand for the second lead. And did you see her pussy pushing out of her bathing suit? It looked bigger than a ballet dancer's cock and balls in tights. If we don't wrap her in a short skirt, we'll never get her past the Hays office."

"How much are we into, A.J.?" Metaxa asked.

"I made a Cinecolor commitment for this picture for seventy-five thousand dollars because that was half the cost of Technicolor. With that and all the other commitments, almost two hundred thousand.' A.J. didn't sound happy.

"If she had an accident," Cohen suggested, "would the insurance companies cover it?"

"Not unless we were in production," A.J. answered. "Besides, we can't take chances like that."

"It was just an idea," Cohen said.

"It's too bad," Ray Stern said. "Joe wrote one of the most literate scripts I have ever read. I was looking forward to doing it. Maybe we can borrow Maria Montez or Yvonne De Carlo from Universal for it?"

"That's not the idea," A.J. answered. "We're committed to the advance sales on a Judi Antoine picture."

Joe looked at him. "We never sold them a story?"

"Never," A.J. said. "We sold them on her pinup pictures."

"Sheena, Queen of the Jungle," Joe said.

"Are you crazy?" A.J. stared at him. "You know Monogram owns that."

"Warrior Queen of the Amazons," Joe said. "Steve and Pat are pilots of a cargo plane that crashes in the jungle and get discovered by a lost tribe of Amazons. We've made that picture a thousand times and it always works. All we need is a screenful of half-naked girls, and Judi is the queen of all of them. She doesn't even have to speak a full line of dialogue. She's like a female Tarzan. You Steve, me Judi, we fuck."

A.J. stared at him, then at the others. "It just might work," he said. "How long would it take you to do a script?"

"Ten days, two weeks, if you want."

A.J. looked at the banker. "What do you think?"

"I know nothing about pictures," Metaxa said. "But I don't like losing money without a shot."

"I'm with him," Cohen said. "Let's take a shot at it."

A.J. turned to Joe. "Start writing."

"This is a new job," Joe said. "What kind of money are we talking about?"

A.J. stared at him. "How can you think about money at a time like this?"

Joe remained silent. He was not really looking for more money. What he was trying to do was collect the balance due for the present script. He had turned in the first draft; now he was at cutoff time. If he didn't rewrite and polish, the last five thousand dollars of the contract didn't have to be paid.

A.J. knew that as well as he did. "You write the new script and I'll pay off the contract and give you an extra thousand when the picture goes on the floor."

"Okay," Joe said. He looked around the room. "If you gentlemen would excuse me, I'll get right back to work.

He made notes on a lined yellow writing pad for almost an hour. He looked down at them, satisfied. He had the basic story line scratched out. He reached for the phone and called the steno pool.

Shirley answered. "Yes, Joe?"

"I need some help, Shirley," he said.

"That's what I'm here for," she replied.

"Can you get me a few scripts of the tits and sand pictures that Universal and Columbia make? I have to study them for style."

"I know what you mean," she said. "Tomorrow morning be soon enough?"

"Great," he said.

Her voice lowered confidentially. The grapevine had already been working. "She tested bad?"

"Worse than that," he answered.

"I'm sorry," she said. "I liked that script you wrote."

"Thank you," he said.

"Hold on a minute," she said, putting him on hold.

She came right back on the line. "A Mr. Cohen is here. He would like to see you in your office."

"Bring him in," he said, putting the phone down and getting up. By that time Shirley had opened the door. Mickey had to step out of the way so that she could close the door behind him. Joe gestured to the chair in front of the desk.

Mickey sat down, glancing around the small room. "They call this an office?" he said. "It's more like a closet."

Joe laughed. "I'm a closet writer."

Mickey smiled. "I guess you wonder what I'm doing here?"

"It's none of my business," Joe said. "You don't have to explain anything."

"I know your father," Mickey said. "We were good friends in the old days in Brooklyn."

"My father's okay," Joe said.

"He still has the chicken market?"

Joe nodded. "The same place."

Mickey smiled again. "Give him my regards."

"I'll do that," Joe answered.

Mickey looked at him. "It's not on the record," he said, "but I'm here as Judi's manager."

"Good enough," Joe said.

"What do you think?" Mickey asked. "Do you think we can pull it off?"

"I'll have the script," Joe answered. "The rest depends on A.J."

"He's already cutting corners," Cohen said. "He got out of the O'Brien agreement with Warner Brothers."

"O'Brien wouldn't make this sort of a movie anyway," Joe said.

"The director bowed out too," Mickey said. "He's not doing that kind of movie anymore."

"There's plenty of directors," Joe said. "That will not create any problem."

"A.J.'s cutting the shooting schedule to twelve days instead of thirty."

"That's about right," Joe said. "The movie shouldn't take more than that."

"Metaxa's worried," Mickey said.

"I can believe that," Joe said. "It's his money and his girl."

"Wrong," Mickey said. "Not his money, not his girl."

Joe looked at him silently.

"You know about the Judge in New York?"

Joe nodded. The Judge was the unofficial arbitrator between all the Mafia families.

"Metaxa is fronting for him. The reason they loaned the studio the money is because that's good business for them. It's legitimate. Clean. I had to get Judi out here because the Judge's wife was getting pissed off."

Joe looked at him. "Does Judi know about that?"

"She knows," Mickey said. "But she doesn't give a shit. The only one she cares about is herself."

Joe was silent for a moment. "You can depend on me," he said. "I'll do the best I can."

Mickey got out of the chair. "You make this work and you have a big marker from us." He reached for the door.

"You keep me informed. Leave a message for me at Dave's Blue Room. Any time, night or day. I'll get back to you."

"Okay," Joe said. Mickey nodded and left the small office. He took a deep breath. Nothing really changes. There's always somebody on top somewhere. He looked down at his scratch pad and wondered if A.J. really thought he was the boss of his own studio.

It was almost eight o'clock by the time he got home. He started up the steps to the bedroom and Rosa called him from the kitchen. "A half-hour for dinner, okay?"

"Okay," he said and walked up the stairs to the bedroom. Motty was just coming from the bathroom as she slipped on a robe. She looked up at him as he bent to kiss her cheek.

"You look tired," she said.

"I am tired," he said.

"You need some food," she said. "I'm having Rosa make veal cutlets."

"Fine," he said unenthusiastically.

She glanced at him. "What's wrong?"

"The picture got fucked."

"It's all off?" she asked. "You're not doing the rewrite?"

"It's off but it's not off," he said. He saw her puzzled look and explained. "Judi's tests were garbage. She can't do anything but look good. No acting, no dancing, no singing—just stand there. A.J. is tearing the rest of his hair out. He said he was out two hundred grand already. There's no way he can make this script."

"I still don't understand," she said. "What is he going to do then?"

"I had an idea," he said. "I remembered one of those stories at *Spicy Adventure* magazine. You know, 'The Warrior Queen of the Amazons.' "

"You told them about the magazine?"

"No, of course not," he said. "I'm not that stupid. I told them as if it was just a new idea that had come to me. And they bought it."

"I can't believe it," she said.

The humor of it finally came to him. He laughed. "I couldn't either. But they bought it, and I have to write it in two weeks."

"Then you're still on the payroll?"

He nodded. "Not only that, but I'm getting another grand when it begins shooting." He took of his jacket and threw it on the bed. "I'll wash up and we can have dinner."

She followed him into the bathroom. "Have you read about the new look in ladies' fashions? It started in Paris. The first important collection since before the war."

"I don't know anything about it," he answered. He turned the hot-water tap and waited for the water to heat up. "What about it?"

"Mr. Marks wants us to be the first store in L.A. to have it. Our dress houses on Seventh Avenue told us they will have knock-offs by next week. He asked if I would go to New York to decide what would work for us."

He looked down and washed his hands without facing her. "Are you going?"

"It's part of my job," she said.

He was silent as he rinsed the soap from his hands and picked up a towel.

"I spoke to your mother," she said. "She said I could stay with them and bring Caroline."

Joe looked at her. "That's a switch." His mother had never spoken to them until the baby was born—and even then, not until they mailed a copy of their wedding certificate to verify that everything was kosher. But she was still cool to him. Fortunately, she no longer felt that way about Motty. After all, the whole thing wasn't Motty's fault—he had taken advantage of an innocent girl. "Did she ask anything about me?" he asked.

"She complained that you never call her."

"I finally gave up," he said. "She always passed the phone to my father or hung up on me. How long will you be gone?"

"About twelve days," she answered. "If I leave on Friday we'll be in New York Sunday night. That leaves the whole week to work and we'd start back home at the end of next weekend. Mr. Marks is being very nice about it. He told me that if I took Caroline he would pay for a sleeperette for us."

"Is he leaving with you?"

She looked at him. "He's leaving before me on Wednesday. His wife is going with him."

Joe nodded. "I guess it's all right."

Motty smiled. "It will be nice, too, that your mother and father will finally see their only grandchild." She breathed a faint sigh of relief as she went downstairs to the kitchen before him. She never told him that Mrs. Marks was leaving for Los Angeles on the Sunday that she and the child would be arriving. She also hadn't told him that Mr. Marks had reserved a room in the Pennsylvania Hotel on Thirty-fourth Street for her just in case she might have to work too late to go home to Brooklyn.

Chapter Nineteen

Nothing succeeds like success. It was almost five months after he had finished the script of *Warrior Queen of the Amazons* that he received a telephone call from A.J.'s office as he sat at his typewriter working on the novel.

"A.J. would like to invite you and your wife to a buffet dinner at his house Friday night. Cocktails at seven, dinner will be at eight," Kathy said.

He was surprised. This was the first time he had ever been invited. "How come A.J. asked me?"

"Don't you read the trades?" she asked. "You have a hit movie. We had a PR junket with Judi to Texas and Florida. Between the Interstate and Wometco circuits, the picture grossed six hundred thousand dollars."

"I don't believe it," he said. "The reviews murdered it."

"But the public bought it," she said. "It looks to be a blockbuster, naturally. That's what counts. The exhibitors are already calling for another picture with her. I have a feeling that's why A.J. called you."

"I'll show up," he said. "But Motty is in New York. She has to go there every three months on buying trips for the store."

"I've been to the store. They've really changed it. Is it doing well?"

"I guess so," he answered. "She's been promoted to head buyer for the whole chain."

"And what have you been doing?"

"I've already finished my novel," he replied. "I've edited about a hundred and forty pages based on Laura's suggestions, but it's hard work. Harder than a screenplay."

"Laura told me it's turning out to be one of the best novels she's ever read."

"She's prejudiced," he said. "But it's the screenplays that pay the rent. Though up to now I haven't received any offers for anything. It seems the minute I wrote *Warrior Queen* all the producers that used to talk to me stopped returning my calls. I guess they all thought it was such a piece of shit they didn't want any part of me."

"They'll be back," Kathy said confidently. "I know this town. They don't read scripts, they read grosses."

He had an idea. "Why don't you come to the party with me?"

"Sorry," she said. "First, I moved in with my boyfriend. Second, A.J. doesn't like the cheap help at his parties."

"He's a cheap prick," he said.

"That's Hollywood," she said laughing. "Why don't you ask Laura? She's never been to a Hollywood party."

"How can I ask her?" he asked. "She's in New York."

"Didn't she call you?" Kathy seemed surprised.

"No," he said. "The last time I spoke to her was a month ago when she sent me her editing suggestions."

"She's right here," Kathy said. "Came in last night. I was sure she'd call you. She's at the Bel Air Hotel, room one twenty-one."

"I'll call her," he said. "Thanks, Kathy."

"Just one thing, Joe," she said. "Don't let Laura know that I told you she was here."

"I don't get it," he said.

"My sister is still pissed off at me because you and I went out a few times."

"Where did she pick that up?" he asked.

"This is Hollywood. Everybody talks here and she has a few friends."

"Okay, Kathy," he said. "I'll play it straight, and by the time I get finished with her, she won't believe anything they told her."

He was dialing Laura at the hotel when he realized after looking at his desk clock that it was almost five o'clock. He put down the receiver. If she was busy she would not return to the hotel until six-thirty or seven o'clock. That was the usual time that Easterners returned to their rooms.

He had an idea. She hadn't called him, so he would surprise her with a visit. Quickly he gathered together a carbon copy of the edited one hundred and forty pages and placed them in an envelope, then called the florist and ordered a dozen roses that he would pick up at six-thirty.

"Rosa!" he called from the balcony as he came out of his tiny study.

She came from the kitchen and looked up at him from the living room. "*Sí, señor?*"

"You have a white linen shirt ready for me?"

"I can iron it in a few minutes," she answered.

"I'm going to have a shower," he said. "You bring it up for me."

"The *señor* is going out for dinner?" she asked.

"I'm not sure," he answered. "Probably." He turned into the bedroom and slipped off his working slacks and underwear and went into the bathroom.

It was five minutes to seven when he knocked on Laura's door, the dozen roses in one hand and a bottle of Dom Perignon in an ice bucket in the other.

Laura opened the door. He smiled. "Welcome to Los Angeles!"

She stared at him in surprise. "How wonderful," she said, taking the flowers.

"I have a bottle of Dom Perignon here also," he said.

"That's too much." She smiled. "Come in."

He followed her into the tastefully decorated room. "You can't imagine how surprised I was when I heard you were in town."

"My sister told you?" she asked.

"No," he said. "I haven't spoken to her since I went off the picture. That was four months ago."

"But somebody had to tell you," she said.

"The trade papers," he said. "They have a daily list of comings and goings from the industry."

"You look good," she said. "Very California-ish."

He laughed. "You look pretty good yourself."

She shook her head. "In this old terry-cloth robe?"

"No complaints from me," he said. "You always look good to me."

"Give me five minutes to get into something more suitable," she said. "Meanwhile you can open the wine."

"I also brought almost a hundred and forty edited manuscript pages," he said.

"That's great," she said.

"What brought you out here?"

"I had to bring a set of contracts to a client," she said. "Now give me a moment or I'll never get ready."

She went into the bathroom and closed the door behind her. A moment later he heard the shower splashing, and he began opening the bottle of champagne. There were two champagne glasses packed in the ice bucket with the wine. He left the bottle open but didn't fill the glasses. There was a radio in the corner of the room. He turned it to his favourite station that played all the pop singers—Sinatra, Crosby, and others—then sat down on the two-seater couch.

In about fifteen minutes she came in from the bathroom, completely made up and dressed. She wore a blue silk shantung dress that clung to her figure.

He looked up at her. "You're already dressed, you must keep everything in the bathroom."

"I'm efficient," she smiled.

He poured the champagne. "Good luck."

She nodded. "Good luck." She sipped the champagne. "This is delicious."

"It's good," he agreed. "Now what would you like for dinner?"

She stared at him. "I have a date with our client and his attorney."

"Put them off until tomorrow," he said.

"I can't do that," she said. "The agency arranged it all before I got here."

"Then we'll make it tomorrow?" he said.

"I'm flying back tomorrow at seven o'clock in the morning."

"What about a late dinner, then?" he asked, refilling the champagne glasses.

"We're going to the client's house to go over the contract in detail," she answered. "I don't know what time we'll get finished."

He looked at her. "Do you have to return to New York? I've been invited to a cocktail party at A.J.'s house. It might be fun and you would meet some important people, directors and producers."

She shook her head. "I'd like to. I've never been to a Hollywood party. But my orders from the agency are explicit. I have to go back."

"Shit," he said. "We won't even have time to discuss the pages I've written."

"I'll read it on the plane and talk to you the day after," she said. She looked at him. "I'm sure you can turn up another date. From what I hear, you do pretty good in the lady department."

"I want you," he said. "Not anyone else."

"I'm running late," she said. "My client will pick me up in the lobby at eight o'clock."

He rose to his feet and met her eyes. "What do I have to do to get a date with you?" he asked. "Wait until our novel is sold?"

"I think you'd better go," she said coldly.

Quickly he put his arms around her and kissed her as he pressed his already turgid phallus against her groin. He saw her face turn white, then flush pink, as she pushed him away.

He walked to the door and turned to her as he opened it.

"Just for your information—I never fucked your sister. It was always you I wanted."

He slammed the door behind him and walked down the corridor to the parking lot.

Chapter Twenty

He was still angry when he walked into his own apartment and up the staircase to the balcony, then to his bedroom. Quickly he took off his jacket, then his tie and shirt. "Bitch!" he said, half-aloud. "Cock-teasing, cold-assed bitch!"

The telephone rang. Laura's voice echoed in his ear. "Joe," she said. "I don't want you to be angry with me."

"How do you expect me to feel when you send me away with my cock in my hand?" he snapped.

"You don't have to speak like that," she said. "You know better. I promised nothing."

"And that's what you gave me," he answered.

"Don't be a fool," she said. "First of all, you're a married man with a child. Second, we have a business relationship, and if my office ever even thought we had a personal one, they would fire me and that would be the end of our opportunities."

He thought for a moment. "Maybe you're right, but it's still shitty."

"You calm down," she said. "I'll read the new pages and telephone the day after tomorrow."

"Okay," he said. "I guess I have no choice. This is the way we have to play it."

"That makes more sense," she said. "I have to go now. Goodbye."

"Have a good flight back," he said. "'Bye now."

He stared down at the telephone. Even the sound of her voice had turned him on. Damn! he thought to himself, then walked out on the balcony. "Rosa!" he called.

"*Sí, señor*," she answered from the living room.

"Can I have some coffee?"

"*Sí, señor.*"

He watched her walking to the kitchen. She still wore the thin cotton dress; underneath he could see the black brassiere and panties showing through. He wondered if she knew how whorish she looked as she moved.

He went through the bedroom to the bathroom. He flipped up the toilet seat and opened his fly. He didn't realize he still had a half-hard until he had finished and turned back toward the bedroom. She had been standing next to the bed, the coffee tray in her hands, watching him. He felt his penis growing in his hand and made no motion to conceal himself.

"Next to the bed?" she asked.

"You can leave it there," he said, still standing in the bathroom.

"*Sí, señor.*" She placed the cup of coffee on the end table next to the bed. "Anything else, *señor?*"

"Nothing."

"Do you want to whip me, *señor?*" she asked, staring at him.

"Why should I want to whip you?" he asked.

"Sometimes my papa wants to do that to me when he is hard like that," she said.

"I'm not your papa," he said.

"But you are a man," she said. "You have four nights without the *señora*. It must be *mucho* difficult for you, *señor*. My papa comes many times when he whips me, then he feels better."

He felt his penis soften. His excitement had gone. "I'm sorry, Rosa," he said wearily. "Go away." He waited until she had gone before he stretched out on the bed.

He stared up at the ceiling. He was angry with himself. He hadn't thought about it until Kathy had called him about A.J.'s party. It had been almost four months since anyone in the business had called him. If it hadn't been for Motty's promotion, they would have been dipping into his savings account just for living expenses. She had been doing well. Now she was up to twenty-four thousand a year. That was more than he had made in his best year.

He sat up and drank his coffee. This was the third trip she had made to New York. The first trip she had taken the kid with her and they stayed at his parent's house; the last two trips, she had stayed at the Pennsylvania Hotel. It was right in the garment district, she had explained. But that wasn't the only thing. Motty had changed—she was no longer that shopgirl he remembered. There was an air of decision about her. Her makeup, clearly professionally arranged, as was her coiffure, and her clothing bespoke the latest fashions. But the real change was in her eyes. Before, they were young and open; now she seemed secretive and guarded, as if she lived in a world he could not penetrate.

He wondered if she was fucking her boss, Mr. Marks. He was being stupid. Of course she was. No way would any girl, no matter how great she was at her job, get the money and promotions otherwise. Even her style of fucking had changed, more sophisticated and reserved than before. Before, she could never stop coming— now one orgasm and she stopped. Then she couldn't wait until she ran to the bathroom to douche and wash away the errant sperm that accidentally might have found its way home inside her. He really had been stupid. The cocksman had been cuckolded by a worm with a gold-plated prick. He slammed his coffee cup down on the plate and the coffee slopped onto the table. "Rosa!" he called.

She appeared immediately in the doorway, her eyes frightened. "*Sí, señor.*"

He pointed to the spilled coffee. "Clean it up."

She nodded and was back in a moment with a washrag. She knelt beside him and began wiping away the coffee. Still on her knees, she turned her face up to him. "No problems," she said.

He pulled out the belt of his pants and let them fall down his legs to the floor. "You'll have to wash them. There's coffee stains on them."

She stared silently up at his genitals.

"What are you staring at?" he snapped angrily. "You want to touch it, don't you?"

Still on her knees, she remained silent.

Angrily he slapped her face. "God damn it! You wanted to touch it!"

Almost reverently, she let her fingers touch his testicles. "*Muy grandes cojones,*" she whispered. Then she clasped her hand around his penis.

He lifted her to her feet. "Not like this," he said harshly. "Undress!"

Silently, not looking at him, she took off her dress, unfastened her black cotton brassiere, and together with her panties let them drop to the floor. She clasped her hands, shielding her pubis. "No fuck," she whispered. "I am virgin."

"Ah shit!" he said, his anger dissipating. "Get dressed." He walked past her to the bathroom. "I'm going to take a shower and go out for a while."

"Fully let out ranch mink jackets for two hundred dollars," Mr. Samuel said. "Real dark ranch, the most popular."

"Where's the bargain? Our stores are in Los Angeles, not New York," Motty said.

"With mink jackets completely lined like this," he said, "you can put them on special sale for four hundred ninety-five dollars and they'll go like hotcakes."

"The price is right, Mrs. Crown," Marks said.

Motty looked at him. "Just remember, Mr. Marks, our fur salons always have been losers. And ground-floor space is too expensive to warrant losers."

"That's because your salespeople are not furriers," Samuel retorted. "A good furrier would make a fortune there."

"I won't argue with you, Mr. Samuel," Motty said. "But we have to work with the people we have. Maybe you have a better idea."

"If you want to keep upgrading your stores," Samuel said, "you have to have a prestigious fur salon."

Motty glanced at Marks, then at the furrier. "What if we gave you the concession? You tell us that you can do better than we do, and I believe you."

"I don't know," Samuel answered carefully. "We're spread a little thin just now. We've already got concessions at Hudson's in Detroit. It comes down to how much money you're talking about?"

"I haven't thought about it," Motty said. She turned to Marks. "What do you think, Mr. Marks?"

"I haven't thought about it either," he said. "How much does the ground-floor space cost us?"

"About ninety thousand in the Beverly Hills store," she answered.

"And the other four stores?"

"About fifteen thousand each. Beverly Hills makes up fifty percent of all our fur sales," she replied.

"It's too expensive," Samuel said quickly. "I'd have to stock a quarter of a million dollars' worth of goods just to build a volume so we could break even."

"We're damned if we do," Marks said. "And we're damned if we don't."

Samuel stared at him. "Are you serious about this?"

Marks nodded. "We're serious."

Samuel nodded. "Okay, then. I'll make you a fair offer. I'll give you fifty thousand for the concessions and twenty percent of the gross sales if you co-op the advertising and carry all the credit sales. If I'm right, we'll all make a lot of money."

"And if you're wrong?" Marks asked.

"We lose a little," Samuel answered. "But you said you always lose anyway."

Marks turned to Motty. "What do you think?"

Motty looked at Samuel. "I have faith in Mr. Samuel. He knows what he's doing."

"Thank you, Mrs. Crown," Samuel said. He turned to Marks. "What do you say, Gerald?"

"We'll do it," he said, holding out his hand.

Samuel shook his hand. "I'll come out there the week after next and we'll begin to make a few changes in the salon." He smiled. "I can see it in the ads now. 'Paul, the Furrier of Beverly Hills.' "

"Not Paul," Motty said.

"Why not?" Samuel asked. "It works at Hudson's in Detroit."

"That's Detroit," Motty replied. "This is Beverly Hills. They need something more impressive."

Samuel stared at her. "You want Revillon, maybe?"

"No," she laughed. "Just call it Paolo of Beverly Hills. The ultimate in furs. Los Angeles is a hick town. They're always impressed with foreign names."

"Paolo of Beverly Hills," Samuel repeated smiling. "The ultimate in furs. I like it. Let's have a drink to it."

It took almost an hour before they closed the door behind Samuel. Motty leaned back on the couch as Marks turned to her. "I'm exhausted," she said. "I thought he would never stop talking."

He looked at his watch. "It's near seven," he said. "Why don't you take a relaxing bath and then get dressed, and we'll go out for dinner?"

"Do we have to go out?" she asked.

"No," he answered. "We can have dinner in the suite."

"I'd like that," she said. "I'm a little tired of having to go out for dinner with people."

"We'll have dinner here, just the two of us." He bent down and kissed her. "I've been waiting to do that all afternoon," he said.

"I did too," she said, putting her arms around him. She kissed him again. "Happy?" she asked.

"Very," he answered. "We're a good team. I think we have a good deal with Samuel."

"Yes," she said. "I only wish that all our problems could be solved as easily."

He smiled, looking at her. "One of them is solved," he said.

She looked at him questioningly.

"I'm a free man," he said. "My lawyer called me. My wife has completed her six weeks in Reno, the divorce has gone through, and now she's my ex-wife."

She stared at him silently.

"You don't seem happy about it," he said.

"I am happy," she said. "But I'm also a little frightened."

"You'll have to tell him sooner or later," he said.

"I know," she said. "But he's been going through such a bad time right now. I just wish he had something to do."

"There'll always be a problem," he said. "From what you tell me, he has enough girls to console him. And since you're not asking for any alimony, child support or community property, he'll recover."

She was silent.

"The divorce should be easy," he said. "You could do it in Tijuana in one day if he'll sign the papers."

She remained silent.

He looked into her eyes. "That is, unless you don't want to marry me?"

She pulled him close to her and slipped her hand over his crotch. She felt his penis growing in her fingers. "Of course I want to marry you," she whispered.

Chapter Twenty-one

His prewar Chrysler Air Flow seemed out of place among the Rollses, Cadillacs and Continentals parked on the street in front of A.J.'s house at the corner of Rodeo and Lomitas in Beverly Hills. The red-jacketed parking attendant gave him a ticket and drove the car away. Joe stood there for a moment before walking to the entrance of the house. He saw the car being driven far down the street, away from the more important cars in front of the house. He smiled to himself. Even automobiles were victims of the caste system.

A Chinese butler in a tuxedo opened the door for him. "Your name, sir?"

"Joe Crown," he answered.

The butler glanced at a list in his hand, then nodded. He gestured toward the living room already crowded with guests.

Blanche Rosen, A.J.'s wife, stood next to the entrance of the living room. She was an attractive woman, looking much younger than her forty years. She smiled, holding out her hand. "Joe," she said in a warm voice. "I'm so happy that you could come."

He shook her hand. "Thank you for inviting me, Mrs. Rosen."

"Call me Blanche," she said. She gestured toward the room: "I'm sure you know most of the people here. You just make yourself comfortable. The bar is set up at the far end."

"Thank you, Blanche," he said, but she had already turned away from him to greet the next guests. He moved toward the bar. He recognized many of the guests, but very few he really knew or had met. A black barman smiled at him. "Your pleasure, sir?"

"Scotch and water," Joe said. He took the drink and moved to the side of the room. A.J. was standing, a circle of people around him, with Judi, dressed in a black sheer see-through sequinned dress, beside him. Everyone in the circle seemed to be talking at the same time.

A mild flurry of excitement came from the entrance to the living room, and A.J. suddenly took Judi by the arm and half-pulled her with him toward it. Joe followed them with his eyes. He saw the woman's hat, and knew at once who she was: Hedda. Her hats were famous, her trademark. She was one of the two most important Hollywood columnists. Photographers suddenly appeared and flashbulbs popped. Even A.J. fawned over the columnist.

Ray Stern's voice growled low in Joe's ear. "I really fucked myself, didn't I?"

Joe turned to the director. "What makes you say that?"

"I could have made that picture and I blew it."

"It's not that important a picture."

Stern looked at him. "Any picture that will gross like that is important."

"I don't see what it's doing for me," Joe said. "I haven't gotten a job since."

"You'll get then now, you'll see," Stern said. "Why do you think A.J. invited you to this party? You're the writer of the biggest-grossing picture out of his studio this year."

Joe looked at him silently.

"He'll probably sign you up for a sequel before the party is over."

"He never even saw me," Joe said.

"Don't you believe it," Stern said. "He sees everything."

Joe shrugged his shoulders. "I don't know." He looked at the director. "What are you working on now?" he asked.

"Nothing," Stern answered. "He let my option drop. I don't know why I've been invited. Probably I was left over on an old party list."

"Come on," Joe said. "It's not that bad."

"The hell with it," Stern said bitterly. "I'll just have another drink."

Joe watched the director move toward the bar. He heard a girl's voice behind him. "Are you Joe Crown?"

He turned. She was a tall girl with blue eyes and long auburn hair almost to her bare shoulders, wearing a soft clinging blue silk dress. "Yes," he said.

She looked at him. "I'm Tammy Sheridan. Don't you recognize me?"

He felt as if he should apologize. "I'm sorry."

"I had the second lead in your movie," she said. "The girl that had the fight with Judi."

"Now I *am* sorry." He smiled. "I never saw the movie."

"Never?" she echoed disbelief. "Not even in a projection room?"

"No one ever invited me," he answered. "And I was off the lot by that time. I'll probably see it when it opens here in Los Angeles."

"But I heard that you were writing the sequel already," she said. "I thought that I could talk you into building up my part a little."

He laughed. "You can talk me into it. But first I have to get the job."

She laughed. He knew she didn't believe him. "Are you alone?" she asked.

"Yes."

"No date with you?"

"No date," he said.

"That's funny," she said. "I heard you were married and that you were balling Judi on the side."

"You hear a lot of stories," he said. "I am married. But my wife has gone to New York, and I am not balling Judi on the side."

"I heard you got her the job."

"I didn't."

"Then how did she get the job?" she asked. "She can't act worth shit. On my worst days I can act like Garbo around her."

He gestured with his hand. "I don't know. I just wrote the script."

Tammy looked across the room at the photographers taking pictures of Judi and Steve Cochran, who had just come in. "She's a fucking whore!" she said jealously. She turned back to him. "Do you have a car?" she asked.

He nodded.

"I came by taxi," she said. "Maybe you can give me a lift home after the party?"

"Sure," he answered.

"You look for me," she said, starting to move away. "Meanwhile I'll try to con some of the photographers into taking a few pictures of me."

He watched her moving in like a bird dog, then turned to the bar and ordered another drink. It was growing warmer in the room and he moved closer to a window to get some cool air. Mr. Metaxa, the banker, came over to him. "Joe," he said jovially, "congratulations."

Joe smiled. "Thank you, Mr. Metaxa. But for what?"

"A good script. Now the movie will make a great deal of money. Maybe two million, distributors' gross. We are very pleased."

"I'm glad, too," Joe said.

Metaxa took him by the arm. "Come," he said. "I have an Italian producer, a good friend of mine, who wants to meet you."

Joe followed him toward a tall, good-looking man with a distinguished head of white hair. Metaxa spoke quickly in Italian, then translated for Joe. "Joe Crown, the *scrittore*," he said. "The great Italian producer, Raffaelo Santini. Signor Santini has made the great success in Rome, *The One-Wheeled Motorcycle*."

Joe had heard about the picture. It was one of the early neorealistic films that had come out of Italy. The critics had loved it. It had almost won the Academy Award as the best foreign picture.

"It's an honor to meet you, Mr. Santini," Joe said.

"It's an honor and pleasure to meet you, Mr. Crown," the Italian said, in Italian-accented English. "I liked your picture. It is most droll and shows that you have a good knowledge of what the movie audience wants to see. We need more knowledge such as that."

"Thank you, Mr. Santini," Joe said.

Mr. Santini nodded seriously. "Maybe someday you will come to Italy with me and we could make a picture together."

"I would like that," Joe said.

A.J. spoke from behind him. "What are you wops plotting behind my back with my number one writer? Trying to steal him away from me?" The smile on his face belied his words.

"Of course not," Metaxa said quickly. "Mr. Santini was only complimenting Joe's work."

"I have a three-picture contract with him," A.J. said.

Joe stared at him. This was the first he had heard of it. He remained silent.

"We have a meeting in the studio Monday morning to discuss the first script," A.J. said. He looked at Joe. "Isn't that right, Joe?"

"That's right, A.J.," Joe answered.

"And what is the title of the new film?" Santini asked.

A.J. stared at him, then turned to Joe. "You can tell him, Joe."

Without hesitation Joe answered the Italian. "*The Return of the Warrior Queen*."

"Of course," Mr. Santini said sagely. "How simple, how clever. Already the title is presold."

"Don't forget. Nine o'clock on Monday morning," A.J. said, moving away and smiling.

The two Italians eyed him. Santini muttered something in Italian to Metaxa in a low voice, then turned again to Joe. "You make a remember what I say, Mr. Crown," he said. "Someday we will make a picture together in Roma."

Out of the corner of his eyes, Joe saw Tammy coming toward him. "Joe!" she called out as if they were old friends. "You must introduce me to Mr. Santini. He's my most, most favorite filmmaker."

"Mr. Santini," Joe said. "Miss Tammy Sheridan."

"I loved your film," Tammy gushed. "I voted for your picture in the Academy Awards. I felt so badly when you didn't get it."

"Thank you, Miss Tammy," the Italian said politely.

"They're announcing dinner," she said. "May I sit with you? I have many questions to ask you about your wonderful movie."

"I am sorry," Mr. Santini said apologetically, "but I am not staying for dinner. I have previous engagement at Chasen's."

"I'm sorry too, Mr. Santini," Tammy said sincerely.

The Italian took her hand and kissed it, bowing. "*Ciao*," he said.

Tammy sighed as she looked at him. "What fucking manners that man has," she whispered. "When he pressed his lips to my hand I could almost feel his tongue tickling my pussy."

"Shit," Joe said. "I can do that."

Tammy looked at him. "Kiss my hand like that?"

"No." Joe smiled. "Tickle your pussy with my tongue."

Chapter Twenty-two

Hollywood parties finished early. The usual excuse was because everyone has to be in the studio at seven o'clock in the morning. Performers usually left even earlier because they had to be in makeup between five-thirty and six. It was eleven when Tammy got into his car beside him. He gave the parking attendant a dollar bill and moved out of the driveway. "Where do you live?" he asked, looking across at her.

"In the Valley," she said. She seemed slightly defiant.

"Okay," he said easily. "Just tell me how to get there."

"Go over Laurel Canyon. I'm two blocks this side of Ventura."

"You've got it," he said, turning onto Sunset.

"It gets so cold at night," she said. "I'm shivering. Could you turn on the heater?"

Silently, he switched it on. Warm air began circulating through the vents.

"That's better," she said, turning to him. "Are you going to do the movie?"

He shrugged. "A.J. wants to see me on Monday."

"You're going to do it," she said with conviction.

"We'll see," he said. "I don't know. He hasn't spoken about money yet."

"He'll take care of it," she said. "That picture is money in the bank."

He smiled at her. "You sound more like an agent than an actress."

She laughed. "I should," she answered. "I've been around this town a long time."

"You're not that old," he said.

"Twenty-six," she answered. "I've been here since I was sixteen."

"You don't look it."

"Makeup," she said, half seriously. "You can guarantee that job for yourself," she added.

"Why do you say that?"

"Mrs. Rosen, A.J.'s wife. She's got eyes for you."

"I didn't notice that," he said. "She barely spoke to me."

"But I saw her watching you. A lot." She waited until the car turned off Sunset onto Laurel Canyon. "Did you know that she used to be his story editor before they were married?"

"No."

"She still reads all the scripts. A.J. never reads. And she likes writers. Especially young ones."

"I don't see how that will guarantee me the job," he said.

"You send her flowers with a thank-you note," she said. "In a day or two she'll call you and invite you to lunch at their Malibu house during the week. That's the way she operates, everybody knows that."

He glanced at her. "You *have* been around."

She nodded. "But not that it does me any good," she said half bitterly. "This is the third studio I've been contracted to but never gotten a lead part."

"They say the third time is lucky," he said.

"I hope so," she said, with conviction.

They remained silent until the road turned and the lights of Ventura Boulevard shone toward them. "Make a right at the third corner," she said. "Second house in."

He turned the car and stopped in front of her house. It was a small house but well kept. "Looks nice," he said.

She looked at him. "I'd invite you in," she said, "but I share the house with two other girls."

"That's okay," he said.

She placed her hand on his lap. "I can give you a little head here in the car," she said.

He smiled. "No. Thanks, anyway."

"I give great head," she said.

"I'm sure," he nodded. "But I can wait."

She leaned toward him and kissed his cheek. "Thanks for the lift," she said. "I'll give you a call at the studio."

"You do that," he smiled. "Good night."

He watched her run to the entrance door of her house then turned the car around and headed for home. He was in bed just after midnight.

"You've become an important man," Shirley said. "The word came down. We've moved you to a corner office."

"I just made the deal with A.J. twenty minutes ago," he said.

"He must have been sure of it," she smiled. "He gave me the order Friday." She picked up a set of keys from her desk. "Come, I'll show it to you."

He followed her to the end of the corridor. The door to this office was solid wood, not inset with a frosted pane of glass whose window would not allow genuine privacy. He opened the door and went in with her. The floor was covered with wall-to-wall carpeting and had paneled wood walls. The couch and two easy chairs were old, but real leather, and the typewriter was on a separate table, not on the desk.

"Like it?" she asked.

He nodded. "At least I feel I can breathe."

"Good," she said. "I've already set up writing paper, carbons, yellow pads and pencils. The telephone is connected directly to the switchboard, and you can make calls and receive calls without going through me. There's a switch next to the phone which you can turn on if you want me to answer when you go out or if you want to have the calls intercepted while you're busy working."

"Seems good," he said.

"How much time do you think the script will take?" she asked.

"Maybe a month for the first draft, another for the rewrite and polish. A.J. wants the picture on the floor in July."

"That doesn't give you much time."

"I'll manage," he said.

"I'll leave you to get settled," she said, turning to the door. "Call me if you need anything."

"Thank you, Shirley," he said.

"Good luck," she said, closing the door behind her. He walked behind the desk and sat down and looked around the office. It really was not bad. There were even several decent framed prints on the wall. He placed a package of cigarettes on the desk and lit one thoughtfully. Despite the better desk and office, A.J. was still a shit. Instead of the three scripts he had promised at the dinner party, he had contracted only this script guaranteed. He did go up to twenty thousand dollars, though. The other two scripts were on option agreements to be agreed on at a later time, after this script had been finished.

The ring of the telephone startled him. He glanced at his watch. It was only eleven in the morning. He picked it up. "Joe Crown."

It was a woman's voice. "Mr. Crown?"

"Yes," he answered guardedly.

"Blanche Rosen," the voice said into his ear. "Congratulations on your new office."

"Thank you, Mrs. Rosen," he said.

"I thought we agreed you would call me Blanche," she said lightly. "I called you to thank you for the lovely flowers. That was very kind of you."

"It was my pleasure," he said. "I really enjoyed the party, and thank you again for inviting me."

"I read many of your works," she said. "Including some of the short stories you've written. You're a very good writer, Joe. Much better, perhaps, than you realize."

"Thank you, Blanche."

"I know what I'm talking about," she said. "I used to be an editor at Doubleday in New York, and then joined A.J. here in the studio as story editor and consultant before we were married. I still read all the scripts that he considers."

"I find that very interesting," he said.

"I know the idea that A.J. has proposed to you and I think I can offer some suggestions that would help you avoid several script problems you may encounter. Why don't we have lunch on Wednesday? I have a small house in Malibu, nothing fancy, but we could be alone there and talk."

"That's very kind," he said.

"Say twelve-thirty?" she asked.

"Twelve-thirty will be fine," he said. "I'll look forward to it."

He put down the telephone. Tammy had been right. She called all the shots.

Tammy's was the second telephone call he received. "Congratulations," she said. "I told you you had the job."

"You were right," he agreed.

"I'd like to come over," she said. "I have a welcome present for your new office. Is now convenient?"

"Come in," he said. "I haven't begun working yet."

"I'll be there in ten minutes," she said and hung up.

The telephone rang again. He picked it up. "You have a busy line," Kathy said.

"Beats me," he said. "I didn't even know that anybody knew I was here yet."

"You told A.J. that you never had seen the picture?"

"That's right," he answered.

"He told me that we're having a sneak at eight o'clock tonight at the Pacific Palisades Theater for the Coast Circuit. He thought you should catch it there. You'll get a better feel of it with an audience in a theater than in a projection room."

"Tell him I'll be there," he said.

A moment later the telephone rang again. This time it was Laura, from New York. "Congratulations," she said. "I hear you're writing a sequel to the Amazon picture."

"News travels fast," he said. "It was just set this morning."

"The studio sent us a teletype with a contract for you. Did you agree to it?"

"Of course," he said. "Twenty grand is pretty good."

"What will that do to your novel?" she asked.

"Slow it up, but only for a month. This script is a piece of cake."

"I hope so," she said. "What you have now is very good, I wouldn't want you to lose your momentum."

"I'll be okay," he said. "I did another fifty pages since you left. I'll send them to you."

"Do that," she said. "I'll be anxious to read them. If it's as good as what I've read so far, you're halfway home."

"I'll do the book, don't worry about it," he said. "But right now twenty grand straightens me out real good."

Her voice softened. "Are you all right?" she said. "I heard you're having domestic problems."

"Where did you hear that?" he asked. "I haven't heard anything like that."

"Some people from the Coast told me that your wife spends a great deal of time away from home."

"That's the fucking rumor factory. That's her job. She's the head buyer and has to travel because of her work."

"Okay," she said. "As long as you're all right."

"Don't worry about me," he said.

"If there's any way I can ever help you, just call me. I'm on your side."

"Thank you," he said. After saying goodbye, he stared at the telephone. People are shitty, all they want to do is make trouble. What business is it of theirs what anyone else does?

There was a knock at the door. "Come in," he called.

Tammy came in and closed the door behind her. She was wearing a tight-fitting cotton sweater and a short skirt. All he could see was tits, ass and long, fine legs. She had it all together like a billboard above Sunset Strip. She glanced around the office. "This is as nice as some of the producers' offices I've seen."

"It's fine," he said.

She placed a small rectangular gift-wrapped box on the desk in front of him. "It's for you."

He opened it quickly, then began to laugh. It was a special dozen pack of lubricated Rameses. "I hope you got the right size," he said. "Usually they're too small."

"Showoff. One size fits all."

"I'll treasure them," he said. "But when are we going to get a chance to use them?"

She turned and locked the door of the office. "I thought it would be nice if I gave you your first fuck. Afterwards you can take me downstairs to lunch."

The first man he saw when he returned to the theater lobby after having seen the movie was Mickey Cohen. They nodded and shook hands. "I liked it," Mickey said.

Joe looked at him to see if he was serious, but he was straight. Joe remained silent.

"The audience loved it," Mickey said. "They were screaming all the time, especially the high school kids in the balcony. I bet it was a three-jerk-off-time movie for them. Judi came off like all pussy."

"I don't get it," Joe said.

"You don't have to," Mickey said. "Just do it again."

"I don't know if I can," Joe answered. "I don't know if I can ever write that badly again."

"For the twenty grand you're getting," Mickey said flatly, "you'll write shit and like it."

Chapter Twenty-three

It was eleven o'clock in the morning, and Judi stormed into his office without knocking. "A.J. said you're giving me a lot more lines in the new movie," she said without even a greeting.

He looked across his desk up at her. "If A.J. said that, that's what you'll get."

"I'd like to see some of the pages," she snapped.

"Don't be a fucking star, Judi," he said. "I've only been working two days on the treatment. I haven't written any dialogue yet."

"I don't believe you," she said.

"Check with A.J.," he answered. "First I have to do the treatment, then the script. That's where the dialogue comes in."

"You're not going to fuck me," she said angrily. "A million-dollar gross tells me that I'm the star. I don't have to suck anybody for a fucking job now."

"That's right," he agreed.

"I've got a contract."

"So have I," he said.

"I can get you off the fucking picture!" she snapped.

"Okay," he said. "Get me off the picture. Then you'll have no movie to be a star in. I'll get paid either way."

She stared at him. "Is that true?"

"Screenwriter Guild rules," he answered.

Suddenly she calmed down. "Then how do I protect myself?"

"Why don't you wait until I finish the script? Then you can bitch all you want."

"You've been fucking Tammy and she's telling everybody that you're giving her more lines than me."

"Everybody believes that you fucked me to get the part in the first picture," he said. "This isn't a movie studio, this is a rumor factory."

She stared at him silently for a moment. "Then how come you never ask me out to dinner?"

He smiled. "I can't afford you. The last time I took you out it cost me two hundred bucks, and A.J. never reimbursed me."

"I'm out of that business now," she said. "You can take me out to dinner for free."

"Then I'll take you out," he said.

"How about Friday night?" she suggested. "Maybe Chasen's or Romanoff. Afterward we can go to the Mocambo."

He shook his head. "That's way out of my league, Judi. I don't make that kind of money. The Brown Derby is the most I can handle."

"Cheap," she sneered.

"I work for a living," he said. "I'm not on any expense account."

"What if I get Publicity to pay for it? They're always hustling me for pictures."

"Just get me the voucher and we'll party all night."

"I'll call you," she said, and she left as she had come in, without a greeting or a goodbye.

He pulled the string to ring the bell inside the door, which was set in a long, closed, slatted wood fence. Blanche's voice answered from behind it. "Who is it?"

"Joe Crown," he said. He glanced at the sun. It was blazing hot.

The door opened and she hid behind it as she let him in. She was wrapped in a large beach towel and every part of her was covered with suntan oil. "You're early. It's only twelve o'clock," she said. She didn't sound angry.

"I'm sorry," he said. "But I've never been out this way before, and I didn't want to be late."

"That's all right," she said agreeably.

He followed her through the small garden off the road, then through the small house, outside to an open wooden sun porch built over the beach. She turned to him. "Would you like to take a swim before lunch?"

"I don't think so," he answered.

"We have swim trunks. I'm sure that you can find your size."

He apologized. "I'm sorry. I never learned to swim."

She laughed. "At least you're honest. Most people find another way to get out of it." She glanced up at the sun. "But you should slip on a pair of trunks. The heat will cook you in all that clothing—even if you stay in the shade."

He found an old straw hat to protect his head from the sun. The swim trunks were all small sizes. He found one that fit over his hips, but even then, his pubic hair could be seen over the top. He saw her looking at him and he knew that was the way she arranged it.

"I made vodka tonics," she said. "That all right?"

"Perfect," he said.

She sat down on a mattress on the wooden floor. She held a glass out to him. "Welcome to Malibu."

"Thank you," he said, sipping the drink. It was icy cold and good.

They clinked glasses, and at the same time her beach towel fell partly away from her and uncovered one side of her from her breast to half of her curly, oily, sun-sparkled pubis. She saw him looking at her. "You're not a prude, I hope."

He shook his head.

She let the rest of the towel fall, then leaning her arms back to the mattress she offered herself up to the sun. "I'm a naturist, a real sun worshipper," she said.

"Beautiful," he said.

She turned to him. "Let me spread some of the suntan oil on you. It will keep you from burning."

"I don't think so," he said.

"Why?" she asked.

"I have a very low boiling point," he said. "I'm having enough trouble right now trying to keep myself straight."

"I'm not blind," she said, looking up at him. "Your prick is sticking out under your trunks. You've probably got the quickest draw in the West. I just hope you don't shoot as fast."

He laughed.

She reached for his penis and pulled him down beside her. "I just want to get in some licks first." She pulled the swim trunks from him and closed a hand around his penis. She looked into his eyes. "Do you know I heard the way Dolores Del

Rio had such perfect skin was that she had a dozen young men jerking off all over her and rubbing it in?"

"I never heard that." He laughed. "You know, you're really a crazy lady."

She laughed at him. "But also really nice. After all, the boss's wife is entitled to some advantages."

"And I thought we were meeting for a story conference," he said.

"This is the story," she said, pulling his penis into her mouth.

Motty walked through the living room of the hotel suite and picked her way through the racks of dresses brought in for them to select. Quickly she calculated there were at least two hundred garments. She looked at Gerald. "We'll never go through all these by tomorrow," she said.

"Maybe we should stay another week," he suggested.

"We can't," she answered. "Paul the Furrier will be in L.A."

"Maybe we can rush through them by Saturday," he said.

"Even so, we can't make the train until Sunday. That will bring us to L.A. on Wednesday morning. Then we'll be in trouble. You know Paul the Furrier, he'll start without us and we'll be screwed."

"I have an idea," Gerald said.

She looked at him.

"Plane," he said. "TWA, United and American all fly to L.A. from New York. They leave at nine o'clock New York time, make two stops en route, Chicago and Denver, and land in L.A. at eleven o'clock at night the same day. We can do that on Sunday."

"I don't know," she said. "That's scary. I've never been on a plane."

"They say it's great," he said. "Free drinks, dinner, good service. They say it's just as if you were in your own living room. And the whole flight is only fourteen hours—you'll be in your own bed by midnight."

She looked at him. "I'd rather be in your bed. After all, I'm not expected home until Monday morning."

"I'd rather you would too. But there's always press at the airport, just as at the train terminal. It'll wind up in the papers. That might mean more trouble for you, because my divorce was already in the papers."

She thought for a moment. "I guess you're right," she said, depressed.

"You'll have to settle things with Joe as soon as you get home," he said. "Until then we'll never be free to do what we want."

She nodded slowly. "You're right, I guess." She paused for a moment. "Do you really think the plane is safe?"

"I wouldn't suggest it if I didn't think so," he answered.

She stared at the rows of garments. "Okay," she said. "You can get the tickets."

"I'll take care of it." He looked at her. "Are you planning to have dinner with your in-laws?"

She nodded. "I promised."

"Okay, if you have to," he said. "But try to return early. I'll miss you."

"I love the matzo balls, Tante," Motty said. "You still make the best chicken in the pot."

Marta nodded, satisfied. "You have to pick out the right chickens, not too much fat."

Phil, as usual, was silent. Then he burped. "It's not that easy anymore," he said. "During the war chicken was king—now everyone wants meat. Steak is king. Good chickens are not easy to buy anymore."

"But we're doing all right," Marta said. "Our customers are loyal. They remember that we took care of them during the war when they couldn't get anything."

"I know that," Motty said, pushing her plate away half empty.

Marta noticed. "You're not feeling well?"

"I'm tired," Motty said.

"Maybe you should give up your job," Marta said. "Taking care of a child is hard enough."

"Rosa takes care of Caroline," Motty said. "I don't have to do anything about her."

Marta looked at her shrewdly. "Joe is working?"

"He just began a new script," she said.

"What about his book?" Marta asked. "The one that he always said he was going to write?"

"He's not been able to get into it," Motty said. "He spends most of his time trying to get scriptwriting jobs."

"He doesn't have to do that," Marta said. "The reason you took your job was so he would have time to work on his book."

"It didn't work out like that," Motty said.

Marta peered at her. "He still runs around?"

Motty didn't look at her. She remained silent.

Marta picked up the plates from the table. She spoke over her shoulder as she placed the plates in the kitchen sink. "He'll never change," she said flatly. "He'll never grow up to face his responsibility as a normal married man."

"That's not true," Phil said, defending him. "He's just not like other boys. We always knew that."

"Boys are not men," Marta said. "Now, my Stevie is a man. He's finished his residency and soon he'll be opening up his own office."

"Fine," Phil said. "But that has nothing to do with Joe. He's creative, not practical."

Marta returned to the table with three glasses of dark brewed tea. She placed a glass before Motty. "Whatever you do," she said, "don't have another baby."

Motty met her eyes. "I don't plan to."

"What are you planning to do?" Phil asked.

Motty didn't answer.

Marta was clever. "Motty has a very good job. She already makes more money than Joe. She doesn't need his money. Maybe she'll divorce him and find another man that is more suited for her."

Phil was angry. "What kind of way is this to talk? Jewish people don't get divorces. It would be a *shanda*."

Marta was smart. She met Motty's eyes evenly. "Not in California," she said. "Lots of Jews get divorced in California. It's not shame there. Read the papers.

Everybody gets divorced in Hollywood. Even Motty's boss, Mr. Marks, got his name in the papers when he got divorced."

Phil looked from one to the other and then back to his glass of tea. His voice was low. "Just remember one thing," he said quietly. "Don't throw out your dirty water until you get fresh."

Chapter Twenty-four

The postman stood in the doorway. He handed Joe the package, marked as usual, "rejected manuscript." He held the delivery book for Joe to initial. "Another one, Mr. Crown," he said sympathetically. "I'm sorry."

"Writers are used to rejection," Joe said philosophically as he returned the delivery book.

He sat down at the coffee table in the living room and opened the package. Jamaica had added an extra in the package. A tinfoil bag of pungent Jamaican ganch, as well as the usual forty envelopes of cocaine. He shook his head. Once again he had forgotten to rent a post-office box.

Rosa came from the kitchen, bringing him a cup of coffee. She placed it on the coffee table in front of him, then glanced at him. "Marijuana," she smiled.

He looked up at her. "You know about it?"

"*Sí, sí.*" She laughed. "*Marijuana Mexicana es la mejor.*"

"You smoke it?" he asked curiously.

She nodded. "Even the children from five, six years. *Para tranquilidad.* Good to sleep."

"Would you like some?" he asked.

"I have," she answered. "If you like, I can bring for you from my family. *Tengo mucho.*"

He laughed. "Thank you. One day I'll take you up on it." He picked up one of the small white envelopes and opened it so that she could look at the white powder. "Do you know this?"

She nodded. "*Cocaína.*"

"Do you use that too?"

She shook her head. *No, señor.* Too nervous, no sleep."

He laughed. "You're smart," he said. "But sometimes for *amor* they say it is very good."

"For *amor,*" she said, "in Mexico we make a tea mixed with peyote and marijuana. Makes many dreams."

"I never knew that," he said.

"It is old Indian *medicina*. My father uses it all the time. *Muy bueno.*"

"How old is your father?" he asked.

"*Curenta y tres años,*" she said. "Like you he has many girlfriends."

"What does your mother say?"

"*Nada*. That is the way with *hombres*."

He picked up the cup and sipped the coffee.

"*Desayuno, señor?*" she asked.

"I don't think so," he answered. "I have to get into the studio."

"Will the *señora* be home on the weekend?"

"Not until Monday," he said.

"Will you have dinner at home those days?"

"Yes," he said. "I plan to work at home on the weekend."

"*Bueno, señor*," she said.

A shaft of sunlight moved into the window behind her. "I gave you money to buy underwear to wear under your dress," he said.

"I was just going to after I brought your coffee, *señor*," she said without expression.

He stared at her. "You're a teasing bitch!"

"No, *señor*," she said without defiance. "I was going to wear it."

He knew she was lying. "Turn your back to me," he said angrily.

Silently she turned around. He raised the back of her skirt over her hips and gave her two stinging slaps, one on each of her buttocks. She made no outcry as his handprint turned white and then bright pink on her skin. "Maybe this will help you to remember."

She looked back at him over her shoulder. Her face was completely expressionless, the skirt still draped over her hips. "You are like my father, *señor*," she said quietly. "But my father hits me harder and more."

He stared at her. "You like it, you bitch!"

"It is part of a woman's duty, *señor*," she said.

He had no answer for her. It was just another way of life.

Keyho came into his office and glanced around. "Very fancy," he said jocularly. "You're becoming a big man. Moving up in the world."

Joe laughed. "You're so full of shit."

"Come on," Keyho said. "This is one of the best of the writer's offices."

"I got lucky," he said.

"Million-dollar grossers do that for you," Keyho said.

"I'd rather they gave me the money," Joe said. "I can do without the office."

"You'll get the money too, in time," Keyho said. "All you have to do is play your cards right."

"Horseshit," Joe said. The telephone rang and he picked it up.

Judi's voice sounded metallically in his ear. "Publicity won't okay a voucher for you," she said. "They said your name don't mean nothing for the papers or the photographers. They want me to go out with the other stars. You know, like Van Johnson, Peter Lawford, even Mickey Rooney."

"I could have told you that," he said. "Then did you get a date?"

"They're working on it, they said," she answered.

"Okay, we'll try it next time," he said.

"You're not angry with me?" she asked. "I don't have any choices. I have to protect my own star status. You understand, don't you?"

"Of course I do," he said, putting down the phone. He looked across the desk to Keyho. "That was Judi," he explained. "Now that she's a star she can only date other stars. The bitch."

"That's Hollywood," Keyho said. "That's what I told you, you'll have to play your cards right."

Joe looked at him. "I'm listening."

"You have to hire a PR agent."

"What for?" Joe asked. "I'm a writer, not a star."

"Writers can be stars, too," Keyho said. "Think about it. Dashiell Hammett, Faulkner, Scot Fitzgerald, Hemingway. They're all writers. And they're stars too."

"I'm not in their league yet," Joe said. "They have a body of work behind them."

"So what?" Keyho said dryly. "A good PR man will make you as well known as any of them. This is a bullshit business but don't underrate it. Bullshitters themselves are the easiest mark for bullshit. They see you in print enough times, they'll believe you're Shakespeare reincarnated."

"I don't know," Joe said dubiously. "Besides, I don't even know a PR man."

"I do," Keyho said. "My sister's son. He works at Columbia Studios as a column planter in the publicity department. He also free-lances for other clients on the side. He's planning to open his own office."

"Is he expensive?"

"It depends on how much you want him to do. Five stories a week, twenty-five dollars; ten stories, fifty bucks; unlimited, a hundred a week."

"That's a lot of money," Joe said. "How do I know he can deliver?"

"How about a line in Winchell's column on Monday?"

"If he can do that, I'll kiss his ass in Macy's window."

"You don't have to do that," Keyho said. "Suppose he slips in a few words in Winchell's Sunday broadcast as well? Go for a hundred up front?"

"You got it," Joe said. He placed the parcel-post package on the desk. "Now how about the merchandise?"

"The same price as the last time," Keyho said. "I'll take a hundred down for my nephew."

"I'll throw in a bag of Jamaican ganch big enough for a hundred five-dollar sticks. You give me the same money. That way we all make a little."

"It's good stuff?" Keyho asked.

Joe opened the tinfoil bag. "You'll get high just smelling it."

Keyho sniffed at it. "You got a deal." He reached for the package.

"When do I get to meet this nephew of yours?"

"How about Monday for lunch? I'll bring Gene over here. You'll like the kid."

"If he doesn't score," Joe said, "don't bring him over. Just give me the extra hundred."

"He'll score," Keyho said definitely. "Another aunt of his is Winchell's number one secretary."

"A.J. wants to talk to you," Kathy said into his phone. "Hold on, I'll put you through to him."

A.J.'s voice sounded pleased with himself. "How's the working going, Joe? When am I going to see some pages?"

"Soon, A.J.," replied Joe. "I'm working on it."

"I know you are," A.J. said. "But that's not the reason for this call. We just got a shipment of New York delicatessen from Barney Greengrass in Manhattan. I thought you might like to come out to our Malibu beach house for brunch about two o'clock Sunday. There'll be some good people there."

"Thank you, A.J.," he answered. "I'd really like that."

"Kathy will give you the address," A.J. said. "See you then. Maybe we can talk some more about the script. I have a few new ideas."

"That's better for me than the deli," he answered. "See you Sunday."

He put down the phone and checked his watch. Twelve-thirty. Time for lunch. He started for the door and the telephone called him back. He picked it up. "Joe Crown."

"What are you doing at your desk?" Blanche asked.

"Working," Joe answered. "That's what I'm supposed to do here."

"I thought you'd be doing something more interesting than that," she said. "Like playing with your prick, for example."

"Not in this fishbowl," he said. "I have the feeling that all the phones coming through the switchboards are tapped."

"No way," she said. "A.J. invited you for Sunday?"

"Yes."

"What are you doing for lunch now?"

"I'm going down to the commissary."

"Why don't you go down on me for lunch," she said.

"I'll never make it back to the studio," he said.

"Don't be crazy, this is Friday," she said. "Nobody ever comes back to the studio after lunch on Friday."

He felt the rush in his loins. "I'll be there in an hour," he said.

Chapter Twenty-five

It was three o'clock in the afternoon and A.J. was on his second bottle of Scotch whisky. If it hadn't been for the fact that his voice was somewhat louder than usual and he had the tendency to repeat his sentences a number of times, one wouldn't realize that he was drunk as a lord. He sat sprawled on a deck chair, looking down at the beach from the deck.

Joe sat on the deck rail beside him. On the beach just below, several tables shaded by sun umbrellas and directors' chairs were occupied with guests wearing swimsuits going to and from the surf. The sun was still hot.

"Good party," A.J. said, holding his drink and gesturing toward the beach. "Good party."

"Very good party," Joe agreed.

"Nice people too," A.J. said. "Nice people."

Joe nodded. He recognized several of the executives from the studio, and there was a sprinkling of film people, actors, actresses, two directors and a producer. Though A.J. had mentioned that Errol Flynn was coming to the brunch, Joe hadn't seen him.

A.J. got up from his chair and leaned over the railing. "Did you see Blanche?" he asked. "Where's Blanche?"

Joe looked down at the beach. "I just saw her a few moments ago," he said. "But I don't see her now."

A.J. sipped at his whisky. "Bitch!" he said. "Bitch!"

Joe remained silent.

A.J. peered out to the surf. "She's nowhere around," he said. "Nowhere. That happens every time we have one of these beach brunches. Suddenly she's gone. Disappeared. Every time."

Joe still remained silent.

A.J. stared at him. "She thinks I don't know what she's doing. But I know. The bitch!" He sipped again at his drink. "She's got some guy in a corner and she's sucking his cock. She's a fucking nymphomaniac." He looked at Joe's face. "You know that, Joe? She's a fucking nymphomaniac."

Joe didn't know what to say. He didn't think it was his place to agree with him.

A.J. shook his head unhappily. "You can't know how a man feels when he knows his wife has probably fucked every man at this party and there's nothing he can even say about it." He looked at Joe. "You haven't fucked her yet, have you?" he asked, then answered the question himself. "Of course not, you haven't been around here long enough. But give her time, she'll get around to you."

He sank back into his chair, refilled his glass and drank morosely. "The fucking problem is there's nothing I can do about it. I can't even divorce her because everything I have is in her name because of taxes. If I divorced her, I'd be wiped out. Not a penny to my name. Not a penny."

Joe felt he had to offer some solace. "It can't be as bad as that, A.J."

"You're nothing but a dumb kid," A.J. said, slurring his words. "How the hell would you know?"

Joe was silent again.

"The whole fucking studio knows about her," A.J. said. "The whole fucking town knows about her. But nobody gives a shit. They all think that I'm getting my share of pussy too. What the hell do they know? I can't even get it up anymore."

"I can't believe that, A.J.," Joe said sympathetically. "You're still a young man. Have you seen a doctor?"

"I've seen a dozen doctors," A.J. said disgustedly. "Zero. They all told me the same thing. It was because of a fever I had about seven years ago when I got a clap from some Chinese whore. That was the end of it."

"Jesus!" Joe exclaimed. "I never heard of anything like that. But now, since the war, they came out with a whole new batch of medicines."

"Not for what I got," A.J. said. "But that isn't the reason she acts like she does. She's been like that all the time. She's always been cock crazy. When I could handle it, it was great, we even used to party together, *ménage à trois* and all that kind of thing. Now I get nothing but shit."

Joe, still sitting on the railing, saw her coming from around the side of the house. She had changed from a swimsuit to a beach caftan. "I just saw her," he said. "She was probably just changing out of her bathing suit. She was probably feeling cold. The sun's going down.'

A.J. came over to the railing beside him and looked down. "It wasn't the sun going down," he said sarcastically. "It was her."

Joe looked at him silently.

"I'm not crazy," A.J. said emphatically. "Look at that satisfied look on her face. I know that look. It's like that every time she gets it off." He went back to the deck chair. He leaned back for a moment then turned up to Joe. "Don't pay attention to me," he said. "I'm a little drunk."

"That happens to us all sometimes," Joe said.

"We won't talk to anybody about it, will we?" A.J. asked, slightly ashamed.

"I don't talk," Joe said. "It's none of my business."

"Good boy," A.J. said, then added in a harsh angry voice, "But if by chance you get to fuck her, give her a good one for me. Bust her ass!"

Joe didn't answer.

A.J. got out of the chair. "I'm tired," he said, his voice suddenly weary. "I think I'll go inside and take a nap."

"I think I'll be going home too," Joe said.

"Have you been working on the treatment over the weekend?" A.J. asked.

"Yes," Joe said. "At home."

"Good." A.J. nodded. He shook Joe's hand. "I'll see you at the studio tomorrow."

Caroline was having her dinner as he came through the door. "Daddy!" she cried, waving her fork and dropping a forkful of spaghetti on the table. "Pasghetti," she exclaimed.

He laughed. She never could pronounce the word. "Good?" he asked.

"Very good," she said seriously. "But I like Tootsie Rolls better."

"After dinner I'll give you some Tootsie Rolls," he promised.

"Good." She lifted another forkful of spaghetti. "When Mommy comes home?" she asked.

"Tomorrow," he answered.

She smiled. "Mommy always brings presents."

"Yes," he said.

"I like Mommy's presents."

That was true, he thought. He wondered why he never thought of bringing a present for her. But then, he never knew what to get her except Tootsie Rolls. He watched her eating. It was strange. He knew that she was his child, of course. But other men always talked about their children and carried their photographs around. He never did. In a way he never thought about her as a child. She was more like a doll or a toy. Maybe it was because he had no way of communicating with her. Perhaps when she grew older and could say more, maybe then he would understand more about her. He loved her, he knew that. But exactly why, he didn't know. Maybe that was one of the things about being a father—not understanding his feeling but only the responsibility she placed on him.

"I went to the park with Rosa," she said.

"Was it nice?" he asked.

"We saw fish in the pool," she said.

"That was nice." He looked across the room at Rosa. "Did she enjoy it?"

Rosa nodded. "*Mucho.*"

"*Mucho,*" Caroline echoed. She pointed to the empty plate with her fork. "All empty," she laughed. "Now, Tootsie Rolls?"

Joe took them from where he always kept them in his pocket. He placed three Tootsie Rolls on the table. "One extra."

"Good." She laughed, already unwrapping one.

"What do you say?" he asked.

She looked up at him. "Thank you, Daddy."

"You're welcome, darling," he said, kissing her on the cheek. He straightened up and looked over at Rosa. "I'll have dinner at eight o'clock, after she's gone to sleep."

"*Sí, señor.*"

He kissed Caroline again on the cheek. "Daddy's going to have a little nap, sweetheart. You have a nice night's sleep.'

"Nighty-night, Daddy," she answered, already chewing on the first Tootsie Roll and unwrapping the second.

He went upstairs to his study and looked down at the typewritten pages of the treatment. Thirty pages. Not too bad. Now that he was getting into it, it was coming easier. Maybe he could have it finished in two weeks.

He turned and went into the bedroom. Quickly he undressed and took a shower. The afternoon in the sun had made him tired. The hot water felt good against his skin. He dried himself with a large bath towel, then stretched out on the bed. It was warm in the apartment. He threw the towel to the floor, rolled over on his stomach and fell asleep.

Then he was in the midst of a strange dream. First, Blanche was sucking him and almost swallowed his testicles in her mouth, and then he was fucking her, ramming into her as if he were an animal, and all the while A.J. was standing over them, screaming at him. "Bust her ass! Bust the bitch's ass!"

A tentative soft hand touched his shoulder. He awoke. Rosa was looking down at him. "It is already nine o'clock, *señor,*" she said softly. "Would you like to have your dinner?"

He shook the cobwebs from his head and began to roll over, then stopped. He felt the urging of his erection against his belly. "First, give me the towel," he said, pointing to it on the floor.

Silently, she handed it to him. He wrapped it around his waist, still conscious of the impression against the towel. "*El señor tiene muchos sueños de amor,*" she said with a faint smile.

He ignored her comment. "Turn on the big radio downstairs," he said. "I'll have dinner on the small table in the living room. I'll be right there."

"*Sí, señor,*" she answered and left the room.

He went into the bathroom and stepped into the shower again. This time, ice-cold water. He dried himself quickly and slipped on his bathrobe and started downstairs.

Walter Winchell's program was already on by the time he sat down at the table.

He sat there silently as Rosa placed the salad in front of him. "Beer, *señor*?" she asked.

"Yes. Beer." He listened to the rapid speech of Winchell. The effect was exciting, as if everything the man said was of life-and-death importance.

It was almost at the very end of the program that Winchell gave the plug that Joe was awaiting.

> *From Triple S studios, usually better known as producers of B movies and quickie pix, comes the sleeper hit of the year*—Warrior Queen of the Amazons—*with Steve Cochran, known only as the poor man's Clark Gable, and Judi Antoine, known only as the star of pinups*—Warrior Queen *has garnered a million and a half dollars in just two weeks . . . That's one and a half million simoleons, Mr. and Mrs. America, and that ain't hay . . . The genius behind this money-grabbing movie is a little up-to-now unknown writer, Joe Crown . . . Joe Crown, who has written two short stories published in the Foley collection of great American short stories, has now written the script of the movie that blends fantasy and adventure that the cognoscenti compare favorably with such box office giants as* King Kong . . . The Lost World . . . Tarzan of the Apes. *Even though helped by the most scantily clad beauties of the silver screen, the triumph belongs only to the genius of Joe Crown . . . Remember that name, Mr. and Mrs. America, Joe Crown . . . You'll be hearing much more about him . . . At this very minute every studio in Hollywood is trying to sign the man to a multimillion-dollar contract . . .*

Almost the moment he had gone off the air the telephone began ringing. A.J.'s was the first call. "Just remember, Joe, we have a contract. Don't let anybody fuck your head around."

"That's right, A.J.," Joe said. "I know that you are always in my corner."

"You bet your ass, son," A.J. answered. "I want to see you in my office first thing tomorrow morning."

"I'll be there, A.J."

The moment he put down the phone it began ringing again. A.J. must have redialed again immediately. "In case I forgot to tell you, son," he said, "I meant to tell you this afternoon at the beach—I'm doubling the figure on your contract to forty thousand instead of twenty."

"Thank you, A.J.," Joe said. He put down the telephone once more. Keyho was right. Bullshitters are the first to believe the bullshit.

For the next two hours the telephone kept ringing. Almost everyone who knew anyone in Hollywood and many who didn't know were calling to congratulate him. It was finally past eleven o'clock when the telephone calls subsided; Joe had never got around to eating his dinner. He walked to the couch and stretched out.

"You didn't eat your dinner, *señor*," Rosa said.

He turned to her. "It's been too hectic," he said. He sat up and looked up at her. "You don't like to wear underwear, is that it?"

"No, *señor*," she said, the secret smile in the corners of her mouth as she looked down at him. "I was getting ready for bed, *señor*."

"Okay," he said. "Just bring me a cup of coffee and you can go to bed."

"*Sí, señor*," she said. She looked down at him again. "I have some *cigarillos*

Mexicanos, señor. Perhaps one would calm you down and you will sleep better."

"Marijuana?" he asked.

She nodded.

He thought for a moment. "What the hell," he said. "Okay." Maybe it would work. He was still too excited to go to bed.

She was back in a moment with a cup of coffee and a thinly rolled cigarette. "Thanks," he said, lighting it. He dragged it deeply into his lungs. It was sweet and soft, not like the Jamaican, which sometimes was harsh and bitter. He dragged on it again. He began to feel better almost immediately.

"*Es bueno, señor?*" she asked.

"Very nice, thank you," he answered. "You can go to bed now."

"I can make you even more calm, *señor.*"

"I feel perfectly calm right now," he said, feeling slightly silly.

She laughed aloud. "*Mire, señor,*" she said, pointing her finger.

He looked down at himself. His prick had never looked so large. It was amazing. He began to laugh. "That's ridiculous," he said. He tried to press it down beneath his bathrobe but the moment he let it go, it sprang up almost slapping against his belly. He laughed louder. He looked up at her. "I'm fucking stoned," he said.

"*Sí, señor.*" She smiled.

"You better go to bed now," he said, trying to be reasonable. "Or I might wind up shoving it up your ass." It was really funny. He couldn't stop laughing.

"Okay in my ass," she said. "But not in there, the other place, I am virgin until marry."

He laughed again. "That makes sense."

She pulled off her dress then backed towards him. "First I must make you wet." She spit into her hand and rubbed the saliva over his penis. "Good?" she asked, looking back over her shoulder at him.

"Very good," he said, taking another drag of the cigarette. "Really very good," he laughed.

Delicately she took the cigarette from his fingers and placed it in an ashtray. Then she carefully spread her buttocks with both hands and backed into him. At the last moment, she grabbed him with one hand and guided him into her. "*Aiee!*" she cried aloud as she sat down completely in his lap.

"Fantastic!" Her anus was as soft as a velvet glove.

She began to spring up and down on him. He grabbed her by the hips. "Hang tight!" he yelled, "or you'll go up through the ceiling!"

There was the sound of a key clicking in the door, and she suddenly froze. In another moment she was gone and racing up the stairs. Motty stood in shock at the door.

He pulled himself to his feet, trying to be serious. "Motty!" he exclaimed. "What are you doing here? You're not supposed to be here until tomorrow."

Motty slammed the door angrily behind her. "I can see that," she said icily.

He pointed his index finger toward her. "You're not going to believe what I'm going to tell you," he said seriously.

She stood there silently.

Then he glanced down at himself. His erection was pointing in exactly the same position as his finger. That was too much—it really was too funny to believe. He began laughing uncontrollably. He fell to the floor rolling back and forth; his sides hurt from the laughter. He tried to sit up but could not. He couldn't stop laughing—tears ran from his eyes.

"It's so funny!" he managed to gasp, between spasms of laughter.

Then the nightmare began.

Chapter Twenty-six

"Is he going to be my new daddy?" Caroline asked. She was more curious than concerned.

Joe looked at her as she stood in front of him. Children came right to the point. What's in it for them and where do they fit? He glanced across the room where Motty, Mr. Marks and the attorneys sat before the small round table, exchanging agreements as several moving men carried out the suitcases and boxes packed with Motty's and Caroline's belongings to the truck outside. He didn't know what to tell the child. "I guess so," he answered doubtfully.

Caroline was puzzled. "Don't you want to be my daddy anymore?"

"Of course I want to be your daddy," he said reassuringly. "But Mommy is moving out and little girls have to live with their mommies."

Caroline shook her head. "I miss Rosa," she said "Mommy doesn't know how to make *huevos rancheros*."

"I'm sure she will find another girl who'll be able to make them," he said.

"I hope so," Caroline said. "And then she can take me to the park too."

Joe nodded.

Caroline stared at him. "Do you like sleeping on the couch, Daddy?"

Joe laughed. "Not really."

"Then why didn't you sleep in bed with Mommy?"

Joe shook his head. This was Friday. He had been spending the nights there since Motty came home on Sunday. The week had been hell. On Monday morning, Motty told him she wanted a divorce.

"That's stupid," he said. "I really was stoned. I never even fucked, not even a little bit."

Motty was adamant. "It was not only Rosa. There were always other girls."

"Shit," he said. "They never meant anything. If I did fuck them it was only a little bit. Friendly. Sociable."

"I don't understand you at all," she said. "You were always like that. I thought you would change once we were married."

"I tried," he said.

"You didn't try hard enough," she said. "You were screwing around even while I was pregnant, the minute you started working at the studio."

"I can't talk you out of it?"

"No."

"You'll have to get a lawyer," he said. "The whole thing's going to take time."

"I have a lawyer," Motty said. "The same one that handled Mr. Marks's divorce."

"What's Marks got to do with it?"

She was silent.

He stared at her, a light dawning in his head. "You're going to marry him?"

She flushed.

"Holy shit!" he exclaimed. "I've been really stupid. You've been fucking him all the time!"

She was angry. "You make things sound so dirty."

"*You* made it dirty," he answered. "At least, I didn't play angel."

She changed the subject. "Are you going to the office this morning?"

"I have to," he said. "I had a meeting scheduled with A.J."

"I'm staying home with Caroline," she said. "I'll tell the lawyer to call you there."

"I'll be home in the evening," he said. "He can talk to me here."

"You're not going to get into the bedroom," she said.

"I can sleep on the couch downstairs," he said. "But I don't see any reason for me to move out. I'm not the one looking for a divorce."

"I'll be moving by the end of the week," she said flatly and walked away from him.

A.J. stared at him across the desk. "I don't know how you did it," he said. "That Winchell plug means another half million at the box office."

"I was lucky," Joe said.

"More than luck," A.J. said. "None of our PR people could ever get a plug in Winchell."

Joe was silent. Somehow he had not felt as elated as when he listened to the man last night. The rest of the night had been a disaster.

A.J. peered at him. "You don't look like you're happy at all. As a matter of fact, you look like a truck ran over you."

"Wife troubles," Joe said.

"Serious?" A.J. asked.

"She wants a divorce," Joe said.

"You talked to her?"

"Until I was blue in the face," Joe said. "She means it. She's going to marry her boss."

A.J. stared at him. "Gerald Marks, the department-store guy?"

Joe nodded. "You know him?"

"I know him," A.J. said. "I heard he just got a divorce."

"What kind of a guy is he?" Joe asked.

"Okay, I guess," A.J. answered. "He's not like us. Very straight, serious. And a lot of money. He's the only heir of his family. Someday the whole department-store chain will belong to him. Your wife is smart."

"Fucking cunt," Joe said bitterly. "She's already lined up a lawyer. Marks's attorney."

"That's serious," A.J. said. "He's going to clean you out."

"What for?" Joe asked. "Marks has money. She'll have all she needs, she won't want any from me."

"You're naïve," A.J. said sagely. "That's not the way it goes. Her lawyer will tell her to go for your throat. You better get yourself a sharp lawyer just to keep yourself alive."

"There's nothing they can take," Joe said. "The furniture cost shit. I got maybe twenty-six, seven grand in the bank."

A.J. stood behind his desk. "They'll take it. And besides that they'll hit you for child support. And wait until they find out about the new contract we're signing. Then you'll see the shit flying."

Joe stared at him. "What do I do about that?"

"First, you get a lawyer. I know a good man for you and he's not too expensive," A.J. said. "Then I suggest we delay signing any new contracts until after the divorce is completed, otherwise they will really wipe you out."

"Motty will never go along with that," Joe said.

"She has no choice," A.J. said. "I put you on week-to-week for seven-fifty, no guarantee. If they get tough, we just agree to lay you off."

Joe was silent.

"Then when it's all over we'll just sign the contract," A.J. said. He looked at Joe, who was still silent. "You can trust me, Joe," he said. "Just remember, I'm on your side. I don't like the idea of a talented kid like you winding up getting screwed."

"Do you really believe she'd do that?" Joe asked.

"All women are bitches," A.J. replied. He looked at Joe. "Do you have a joint account?"

Joe nodded.

"You better grab your money out before she does."

"She won't do that," Joe said.

"No?" A.J. said pointedly. "Call your bank and put a hold on your account. You can use my phone."

Joe picked up the telephone and dialed the bank. An assistant vice president answered. Joe asked him to put a hold on the account, then waited.

After a moment, the bank officer came back on line. "I'm sorry, Mr. Crown," he said, "but Mrs. Crown was just here this morning, withdrew all the funds and closed the account."

Joe put down the receiver and stared at A.J. "She took out all the money," he said in a stunned voice.

A.J. shook his head. "I told you."

"But all the money," Joe repeated, still stunned.

"Like I said," A.J. answered. "When it comes to money, all women are nothing but bitches and whores."

"What do I do now?" Joe asked.

"I'll make an appointment for you with the lawyer," A.J. said. "You better see him right away."

Joe pulled two Tootsie Rolls from his pocket and gave them to Caroline, then glanced over at the table where Motty and Marks sat with the lawyers. Joe's attorney, Don Sawyer, was a young man, a nephew of A.J.'s. Whether he was capable or not Joe could not judge, because everything seemed very cut-and-dried. At the end of it all, Joe had no choice. Motty held all the cards—she had been well prepared.

His attorney gathered a stack of papers and placed them on the coffee table in front of Joe. "It's simple," he said. "Only four agreements. You sign them and it's all over."

Joe looked down at them as Don pulled a chair opposite him. "What are they?" he asked, feeling stupid.

Don nodded. "First is the agreement for not contesting the Mexican divorce; second, the agreement about the community property; third, you waive your visitation rights concerning the child in exchange for no payment of either alimony or child support; and fourth, you accept the return of ten thousand dollars formerly in your joint bank account, and the furniture and accessories to the furnishings in the apartment belong to you and will be turned over to you the moment the divorce is finalized. That should be sometime next week."

"What happens if she does not go through with the divorce?" Joe asked.

"She'll go through with it," Don said confidently. He lowered his voice so that he could not be overheard. "They're hotter for the divorce than you are."

"Shit," Joe said. He stared down at the papers. "I guess I have no choices."

"Unless you want to fight," Don said. "And even if you do, you're going to lose. The California courts and laws are all against you."

Joe looked across the room at Motty. Motty kept her face turned away from him. He turned to Don. "Lend me your pen," he said. "I'll sign."

Quickly he signed the agreements, and Don took them back to Motty's attorney. Motty looked at her attorney. "Can I leave now?" she asked.

He glanced at the agreements. "Everything's been signed. You can leave whenever you're ready."

She crossed the room and took Caroline by the hand. "Come, Caroline," she said. "We're going now."

The child looked at Joe. Her face was already smeared with chocolate. "Bye-bye, Daddy," she said calmly.

Joe started to get up from the couch. "Goodbye, baby," he said, his voice strained. He turned to Motty. "Happier now?" he asked bitterly.

She didn't answer, her face flushing. She started toward the door, pulling the child along with her.

Joe stared at her. There was something in her face, something about the way she walked. It was nothing new. He had seen that before. Then he remembered. "You're fucking pregnant!" he shouted.

She rushed out the door with the child. He turned and looked at Marks, who was hurrying after her. "Asshole!" he shouted. "I'm not the only asshole in the world! That's the same way she nailed me!"

But Marks was already outside the door. Joe turned to his attorney. "No wonder they were in such a rush," he said. "We were stupid. I should have guessed!" Then his anger dissipated as quickly as it had come. He smiled wryly. "I've been outfucked and outsmarted. But maybe I got away lucky."

Don nodded. "It could have been worse."

"Yeah," Joe said. "I could have been fighting over two kids, not one. And one of them not even mine!"

Chapter Twenty-seven

It was nearly six o'clock by the time the attorney gathered up all the agreements and placed them in his briefcase. "I'll be on my way," he said. "My in-laws are coming over for dinner."

Joe nodded. "Fine."

Don looked at him sympathetically. "Would you like to join us?"

"I don't think so," Joe said. "But thanks anyway."

"You ought to go out for dinner, maybe catch a movie. It won't be much fun for you to be sitting around here alone. The first night after the divorce papers is a bitch."

Joe looked at him curiously. "You know?"

Don nodded. "I've been through it. I'm on my second marriage."

Joe thought for a moment. "I guess everyone thinks that they were the only one it ever happened to."

Don smiled. "It's almost like a way of life out here."

Joe nodded, and shook his head. "I'll be okay," he said. "Thanks for everything."

"I'll call you at the beginning of the week," Don said. "Just as soon as they return the official agreements to me."

Joe closed the door behind the attorney and then opened a bottle of Scotch. Quickly he drank three straight shots. He felt the liquor burning its way down his throat and coughed. "Shit!" he said, then turned on the radio and slumped into the couch. He spun the radio dial until he found a station that broadcast only music—he was in no mood for the news program that usually came on at this time. He had another drink, then leaned his head back against the cushion. Suddenly, he felt exhausted. His eyes were burning and he rubbed them slowly. It was not tears he felt; he never cried. Then he fell asleep.

He thought he heard a baby crying and opened his eyes. The room was dark. The sound was the buzzing of the radio after the station had gone off the air. He switched off the radio and turned on the lamp next to the couch. The half-empty bottle of Scotch stared up at him from the coffee table. He shook his head, trying to clear it. He hadn't realized he had drunk that much. He checked his watch. It was after one in the morning.

He looked around the room. It was strange—not familiar at all. Then he realized that it was the silence. There always had been some sound in the apartment. Now, nothing. He lit a cigarette. The scratch of the match echoed loudly in his ear. He took a deep drag of the cigarette and let it out slowly through his nose. He stared at his hands, which were trembling. He dragged again on the cigarette. Besides his shaking hands, he had the granddaddy of all headaches.

Slowly he pulled himself to his feet and walked into the kitchen. He took a bottle of Pepsi from the refrigerator and then a tin of Bayer from a shelf. He popped three aspirin tablets in his mouth and swallowed them with the Pepsi. He finished the bottle of Pepsi and went up the steps to the bedroom.

He turned on the light and stood in the doorway looking into the bedroom. It was a mess. Motty's closets were open, clothes hangers strewn on the floor; the dresser drawers and cabinet doors had been emptied and left open. Looking through the bathroom door, he saw that the medicine cabinet doors were also thrown open, and only his shaving cream and razors remained. Inexplicably, even his toothbrush and toothpaste had disappeared.

He turned from his bedroom door to Caroline's room. Her small bed and other furniture were gone and the room seemed bare with only the narrow cot and small cabinet that had been assigned to Rosa and her few belongings. He wondered whether Rosa had taken her things with her when she had run out of the house that night. He didn't trouble to check the cabinet. It didn't matter anyway. She had not returned since.

He closed the door and walked into his study. He walked to his desk. His manuscript papers were still neatly piled on the desk top. There was a sheet of paper on the typewriter. He picked it up. It was in Motty's handwriting.

Fuck you! You're nothing but a fucking fake. You can't write. Not one thing you've ever done was worth a shit. You can't even write a lousy comic strip. Not only that you can't write, you can't fuck. Now that I have a real man, I really know what fucking is. You will take a hundred years to do what he can do in a minute. And if you think you have such a great big prick, forget it. His is twice the size of yours and he can do more things with it than you can ever imagine. You're a kid, not a real man, all you're good for is jerking off.

Love, Motty

Angrily he crumpled it into a ball and threw it across the room. "Bitch!" he exclaimed. Then he picked it up from the floor, straightened it and placed it on the desk in front of him. Then he stared at it and began to smile. Dumb cunt, he thought. She signed it "Love."

He picked up the framed eight-and-a-half-by-eleven photograph standing at the far end of the desk and looked at it. Quickly he slipped the glass off the frame and then, carefully folding the note so that it covered the bottom portion of the photograph, placed it so that her downcast eyes seemed to be looking at the note. He smiled as he replaced the glass and put the frame back on the desk. If ever he needed a reminder of how a woman could screw him, he would always have it.

He began to feel hungry. He hadn't eaten since lunch the day before. He went back to the kitchen. The refrigerator was empty; a half-empty bottle of milk, some bottles of Pepsi and two beers—nothing else. He scratched his head. Tomorrow he would have to go to the market and stock up.

He left the apartment, got into his car and drove to the all-night drive-in on Sunset and Cahuenga. It was after two in the morning and the drive-in was almost empty. He headed the car into the curb, turned off the engine and rolled down his window.

A moment later, a cute little blond wearing a French sailor hat with a red pompom and a little flared-out, short-sleeved cotton shirt that barely covered her tight little shorts, came toward him in her red high-heeled shoes. She placed the clip tray over the car door. "Coffee?" she asked, the filled paper cup in her hand.

"Please."

She placed the cup with two lumps of sugar and a thin wooden spoon on the tray. "Our special tonight is two beef dogs on a roll with chili and french fries."

"Sounds good to me," he said. "How about a beer?"

"It's after two o'clock," she answered. "Regulations. No wine or beer on the premises after that."

"Could I have a glass of water?" he asked.

"Sure. But we have Coke and any soft drink you want."

"I brought my friend with me," he said, picking up the Scotch bottle next to him so that she could see it. "Johnnie."

She laughed. "Johnnie Walker's everybody's friend. Even me."

"Bring an extra glass and I'll introduce you."

"Not on the job," she said. "They'll have my ass for that."

"We can fake it," he said. "Just bring the extra glass."

He watched her go behind the serving counter as he turned on the car radio. The only station that was on the air was playing Mexican music. Good enough, it went with the chili. There were two water glasses on the tray she brought back. The chili dogs were on a paper plate with a wooden fork, the french fries in a square paper container. A half-dozen foil envelopes held the ketchup and mustard.

He poured the whisky into one of the glasses. As he lifted it up to the tray he knocked over the container of french fries. "I'm sorry," he apologized, holding the Scotch bottle in his hand outside the car, pointing down toward the french fries.

She smiled and knelt to pick up the container. At the same moment she took the drink and swallowed it in one gulp. She came up with the paper container. "No problem, sir," she said, the liquor flushing her face. "I'll get you another."

He had eaten half the first chili dog by the time she returned with the fries. "Very smart." She grinned.

"Where there's a will there's a way."

"I needed it," she said.

"How much time do you put in?"

"Six hours," she answered. "Another fifteen minutes, then I can go home."

"Do you have to go home?" he asked.

"I should," she said. "My husband likes me home when he gets in. He works the night shift at Hughes Aircraft and he's in by five usually."

"That's two and a half hours," he said. "Johnnie's got a twin brother at my place and he's not even been opened yet."

"I don't know," she said hesitantly. "I don't have a car. I only live two blocks from here. That's why I took this job."

"I'll get you home in time," he said. "You and me and Johnnie will make up a great *ménage à trois*."

"I don't even know your name," she said.

"I don't know yours," he replied. "But what difference does it make? Let's leave it at that."

"You're so bad." She smiled. She looked back to the drive-in and then at him. Silently she placed the ticket on the tray. He threw a five-dollar bill on it. "Keep the change."

She took the ticket and the money. She looked at him for a moment. "What do you work at?"

"I'm a screenwriter."

"At a studio?"

"Triple S."

"Maybe you can get me in for an interview?" she asked. "I was in all my high school plays."

"Maybe," he said.

She stared at him again. "I'll change out of my uniform. Another girl will take your tray away. You can pick me up on the next block."

He watched her return to the serving counter and walk into the back of the drive-in. He had finished almost half the second chili dog when he saw her leave from the side door. He honked the car horn and another girl took the tray away almost immediately. Carefully he backed out into the street and followed the blond. She was exactly in the middle of the next block. He pulled the car over to the curb and opened the door.

She got into the seat beside him. The bottle of Scotch pressed hard between them. She picked it up and laughed. "If you're as hard as our friend Johnnie," she said, "we're going to have a hell of a party."

He watched her uncork the bottle and bring it to her lips. "Good whisky," she said, offering him the bottle. "Black Label. The best."

He waved it away. "Not while I'm driving."

"Very smart," she said, nodding owlishly. She raised the bottle to her mouth again. By the time he drove to his apartment, the bottle was empty and she was pissed drunk. When he opened the door to let her out of the car, her legs gave beneath her and she slipped onto the small lawn in front of the sidewalk.

He lifted her up from under her arms and placed her back into the car. "I'd better take you home," he said.

"I'll be okay," she said. "All I need is a little food. I never eat at the restaurant, I hate the crap they serve there."

"But I haven't anything to eat in the house," he said. "That's why I went to the drive-in."

"Too bad," she said. "Too bad."

"Where do you live?" he asked.

"Two blocks from the drive-in," she said.

He got back into the car and turned on the motor. It didn't take long to drive her home; it took ten minutes to get her from the car to her door.

She leaned on her door, weaving slightly. "Thank you for a lovely evening," she said politely.

"You're welcome," he said and went home.

The apartment was still as silent as when he had left it. Crazy. He'd never thought he could feel so alone. He took three more aspirin and two more drinks and went upstairs to his bedroom. He looked into the study room for a moment, then took the framed photograph and letter from the study, and walked into the bedroom and put it next to the night table beside him.

He watched it while he undressed and by habit placed his clothes away neatly. Then he got into bed and turned off the light. But sleep evaded him. He tossed and turned; the strange silence was too much for him.

He turned on the radio, but found only the same Mexican station. He sat up in bed, smoked a cigarette and stared at the photograph. Then he put out the cigarette and reached to turn off the lamp. The photograph still stared at him. Suddenly he was angry. "Fucking cunt!" he shouted and threw the frame and photograph across the room. The tinkling sound of the broken glass took his anger away. It was the same sound he had heard when he smashed the glass under his foot on their wedding day. It was only right that the marriage should be ended with the same ancient ceremony. He fell asleep immediately.

He heard the telephone ringing in the distance. He rolled over in bed and opened his eyes. Nine o'clock in the morning. He pushed himself erect and reached for the telephone. "Hello."

"Joe? It's Laura Shelton from New York."

"Good morning," he said.

"Did I wake you?" she asked. "I'm sorry about the news of your divorce," she went on. "But if you're feeling down, maybe a little good news will lift you up."

"Good news will help," he replied, lighting a cigarette. He thought he smelled the aroma of coffee coming from downstairs. But it had to be an illusion.

"Santini, the Italian producer, wants you for two pictures in Europe. Guaranteed pay or play, thirty-five thousand each and five percent of the net. I've already received the contract and a deposit check of ten thousand dollars if you sign."

"I thought it was cocktail-party talk," Joe said.

"He obviously meant it," Laura said. "I spoke to him in Rome; he's anxious for you to begin right away."

The aroma of coffee was not an illusion. Rosa appeared in the bedroom door, a tray of coffee and sweet rolls in her hands. He looked at her silently as she placed the tray on the bed beside him and left the room. He took a sip of coffee. It was hot, and it warmed him.

"Right away?' he said to Laura. "What about my agreement with A.J.?"

"I have a feeling that A.J. is going to pull out of it," Laura said. "Kathy tells me that Steve Cochran won't do the picture and Judi told A.J. that she would not do the picture unless she got a new contract with a lot more money. A.J. has already placed her on suspension."

"Where does that place me?" he asked. "I have the treatment almost ready."

"How long will it take you to finish it?"

"Another week."

"You have no signed contract," she said. "You can turn the treatment in and go on your way. As a matter of fact, I have a feeling that A.J. will be relieved."

He sipped at the coffee again. If he had no deal with A.J., he had nothing to tie him down here. The only life he had here was wrapped around the industry. He had no real friends. "You sound like you know something," he said. "Have you spoken to A.J. already?"

She hesitated for a moment before answering. "I'm a good agent," she said. "I don't want you to get screwed on anything. A.J. said he wouldn't stand in your way."

He was silent.

"And another thing," she added. "I spoke to the chief editor at Rinehart. They're interested in your novel."

"You've been busy."

"I'm your agent," she said. "I was testing the waters with Rinehart. The manuscript is at Doubleday right now. They can come up with a lot more money with all the book clubs they own."

"I'm feeling better already, Laura. What you're doing is above and beyond the call of duty."

"Not duty, Joe." There was a pause. "I think you've got two good opportunities. You can take advantage of both of them. What do you say?"

He took a deep breath. "Let's do them."

"Good. I'll have the papers and tickets here in New York for you. You can sign them on your way through."

"I'll see you then, say, a week from today. Okay?"

There was another pause. "My office will handle it, Joe. Just papers to sign—everything will be in order."

"You don't *want* to be there?" he asked.

"It's not a question of wanting or not wanting, Joe. It's a tangle of feelings about you that I don't know how to handle. I'm working for you, but I sincerely believe that I'd feel safer if we don't meet just now."

He stared at the phone for a moment. "You scare me, Laura."

"You've got a fine director to work with, a new film world. You've got a book that one publisher will put up money for—it's a whole new world. Enough to scare anyone, so why add another mixed-up lady? You've had your share of them too, haven't you? Work is the answer right now, not romance."

"Now you really sound like an agent."

"Not like an agent, Joe. I really care about you—not only about your talent and the money you will make, but about you. 'Bye for now, Joe."

He put down the telephone. "Rosa!" he called.

He heard her footsteps on the stairs then she appeared in the doorway. "What are you doing here?" he asked.

"I came for my clothes, *señor*," she said. "When I saw you were asleep and there was nothing in the kitchen for breakfast, I went to the market to bring something in."

"Thank you," he said. He looked at her closely. Her face showed several faint bruises and the remnant of a black eye. "What happened to you?" he asked.

"My papa beat me for losing my job," she said simply. "I must have another job or he will send me back to Mexico to my mother."

"I'm sorry," he said.

"It is not your fault, *señor*," she said. She looked at him. "Perhaps I could be your housekeeper. I would cook and clean as I did before and I would ask only twenty dollars a month."

He stared at her. That was ten dollars less a month than she had been paid before, including taking care of the child. "I wouldn't change your salary," he said. "But I will not be here for long. I am going to Europe very soon to work."

"Even working for one week would help me, *señor*," she said. "Perhaps by that time I could find another job."

He thought for a moment. She would be a great help to him. There was no way he could handle the apartment by himself. "Okay," he said.

She came to him and kissed his hand quickly. "Thank you, *señor. Mil gracias*."

"It's all right," he said.

"I am sorry for what happened, *señor*," she said.

"That part is over," he said. "Now we both must look forward to tomorrow."

Part Three

1949

Chapter Twenty-eight

"*Belle Starr and Annie Oakley*," Santini said. "The title alone is worth a million dollars."

"I still can't believe it," Joe said as they came from the projection room. "The picture is not bad."

"It's a work of genius," Santini said with his Italian superlatives and enthusiasm. "And it was all your idea. You were the one who talked Judi Antoine into coming here to co-star with Mara Benetti in a Western. I don't know how you ever thought of it."

"It was John Wayne and Gary Cooper in drag," Joe laughed. "And it worked. But you were the genius. I never thought two big pair of tits like that would fit on the screen at the same time in Cinescope."

"We're Italian," Santini smiled. "We're used to big tits. All Italian women have them." He turned to the small man that always followed behind him. Giuseppe was the ultimate flunky. "Giuseppe, *il carro*." He snapped his fingers.

"*Si, maestro*." Giuseppe bowed and ran out.

Santini turned back to Joe. "Now, my friend, what is the next project your genius will propose for me?"

"I thought I might rest a little from movies for a while and work on my novel," Joe said. "I'm hoping that you will be able to give me the balance of the fees from the picture to carry me."

Santini smiled. "No problem," he said. "I will make a distribution deal for the States in another week; then I will send you the money."

Joe stared at him. That was what he had said when they finished the first movie he had written for him, *Shercules*. It had been a rip-off of *Warrior Queen*. But the Italian actress Santini had discovered was even more exciting than Judi. It was a very successful drive-in movie in the States and set up the girl for this movie. Yet, even with that, Joe had not received the balance from the first picture until he began working on the second. As far as profit shares—zero. Italian accounting was even more dishonest than American. "I could use five thousand dollars right now," he said diplomatically. "I have many bills to pay."

Santini took out his checkbook and a pen with a flourish. "I will do that immediately." He wrote the check and handed it to him.

Joe looked at the check. It was for five thousand dollars. He kept his face expressionless. They both knew that the check was made of rubber. "Thank you, *maestro*," he said politely.

"What are you doing for the month of August?" Santini asked, equally politely. "At the Lido in Venice as you did last year?"

"I haven't made up my mind," Joe said. "It's too expensive for me right now. Besides, last year, I met this beautiful girl, unbelievable. She stayed with me all three weeks I was there. Then when I was ready to leave, her father showed up and shook me down for a bundle. I thought the girl was at least twenty—she was fourteen. Not only that, she left me with the clap."

Santini laughed. "Summer romances. It's always like that. Love and disillusionment." He looked at him. "Was she good in bed at least?"

Joe laughed. "The best."

"So it was not so bad," Santini said. Looking toward the street through the glass doors, he saw his car pulling up to the curb. "I have an appointment." He waved to Joe as he left. "I will call you at the beginning of the week. *Ciao*."

"*Ciao*," Joe said. He watched the car move away, then looked at the check. Carefully he folded it and put it in his wallet. He knew the routine. The bank would bounce it. Then he would have to get in touch with Metaxa in New York to collect it for him. If he was lucky, he might collect it in three or four months. Slowly he left the building and walked up the side street to Via Veneto.

It was six o'clock, and the heavy, humid heat of Rome pressed wearily against the pavement. The tourists were already returning from the museums, the Vatican and other sightseeing attractions. Now they were looking in the shop windows or seating themselves at the tables at the sidewalk cafés for ice cream or coffee and pastries. He stopped at his usual table on the sidewalk in front of the Café Donay. He glanced at the entrance of the Excelsior Hotel and then across to the newsstand on the opposite corner of the street where they sold all the foreign magazines, newspapers and books. Someone once said that if you sat here long enough you would see everyone you knew in the world walk by. Maybe not in the whole world, but at least everyone you knew in Rome.

His usual waiter suddenly appeared. Old, thin-haired, with old-fashioned gold-rimmed glasses. He placed the usual espresso before Joe and took the "reserved" card away. "*Buon giorno, Signor* Joe." He smiled with his nicotine-stained, crooked teeth.

"*Buon giorno*, Tito," Joe answered.

"I heard you saw the new movie," Tito said. "Is it good?"

Joe looked up at him. There were no secrets in this town. Especially from waiters. He shrugged. "*Così, così.*"

Tito nodded. "I have a friend who works at the laboratory. He said there is one scene where the two girls fight in the mud of the street and that it was just as if they were both *nuda*."

"That's right, Tito," Joe said. He put a cigarette in his mouth. Tito held a light for him. "They both have great bodies."

Tito smacked his lips. "I would like to see that."

"As soon as they have prints made, I will invite you to a private screening," Joe said. "But that will not be until September. All the laboratories are closed for the month of August."

"Italy, Italy," Tito sighed. "No one wants to work. But I will be patient, *Signor* Joe, and I thank you for your invitation."

Joe pressed a thousand-lire bill in the waiter's hand. "Thank you, Tito."

A group of tourists came toward a table next to Joe. Quickly the little waiter moved them away to a further table. "*Scusi, reservato, reservato,*" Tito said and then took their orders as they sat down.

Joe glanced at the Excelsior entrance. There were the usual hustlers and guides standing there, but also a number of paparazzi, their cameras slung around their necks and shoulders. One of them, a young man, glanced back over his shoulder at Joe. Joe gestured his arm in invitation.

The paparazzo nodded and came toward him. "*Ciao,* Joe," he said.

"*Ciao,* Vieri," Joe answered. "Have a drink with me."

The young man looked back at the hotel entrance but the offer of a drink was too much for him. He slipped into a chair. "Cognac, *francese,*" he said.

Joe nodded. That was normal—the most expensive drink he could order. He signaled to the waiter, who had already heard. Joe turned to Vieri. "What's all the excitement about?"

"You haven't heard?" Vieri asked. "Ingrid Bergman and Rossellini have just returned from shooting their film on Stromboli and they are in the hotel."

"You saw them?" Joe asked.

"Not yet," Vieri answered. The waiter placed a snifter containing the cognac on the table, along with a glass of water. Vieri swirled the cognac and held it under his nostrils. He breathed its scent lightly. "The perfume of the gods," he said.

"*Salute,*" Joe said.

"*Salute,*" Vieri replied and took a sip of the cognac. "My friend saw them when they came out of the airport. He said she was pregnant as a house."

Joe didn't understand the simile. "I thought Rossellini had a home in Rome."

"He does," Vieri said. "But his wife is living in it."

"Oh," Joe said.

"You saw your picture today," Vieri said, then without waiting for an answer, "Did Santini pay you your money?"

Joe laughed. "Of course not."

"The prick," Vieri said. "He owes me for some photographs I made for him five months ago."

"It's a way of life for him," Joe said.

"For all the Italian producers and directors," Vieri said sarcastically. "They think they are above all things like that. But not above their own money. That they get first."

Joe shrugged and sipped his espresso.

"What are you doing this summer?" Vieri asked.

"I don't know," Joe said. "I thought I'd go back to the States and work on my book. There are no jobs over here."

"The Americans," Vieri said. "The big companies are planning important movies. There's a lot of building going on at Cinecittà and the money is coming from the States. And I also hear that many American stars are coming over. Audrey Hepburn, Gregory Peck, Elizabeth Taylor, Robert Taylor. Production costs are less than in Hollywood."

"It doesn't do me any good," Joe said. "Nobody contacted me."

"Maybe they will," Vieri said. "After all, you've been here almost two years already. You have the experience and know how things are done here."

"I can't hang around without money," Joe said. "I have to produce."

"Are you going to the Contessa Baroni's party tonight?" Vieri asked.

"I haven't made up my mind yet," Joe answered. "I don't know whether I'm up to dressing in a tuxedo tonight with this heat."

"You should go," Vieri said. "It's her annual event. Always on the last Friday in July. Everyone will be there. Then she spends the month of August in her villa at Cap Antibes on the French Riviera. She always invites five or six people to stay with her."

"She didn't invite me," Joe said.

"She never does until the night of this party," Vieri said. "But I hear they have a ball over there. That's where all the action is. She has a yacht and there's a gala every night. Monte Carlo, Nice, Cannes, Saint-Tropez. The most beautiful girls from all of Europe flock there next month. And they're all looking for a good time and a place to stay."

"That leaves me out," Joe said. "The contessa is very possessive."

"She swings both ways, I hear," Vieri said.

"So?" Joe shrugged. "Then she'll get the girls, not me."

"You'll get seconds. That's not too bad."

Joe laughed. "She'll never invite me. I'm not important enough for her."

"You've been out with her a number of times," Vieri pointed out. "You fucked her, didn't you?"

"She's fucked everybody," Joe said. "That doesn't mean anything."

"She's got it all," Vieri said. "Money, dope, champagne, parties. You should go tonight. Maybe you'll get lucky."

"Are you going?" Joe asked.

"I'm not invited, but I'll be there," Vieri answered. "Outside. Trying to grab a few pictures. If you go, I'll take a few shots of you."

"Don't waste your film," Joe said. "You won't be able to sell any of the pictures."

"You hang around until a pretty girl or a star shows up, then get next to them, and I'll get the shot."

"That's not my style," Joe said.

"Go to the party anyway," Vieri said, standing up. "I've got to get back to work. Thanks for the cognac. *Ciao*."

"*Ciao*," Joe said, watching him walk to the hotel entrance. He held up his hand for the check. Then he went back to his hotel near the foot of the Spanish Steps.

His small apartment seemed cool, protected from the heat outside by the louvered wooden window shutters. Quickly he pulled off his shirt damp with perspiration and dropped his slacks across a chair. He bent over the sink and splashed water over his head and face, then took a deep breath. Slowly he dried himself with a coarse face towel. He looked at himself in the mirror over the sink and shook his head. It was no wonder people ran away from Rome in the August heat. It was a real bitch.

The telephone began to ring. He walked to the little desk in the living room and picked it up. "*Pronto*," he said.

It was Laura Shelton, calling him from New York. "How are you?" she asked.

"Hot."

"It's hot here too," she said.

"Nothing can be as hot as heat in Rome."

"Have you seen the movie?" she asked.

"Today," he said.

"What did you think of it?"

"It's okay," he said. "If you like big tits on a big screen and a lot of them."

She laughed. "I thought that was your thing."

"Not in movies," he said. "Seeing is not always believing. A little more story would have helped."

"Did Santini pay you?"

"One rubber check for five thousand, if you can count that. Otherwise, he said he'll pay me the rest when he makes his distribution deal in the States. He said the picture will gross a million dollars."

"I heard from the Coast that several companies are interested in it. Apparently he shipped two prints out there before he showed it in Italy. Kathy told me A.J. might take it on."

"Good," he said. "Then I may get my money."

"You'll get your money," she said confidently. "I'm turning your account over to Paul Gitlin, he's an attorney who will act as your agent as well. I've known him a long time and he's very good."

"What are you going to do?" he asked in surprise.

"I said I wanted to be an editor and I finally got a job at Doubleday. So we'll still be in touch, only I'll be your editor, not your agent."

"How does the agency feel about that?" he asked.

"Okay," she said. "They never liked you as a writer anyway. You were not genteel enough for them."

"How did you wind up with that job?"

"Doubleday likes you," she said. "They were satisfied with the sales of your first book. They told me that they will come out with between thirty and forty thousand books, the Doubleday Book Club pushed out one hundred and twenty-five thousand copies, and they made a paperback deal with Bantam for forty thousand dollars—that's not so bad. They get half of it, that's twenty thousand."

"Where does all that fit in with you?"

"You're one of my authors. All you have to do is turn out another book in a year or so. They already are willing to up the terms for the second book."

"I haven't started to write it yet," he said.

"Then start now while you have time," she said. "I know you have the story, you told me about it."

"I'll need help," he said. "You're my editor—meet me here and we'll block out the novel together."

She laughed. "I still have work to do."

"What work?" he asked.

"It will take me about two weeks to clean up my desk here. Doubleday wants me on the first of September."

"You can still spend the last two weeks of August with me," he said. "I'll pick up a car and we'll travel along the French Riviera. I hear that it's fantastic."

She laughed again. "You're really crazy. Do you know how much money that would cost?"

"I can afford it," he said. "Besides, I would like to see you."

"I don't know," she said hesitantly.

"Look you don't have to worry about that goddamn agency spying on you all the time. You're the boss now. We'll have a real ball. I'll send you the ticket."

She was silent for a moment. "Would you give me a little time to think it out?" she asked.

"How much time?" he asked.

"Call me on the tenth," she said. "Maybe I'll feel better about it then."

"I'll call you on the tenth, but I'll send the ticket now," he said.

"Where will you be?" she asked.

"I'll be traveling but the ticket will be open. I'll be wherever you are when you give me the okay."

"Don't send me a ticket. I can afford my own," she said. "And call me at home, not at the office."

"Gotcha. Have you ever been to Europe before?"

"I spent two years in college in Paris."

"Then you speak French?"

"Yes," she said.

"Then you have to come over," he said. "You'll be able to take me around."

She laughed. "Just call me on the tenth and start thinking about the new book."

"I can think of more fun things than a new book," he said.

"Don't play games with me," she said. "I'm a very serious person."

"I'm being very serious," he replied. "You just tell me that you're joining me and you'll find out just how serious I can be."

He stared down at the telephone for a moment, then placed his monthly call to his parents. He put down the receiver and checked his watch. It was six hours earlier in New York than it was in Italy. The chances were that there would be no answer on their end. But he was wrong. Miraculously, the call went through in ten minutes.

His mother answered. "Hello?"

"Mama, how are you?" he asked.

"Where are you?" she asked suspiciously. "You sound like from the corner."

"I'm still in Rome," he said. "How's Papa?"

"Papa's all right. He takes care of himself and he is all right. When are you coming home?"

"I don't know," he said. "There is another job on the way and I'm taking a month's vacation in France."

"In France," she said. "You're becoming so fancy-shmancy. France has nothing but the most expensive whores."

He laughed. "You'll never change, Mama."

"What should I change? When your book came out I thought you had some respect. But instead, all our friends that read it said they never read so much filth like that. I don't understand, it was on the best-seller list for fifteen weeks."

"Did you read it?"

"I should read filth like that?" she asked. "I don't even tell anybody that you're my son, I'm so ashamed."

"You're never going to change," he repeated. "Is Papa home?"

"No," she said. "He went to the market today, just for a few hours."

"Then tell him that I called." He put down the phone.

It was no use. He could never win with her.

Chapter Twenty-nine

He left the bathroom door open so that he could hear the telephone ring as he slid into the comfort of the large, deep Italian bathtub filled with lukewarm water. He lit a cigarette and leaned back in the curve of the bathtub. It was almost nine o'clock and still bright daylight. He hadn't yet made up his mind about the party tonight. There was no rush. Italian parties didn't start until midnight.

He heard a knock from the living-room door. He shouted from the bathroom. "Who is it?"

"Marissa," the girl's voice came through the door. "I've brought all your files from the office."

Marissa was the black girl who had acted as his secretary while he worked on the scripts for Santini. She was the daughter of an Italian consulate attaché in New York who had married a black American woman, and when he was recalled to Italy in 1940, he brought his wife and daughter, Marissa, then fifteen, to Rome with him. She had worked as an interpreter for the American Army when they came to Rome during the war, and afterwards she had worked at various jobs, winding up as secretary-interpreter for various Italian film producers.

"Come in!" he yelled from the tub. "The door is open."

He looked into the small living room. She was carrying a large olive-drab canvas army surplus duffel bag, which she dropped on the floor. "What the hell have you got in there?" he called.

"My clothes," she replied. "I need a place to stay for a few days."

"What happened?"

"Santini closed the office for August without paying me. My *pensione* is very strict about the rent. I'm out of money, so I thought I would get my things before they locked me out."

"The cheap bastard screwed you too?" he exclaimed.

"Did he pay you?" she asked.

"You gotta be joking," he answered. "He said he'd pay me as soon as he made a distribution deal for the States."

"I also brought over your files," she said.

"Thanks," he said.

She came to the bathroom doorway. "Do you have a cigarette?"

He gestured. "On the shelf under the mirror." He watched her light a cigarette. There were sweat stains under her armpits and the silk blouse seemed glued across her strong breasts. "How long would you need to stay here?"

"Just the weekend," she said. "My girlfriend will give me her apartment for the month of August. She's going to Ischia with her boyfriend."

He looked up at her. "Okay."

"You're wonderful!" She bent over to kiss his cheek. "I won't be any problem," she added. "If you have anybody over I can sleep on the couch."

"I don't have any plans," he said, glancing down the open neckline of her blouse. Her nipples were dark lavender against the lighter tan of her breasts. Beads of perspiration rolled down the valley of her chest. "You're sweating bullets," he said. "Why don't you get into the bathtub with me?"

She dragged on the cigarette. "I stink that bad?"

"No." He laughed, holding his erection out of the water so that she could see it. "I just want to fuck."

She began taking off her clothes. "Great!" she said. "I'm always horny." In a moment she was naked. She stepped into the tub, standing erect over him. Quickly she masturbated her vulva, then spread her vagina with two fingers so that the small purple clitoris peeked out between her labia. "How about that?" she laughed, looking down at him.

"Fantastic!" He held his erection and arched his back to meet her. "Get on it."

"In a second," she said, reaching for a bar of soap. Quickly she soaped and rubbed his phallus until he thought every nerve was burning through to his testicles, then she held him tightly and, sitting on her haunches, brought him into her.

He gasped for breath. It felt as if he had been dipped into a vat of burning oil. He grasped her buttocks to bring her closer to him as she leaned over his face, her breasts smothering him.

He felt himself slipping back down into the tub, the water beginning to reach his face. "You're going to fucking drown me."

"Don't worry." She laughed. "I'll save you. I have a lifeguard's certificate." She began writhing and bringing him more inside her, never letting him slip out. "Just relax." She smiled, sure of her power. "Let me do all the work. Just think as if I'm a propeller spinning on your shaft."

He looked up at her. "I never knew you could fuck like this when we were in the office."

"Office fucks are never the best," she said. "They're always quickie duty fucks. You can never be creative. Just get your rocks off and run."

"Hallelujah!" he cried.

Suddenly she held him still. "Don't move!" she ordered.

He glanced up at her. "What's wrong?"

"Nothing," she said. "I'm starting to pee. Ooh," she whispered ecstatically. "Now you do it inside me."

"I can't pee through a hard on," he said.

"Yes, you can," she said. "I'll show you." Quickly she placed a finger under his testicles and pressed a nerve. His urine came pouring forth like a spout. At the same time, she took his phallus from her and lifted it, still urinating, onto her face and gulped as much of it as she could catch in her mouth. When the urine had stopped she replaced him instantly inside her. She moved her face close to him. "I love the taste of your pee," she said. "It's like sweet sugar."

He felt her exciting writhing again. "Where did you ever get into that?" he gasped.

"From the American soldiers during the war," she said huskily. "They all wanted to give me golden showers, and after a while I really got into it."

"Christ," he said.

"That wasn't all," she said. "The Americans were more fun than the Germans. The Boche were straight fuck and suck. The Americans even loved to stick Mars Bars and Baby Ruths up my ass and cunt."

"Then what did they do?" he asked.

"Either they ate it or I did," she said.

"Shit," he said.

"That, too," she answered. "When you're on the losing side you do what they tell you. Otherwise you're out. Nothing to eat, no jobs, no favors."

"Is it that way now?" he asked.

"In a kind of way," she said. "You don't get any kind of job unless you fuck for it."

"You didn't have to fuck me for the job."

"You didn't hire me," she said. "Santini did." She looked down at him. "You're losing your hard," she said. "That's what happens when you think too much and talk too much."

He stared at her silently.

"Don't worry about it," she said. "I'll get it back for you in a moment." She moved slightly to one side and passed her hand over his buttocks. A moment later she slipped two fingers into his anus and began lightly pressing and massaging his prostate. His erection was instantly resurrected.

"Now, you motherfucker," she cried. "Do it! Do it hard!"

He was half dozing on top of the bed when the telephone began to ring. Sleepily he looked across the room toward Marissa. Nude, she was moving around the living room, unpacking her clothes. She glanced at him questioningly.

"Answer it," he said.

She picked up the telephone. "*Pronto.*"

He could hear an Italian woman's voice in the receiver. She listened for a moment, then called to him. "It's Mara Benetti," she said. "She wants to know if you are going to the contessa's party?"

"I haven't made up my mind yet," he said.

"It's after ten o'clock," she pointed out.

"So what? Nobody ever gets there until midnight," he answered.

Marissa spoke to the actress in Italian, who then fired a number of words at her. "She wants you to escort her," she told him.

"What happened to Santini?" he asked. "He was supposed to take her."

More words spewed from the telephone. "Santini screwed her," Marissa explained. "He's taking the American actress instead. Her boyfriend said he'd give her a limousine to use tonight, if you'd take her."

"Why doesn't *he* take her?"

"He's a Mafioso," Marissa said flatly. "He's maybe got other things to do."

"He'll blow my fucking head off after the party," he said.

"Not if you bring me along with you," Marissa said shrewdly. "That will show him that you respect him."

"You'd like to go?" he asked curiously.

"Of course. It's the big party of the season," she answered. "And I stole a great dress from the wardrobe in the studio just for a chance like this."

Joe shrugged. "Ask her if she would mind if I brought you along?"

"I'll explain it," she said. "After all, you don't speak Italian, I'm your secretary and you need me to interpret for you. Also, she knows me."

"Okay."

Marissa turned to the telephone again and spoke quickly in Italian. "She said okay. The car will be here to pick us up."

Chapter Thirty

He was just taking his white dinner jacket from the closet when she came from the bathroom. He stared at her.

She smiled. "You like?"

"Beautiful," he said. "But you look naked under your gown."

"I *am* naked," she answered. "Flesh-colored sheer form-fitting chiffon sprinkled with bugle beads."

"I can see your pussy and the crack of your ass as you turn around. Even the purple-red color of your nipples."

She laughed. "That's makeup. I also dusted some silver sprinkles over me. I think it's exciting."

He looked at her. She was completely made up with mascara, blue and gold eye shadow, rose rouge highlighting her cheekbones, and scarlet lips. A soft black curled long-haired wig covered her own tightly crinkled hair. "You look like a Harlem hooker I used to know."

"Sexy?"

"Very," he answered. "Mara's going to blow her mind. I don't think she expected this kind of competition."

She laughed. "I told her what I was wearing. She said it would be okay. She's wearing a black dress, lace, open-cut down between her breasts to her pussy in front and down her back to the middle of the crack of her ass. She said that between us we'd put the American actress away."

"I'll never understand you women," he said.

"You don't have to," she said. "Just enjoy it."

The paparazzi were having a field day. Vieri came over to Joe. "How did you manage it?"

Joe held out his hands. "It just happened."

"You're fucking both of them?" he asked.

Joe smiled without answering.

"Lucky bastard," Vieri said. "These have to be the best pictures of the night. I'll be able to sell them all over Europe."

"Good," Joe said. He looked at the photographer. "Did Santini show up yet?"

"Yes. About a half an hour ago. The American girl is stupid. She wore a simple white organza dress. Nothing but big tits and ass, not sexy at all, and the white doesn't photograph well.'

Joe laughed.

"Mara's boyfriend know you took her out?" Vieri asked.

"He arranged it," Joe said. "It's his car that we're using."

Vieri nodded. "Good," he said. "I was worried that you might get into trouble. He's a tough man."

"It's okay," Joe said. He walked toward the girls still standing at the steps posing for the photographers. "I think we'll go in now."

"Just stop a moment at the top of the steps," Vieri said. "That way I can shoot up and get a shot of the girls with their pussies showing right through their dresses."

"You've got it," Joe said. He walked up with the girls, held still for a moment, then turned as the footman opened the door.

The foyer of the house was almost as large as a ballroom and crowded with people. Joe vaguely recognized many of them, but didn't know their names. Whispering behind her hand, Marissa identified them for him. He looked at her gratefully. She was a perfect secretary.

Slowly they moved through the foyer; the girls' hands were kissed again and again. He handed his card to the butler, with both their names beneath his.

The butler called out, "*Dottore* Joseph Crown and *Signorina* Mara Benetti and *Signorina* Marissa Panzoni."

They walked down the steps to the ballroom. A waiter walked toward them with a tray of champagne glasses. Joe handed a glass to each of the girls, "*Salute.*"

Mara was smiling. She felt good. She knew that everyone had been looking at them. "*Salute,*" she said to Joe, and in her accented English, her eyes glancing across the room, "Have you seen that son of a bitch yet?"

"Not yet," Joe smiled.

"I will tear his eyes out," Mara said sweetly. "And that *putana* with him."

Joe laughed. "You don't have to worry about them. Everyone has already forgotten them, blinded by the dazzle of your beauty."

Mara nodded seriously. "I am much more beautiful than her?"

"Without question," Joe said quickly. "You're the most beautiful woman in this party."

Marissa nodded in agreement. "If I were a man I would throw myself at your feet."

"You're so sweet," Mara smiled. "And Joe, too. I am so glad I invited you both to this party."

Marissa and Joe glanced at each other. Who invited who, who was invited by who? They smiled. "I am happy too," Joe said.

At the far end of the ballroom an orchestra played and people began dancing. The cool night air was coming in through the large French doors. In the next room was a long buffet table laden with food and a long line of guests queuing up for dinner.

Another uniformed footman came toward him. "*Dottore* Crown?"

Joe nodded.

The footman spoke to him in Italian. Joe glanced at Marissa, who translated. "The contessa would like you and your guests to come to her private apartment."

Again Joe nodded and they followed the footman through the dining room and a narrow hallway, then up a staircase and through another corridor. He opened large double doors and closed the doors behind them as they entered.

The contessa was seated on a large thronelike chair at the head of a table also laden with food. The contessa was a beautiful woman with an imperious manner. She gestured for Joe to come to her. "Joe," she said laughing. "My brilliant American writer."

Joe kissed her outstretched hand. "*Eccellenza*," he murmured. He straightened up. "You know my friends. *Signorina* Mara Benetti, the star of my movie, and my assistant, *Signorina* Marissa Panzoni."

The contessa nodded. "Very beautiful children," she said, then turned back to Joe. "You are fucking with both of them?"

Joe laughed.

"Don't be embarrassed. You should be proud. I would love to see the three of you making love. It would be most exciting." She leaned from her chair and ran her hands across each girl's body. "Beautiful, beautiful," she murmured. "So firm and strong and sexual."

The two girls were used to it—but then, they knew the contessa better than Joe did. "Thank you, *Eccellenza*," they answered in unison.

The contessa snapped her fingers. A footman came toward them with a small covered silver sugarbowl, which he opened before them. Quickly the contessa picked up a gold coke spoon and took two big snorts in each nostril. She then offered it to them.

Joe took it first. The coke exploded in his head. It was top quality. The coke that Joe bought on the streets in Rome was like shit next to this. This was a real buzz.

Mara snorted it cautiously, but Marissa was like a steam shovel—four heavy snootfuls in each nostril. Her eyes lit up like electric bulbs. "*Mamma mia!*" she laughed. "I think I'm coming already."

The contessa laughed and put her hand under Marissa's dress. "It's true!" she shouted, taking out her fingers and licking them. "You're soaking wet."

Mara looked down at the contessa. "Pardon me, *Eccellenza*, have you seen Maestro Santini this evening?"

The contessa gestured with her hand. "He is downstairs with his American girl. She has no class, very common. I left them downstairs with the hoi polloi." She turned to Joe. "Do you think his movie will make some money?" she asked. "I have invested one hundred thousand of my dollars into it."

"I think you have a good chance," Joe said loyally. After all, he had a stake in that movie too.

"Has he paid you?" she asked shrewdly.

"Not yet," he answered.

The contessa laughed. "He is such a crook, not even a charming scoundrel. He told me that he had paid everybody off."

Joe was silent.

The contessa turned to Mara. "And you? Has he paid you?"

Mara nodded. "My gentleman friend arranged that."

"That makes sense," the contessa nodded. "He will not have any trouble from your friend."

"He even owes me twenty thousand lire," Marissa added.

"Cheap," the contessa said. "Cheap." She turned to the footman. "Give the *signorina* twenty thousand lire."

"No, *Eccellenza*," Marissa protested. "It is not your responsibility."

"You are my friend," the contessa said firmly. "And also you have a very sweet pussy."

Another footman brought a tray of champagne and they all took one, while still another footman came with a tray of cigarettes. As Joe lit the first cigarette, the heavily perfumed hash oil laid on the tobacco came through the room.

The contessa laughed. "It's a lovely party." She turned to one of the footmen. "Lock the doors to my suite. We'll have our own party."

Mara hesitated. "*Eccellenza*, I must beg your pardon, but my gentleman friend would not approve of this for me."

The contessa laughed. "He will not object, my dear. After all, I am his sponsor in Rome. He knows that you are joining me. Wasn't it his idea that he give you his limousine?"

Mara stared at her.

The contessa smiled. "Enjoy a cigarette and relax. Then we will all have dinner together. I will have your breasts for dessert. I will lick them as if they were the sweetest Devonshire cream."

Joe glanced around the room. So far only they and the contessa were in the private apartment. A moment later two couples entered from a rear door. The men were dressed in Indian turbans, short brocaded vests and blousy harem cotton pantaloons tied by a string around the waist. The girls were wearing harem-type softly twisted brassieres and beribboned, flared silk skirts, open to reveal their bodies from legs to waist. Soft music came from between the curtains and the room lights began to dim.

"We can change our clothes here," the contessa said huskily. "We have more costumes for all of us." She looked at Mara and Marissa. "Each of those men has cocks at least twenty centimeters large, and all of them, the men and the women, are trained in the Eastern arts of pleasure."

She reached for the sugar bowl and took two more snorts from the golden spoon, then rose from her chair. Her dress had not been fastened, and it fell to the floor as she moved forward. Her body was large and firm. Slowly one of the men began to wrap a costume around her.

Joe turned to the two girls. They returned his glance silently. Then he picked up the sugar bowl and helped himself before he began to undress. Marissa followed suit immediately, and a moment later Mara began to slip her dress from her shoulders.

The contessa raised her champagne glass. "*A la dolce vita!*"

Chapter Thirty-one

It was almost eight o'clock in the morning when they left the contessa's palazzo and got into the car. "We can have some coffee at my hotel," he said. "The kitchen is already open."

Mara looked at him. "I think I'd better go right home."

"We could all use some coffee," Joe said.

"I'll drop you off," she said. She lit a cigarette. "It's been a long night."

"As you like," Joe said.

Mara looked at them. "You won't tell my friend what we did?"

"I don't know anything," Joe said. "I don't even know him."

"He is very jealous," Mara said. "If he thought that I had been with another man he would kill me."

"And what about the contessa?" he asked.

"He knows about her," she said. "Besides, women don't count."

"Okay."

The limousine pulled up in front of his hotel and he and Marissa got out. "Thank you," Joe said.

"It's nothing," Mara answered. "Will you stay in town this month?"

"I don't know yet."

"I will call you," she said. "*Ciao. Ciao*, Marissa."

The limousine drove off and they went into the hotel. He placed his order for breakfast with the concierge before he went up to his apartment. Marissa was out of her dress and into an old army surplus T-shirt before he had even taken off his jacket.

"*Jesù Cristo!*" she said. "That contessa is too much."

He took off his shirt and threw it on a chair. "She's something else."

"I never knew anyone could eat pussy like that," she said. "One time I thought her tongue would go through my cunt to my asshole."

He looked at her. "You liked it?"

"She was the best. I heard that lesbians were the best, but I never believed it until now."

There was a knock at the door and the waiter brought in the tray with coffee and rolls. She waited until the waiter had gone. "She left me forty thousand lire, not twenty."

"Not bad," he said.

"She gave you something," Marissa said. "I saw her."

Joe laughed and took out a small wax-paper bag. "Cocaine."

"She's a real lady," Marissa said. She filled the coffee cups. "Was she a good fuck?"

"I'm not complaining," he said.

"My cunt is so sore," she said, "it burns when I pee."

He laughed and sipped his coffee. "It'll get better."

She looked at him. "Do you want me to sleep on the couch?"

"You can sleep in the bed," he said. "Just don't wake me up if you have to move around."

"I'll be quiet," she said. "Do you have any plans for tomorrow?"

"I might look for a car in the afternoon," he answered. "There's an Alfa convertible I have an eye on."

"You'd better take me with you," she said seriously. "You're American, they'll steal your eyeballs. Let me do the talking and it will cost you less."

"I'll think about it when we wake up," he said. He dropped the rest of his clothing and crawled naked into bed.

She looked down at him. "Do you mind if I shower? I have to take off my makeup and get the shiny sprinkles off me, or they stick all over the bed."

"Go ahead," he said. "But turn out the lights in here. I want to sleep."

"Okay," she said. The lights went off and she closed the bathroom door behind her. A moment later he heard the soft running of the shower. He closed his eyes.

La dolce vita, he thought. The contessa was right when she called it that. It would make a good title for a movie, but not for him. It really was another world. He could enjoy it, but he could not begin to understand it. Then he was asleep.

The sound of voices came through the closed bedroom door. Slowly he opened his eyes. Marissa was not there. He heard her voice from the living room. He sat up and put on his wristwatch. It was four o'clock in the afternoon. He lit a cigarette and listened to the other voices—a man's and another woman's.

Quietly he went into the bathroom, splashed cold water on his face and slipped on a bathrobe. Still barefoot, he opened the bedroom door.

Marissa, Mara, and a man he didn't know were seated at the small table; the waiter had just served coffee. "*Buon giorno*," Joe said.

The man sprang to his feet. He was a strong-looking man of medium height, his black hair slicked back in the fashion of the time, with dark brown eyes, a large Roman nose over full lips, and a square chin. He bowed to Joe. "*Signor Dottore*," he said.

Joe looked at him, then at Marissa. Mara spoke quickly. "This is my friend, Franco Gianpietro. He has much honor and pleasure to meet with you."

Joe nodded and held out his hand. "It is my honor."

They shook hands European style, pumping hands up and down twice. The man said something quickly in Italian. Marissa translated. "Signor Gianpietro apologizes for the intrusion. If you want to return to bed, he would be pleased to come back at your convenience."

"It's okay," Joe said. He gestured. "Please sit down."

The Italian nodded. "My English is not too good," he said. "But with *permesso*, I will try."

Joe smiled. "It's very good." He took the coffee that Marissa had placed before him and leaned back in the couch. The coffee was strong and black. That woke him up. "What can I do for you?" he asked.

"You are a very important *scrittore*," Gianpietro said. "Mara tells me that you are the best in America."

"She is very kind," Joe said.

She smiled. "*Vero*. True."

"Santini is a prick," Gianpietro said.

"I won't argue about that." Joe laughed.

"Mara thought that you perhaps write a movie for her. She feels that Santini screwed her in this picture, he gave all the good scenes to the American girl." Gianpietro looked at him.

"It would be an honor," Joe said. "But there are some problems. One, I have no producer; two, I have no story suitable for her."

"The producer I can obtain," Gianpietro said. "And maybe there is a magazine story that she read might be good for a movie. It is a well-known story in Italy, has been very well received. *La Ragazza Sulla Motocicletta*."

"I know the story," Marissa said. "It's good. It's about a girl from a poor family who steals a big motorcycle, then runs all over Rome fucking and stealing in order to feed her family. It has an exciting ending where the police chase her through the streets in the city, and she is killed because she will not run over a little child that was crossing the street."

"It sounds interesting," Joe said. "But I'd have to read the story. Is there a translation around?"

"I can do one for you in a day," Marissa said.

Gianpietro nodded. "With me, you would get all your money. I am a man of honor, not like Santini. Also, I have heard that you would like to spend August in the south of France. I have a large villa just outside of Nice where Mara and I will be. There is a nice guest house, and you could live there in comfort. I even have a car for your personal convenience."

"That sounds good," Joe said. "But I would have to read the story first. Perhaps I am not the right writer for it. I don't know that much about the people here."

"Mara and Marissa can tell you everything you need to know," Gianpietro said. "And I know how much fees you command. I will pay you the thirty-five thousand and expenses in full when you've finished the script. You don't have to wait for the movie to be made."

"You are more than generous," Joe said. "But I do think I should read the story first. I don't want to cheat you and say I can do it if I can't."

Gianpietro looked at him for a moment, then took a roll of bills out of his pocket. Slowly he counted out a number of one-thousand-dollar bills. "That's twenty thousand dollars," he said as he finished counting and replaced the roll in his pocket.

"What's that for?" Joe asked. "I haven't agreed to do the script yet."

"This has nothing to do with the script. This is the money I collected from Santini for you."

Joe stared at him.

"It's okay," Gianpietro said. "The contessa asked me to take care of it."

"But Santini wouldn't give it to me," Joe said. "He said he did not have the money."

Gianpietro smiled. "It's surprising how quickly a man like this finds that he has the money, especially when you squeeze his balls a little."

Joe looked at him, then picked up the money and put it in his bathrobe pocket. "Thank you."

Gianpietro nodded. "I have given a copy of the story to Marissa, and perhaps Tuesday night after you've read it we could have dinner and discuss it."

"It will be my pleasure," Joe said.

Gianpietro rose and Mara joined him. She looked at Joe. "You will make a very big star of me. More of a star than that *putana*."

He kissed her on the cheek and shook hands with the Italian. "Tuesday night for dinner," he said.

He turned to Marissa after they had gone. "Did you know anything about this?"

"I heard Mara and the contessa speaking, but we were all kind of spaced out so I didn't think anything about it." She laughed. "Maybe we got lucky."

He looked at her silently. "You sure you didn't put them all up to this?"

"I'm just nothin' but your nigger secretary. Nobody would pay any attention to me."

"I'm not that sure," he said.

She changed the subject. "The American Express office is still open," she said. "We better get over there and you can turn your money into traveler's checks. It's too much cash to carry around."

It took Marissa almost two days to translate the story and only two hours for Joe to read it. He threw the manuscript on the table and stared at it. Then he looked at Marissa. "It's pure shit," he said. "There's no what I can write this script."

Marissa lit a cigarette. "There must be some way you can save it."

He shook his head. "No way. It's pure pulp. On top of that, it's not even entertainment. It's childish."

"Gianpietro will be disappointed."

"I'd rather he be disappointed with the truth than lead him down the garden path. He's not stupid. Sooner or later he would figure out that I took him for the money. I would not like him to get angry with me. I wouldn't think I'd like him squeezing my balls a little."

"You'll have to be very diplomatic," she said. "He's got his mind set on making Mara a star."

"I'll explain it to him. We have to find a better vehicle for her."

"You know what you're doing," she said, disappointed. "There goes our spending the month on the French Riviera."

"I'm going anyway," he said. "My agent is coming over in a couple of weeks."

"I'm going to have to sweat it out here in town," she said, meeting his eyes.

Joe smiled at her. "You're a fucking hustler. I guess you think I'll feel sorry for you."

"Don't you? Just even a little?" Her eyes were wide. "How would you feel if you were stuck here?"

"Hustler!" Joe laughed.

"I have an idea," she said.

He looked at her.

"Why don't you tell him that we'll spend the two weeks with them and try to come up with a story that would be right for all of us?"

"That's a real con," he said.

"Not really," she said. "Who knows? You might come up with something that will work."

"You've gotta be joking, you know that cunt can't act. I wouldn't know what would work for her," he said.

"You said you don't need the money," she pointed out. "Tell him it's for free, all you promise is to try for two weeks. All it will cost him is the house expenses, which he is spending anyway."

"And you get your vacation?"

"Of course," she said. "And it wouldn't cost you anything. Also, you don't have to pay me any salary."

He laughed. "You want it that bad?"

She met his eyes. "Yes. For a girl like me, the French Riviera is the top of the world. Who knows what opportunity I may find? All the rich people are there. I might get very lucky."

Joe looked at her seriously. After a moment he said, "Okay. I'll suggest it to him. But if it doesn't work, don't blame me."

She kissed his cheek. "I won't blame you. And I'll get off your back at the end of the two weeks, but you'll have to be careful."

"Careful of what?" he asked.

"Mara," she said. "She's got the hots for you and he has to stay in Rome during the week and only comes over on the weekends."

"What makes you think that?" he asked in surprise. "She's not stupid. She knows on which side her bread is buttered."

"True," she answered. "But she wouldn't mind a little partying with you on the side."

Chapter Thirty-two

It was a typical old-fashioned Mediterranean villa situated on a small knoll above the sea in Villefranche. Just slightly in front of the main house was the small guest house Gianpietro had offered him. It was not decorated in the same manner as the main house—in former times, Joe thought, it had been assigned to the servants. But it was comfortable despite the tiny rooms, and it was far enough away from the villa so that sounds did not carry. There was a private staircase that led down to the pebble beach.

Joe placed his typewriter on a table in front of the large window through which he had the view of the whole bay of Villefranche across to the end of St-Jean Cap Ferrat. He looked toward the villa. He could see a corner of the staircase that a guest in the main house could use to go down to the beach. In front of the beach was a dock to which was tied a small Riva.

Late the same afternoon Joe had arrived, Gianpietro came down to the guest house. "You like it?" he asked.

Joe smiled. "It's perfect, thank you."

The Italian smiled. "I thought you would like it. Here you have the privacy you need to work. No one will disturb you."

"Thank you again."

"I have a favor to ask of you," Gianpietro said.

"Just ask," Joe answered.

"Mara wants to speak American," he said. "It is difficult to find a tutor for just a month here. Marissa said that she could help her and stay for the month even when you leave."

"That's okay with me," Joe answered.

"Thank you, Joe," Gianpietro smiled. He waved his hand out, gesturing to the bay. "What do you think of the Côte d'Azur?"

"What I see right now is beautiful."

"It is the garden spot of the world," Gianpietro said. "Get yourself organized, then come up to the villa at six o'clock. We will have drinks, then at nine o'clock we will have dinner at the Hotel de Paris in Monte Carlo. After that we'll go to the casino and maybe to a nightclub."

Joe laughed. "You're not wasting any time."

"I only have the weekend, then I must go to Rome and work. I will return here every Friday night."

"You should spend more time here," Joe said.

"I can't." He shrugged expressively. "Even on the weekend here I have business. This evening I have some associates, Frenchmen from Marseilles, who will be joining us for dinner."

Joe nodded. "I understand."

He looked at Joe. "Do you think Mara has the talent she needs to become a star?"

Joe returned his gaze honestly. "Nobody knows. She has the look, but the rest of it is in the lap of the gods. She has one thing going for her in any case. She is not afraid of hard work."

Gianpietro nodded seriously. "That is true. But I would prefer that she relaxes and we have a baby. That is what I really want."

"Then why doesn't she do it?"

"She said not until we marry. She does not want the reputation of being a *putana* like many other actresses we know."

"Marry her then," Joe said.

Gianpietro smiled wryly. "It's so easy for Americans, but not for Italians. I am already married, and even though I have not been with my wife for more than ten years I cannot obtain a divorce."

"I'm sorry," Joe sympathized.

Gianpietro laughed. "It's not that bad. Being married, I cannot become married. And in the last ten years, Mara is the fourth girl I have fallen in love with. Perhaps next year I might fall in love with another girl. It is easier to get rid of a girlfriend than a wife."

"I didn't think about that," Joe said. "But I guess you are right."

"I am right," Gianpietro said. "Think of the problem that Rossellini and Bergman are having. And, now, Ponti and Loren. His wife will not allow him a divorce either. And Vittorio de Sica, with one legal wife and another illegal wife, each living on the same grounds, one house behind the other, each with her own family of his children."

"Do they know about each other?"

He shrugged. "Who knows? Probably they do, but no one ever discusses it. No wonder sometimes he seems as if he is going crazy and spends his spare time gambling all his money at the casino."

"Do you know De Sica?" Joe asked.

"Very well," he answered.

"Do you think he would do a picture with Mara?"

"He always needs money," Gianpietro said.

"If I had an idea for a story," Joe said, "not a script—he could select his own scriptwriters—could you give it to him?"

Gianpietro nodded. "Of course. And if he likes it, he would make it with Mara."

"You're sure of that?" Joe asked.

Gianpietro laughed. "There are many ways a man can get his balls squeezed. De Sica already owes me almost seventy thousand dollars." He paused for a moment. "You have an idea for him?"

"I'm not sure," Joe said. "De Sica is a classy director. I don't know whether he would work with a writer like me."

"He owes me seventy thousand dollars," Gianpietro repeated. "For that kind of money he'll work with a monkey in the zoo."

"I'm feeling a different kind of love story. Usually the American soldier has a baby and leaves the baby with the girl. This asshole wants the baby for himself and takes it to the States. The girl fights her way by hook or crook and tracks him down to a small town in the Midwest. Finally, when she sees that the child is really having a good life, one better than she could have given him, she leaves the baby with the father and returns to her home in Italy."

"De Sica will do it. Of course, he will want you to collaborate with his own writers, but that is nothing. He will feel more secure with their Italian idiom. Within a few days I will arrange for him to meet with you."

"And if he doesn't like it?" Joe asked.

"Fuck him. There's always Ponti or Rossellini plus a dozen others who owe me a lot of money." He walked to the door. "Just leave it to me. All you have to do is get dressed for dinner tonight."

The Hotel de Paris restaurant extended outside the huge great french doors to a terrace on a carpeted platform that reached almost to the edge of the sidewalk.

The outside walls were a bank of beautiful flowers that prevented the tourists and hoi polloi from looking at the crowds of shapely ladies and the men who exuded riches and power. Each table was covered with beautiful linen and crystal and centered with artfully arranged flowers.

Gianpietro had reserved a table seating for ten placed against a corner in a secluded location. Besides himself, Mara, Marissa and Joe, three Frenchmen and their ladies were his guests. Unfortunately, none of them could speak, or pretended not to speak, English. They made the usual French handshakes of introduction, and after that, it seemed as if Joe did not even exist. The men spoke always in monotone, the women never at all. There was no laughter, and it did not take long for Joe to see that this was a business meeting, not a dinner. Joe smiled at Marissa and paid attention to his dinner for the food was superb. Joe was not unhappy.

Dinner was served quietly and quickly. Joe had the feeling that it had been arranged in advance because when the dinner was completed, the Frenchmen and their ladies said their goodbyes.

Gianpietro stood at the table until they had gone, then returned to his chair. "The French are always the same. They have no manners."

Mara spoke to him in Italian. She sounded angry.

Gianpietro shook his head. "It's business," he said.

She was still angry. "You're not going to leave me alone here this summer while you run around doing your business."

"Just two weeks," he said. "Then I'll be back." He called for the bill and turned again to her. "We can do our talking in the car on the way home. This is no place to allow anyone to hear what we speak about."

"We're not going directly home," she said. "I thought we were going to the casino."

"I have no time for that just now," he said. "I'm leaving at six in the morning on the Rome Express from Nice."

Chapter Thirty-three

Joe and Marissa headed down the path to their small bungalow. It was almost one-thirty in the morning when they closed the guest-house door behind them. He asked Marissa what was happening.

She began slipping out of her gown. "It was simply business," she answered. "The French want Gianpietro to get two hundred tons of raw untreated heroin from Sicily and deliver it to Marseilles, where they have just set up laboratories. If he can do this for two weeks, his share will be two million dollars."

"Then what is Mara so pissed off about? She should know that Gianpietro will take good care of her."

"She wants to show herself around the Riviera playing the star. He won't be around, so who is there to show her off? She's simply a selfish bitch."

Joe had taken off his jacket and thrown his black tie and shirt on a chair when there was a knock at the door of the bungalow. "Come in," he called.

Marissa had just slipped on her dressing gown when Gianpietro came into the room. He turned directly to Joe, not even looking at her. "I need your help, my friend," he said.

"How can I help you?" Joe asked.

"As you probably realize, I have to go away for several weeks on business. Mara became very angry, but I have finally been able to calm her down. First, and most important, she wants you to continue the script for her. Second, she doesn't want to stay alone in the big house. She said that she would feel more secure if Marissa moved up there with her. I also arranged for her to have enough money so that she could shop and go out several times during the week for dinner and amusement. She also wants to speak only in English with Marissa so that she becomes very expert and fluent."

Joe looked at him. "I agree with you, of course, but don't you think it would be more discreet if I returned to Rome with you? After all, Mara is a very attractive lady and people will talk, as they always do."

"Let them think what they will, fuck them. You are my friend and a gentleman. I know in my heart that there will not be any improper behavior between you."

Joe turned to Marissa. "What do you think?"

"I agree with Franco," she said. "This is, of course, the correct way to handle the situation."

Joe held out his hand. "Then it will be done."

The Italian embraced him. "Thank you, my friend. Thank you."

Despite the heat in the small room, he slept as though he were dead. But then a strange new aroma filtered to his nostrils. It was a new scent, not Marissa's—he was familiar with hers. Slowly he opened one eye and looked at his watch. It was one o'clock in the afternoon. Then he opened the other eye and looked across the bed.

Mara was seated on a chair next to the bed, naked, her legs apart. She smiled at him. "I thought you would never wake up."

He stared at her. "What did you do? It looks like you shaved off ninety percent of your pussy."

She laughed. "You have a good eye. But this is the big style in the south of France. The new bikinis are so tiny that any hair will make you look like you're wearing a beard down the sides of your thighs."

Suddenly he was completely awake. "You're speaking English?" he questioned. "I thought you knew only a few words."

She met his eyes. "It makes more sense this way. People prefer it, they think that you are more stupid, and because of that they say many things that they expect you not to understand."

Marissa came in from the bathroom. She was drying her naked body with a towel. She laughed at Joe. "How do you like it?" she asked. "I did a pretty good job on Mara. Maybe I should become a cunt coiffeuse."

"I could do it better," Joe laughed. "And I wouldn't need scissors, I could nibble at it with my teeth."

"Don't be a wise guy," Marissa said. "Grab yourself a shower, then throw some shirts and slacks into a valise. We're on our way to Saint-Tropez for a few days."

"Saint-Tropez? Where the hell is that?"

"About fifty miles down the coast," Marissa told him. "It's the fun place of the Riviera. Not with old people like Monte Carlo, but all the young rich and fun people. All day on the beaches and parties all night long."

"And Franco left me with money," Mara added. "He already knows that an old friend of mine invited us to his house. He has one of the biggest homes near the beaches."

"I don't know," Joe said cautiously. "Franco never told me about a setup like this."

"There'll be nothing wrong," Mara said. "He knows my friend is a *peole*. As long as Marissa stays with me teaching me English, and you keep writing, it's okay. Besides, we'll be home long before he returns."

Joe looked at her. "But how are you going to explain the trimmed pussy?"

"My hair grows fast enough," she said. "Besides, he's a true Italian. He wouldn't go down on a pussy even if he had a nose as big as Pinocchio's."

"I still don't know," Joe said doubtfully. "I would not want Gianpietro to be angry with me. He's a tough one."

Mara laughed. "That's just his act. He's really a sweet man.

Joe stared at her quizzically.

She rose from her chair, went to the bed and pulled his hand to follow her to the bathroom. "Get into the shower," she said. You'll feel better, especially when I wash your prick and balls with my own perfumed soap."

A two-hour drive in the small Renault brought them to Saint-Tropez. Mara and Marissa took turns driving. Joe scrunched into the rear seat among the luggage. Most of the drive was interesting, Joe thought, as they rode along the RN 7, the coast road through Nice, Antibes and Cannes. After Cannes, the road became uncomfortable, but the narrow asphalt-and-dirt trail was the only road between the mainland and the peninsula that connected Saint-Tropez to the mainland. That road was the only passage on land—there was neither railroad, bus service nor taxis, although during the day there were several sixty-passenger ferries that traveled from eight in the morning until eleven at night. Saint-Tropez was in the process of changing from a small village surrounded by vineyards that produced cheap table wines, to a fashionable resort for the young, playful, monied French and other knowledgeable Europeans.

Mara turned the car away from the port of the village, where the lights allowed them to see that many people were still in the streets and the restaurants were still busy. She took the car up a dirt road and turned finally into the driveway of a large villa where lights were shining.

Joe got out of the car feeling very much like a sardine pried from its can. Mara led them to the large, open doors. The house was silent but in a moment a majordomo arrived.

He bowed politely. "I am sorry, mademoiselle, that Monsieur Lascombes and his guest have gone out."

"I would guess that." Mara spoke in French. "But he has invited myself and my friends to join him here in the villa." He glanced down at the sheet of paper and read out Mara's name.

"Correct," Mara said. "The lady and the gentlemen are my guests. I will arrange it with Monsieur Lascombes in the morning."

"*D'accord*, mademoiselle," he said. "For the moment I will assign the two ladies to room twelve and the gentleman will occupy room nine across the hall from you. Each room is on the second stage."

"Thank you," Mara answered.

"I apologize," said the majordomo, "that the porters have already departed for the night, but we will bring the luggage in first thing in the morning."

"I understand," she said. "We'll take the things we need for the moment and we'll manage." She opened her purse and handed him a five-hundred-franc note. "Meanwhile, if you would be kind enough to show us to our rooms, we will be content."

The second floor in a French house is two flights up—this equals the third floor in the States. The girls' room didn't seem too bad; there was a large bed and a private bathroom. Joe's room was a horror. It had to be a maid's room—a small uncomfortable bed, and in the corner only a bidet and a washbasin. But he was too tired to complain. Quickly he got out of his clothes and passed out bare-assed on the bed.

He felt he had slept less than an hour when Marissa touched him on the shoulder. "Joe," she said in a low voice, "wake up."

"I'm sleeping," he said. "Wake me in the morning."

"It *is* morning," she said. "Get up. We have a problem."

He opened his eyes and rubbed them as he sat up in bed. The gray morning light came through the window. "What's happening?"

"You'll have to get out of here," she said.

He stared at her. "How can I do that?"

"I'll drive you over to Saint-Raphael. You can get a taxi there to take you back to the villa."

"That doesn't make sense," he said. "Mara said everything would be arranged."

"She fucked up," Marissa said.

He got out of bed and pulled on his pants. "Let me talk to her."

"It won't help," she said. "She took two Nembutal and she'll sleep until the middle of the afternoon."

"How did you find out I have to go?"

"Lascombes came into our room. He said this room has been promised. Mara never told him that you were joining us. He doesn't want any hassle from Gianpietro, so you have to go."

"Shit!" he exclaimed. "I might have figured that she was a nut. I wanted to stay at the villa. I'm sorry I let her talk me into it." He looked at her. "Can't I move into a hotel in Saint-Tropez?"

"I checked all the hotels. They're booked up. There's not a room in the town."

He looked at her. "Then you're staying here?"

"If it's okay with you," she said. "Gianpietro is paying me for the month to stay with Mara. But I'll go back with you if you want."

He thought for a moment. "No, it's okay, I'll manage."

"You'll be more comfortable at the villa anyway," she said.

"Sure," he said. "How much time to get ready?"

"I'm ready right now," she said.

He nodded slowly. "Give me ten minutes. I'll meet you downstairs."

She looked up at him. "I'm sorry, Joe."

He smiled wryly. "That's the way it goes. You can't win them all."

Chapter Thirty-four

It was four days later that he waited in the Nice Airport for Laura to arrive on her connecting flight from Paris. An airport announcement bell echoed before a girl's voice came from the loudspeakers, first in French, then in English. Laura's flight would be delayed by two hours because of weather conditions in Paris.

Joe looked up at the flight departure and arrival board below the giant clock. It was nine o'clock. The flight arrival that had been scheduled for nine-thirty was now posted for eleven-thirty. He swore to himself, headed for the small restaurant and bar and sat down at a table. Carefully he placed the two dozen roses he had brought for her on the table and looked up at the waiter. "Scotch whisky and water," he said.

The waiter shook his head. "Sir, at the tables one must always order food."

"I had breakfast already," Joe said. "What do you suggest?" Automatically he gave the waiter a hundred-franc note.

"In that case, monsieur," the waiter said, "I will bring you a double Scotch and water."

"Beautiful." He looked out at the airport. A crowd was already waiting for the Paris flight to arrive. They waited patiently, apparently used to delays.

The waiter brought his two Scotches and water, and placed them on the table. Joe stared at them. He lifted one of the glasses and tasted the Scotch. It was strong. By the time Laura arrived he would be completely bombed. He decided to nurse the drinks as he reflected upon his last few days.

It had been two o'clock in the afternoon when he returned to Gianpietro's villa from Saint-Tropez. The houseman came out as he descended from the taxi. "*Bonjour*, Monsieur Crown," he said in greeting. "Monsieur Gianpietro is on the telephone for you."

Joe paid off the taxi and followed the houseman to a telephone in the hall of the main house. "Franco," he said.

"Joe, my friend," Gianpietro said. "The houseman said that you had gone with the girls to Saint-Tropez."

"It was not my cup of tea," Joe said. "There was no way I could work there."

"You will be more comfortable at the villa," Gianpietro said.

"Probably," Joe said. "But I have been thinking about your kind offer and I feel I can't give you the kind of story you need for Mara. So I have decided to leave and begin work on my next book."

"You are probably right," Gianpietro agreed, a note of relief in his voice. "Mara is a cunt. She is not serious about her work. All she wants is people to do it for her."

"You don't sound very happy with her," Joe said. "I hope I am not the reason for that."

"Not at all," Gianpietro said reassuringly. "As a matter of fact, there is another girl I have had my eye on for a long time. I think that Mara will have a surprise quite soon."

"I'm sorry," Joe said. "May I have your permission to telephone my editor in the States? Also, I will be leaving the villa tomorrow."

"Anything you want, you know that, my friend," Gianpietro said. "If there is anything you need, please call on me."

"Thank you, Franco. *Arrivederci*." Joe put down the telephone and turned to the houseman. "*S'il vous plaît*," he asked, in about all the French he could speak, "would you place a telephone call to New York for me?"

The houseman nodded. "*Avec plaisir*," he said handing a small paper pad and pencil to Joe. "Write the number for me, please," as he picked up the phone.

Joe wrote Laura's telephone number on the pad and returned it to him. Quickly, the houseman spoke to the operator and waited for a reply. Joe heard the scratch of a girl's voice from the receiver. "The circuits are occupied just now. It will take about two hours to place your call."

"That's okay," Joe said. "I'll wait."

The houseman spoke a few words into the telephone, then replaced the receiver. "Is there anything else, monsieur?"

"I'm leaving the villa tomorrow," Joe said. "What is the best hotel in Nice?"

"The Negresco, monsieur."

"Can you get me a double room there for a few days?"

"It will be difficult, monsieur. This is the height of the season and they're usually *complet*."

"Damn," Joe said. "Is there any way you can help me?"

"My brother-in-law is in the conciergerie. Perhaps he can arrange something?"

"Talk to him," Joe said. "Tell him that I will give him fifty dollars if he can get a room for me."

"I will try my best, monsieur," the houseman said.

"Thank you," Joe said, pressing a ten-dollar bill into the man's hand. "I'll be down at the guest house and begin my packing. When the New York call comes through, call me there."

By the time he had gone into the guest house, the telephone rang. It was the houseman. "I have already spoken to my brother-in-law and your room is confirmed."

"That's wonderful," Joe said. "Thank you very much.'

"It is my pleasure, monsieur," the houseman said. "I will be pleased to drive you to the hotel tomorrow."

"Thank you again," Joe said and put down the phone. He went to the large armoire and took out his valise. He carried it to the bed, then stared at it. Suddenly he felt very tired. It was a long drive from Saint-Tropez and the heat had already dragged him down. Almost automatically he stretched out on the bed and went to sleep.

The sun flooded in from the west window opposite his bed, awakening him. He looked at his watch. He had been sleeping almost an hour and a half. He splashed some water on his face and began to feel better. He picked up the telephone. The houseman answered. "Any reply on my New York call yet?" Joe asked.

"No, monsieur." The houseman was polite. "Would monsieur like something to eat or drink?"

Suddenly Joe realized that he had not had lunch. "Yes, I would like something."

"I have prepared several sandwiches, one chicken, one *rosbif*. What do you prefer to drink, wine or beer?"

"Do you have any Coca-Cola?"

"Of course, monsieur." The houseman sounded slightly surprised.

"That's great," Joe said. "With lots of ice. Very cold."

"I will bring it immediately, monsieur."

Joe put down the telephone and began unbuttoning his shirt. It was damp with perspiration. Before he had the shirt off, the telephone rang.

"La Contessa Baroni, monsieur," the houseman said.

Joe was puzzled. "For me?"

"She asked for you, monsieur."

"Okay," Joe said. He heard the click in the receiver as the call was transferred. "Hello?"

"This is Anna Baroni," the contessa's voice echoed in his ear. "What are you doing living with that gangster down there?"

"I was trying to think of a movie idea for his girlfriend," Joe said. "But I can't make it so I'm leaving in the morning. I'm planning to meet my editor so that I can begin working on my next book."

The contessa laughed into the telephone. "Is your editor a man or a woman?"

"A woman," Joe smiled.

"I might have guessed," the contessa said. "Is she pretty?"

Joe thought for a moment. "More than that," he said. "She has style."

"Spoken like a writer," she said. "By the way, in case you don't know it, I am your publisher in Italy. I own the company that is putting out your novel in Italy."

"Have you read it?" he asked.

"No," she answered honestly. "I do not have the patience. I called to invite you on my yacht for a long weekend."

He hesitated. "I would love to join you, but my editor is very conservative."

The contessa laughed again. "There is a quiet group on the boat. Your editor might even enjoy it. The managing director of my publishing company and his wife will be along."

"Thank you," he said. "But I haven't received her arrival date yet. It might be too late for you. She's expected either the day after tomorrow or the weekend."

"Either way, call me," she said. "You can reach me on my yacht, just telephone the captain's office at Port d'Antibes. They will transfer the call to my boat."

"Okay," he said. "You will hear from me on Friday. And thank you again."

"*Ciao*," she said and hung up.

It took two hours for the call to Laura to go through. By that time he had everything packed and his valises closed. Laura's voice sounded half asleep.

"Did I wake you?" he asked.

"Yes," she said. "It's after midnight here." Now she was awake. Her voice sounded concerned. "Is there anything wrong?"

"Nothing is wrong," he answered. "Yes, everything is wrong. You're not here."

"It's not the tenth yet," she said. "I told you to call me on the tenth."

"It's the fifth," he said. "I'm sure you know what you want to do. I'm in Nice and it's taken six hours for the circuits to clear so I could make this call to you. I want you to come now. The tenth will turn to the fifteenth before you get here, then before we know it, we'll have no time together."

"Have you done any work on the book?"

"No," he answered. "I've been farting around with an Italian producer. Finally, I decided there was nothing in it for me. I'd rather work on the book, but I need your help to get it started."

She was silent.

"Besides, I want to be with you," he said.

She took a deep breath. "I don't want to be just another girl with you."

"You're not just another girl," he said. "You're someone special to me. I know that now. All the others were yesterday, I was playing with myself. I called you because I need you. I don't know what I can do, but I do know that I don't want to write any more scripts. I want to be a real writer. And I need you, not only for myself but to help me work."

"You really mean that?" she asked softly.

"Yes," he said.

"When do you want me to be there?" she asked.

"I'd like tomorrow."

"This is Tuesday," she said. "How about Friday?"

"I'll settle for that," he said. "I'll pick you up at the Nice Airport. I'll be at the Negresco Hotel when you get the tickets. Hurry."

"Joe," she said. "I don't want to make any mistakes."

"You won't," he said. "I promise."

The houseman's brother-in-law had the right connections. Joe was given one of the best rooms in the hotel, on the fifth floor, with two wide glass doors leading to a narrow balcony over the broad expanse of the beaches and the Mediterranean. Joe looked at the twin beds.

The room clerk who had ushered him to the room, smiled. "*A l'Amérricaine*," he said. "Most of our American clients prefer twin beds."

Joe smiled. "Doesn't bother me." He gave the clerk a hundred francs and nodded as the clerk thanked him. The clerk had just gone when the porter came in with the valises, and right behind him the valet, who unpacked everything. Joe watched his twenty-franc notes flying like paper airplanes. But he had a good feeling. The service was great, even if it cost.

He opened his portable typewriter and placed it on the desk near the window. He took several sheets of paper from his brief case. He had an idea for the novel. He didn't care that everyone said there were too many novels about Hollywood; this would be a story that no other writer had written—a story of booze, dope and broads. It had nothing to do with the movie business.

The telephone rang. It was Laura. "Friday morning okay with you?" she asked.

"Perfect," he said.

"What are you doing?" she asked after she had told him about her flight.

"I'm trying to have something on paper to show you," he said. "I didn't want you to feel that I was screwing off."

"That's good," she said.

"This is the height of the season," he said, "and everything is filled up. But I was lucky. I got one of the best large rooms in the hotel, looking out on the sea."

"Sounds beautiful," she said.

"Only one problem," he said. "It has twin beds."

She was silent for a moment. "Remember, I spent two years in France; I can handle it."

He laughed. "I hope I can. But I'll be at the airport waiting for you. I'm really very excited."

"So am I," she said.

He put down the phone and then looked at the typewriter. He had already written four pages. He looked at his watch. It was eight o'clock at night and the sun was still shining. Suddenly he felt hungry. He hadn't eaten any lunch. He called down to the concierge.

The concierge recognized his voice. "Monsieur Crown, this is Max. We met when my brother-in-law brought you here."

"Max, of course," he said. "What restaurant do you suggest for dinner?"

"The restaurant in the hotel is very good, monsieur," Max answered.

"Fine," Joe said. "Can you reserve a table for me at nine o'clock?"

"Of course, monsieur. You will be alone?"

"Yes," Joe answered.

"Very well, monsieur. Thank you." The receiver clicked off and Joe put down the telephone. He showered and dressed and was ready to go downstairs when the telephone rang.

"Joe?" It was Marissa.

"Yes," he said.

"Mara wants you to return to the villa."

"Tell her to fuck herself," he said.

"She said Gianpietro will be angry," Marissa said.

"She's lying," he said flatly. "I already spoke to him and he said it was okay for me to leave."

She was silent for a moment. "What are you going to do?" she asked.

He lied a little. "My editor will arrive from New York tomorrow morning, then we're beginning work on my next book."

"I'm sorry, Joe," she said. "I really like you. I'm sorry that it's ended like this."

"I still like you too," he said. "But we had a good run. Maybe there'll be another time."

"I hope so," she said sincerely. "Good luck."

"And good luck to you," he said. "*Ciao*."

He went down to dinner.

The airport announcement bell echoed. Quickly, Joe paid for the Scotches. Laura's flight was on the ground.

Chapter Thirty-five

She walked through the hotel room and out on the narrow balcony while the porter placed her valises on the luggage racks and left. Joe stood in the middle of the room watching her. She turned back to him. "I still can't believe that I'm really here," she said.

"You can believe it," he said, moving to the small table on which there was a bottle of champagne that stood in a silver ice bucket. Quickly he popped the cork out and filled a glass for each of them. "Welcome to the Riviera," he toasted.

She tasted the champagne. "It's lovely," she said. She met his eyes. "You've done everything. Roses at the airport, champagne in the room. Do you know that you're a romantic?"

He laughed. "I never thought that. I was just happy that you came."

"I'm happy too," she said. She came to him and kissed him lightly. "Thank you."

He shook his head silently.

"I've got to take a shower," she said. "I have a feeling that my clothing is stuck to me. Eighteen hours on the plane isn't the most relaxing way of traveling, only the fastest."

He held up his glass. "To modern speed," he said. "You take your shower. You'll feel better then."

She looked down at the beds. "Which one is mine?"

"Take your pick," he said. "It doesn't matter to me."

"I'll take the one nearest the bathroom," she said. She placed the champagne glass down. She opened one of her valises and took out a small box that held her cosmetics. "Is there an extra bathrobe in the bathroom.?"

He nodded.

"Good," she said, going to the bathroom. "I won't be too long."

"I'll be here," he said. He sat at the desk and looked down at the pages he had written. Twenty-seven pages, single-spaced. That was pretty good. She had to be pleased. Then he heard the water running in the shower. He closed his eyes. In his mind he could see her nude body, the water pouring over her. He felt the excitement throbbing through his erection. Quickly he walked out on the balcony and looked out toward the sea. He cursed to himself at the way the Italians cut their slacks—all that was needed was a half hard, and it showed against the material.

A few minutes later, she was beside him on the balcony. "What are you watching?"

"Nothing," he said. "It's just that it's warm and there's no fan in the room."

"I think it's great," she said. "We had nothing but rain the last few weeks in New York."

He turned to her. She was wearing the terry bathrobe supplied by the hotel. "How was the shower?"

"I feel a lot better," she said. "But I'm still tired."

"That's normal," he said. "Why don't you have a siesta? There's no rush."

She looked up at him. "What are you going to do?"

"The same thing," he said. "I was too excited to sleep well."

He followed her into the room and hung a "Do Not Disturb" sign outside the door. Then he took down her bedcover and threw it on a chair. "*Violà*," he said.

"That looks good," she said, turning back the blanket. She stretched out on the bed and covered herself with the sheet.

He sat at the end of his bed and took off his shoes. "Okay if I undress and rest in my undershorts?"

"Don't be silly," she said. "It's too warm to sleep with your clothes on." She wriggled under the sheet. A moment later she had the bathrobe out from under it and at the foot of the bed. She looked at him. "I'll just rest a little while. Then we can talk."

He undressed with his back to her. He still had his wet hard and didn't want her to see the wet spots on his shorts. He pulled the drapes across the window and the room turned dark. He stretched out on his bed and closed his eyes. But he couldn't sleep; he was listening to the soft breathing from the other bed. He became annoyed at himself because his erection wouldn't relax. He turned on his side, away from her, and tried to clear his mind. Then the telephone rang.

Quickly he rolled over and picked up the telephone before it could ring again and wake her. "Hello," he said in a low voice.

"Joe." It was the contessa. "Did your editor arrive?"

"Just this moment, Contessa," he said.

"I wanted to remind you that you are both invited for a long weekend on my yacht. We will be sailing at noon tomorrow."

"May I call you at seven o'clock this evening?" he asked. "I will be able to let you know by then."

"Okay," she said. "*Ciao*."

As he replaced the receiver, Laura turned on the lamp on the night table between them. She was unaware that the sheet had slipped half away from her. "Who was calling?" she asked.

"The Contessa Baroni," he said. "She's invited both of us for a long weekend on her yacht." He felt himself growing more erect and rolled over on his stomach to cover himself.

"Contessa Baroni?" she said reflectively. "I know that name."

"Baroni—that's the name of the publishing company that bought the Italian rights to my book. She owns the whole company and many other things I don't even know about." He tried to burrow deeper into the bed. "She also financed the last picture I did for Santini and arranged for me to collect all the money he owed me."

"How did you meet her?" Laura asked. "At one of her parties? She also has a reputation for being a great hostess."

"Santini introduced us and for some reason she seemed to like me. I have a feeling that she gave her publishing company orders to buy my book. She told me that the managing director of her book company will be on the yacht on the weekend with his wife."

She met his eyes. "Did you have an affair with her?"

"Jesus!" he exclaimed, automatically sitting up. "I'm not her type. She's into young girls."

She stared at him, her eyes looking at his erection, the front of his shorts bulging, a large wet stain half covering the fly. "But she did that to you on the phone?"

"That's stupid," he snapped. "I've had this hard on from the moment you came off the plane. Besides, looking at you half naked right now doesn't make it any easier for me."

She glanced down at herself, the sheet falling off. She didn't pick it up. "I did think, several times, that you were looking uncomfortable."

"You were right," he said.

"Take off your shorts," she said suddenly, "before you get a hernia."

He swung himself off the bed and dropped his shorts to the floor. His phallus slapped up against his stomach.

She looked at him. "You have a large penis, almost up to your bellybutton," she said softly. "Like eight or nine inches."

"I never measured it," he said.

She took a deep breath. "I love big pricks. That's why I kept away from you. I wanted it to be only business. I had a feeling that you would be like that."

"Is that what you want now? Only business?" he asked.

She looked up at him and laughed. "Now you're the one who's crazy. I didn't fly half-way across the world only to help write a book."

"I don't get it." His surprise echoed in his voice. "You were always so cool. What made you change your mind?"

"Eight years in that damn agency with all their stupid rules." She looked up at him. "And you know something? It would be the same in the new job so I quit it before I started."

"What are you going to do then?"

She reached and clasped his phallus in her hand. "This," she said. "And I want to live free. Like you. You do anything you want. You seem to always be having a ball. What I read in the papers, you are always where the action is. People. Parties. My life is just boring."

He sat down on the side of the bed and placed his hand between her legs. "Your cunt is soaking," he said huskily.

"I want you to kiss it," she said. "I was engaged to a lawyer for almost six years and he never did anything but fuck me, and that was always with a condom. I never had a man kiss me there."

"You came to the right man," he said. "Eating pussy is my thing." He bent his face into her. He could hear her moaning as he moved around and into her. He felt her clitoris grow larger in his mouth. "My God!" he exclaimed. "You've got the biggest clit I've ever seen. It's like a little prick."

She grabbed his hair and pulled his face tighter into her. "Stop talking when I'm coming in your mouth!" she said gasping, shaking her head wildly from side to side.

He glanced up at her. Her eyes were tightly closed. Quickly he pushed her legs back, his hands under her knees until she was opened wide to him. He slammed himself deep into her. Her mouth gaped open as she half screamed. "Is this prick large enough?" he growled.

"I feel it in my throat," she cried. "I love it! I love you! Just love me like this, forever and ever."

Chapter Thirty-six

The soft sound of the ship's engines awakened him. He checked the radium dial of his wristwatch. It was just past seven o'clock in the morning. Carefully he slipped out of the small three-quarter-size bed in the cabin and glanced at Laura. She was fast asleep, with the bedsheet draped over her head. Quickly he stepped into his bermuda shorts and pulled on a shirt. Quietly he left the cabin and closed the door without making a sound.

He walked up the small circular staircase past the main deck and made his way to the dining salon. Already there was a small buffet set out for breakfast. He picked up a glass of tomato juice and sipped it slowly. Through the windows he saw the land slipping behind them as the ship moved forward.

"The girl is going to marry you," the contessa said behind him.

He turned in surprise. The contessa was wearing a silk robe over a tight bathing suit. "What makes you think that?" he asked.

"There are some things I know," she said. She held out her cheek for him to kiss. "*Buon giorno.*"

"*Buon giorno,*" he said, kissing her. "Are you psychic?"

"No," she said. "But we have been together three days now. That's enough to tell. But do not be afraid. She will be very good for you."

He was silent.

"Is she a good fuck?" the contessa asked.

Joe nodded. "Very good."

"I thought so," the contessa said. "I felt she was a woman who had kept her sex bottled inside for a long time, and now this is the first time she feels free with herself."

"What else do you have to tell me, O wise lady?" He smiled.

"I would like to eat her pussy," the contessa said. "And I am sorry that will never happen. This kind of sex is not a part of her. She loves you, Joe. That is the simple truth of it."

"Where is your little Danish girlfriend?" he asked.

"Still asleep," she said. "But I am bored with her. She has no imagination. I am also bored with Enrico and his wife. So much discussion of business does not make for a good time. This has to be done once a year. It is important to keep in touch with my business affairs."

"You have many," he said.

"My father didn't have a son so I had to take care of all his business after he died." She pulled a cord to summon the steward. "Would you like some American breakfast?" she asked. "Eggs and bacon?"

"That would be nice."

The steward in his immaculate white jacket appeared. She spoke to him in Italian and he left the salon. She gestured for Joe to follow her to the breakfast table. She sat at the head of the table and placed him to her right. Silently she poured a small cup of coffee for herself from the silver carafe and poured another cup for Joe. She drank the coffee slowly. "Dull," she said. "Nothing but dull."

Joe was silent.

She looked at him. She took out a vial of cocaine and a small gold spoon from the pocket of her silk robe. "I need a lift," she said, taking two deep snorts and holding it out to him.

He shook his head. "It would make me crazy in the morning."

She laughed. "Then let me put some on your fingers, and stick your hand in my cunt."

He broke up. "Anna," he laughed, calling her by name for the first time. "You really are too much. We're here in the dining salon. The steward is bringing breakfast, and who else do we know that might show up?"

"Nobody will see even if they came up," she said. She lifted the edge of the tablecloth and spread open her legs. "It will only take a moment. My cunt is on fire. Cocaine will cool it off."

"What about your bathing suit? You can't take that off?"

"Let me worry about that," she said, taking his fingers and sprinkling the cocaine across them from the vial. "Now put your hand under the tablecloth."

He looked at her and did as she had suggested. He felt her hand grasp his hand and pulled it toward her pussy. Surprised, he felt the seam under her bathing suit open. She slid forward in her seat and then strongly pulled his hand into her already soaking pussy, her cunt almost covering his knuckles. "Now!" she said, gasping. "Twist it twice then pull it out!"

He could feel the juices running over his hand as he took back his hand. He looked at her. For a moment she was flushed, then the perspiration broke out on her forehead. She let her breath out in a slow sigh and smiled slowly at him. "You can wash your hand in the fingerbowl on the table next to you. It is scented with fresh lemon."

Quietly he splashed the water over his fingers, then wiped himself with a napkin. "Better now?" He smiled.

She dabbed her face with her napkin. "Didn't ruin my makeup?" she asked.

"You look perfect," he said.

She leaned across the table and kissed his cheek. "You are a very sweet man," she said. "Believe me, that girl is very lucky."

He was staring in wonder at her as the steward came into the salon with his breakfast. He waited until the man had left. "Anna, tell me. Why?"

There was a strange sadness in the back of her eyes. "Life is so fucking dull, darling," she said, sounding almost angry at herself. "Sometimes you have to do something crazy."

The last day of the weekend on the yacht ended with the fireworks display in the bay of Cannes on Tuesday night. The contessa's yacht was surrounded by boats, large and small, as the fireworks exploded above them. Joe and Laura had gone up to the sun deck to look at the sky. The others had remained on the afterdeck close to the buffet dinner placed on a long table. The contessa had invited about thirty guests to join her on the yacht.

"I've never seen fireworks like this," Laura said, staring up at the exploding lights in the night sky.

"Neither have I," Joe said. "Last summer I spent at the Lido in Venice. They never had anything like it."

She glanced over the railing toward the afterdeck. "I don't think any of them down there are even watching."

"They are more interested in drinking and eating," he said.

"I thought I caught a sniff of marijuana near some guests."

Joe laughed. "It's not marijuana, it's hashish. They don't have any ganch here. But the contessa has everything. Cocaine, hash, absinthe, opium. All you have to do is ask."

"Kathy told me you always had coke and ganch," Laura said.

"I did in Hollywood," he said. "But here I don't have any connections."

"I've smoked with Kathy a few times," she said. "But I never had any cocaine. Sometime I think I would like to try it. What does it do for you?"

"It's a big high," he said. "Goes right through your head. But you can't use too much of it. Then it's a big downer."

"It might be fun if we could try it together."

"I'll check with the contessa," he said. "Maybe she'll give me a little."

She looked down again over the railing. "I don't know how the contessa got all these people together at one time." She turned back to Joe. "I saw Ali Khan and Rita Hayworth and Rubirosa and Zsa Zsa Gabor. There were also a lot of faces that I recognized but I couldn't connect their names."

"The contessa collects them all," he said. "She can afford it."

An explosion of white Roman candles turned the night into day. "Do you like my dress?" she asked.

"Beautiful," he said. The black silk dress clung softly to her lush figure.

"I bought it in a store on the Rue d'Antibes today," she said. "When I heard there would be a party, I realized I didn't have an evening dress with me that would be appropriate."

"It's just great," he said.

"It was two hundred dollars," she said. "I never spent that much money on a dress."

He laughed. "I'll pay for it. It's worth it just seeing you in it."

She kissed him quickly. "I had another idea while I was walking around in Cannes. It's a much smaller and quieter town than Nice. I found a small one-bedroom apartment on La Croisette, just across from the beach. The hotel would cost like fifty, sixty dollars a day. I can get the apartment for two hundred dollars for two weeks. It has everything. Bathroom. Kitchen."

"You planning on cooking?"

"I'm a good cook," she said. "And we can save some money while you're working."

He was silent.

"I've already gone through your twenty-seven pages. You have the whole book there. I can help you block it out into chapters, then I will write a few pages of outline I know would sell if you write five chapters to go with it. I know I can get this book sold, for a crazy deal."

He stared at her. "Then what's going to happen to our fucking?"

She moved closer to him. Quickly she opened his fly and held his phallus. It went hard almost immediately. She squeezed him. "I always know where to find it." She laughed.

He held up his hands in mock surrender. "You win. I'll tell the contessa that we'll get off here in the morning."

She took his handkerchief from his jacket pocket. She wiped her hand, then handed it to him. "You'd better dry yourself. Your cock is dripping like a leaking faucet."

Chapter Thirty-seven

It was almost two o'clock in the morning when he finished the last page of chapter three. He pulled the page from the typewriter and read it, then glanced down at the table that he used as a desk and studied the chapter block-out that he and Laura had worked out. He needed two more chapters to submit to a publisher in New York. Laura had finished the outline of the book and he had to admit to himself that she, with her experience as editor and agent, had written a better outline than he could have ever done.

A look at that last page, and he realized that it worked well. But it was not going as quickly as he would like. The two chapters he had to finish would take more than the two days left of the two-week lease of the apartment, and they had already been notified that the apartment would not be available after the lease expired.

He rose from the table and turned off the light. He walked into the darkened room and looked out of the window. Across La Croisette he saw people entering and leaving the casino. Near the other corner he watched the whores offering their wares. The way he had it figured, business was not very good. But then, the end of the season was approaching.

He heard the rustle of silk and turned. Laura had come from the bedroom in a short silk robe and joined him at the window. "Finish the chapter?" she asked.

He nodded. "But it's only the third. I'll never make the five chapters in the two days we have left here."

"We can find another apartment," she said. "The season is over and there are plenty of vacancies."

He shook his head. "I've had enough of these places. The French aren't very cooperative with their tenants. Besides the rent, they charge you for towels and sheets, they murder you with a deposit on the telephone—which you'll probably never collect once you're gone."

"What do you want to do then?" she asked. "Do you want to go back to Rome?"

"That won't help," she said. "I have nothing there except some trunks in storage."

She looked up at him. "I know you," she said. "You have an idea."

He nodded. "Our lease is over Wednesday. Every Wednesday an Italian liner stops at Cannes to pick up passengers on the way to New York. The trip takes eight days. I can finish the next two chapters on the boat. And we'll be home."

"An ocean voyage is very romantic," she said. "But it's also very expensive. Could we afford it?"

He laughed. "If it's good it's automatically expensive."

"But you have to wear an evening dress at dinner every night. I have only the one I bought for the contessa's party," she said.

"So buy a few more. They should be cheap enough, it's the end of the season."

"Are you sure you'll be able to work on the boat?"

"I'll be able," he said. "We should have everything together so that you and the lawyer can work out a deal for the book."

"Then what are you going to do?" she asked.

"Write the book and get rich."

She looked up at him. "And what plans do you have for me?"

He took her in his arms and bent down to kiss her. "You come with me," he said.

"I don't believe it," she said angrily. "They told me the boat is completely booked up. Not a stateroom or cabin available. Maybe next week they might be able to accommodate us."

Joe glanced at his watch. It was just after eleven in the morning. "Who did you talk to?" he asked.

"There are only two people in their offices—the manager and his secretary. They were polite, but that's all."

"Money talks," he said. "Did you offer them a gratuity?"

"I'm not stupid," she said. "Of course I did. It didn't help."

"Okay," Joe said. "We have friends. Let's see what they can do. Let's get the contessa on the telephone."

Laura picked up the phone and gave the operator the contessa's number. She spoke quickly in French, then put the phone down. "The contessa is on her yacht on the way to Capri and cannot be reached."

"I have one more chance," Joe said, reaching for the phone and calling Gianpietro's villa. The houseman called Gianpietro to the phone.

"Joe, my friend," Gianpietro said. "I am happy to hear from you. Are you well?"

"Okay," Joe said. "And you, Franco?"

"Much better," the Italian said. "I have a new girl. She is Swedish and a model, and best of all she does not want to be a movie star."

"What happened to Mara?" Joe asked.

"I have sent her back to Rome with your former secretary. Mara cried a lot but when I gave her money, her tears were dried." Gianpietro laughed. "I was lucky—everything went well."

"Congratulations," Joe said. "I wonder if you have any connections at the Italian Lines? I'm trying to board the Wednesday voyage to New York, but they tell me they are all booked up."

"What do you need, my friend?" Franco said.

"A good double cabin, large if possible, because I plan to write on the voyage."

"Your editor is with you?"

"Yes," Joe said. "We rented an apartment in Cannes."

"Give me your telephone number," Franco said. "I will call you back in less than a half-hour."

"Thank you," Joe said.

"*Ciao*," Franco said.

Laura looked at Joe as he put down the phone. "Who is he?"

"Gianpietro," he said. "I guess we could call him a banker. He has financed many Italian pictures, and he partnered with the contessa the one I did for Santini. As a matter of fact, he was the one who brought me the money from Santini."

"Why would he do all that for you?" she asked.

"He had an idea that I could write a script for his girlfriend. He offered me good money, but I didn't have any ideas for them. Besides, I wanted to be with you."

"He sounds like Mafia to me," Laura said.

"He probably is." Joe smiled. "But then, all Italians seem like Mafia to me."

"What if we don't get on the boat?"

"Then, plane," he said. "I've had enough of these French apartments. I can get a good hotel apartment in New York and work there."

She looked at him. "What would be wrong with my apartment?" she asked.

"What about your mother?"

"My mother passed away two years ago."

"I'm sorry, I didn't know."

"I kept the apartment," she said. "There's plenty of room."

"That's what we'll do then," he said. The telephone rang and he picked it up. "Hello."

"Joe," Gianpietro said. "You have your stateroom, first class, very good. Can you go immediately to the office of the Italian Lines? It is all arranged."

"That's wonderful, Franco," he said. "I'm sure that no one but you could do that. I don't know how I can thank you."

"You are my friend," Gianpietro said. "That's what friends are for. To help each other."

"I don't know what to say," Joe said.

Franco spoke quietly. "You have nothing to say. Only good luck to you. And bon voyage." The phone clicked off.

Joe put the phone down and looked up at Laura. "We have the reservations and we have to get over to the Italian Lines office right away."

She stared at him. "I can't believe it."

Joe laughed. "Let's get our ass over there and grab our tickets before someone else gets them."

Second dinner setting was at nine o'clock. This was for the first-class passengers. Second-class passengers were served in the same dining room but they were seated at seven o'clock. The maitre d' turned to Joe and Laura as they came to the dining-room entrance. He bowed. "Mr. and Mrs. Crown?"

Joe smiled. "That's right," he said. The ship's personnel had everything organized. The maitre d' knew that they were not married but he was schooled in old-fashioned diplomacy.

"We have several tables that you might choose," the maitre d' said. "A table for two, or other tables with guests seated for six."

"A table for two," Joe said, handing him a ten-dollar bill.

"A good choice." The maitre d' bowed. "We have a lovely table for you." He gestured to a table captain. "Table sixty-nine."

They followed the captain to a side of the dining room, under one of the large portholes. He pulled the table out for them as they seated themselves on the comfortable banquette. With a flourish he placed the napkins on their laps and gave them the menu. He bowed, "I recommend the caviar most highly," he said. "Malossol gros grain and we serve it with vodka russe."

Joe turned to Laura. "I love caviar," she said.

Joe gestured approval to the captain, who bowed and walked away. Joe turned back to her. "I love this table too," he said. "Sixty-nine is my favorite number."

It was more than an hour and a half before they left the dinner table. He turned to her as they stood a moment in front of the dining-room entrance. "Back to the stateroom, or would you like a walk on the promenade deck?"

"A little walk, please," she answered. "I've never eaten so much in my life."

Apparently many of the passengers felt the same way because the promenade deck was crowded. They made their way to the aft-deck railing and leaned against it looking down at the water sparkling in the moonlight behind the ship.

Laura looked up at the sky. "It's a full moon."

Joe nodded. "They tell me that a full moon makes women horny."

She laughed. "Who told you that?"

"I don't remember," he answered.

"You made it up," she accused.

"Maybe," he said. "But I'd better believe that all the food you ate does it. Caviar, pasta, fish, sorbet, lemon veal scaloppine, chocolate cake and ice cream."

"Don't remind me about it. This is only the first night on board and we have seven more in front of it. I'll gain forty pounds," she said.

"You'll have to exercise," he said. "There is a gym on board."

"I never liked exercise even at school," she said.

"Then let's go to the stateroom. Maybe I can suggest another kind of exercise you might like."

He held the door open for her as she entered the stateroom. "I don't believe it!" she exclaimed as she closed the door.

"What?" he asked feigning innocence.

"Look at the bed," she said. "The maid has placed a sheer black nightgown on my side. I've never owned a black nightgown."

"I bought it for you yesterday and left it with the steward when we came aboard."

Then she gestured to the small breakfast table. "Champagne and roses! No one can ever tell me that you are not romantic. Will you always be like this every time we go anywhere?"

He held up a small vial in front of her. "Cocaine." He smiled. "You said you might like to try it."

She stared at him. "Will it make me crazy?"

"Happy crazy," he laughed. He filled the champagne glasses. "Bon voyage, darling."

"Bon voyage, darling." She sipped, then put her glass down. "Let me undress quickly," she said. "I can't wait to put on my new nightgown."

"First this," he said, lifting up a coke spoon. "It's done like this." Quickly he snorted a hit in each nostril, then held it out to her.

She looked at him apprehensively.

"It won't hurt you," he said. "Sniff hard."

She did exactly as he told her. Then she sneezed. "It burns," she said.

"Give it a moment," he said. Then he saw her eyes begin to brighten and sparkle. "How does it feel now?"

"Wonderful. Suddenly I don't feel dull or tired anymore."

"Then let's get undressed,' he said. He took off his tie and jacket and shirt and turned to her.

Her dress was on the floor and she lay naked on the bed, not wearing her nightgown but holding it between her breasts and down her body between her legs.

"Jesus!" he exclaimed. "You look exactly like a French whore!"

She laughed. "That's what I always wanted to be," she said. "Now get your pants off and fuck me."

Chapter Thirty-eight

"The outline and the five chapters of the new book are very exciting. I'm sure that we can develop a very strong deal for it. I personally know several publishers who will go all the way with it." The attorney nodded very judicially. "I must congratulate you."

Joe glanced at Laura. "It's not me alone," he said. "If it were not for Laura's editing and advice, it would not be even half as good."

Laura smiled. "Thank you, Joe. But don't forget that it was you who did the writing. I am not a writer."

"You make a good team," the lawyer said, smiling. Then he turned to Joe and said seriously, "Meanwhile we do have a real problem. According to the records that I have gone through, you have not filed your Federal income taxes for the last two years."

"I didn't think I had to," Joe said. "I've been working in Europe all that time."

"You are still responsible for filing income taxes."

"Have they called me on it yet?" Joe asked.

"Not yet," the attorney answered. "But they will soon. I know how they operate."

"Why don't we wait until they come after it?"

"If they do that, it will be too late. They'll come down on you like a vulture. They'll strip you clean. Not filing a return is a criminal offense. Filing and not paying is simply a collection job for Internal Revenue."

"Then what do I do?" Joe asked.

"I will prepare your returns and we will file them with the excuse that you were working outside the country and didn't realize that you had to file. That way, all you will have to do is pay interest and a small penalty on the tax."

Joe stared at the lawyer. "About how much will that cost me?"

"Thirty-five or forty thousand dollars," the lawyer said.

"Shit!" Joe said disgustedly. "That will almost clean me out. It's more than sixty percent of what I have in the bank."

"It's better this way than if they catch you. Then they'll lien everything you have—not only the bank accounts but the monies your publishers have to pay you in royalties." The attorney nodded emphatically. "Just pay the man the two dollars."

Joe laughed. That was the first time he realised that the attorney had a sense of humor. "Okay," he said. "I'll leave it up to you. But we better make a quick deal on the new book."

"The important thing is to get a good deal," the lawyer said.

Joe turned to Laura. "How do you feel about it?"

"He's right, Joe," she said. "Let him do his job and you continue to do yours. Write the book."

"Don't worry, darling. I'll write the book. I just hope we get the kind of deal we want." He glanced at his watch. "Jesus, it's after two o'clock already and I promised my parents I would meet them at the market before three. My father is selling his share of the market this afternoon and they want me to be there. They've already sold the house and Saturday they move out. My brother has a practice in Fort Lauderdale and he found an apartment for them in North Miami."

"They're flying?" Laura asked.

He laughed. "You don't know my mother. She won't fly. She won't even take the train. They're going to drive down."

"Is that good, with your father's heart condition?"

"They're going to take it slow. Only five hours a day on the road, and probably she'll be driving most of it." He rose from his chair. "I'll be running now."

"Are you having dinner with them?" Laura asked.

"No,' he said. "My mother said she'll be too busy to do anything except pack. I should be at the apartment by about seven or eight o'clock."

"I'll have something for dinner for us," she said.

"Don't trouble yourself." He kissed her cheek. "We'll go out for dinner."

The attorney waited until Joe had left, then looked at Laura. "I haven't heard anything about your plans."

Laura met his eyes. "I haven't made any plans."

"Is that wise?" the lawyer asked. "He can walk out on you any time. It's not as if you were married."

A secret smile lurked deep in her eyes. "I'm not worried about that. A piece of paper never kept anyone, man or woman, together if they wanted to go."

"But you *do* want to marry him, don't you?"

She laughed. "Even the wisest men are stupid when it comes to women. And I'm surprised at you, Paul. He may not know it yet, but he will marry me. Not because I want him to but because *he* wants to."

It was just a little after three-thirty as Joe hurried out of the subway. The streets and stores were crowded as Joe turned down the block to his father's market.

His father's car was in front of the door and the Italian had parked his truck in the alley. Joe opened the door and went inside. His mother and father were closing a brown envelope and were tying envelopes in batches.

His mother looked at him. "You're late already, your father and me have been here since six o'clock in the morning."

"But I'm here now," Joe said. "What do you want me to do?"

"Take those batches of envelopes, we're putting them into the trunk of the car," she said.

"Okay," he said. He saw his father sit down in his desk chair. "Are you all right?" he asked.

"A little tired," his father said. "But I'm all right."

"When is the Italian bringing over the money?" Joe asked.

"He's out of it," his father said. "The Mafia wanted him out too. They are going to change the place into an auto-mechanic yard and garage."

"I thought he wanted it for himself."

"He did but the others have the right connections. He's loading his chickens and going down to his brother-in-law's stall in the market on Atlantic Avenue. He's going to be only in the wholesale business. He'll get along."

Joe was silent. He began to load the car. It took only a half an hour to get everything out. He looked at his father. "What about the furniture and fixtures?"

"It's all old junk," Phil said. "They can have it." He took out his pocket watch. "They should be here any minute. They're supposed to be here at four o'clock."

"You have the papers?" Joe asked.

"I have them ready to sign," Phil said. "They're giving me the money right away. All in cash—no check."

"That makes me feel a little more comfortable," Joe said.

The buyers were exactly on time. Of the three men, two seemed really tough; the other man introduced was their lawyer. Quickly they signed the papers and one of them handed an envelope to Phil. Phil opened it and checked the bills. He looked up at them. "I was supposed to get five thousand. This is only four five."

"Five hundred for the lawyer's fee," one of the men said.

"But I was never told about that," Phil protested. He began to get angry.

"That's normal," the man said. "The seller pays all the bills."

Joe looked at him and then at his father. "That's right Papa," he said. "Let it go. It's done now. You already signed the papers."

Phil was silent for a moment. "Okay." Then, without saying another word, he walked out of the store and got in the car.

Joe stood next to the window of the car and looked at his father. "Do you mind if I drive?"

"No," Phil said.

Joe opened the rear door for his mother. She looked up at him. "Before we go home," she said, "stop at the East New York Savings Bank on Pitkin Avenue. I want to put this money in the bank right away."

"Okay," Joe said. He slipped into the driver's seat, started the car and moved out into the traffic.

When she returned from the bank, Joe asked. "What about your plan for Florida?"

"We took the offer of thirty-five thousand for the house, but you know your father, he says we should have gotten forty."

Joe looked at his father. "Thirty-five is good."

"Moving the furniture down there would cost five thousand, along with other things," his father said.

"You're planning to move into an eight-room house there?" Joe asked.

His mother spoke from the back seat. "No, Stevie has found us a four-room apartment near the beach. My friend Rabinowitz who moved there six months ago told me everything is dirt cheap. You can buy furniture for a whole apartment for fifteen hundred dollars."

"It doesn't make sense to move your furniture," Joe said. "You ship only your linen and kitchenware. You'll probably get more than a thousand dollars from a secondhand furniture dealer."

Joe stopped the car to allow the traffic on Pitkin Avenue to pass so that he could turn into the lane. He glanced in the rearview mirror and saw the sign on the fence around his father's market. They were already taking it down. He looked at his father. His father's face was sad and it seemed as if there were tears in his eyes. Joe reached over and touched his father's hand. It was trembling. "Don't feel bad, Papa," he said. "You did the right thing. Life will be a lot more comfortable from now on."

"I remember when we made that sign. It was almost thirty years ago, just after you were born. We had such great hopes then," Phil said.

"You made them all happen, Papa. You have enough money in the bank to live comfortably. It's time now that you leaned back and took it easy."

"That's what I mean," Phil grumbled. "I don't know what to do with myself."

Joe looked at his father. He smiled. "What does Rabinowitz do?"

"He goes to the beach and looks at the girls."

Joe laughed. "There's nothing so bad about that."

"I'll kill him," his mother said. But even she was laughing.

He pressed the bell of Laura's apartment. She opened the door for him. He was carrying two cardboard boxes, which he placed on the foyer floor. He bent over and kissed her.

"What's in the boxes?"

"Books," he said. "My mother gave them to me. I have had them since I began to read. She saved them for me because she thought I might want to keep them."

She looked up at his face. "Are your parents all right?"

He nodded. His face was tight and hurting.

"You need a drink," she said quickly.

He followed her into the living room and sank into the couch. She poured a heavy Scotch on the rocks. "Drink it," she ordered.

He swallowed half the drink, then looked up at her. "You know, sometimes you see people but you never really see them. It's like they have always been there. They always look the same."

She said nothing.

"Suddenly I saw my father, and I realized I'd never really seen him. And my mother too. Suddenly, overnight, they had grown old. They were not the young and angry parents I had always known. They were old and apprehensive people moving to a world they've never known, facing dangers they could never imagine." He felt the tears welling in his eyes and tried to hold them back. "I don't know if they really know how much I love them. Maybe I haven't told them enough times. Usually we were so busy arguing that we didn't have the time."

She said softly. "They know, just as you know. Sometimes you don't have to say the words. Love is just there."

"I watched my father's eyes when they tore down the sign over his market. He put it up there when I was born. Thirty years ago. And I saw thirty years of his life blow away." He looked up at her. "Is that the way it's supposed to be? Thirty years from now, will I see my life blowing away like that?"

She knelt on her knees before him and placed her hands on his cheeks. "It won't be like that," she said gently. "Thirty years from now, the book you wrote two years ago, the book that you're writing now, and all the books that you will write in the future will still be there. Just as your father will live always in his world, you are a writer and you will always live in your world."

She drew him down to her breasts and cradled his head against her. "Don't be afraid to cry, lover," she whispered. "Tears are part of loving."

Epilogue

I was first in line to debark from the 747 as the passenger hatch rolled open. I had to wait for a moment for the immigration officer to take the passenger list from the chief steward and then step out onto the ramp. An Air France service manager came toward me. "Welcome home, Mr. Crown." He smiled as he took my attaché case from my hand and lead me into the terminal. "Was it a good flight?"

I shook his hand, even though I did not know his name. "Very good, thank you." I followed him quickly, not using the cane I always carried. It was more than a year since I had been in the hospital with a broken hip.

"If you would give me your baggage claim checks," he said, "I'll take you through customs quickly. Your car and chauffeur are already waiting."

"No baggage," I said. "I keep a complete wardrobe here and in France. It saves time."

"Very wise." He nodded. "Then I'll take you directly to customs."

The customs officer was a woman, I passed my declaration card and passport to her. She glanced at me. "You're Joe Crown, the writer?"

"That's right," I said.

"I'm happy to meet you," she said. "I just finished your new book. It's number one on the best-seller list already." She laughed. "It's wild, really wild!" she added.

"A little bit," I answered.

Then she turned serious. "Where's your luggage?"

I placed the attaché case on the counter and opened it. "Here it is."

"Nothing else?" she asked.

"No," I said. "I have all the clothes I need here at home."

She was silent for a moment, then punched some numbers in the computer in front of her. "Nothing else to declare?" she asked. "Gifts, jewelry, perfume?"

"Nothing," I said. "I travel light."

She punched the computer again, then turned to me, returned my passport and initialed the custom declaration. "Leave the declaration at the door as you walk out. I love your books, I really do. They're very exciting."

"Thank you," I said.

She looked at me. "Didn't I read in the papers that there is a party tonight to celebrate your silver anniversary on the best-seller list?"

"That's right," I answered.

"It must be wonderful," she said. "You go all over the world, with parties and exciting happenings."

"It could be worse." I laughed.

"Good luck," she said.

"Thank you again," I said and walked out. I thanked the Air France service manager. I looked for my car. LAX air was never the best, maybe 80 percent carbon monoxide on a good day. This was a good day. I choked only a little.

The silver-and-blue Rolls convertible cut into the traffic and stopped in front of me. Larry jumped out and ran around the car to open the door for me. "Welcome home, boss," he smiled. "I would have been waiting here for you, but one of the cops chased me away from the curb. But it wasn't bad. Only twice around the airport."

I got into the seat beside him. "Close the convertible top and turn on the air conditioner," I said. "The air stinks and it's as hot as a bitch."

Larry had it together in a moment; then we moved out into the mainstream of traffic. He looked at me. "You're lookin' good," he said. "How's the walking?"

"I'm doing good," I said. "No problems now."

"That's good," he said.

"Where's Mrs. Crown?" I asked.

"She's down at the restaurant putting the finishing touches on the party," he said. "Then she'll be home. The hairdresser and the makeup men are due there at five-thirty."

"That figures," I said.

"Your doctor called you. He wants you to call him the minute you get in," Larry said.

"Okay." I picked up the telephone and called. The nurse answered. "Joe Crown returning his call." There was a click as Ed came on the phone.

"How the hell are you?" he asked.

"I'm alive. And I don't know how but I made it."

"You home already?" he asked.

"No," I said. "I'm calling from the car. We're just leaving the airport."

"I'll meet you in half an hour," he said. "I want to have a quick look at you."

"Good enough," I said. "I'll be there.'

"And by the way," he said, "congratulations on the new book. I see it's number one already."

"I got lucky," I said.

"Great," he said. "See you."

I put down the phone and looked over at Larry. "How've you been doin'?"

"Okay," he said. "There's not much going on when you're away." He glanced at me as he moved the car onto the freeway. "I read in the *Enquirer* that the girls dancing in the French discos are all topless, that true?"

"That's true," I said.

"Jesus!" he exclaimed. "How can you stand it? If'n I walked on the floor to dance I'd have such a big hard on I'd pop the zipper on my pants."

I laughed. "I don't have any problems. Don't forget, I can walk pretty good but I'm not up to dancing yet."

Traffic was heavy on the freeway and Ed beat me to the house. He was in the bar nursing a Scotch and water. He watched me as I walked toward him. "You're walking real good, sport," he said, standing up and hugging me."

I hugged him too. "I feel good," I said.

"Why the cane?" he asked, taking it from me and studying it.

"When I get real tired, I ache a little."

"That's normal," he said. He felt the metal head of the cane. "Real gold?"

I nodded. "What would you expect me to have? Stainless steel? It would ruin my reputation."

"Where did you get it?"

"A girl gave it to me in France," I said.

"Laura?" he asked.

"Who else?" I answered.

He handed the cane back to me. I walked behind the bar and mixed a Scotch and water for myself, then sat down behind the bar opposite him. "Cheers," I said.

"Cheers," he replied. "How was the summer in France?"

"Okay," I said. "I thought you were going to come over."

"I couldn't make it," he said. "Too busy."

"I heard you got a divorce," I said. "Divorces keep you busy."

"Shit," he said. "I'm not lucky with women."

"Maybe you were lucky to get rid of this one," I said. "Look at it that way."

"I'd like to find a nice lady and just be happy," he said.

"That's easy," I said. "But you don't have to marry them."

"You're still married. How do you manage with all the trouble you get into?"

I smiled at him. "I always go home to Mama," I said. "And she knows it."

"You're wheezing," he said.

"Eighteen hours in planes, and the shit they call air at LAX is enough to croak anybody. Especially me with my asthma."

He took his stethoscope from his pocket. "Take your shirt off and let me listen to your chest."

"Playing doctor again?" I grumbled.

"I am a doctor," he said deadly serious. "Now do what I say."

I took off my shirt and we played the breathing-in-and-out routine. "And by the way," he said, "I keep telling you it's not asthma, it's emphysema. And that you don't get better. You still smoking?"

"Yes."

"Stop now and you pick up five years more living. I'll guarantee it."

"Five years or fifty thousand miles?" I laughed.

"I'm serious," he said. "You're just getting along now. From here on it can get worse."

"I'll think about it," I said, putting my shirt back on. "But whenever I begin writing I reach for a cigarette."

"Relax," he said. "Work less. You don't have to do all that. The money isn't that important now. I know that you have everything straightened out."

"You don't understand," I said. "There's no way a writer can stop working—not as long as there is an idea in his head. And I will never live long enough to write every story I want to write. Not even if I lived to be a hundred and fifty."

His face softened. "You know you're crazy, don't you?"

"Yes," I said. "But there's always another mountain I have to climb. Thank you for trying, though."

"Come into my office on Friday," he said. "Just for a regular checkup."

"Okay."

"And I'll see you tonight," he said, getting up. "Try to get a little sleep before the party. You've already had a long day."

I looked through the window and watched his car go down the driveway. Then I went upstairs to the bedroom, lay down and closed my eyes. Sleeping wasn't bad at all, but I could hear the jet engines in my ears.

I felt a light hand on my shoulder. "Hi, baby," I said without moving. "I'm sleeping."

Her soft cheek pressed against mine. "I'm sorry, lover, I didn't want to wake you, but it's six o'clock and you've been sleeping for four hours. I have the barber and manicurist waiting for you. We have to be at the party before eight o'clock when the guests arrive."

"Fuck 'em," I said. Then an unfamiliar scent came to my nostrils. "Jesus!" I said. "I wound up in the wrong house."

She laughed. "I was trying out a new perfume. Now, stop faking it and get your ass out of bed." She took my hand and placed it between her legs. "Now, tell me that you're in the wrong house."

I pulled her down and kissed her. "Hello, Mama."

"You awake now?" she asked.

"Yes," I said.

She got up. "Then get started. After all, it's your party."

I followed her into her bathroom. She was nude. I stared at her. "What did you do to yourself?" I asked. "I saw you only three days ago in France and suddenly you got skinny."

"I didn't get skinny," she laughed. "I got bloated in France from eating too much and drinking too much. So I had a couple of body wraps. It's magic—I sweated out nine pounds of water. Do you like it?"

"Do we have time for a fuck?" I asked.

She laughed. "After the party," she said. "Now get over to your bathroom and let the barber and manicurist work on you."

Upstairs at the Bistro all was silver and white. Even the flowers were sprayed silver. The place cards at the tables were embossed in silver, and silver-and-white ribbon covered the ceiling. In the large barroom outside the dining room silver letters were painted on the mirror behind the bar. SILVER ANNIVERSARY—JOE CROWN—25 YEARS ON THE BEST-SELLER LISTS.

Gene, who directed my public relations, smiled at me. "It's going to be the best of all of your parties. We've got two bands, one rock, one middle-of-the-road. After dinner we have a show with a dozen girls we brought in from the Casino de Paris in Las Vegas. And we've got the best guest list in town. All A's. From movies and TV to politicians and socialites. One hundred guests. And I even squeezed in two tables of press. We'll be covered all over the world. Newspaper, radio and TV. Laura and I broke our asses to set the place cards at the right tables. Do you like it?"

I laughed and hugged him. "Don't you even say hello?"

He looked at me and laughed. "You look great," he said. "What did you do to yourself?"

I smiled. "Makeup," I said. "But you were right. It's just the greatest."

Three-quarters of the way through dinner I looked across the room. Gene was right—everyone was there. And my voice was hoarse and almost gone, what with the greetings and all the interviews I had hurried through. But I was getting tired. The long day was catching up with me.

Across the room I could see Kurt Niklas whispering into Gene's ear; then Gene came toward me. He bent close and in a low voice said. "Kurt tells me there's a very distinguished old black man downstairs. He said he was an old friend of yours. He also said that the old man is wearing a beautiful tuxedo and the largest diamond rings and cufflinks this side of Sammy Davis. He said he was from Jamaica or something."

"Jamaica?" I asked curiously.

Gene nodded.

"Bring him up," I said.

"He's got a wild black chick with him," Gene said.

"Bring them both up and have the waiter bring two chairs over here beside me," I said.

"What is it?" Laura asked me as Gene walked away.

"A very old friend of mine," I said. "I don't remember whether I had ever mentioned his name to you."

The waiters were placing dessert and coffee on the tables as Gene led Jamaica and the girl to our table. I was on my feet already. We hugged each other. I looked into his face. Scarcely anything about him had changed—not a wrinkle showed. But the full head of kinky black hair had turned to white. I looked into his eyes. He was crying. "Jamaica", I said.

"Joe," he said softly. "Joe, my man. I didn't even know if you'd remember me."

"Crazy bastard," I said. "How could I not remember you?" I turned to Laura. My voice was really almost gone. "Laura, this is my old friend Jamaica. Jamaica, this is my wife, Laura."

She stood up and held out her hand. Gently he took it in his and bent to kiss it. "Laura, thank you for doing good for my man. He was a good boy an' I loved him truly."

"I'm happy to meet you," Laura said. "Please sit down with us."

"No, no," Jamaica said. "I don't want to butt into your party. I just wanted to see my man once again and tell him how proud I was of him."

"Please, sit down," Laura insisted. "Besides, the lights are going out and the show will be starting. Sit right down there right next to Joe."

Jamaica bowed. "Thank you, Laura." He gestured to the girl with him. "This is my youngest girl, Lolita."

"Hi," the girl said.

I remembered the edge in Jamaica's voice. Time hadn't robbed it from him. "Now, Lolita," he said softly, "you say a polite how-de-do to my friends, just like your mama taught you."

"How do you do, Mrs. Crown, Mr. Crown," Lolita said. She made almost a half-curtsy.

I was smiling as they sat down. All the lights in the room went out. Then a young man in white-and-silver tails came out on the small stage. "Ladies and gentlemen, since Mr. Crown has just arrived this day from France, the Casino de Paris of Las Vegas has the pleasure of bringing their girls here tonight to perform a genuine version of the Can-Can."

The orchestra struck up the music and the girls came flying out on the stage. I whispered to Jamaica, "Where the hell did you come from?"

"I retired to Cleveland," the old man whispered back. "I have an apartment in Honolulu for the winter. These old bones cain't take the cold weather. I jes' heard about your party on the television in the hotel. I was here on the plane layover."

"I'm happy to see you," I said.

"I read all your books," he said. "When I retired I had the time to read them. Even the first one when you wrote about me."

"Watch the show," I laughed. I found Laura's hand and held it tightly. "I was working for him when you sold my first short story."

"Then he was the—"

"Yes," I whispered. "The one in the book."

Then the fanfare sounded and the standard finale of the dance began. The girls locked arms on the stage and kicked in precision twelve times, then suddenly they turned around, their backs to the audience and flounced their skirts back up over their derrieres. The audience began to applaud wildly. Each bared bottom was imprinted, one letter on each cheek—and a twinkling exclamation point on the last bottom—in sparkling silver. Together they spelled out the words CONGRATULATIONS JOE CROWN! Then the stage went dark as the girls ran off.

The applause was still ringing as the lights came on. I leaned over and kissed Laura. "Thank you," I said. Then I turned to Jamaica. But the old man had gone.

I started to get up and go after him. Laura held my hand. "Let him go," she said softly. "He wanted to share a memory with you, and you both did. Now you can let it go."

"But—"

Laura interrupted. "It was another world then. Don't spoil it for him. This is not his world."

I was silent. "Is it mine?" I asked.

"Your world, lover," she said, "is whatever you want to make it be."

The Pirate

To my daughters,
Caryn and Adréana . . .
May their world be filled
with understanding, love
and peace.

In the name of Allah, the Beneficent, the
Merciful.
Abundance diverts you.
Until you come to the graves.
Nay, you will soon know,
Nay, would you knew with a certain
knowledge!
You will certainly see hell.
THE HOLY KORAN
From Chapter 102
The Abundance of Wealth

Prologue–1933

It was the eighth day of the storm. There had never been a storm like this one before. Not even in the memory of old Mustapha, the camel keeper, who was himself an old man when all the others in the caravan were boys.

Holding his ghutra close to his face, he made his way laboriously toward the tent of Fouad the caravan master, pausing every few moments to peer through the narrow cloth slits, to make sure he did not lose his bearings and wander away from the tiny shelter of the oasis out into the ripping, swirling sand of the open desert. Each time he stopped, the grains of sand tore into his face like so many shotgun pellets. He hawked and summoned up his spit to clear his throat before he entered the small tent. But there was no moisture, only the grainy dryness of the sand.

Fouad looked up at the camel keeper from his chair next to the small table on which the oil lamp flickered, lending only shadows in the darkness. He did not speak. A giant of a man, he was not much given to words.

Mustapha drew himself up to his full height of almost five feet as he always did when talking to the caravan master. "There is sand in the eyes of God," he said. "He is blind and has lost sight of us."

Fouad grunted. For once he found words. "Ass," he said. "Now that we've made the journey to Mecca, do you think He would lose sight of us on our way home?"

"There is death in the air," Mustapha said stubbornly. "Even the camels can smell it. For the first time they are nervous."

"Put blankets over their heads," Fouad said. "If they cannot see, they will dream their camel dreams."

"I have already done that," Mustapha said. "But they toss the blankets away. I have lost two blankets in the sand."

"Give them some hashish to chew on then," Fouad said. "Not enough to make them crazy. Just enough to make them quiet."

"They will sleep for two days."

The caravan master looked at him. "It does not matter. We are not going anywhere."

The little man stood his ground. "It is still a bad omen. How goes it with the master?"

"He is a good man," Fouad answered. "He does not complain. He spends his time tending to his wife, and his prayer rug is always turned toward Mecca."

The camel keeper smacked his lips. "Do you think their prayers will be answered now that they have made the pilgrimage?"

Fouad looked up expressively. "All is in the hands of Allah. But her time is growing very near. Soon we will know."

"A son," Mustapha said. "I pray Allah to give them a son. Three daughters are enough of a burden. Even for such a good man as he."

"A son," Fouad repeated. "Allah be merciful." He rose from his chair, towering over the little man. "Now, donkey," he suddenly roared. "Go back and tend your camels or I will bury your old bones in their dung."

The large tent pitched in the center of the oasis between the four giant palm trees was aglow with light from the electric lamps placed strategically in the corners of the main room. From behind one of the curtains came the faint sound of the small gasoline-powered generator that supplied the electricity. From behind another curtain came the sweet smell of meat roasting on tiny charcoal braziers.

For the twentieth time that day Dr. Samir Al Fay lifted the curtain and went to the outside wall of the tent and peered out into the storm.

The sand tore at his eyes through the tiny crack and he could not even see to the tops of the trees fifteen feet above the tent nor to the edge of the oasis where the swirling sand seemed to form a wall that climbed up into the sky. He closed the opening and rubbed the sand from his eyes with his hand as he walked back into the main chamber of the tent. His slippered feet moved soundlessly as they sank into the soft woven rugs that completely covered the sand floor.

Nabila, his wife, looked up at him. "No better?" she asked in her soft voice.

He shook his head. "No better."

"When do you think it will stop?" she asked.

"I don't know," he answered. "At any rate there are no signs of it letting up."

"Are you sorry?" Her voice was gentle.

He crossed to her chair and looked down at her. "No."

"You would not have made this pilgrimage if I had not insisted."

"It was not because of you that I made this pilgrimage. It was because of our love."

"But you did not believe that the pilgrimage to Mecca would change anything," she said. "You told me that the sex of a child is determined at its conception."

"That is because I am a doctor," he said. "But I am also a believer."

"And if the child is a girl?"

He did not answer.

"Would you then divorce me or take a second wife as your uncle, the prince, wishes?"

He took her hand, "You are being a fool, Nabila."

She looked up into his face, shadows darkening her eyes. "It is almost time. And I am growing afraid."

"There is nothing to be afraid of," he said reassuringly. "Besides, you will have a son. Did I not tell you that the child's heartbeats are those of a boy's?"

"Samir, Samir," she whispered. "You would tell me anything to keep me from worrying."

He raised her hand to his lips. "I love you, Nabila. I do not want another wife, another woman. If we do not have a son this time, it will be the next."

"There will be no next time for me," she said somberly. "Your father has already given his word to the Prince."

"We will leave the country. We can go to England to live. I went to school there, I have friends."

"No, Samir. Your place is at home. Our people need you. Already the things you have learned are helping them. Who could ever have dreamed that the generator you brought from England to light your surgery would lead to a company that is bringing light to our land?"

"And more wealth to our family," he added. "Wealth that we do not need since we already own everything."

"But it is only you who can see to it that the wealth is used for the good of all rather than just a few. No, Samir, you cannot leave. Our people need you."

He was silent.

"You must make a promise to me." She looked up into his eyes. "If it is a girl, you will let me die. I cannot bear the thought of life without you."

"The storm," he said. "It has to be the storm. There is no other explanation for the crazy thoughts you have in your head."

Her eyes fell before his gaze. "It is not the storm," she whispered. "The pains are already beginning."

"You're sure?" he asked. According to his calculations, it was about three weeks early.

"I have had three children," she said calmly. "And I know. The first one was about two hours ago, the last one just now while you were looking out into the storm."

Mustapha was sleeping, sheltered from the storm by the three blankets over his head and warmed by the heat of the camels on either side. He dreamed of paradise filled with golden sunshine and lovely houris of the same golden color, with fat breasts and bellies and buttocks. They were beautiful hashish dreams, for he would not have been selfish enough to refuse to share the hashish he gave his camels and let them wander alone into paradise without his guidance. Without him the poor creatures would be lost.

Above him the storm raged and the sand blew on his blankets, and then blew off as the wind changed. On the edge of paradise a camel shifted and a sudden cold crept through to his old bones. Instinctively, he moved toward the heat of the animal but it moved farther away from him. Pulling the blankets around him, he moved toward another camel. But that one, too, had shifted and now the cold was attacking him from all sides. Slowly he began to awaken.

The camels struggled to their feet. As usual, when they were nervous, they began to defecate, then urinate. The spatter from one of them on his blankets brought him wide awake. Swearing angrily at having been torn from his dream, he scrambled away from the hot acidy stream.

Raising himself on hands and knees, he peered out from beneath the blankets. Suddenly the breath froze in his throat. Out of the wall of sand came a man riding toward him on a donkey. Behind that man was another donkey whose saddle was empty. The rider turned to look at him.

It was then that Mustapha screamed. The man had two heads. Two white faces on one body fixed him with their baleful glare.

Mustapha leaped to his feet. Forgetting the sand that bit at his face, he ran toward the caravan master's tent. "Ai-yee! Ai-yee! It is the angel of death coming for us!"

Fouad came out of his tent like a thunderbolt, caught Mustapha in his giant arms and held him in the air, shaking him as he would a child. "Shut up!" the caravan master roared. "Has not our master enough on his mind with his wife in labor to listen to your dope-ridden dreams?"

"The angel of death! I saw him!" Mustapha's teeth were chattering. He pointed. "Look. By the camels!"

By now several of the other men had run up to them. They all turned to look in the direction of Mustapha's pointing finger. A collective sigh of fear was released as the two donkeys came out of the darkness and blinding sand. And on the first donkey was the man with two heads.

Almost as quickly as they had come, the other men disappeared, each vanishing into his own private shelter, leaving only Mustapha still struggling in Fouad's arms. Involuntarily, Fouad loosened his grip on the camel keeper, and the little man slid from his grasp and dived into the tent, leaving him alone to face the angel of death.

Almost paralyzed, Fouad watched the donkeys come to a stop before him. A man's voice came from the rider, "As-salaam alaykum."

Automatically, Fouad answered. "Alaykum as-salaam."

"I beg your help," the rider said. "We have been lost in the storm for days and my wife is ill and near her time."

Slowly, carefully, the rider began to dismount. It was then that Fouad saw that the rider's blanket had been covering two people. He moved forward quickly. "Here," he said softly. "Let me help you."

In the darkness Samir appeared clothed in a heavy beige mishlah. "What is happening?' he asked.

Fouad turned, the woman lying like a feather in his arms. "Travelers who have been lost in the storm, master."

The man stood leaning weakly against his donkey. "I don't know how many days we have been out there." He began to slip toward the ground.

Samir caught him and slipped an arm under the man's shoulders. "Lean on me," he said.

The man slumped against him gratefully. "My wife," he whispered. "She is ill. Without water."

"She will be all right," Samir said reassuringly. He looked at the caravan master. "Bring her to my tent."

"The donkeys," the man said.

"They will be taken care of too," Samir said. "You are welcome in my house."

The man's face was scraped and bleeding from the windblown sand and his lips swollen and blistered. The scarred hands completely hiding the small teacup he clutched in them. He was tall, taller than Samir, almost six feet with a large nose and piercing blue eyes that were hidden behind puffed lids. He watched Samir as the doctor straightened up from the pallet on which the man's wife lay.

Samir turned to him. He did not know what to say. The woman was dying. She was almost completely dehydrated, with a faint, erratic pulse and an alarmingly low blood pressure. "How many days were you in that storm?" he asked.

The man stared at him. He shook his head. "I don't know. It seemed forever."

"She is very low," Samir said.

The man was silent for a moment. He stared into his teacup. His lips moved but Samir could hear no sound. Then he looked at Samir. "You're a doctor?"

Samir nodded.

"Will she live?"

"I do not know," Samir said.

"My wife wanted our child to be born in the holy land," the man said. "But the British would not give us visas. So we thought if we could cross the desert, we could enter from the rear and slip into the country."

The shock showed in Samir's voice. "With just two donkeys? You have still almost six hundred miles of desert to cross."

"The storm came and we lost our supplies," the man said. "It was a nightmare."

Samir turned back to the woman. He clapped his hands and Aida, his wife's serving woman, came into the room. "Prepare some sugared water," he told her. As she left the room, he turned back to the man. "You must try to get her to swallow some," he said.

The man nodded. For a moment he was silent, then he spoke. "You know, of course, that we're Jews."

"Yes."

"And still you are willing to help us?"

"We are all travelers on the same sea," Samir said. "Would you refuse me if our positions were reversed?"

The man shook his head. "No. How in the name of humanity could I?"

"Then it is so." Samir smiled and held out his hand. "I am Samir Al Fay."

The man took his hand, "Isaiah Ben Ezra."

Aida came back into the room with a small dish and spoon. Samir took it from her. "Bring a small clean cloth," he said.

He sat down beside the pallet with the cloth she gave him. He soaked the cloth in the warm water and pressed it against the woman's mouth. "Here, watch what I am doing," he said to the man. "You must gently force her lips apart and let the drops trickle into her throat. It is the only substitute I can think of for glucose intravenous feeding. But very slowly, for she must not gag."

"I understand," Ben Ezra said.

Samir rose to his feet. "Now I must tend to my own wife."

Ben Ezra looked up at him questioningly.

"We are on our way home from a pilgrimage to Mecca and the storm caught us here. Like you, we wanted our child to be born at home but now it is not likely to be. She has begun labor three weeks early." Samir made an expressive gesture. "The ways of Allah are mysterious. Had we not gone to Mecca to ask Him for a son, had you not wanted to have your child born in the holy land, neither of us would have ever met."

"I thank the Lord you are here," Ben Ezra said. "May He grant you the son you pray for."

"Thank you," Samir replied. "And may Allah stand guard over your wife and child."

He left the curtained chamber that separated the rooms, as Ben Ezra turned back to his wife and began pressing the moistened cloth to her lips.

It was in the hour just before dawn that the storm reached its zenith. Outside the tent the wind roared like the echo of distant cannon and the sand beat against the tent like hailstones flung from an angry sky. It was at that moment, Nabila screamed in pain and fear. "The child within me is dead. I can no longer feel its life and movement."

"Hush," Samir said gently. "All is well."

Nabila reached for his arm. There was a note of desperation in her voice. "Samir, please. Remember your promise. Let me die."

He looked at her, the tears beginning to blur his vision. "I love you, Nabila. You will live to give me a son." He was swift, so swift that she never felt the hypodermic needle find her vein, only the sweet surcease of the pain as the morphine took her.

He straightened up wearily. For more than two hours now he had not been able to find the child's heartbeat with his stethoscope. All the while, Nabila's pains had been increasing but there had been little dilation.

"Aida," he said to the old serving woman. "Call the caravan master. I will need his help to take the child. But have him wash thoroughly before he enters the tent."

She nodded and fearfully ran from the chamber. Quickly Samir began to lay out the instruments on the clean white cloth next to the bed.

Suddenly Nabila shuddered and blood began pouring from her. Something was seriously wrong — Nabila was hemorrhaging. Her heaving body seemed to be trying to push the child out. But Samir could not feel the baby's head. He knew now what the trouble was. The afterbirth was blocking the outlet of the womb.

The stain on the sheets was growing rapidly and Samir worked madly against a quickening fear.

With his hand he went into Nabila and dilated her cervix so that he could pull out the afterbirth. When he'd removed the bloody tissue, he broke the water bag and guided the baby down and out of her body. Swiftly he cut away the umbilical cord and turned back to Nabila. He held his breath for a moment, then let go a sigh of relief as the bleeding stopped. Now, for the first time, he looked at the child.

The baby was a girl and she was dead. He knew that even without touching her. The tears rushed to his eyes as he turned and looked down at Nabila. Now she could never bear him a son. Nor any child. He would see to it that she would never become pregnant — the threat to her life would be too great. He felt a flood of despair. Perhaps she had been right. Death might have been preferable.

"Doctor!" Ben Ezra stood at the curtained door.

He stared at the Jew; his eyes blurred. He couldn't speak.

"My wife, Doctor." Ben Ezra's voice was frightened. "She stopped breathing!"

By reflex, Samir picked up his medical bag. He looked again at Nabila. The morphine had done its work well. She was sleeping comfortably. He went quickly into the other chamber.

He knelt over the silent woman, searching for her heartbeat with his stethoscope. There was no sound. Quickly, he prepared an injection of adrenalin and shot it directly into the woman's heart. He forced open her mouth and tried to breathe some air into her lungs but it was of no use. Finally, he turned to the man. "I'm sorry," he said.

Ben Ezra stared at him. "She can't be dead," he said. "I see her stomach moving."

Samir looked down at the woman. Ben Ezra was right. The woman's stomach seemed to be heaving. "The child!" Samir exclaimed. He reached into his bag and took out a scalpel.

"What are you doing?" Ben Ezra demanded.

"The child," Samir explained. "It's not too late to save the child."

Samir had not time to open the woman's clothing. He cut it away swiftly. Now the woman's belly was exposed, blue-tinged and swollen. "Now, close your eyes — do not look," Samir said.

Ben Ezra did as he was told. Swiftly Samir made an incision. The thin skin cracked with an almost popping sound. Samir opened the abdomen and a moment later he had the child in his hands. Quickly, he cut the cord and tied it off. Two sharp slaps on the child's bottom and the healthy wail of the baby filled the tent.

He looked at the father. "You have a son," he said.

Ben Ezra stared back at him with a strange expression. He didn't speak.

"You have a son," Samir repeated.

Ben Ezra's eyes filled with tears. "What will I do with a son?" he asked. "With no woman and six hundred miles of desert still to cross. The child will die."

"We will give you supplies," Samir said.

The Jew shook his head. "It won't work. I am already hiding from the police. There is nothing I have to offer the child."

Samir was silent, still holding the child in his arms.

Ben Ezra looked at him. "Your child?" he asked.

"Dead," Samir answered simply. "I guess Allah in His wisdom saw fit not to answer our prayers."

"Was it a son?" the Jew asked.

Samir shook his head. "A girl."

Ben Ezra looked at him. "Maybe Allah is wiser than both of us and that is why He brought us together in the desert."

"I don't understand," Samir said.

"If it were not for you, the child would have died with the mother. You are more his father than I."

"You're mad," Samir said.

"No." Ben Ezra's voice seemed to gain strength. "With me, he will die. And the burden of taking him could well lead to my death also. But Allah has answered your prayer for a son. With you, he will grow safe and strong."

Samir looked into the Jew's eyes. "But he will be Muslim, not a Jew."

Ben Ezra stared back at him. "Does it really matter?" he asked. "Did you not tell me that we are all travelers on the same sea?"

Samir looked down at the tiny boy-child in his arms. Suddenly he was filled with a love such as he had never felt before. Truly Allah had in His own way answered their prayers. "We must be quick," he said. "Follow me."

Samir carried the baby into his chamber. "Take the other child."

Ben Ezra picked up the stillborn baby and went back through the curtain. Samir placed his son on the table and wrapped him in a clean white sheet. He had just finished when Aida and Fouad came in.

He looked at the woman. "Clean and wash my son," he commanded.

The woman stared into his eyes for a moment, then her lips moved. "Allah be praised."

"There will be time for that at morning prayers," he snapped. He looked up at the caravan master. "You come with me," he said, leading the way through the curtain.

As suddenly as it had come upon them, the storm had gone. The day dawned bright and clear. The two men stood at the side of the new graves at the edge of the oasis. Beside Ben Ezra were his two donkeys, one loaded down with water and supplies, the other with the old worn leather saddle. Ben Ezra and Samir looked at each other awkwardly. Neither knew what to say.

Isaiah Ben Ezra held out his hand.

Silently, Samir took it. There was a warmth and bond between them. After a moment they let go and the Jew swung up into the saddle. "Khatrak," he said.

Samir looked up at him. With his right hand, he made the traditional gesture. He touched his forehead, his lips and finally his heart. "As-salaam alaykum. Go with peace."

Ben Ezra was silent for a moment. He looked at the graves, then at Samir. The eyes of both men were filled with tears. "Aleichem sholem," he said and turned the donkeys away.

For a moment, Samir stood looking after him, then slowly walked back into his tent. Aida was waiting at the entrance for him, an excitement in her voice. "The mistress is awakening!"

"Did you tell her?" he asked.

The serving woman shook her head.

He went through the curtain and picked up the child. He was standing next to his wife when she opened her eyes. Smiling, he looked down at her.

"Samir," she whispered. "I'm sorry."

"There's nothing to be sorry about," he said softly, placing the child in her arms. "Allah has answered our prayers. We have a son."

For a long moment she looked down at the baby, then she turned her face up to him. Her eyes began to fill with tears. "I had the most terrible dream," she half-whispered. "I dreamed that the baby had died."

"It was a dream, Nabila," he said. "Just a dream."

Nabila looked down at the child, her fingers moving the white sheet away from the infant's face. "He's beautiful," she said. Then a startled expression came into her face. She looked up at him. "Samir," she exclaimed. "Our son has blue eyes!"

He laughed aloud. "Woman, woman," he said. "Will you never learn? All new-born children have blue eyes."

But Allah had really performed a miracle. For Baydr Samir Al Fay grew up with dark, almost violet, blue eyes, the colour of the sky over the desert at night.

BOOK ONE

The End of Spring 1973

Chapter One

The needlepoint spray of the shower on his scalp drowned out the sound of the four big jet engines. Steam began to fog the walls of the narrow shower stall. Quickly, he rubbed the rich soap into a perfumed lather over his body, then rinsed and cut the water from hot to ice cold. Instantly, fatigue left him and he was wide awake. He turned off the water and stepped from the shower stall.

As usual, Jabir was waiting, the heavy terrycloth robe and thick towels over his arm. He draped the towels over his master's body. "Good evening, master," he said softly in Arabic.

"Good evening, friend," Badyr said, rubbing himself vigorously. "What time is it?"

Jabir glanced at the heavy stainless steel Seiko chronograph that his master had given him. "It's nineteen hours, fifteen minutes, French time," he said proudly. "Did the master spend a restful time?"

"Yes, thank you," Baydr said, dropping the towels and slipping into the robe being held for him. "Where are we?"

"Over the English Channel," Jabir answered. "The Captain has asked me to inform you that we will be in Nice at twenty hours and forty minutes."

"Good," Baydr said.

Jabir held the door of the small bathroom open as Baydr went through into his cabin. Though the master cabin was large, taking up almost one-third of the interior of the Boeing 707, the air was heavy and overladen with the pungent scents of hashish and amyl nitrate.

Baydr paused for a moment. He didn't mind the odors while he was using them but afterwards they were distasteful to him. "It stinks in here," he said. "Too bad we can't open a window and air the room out. But at thirty thousand feet that might prove embarrassing."

Jabir didn't smile. "Yes, sir." He went through the cabin quickly opening all the air jets, then picked up a perfumed aerosol spray and sprayed the room. He came back to Baydr. "Has the master decided on his costume?"

"Not yet," Baydr answered. He looked down at the giant king-sized bed that took up almost half the cabin.

The two girls lay in each other's arms, their naked bodies gleaming in the soft golden light of the cabin. They were dead to the world. Baydr's memory of what had happened hours before was as vivid as if it were happening now.

He had been standing at the side of the bed, looking down at them making love. Their heads were between one another's legs, their mouths and tongues viciously devouring each other when suddenly they rolled over one on top of the other and the twin half-moons of a pair of white buttocks were shining up at him. He felt the excitement race through him and glancing down saw his erection, hard and pulsing. Moving quickly, he scooped up the amies from the table and, kneeling over the girl, placed his penis at the opening of her anus. He slipped one strong arm under the girl's belly and held her tightly against him. He reached down with his hand until he felt her mound. The other girl's tongue, licking her clitoris, touched the edge of his fingertips. Savagely, he pulled her back against him and with a powerful thrust pushed himself deep into her anus.

The girl froze for a moment at the unexpected assault, then opened her mouth to scream. As she sucked in her breath for air, he broke two capsules under her face. Instead of screaming she climaxed in a frenzied spastic orgasm. A second later, he cracked an amie for himself and exploded in an orgasm he thought would never end. The room began to reel around him and he slipped into the dark. His next conscious act was awakening and going into the shower.

Now he stood at the side of the bed looking down at them once again. But this time he felt nothing. It was over. They had been used, and served their function. They had eased the boredom of the long flight from Los Angeles. Now he could not even remember their names. He turned away and went to the cabin door. He turned to Jabir from the doorway. "Wake them and tell them to dress," he said, and closed the door behind him.

He walked through the narrow corridor past the two guest cabins into the main salon. Dick Carriage, his executive assistant, was in the office at the forward end of the salon, seated at the desk, next to the telephones and telex. As usual, the young attorney was formally dressed: white shirt, tie, dark suit. Baydr could never remember having seen him in his shirt-sleeves.

Carriage got to his feet. "Good evening, chief," he said formally. "Have a good rest?"

"Thank you, yes," Baydr said. "And you?"

The young attorney gave a brief grimace, the most expression he would allow himself. "I've never learned to sleep on planes."

"You will," Baydr smiled. "Just give yourself time."

Carriage didn't smile. "If I haven't learned in two years, I'm afraid I never will." Baydr pressed the service call button. "Anything happening?"

"Everything's quiet," Carriage answered. "Weekend, you know."

Baydr nodded. It was Saturday. He hadn't expected any action. By the time they'd left Los Angeles it had been one o'clock in the morning.

Raoul, the chief steward came from the galley. "Yes, sir?"

"Coffee," Baydr said. "American coffee." His stomach wasn't quite up to the harsh filter coffee the steward preferred to serve. He turned back to Carriage. "Have you been in touch with the yacht?"

Carriage nodded. "I spoke with Captain Petersen. He has everything set for the party tonight. The Rolls and the San Marco will be at the airport. If the seas are good, he says the San Marco can get you to Cannes in twenty minutes. The car will take over an hour because of the film festival traffic."

The steward came back with the coffee. While he filled a cup, Baydr lit a cigarette. He took a sip of coffee. "Would you care for something to eat?" the steward asked.

"Not just yet, thank you," Baydr said. He turned to Dick. "Is my wife aboard the yacht?"

"The captain told me she was at the villa. But Youssef came down from Paris and is already aboard. He asked me to inform you that he has some sensational talent lined up for tonight."

Baydr nodded. Youssef Ziad was chief of his Paris office. He had one in every country. Bright, charming, educated young men who loved money and being next to the seat of power. Their main function was pimping and finding pretty girls to decorate the parties that Baydr gave in the course of business. "Get Mrs Al Fay on the phone for me," he said.

He walked back to the dining area and sat down at the round mahogany table. Raoul refilled his cup. Baydr was silent as he sipped his coffee. A moment later the phone buzzed. He picked it up.

Carriage's voice came through. "Mrs. Al Fay is not at home. I just spoke with her secretary, who informed me that she went to a film and said she would proceed directly to the yacht from there."

"Thank you," Baydr said, putting down the phone. He was not surprised. He hadn't expected Jordana to be at home — not when the film festival was on or there was a party going. She had to be where the action was. For a moment he was annoyed, then it passed. After all, it was that which had attracted him to her in the first place. She was American, not Arabic. American girls did not stay at home. He had once tried to explain it to his mother but she never really understood. She was still disappointed that he hadn't married another Arab girl after he had divorced his first wife.

The phone buzzed again. He picked it up. It was the pilot, Captain Andrew Hyatt. "With your permission, sir," the pilot said. "I'd like to have Air France service the plane if we'll be in Nice long enough."

Baydr smiled to himself. It was the captain's polite way of finding out how much ground time he could give the crew. "I think we can plan on remaining here until Wednesday. Will that be time enough, Andy?"

"Yes, sir."

"It's been a good flight, Andy. Thank you."

"Thank you, sir," the pilot's voice was pleased as he rang off.

Baydr punched the button for Carriage. "Book the crew into the Negresco until Tuesday."

"Yes, chief." Carriage hesitated. "About the girls, shall we invite them to the party?"

"No." Baydr's voice was flat. Youssef had already taken care of that item.

"What shall we do with them?"

"Check them into the Negresco with the crew," he said. "Give them each five hundred dollars and a return ticket to Los Angeles."

He put down the telephone and stared out of the window. It was almost dark and far below him lights were beginning to twinkle in the French countryside. He wondered what Jordana was doing. It had been almost a month since he had seen her in Beirut with the children. They had arranged to meet in the south of France on her birthday. He thought of the diamond Van Cleef necklace and wondered whether she would like it. He just didn't know. Everything was tie-dyed jeans and fake jewelry now. Nothing was real anymore, even the way they felt about one another.

Jordana got out of the bed and started for the bathroom, picking up her clothing as she went.

"What's the hurry, darling?" the man's voice came from the bed.

She paused in the bathroom doorway, and looked back at him. "My husband's coming in," she said. "And I have to be on the boat in time to change for the party."

"Maybe his plane will be late," the man said.

"Baydr's plane is never late," she said flatly. She went into the bathroom, closing the door behind her. She bent over the bidet and turned the taps, balancing the flow of hot and cold water until it was just the temperature she liked. Opening her purse she took out a plastic container of her own soap and straddling the bidet began to wash. "Someday I just won't wash," she thought. "I wonder if he would know when he ate me."

She rejected the idea, laughing to herself. Men were so obsessed with the idea of the irresistible power of their invincible cocks they couldn't imagine that any woman they penetrated would do anything but have orgasm after orgasm. She could almost count the number of times she had truly climaxed on the fingers of both hands. But of one thing she was sure. If they ever got around to handing out Academy Awards for acting out orgasms, she would win one every year.

She pressed the plug and stood up, drying herself as the water gurgled down the drain. French hotel bidets always sounded the same whether in Paris, Cannes or the Provinces. Glug, glug, pause, glug, glug glug. Dry now, she put some perfume on her fingertips and brushed it lightly across the silky soft pubic mound. Then quickly she dressed and came out of the bathroom.

The man was sitting up, naked in the bed, playing with his penis, which was erect again. "Look what happened, darling."

"Goody for you," she said.

"Suces moi," he said. "Pas partir comme ça."

She shook her head. "Sorry, darling, I'm running late."

"Perhaps later at the party," he said. "We can find a quiet corner, away from the crowd."

She met his eyes. "You're not coming to the party."

"But darling," he protested. "Why not? I have been on the boat with you all week."

"That's why," she said. "Baydr is no fool."

"Then when will I see you?" he asked, his penis already beginning to droop.

She shrugged her shoulders. "I don't know." She opened her purse and came out with a small envelope filled with hundred-franc notes. She dropped it on the bed beside him. "This should cover your hotel bill and expenses," she said. "With something left to tide you over until you can make another connection."

The man's voice was hurt. "But, darling, do you think it was only for the money?"

She laughed. "I hope not. I would hate to think I was that bad."

"I will never find another woman like you," he said sadly.

"You just look," she said. "There are a lot of us around. And if you need any references, you just tell them that I said you were the best."

She was out of the room before he could answer. As she stood in the hallway waiting for the elevator, she looked at her watch. It was a quarter to eight. She would just have time to get to the boat and take a hot tub before dressing for the party.

Chapter Two

Youssef noticed Jordana's white Corniche convertible parked in front of the Carlton Hotel when he got out of his taxi. He looked for her as he paid the driver but all he saw was her chauffeur, Guy, talking to some other drivers. He turned and went into the lobby.

It was the day before the official opening of the film festival and already most of the signs were in place on the posts and the stands of the smaller film vendors. He paused for a moment to look at them.

The most prominent display was the giant banner overhanging the entire lobby. ALEXANDER SALKIND PRESENTS THE THREE MUSKETEERS. Slowly he read the list of credits: Michael York, Oliver Reed, Richard Chamberlain, Raquel Welsh, Charlton Heston, Faye Dunaway. It was truly an all-star cast. Even he, a film fan from the time he had been a child, was impressed. He turned toward the concierge's desk.

Elie, the chief concierge, smiled and bowed. "Monsieur Ziad, so good to see you again."

Youssef returned his smile. "It is always good to be here, Elie."

"And what can I do for you, Monsieur Ziad?" the little man asked.

"I am to meet Mr. Vincent here," Youssef said. "Has he arrived?"

"He awaits you in the little bar," Elie said.

"Thank you," Youssef said. He turned away and then back as if with an afterthought. "By the way, have you seen Madame Al Fay?"

Without hesitation, Elie shook his head. "I have not. Would you like to have her paged?"

"It's not important," Youssef said. He turned and walked toward the little bar near the elevators.

Elie picked up a telephone from behind the counter and whispered a number into it. The operator in the descending elevator answered. A moment later he put down the telephone and turned to Jordana.

"Monsieur Elie suggests that Madame might like to descend by the elevator at the Rue de Canada side of the hotel. He has sent a man there to pick you up on the mezzanine floor."

Jordana looked at the operator. The man's face was blank; the elevator was already stopping at the mezzanine. She nodded. "Thank you."

She stepped out and walked down the corridor to the far corner of the hotel. True to his word, Elie had a man waiting there in the small old-fashioned cage elevator that still served that end of the building on special occasions.

She left the hotel through the Carlton Bar and walked out onto the terrace and then up the driveway to the hotel entrance. Guy, her chauffeur, saw her and sprang to the door of the Rolls. She turned and looked into the lobby before she went down the steps. Through the crowd of people in front of the concierge, she caught Elie's eyes. She nodded her thanks. Without changing expression, he bent his head forward in small bow.

Guy held the car door as she got into it. She didn't know why Elie had flagged her down but it was enough that he had. The concierge was probably the wisest man on the Riviera. And probably the most discreet.

The little bar was crowded but Michael Vincent had a table away from all the others between the bar and entrance. He got to his feet as Youssef entered and held out his hand.

Youssef took it. "Sorry to be late. The traffic on the Croisette is just awful."

"No problem," Michael answered. It was amazing to hear the gentle voice emerging from a six-foot-four giant of a man. He gestured to the young women seated at the table with him. "As you can see, I have been most pleasantly occupied."

Youssef smiled. He knew them. They were part of the group he had brought down from Paris. "Suzanne, Monique," he murmured as he sat down.

The girls rose almost immediately. They knew the signals. This was a business meeting. They had to go to their rooms and prepare for the party that evening.

The waiter hurried over with a bottle of Dom Pérignon and held it out for Youssef's approval. Youssef nodded. The waiter quickly opened the bottle and offered the glass for him to taste. Again Youssef nodded and the waiter looked at Michael Vincent.

"I'll stick with the Scotch," the producer-director said.

The waiter finished filling Youssef's glass and left. Youssef raised the wine. "I trust your accommodations are to your liking."

The big man smiled. "The best suite in the place and you ask if I like it? What I want to know is how you did it. Two weeks ago when I called there wasn't a room available anywhere in town during the film festival. And you call one day in advance and, like magic, there is room."

Youssef smiled mysteriously. "Let us say that we are not without influence."

"I'll drink to that," the American said. He finished his whiskey and signaled for another.

"Mr. Al Fay asked me to express his appreciation for your trouble in arranging to be here. He is very much looking forward to your meeting."

"So am I," Vincent said. He hesitated a moment then spoke again. "I find it almost too much to believe."

"What is that?" Youssef asked.

"The whole thing," Vincent said. "It took me more than five years to raise the money to make *Gandhi* and here you come to me with ten million dollars and ask if I am interested in doing the life of Muhammad as a film."

"It is not surprising to me," Youssef said. "And it won't be to you when you meet Mr. Al Fay. He is a man of great instincts. And after seeing your films of the great philosophers — Moses, Jesus Christ and Ghandi — what could be more natural than his turning to you, the one man who could possibly bring this great story to life."

The director nodded. "There will be problems."

"Of course," Youssef said. "There always are."

Vincent frowned. "It will not be easy to get a release. There are many Jews in the film business."

Youssef smiled. "We will worry about that when we get to it," he said smoothly. "Perhaps Mr. Al Fay will buy one of the major companies and distribute the film himself."

Vincent took another sip of his Scotch. "He must be quite a man this Mr. Al Fay of yours."

"We think so," Youssef said quietly. He studied the film maker and wondered if the man would feel the same way if he knew how carefully he had been investigated before Baydr chose him. Every thing Vincent had done since he had been a child was in a dossier on Baydr's desk. No element of the man's private life was unknown. The girls, the women, the drinking, even his membership in the secretive John Birch Society and certain other subtly anti-Semitic groups. It was all there. Down to an analysis of why he was persona non grata in the film industry. Anti-Semitism was hard to hide in an industry as sensitive as the film business. It had been five years since *Gandhi* had been made and it had not yet been released in the Western world. And not a single new project had materialized for the man since then. He had been living on friends and promises for the last few years. And the whiskey bottle.

Youssef didn't tell him that Baydr had approached many others before coming to him. But they had all turned down the offer. Not because they did not agree that the Prophet was a good subject for a film, but because they thought its purpose at this time would be more propagandistic than philosophical. All of them knew better. It was the Jews they feared; the Jews had a stranglehold on the business and they were afraid to antagonize them.

He glanced at his watch and rose to his feet. "I'm sorry but I must be off. There are some important matters that I must attend to."

Vincent looked up at him. "Of course, I understand. Thank you for looking in on me."

"It was my pleasure." Youssef looked down at him. "The yacht will be in the bay in front of the hotel. From ten-thirty on there will be a fleet of speedboats at the end of the Carlton pier to ferry you out to the boat. You're welcome any time after that."

The waiter came up with the check. Youssef signed it as Vincent rose. The two men shook hands and Youssef left the bar as Vincent ordered another Scotch.

He noticed that Jordana's car was gone when he came out of the hotel. He glanced at the Piaget on his wrist. It was a few minutes after eight o'clock. He went down the steps and turned toward the Martinez. Already the curious were gathering. There would be a mad scene every evening during the next few weeks as people came from all over to gawk at the celebrities and movie stars. He walked rapidly through the crowd, looking neither left nor right. He had at least another hour to spare before he had to return to the boat and meet Baydr.

The Martinez lobby was not as crowded as the Carlton had been. He went directly to the elevator and rode to the top floor. From the elevator, he walked down the corridor to the corner penthouse suite. He pressed the button. Inside a chime rang softly. He waited a moment, then impatiently pressed the button again.

The husky resonant voice came through the closed door. "Qui est là?"

"C'est moi. Ouvrez la porte."

There was the sound of the chain being removed, then the door swung open revealing a tall blond young man. He looked at Youssef truculently. "You're late," he accused. "You said you'd be here an hour ago."

"I told you that I had some business," Youssef explained, walking past him into the suite. "I have to work for a living you know."

"You're lying!" The young man's voice was angry as he shut the door. "You were with Patrick."

"I told you Patrick's in Paris," Youssef said. "I didn't want him down here."

"He's here," the blond young man said flatly. "I saw him on the plane this afternoon. He was with that Englishman who owns the department stores."

Youssef was silent, controlling the anger that seethed inside him. He had given Patrick express orders to stay in the hotel and not come out until tomorrow. "The bitch!" he swore. "I'll take care of him when I see him."

He crossed the room to the table, where a bar had been set up. There was an open bottle of Dom Pérignon in an ice bucket. He poured a glass for himself and turned to the younger man. "Would you like some wine, darling?"

"No." The young man was sullen.

"Come on, Jacques," Youssef said placatingly. "Don't be like that. You know the plans I have for you."

For the first time since he had entered, Jacques looked at him. "When am I going to meet her?" he asked.

"This evening. On the yacht," Youssef said. "I have it all arranged."

"I am going with you?" Jacques asked.

Youssef shook his head. "No. You do not even know me. If she suspects that we are friends, you will have no chance. I have arranged that you will escort the Princess Mara to the party. She will present you to the hostess."

"Why Mara?" Jacques protested. "You know I can't stand her."

"Because she will do what I say," Youssef answered flatly. "She will take Jordana aside sometime during the evening and tell her how great you are in bed and what a magnificent cock you have."

Jacques looked at him. "And that will make the lady fall in love with me?"

"No," Youssef answered. "That is up to you. But Jordana is still enough of an American to be impressed when a woman as experienced as Mara recommends you. Besides, Jordana is cock crazy."

The younger man was silent as he crossed to the bar and poured himself a glass of champagne. "I hope you're right," he said as he took a sip. "But what if there's someone else she's interested in?"

"There was," Youssef said. "I picked that up from the crew on the boat. But if I know Jordana, she has gotten rid of him because she will have no complications while her husband is around."

"What if she doesn't like me?" Jacques asked.

Youssef smiled and put down his glass. He walked over to the young man and pulled the sash that held his bathrobe. The robe fell open. Youssef took Jacques' penis in his hand and stroked it gently. "Ten beautiful inches," he murmured. "How can she not help liking it?"

Chapter Three

The teletype began to clatter as soon as the plane came to a stop at the west end of the field near the warehouses. Dick Carriage unfastened his seat belt and walked over to the machine. He waited until the sound ceased, then he tore the message from it, sat down at the desk and opened the code book he always carried with him.

Baydr glanced at him, then turned back to the two girls. They were already unbuckled and getting to their feet. He rose with them and smiled. "I hope you enjoy your stay on the Riviera."

The blond girl returned his smile. "We're very excited. It's our first trip here. The only thing we're sorry about is that we won't see you."

He gestured vaguely. "Business. Always business." His mind was on the message. It had to be important if the teletype worked on the weekend. "But if there's anything you need, just call Carriage; he will take care of things."

"We will," the dark girl said. She held out her hand formally. "Thank you very much for a lovely trip."

The blond girl laughed. "It was a real trip."

Baydr laughed with her. "Thank you for coming along."

Raoul approached them. "The ladies' car is waiting at the gate."

Baydr watched the girls follow the steward to the exit and turned back to Carriage. A moment later the young man finished decoding the message. He tore it from the pad and handed it to Baydr.

TEN MILLION £ STERLING DEPOSITED YOUR ACCOUNT BANQUE DE SURIE GENEVE ACCORDING TO AGREEMENT. CONTACT ALI YASFIR MIRAMAR HOTEL CANNES FOR FURTHER DETAILS.

(signed) ABU SAAD.

Baydr looked at the message impassively, then carefully tore it into shreds. Carriage did the same with the teletype and put the pieces in an envelope. He walked back to the desk and, from under it, pulled what looked like an ordinary wastepaper basket with a slotted cover. He opened the basket and threw the papers into it, closed it and pressed a small button on its side. The button glowed bright red for a moment, then faded to dark. He opened the container and looked in. All that was left of the papers was crinkly gray ashes. He nodded and went back to Baydr.

"When would you like to see Mr. Yasfir?" he asked.

"Tonight. Invite him to the party."

Carriage nodded and went back to the desk. Baydr leaned back in his chair, thinking. It was always like this. No matter how carefully he planned his holidays, something always came up that interfered. But this was important and had to be attended to. Abu Saad was the financial agent for Al-Ikhwah, one of the most powerful of the Fedayeen splinter groups, and the sums of money that passed through his hands were astronomical. Contributions came from the rulers of oil-rich sheikdoms and monarchies like Kuwait, Dubai and Saudi Arabia that were anxious to keep their images in the Muslim world intact. And with typical Middle Eastern caution, part of the money was set aside for investment and safekeeping in case the movement should fail. Perhaps no more than 50 per cent of the total amounts received were funneled back into the struggle for liberation.

Baydr sighed gently. The ways of Allah were strange. Freedom had always been an elusive dream for the Arab world. Perhaps it was written that it would always remain so. Certainly there were those like himself upon whom He smiled, but for the others there was only bleak existence and struggle. But the gates of paradise were open to all who believed. Someday they would reach those gates. Maybe.

He rose to his feet and walked over to the desk. "Get the necklace from the safe," he told Carriage. He slipped the velvet-covered box into his jacket pocket and walked to the door of the aircraft. He looked back at Carriage. "I will see you on the boat at eleven o'clock."

Carriage nodded. "Yes, sir."

Jabir was waiting for him at the foot of the ramp. "The car is waiting to take you to the speedboat, master."

The big black Cadillac limousine was on the field beside the plane. Standing next to the car was Raoul and a man in the uniform of the French customs service. The man touched his cap in a semi-salute. "Vous avez quelque chose pour déclarer, monsieur?"

Baydr shook his head. "No."

The douanier smiled. "Merci, monsieur."

Baydr got into the car. Jabir closed the door behind him and got into the car beside the driver. The motor started and the car swung around and headed for the western tip of the airfield.

The San Marco was there, tied to a rickety old pier. Two sailors and the first officer of the yacht were waiting for him. The first officer saluted as he got out of the car. "Welcome back, Mr. Al Fay."

Baydr smiled. "Thank you, John."

A sailor held out his hand and Baydr took it as he stepped down into the speedboat. Jabir followed, then the sailors. Baydr moved forward and stood behind the controls.

The first officer held up a yellow slicker and cap. "I have some wet gear here, sir. There's a bit of wind and this baby kicks up quite a spray."

Silently, Baydr held out his arms as the sailor helped him into the slicker. Jabir picked up a slicker and got into it, as did the sailors. Baydr turned back to the controls and touched the starter button. The engine sprang into life with a roar that shattered the night. Baydr looked back over his shoulder. "Cast off."

The sailor nodded and snapped the tie line. The rope jumped up from the post like a rippling snake and the sailor pushed the boat away from the pier. "All clear, sir," he said, straightening up and coiling the rope at his feet.

Baydr threw in the clutch and the big speedboat began to move slowly forward. Gently Baydr advanced the throttle and headed the boat out to sea. Effortlessly, it slipped through the water. Baydr sat down and fastened the seat belt across his lap. "Tie yourselves in," he said. "I'm going to open her up."

There was the sound of movement behind him, then the first officer's voice shouted over the roar of the engine. "All ready, sir."

Baydr moved the throttle all the way up. The boat seemed to climb out of the water in a sudden forward surge and the spray from the bow made an incandescent arch over their heads. The wind whipped his face and he bared his teeth in a grimace as he caught his breath. A glance at the speedometer told him they were already doing forty knots. He almost laughed aloud as he turned the wheel gently to head the boat for Cannes. The strength of three hundred and twenty horses at his fingertips, and the wind and water tearing at his face. In some ways it was better than sex.

The telephone began to ring in Ali Yasfir's apartment. The pudgy Lebanese waddled to the telephone and picked it up. "Yasfir."

The American voice crackled in his ear. He listened for a moment, then nodded. "Yes, of course. It will be my pleasure. I am looking forward to meeting with his excellency." He put down the telephone and waddled back to his friends.

"It is done," he announced with satisfaction. "We are to meet on his boat tonight."

"That is good for you," the slim, dark Frenchman on the couch said. "But it still does not solve our problem."

"Pierre is right," the American in the brightly coloured sport shirt said. "My contacts in America have a greater problem."

Ali Yasfir turned to him. "We understand and we're doing all we can to resolve it."

"You're not doing it fast enough," the American said. "We're going to have to do business with other sources."

"Damn!" Pierre said. "Just when he had the processing plants operating smoothly."

"And there has been no shortage of the raw material," Ali said. "The farmers have come through. The harvest has been good. And deliveries to the plants here have been without interference. It seems to me, Tony, that we're bearing the brunt of a breakdown in your own delivery system. The last two major shipments from France have been intercepted in the United States."

The American's face hardened. "The leaks came from here. Otherwise the Feds never would have got on to them. We're going to have to find another route into the country."

"From South America," the Frenchman said.

"It won't help," Tony said flatly. "We did that the last time and it was picked up. If it starts here, we're in trouble."

Ali looked at the Frenchman. "The leak has to be in your organization."

"Impossible," the Frenchman said. "Every man working for us has been checked and rechecked."

"We may have no choice," Ali said. "We cannot keep financing your operation if the merchandise can't get to the market."

The Frenchman was silent for a moment while he thought. "Let's not be hasty," he said finally. "We have a shipment leaving this week. Let's see what happens."

Ali Yasfir looked at the American. The American nodded. Ali turned back to the Frenchman. "D'accord, Pierre. We will wait and see."

After the Frenchman had gone, Tony looked at Ali. "What do you think?"

Ali shrugged. "Who knows what to think?"

"He could be selling us out," Tony said. "The stuff's still getting into the West Coast. We're paying premiums to the mobs out there just to get enough to keep us in business."

"Their merchandise comes from Indochina?" Ali asked.

Tony nodded. "And it's cheaper than ours."

Ali shook his head. "With good reasons. Our costs would be lower too if we were financed by the C.I.A."

"That's only part of the problem," Tony said. "The hot item in the States now is coke. And that's where we're weak."

"We've been looking into that," Ali said. "I have some contacts in Bogotá and will be going there myself next week."

"The boys will be glad to hear that. We'd rather stay in business with you than go looking for new partners."

Ali rose to his feet. The meeting was over. "We're going to be in business together for a long time."

He walked to the door with the American. They shook hands. "We will meet in New York at the beginning of next month."

"I hope things will improve by then."

"I'm sure they will," Ali replied. He shut the door behind the man, bolted it and placed the chain across the latch. He went from the door directly to the bathroom, where he fastidiously washed his hands and dried them. He then went to the bedroom door and knocked softly.

The door opened and a young girl stood there. Her olive skin, dark eyes and long black hair belied her modern St. Tropez studded jeans and shirt. "Is the meeting over?" she asked.

He nodded. "Would you like a cold drink?"

"Do you have a coke?"

"I'm sure," he answered. He went into the kitchen and brought a Coca-Cola from the refrigerator. He poured it into a glass and handed it to her.

She drank thirstily. "When will we be leaving?" she asked.

"We're booked on tomorrow's plane for Beirut," he answered. "But there might be a delay."

She looked at him questioningly.

His eyes met her gaze directly. "I have a meeting with your father tonight."

A startled expression came into her eyes. "You're not going to give me away?" She put the drink down. "They promised me he would not know. I would not have left the school in Switzerland otherwise."

"It has nothing to do with you," he reassured her. "Your father suspects nothing. We have some business with him."

"What kind of business?" Her tone was suspicious.

"Your father handles many investments for us. He has entrée into areas that we could not penetrate otherwise. He can also purchase supplies and matériel that we cannot."

"Does he know that it is for the cause?"

"Yes."

A strange expression crossed her face.

"He is a sympathizer," Ali said quickly.

"I don't trust him!" She was vehement. "My father sympathizes with nothing but money and power. The suffering of people and justice mean nothing to him."

"Your father is an Arab," he said stiffly.

She stared at him. "He is not! He is more Western than Arab. Otherwise he would not have divorced my mother to marry that woman. It is the same with his business. How much time does he spend with his own people, in his own land? Two weeks out of the year? It would not surprise me to discover that he even trades with the Israelis. He has many Western friends who are Jewish."

"In his own way your father has done much for the cause." Ali found himself defending a man he had never met. "Our battle cannot be won by soldiers alone."

"Our battle will be won by those who are willing to spill their blood and give their lives, not by men like my father whose only interest lies in the profits he can make." Angrily she stamped back into the bedroom and slammed the door behind her.

He knocked on the door. "Leila," he said gently. "Leila, would you like me to order some dinner?"

Her voice came faintly from the room. "Go away. Leave me alone. I'm not hungry!" A faint sound of sobbing came through the wooden panels of the door.

He stood there indecisively for a moment, then went to his bedroom to dress for dinner. The young were filled with ideals. To them everything was black or white. There were no shadings in between. It was good and it was bad.

But he was not in the business of passing judgment. Causes were not run on ideals alone. The young never knew that it took money to make things happen. Money to buy their uniforms, to feed them, to give them guns and weapons and training. Modern warfare, even guerilla warfare, was expensive. And that was the real reason so much time had been spent indoctrinating her. They had used her resentments against her father until she had reached the point where she was ready to commit herself physically to the Fedayeen. It was not just what she herself could do. There were many other girls who could have performed as well.

But none of the others had a father who was among the richest men in the world. He felt a sigh escape his lips. By the day after tomorrow she would be in a training camp in the mountains of Lebanon. Once she was there and under their control perhaps Baydr Al Fay would be more amenable to some of the plans he had already rejected. She would be better than a gun pointed at his head.

Chapter Four

"Your call to the United States is ready, Mr. Carriage," the hotel operator said in English.

"Thank you," Dick said. There was a whine and series of clicks, then a voice came on. "Hello," Dick said.

There were more clicks, then a buzzing sound. "Hello, hello," he shouted. Suddenly the line cleared and he heard his wife's voice. "Hello, Margery?" he shouted.

"Richard?" she sounded doubtful.

"Of course, it's Richard," he snapped, strangely annoyed. "Who did you think it was?"

"You sound so far away," she said.

"I am far away," he said. "I'm in Cannes."

"What are you doing there?" she asked. "I thought you were working."

"Jesus, Margery, I am working. I told you the chief was planning to spend the weekend here for his wife's birthday."

"Whose birthday?"

"His wife's," he shouted. "Oh, forget it, Margery. How are the kids?"

"They're fine," she said. "Only Timmy has a cold. I kept him out of school today. When are you coming home?"

"I don't know," he said. "The chief's got a lot of things going."

"But you said it would only be for three weeks this time."

"Things piled up. It's not my fault."

"We were better off when you worked for Aramco. At least then you came home every night."

"I also made a lot less money," he said. "Twelve thousand a year instead of forty."

"But I miss you," she said; there was the faint edge of tears in her voice.

He softened, "I miss you too, darling. And the kids."

"Richard," she said.

"Yes, dear?"

"Are you all right?"

"I'm just fine," he said.

"I worry all the time. It seems to me that you're always flying, that you're never in one place long enough to get proper rest."

"I've learned to sleep on the plane," he lied. "I'm just fine." He reached for a cigarette with his free hand and lit it. "At any rate we'll be here until Wednesday. I'll be able to catch up by then."

"I'm glad," she said. "Will you come home soon?"

"As soon as I can," he said.

"I love you, Richard."

"I love you," he said. "And give the kids a big kiss for me."

"I will," she said. "Goodbye."

"Goodbye, darling." He put down the phone and took a long drag at his cigarette. He looked around the hotel room. It seemed strangely empty and sterile. Hotel rooms everywhere in the world were alike. They were designed so that you could not feel you belonged.

He wished he were more like Baydr. Baydr seemed to belong anywhere he put himself down. Strange rooms and strange places seemed to have no effect on him. Of course, he had his own homes or apartments in most of the major cities. New York, Los Angeles, San Francisco, Paris, London, Geneva, Beirut, Teheran. But even when he did stay in a hotel he had a way of changing the room to fit his own style.

Perhaps it was because he had spent all of his life in foreign lands. As a boy his father had sent him to school in England, then to college in the States, first Harvard Business School, then Stanford. In a curious manner, his life had been planned for him even before his birth. A first cousin to the reigning Emir and the only male descendant of his family, it was only natural that they would entrust him with their business affairs. With the development of the oil leases, the money had begun to flow into their coffers. And the family's investments were turned over to Baydr because they could not bring themselves to trust the Westerners. In addition to the basic differences in philosophy and religion, there had been too long a history of colonial oppression. Rich to begin with, Baydr became even richer. Just on commissions alone his income began to run in excess of five million dollars a year and he controlled an international investment fund of over five hundred million dollars. And perhaps the most curious part of it all was that he conducted his business without a centralized organization. In each country there was a small group of employees reporting directly to him. In the end he made all the decisions. He was the only one who knew where it was all going. Now after two years, Dick was beginning to get a feel of the scope of the operation but still he found each day would bring some new development that would take him by surprise.

The first time that he realized that Baydr might be involved in Al-Ikhwah was when he had seen the cable signed by Abu Saad, the group's financial representative. He had always thought that Baydr, with his basic conservatism, frowned upon the Fedayeen's course of action, that he had thought it more harmful than helpful to the Arab cause. Yet, he appeared to be doing business with them. Carriage was bright enough to know that there had to be a reason. Something was happening of which only Baydr was aware. He wondered what it could be. But there was no way he could guess. In time, he would find out. When Baydr was ready to disclose it.

Carriage looked down at his wristwatch. It was almost ten o'clock. Time to get dressed and go to the yacht. Baydr liked him to be around when there was business being done.

Baydr stopped at the connecting door between their staterooms. He stood for a moment in thought, then walked back to his dressing table and picked up the velvet-covered jewel case. His slippers were noiseless in the deep pile of the rug. The only sound was the rustle of his polished cotton jellaba as he crossed into her room.

The room was in total darkness except for the light spilling through the open doorway. He saw her huddled form hidden beneath the sheets. Softly, he closed the door and went to the bed and sat down. She didn't move.

After a moment, he spoke. "Jordana."

There was no sign that she had heard him.

"Are you awake?" he whispered.

There was no answer. He leaned forward and placed the jewel case on the pillow beside her head, then got to his feet and started back to the door. As he reached for the knob, the lights suddenly came on. He blinked and looked back.

She was sitting up in the bed, her long blond hair spilling down over her white shoulders and full rose-tipped breasts. She didn't speak.

"I thought you were asleep," he said.

"I was," she answered. "Did you have a good flight?"

He nodded. "Yes."

"The boys will be glad to see you," she said. "Will you be able to spend some time with them this trip?"

"I plan to be here until Wednesday," he said. "Perhaps tomorrow we can take them down to Capri and spend a few days there."

"They would like that," she said. She threw off the sheets and stepped out of bed. Her robe lay over a chair and she picked it up. In the mirror at the far end of the stateroom, she saw him watching her. "I have to dress for the party," she said, turning toward him as she slipped into her robe.

He didn't answer.

"You'd better dress too."

"I will," he answered.

He watched her walk into the bathroom and close the door behind her, then he turned back to the bed. The black velvet case still lay there on the pillow. She hadn't even noticed it.

He walked back to the bed and picked it up, then quietly went back into his own stateroom. He pressed the button for Jabir.

Jabir appeared as if by magic. "Yes, master?"

Baydr held out the jewel case. "Have the captain place this in the safe. We will return it in the morning."

"Yes, master," he replied, putting the jewel case in his pocket. "I have prepared the blue shantung dinner jacket for this evening. Will that be satisfactory?"

Baydr nodded. "It will be fine."

"Thank you," Jabir said. He bowed and left the stateroom.

Baydr stared at the door the servant had closed behind him. It was impossible. She could not have failed to see the jewel case on the pillow beside her. She had chosen to ignore it.

Abruptly, he turned and went back into her room. She was seated at her dressing table, looking into the mirror. She saw his reflection there and turned toward him.

His open palm caught her across the face. She crashed from the chair to the floor, her arm sweeping the dressing table almost clean and the perfume and assorted bottles of cosmetics off the dressing table. She stared up at him her eyes wide, more in surprise than fear. She touched her cheek and could almost feel the imprint of his hand. She made no move to get up. "That was stupid of you," she said, almost impersonally. "Now I won't be able to come to my own birthday party."

"You'll come to the party," he said grimly. "Even if you have to wear a veil like all good Muslim women."

Her eyes followed him as he walked back to the door. He paused and looked down at her "Happy birthday," he said, and closed the door behind him.

Dick stood near the bar looking across the deck at his employer. Baydr was standing with Youssef and several other people, listening in his quietly attentive manner as Youssef told one of his interminable stories. Dick glanced at his watch. It was almost one o'clock. If Baydr was disturbed that Jordana had not yet appeared, he did not show it.

The music came through the loudspeakers that had been placed above the canopy over the sundeck. Several couples were dancing, their bodies fluid in the lights that had been strung across the ship for the party. Other couples were seated on the banquettes along the railings and at small cocktail tables around the dance floor. The buffet had been set up on the main deck below, but Baydr had not yet given the signal for dinner.

Ali Yasfir came toward him. The pudgy Lebanese's face was shining with perspiration despite the coolness of the evening. "This is a beautiful ship," he said. "How big is it?"

"A hundred and eighty feet," Dick said.

Yasfir nodded. "It seems larger." He glanced across the deck at Baydr. "Our host seems to be enjoying himself."

Carriage smiled. "He always does. I know no other man who can combine business and pleasure in the same way that he does."

"Apparently pleasure comes first." Yasfir's voice was faintly disapproving.

Carriage's voice was polite but cold. "This is Madame's birthday after all and he did not expect to do business this trip."

Yasfir accepted the implied rebuke without comment. "I haven't met the lady yet."

Carriage allowed himself a smile. "It's her birthday and you know how women are. Perhaps she's planning a grand entrance."

Yasfir nodded solemnly. "Western women are very different from Arab. They take liberties our women would never dream of. My wife—" His voice trailed off as he stared at the stairway from the lower deck.

Carriage followed his gaze. Jordana had just made her appearance. All sounds of conversation faded away. Only the music blared from overhead, and abruptly it changed to the wild strains of "Misirlou".

A light seemed to envelop Jordana as she moved to the center of the dance floor. She was dressed as an Oriental dancer. A hammered gold brassiere covered her breasts, below which she was bare to the jeweled band from which hung the multicolored panels of sheer chiffon that made up her skirt. On her head, she wore a coronet and her long golden hair flowed down over her shoulders. A silken veil covered her face so that only her seductive eyes were visible. She raised her hands over her head and stood poised for a moment.

Carriage heard the Lebanese catch his breath. Jordana had never looked so beautiful. Every line of her magnificent body was revealed. Slowly, Jordana began to sway with the music.

First the finger cymbals on her hands picked up the rhythm, and as the beat became more pronounced, she moved into the dance. Carriage had seen many belly dancers in his time. He came from a Middle Eastern family and had known the dance since he was a child. But he had never seen it performed like this.

This was the height of sexuality. Her every movement brought back memories of the many women he had known, all concentrated in the eroticism of her dance. Deliberately he tore his eyes away from her and looked around the deck.

Everyone there felt it, man and women alike. Their passions and hunger were revealed in the way they looked at her as the dance thrust wildly toward its end. All except Baydr.

He stood there silently watching her every move. But his face was impassive, his eyes withdrawn. And his expression did not change even as she moved in front of him and kneeling made him the classic offering movements. The music crashed to its climax and she sank to her knees before him, her forehead touching his feet.

For a moment there was silence, then applause. There were cries of *brava* mixed with the Arabic *ahsanti*. Still Jordana did not move.

After a moment, Baydr bent over her, taking her hand in his, raised her to her feet. They were still applauding as he turned toward them. He raised a hand to still them. The applause died away.

"On behalf of my wife and myself we thank you for being with us on this joyous occasion."

There was more applause and cries of Happy Birthday. He waited until they were silent again. "Now, there is nothing more we can say, except that . . . dinner is served."

Still holding her hand, he led her to the staircase and they began to descend. Once again the sounds of conversation began to fill the night as the others moved to follow them.

Chapter Five

Uniformed stewards were standing at the buffet table to help the guests. The table was laden with food—roast beef, baked hams, turkeys and a giant loup caught fresh that day in the Mediterranean. The centrepiece was a huge fish carved of ice on the top of which was set a crystal bowl holding five kilos of Malossol grosgrain beluga caviar.

Many of the tables and banquettes were already occupied by hungry guests when Carriage saw Baydr excuse himself and cross to the salon doors. He turned and looked back at Carriage, then nodded in the direction of Yasfir, who was still waiting in line for the buffet. Baydr turned and entered the salon without looking back.

Carriage crossed to the Lebanese. "Mr. Al Fay waits at your convenience."

Yasfir looked at the buffet table, then at Carriage. The little man's stomach had begun to rumble at the sight of food. Reluctantly, he began to put down the empty plate he had been holding.

Dick took the plate from his hand. "I will arrange for a steward to bring you dinner."

"Thank you," Ali said.

Dick gave the plate to a steward and instructed him to bring it to Mr Yasfir in the study, then turned back. "If you will follow me."

Yasfir followed him through the salon into the corridor which led to the state-rooms. Midship, he paused at a mahogany door and knocked.

Baydr's voice came from inside. "Enter."

Carriage opened the door and stepped aside to allow Yasfir to precede him into the study. He did not enter. "Will there be anything further, sir?" he asked.

"Turn your beeper on," Baydr said. "I may want you later."

"Yes, sir." Carriage answered. A steward arrived with Yasfir's dinner plate. "Place it inside," he directed. When the steward came out he closed the door. He heard it lock as he went back down the corridor.

"I apologize for the inconvenience," Baydr said.

The Lebanese was already seated and eating. "It is no problem," he said, between mouthfuls of caviar. A black driblet escaped from the corner of his mouth and he patted it delicately with his napkin.

Baydr walked over to the small desk and took out a folder from the center drawer. He placed it on the table next to Yasfir's plate. "In accordance with my discussions with your principals," he said, "I have prepared a portfolio of invest-ments, comprising blue chip stocks and real estate, which we conservatively estimate should throw off a return of twelve percent annually over a ten-year period. This includes a growth rate of six percent and cash dividends in the same amount. It means that at the end of the ten-year period we will have received a cash return of better than forty percent, or ten million pounds sterling, while our principal will double in value."

"That's very good," Yasfir said, his mouth working on a piece of chicken.

"All I need to put the plan in operation is approval from your principals," Baydr said.

Yasfir made no move to look at the folder. He put the chicken bone back on the plate and smacked his lips politely to show how much he had enjoyed the food. "May I wash my hands?" he said.

Baydr nodded. He took the Lebanese to the small lavatory just off the study. When the little man returned, Baydr was sitting behind his desk. The Lebanese left the folder on the table next to his empty plate and took a chair opposite the desk. Baydr waited politely for him to speak.

"Man proposes, God disposes," Yasfir said.

Baydr was silent.

"Circumstances necessitate a change in our plans," Yasfir said. "I am afraid we will not be able to go forward with the investment plan."

Baydr's face was impassive. He did not speak.

"Other commitments had to be made for the funds," the Lebanese said.

"I understand," Baydr said quietly. "I will arrange to have the ten million pounds returned to you immediately."

"That will not be necessary," Yasfir said quickly. "We see no reason why you cannot handle this affair for us. At your usual rates of commission, of course."

Baydr nodded silently.

"As you know, Israel is growing more powerful every day. And more oppressive. The suffering of our people under their domination continues to increase. They cry out to their brothers for help. Time is growing short. Soon we must move or all will be lost forever." The Lebanese paused for breath. "We have entered into certain arrangements with the Société Anonyme Matériel Militaire for supplies in the amount of six million pounds. Because of the trust we have in you, we have agreed that you would be an approved purchasing agent. For this we are prepared to pay you your usual ten-percent commission above the expenditure."

Baydr was silent.

"For the balance of three million four hundred thousand pounds left after that purchase, we have ear-marked a million pounds for investment in Colombian farmlands, coffee plantations, of course."

"Of course," Baydr said. But both realized that he knew better. "That leaves two million three hundred."

Yasfir smiled. The little man was pleased. He knew that once the money had been placed in Baydr's account, there would be no problem in securing his assistance. No matter how rich he was, he always wanted more. "We have made no plans for the balance," he said. "We thought perhaps that you might prepare a portfolio for that amount and we would give you a list of certain numbered accounts in Switzerland and the Bahamas to which it would be credited."

"I see," Baydr nodded.

"You would, of course, receive your ten-percent commission on that balance also," Yasfir said quickly. "That means you would receive almost a million pounds just to clear the money through your account."

Baydr looked at him. This was the weakness of the Arab world. Corruption and graft had almost become an integral part of their commerce. Out of ten million pounds, only six million pounds were going to be used for the benefit of the people. And that benefit was highly questionable. What the people needed was food and education, not guns. And certainly they did not need to enrich their leaders at their own expense.

The Lebanese took his silence for assent. He rose to his feet. "Then I can inform my principals that you will attend to the matter for them," he said with satisfaction.

Baydr looked at him. "No."

Yasfir's mouth fell in surprise. "No?" he echoed.

Baydr got out of his chair. He looked down at the little man. "The money will be returned when the banks open Monday morning," he said. "You will express to your people my regrets at not being able to be of service to them. But I am not equipped to function in that sort of capacity. I am sure they will find others more qualified in those matters than I."

"It is written that a decision made in haste is often regretted," the little man said.

"It is also written," Baydr quoted pointedly, "that an honest man lives his life without regret." He pressed on the signaling device built into the digital clock on his desk. He started for the door.

"Mr. Al Fay," Yasfir said.

Baydr turned to him. "Yes?"

"There will be war before the winter comes." The Lebanese spoke in Arabic for the first time. "When it is over we will be in control of the Middle East. Israel will no longer exist because we will force the world to its knees. The old order is changing — a new force is coming from the people. If you join us now, you will be with the victors."

Baydr didn't answer.

"The sands of the desert will turn red with the blood of our enemies," Yasfir added.

"And our own," Baydr answered. "And when it is over, nothing will be changed. A few hundred yards here, a few hundred there. We are merely pawns in the hands of greater powers. Russia and America cannot afford to let either side win."

"They will have to listen to us," Yasfir said. "We control their oil supply. If we turn it off they will come to their knees."

"Only to a point," Baydr said. "Then they will force us to our own knees."

There was a knock at the door. Baydr unlocked and opened it. "Please escort Mr. Yasfir back to the party," Baydr said to Carriage. He turned back to the Lebanese. "If there is anything you should require to make your visit more pleasurable, we are at your disposal."

Yasfir stared at him. The bitterness of his disappointment rose like gall in his throat. But he forced himself to smile. Things would change quickly once Baydr discovered they had his daughter with them. "Khatrak," he said. "With your permission?"

"Go with peace," Baydr said formally in Arabic. He closed the door behind them and crossed to the table and picked up the portfolio. He looked at it for a moment, then dropped it into a waste-basket.

It had merely been a ploy to involve him. They had never intended to go through with the portfolio. He knew that now. He also knew that they would not give up. They would not rest until they dragged the world down to their own level. Or, failing that, destroyed it.

Suddenly weary, he went back to his desk, sat down and closed his eyes. He saw the gentle, earnest eyes of his father looking into him, almost to his very soul. The scene was one from childhood. He had been ten years old at the most.

The children had been playing at war and he had been beating his playmate with a wooden scimitar, shouting at the top of his lungs, "Die, infidel, die! In the name of the Prophet die!"

He felt the scimitar snatched from his hand and turned in surprise to see his father. His playmate was sniffing and crying. "Why did you stop me?" he asked angrily. "Ahmed was pretending to be a Jew."

His father knelt so that their faces were on the same level. "You were blaspheming," he said gently. "You were taking the name of the Prophet to justify your own actions."

"I was not," he retorted. "I was defending the Prophet."

His father shook his head. "You forget, my son, that the Prophet you try to defend by an expression of violence is also known as the Messenger of Peace."

That had been thirty years ago and now other yesterdays crowded and fought their way into his memory.

Chapter Six

The airstrip shimmered in the heat of the noonday sun as the twin-engined DC–3 circled the field at the edge of the desert in preparation for its landing. Baydr looked down from the window at the field as he heard the landing gear lock into place. At the far end of the airstrip, there were several large black Cadillac limousines waiting; beyond them, resting in the shade of a cluster of palm trees, were some camels and their drivers. The grinding sound of the flaps signaled that the plane was on its final approach.

Baydr turned back to the cabin. The stewardess was already in her seat with her seat belt fastened. Opposite him, Jabir, too, was strapped in. He fastened his own belt as the plane dropped smoothly toward the desert.

The sand was rushing below his window and it seemed as if the pilot were about to land on the desert floor. Then the concrete landing strip raced beneath him and a shudder ran through the plane as the wheels touched down. A moment later, the pilot hit the brakes and Baydr felt himself thrust against the seat belt. Abruptly, the pressure ceased and the plane rolled gently toward the end of the airstrip. The noise of the motors lessened in the cabin and the stewardess rose from the seat and came down the cabin toward him.

A blond American, she had the same impersonal, professional smile that stewardesses seemed to cultivate no matter what airline they worked for. The fact that this was his father's private plane seemed to make no difference in her attitude. "I trust you enjoyed the flight, Mr. Al Fay."

He nodded. "It was fine, thank you."

"We made good time," she said. "Only eighty-seven minutes from Beirut."

"Very good time," he said.

The plane came to a stop. Through the windows he could see the limousines begin to move in closer. A number of men dressed in semi-uniforms emerged from the first car. Each carried a submachine gun, and they ran to take up their assigned placed around the plane. The doors of the second limousine remained shut. Baydr could not see into it because of the heavily shaded brown sunglass. The landing ladder rolled toward the plane pushed across the airstrip by four workmen.

Baydr pulled the buckle and got to his feet. He started toward the door. Jabir held out a restraining arm. "If the master would be kind enough to wait for a moment."

Baydr nodded and let the servant advance toward the door in front of him. The co-pilot had come from the flight cabin and was standing with the stewardess at the exit. They made no move to open it. Jabir opened his jacket and from under his sleeve withdrew a heavy Luger automatic. He pulled back on the safety and held the gun at the ready.

A knock came at the door. One, two, three. The co-pilot raised his hand. He looked at Jabir.

"One, two," the servant said. "They should answer with one, two, three, four. Anything else and we leave."

The pilot nodded. His fist rapped on the door. One, two.

The reply was instant and correct. The pilot pulled the latch on the door and it swung open. Two guards with guns were already at the top of the landing ramp and two more were at the foot of the stairs.

Baydr started for the door but again Jabir held out his hand. "With your permission, master."

He stepped out onto the ramp and exchanged a quick word in Arabic with one of the guards, then turned back to Baydr and nodded.

The intense heat of the desert hit the young man even before he reached the doorway. Baydr stepped out into the sun, blinking his eyes in the white light. He started down the ramp just as the door of the second limousine opened and his father emerged.

His father stepped out in front of his guards and slowly walked to meet Baydr. He wore the soft traditional robes of the desert sheik, and his head and neck were protected from the hot rays of the sun by his ghutra. Baydr moved quickly to his father and took the outstretched hand and pressed it to his lips in the traditional gesture of respect.

Samir reached out and raised his son's head. For a long moment, his eyes searched the young man's face, then he leaned forward, to embrace him and kiss him on each cheek. "Marhab. Welcome home, my son."

"Ya halabik. I am happy to be home, my father." Baydr straightened up. He was a head taller than his father.

Samir looked up at him. "You have grown, my son," he said proudly. "You have become a man."

Baydr smiled. "It is 1951, father. One does not remain a boy forever."

Samir nodded. "We are proud of you, my son. We are proud of your achievements in the American schools, proud that you have been accepted in the great University of Harvard in Boston, Cambridge, Massachusetts."

"I only seek to bring honor and pleasure to my parents," Baydr said. He looked toward the car. "How are my mother and sisters?"

Samir smiled. "They are well. You will see them soon enough. Your mother awaits you eagerly at home and tonight your sisters and their husbands will come and join us for dinner."

If Baydr felt disappointed at their not being at the airfield to greet him, he knew better than to show it. This was not the United States, where he had been living the past five years. Arab women did not appear in public, at least not the respectable women. "I look forward to seeing them," he said.

His father took his arm "Come, get into the car. We will be cool in there. It is the latest model and air-conditioned against this unbearable heat."

"Thank you, Father," Baydr waited politely until his father got into the car before he entered.

A guard with a submachine gun ran quickly to the car and closed the door behind them, then got into the front seat beside the driver. Other guards piled into the limousine in front of them. As the cars began to move away, Baydr saw the drivers beating the pack camels toward the plane to collect the luggage and supplies. The car left the airfield and turned onto a concrete road that led to the mountains a few miles distant. An armored Land Rover with a mounted machine gun fell into the lane behind them.

Baydr looked at his father. "The war has been over these many years, I thought guards would no longer be necessary."

"There are still many bandits in the mountains," his father said.

"Bandits?"

"Yes," his father said. "Those who slip across our borders to steal, rape and kill. There are some who think they are Israeli guerrillas."

"But Israel has no borders near here," Baydr said.

"True," the older man replied. "But they could be agents in their employ. We cannot afford to relax our vigilance."

"Have you ever been bothered by these bandits?" Baydr asked.

"No. We have been fortunate. But we have heard of others who have." Samir smiled. "But let us talk of other pleasant matters. Have you heard that your eldest sister is expecting a child in a matter of weeks?"

The automobiles began to climb into the mountains. After a few minutes Baydr saw the first hint of green on the sides of the road. Cacti gave way to scrub pine, then to flowers, bougainvillea and green grass. His father reached over and pressed the button to let down the windows. The fresh scented air flowed into the car, replacing the stale, cooled air of the machine.

His father took a deep breath. "There are many inventions of man but they cannot duplicate the scent of mountain air."

Baydr nodded. They were climbing rapidly to the crest of the mountain. Their home was on the far side overlooking the sea. He wondered if it was as he remembered it.

The house came into view as they turned at the top of the hill and started down. Baydr, looking from his window, saw the white roofs of the house below him. It was larger than he remembered. More buildings had been added. A large swimming pool had been built at the far end of the property, looking out toward the sea. There was something else he had never seen before. A high wall had been erected all around the complex, and stationed on top of that at approximately fifty-yard intervals were small sentry booths, each manned by a guard with a machine gun.

The house itself was hidden by trees. Baydr turned back to his father. "Are all the homes like this?"

His father nodded. "Some have even more guards. The Prince has more than one hundred men at his summer estate."

Baydr didn't comment. Something had to be wrong if men had to make prisoners of themselves in order to feel safe. The car turned off the road onto the driveway leading to the house. A moment later, they passed the trees that concealed it from the road and came to the giant iron gates in the wall. Slowly the gates, powered by silent electrical motors, began to swing open. Without stopping, the automobiles rolled through. A quarter-mile farther, they stopped in front of the huge white house. A servant ran to open the doors of the car. His father got out first. Baydr followed.

His eyes looked up the giant marble steps that led to the door. It was open. A woman, unveiled but wearing a headcloth and a long, white tob appeared in the doorway.

"Mother!" he cried, running up the steps and taking her in his arms.

Nabila looked up at her son, tears in the corners of her eyes. "Forgive me, my son," she whispered. "But I could no longer wait to see you."

Since it was not a formal occasion and only members of the family were present, they all ate together. On formal occasions the men dined alone, and the women ate afterwards or not at all.

Baydr looked down the table at his sisters. Fatima, three years older than he, her face round and body heavy with child, was beaming as she sat proudly next to her husband. "It will be a boy," she said. "There have been nothing but boys in Salah's family and they all say that I look just like his mother did when she was carrying him."

Her father laughed. "Old wives' tales. Not very scientific but until we do find a way that is more exact, I'm willing to go along with it."

"I will give you your first grandson," Fatima said pointedly, looking at her sister Nawal whose first child had been a girl.

Nawal said nothing. Her husband, Omar, a doctor who worked in his father-in-law's hospital, was also silent.

"Boy or girl," Baydr said, "it will be the will of Allah."

To that they could all agree. Samir rose to his feet. "The Westerners have a custom," he said. "The men retire to another room to enjoy a cigar. I find that very pleasant."

His father led the way to his study. Baydr and his brothers-in-law followed. A servant opened and closed the door behind them. Samir opened a box of cigars on his desk. He took a cigar and sniffed it with satisfaction. "Cuban cigars. They were sent to me from London."

He held out the box. Salah and Omar each took one but Baydr shook his head. He took a package of American cigarettes from his pocket. "I'll stick to these."

Samir smiled. "Even your language is more American than Arabic."

"Not to the Americans," Baydr said. He lit his cigarette and waited while the others lit their cigars.

"What do you think of them?" Samir asked curiously.

"In what way?" Baydr asked.

"They are mostly Jews," Salah said.

Baydr turned to him. "That is not true. In proportion to the whole population they are very few Jews."

"I have been to New York," Salah said. "The city is crawling with Jews. They control everything. The government, the banks."

Baydr looked at his brother-in-law. Salah was a heavy-set, pedantic young man whose father had made a fortune as a money lender and now owned one of the major banks in Beirut. "Then you deal with Jewish banks?" he asked.

An expression of horror crossed Salah's face. "Of course not," he said stiffly. "We deal only with the biggest banks, the Bank of America, First National and Chase."

"They're not Jewish?" Baydr asked. Out of the corner of his eye he caught his father's smile. Samir had already gotten the point.

"No," Salah answered.

"Then the Jews do not control everything in America," Baydr said. "Do they?"

"Fortunately," Salah said. "Not that they wouldn't if they had the opportunity."

"But America is pro-Israel," Samir said.

Baydr nodded. "Yes."

"Why?"

"You have to try to understand the American mentality. They have sympathy for the underdog. And Israel has very successfully played upon that in their propaganda. First against the British, now against us."

"How can we change that?"

"Very simply," Baydr said. "Leave Israel alone. It is only a tiny strip of land in our midst, no bigger than a flea on an elephant's back. What harm can they do us?"

"They will not remain a flea," Salah said. "Refugees from all over Europe are coming in thousands. The scum of Europe. They will not be content with what they have. The Jews always wants it all."

"We do not know that yet," Baydr said. "Perhaps if we welcomed them as brothers and worked with them to develop our lands, rather than opposing them, we would find out differently. A long time ago it was said that a mighty sword can fell an oak tree with one blow but cannot cut a silken scarf floating in the air."

"I'm afraid it is too late for that," Salah said. "The cries of our brothers living under their domination are ringing in our ears."

Baydr shrugged his shoulders. "America does not know that. All they know is that a tiny nation of a million people is living in the midst of an enemy world which surrounds and outnumbers them one hundred to one."

His father nodded solemnly. "There is much thinking to be done. It is a very complex problem."

"It is not complex," Salah said heavily. "Mark my words, in time you will all see what I tell you is true. Then, we will unite to destroy them."

Samir looked at his other son-in-law. "What is your opinion, Omar?"

The young doctor cleared his throat with embarrassment. He was inordinately shy. "I am not political," he said. "So I really do not think of these matters. In the foreign universities of England and France where I studied, there were many professors who were Jews. They were good doctors and good teachers."

"I also," Samir said. He looked at Baydr. "I trust you have made no plans for tomorrow."

"I am home," Baydr said. "What plans do I need to make?"

"Good," Samir said. "Because tomorrow we are to have dinner with his excellency, the Prince Feiyad. He wishes to celebrate your eighteenth birthday."

Baydr was puzzled. His birthday had passed some months before. "Is his excellency here?"

"No," Samir said. "He is in Alayh, enjoying a holiday from his family and duties. We are invited to join him tomorrow."

Baydr knew better than to ask the reason. His father would tell him in his own good time. "It will be my pleasure, Father," he said.

"Good," his father smiled. "Now shall we rejoin your mother and sisters? I know they are waiting eagerly to hear more of your stories about America."

Chapter Seven

Alayh was a tiny village in the mountains thirty miles from Beirut. There was no industry, no trade, no farming. It had only one reason to justify its existence. Pleasure. Both sides of the main street that ran through the center of the village were lined with restaurants and cafes which featured Oriental dancers and singers from all over the Middle East. Western tourists were discouraged and seldom if ever seen here. The clientele were the rich sheiks, the princes and businessmen, who came here to escape the rigid moralities and boredom of their own world.

Here they could indulge in all the things that were not acceptable at home. They could drink the liquor and taste the foods and delights that strict Muslim law forbade them. And perhaps most important was the fact that here they were anonymous. No matter how well one man knew the other, he did not recognize him, or speak to him unless invited to do so.

It was after ten o'clock the next evening that Samir's limousine rolled to a stop in front of the largest cafe on the street. In keeping with his importance, Prince Feiyad had taken over the entire establishment for the night. It would not be proper for him to mix with the casual visitor. He was absolute monarch of a thousand square-mile piece of land bordering on four countries, Iraq, Saudi Arabia, Syria and Jordan. That his land infringed somewhat into each of these countries did not matter because it served a useful purpose. It was to his country that each could come with impunity and in safety to work out disagreements and problems between them. Baydr's grandmother was the sister of Prince Feiyad's father and as cousins to the royal family the Al Fays were the second most important family.

It was to Baydr's father that the Prince had given the rights to all public utilities, The electric and telephone companies were owned by Samir and in return, the family had built schools and hospitals where free care was provided for all who sought it. They had been rich to begin with, but with the grants they had grown even richer almost without effort.

It was a great disappointment to the whole family that the Prince had no male heirs to whom he could pass the throne. He had married a number of times and always performed his duties. And as each wife failed to produce the required heir, he had divorced her. Now, sixty years old, he had long ago decided that if it was the will of Allah that he should have no direct heir, he would see to it that his cousin would provide one for him.

It was for this reason that eighteen years earlier, Samir had made his pilgrimage to Mecca. His prayers had been answered with the birth of Baydr. But, despite his promise, Feiyad had still not designated the boy as his heir. Instead, he had insisted that Baydr be educated in Western ways and live and learn about the Western world. In many ways, Samir had been pleased. His son would become a doctor as he had been and together they would work, side by side.

But the Prince had other ideas. There were others who could become doctors. Baydr had to be educated in more important matters — trade, investment. It was only through increased sophistication in commerce that the country, meaning himself and his family, would continue to grow in wealth and stature. He had the basic

Arab distrust of the Western people he did business with: he felt they regarded him as somehow inferior, almost childlike in his lack of knowledge. And so it was that he decided that Baydr would not go to England to follow in his father's footsteps, but to America, where business was the admired and respected profession.

Samir looked proudly at his son as he stepped from the limousine. Dressed in traditional Arab clothing, the ghutra falling down his neck, the robes clinging to his tall lean frame, he was a handsome figure. The strong chin, prominent nose and blue-black eyes set deeply into high-boned, olive cheeks gave promise of the strength and character of the young man. The Prince would be pleased. Perhaps, now, he would designate Baydr as his heir.

Mentally he begged Allah's forgiveness for his earthly hopes and vanities. It was enough of a miracle that he had brought a son to him in the desert. With that he should be content. Allah's will be done.

He gestured to Baydr, who followed him up the steps into the cafe. The Prince's major-domo was at the door with two armed guards. He recognized Samir. He bowed in the traditional greeting. "As-salaam alaykum."

"Alaykum as-salaam," Samir replied.

"His excellency has been awaiting the arrival of his favorite cousin with great anticipation," the major-domo said. "He has requested that I bring you to him as soon as you arrive. He is in his apartment upstairs."

They followed the major-domo through the empty cafe to the staircase at the rear of the great room. The cafe itself was quiet. The usually busy waiters stood around in clusters gossiping with one another, and near the stage, the orchestra sat smoking and talking. None of the singers or dancers was visible. Nothing would begin until the Prince gave the signal.

The apartments over the cafe were reserved for very special clients and their guests who, after a night of amusement in the cafe, might be too tired to make the journey home or who wished to stay and partake of further pleasures that could be provided by the management. The major-domo paused in front of a door and knocked.

"Who ith it?" a young boy's voice answered.

"The Doctor Al Fay and his son are here to see his excellency," the major-domo replied.

The door was opened by a young boy clothed in silken shirt and trousers. His eyes were heavily made up and his cheeks rouged and his fingernails long and painted. "Pleathe come in," he lisped in English.

Baydr and his father entered the room. The faintly sweet odor of hashish hung in the air. The room was empty. "Pleathe be theated," the boy said, indicating the sofas and chairs. He left them and went into another room.

Baydr and his father looked at each other without speaking.

The boy came back into the room. "Hith exthellenthy will be with you in a moment. Ith there anything I can do for you? A thweet? A refrethment perhapth? We have Englith Whithkey if you prefer."

Samir shook his head. "No, thank you."

The door opened again and Prince Feiyad entered. He was fully dressed in his royal robes, his head covered in white muslin. He crossed the room to his cousin. Samir and Baydr rose and made the traditional obeisance to their monarch.

Feiyad brushed Samir's arms aside with a smile. "Is that a way for cousins to meet after they had not seen each other for a long time?" He put his arms on Samir's shoulders and kissed him on each cheek then turned, still smiling, to Baydr. "And this is the little boy who cried when he went away to school?"

Baydr felt himself flushing. "That was a long time ago, your excellency."

"Not too long," the Prince said and laughed. "I think you were six then."

"He's eighteen now," Samir said. "And a grown man, praise be to Allah."

"Al-hamdu li-llah," the Prince echoed. He looked up at Baydr, who stood a head taller than either of them. "He is tall, your son. Taller than anyone I remember in our family."

"It is the diet, your excellency," Samir said. "The food in America is enriched with many vitamins and minerals. The entire younger generation is growing taller than their parents."

"What miracles your scientists perform," the Prince said.

"The miracles are Allah's," Samir said. "We are nothing but His instruments."

The Prince nodded. "We have much to talk about, my cousin," he said. "But we can do that in the morning. Tonight we must enjoy the pleasure of our reunion and each other's company." He clapped his hands, "I have had a suite made ready for you so that you may freshen yourselves after your journey. At midnight we will gather in the cafe below, where a feast has been prepared for us."

Samir bowed. "We are most grateful for the kindness of your hospitality."

The young boy appeared again. "Show my cousins to their apartments," the Prince commanded.

The boy bowed. "It will be my pleathure, your exthellenthy."

Baydr's room was separated from his father's by a large living room. He left his father and went into his bedroom which was luxuriously furnished in rich silks and satins. The couches were covered with velour cushions. No sooner than he had entered, a soft knock came at the door. "Come in," he called.

A young maidservant came into the room. She bowed her head respectfully. "May I be of service to the master?" she asked in a soft voice, her eyes properly averted.

"There is nothing I can think of."

"Perhaps I can draw the master a hot bath so that he may wash away the fatigue of his journey?" she suggested.

"That would be nice," he said.

Baydr looked after her thoughtfully. Now he knew he was home. Service was not like this in America.

The noise of the kanoon and the drums flooded the cafe. On the small stage a dancer whirled, her multicolored scarves floating around her, the silver metal of her brassiere reflecting the sparkling lights. At a horseshoe-shaped table at the front of the stage, the Prince's party watched intently.

The Prince was seated at the center of the table, Samir in the place of honor on his right, Baydr on his left. Behind the Prince, on small stools, were several young boys, all wearing the same elaborate make-up as the young boy who had greeted them in the Prince's suite. Standing behind them was the major-domo, who supervised the service of the waiters and other members of the staff. There were bottles of champagne in buckets near each guest and their glasses were constantly filled. The table was covered with more than fifty varieties of hors d'oeuvres and delicacies of the region. The guests ate with their fingers, and a servant delicately wiped their hands after each mouthful with a fresh warm damp cloth. At the door and against the wall stood a dozen of Feiyad's personal guard, who never took their eyes from the Prince.

The music reached a crescendo and the dancer sank to her knees in finale. The Prince led the applause. At a gesture from him, the waiters snatched bottles of champagne from their buckets and kneeling before the stage popped the corks from bottle after bottle, shooting them high over the kneeling dancer's head. Idly, the Prince picked up a bank note from a pile in front of him and, crumpling it in his hand, threw it onto the stage in front of the girl.

With a fluid graceful motion, the dancer picked up the money and placed it in her belt just below her navel. She bowed again and smiling seductively backed off the stage.

The Prince signaled the major-domo and whispered in his ear. The major-domo nodded. He turned and made a gesture to the boys sitting behind the Prince, then signaled the orchestra to begin again.

At the first sound of the music, four girls came on the stage and began their dance. Gradually, the lights went down until the room was in almost total darkness, with the exception of tiny blue spots on the dancers. As the music grew wilder, the spotlight would lose a dancer, then find her moving more excitingly than ever before. The dance lasted more than fifteen minutes, and when it was finished, the girls seemed to be in a frenzy, finally falling to the floor as the stage went completely dark.

For a moment there was silence, then for the first time the Prince began to applaud enthusiastically. Slowly the lights came up. The dancers still prostrate on the floor, began to rise to their feet. Baydr stared unbelievingly. The dancers on the stage were not the girls who had begun the dance. Instead, their places had been taken by the boys who had been seated behind the Prince.

This time the Prince didn't bother to crumple the bank notes. He threw the money on the stage in handfuls while the champagne corks popped wildly.

Baydr glanced at his father. Samir's face was impassive. He wondered what his father thought of the evening. Those were one-hundred-pound notes that the Prince was so carelessly throwing at the dancers. More money than the average workman earned in a year.

The Prince looked at Baydr and spoke in French. "C'est beau, c'est magnifique, non?" Baydr met his eyes. They were watchful and appraising. "Oui." He hesitated for a moment. "C'est tout pédéraste?"

The Prince nodded. "Vous aimez? Choisissez quelqu'un pour votre plaisir."

Baydr still looked into the older man's eyes. He shook his head. "Merci, non. Pas pour moi. Je préfère les femmes."

The Prince laughed aloud and turned to Samir. "Your son is lovely, and he has sound taste," he said. "He is also very American."

Samir looked at his son and smiled proudly. Somehow Baydr knew that he had passed the Prince's first test.

It was five o'clock in the morning and dawn was breaking in the mountains when Baydr bid his father good night and went into the bedroom. The drapes were drawn and the room was dark. He reached for the light switch.

A hand stopped his arm. The woman's voice was soft and held the faintest Egyptian accent. "We will have candles, your excellency."

The faint scent of musk came to his nostrils as she moved away from him. He stood very still in the darkness, his eyes trying to make her out, but he could see nothing until the match scratched and glowed. Then her dark, heavy-lashed eyes smiled at him and she turned to the candle.

The soft yellow light spilled into the room. He recognized the woman as one of the dancers who had performed earlier that evening. The only portion of her costume that had been changed was her brassiere. Her breasts were no longer contained by the silver metal plate. Instead, they were covered by a diaphanous silken scarf through which the dark areola of her nipples could clearly be seen. She smiled again at him. "I have had a warm bath prepared in case his excellency should be weary."

He didn't answer.

She clapped her hands. Two more women came from the corners of the room where they had been standing in the shadows. They wore even less costume than the first. Only the thinnest of veils covered their breasts and fell from their hips around their legs. As they moved toward Baydr, they crossed in front of the light, and he could clearly see the shape of their nude bodies and their carefully depilitated hair-free mounds. Only their lower faces were hidden by the traditional Muslim veil.

The first woman clapped her hands again and still another woman came from a far corner. She turned on a record player and the soft sound of music began to come into the room. She began to sway gently to the rhythm.

The two women took his hand and led him toward the bed. Their touch was light and swift as they undressed him. He still hadn't spoken.

The first woman lit a cigarette and gave it to him. He took a drag. The faintly sweet pungent odor of hashish floated into his nostrils, and he felt a gentle rush of warmth. He took another deep puff and gave back the cigarette.

He looked at her. "What is your name?"

"Nadia, your excellency," she said, making the gesture of obeisance.

He smiled at her, feeling the surge of sex rising within him. He stretched out on the bed. "Must we bathe?" he asked.

The woman laughed. "Whatever your excellency desires."

He looked around at them. He could feel the hashish in his loins. He looked down at his phallus, long and lean and hard against his belly, then back at the first woman.

"I desire all of you," he said.

Chapter Eight

He awoke with the sunlight spilling into the room and Jabir standing next to his bed, with a cup of hot steaming Turkish coffee. He took a sip. It scalded his mouth. "What time is it?" he asked.

"It is noon, master," the servant said.

He looked around the room. He could not remember when the girl had gone. His last memory of them was a wild tangle of bodies and warmth. He had been lying on his side. One of the girls had anointed his entire body with oil and they were all licking at him with their tongues, at his anus, his scrotum, his nipples, his phallus, his belly until the sensation had become so exquisite that the juice burst from him in a final exhausting geyser. Then he had fallen asleep.

He took another sip of the scalding coffee and shook his head. "Is my father awake?" "Yes, master. He is with the Prince and they await you for breakfast."

He took another gulp of the coffee and got out of bed. "Tell them I'll grab a shower and be right there."

He let the water run cold, then hot, then cold again. In a moment he was wide awake. He ran his fingers quickly over his chin and decided that he could shave later. When he came out of the bathroom, Jabir had laid out shirt and slacks for him.

The Prince and his father were still seated at the breakfast table when he came into their room. The major-domo was just clearing away the breakfast dishes.

Baydr kissed his father, then the Prince's hand. At the Emir's gesture he sat down. "Would you like something to eat?" the Prince asked politely.

"No, thank you," Baydr said. It would have been impolite for him to eat after they had finished.

"Some coffee then," the Prince said.

"Thank you," Baydr nodded.

The major-domo hurried to fill his cup. Baydr tasted it. It was thick and sweet. He waited quietly, respectfully. Though the shades were drawn so that the sunlight could not enter the room, the Prince still wore dark sunglasses, behind which his eyes could not be seen. He waited until Baydr put down his cup. "Your father and I have been discussing your future."

Baydr bowed his head. "I am your servant."

The Prince smiled. "First, you are my cousin, my blood."

Baydr didn't speak. He was not expected to say anything.

"The world is changing rapidly," the Prince said. "Many things have happened since your birth. Our plans must change accordingly." He clapped his hands sharply.

The major-domo withdrew from the room, silently closing the door behind him. They were alone in the room.

The Prince waited for a moment. His voice dropped almost to a whisper. "You know that I have always looked upon you as my heir and believed that someday you would take my place as ruler of our country."

Baydr glanced at his father. Samir's face was expressionless. He turned back to the Prince.

"But times have changed," the Emir said. "There are other, more important matters that confront us. All through the Middle East the tide of the future flows from beneath the sands of the desert, promising riches such as we have never envisioned. The source of this wealth is oil. The lifeblood of the modern industrialized Western world. And our little country sits upon some of the greatest pools of oil ever known to man."

He paused for breath, raising his coffee cup to his lips to taste the hot sweet mixture. "I have this past month concluded an agreement with several American, British and European companies to develop this resource. For exploration rights, they have agreed to pay us ten million dollars. If oil is discovered, they will pay us additional sums for each operating well and a royalty on the oil that is exported. They have also committed themselves to build refineries and help develop the country. All of this has great promise but I am still not at ease."

"I don't understand," Baydr said. But he did. It was for this reason that he had been sent to learn the ways of the Western World.

"I think you do," the Emir said shrewdly. "But let me continue in my own way. Though the world has renounced imperialism and colonization as a way of life, there are other ways to enslave a country and its people. By making them economically dependent. I do not intend to let the West do that to us, but it suits my plan to let them pay for our progress."

Baydr nodded. He began to feel new respect for the Prince. Behind all the strange and peculiar ways lurked a man of thought. "How can I be of help?" he asked. "I am yours to command."

The Prince looked at Samir and nodded approvingly. Samir smiled. The Prince turned back to Baydr. "I have a more important task for you than to succeed me. I want a man who can walk in the Western world and take these riches they grudgingly give to us and use them in the Western way to acquire even more riches. And if you will undertake this task for which you have been trained and will be trained even further, I promise you that your first-born son will become my heir and the next Prince."

"I need no promise from my sovereign prince," Baydr said. "I will take my joy in carrying out his wishes."

The Emir rose to his feet and embraced Baydr. "My own son could not do more for me."

"I thank your excellency for your trust. My only prayer is that Allah sees fit in His wisdom to make me worthy of it."

"It will be as Allah wills," the Prince said. He returned to his seat. "You will return to America to school. Only now your education will be in the hands of certain men recommended to me by the American oil companies. You will not take the ordinary schooling. Your education will be specialized and completed within a three-year period."

Baydr nodded. "I understand."

"And now there is just one further matter to be arranged," the Prince said. "Your marriage."

Baydr stared at him in surprise. This was something he had not expected. "My marriage?" he echoed.

The Prince smiled. "You need not be surprised. From the reports I have had about last night, you should provide me with many sons."

Baydr was silent.

"Your father and I have been discussing the matter very carefully and after a great deal of thought have selected a bride for you of whom you can be very proud. She is young and beautiful and comes of one of the best families in Lebanon. Her name is Maryam Riad, daughter of Mohammed Riad, the famous banker."

"I know the girl," his father said hastily. "She is indeed very beautiful. And very devout."

Baydr looked at his father. "How old is she?"

"Sixteen," Samir answered. "Though she has never been abroad, she is very well educated. At the present time she is attending the American Girls College in Beirut."

"Sixteen is young for marriage," Baydr said.

The Emir began to laugh. "I have chosen wisely. Perhaps in America a maiden of sixteen is young. In our lands she is just ripe."

Baydr was silent in the car on the drive back to Beirut. It wasn't until they were at the outskirts of the city that Samir spoke to him. "What is it, my son?"

"Nothing, Father."

"Are you disappointed that you are not to be the Prince's heir?"

"No."

"Then is it the thought of your impending marriage?"

Baydr hesitated. "I don't even know the girl. I never heard of her before this afternoon."

Samir looked at him. "I think I understand. You wonder why we go to all the trouble to educate you in the Western ways and then revert to our own in arranging your marriage. Is that it?"

"I guess that's it. In America, at least, you get to meet the girl first and find out if you like each other."

"That happens here too, son," Samir said quietly. "But we are not ordinary folk. We have responsibilities that go beyond our own personal feelings."

"But you and Mother knew each other before you were married. You practically grew up together."

Samir smiled. "That's true. But our marriage had been arranged while we were still children. Somehow we knew that and it brought us closer together."

"Would you have married someone else if it had been arranged? Knowing how you felt about Mother?"

Samir thought for a moment, then he nodded. "Yes. I might not have liked it but I would have had no choice. One must do what one must do. It is the will of Allah."

Baydr looked at his father, and sighed. The will of Allah. That covered it all. Man himself had very few options. "I would like to meet the girl," he said.

"It is already arranged," Samir replied. "Her family has been invited to spend the weekend with us in the mountains. They will arrive the day after tomorrow."

A sudden thought crossed Baydr's mind. "You have known about this for a long time?"

"Not long," his father answered. "The Prince just told me of his decision last week."

"Does mother know?"

"Yes."

"Did she approve?"

"Of the marriage? Yes."

"You seem to hesitate," Baydr said.

"Your mother had grand dreams of you becoming the prince." Samir laughed. "Women aren't always practical."

"And you Father, were you disappointed too?"

Samir looked into his son's eyes. "No." He thought back to the night his son was born. "You always were and always will be my prince."

Chapter Nine

Maryam Riad, like most Lebanese girls, was small, no more than five feet tall, with large dark eyes. Her black hair was worn high on her head in the latest Paris fashion to give an illusion of greater height. Her skin was pale olive and she had a tendency toward plumpness, which she continually fought by dieting, much to the despair of her parents, who preferred the roundness traditional of the Arab woman. She spoke French fluently and English uncomfortably, hated going to the American Girls College and made a point of continually letting her parents know that she felt she should have gone to Swiss or French schools like the children of other well-to-do families.

To this complaint her father had one answer. Girls had no need of education because after they were married they had only to run a house and bear children. Bitterly, Maryam had watched her brothers go away to school while she herself remained at home without ever being allowed the freedom that many of her friends who attended the school enjoyed. She had to be home immediately after classes, was never allowed dates and could not go out unless chaperoned under circumstances approved by her father.

In the limousine with her parents on the way to Badyr's home, her father looked at her with satisfaction.

"Now, my daughter," he said in his heavy manner, "perhaps you understand why your parents looked after you the way we did. Perhaps now you will appreciate us more."

She turned from the window. "Yes, Father," she said obediently.

"Do you think you would have been chosen for this marriage by the Prince himself if you had been away in foreign schools?" he asked. "No," he said, answering his own question. "What he wanted was a true Arab woman, not one who had been tainted by foreign influences."

She glanced at her mother, who was silent. Her mother never spoke when her father was near. "Yes, Father," she said again.

"Now I want you to remember your manners," her father said. "Above all, be respectful and decorous. I want none of the frivolous ways that you learned from friends at the college."

"Yes, Father," she said wearily for the third time.

"This marriage will be the most important in the country," her father said. "Everyone knows that your first son will become heir to the Prince."

She glanced at her father out of the corner of her eyes. "But what if I have nothing but girls?"

Her father was shocked. "You will have sons!" he shouted, as if saying it would make it so. "Do you hear me? You will have sons!"

"If it pleases Allah," she said with a secret smile.

"His will be done," her mother said automatically.

"It is the will of Allah," her father said with conviction. "Why else would He have arranged this marriage?"

Maryam was very impressed by what she saw as the car drove through the gates of the vast estate. She had known wealth, but nothing like this. Compared with Samir, her father, who was one of the richest men in Beirut, was just comfortable. Here there were endless servants and guards. It was like another world.

In honor of the occasion, the family wore traditional clothing but in their suitcases were the latest Paris clothes, into which they would change for the grand dinner that evening.

"Adjust your veil," her mother said as the car came to a stop and a servant advanced to open the door.

Quickly, Maryam covered her face so that only her eyes were visible. Looking up the steps she saw Dr. Al Fay descending toward them. A half-step behind him was Baydr. Her breath caught in her throat. They, too, wore traditional clothing and there was something in her fiancé's bearing that bespoke a desert heritage. Only a true sheik could look like that.

Her father got out of the car. Samir advanced toward him, arms outstretched. "Ahlan, Ahlan."

"Ahlan fikum.' The two men embraced, kissing the other on each cheek.

Samir turned and introduced his son. Baydr made the gesture of obeisance and respect, bidding his future father-in-law welcome. Then he held out his hand, Western fashion.

They shook hands and turned back to the car. Mrs. Riad got out of the car and was greeted by Samir. A moment later Maryam descended. Her father held out his hand toward her and led her to the doctor. "You remember Dr. Al Fay?"

She glanced up for a moment, then averted her eyes as was proper. She nodded and made the gesture of obeisance.

Samir took her hand. "My child," he said. "Welcome. May our home forever be your home."

"Thank you," she whispered. "May it be the will of Allah."

Samir gestured and Baydr came forward. Decorously, she kept her eyes down so that all she saw were the tips of his shoes under the flowing jellaba. "Máryam," he said. "May I present my son, Baydr, your future husband?"

She made the gesture of obeisance before looking up, then she raised her head. For a moment, she was startled. No one had ever told her that his eyes were blue. Then her heart began to beat and she could feel the blush creeping up under her veil. There were so many things that no one had ever told her about him. He was so tall. And so handsome. Her eyes fell and she could hardly hear his words of welcome, the sound of her heart was pounding so strongly in her ears. For the first time in her life she was truly grateful that her parents had not sent her abroad to school. She was hopelessly in love.

Dinner was a formal affair. Samir had ordered the French chef to come from their house in Beirut to prepare it. Instead of the usual Lebanese mezzeh, the hors d'oeuvers were pâté de foie gras and grosgrain Iranian caviar. Rather than the customary mouloukhieh, rabbit and rice, the entrées were coq au vin and gigot, but the dessert was typical — baklava in more than twenty of its honey-sweet variations.

Champagne was served throughout the meal — the single exception to Muslim law. The women in their long Paris gowns and the men in dinner jackets carried on casual, polite conversation as the two families became acquainted.

As the meal drew to its close, Mr. Riad rose to his feet. "If I may be permitted," he said in his most important manner, "I would like to propose a toast to our most gracious host, the good doctor Al Fay. May Allah shower His blessings upon him and his family."

He raised his glass and took a sip of the champagne. "And another toast," he said quickly, still holding his glass. He smiled down the table at Baydr. "To my future son-in-law, whom I already think of as my son, and to my daughter. May Allah bless their union with many sons."

Maryam felt herself blushing at the sound of the warm laughter. She did not dare look across the table at Baydr. Her father was speaking again.

"And though the question of dowry never arose between our families, I would not like to lose sight of this ancient and honored custom. For in what other manner can a man show his affection for his daughter and appreciation of her husband?"

Samir rose protestingly. "No, Mohammed, the gift of your daughter is riches enough."

"My dear doctor." The banker smiled, overriding him. "Would you deny me this simple pleasure?"

"Of course not," Samir returned to his chair.

"My son," Riad said, turning to Baydr. "On the day of your wedding, an account will be opened in your name at my bank in Beirut in the amount of one million pounds Lebanese. It will be yours to do with what you wish."

Baydr glanced across the table at Maryam before he rose to thank his father-in-law. Her face was flushed and she did not look up from the table. He turned to the banker. "My honored father," he said slowly, "may Allah be witness to your generosity and kindness. There is only one thing more that I ask and that is that you give me guidance so that I may make wise use of your great gift."

"You shall have it," Mohammed said quickly. He was pleased. It was working as he had planned. He was sure that his account was only the beginning of the business his bank would be doing with the Al Fay family.

Samir rose to his feet. Dinner was over. He looked at Baydr. "It would be nice if you showed your fiancée the gardens," he said, "while we go into the library to relax."

Baydr nodded, went around the table and held Maryam's chair as she rose. He smiled at her. "They seem to want to get rid of us."

She nodded. He took her arm and they started for the garden doors.

As they went through the doors, Mrs. Riad turned to Nabila. "Don't they make a beautiful couple?" she asked.

They had reached the pool at the far end of the garden before either of them said a word. Then they both began speaking almost at the same time.

Maryam stopped, "I'm sorry."

"It's my fault," Baydr said quickly. "What was it you wanted to say?"

"Nothing important," she said. "What was it you wanted to say?"

They laughed, each a little embarrassed for the other. He looked down at her. "I was wondering how you felt. I mean about our getting married?"

Her eyes fell. She didn't answer.

"You don't have to answer that," he said quickly. "It wasn't fair of me. You don't have much choice, do you?"

Her eyes came up. "Do you?"

It was his turn not to answer. His fished in his jacket pocket and came out with a packet of cigarettes. He held them toward her. "Do you smoke?"

She shook her head.

He lit one and drew a deep breath. He let the smoke out slowly.

"It's kind of old-fashioned, isn't it?"

"Yes."

"In America I almost forgot how we do things."

"I always wanted to go abroad," she said. "But my father wouldn't let me. Did you like it?"

"Yes," he answered. "People are simpler there. Most of the time you know exactly what they are thinking."

She hesitated. "Did you have a girl there?"

"Not one special girl. But we had lots of dates. And you?"

"My father is very strict. I wasn't allowed out much. There was even a fight when I wanted to go to the college."

They fell silent again. He looked at the glowing tip of his cigarette. This time it was she who spoke first. "You have blue eyes."

"Yes," he said. "My father says it goes all the way back to the holy wars. Ever since then blue eyes show up in the family now and then."

She turned away and looked out to the sea. Her voice was very low. "I must be a great disappointment to you after all the Western girls you have known."

"That's not true," he said quickly. "I could never take them seriously. They're too empty-headed. Not like us."

"Still they're very beautiful. They're tall."

"Maryam," he said.

She turned toward him.

"You're very beautiful too."

"I am?" she asked. "Do you really think so?"

"I think so." He reached for her hand. "Would you still like to go abroad?"

"Yes."

He smiled. "Then we'll go to Europe on our honeymoon."

And that is what they did. Married, at the end of July, they spent the month of August traveling the Continent. In September when Baydr brought Maryam back to Beirut and left her to return to school in America, she was already pregnant.

Chapter Ten

Dancing had resumed on the upper deck when the guests wandered back after dinner. As usual, Baydr had disappeared as soon as the food was served. It was his habit to hold his meetings while everyone was eating so that by the time they were finished he would come out again and join the party. In that fashion he would not be missed.

Jordana joined one of the tables and seated herself so that she could watch for Baydr's reappearance in the salon. He was still strange to her, even after nine years of marriage. There was something about him she would never understand. At times it seemed as if he were completely unaware of her and then, suddenly, out of nowhere, he would bring her up short and she would realize that there was very little about her that he was not aware of.

Like tonight. She had seen the Van Cleef box on the pillow but for some perverse reason which even she did not fully understand, she had decided not to acknowledge it. Perhaps it was just that he could not excuse his comings and goings with another gift. Unlike American men she had known, she could not manipulate him with guilt. He was the way he was and there was nothing anyone could do about it. His reaction was direct and simple. The savage roared out of the darkness within him.

It was her own reaction that surprised her. There was something comforting in his violence. It was as if she had been a child provoking a parent into punishment so that she could be reassured of his love. Her own guilts were clarified and she began to think of ways to win back his pleasure.

No sooner had the door slammed behind him than she rose and looked in the mirror. His handprint was turning bright on her cheek. She pressed the button for her secretary and asked for an ice pack, then sat in her room for over an hour holding the cold pack to her face until the swelling was gone.

It was then that she decided on her costume. She would be a Muslim wife if that was what he wanted. A wife, a houri, a slave. Wasn't that what Allah promised when they entered the gates of paradise?

She raised a glass of champagne to her lips as she watched the salon doors. Baydr had not yet come out.

"Jordana, darling," a voice gushed in her ear. "Your dance was so beautiful."

She turned to the speaker, recognizing the voice. "Mara," she said, holding up her cheek for the customary kiss. "You're more than kind."

"No, darling," the Princess said quickly. "It's true. It was the most érotique thing I have ever seen. Had I been a man I would have raped you then and there." She laughed and added, "As a matter of fact I still might."

Jordana laughed with her. "That's the greatest compliment of all, Mara."

The Princess bent her head closer to Jordana's ear. "What you did was unbelievable. Did you notice the young man I brought with me? He went out of his mind. I thought he would burst his trousers."

Jordana looked at her. It was not like Mara to be so effusive. "Really, darling?"

"Really," Mara answered. "And he's dying to meet you. Do you have a moment?"

Over the Princess's shoulder, Jordana saw Carriage coming out of the salon with Mr. Yasfir. "Not just now," she answered. "Baydr should be coming out soon."

Yasfir made his way directly to her. "Madame Al Fay." He bowed.

"Mr. Yasfir," she said formally.

"I wish to express my thanks for a gracious evening and present my apologies for leaving so soon but I have pressing affairs ashore."

She held out her hand. "I'm sorry too."

He kissed her hand.

"Perhaps next time we will have the opportunity to become better acquainted," she said.

"I will look forward to that," he said. "Bon soir, madame."

As Yasfir made his way down the deck to the ladder that led to the speedboat which would take him back to shore, she saw Carriage go over to Youssef. Youssef and the American film director Michael Vincent followed Carriage into the salon and down the corridor leading to Baydr's study.

"Another meeting?" Mara asked.

Jordana shrugged silently and raised her champagne. The Princess slipped into the chair beside her.

"One of my husbands was like that. I forget which one. Always meetings. It was so boring, I divorced him."

Jordana smiled at her. "Baydr may be many things but he is not boring."

"I did not say he was. But some husbands do not realize there are other things in life besides business."

Jordana did not answer. She sipped at her champagne. Suddenly she was down. Nothing seemed to work for them anymore.

"Come, darling," the Princess urged. "Meet my young man. It will make him happy and may amuse you for a few minutes."

"Where is he?"

"Over there. The tall blond one standing near the steps."

Jordana glanced at him. "He seems young."

The Princess laughed. "He is young, darling. Twenty-five and with the staying powers of an ox. I have not known a man like him since Rubi was in his prime."

"Gigolo?" Jordana asked.

"Of course, darling," Mara said. "Aren't all the beautiful young men? But that makes life simpler. When you get tired of them. Give them a few francs and they go away. No complications."

"Tired of him already? Is that why you're giving him away?"

Mara laughed. "No, darling. It's just that he exhausts me. I can't keep up with him. He keeps sticking his big beautiful cock at me and I'm not as young as I used to be. I'm exhausted."

"At least you're honest."

Mara's voice was hurt. "I'm always honest. Now will you meet him?"

Jordana glanced toward the salon. Carriage was coming back alone. Youssef and Vincent had remained with Baydr. She shrugged her shoulders. "All right," she said, "Bring him over."

Baydr handed the Scotch and water to Vincent and gestured him to a seat. Youssef retired discreetly to a corner of the room as Baydr sat down opposite the American.

"I have been an admirer of your work for a long time, Mr. Vincent," Baydr said.

"Thank you, Mr. Al Fay. I'm truly flattered."

"I'm sure I'm not alone," Baydr said, and decided to come right to the point. After all the man was American and he didn't have to beat around the bush. "That is why I decided to ask you if you would be interested in doing a film based on the life of the Prophet. Have you ever thought about it?"

The director pulled at his drink. "Honestly, Mr. Al Fay, I never have."

"Any particular reason, Mr. Vincent?"

Vincent shook his head. "It just never occurred to me. Maybe it's because we Americans know very little about Muhammad."

"But there are more than four hundred million people who do," Baydr said.

Vincent nodded. "I know that now. Mr. Ziad very carefully explained that to me. He also gave me several biographies of the Prophet and I must admit that I was fascinated with the idea."

"Do you think there is a film there?"

"I do, a very good film."

"One that could be successful in the Western world? One that could help them understand that we have a civilization founded on morality much like their own?"

"Successful? I don't know. There will be problems in exhibition," the director answered. "In terms of understanding, I would say, yes. Conditional, of course, on the film being shown."

Baydr nodded. "I understand that. But suppose that were possible. What is the first step we would have to take to get the film made?"

"All films begin with a script."

"You've written the scripts for your other films. Would you consider writing this one?"

"I would if I knew enough, but I'm afraid I lack knowledge."

"If you could obtain the help you need, would you then consider it?"

"If I were sure that when I was finished with the script a picture would be made."

"And if I guarantee that the picture will be made?"

Vincent looked at Baydr and took a deep breath. If he said yes and the picture were abandoned, he would be finished in the industry. The Jews would see to that.

But if it were made, and it was good, they would even play it in their theaters. They didn't care what the film was if it brought money into the box office. "I'm expensive," he said. "I don't come cheap."

"I already know that, Mr. Vincent. Would a fee of one million dollars plus a share in the profits of the picture be too little?"

The music that came through the loudspeakers was slow and romantic and the floor was crowded as Jacques took the glass of champagne from her hand, put it down and led her onto the floor. He smiled down at her. "I have waited a long time for just the right music so that I could ask you to dance."

Jordana felt the champagne buzzing in her head. She smiled back at him. "How nice."

He pulled her close to him. "You Americans. Is that all you can say? 'How nice'."

She looked up into his face. "American? I'm not American. Can't you tell from my dress?"

"Don't think," he said. "Just dance." He moved her head against his shoulder and with his other hand in the small of her back pressed her hips tightly against him. He moved very slowly in time with the music, allowing her to feel his growing erection.

After a moment, he looked down at her. Her eyes were closed. He let the hand that held her drop to his side, then moving toward the railing where no one could see what they were doing, he began to rub her hand against his rock-like shaft. "I have buttons on my trousers," he whispered. "Not zips. Open them."

She stared up at him, her eyes wide. "You're crazy!" she whispered. "There are people watching!"

"No one can see!" he whispered fiercely. "We have our backs to them. I have already masturbated twice since your dance. This time I must have you touch me!"

Still looking into his eyes, her fingers found the buttons and opened them. He wore no undershorts and his phallus leaped out into her hand. He pressed her head against his chest so that she would have to look down at him. "Pull it!" he commanded.

The palm of her hand covered no more than one-third of its length. In the dim lights she could see the glistening red glans bursting from the foreskin. She felt the moisture fill her palm.

"Harder!" he said.

She no longer heard the music. The only rhythm was that of her hand moving back and forth, back and forth over the length of him.

"Now!" he whispered. "Through the railing into the sea!" He let it come.

Staring down, she could see the spurts of semen as they shot from his shuddering penis. Then it was over. She looked up into his face.

"Thank you," he said, smiling. He took the handkerchief from his breast pocket. "Dry your hands."

She took the handkerchief and rubbed it against her palm, then gave it back to him.

He shook his head. "Dry me too."

She wiped him and he slipped himself back into his trousers. "You can throw the handkerchief away," he said.

The handkerchief fell toward the sea and they moved from the railing back onto the crowded dance floor. "I must see you again," he whispered. "Where can I call you?"

"You can't call me. I will call you."

"I'm at the Martinez. You will call? You promise?"

She nodded. The music stopped just as she saw Baydr followed by Youssef and the American director to the top of the stairs. "My husband," she whispered. She began to leave him but he held onto her hand.

"Tomorrow?" he whispered.

"Yes!" She pulled her hand free and made her way across the floor toward Baydr. Her face was flushed and she felt as high as if she had just finished a joint of hash.

"Darling!" she exclaimed. "What a lovely birthday party. How can I ever thank you enough?"

Chapter Eleven

It was past midnight and Leila was getting bored with sitting in her room. She stood at the window looking out at the Croisette. The crowds were still milling back and forth in he warm night. The lights on the billboards on the center islands were still advertising the films that were to be shown during the coming festival and there was a bright, gay feeling in the air.

She turned from the window. She had had enough. She had to get out for a walk or she would go crazy. She picked up her denim jacket and her key and went out into the hall. She put on her jacket while waiting for the elevator and when she emerged from the building she looked much like the other young women wandering the night in their jeans and shirts.

She stared down toward the Carlton, stopped and bought an ice cream on the corner of the Rue du Canada, then crossed the street to the beach side, where the crowds were less. Opposite the Carlton, she sat down on the slanting concrete railing along the esplanade and watched the people entering and leaving the hotel.

She finished the ice cream, ate the sugar sweet cone down to the last tiny fragment and then licked her fingers clean. She heard the noise of a motor and turned around to look.

A big Riva was pulling up to the Carlton dock. It was empty except for two uniformed sailors in white T-shirts and duck trousers. One leaped up on the dock and tied the line to a small stanchion. A moment later the other sailor climbed up beside him, then both stood idly smoking and talking.

She looked past the speedboat. Her father's yacht was anchored several hundred yards out in the bay; the party lights across the upper deck twinkled in the night.

The faint sound of music drifted toward the shore. She took out a cigarette and lit it.

She glanced back at the hotel. Nothing was happening there. She dragged on the cigarette. A small car going by on the Croisette slowed down, then stopped opposite her. The driver leaned across the seat, rolled the window down and yelled something at her.

She didn't hear what he said but she knew what he wanted. Contemptuously, she shook her head and, getting to her feet, turned her back on him. The driver hooted his horn in reply and drove off with a clashing of gears.

Impulsively she started down the steps to the beach and walked out on the jetty. Automatically, the sailors began to come to attention, but when they saw her, they relaxed and continued smoking. Their eyes watched her as she approached.

She halted on the upper portion of the pier and looked down at them. She didn't speak.

"Bon soir," the taller sailor called to her.

"Bon soir," she replied. She studied the Riva. It was the big one, elaborately furnished with radio telephone and stereo tape deck. There was no doubt in her mind that it belonged to her father. He was into all the American toys.

"No business tonight?" the shorter sailor asked slyly in French.

She ignored him.

The taller one laughed. "Come down here," he said. "We'll pay you ten francs each for a quickie."

She stared at him. "What's the matter?" she asked tauntingly, gesturing toward the yacht. "The girls out there too expensive for you?"

The taller sailor was undaunted. "Twenty francs each. That's our top offer."

She smiled at him. "I'll give it to you for free if you take me out there."

The two sailors looked at each other then at her. "We can't do that," the taller one said.

"Afraid you'll lose your jobs?" she taunted. "What's going on out there that's so important?"

"It's the birthday of the wife of our patron, the Sheik Al Fay," the smaller one said.

Teasingly, she undid the buttons of her denim jacket and let it fall open. She put her hands under her full breasts and held them out so that they could see them. "Regardez ces tétons," she said. "How would you like one of these beauties in your mouth?"

They shook their heads almost sadly. "Twenty-five francs," the taller one said finally.

"Sorry," she said. Quickly she did up the buttons. She began to turn away. "You had your chance."

"Tomorrow," the tall one called after her. "Come to the old port. We'll take you out then."

"Tomorrow I won't be here."

"Wait!" the shorter one called. He said something quickly to the other that she could not hear, then turned back to her. "Okay. Out there and once around the yacht, then back. Agreed?"

"Agreed." She climbed down to the boarding jetty while the taller sailor jumped into the speedboat. The roar of the engine filled the night. The shorter sailor held out his hand to help her down into the boat. She stepped in without his assistance, and went to the back and sat down.

The shorter sailor cast off the line and stepped down into the moving speedboat. He turned to her. "Better come forward. You'll get soaked with spray back there."

She smiled up at him. "I don't care," she said. "I love the water."

As the Riva picked up speed he came and sat beside her. He reached over and undid the two buttons on her blouse. A calloused hand cupped her breast roughly. "Magnifique," he said. "Epatant."

"What's your hurry?" she asked. "There's plenty of time."

He bent forward and placed a greedy mouth on her nipple. His teeth were rough against her skin. She pushed him away. "Wait," she said angrily. "When the ride is finished."

He stared at her, his face flushed.

She smiled sweetly at him. "I won't cheat you, don't worry." She took off her jacket and handed it to him. "You can hold that as collateral."

He stood there stupidly holding the jacket and looking at her. "What kind of a game are you playing?"

The radio telephone buzzed before she could answer. The taller sailor picked it up. A voice crackled angrily. He put it down and looked back at them as he turned the boat in a wide arc. "We have to go back to the dock," he said. "The captain is pissed at us. There are people waiting there to come aboard."

"Damn!" the shorter sailor said. He gave the jacket back to her. "Put it on."

"I told you we shouldn't have done it," the taller sailor said.

"Merde!" the shorter sailor snapped.

Silently, Leila buttoned her jacket. She looked at the dock where some people were standing, dressed in elaborate evening clothes. The sailor cut the engine and the boat drifted in toward the dock.

Smartly, the little sailor, holding the line in his hand, leaped to the dock and fastened it. The taller sailor remained in the boat.

There were two men and two women. They stared curiously at her as she got out of the speedboat but didn't speak. She climbed to the upper portion of the pier before she turned around. The smaller sailor was helping the ladies down into the Riva with exaggerated solicitude. Suddenly he looked up at her.

"C'est la vie," she called down to him with a smile.

The men were already in the speedboat and it began to move away slowly. The smaller sailor leaped into the boat and turned back to her. Then he laughed and held up his hands in a typically Gallic gesture of helplessness.

Leila started down the pier to the beach when he suddenly appeared out of the shadows under the cabanas. "What's the matter with you?" he shouted. "Have you lost your mind? You could have given everything away!"

She was startled. "I didn't see you come from the boat."

"When I got to the apartment and saw you weren't there," Ali Yasfir said, "I almost went crazy. You know you weren't supposed to leave the rooms."

"I was bored," she said.

"So you were bored," he repeated sarcastically. "So you had to come out and take a ride on a boat?"

She stared at him. "Why shouldn't I?" she asked. "Who has a better right? After all, it belongs to my father."

It was after four o'clock in the morning when the last of the guests boarded one of the speedboats to go ashore. Jordana was bidding good night to the Princess Mara and Jacques when Youssef crossed the deck to Baydr, who was standing alone. "Shall I leave the girls?" he asked, gesturing to the two actresses who were standing with Vincent.

Baydr shook his head.

"Do you want me to stay aboard?"

"No. I'll reach you at the hotel in the morning."

"Okay." Youssef smiled. "Good night."

"Good night."

Baydr was gone when Jordana turned back from the ship's ladder. Slowly she went into the salon.

A steward came up to her. "Anything I can get madame?"

"Nothing, thank you," she said. "By the way, have you seen Mr. Al Fay?"

"I believe he's gone to his stateroom, madame," the steward said and left the salon.

She went down the corridor to her stateroom. Only the lamp at the side of the bed was on; her nightgown and robe were already laid out. Slowly she undressed. Suddenly she felt drained and exhausted. Her face where he had slapped her began to ache again.

She went into the bathroom, opened the medicine cabinet and took out a bottle of Percodan. She tossed two of the yellow tablets back into her throat and washed them down with a swallow of water. She looked into the mirror. She thought about taking off her makeup but it was too much effort.

She went back into the bedroom and slipped into her nightgown. Wearily she got into the bed and, turning off the night lamp, sank back against the pillows.

The light spilled into her room from the crack under his door. He was still awake. She closed her eyes as the pain began to subside. She was almost asleep when his door opened suddenly. Her eyes flew open.

He stood in the doorway, still fully dressed. For a long moment he didn't speak. "I want the children on board by nine o'clock in the morning," he said finally.

"Yes, Baydr," she said. "I'll see to it. It will be nice. It's been a long time since we've been together with the children."

His voice was cold and expressionless. "I asked for my sons. Not you."

She was silent.

"I'll return them on Sunday."

"You can't make it to Capri and back by then."

"We're not going to Capri. I have to be in Geneva early Monday morning. We'll just go up to St. Tropez and the Porquerolles."

The door closed behind him and again the room was dark. She looked at the illuminated dial of the digital clock on the table next to her. It was after five.

She reached for a cigarette and lit it. Too late to go to sleep here if she had to have the children at the boat by nine o'clock. Wearily she turned the light on and pressed the signal button for her maid.

She might as well dress and go back to the villa now. By seven o'clock the children would be awake. She could catch up on her sleep after they had gone.

Chapter Twelve

Michael Vincent came into the dining room of the hotel. His eyes were puffed from lack of sleep, his face lined and whiskey worn. He peered through the morning sunlight looking for Youssef. He found him at a table near the window. Youssef was freshly shaven. His eyes were clear. On the table next to his coffee was a pair of binoculars. "Good morning," he smiled.

"Morning," Vincent grumbled as he sat down. He blinked his eyes. "How do you do it? It had to be six o'clock before you got to bed. Yet here it is only nine-thirty and you call for a meeting."

"When the chief's around, nobody sleeps," Youssef said. He picked up the binoculars and gave them to the director. "See for yourself. He's out there water-skiing already."

Vincent peered through the binoculars adjusting the glasses until the view of the yacht was clear and sharp. He picked up the Riva as it raced across the bay. Behind it, holding on to the tow lines with one hand, was Baydr; the other hand held a small boy sitting on his shoulders. "Who is the boy?" Vincent asked.

"The chief's younger son, Samir," Youssef answered. "He's four and named after his grandfather. The older son, Prince Muhammad, is skiing off the Riva just behind his father. He's ten."

Vincent, who had been following Baydr hadn't noticed the second speedboat. He swung his glasses and picked up the boy. The ten-year-old was a miniature of his father; slim and strong, he too held the tow with one hand. "Prince Muhammad?" he questioned. "Is Baydr a—"

"No," Youssef said quickly. "Baydr is first cousin to Prince Feiyad, the reigning prince. Since he has no male heirs, he has indicated that Baydr's son will be the successor to the throne."

"Fascinating," Vincent said. He put the glasses down as the waiter came to the table. "Is it too early to get a Bloody Mary?"

"Not here," Youssef smiled. "Bloody Mary."

The waiter nodded and disappeared. Youssef leaned toward the director. "I apologize for disturbing you so early but the chief called me this morning and I must leave with him for a few days, so I thought it important that we conclude our business."

"I thought everything was agreed on last night," Vincent said.

The waiter returned with the drink. Youssef waited until the man left and Vincent had taken his first sip. "Almost everything," he said smoothly. "Except the agent's commissions."

"I have no agent," Vincent said quickly. "I always conduct my own negotiations."

"You have this time," Youssef said. "You see, it's a matter of custom. And we are great people for custom."

Vincent was beginning to understand but he wanted to hear Youssef say it. "And who is my agent?"

"Your greatest fan," Youssef said urbanely. "The man who recommended you for the job. Me."

Vincent was silent for a moment, then he took another sip of the Bloody Mary. He felt his head beginning to clear. "The customary ten percent?" he asked.

Youssef shook his head, still smiling. "That's the Western custom. Our custom is thirty percent."

"Thirty percent?" Vincent's voice expressed his shock. "That's an unheard-of-amount."

"It's not unfair in view of your fee for this film. A million dollars is an unheard-of-amount. I happen to know it's five times what you received for your last film. And you would not have been offered that if I hadn't known that this picture had been a dream of Baydr's for a long time and that he should make you an offer that would ensure your cooperation."

Vincent studied Youssef's face. The Arab was still smiling but behind the smile his eyes were deadly serious. "Fifteen percent," he offered.

"I have many expenses," Youssef said. He spread his hands in a deprecating gesture. "But you are my friend. I will not bargain with you. Twenty-five percent."

"What expenses?" Vincent was curious. "I thought you worked for Baydr. Does he not pay you well?"

"Well enough for a good existence. But a man must think of the future. I have a large family to support and must put a few dollars aside."

Vincent fished in his pocket for cigarettes. Youssef anticipated him. He clicked open a gold cigarette case and held it toward the director. "That's a beautiful case," Vincent said, taking a cigarette.

Youssef smiled. He placed it on the table in front of the director. "It's yours."

Vincent stared at him in surprise. He just didn't understand this man at all. "That's solid gold. You just can't give it to me like that."

"Why not? You admired it."

"Still that's not enough reason," Vincent protested.

"You have your customs, we have ours. We consider it a blessing to give gifts."

Vincent shook his head in resignation. "Okay. Twenty percent."

Youssef smiled and held out his hand. "Agreed."

They shook hands. Vincent put the cigarette in his mouth and Youssef lit it with a gold Dupont lighter. Vincent dragged on the cigarette, then laughed. "I don't dare admire your lighter or you'll give that to me too."

Youssef smiled. "You learn our customs quickly."

"I'll have to," Vincent said, "if I'm going to make this picture."

"Very true," Youssef said seriously. "We will work very closely together on this film and when the time comes I think I can show you how we both can make a great deal of money."

Vincent picked up his Bloody Mary and sipped it. "In what way?" he asked.

"The money they would ask you to pay for services and material is much more than they would ask from me," Youssef said. "Together we might be able to save the chief a great deal and at the same time find some reasonable benefit for our diligence."

"I'll remember that," Vincent said. "I'll probably call on you a great deal."

"I am at your disposal."

Vincent looked across the table. "When do you think the contracts will be ready for signature?"

"Within the week. They're being drawn in Los Angeles and will be telexed here when completed."

"Why Los Angeles? Aren't there good lawyers in Paris?"

"Of course there are, but you have to understand the chief. He demands the best in everything. And the best film attorneys are in Hollywood." He glanced at his watch "I must go," he said. "I'm late. The chief wants me to gather up the girls and bring them on board with me."

Vincent rose with him. He was puzzled. "The girls? But won't Mrs. Al Fay object?"

"Mrs. Al Fay has decided to remain in the villa in order to give the chief more time to spend alone with his sons."

They shook hands and Youssef walked out into the lobby. Vincent sank back into his chair. There was so much about these people he would have to learn. They were not quite as simple as they had seemed at first. The waiter came up and he ordered another Bloody Mary. Might as well start the day right.

The actresses and Patrick were waiting in the lobby with their luggage when he came out of the restaurant. He asked Elie to have the bagagiste carry the bags to the pier and place them on board the Riva.

"You go ahead," he told them. "I'll be with you in a minute. I have one more call to make."

He made his way up the small landing to the telephones and placed a call to Jacques at the Martinez. The telephone rang ten times before the sleepy voice answered.

"C'est moi, Youssef," he said. "Did I wake you?"

"Yes." Jacques' voice was surly.

"The chief has asked me to go on the boat with him for a few days and I am leaving now. I wanted to know how you left it with her."

"She is supposed to call me."

"Do you think she will?"

"I don't know. I didn't have much trouble getting her to whack me off."

"She will call then," Youssef said with satisfaction. "The first step in getting it between her legs is getting it in her hands."

"When will you be back?" Jacques asked.

"Sunday evening. The chief is leaving for Geneva that night. And if you haven't heard from her by then, I will give a dinner party for the American director and you will meet her then."

"I don't have to come with that Princess Mara again, do I?" Jacques asked. "I can't stand that woman."

"No. This time you will come alone." Youssef came out of the booth and gave the telephonist a few francs tip. He fished in his pocket for the cigarette case, then remembered he had given it away. He swore to himself, then smiled as he went down the steps toward the street. It wasn't too bad a deal. The three-hundred-dollar cigarette case got him the last five percent. And fifty thousand dollars was not to be laughed at.

She was standing at the window looking out at the sea when he came into her room. "Are you packed?" he asked.

"Yes," she said without turning back to him. "My father's boat is leaving."

He came to the window and looked out. The yacht was turning and moving out to sea toward the Estérel. The sky and the water were a matching blue and the sun was bright. "It will be warm today," he said.

She still didn't look at him. "He was water-skiing with his sons."

"Your brothers?"

Her voice was bitter. "They are not my brothers! They are his sons." She turned back into the room. "Someday he will find out."

Ali Yasfir was silent as he watched her cross the room and sink into a chair near the bed. She lit a cigarette. She didn't realize how much her father's daughter she really was. That slim strong body was not her mother's lineage. Her mother, like most Arab women, ran to weight.

"I remember when I was little he would take my sister and me water-skiing with him. He was very good and it was such fun. Then after he divorced my mother, nothing. He never even came to see us. He threw us away like old shoes."

Despite himself Ali found himself defending Baydr. "Your father needed sons. And your mother could bear no more children."

Leila's voice was contemptuous. "You men are all alike. Maybe someday you will learn that we are not just creatures of your convenience. Even now, women are giving more to the cause than most men."

He didn't want to argue the point with her. That wasn't his job. His job was to get her to Beirut and then into the mountains to the training camp. After that she could argue all she wanted to. He pressed the button for the porter.

"What plane are we making?" she asked.

"Rome via Air France, then M.E.A. to Beirut."

"What a drag," she said. She got out of the chair and walked back to the window and looked out. "I wonder what my father would think if he knew I was here?" she asked.

Chapter Thirteen

Baydr looked at his wristwatch. "We have five hours before the market opens in New York," he said.

"That doesn't leave us much time to refinance ten million pounds sterling, Monsieur Al Fay," M. Brun, the Swiss banker, said. "And it's too late to recall the buy orders."

John Sterling-Jones, his British associate, nodded in agreement. "It will be impossible. I suggest you reconsider your position, Mr. Al Fay."

Dick Carriage watched his employer from the far side of the room. No expression crossed Baydr's face though he knew what the British banker was suggesting. It would be simple enough to pick up the telephone and let Abu Saad know that he would go along with their new proposition. But once he did that they would own him. And he was not about to let that happen. Not after all the years he'd spent building his independence. No one could own him now. Not even his sovereign prince.

"My position remains the same, Mr. Sterling-Jones," Baydr said quietly. "I do not intend to go into the armaments business. If I had, I would have done so years ago."

The Englishman didn't answer.

Baydr turned to the Swiss. "How much can I cover from here?" he asked.

The Swiss looked down at his desk. "You have a free cash credit balance of five million pounds, Monsieur Al Fay."

"And a borrowing credit?"

"Under the present circumstances?" the Swiss asked.

Baydr nodded.

"None," the Swiss said. "Unless you alter your position. Then, of course, you can have any amount you want."

Baydr smiled. Bankers were always the same. "If I did that, I wouldn't need your money. Monsieur Brun," he reached into his pocket and took out a checkbook, "may I borrow a pen?"

"Of course, Monsieur Al Fay." The Swiss handed over his pen with a flourish.

Baydr placed the book on the corner of the desk and quickly wrote a check. He tore the check from the book and pushed it together with the pen back to the banker.

The banker picked up the check. "Monsieur Al Fay," he said in a surprised voice, "if we pay this check for five million pounds it would empty your account."

Baydr rose to his feet. "That's right, Monsieur Brun. And close it. I'll expect a copy of your transfer advice to my bank in New York at my hotel within the hour." He walked to the door. "You will also receive instructions on the disposition of the funds in the other trustee accounts under my jurisdiction before the morning is over. I trust you will give the same attention to the closing of those accounts as you did to their opening."

"Monsieur Al Fay," the banker's voice rose to a squeak. "No one has ever withdrawn forty million pounds from a bank in one day."

"Someone has now." Baydr smiled, then gestured to Carriage, who followed him out the door. They started through the bank toward the street.

They were almost at the street entrance when Sterling-Jones caught up with him. "Mr. Al Fay!"

Baydr turned to look at him. "Yes, Mr. Sterling-Jones?"

The Englishman almost stammered in his haste to get the words out. "Monsieur

Brun and I have reconsidered your position. What kind of bankers would we be if we did not grant a loan of five million pounds?"

"Ten million pounds. I see no reason why I should have to use any of my own money."

The Englishman stared at him for a moment, then nodded. "Ten million pounds."

"Very good, Mr. Sterling-Jones." He turned to Dick. "You go back with Mr. Sterling-Jones and collect the check I just gave them. I'll go on to the Aramco meeting and you catch up with me there."

"Yes, sir."

Baydr nodded pleasantly to the banker and without saying goodbye went out through the doors to the curb, where the limousine was waiting. The chauffeur leaped out of the car to open the door for him.

Baydr sank into the comfortable seat with a sigh of relief. What the bankers did not know was that it all had been a bluff. There was no way he could close the trustee accounts without the consent of the principals. But that check for five million pounds had made them forget that.

He lit a cigarette. By tomorrow it wouldn't matter. Chase Manhattan in New York would give him seventy percent of the market value on the stock as collateral. He would return that to the Swiss bank because the New York bank's interest rates were much lower. That would leave his exposure here at only three million pounds, which he could cover from his own account if necessary.

Meanwhile it wasn't all bad. Perhaps he really owed Ali Yasfir a note of thanks. Because of the withdrawal of their support, he had wound up as the controlling stock-holder of a small bank in La Jolla, California, a mail-order insurance company based in Richmond, Virginia, and a home-loan and finance company with forty branches in Florida. The three companies alone had assets of over sixty million dollars, of which at least twenty million was in cash with an annual profit of ten million dollars after taxes.

Abruptly, he decided not to go to the Aramco meeting. There was really nothing to be accomplished. Production and sales quotas for the year were being met. Instead, he directed the chauffeur to take him back to the President Wilson Hotel, where he maintained a suite.

He picked up the phone and called Aramco, apologized for cancelling the meeting at the last minute and asked that Carriage be sent to the hotel when he got there. Then he called his pilot at the airport and asked him to prepare to depart for the States immediately.

He went into the bedroom, took off his jacket and stretched out on the bed. Jabir appeared, almost immediately, from his little room behind Baydr's.

"Would the master like me to draw him a bath?"

"No thanks. I just want to lie here and think."

"Yes, master." Jabir turned to leave.

Baydr called him back. "Where is the girl?" He had almost forgotten that he had brought Suzanne, the little red-headed French actress that Youssef introduced to him in Cannes.

"She went out shopping, master," Jabir answered. "She said she would return shortly."

"Good. See to it that I am not disturbed for at least an hour."

"Yes, master. Shall I draw the drapes?"

"Good idea." When the servant left, Baydr closed his eyes. There was so much to do and so much to think of and so little time. It was hard for him to believe that just yesterday afternoon he had been water-skiing with his sons.

He had spent every hour of daylight with the boys. They had gone to beaches, looking for shells which they never found, rented paddle boats at St. Tropez, snorkeled off the Porquerolles, picnicked on the Isle of Levant. In the evening after their dinner they watched the Disney films he kept for them in the film library on the boat. He also had other films but they were not for children.

But it hadn't been until they were on their way back to Cannes on Sunday evening that he realized something had been troubling him.

They were in the salon watching *Snow White and the Seven Dwarfs* when it came to him. He looked down at their rapt faces watching the screen. He held up his hand, signaling the steward who was performing as projectionist. The film stopped and the salon lights came on.

The boys looked at him. "It's not bedtime yet, Daddy," Muhammad said.

"No, it's not," he answered in Arabic. "It's just that I realized we've been so busy having a good time we haven't had time to talk."

"Okay, Daddy," the boy said agreeably. "What shall we talk about?"

Baydr looked at him. Muhammad had answered him in English. "Supposing we talk in Arabic," he said with a gentle smile.

An uncomfortable look crossed the boy's face but he nodded his head. "Yes, Baba," he answered in Arabic.

Baydr turned to his youngest son. "Is that all right with you, Samir?"

The little one nodded without speaking.

"Have you both been studying your Koran?" he asked.

They both nodded.

"Have you come to the Prophecies yet?"

Again they nodded without speaking.

"What have you learned?" he asked.

"I have learned that there is but one God," the older boy said haltingly. "And that Muhammad is His prophet."

From the child's answer, Baydr knew that he had forgotten his lessons. Indulgently, he turned to Samir. "And what have you learned?"

"The same thing," the little one replied quickly in English.

"I thought we were going to speak Arabic," he said softly.

The little one met his eyes. "It's hard to say, Daddy."

Baydr was silent.

A look of concern came over Samir's face. "You're not angry with me, are you, Daddy?" he said. "I know the words in French — la même chose."

"I'm not angry with you, Samir," he said gently. "That's very good."

The little one smiled. "Then can we go back to watching the movie?"

He nodded and signaled the steward. The salon lights went down and the picture came back on the screen. A few moments later they were again lost in Snow White's adventures. But there was a hint of tears in Muhammad's eyes.

He reached over and drew the boy to him. "What is the trouble, my son?" he asked in Arabic.

The boy looked up into his face for a moment, then the tears began to roll down his cheeks. He tried to stifle his sobs.

Baydr felt helpless. "Tell me, my son."

"I speak so badly, Father," the boy said in Arabic with a heavy English accent. "I feel you are ashamed of me."

"I'll never be ashamed of you, my son," he said, holding the child close to him. "I'm very proud of you."

A smile burst through the boy's tears. "Really, father?"

"Really, my son. Now watch the movie."

After the children had gone to bed, he sat in the darkness of the salon for a long while. Youssef and the two French women came into the room and Youssef turned the lights on before he realized that Baydr was there.

"I'm sorry, chief," he apologized. "I didn't know you were in here."

"That's all right," Baydr said, rising. "I was just going to my room to change." A thought flashed through his mind. "You were here when Jordana and the children arrived from Beirut?" he asked in Arabic.

"I saw them through customs."

"Was their Arabic tutor with them?"

Youssef reflected for a moment. "I don't think so. Only the nanny."

"I wonder why Jordana didn't bring him."

"I don't know, chief. She never said anything to me."

Baydr's face was impassive.

"But then, Jordana and I don't have much chance to talk. She's always busy. There are so many parties here."

"I guess so. Remind me to cable Beirut in the morning. I want my father to send a tutor on the next plane."

"Yes, chief."

Baydr started for his room.

"Mouscardins okay for dinner at ten o'clock in St. Tro?" Youssef asked.

"Les Mouscardins will be fine." Baydr went down the corridor to his room. Leave it to Youssef. Les Mouscardins was the finest restaurant in St. Tropez and Youssef wanted nothing but the best.

Baydr called Jordana from the airport the next morning before the plane took off for Geneva. "What happened to the Arabic tutor?" he asked. "I thought he was coming with you."

"He was ill, and there was no time to get another."

"No time?" he said sarcastically. "You could have called my father. He would have found one and sent him right out."

"I didn't think it was important. After all, it is their summer vacation. They shouldn't have to study."

His voice was cold with anger. "Not important? What gives you the right to decide what is important and what is not? Do you realize that Muhammad is going to be the ruler of four million Arabs and he cannot even speak his own language?"

She was silent.

"I see I've left too much in your hands," he said. "I've cabled my father to send a tutor and when they return this fall, I'm sending them to my parents' home to live. Maybe there they'll be brought up properly."

She was silent for a moment. When she spoke there was hurt in her voice. "And me?" she asked. "What plans have you made for me?"

"None at all," he snapped. "You can do anything you goddamn well please. I will let you know when I need you."

Chapter Fourteen

Jordana was drunk, drunker than she had ever been in her life. It was the kind of peculiar drunken high that comes only after a deep depression, a high that let her watch herself as if she were outside her own body. She was being gay, charming, witty and brilliant all at the same time.

She had been down all day after Baydr's call that morning. The two things she truly loved in all the world were her sons. Once she thought she had loved Baydr like that. But now she did not know how she felt about him. Maybe it was because she did not know how he felt about her.

For the first time, she had been pleased to receive Youssef's invitation. She didn't like Youssef, but then she never had liked any of Baydr's full-time flunkies and part-time pimps. She never understood Baydr's need to surround himself with those kind of men when he could get any woman he wanted with just a snap of his fingers. He was still the most exciting and attractive man she had ever met.

When Youssef had explained that he was giving a small dinner party for Michael Vincent, the man who was to direct Baydr's film, The Messenger, she had agreed that it would be a nice gesture if she were to act as hostess. Especially when Youssef had hinted that Baydr would be very pleased by her action.

Youssef's small dinner party was for twenty people at La Bonne Auberge, a restaurant halfway between Cannes and Nice. As hostess, she was seated at the head of the table with Vincent, the guest of honor on her right. Youssef sat on her left. Since Baydr was not there the foot of the table was left significantly vacant. Half-way down the table, between two pretty women, sat Jacques, the blond gigolo whom Princess Mara had introduced to her the night of her birthday party. Idly, she wondered who he was with.

The dinner, ordered by Youssef, was superb. And the Dom Pérignon came in a never-ending flow. She knew from the very first sip that she was going to feel the wine. But tonight she didn't care. Michael Vincent was a bright man even though he drank nothing but Scotch, and also he was an American with whom she could share jokes that no one else at the table really understood.

Halfway through dinner, she became aware that Jacques had been watching her continually. Each time she would look down the table, his eyes would try to fix her gaze. But they were too far away from one another to engage in conversation.

After dinner, Youssef suggested that they all go to a discotheque to continue the party. By that time, she was high enough to think it was a wonderful idea. She loved to dance. It was not until they had been at Whisky for almost an hour that she looked up and saw Jacques standing in front of her.

He bowed almost formally. "May I have this dance?"

She listened to the music responding to the hard driving beat of the Rolling Stones. She looked at Vincent. "Excuse me," she said.

He nodded and turned to Youssef, who was sitting on his other side. She was dancing even before she was on the floor.

Jacques turned to face her and began to dance. For a moment she looked at him critically. Rock really wasn't a Frenchman's style. He danced with the uptight stingy movements that to a Frenchman passed for cool. He would be better off if he stayed with ballroom numbers. But she soon forgot about him as she lost herself in her own dancing.

His voice rose over the sound of the music. "You said you would call me."

She looked at him. "I did?"

"Yes."

"I don't remember," she said. She honestly didn't.

"You're lying," he said accusingly.

Without a word she turned and started off the floor. His hand caught her arm, pulling her back.

"I apologize," he said earnestly. "Please dance with me."

She stared at him for a moment, then let him lead her back to the floor. The record changed from rock to ballad. He took her into his arms and held her tightly against him.

"For the past three days I have not been able to eat or sleep," he said.

She was still cool. "I don't need a gigolo."

"I, better than anyone else should know that," he said. "Someone as beautiful as you. I want you for myself."

She looked up at him skeptically. His hardness pressed into her. "Feel how much I want you," he said.

Her eyes closed and she rested her head against his shoulder. She allowed herself to enjoy the pressure. The high inside her head seemed to take on a rosy hue. Maybe he was telling the truth after all.

What she didn't see was the smile that passed between him and Youssef.

The coarse cotton khaki of her shapeless shirt and trousers scratched at her skin as she followed the five other new women into the barracks of the commanding officer. The stiff leather boots clumped heavily on the wooden floor. The yellow light of the oil lamps cast an unsteady glow in the room.

The commanding officer sat at a table at the far end of the room, a uniformed soldier seated on each side. She was studying a paper on the table and did not look up until they came to a halt in front of her.

"Attention!" their sergeant barked.

"An-nasr. Victory," they shouted as they had been trained to do on the very first night they arrived in camp a few days before.

Leila felt her brassiere pull tight against her breasts as she snapped her shoulders back. The brassiere too was made of coarse cotton. She looked straight ahead.

Slowly the commanding officer rose to her feet. Leila saw that she wore the equivalent of a colonel's pips on the shoulders of her blouse. She stared at them silently for a moment, then abruptly in a surprisingly strong voice she shouted, "Ibdah al-adu!"

"Slaughter the enemy!" they yelled back.

She nodded, a faint smile of approval coming to her lips. "At ease," she said in a more normal voice.

There was a rustle of the coarse cloth as the women settled into a more relaxed position. The C.O. came around the front of the desk.

"In the name of the Brotherhood of Palestinian Freedom Fighters, I welcome you to our holy struggle. The struggle to free our peoples from the bondage of Israel and the enslavement of imperialism. I know that each of you has made many sacrifices to come here, estrangement from loved ones, perhaps ostracism from your own neighbors, but I can promise you one thing. At the end of our struggles lies a freedom greater than has ever been known.

"And because of this, your struggle is only beginning. You will be called upon to make many more sacrifices. Your honor, your body, even your life may have to be given to win the freedom we seek. For we will have victory.

"Here, you will be taught many things. Weaponry. Guns, rifles, knives. How to make bombs. Small and large. How to kill with your bare hands. How to fight. All so that together with our men, we can drive the Zionist usurpers back into the sea and restore the land to its rightful owners, our people.

"You have already, each of you, taken the sacred oath of allegiance to our cause. And from this moment on your real names will be forgotten and never used in this camp. You will answer only to the name assigned to you and in this manner, in the case of unforeseen capture, you will never give away the names of your comrades. From this moment on your only loyalty is to your cause and your brethren in arms."

The commanding officer paused for a moment. The women were silent in rapt attention. "The next three months will be the most difficult any of you have ever known. But at the end you will be able to go forth to take your place beside Fatmah Bernaoui, Miriam Shakhashir, Aida Issa and Leila Khaled as well as others of our sex who have proven themselves the equals of their brothers in the struggle."

She walked back around the table and took up her position between the two men. "I wish you luck."

"Attention!" the sergeant barked.

"An-nasr," they yelled, straightening up.

"Idbah al-adu!" the C.O. cried.

"Idbah al-adu!" they shouted back.

The commanding officer saluted. "Dismissed."

They broke ranks and followed the sergeant back out into the night. "Get to your barracks, girls," the sergeant said drily. "Your day begins at five tomorrow morning."

He turned and went off to the men's section of the camp as they started for their own small building. Leila fell into step with the young women who occupied the bed next to hers.

"Wasn't the C.O. wonderful?" Leila asked. "For the first time I feel my life has a meaning."

The woman looked at her as if she were a creature from another planet. "I'm glad you feel that way," she said in a common-sounding voice. "The only reason I came here is to be near my boyfriend. But I haven't even been able to get anywhere near him and I'm getting so horny that I wouldn't be surprised to find myself in your bed eating your pussy tonight."

Thirty-five thousand feet over the Atlantic Ocean in a dark blue star-filled sky, Baydr slept as his plane raced time on its way to New York. Suddenly he awoke with a start. He sat up in the bed, his eyes wet with tears.

He brushed them away with his fingers and reached for a cigarette. It must have been a bad dream. But there was a presentiment of dread within him, a curious foreboding that lay heavily on his heart.

The girl beside him stirred. "Q'est-ce que c'est, chéri?" she asked in a sleepy voice.

"Rien," he said. "Dors."

She was silent and after a while the drone of the engines made him drowsy. He put out the cigarette and went back to sleep.

Another Place: June 1973

The black Cadillac limousine bearing diplomatic plates rolled to a stop in front of the administration building and three men got out—two men dressed in civilian clothing and an American Army colonel. They started up the steps toward the building. The Israeli soldiers standing guard at the entrance presented arms. The colonel saluted and the three men went into the building.

The senior staff sergeant at the reception desk rose from his chair, saluting. The colonel returned the salute. The sergeant smiled. "You know where to go, colonel?" It was more a statement than a question.

The colonel returned his smile, nodding. "I've been here before, sergeant." He turned to the other two men. "If you'll follow me—"

He led them down a corridor to an elevator and pressed the call button. The doors opened silently and they boarded the car. He pressed a button on the panel and the elevator began its descent. Six levels underground it stopped and the doors opened again.

The colonel led them out into another reception area, where another senior staff sergeant sat. This time the sergeant did not get up. He looked at them, then down at the list on his desk. "Please identify yourselves, gentlemen?"

The colonel spoke first. "Alfred R. Weygrin, Colonel. United States Army."

The civilian in the three-button suit: "Robert L. Harris, United States Department of State."

The man in the rumpled sports jacket: "Sam Smith, American Plumbing Supply Company."

The sergeant didn't crack a smile at the absurd cover name for the C.I.A. agent. He ticked the names off the list and gave each of the men yellow plastic identification cards, which they affixed to their lapels. He pressed a signal button on his desk and a corporal appeared from a door on his right. "Please escort these gentlemen to Conference Room A."

Conference Room A was at the end of a long narrow gray corridor, guarded by two soldiers and still another sergeant at a desk. The corporal halted in front of the desk while the sergeant checked their plastic I.D. cards then pressed a signal button which opened the electronically controlled doors. The visitors went into the room and the doors shut automatically behind them.

There were approximately nine men already in the room, only two of whom were in the uniform of the Israeli Army, one a brigadier general, the other a colonel. The brigadier came forward, his hand outstretched. "Alfred, it's good to see you again."

The American smiled as he shook his hand. "Good to see you, Lev. I'd like you to meet Bob Harris of State and Sam Smith. Gentlemen, General Eshnev."

They exchanged handshakes. The general introduced them to the others and then gestured to a large round table set at the far end of the large conference room. "Supposing we find our seats, gentlemen."

Printed nameplates indicated their places, and when they had all been seated there was only one vacant chair remaining at the table. It was positioned just to the left of the Israeli general, and inasmuch as he was the highest-ranking officer it meant that the vacant place belonged to his superior. The Americans glanced at the nameplate curiously but without comment.

General Eshnev caught the glance. "I'm sorry for the delay, gentlemen, but I am informed that General Ben Ezra is on his way. He has been tied up in traffic and should be here at any moment."

"Ben Ezra?" Harris whispered to the colonel. "I never heard of him."

The soldier smiled. "I'm afraid he was a little before your time, Bob. The Lion of the Desert is almost a legendary figure. Honestly, I thought he was long since gone."

General Eshnev caught the tail end of the remark. "Was it your MacArthur who said, 'Old soldiers never die, they just fade away'? Ben Ezra proves how wrong that statement is. He refuses to die or to fade away."

"He must be in his seventies by now," the C.I.A. man said. "The last we heard he had gone back to his kibbutz after the sixty-seven war."

"He's seventy-four," the Israeli said. "And as far as the kibbutz is concerned, there's no way we have of knowing just how much time he actually spends there. He's got the whole kibbutz under his spell. Not even the children will tell us about him. We never know whether he is in or out."

"It would seem to me if you wanted to know what he's up to, you'd keep him in Tel Aviv," Harris said.

"It could become embarrassing," Eshnev said, smiling. "The Lion of the Desert was never known for his tact. It seems your President still remembers his comments when Eisenhower stopped the British and French takeover of the Suez Canal in fifty-six. You know he planned that operation for the British."

"I didn't know that," Harris said. "But why should the President be angry? He wasn't President then."

"He was Vice-President and Ben Ezra was very outspoken on the subject of his support of certain Arab elements which he held responsible for Eisenhower's decision. Ben Ezra even went so far as to advise the British to tell Eisenhower to mind his own affairs, and I'm afraid his language was not very diplomatic. After that embarrassment, Ben Gurion had no choice but to accept his retirement. That's when he went to the Sinai to live in a kibbutz."

"You mentioned that he came out in sixty-seven?" Harris asked.

"Yes. But not officially. And that proved to be another embarrassment. He didn't want us to stop until we reached Cairo and got a total surrender. He said his own intelligence could prove that if we didn't we would have to do it all over again within seven years."

"What makes him feel that his sources are superior to our own?" the C.I.A. man asked.

"His mother was an Arab and there are still some who maintain he's more Arab than Jew. At any rate, he lives out there among thousands of them and in a strange manner they seem to trust him and come to him for justice. The Arabs call him 'Imam' — holy man, reader, a man who lives by the honored principles. He crosses borders with impunity and alone."

"Was he married?" Harris asked.

"Twice," General Eshnev replied. "Once when he was a young man. His first wife died in the desert giving birth to a child, who also died while they were trying to slip through the British lines into Palestine. The second time was after he had retired. He married an Arab girl and as far as I know she is still alive and living with him in the kibbutz. They have no children."

"Does his coming here mean that you expect trouble then?" Colonel Weygrin asked.

The Israeli shrugged. "We Jews always expect trouble. Especially when there are things happening we don't understand."

"Such as?" Harris asked.

"That's why we're meeting," Eshnev said. "Let's wait for Ben Ezra. He just appeared after two months of dead silence and called for a meeting."

Harris' voice was slightly disdainful. "And the old man gets it, just like that?"

"Not quite like that. First he had to convince Dayan that he had something. Dayan then went to the Prime Minister. It was she who gave approval for the meeting."

"You would think after being so insistent, he would at least be on time," Harris said.

"He's an old man," Eshnev said apologetically. "And he insists on using his own car, an old Volkswagen that keeps breaking down. He won't take one of ours. If I didn't leave special word outside I'm sure they wouldn't even let him into the parking lot." The telephone in front of him buzzed. He picked it up, nodded and put it down. "The general is on his way, gentlemen."

The electronic doors opened silently and every head turned. The man who stood there was tall, over six feet, and clothed in dusty sand-encrusted bedouin robes. The white hair and beard covering his lined, sun-blackened face made him look more Arab than Jew. Only the startling dark-blue eyes denied Arab heritage. His walk was firm and proud, as he moved toward General Eshnev. His voice was raspy as if eroded by time and the desert sand. "Lev," he said, holding out his hand.

"General," Lev Eshnev replied, rising. They shook hands. "Gentlemen, allow me to introduce General Ben Ezra." He then introduced each man beginning counter-clockwise from the old man's right.

Ben Ezra looked directly into each man's eyes and repeated his name. When the introductions were completed, they sat down.

Eshnev turned to the old man. "It's your meeting, general."

"Thank you." The old man spoke in unaccented English. "I suppose you have all been made aware of the buildup along the Suez Canal by the Egyptians and by the Syrians along the Golan Heights. And I suppose you are also aware of the new military equipment that is arriving in greater quantities than ever before from Russia and China. I suppose you realize that if this rate of supply continues they will soon achieve a military parity and perhaps a strike potential in excess of our own within a very short time."

"That's true," Eshnev said. "We know all that."

"I'm sure you also know of the heavy influx of North Korean fighter and bomber pilots."

"Yes," Eshnev said. "But we also know that Sadat is under heavy criticism from the moderates about the Russian influence."

Ben Ezra nodded. "But we can't allow that to lull us into a false sense of security. For the first time they are building a capable war machine. And that's something you don't do unless you intend to use it."

"Granted," Eshnev said. "But it could be another year and a half before they are ready."

"No," Ben Ezra said. "They are ready now. They can strike anytime."

"Then what are they waiting for?" Eshnev's voice was polite but there was a faint note of impatience. "So far you've told us nothing we do not know."

Ben Ezra was unruffled. "This time, we cannot evaluate their decisions simply on a military basis. Other factors outside the military play a part in their plan. They have been infiltrating the Western world through financial investments. In addition, they are lining up the oil-producing countries to create an economic force that can be used to reduce the support we've been getting from the technological countries. They will strike when they have those plans worked out and not before."

"Do you have specific information on that?" Eshnev asked.

"No. All I know is what I have picked up in my wanderings. There are rumors in the Sinai that the Fedayeen are exerting pressure on the moderates. They are selecting targets among the Arabs themselves in order to coerce cooperation from the rich oil producers."

"Any specifics on that?"

The old man shook his head. "That's why I asked for this meeting." He looked across the table at the Americans. "I thought our busy friends might have some knowledge of that pressure."

Harris looked at his companions. "I wish we did," he said. "But there is very little we do know."

Ben Ezra's face was inscrutable. "You're State Department?"

Harris nodded.

"That's understandable," Ben Ezra said. He looked directly at the C.I.A. man. "How about you?"

Smith was uncomfortable. "We're aware of their economic plans."

"Yes?"

"But we haven't been able to tie them together," Smith said. "The economic thrust seems to be under the direction of one man, Prince Feiyad's personal representative, Baydr Al Fay. But he appears to be completely independent, a known conservative and an advocate of rapprochement with Israel. Not because he likes you but because he thinks it would bring about an economic solution that would benefit the entire Middle East. But we have no way of knowing for sure. We haven't been able to infiltrate his organization so far."

Eshnev looked at him. "You haven't?"

The American shook his head. "No."

Eshnev smiled with faint triumph. "Then maybe we can be of help. We have a man in there."

There was a moment's silence around the table. It was Ben Ezra who broke it. "So?" he asked.

Eshnev's voice was calm. "Al Fay's principal interest at the moment seems to be his desire to make a film based on the life of Muhammad, to be called *The Messenger*. We also know that he has rejected a proposal by Al-Ikhwah to handle certain purchases for them."

Ben Ezra looked at him. "Was Ali Yasfir involved in that proposal?"

It was Eshnev's turn to be surprised. "How did you know that?"

"I didn't," the old man said. "But Yasfir just turned up in one of the Al-Ikhwah training camps in Lebanon with what they call the most important recruit they ever made. The daughter of the richest man in the Arab world. Does this man have a daughter?"

"He has two," Eshnev said. "One is married and lives in Beirut near her mother, Al Fay's former wife. The youngest is in a school in Switzerland."

"You're sure of that?" Ben Ezra asked.

"We've had no word to the contrary," Eshnev said. "But we can check on that easily enough."

"He has other children?"

"Yes. Two sons with his present wife, an American. The eldest son, now ten, is to be appointed by Prince Feiyad as heir to the throne."

"Then if they have the girl, they may have the key to Al Fay," Ben Ezra said.

"Possibly."

"I'll see what can be found out in the Sinai," Ben Ezra said. "You people pursue your sources."

"We'll do that," Eshnev said.

"Agreed," Smith added.

"That still leaves us with the important question," Eshnev said. "When do you think they will attack?"

Ben Ezra looked at him. "Right after the feast of Ramadan." he said flatly.

Eshnev could not keep the shock from his voice. "But that's around the High Holy Days. They wouldn't do that. Respect for the laws of Moses is still an important part of their religion."

Ben Ezra got to his feet. "Not as much as it is of ours."

Eshnev looked up at him. "If they come we'll be ready for them."

"I hope so," the old man said. "But there are better ways."

"Preemptive strike?" Eshnev asked, but didn't wait for an answer. "You know we can't do that. Our allies won't permit it."

Ben Ezra looked at him, then at the Americans. "Maybe they will if they realise that without us they lose their power in the Middle East. The Sixth Fleet can't cross the desert and occupy the oil fields."

"It is the belief of the State Department that there will be no attack by the Arabs in the foreseeable future," Harris said stiffly.

Ben Ezra smiled. He looked at the C.I.A. man. "Is that also your opinion?"

Smith didn't answer. It was not his place to make official statements.

Ben Ezra turned to the American soldier. "Installation of the latest Russian ground-to-air missiles have been completed in the Suez and on the Golan Heights. I've seen them with my own eyes. Don't you agree that the time to attack has come when your own defenses are set?"

Weygrin nodded. "I would think so."

Ben Ezra looked around the table. "Then they're ready." He paused for a moment. "All they're waiting for now is to get their house in order."

"How will we know when that is?" Eshnev said.

"We won't," the old man shrugged. "Until they attack. Unless—"

"Unless what?"

A thoughtful expression came into the old man's eyes. He seemed lost for a moment in memory, then his eyes cleared. "It may sound strange to you but in an old man's bones there is a feeling that we may find the answer in Al Fay. The winds that blow across the desert no longer originate in the East — they come from the West. The Arab sheiks have awakened to the power of their wealth. That will be the real end of Russian influence. Communism has no answer for them. And control of the Middle East is only the beginning. If they invest their wealth wisely they may soon be able to control the world without ever firing a shot."

He looked around the silent table. "I hate to disillusion you, gentlemen, but the fact is that we are no longer important to Islam except to their pride. They must achieve some victory no matter how minor just to regain face. The big thrust will come after the battle is over."

He turned to the Americans. "We will need your help. For now. Later, you will need ours."

Harris was polite but disdainful. "What makes you think that?"

"Because we, more than anyone in the world, understand them," the old man said, his face settling into grim hawklike lines. "And because you, not we, are the real target."

Again there was silence. Finally Eshnev spoke. "You will continue to keep us informed of what you learn?"

The old man nodded. "Of course. I would also appreciate a favor."

"If I can do it, it will be done," Eshnev answered.

"I would like a complete dossier on Al Fay. His whole life. Everything — personal and business. I want to know all about him."

Eshnev looked around the table. There were no objections. He nodded. "It will be done immediately."

"You will relay my opinion to the Prime Minister?" Ben Ezra asked.

"Yes, I will."

"Also give her a kiss for me," Ben Ezra said, smiling. "I think she could use it."

There was a polite murmur of laughter around the table. The telephone rang and Eshnev picked it up. He listened for a moment then put it down. "There's been another hijacking," he said. "A Lufthansa plane out of Düsseldorf. It's on its way to Beirut."

Ben Ezra shook his head sadly. "How sad. How stupid." He looked at the Americans. "The net effect is nothing but headlines. And while we are distracted by the news, quietly, under our very noses, without anyone really being aware of it, they are hijacking the world."

BOOK TWO

The End of Summer 1973

Chapter One

Youssef entered the restaurant at the Tahiti Plage through a roadside door. He looked out of place in his dark suit, white shirt and tie as he threaded his way through the half-naked men and women to the beach. He blinked his eyes as he came out into the bright sunlight once again. Squinting, he looked around at the tables. After a moment he saw him, seated near the frond-covered beach bar. He was talking earnestly to a good-looking young black man.

Jacques looked up as Youssef's shadow fell across him. "Youssef," he said in French, rising. "What a pleasant surprise. We weren't expecting you."

Youssef didn't return his smile. "I can see that," he said coldly. "Tell your petit ami to get lost."

A sullen look crossed Jacques' face. "What right have you—"

Youssef didn't let him finish. "I own you, you cunt!" he snarled. "Now tell him to get lost, or I'll throw you back into the gutters of Paris where I found you! Hustling tourists for ten-franc blow jobs!"

The black man got to his feet, the muscles tensing in his arms as he tightened his fists. "Do you want me to get rid of him for you, Jacques?"

Youssef stared at Jacques. Jacques' eyes fell after a moment. "I think you better go, Gerard." He didn't look at the black.

Gerard's lips curled contemptuously. "Poule!" he snapped at Jacques then turned his back on them. He dropped to the sand a few feet away and covered his eyes with his arm, seeming to pay no attention to them.

The waiter came up as Youssef sat down in the chair the black had just vacated. "Monsieur?"

"Coca. Beaucoup de glace." He turned to Jacques, who was sinking back in his chair. "Where is she?"

Jacques didn't look at him. "How the hell should I know?" he retorted sullenly. "I've been waiting here on the beach for her almost two hours."

"You're supposed to know!" Youssef snapped. "What the hell do you think I am paying you all this money for? To fuck around with petit négres on the beach?"

The waiter put the Coca-Cola on the table and went away. Youssef picked it up and drank thirstily. "Were you with her last night?" he asked.

"Yes."

"The pictures? Did you get them?"

"How could I?" Jacques asked in return. "She never came to the apartment. She left me in the disco at three o'clock and told me to meet her on the beach today at noon."

"Were you with that black all night?"

"What was I supposed to do?" Jacques answered defensively. "Save myself for her?"

Youssef reached into his side coat pocket and took out his new gold cigarette case. He opened it slowly and carefully took out a cigarette. He tapped the cigarette on the cover of the case. "You're not very smart," he said, placing the cigarette between his lips and lighting it. "Not smart at all."

Jacques stared at him. "How can I get the pictures when she does not come to the apartment? Never. Always we do it where she chooses." He looked over Youssef's shoulder at the sea. "Ah, she is coming now."

Youssef turned to look. The big San Marco was heading toward the shore from the open sea. He reached into his jacket and threw a key on the table in front of Jacques. "I have an apartment reserved for you at the Byblos. All the equipment is there. The room is bugged and a photographer will be waiting in the next room for you to let him in. You get her there. I don't care how you do it but you get her there. You have only this night left."

Jacques stared at him. "What is the sudden rush?"

"I have a telegram in my pocket from her husband. Tomorrow afternoon she will be on a plane to California."

"What if she does not want to stay? What am I supposed to do, hit her on the head? If it is like last night, she will leave at three o'clock in the morning, return to the San Marco and go back to Cannes."

Youssef got to his feet and looked down at Jacques. "I will see to it that the San Marco will have engine trouble. The rest is up to you." He glanced over his shoulder at the sea. The San Marco was trolling slowly into the shallow waters near the beach. "Go down to the water, lover boy," he said sarcastically, "and help the lady ashore."

Silently, Jacques got out of his chair and started toward the beach. Youssef watched him for a moment, then turned and made his way back through the restaurant to the road where he had parked his car.

He got into the car and sat there for a moment before turning the key in the ignition. If only Jordana didn't hate him. Then none of this would be necessary. But he knew how many times she had tried to turn Baydr against him because she resented their relationship. And after all, he was only an employee while she was the boss's wife. If it came to a showdown there was no doubt in his mind who would be the victor. She would win hands down. But if Jacques came through tonight that would never happen. The threat of presenting Baydr with proof of her indiscretion would be enough to keep her in line. Youssef knew that the best ally was a conquered enemy.

Jordana opened her eyes the moment the heavy roar of the engines died down to idling speed. She glanced at her watch. It was forty minutes since she had left Cannes. By road, with all the traffic, it could have taken an hour and a half. This was not only faster but the sea had been smooth and she had slept all the way.

She sat up, reaching for her bikini top and shirt. She looked down at herself as she fastened the brassiere. Her breasts were as tanned as the rest of her body, a golden nut brown, and her nipples were a purple plum color instead of their normal red rose. She was pleased with herself. Her breasts were still firm. She hadn't yet begun to sag like so many women her age.

Instinctively she glanced over her shoulder to see if the two sailors at the helm of the speedboard had been looking at her. Their eyes were studiously turned away but she knew that they had been watching in the rear-view mirror mounted on the windscreen in front of them. She smiled to herself. To tease them, she cupped her breasts with her hands suggestively so that her nipples hardened. Then she fastened the bra.

A paddle boat came by with two topless girls. They looked at the seventy-thousand-dollar San Marco with undisguised hope and curiosity. Again she smiled to herself as the look of disappointment crossed their faces when they saw that she was the only passenger. They were so obvious. The pedalo turned away slowly.

" 'Allo!" The call came from the other side of the boat.

She turned. Jacques had come out in a small dinghy with an outboard motor. His blond hair had completely whitened in the summer sun, making his tan even darker by contrast. She waved without speaking.

"I've come to take you ashore," he shouted. "I know how you hate to get your feet wet."

"I'll be right with you," she called. She turned to the sailors. "Wait out here," she told them in French. "I'll call you when I'm ready to leave."

"Oui, Madame," the sailor at the helm replied. The other sailor started back to help her over the side. She gave him the large beach bag she always took with her. Inside were her shoes, a change of wardrobe for the evening, the walkie-talkie for communication with the speedboat, as well as cosmetics, cigarettes, money and credit cards.

The sailor reached over the side and pulled the dinghy close to the speedboat. He dropped the bag into Jacques' hands, then held Jordana's arm as she stepped over. He cast the dinghy free as soon as she sat down.

She sat facing the rear of the dinghy. Jacques sat at the tiller of the outboard motor. "Sorry to be late," she said.

"That's all right," he smiled. "You sleep well?"

"Very well. And you?"

He made a moue. "Not too well. I was too—how you say?—frustrated."

She looked at him. She couldn't quite figure him out. Mara had said he was a gigolo but the several times she had given him money he had returned it with a hurt look. This was not business, he had said. He was in love with her. But it still didn't make sense. He had taken an expensive apartment in the Miramar, right on the Croisette in Cannes, and a brand-new Citroën SM and never seemed short of money. He never let her pick up a check as so many others did, gigolo or no. Several times she had seen him eyeing some boys but he had never made any overt moves while she was around. At one point, she was fairly sure that he was bi and that perhaps his real lover was a man who had sent him down to the Côte d'Azur for the summer, but that didn't disturb her. She had long ago come to the conclusion that bisexual men made the best lovers.

"With all the talent available in that discotheque?" she laughed. "I wouldn't have thought you would have any problems."

"I didn't," he said to himself, thinking of his night with Gerard. He felt himself growing hard as he thought of the black towering over him, and peeling the foreskin back on his giant black shaft to expose the reddish purple swollen head. He remembered going down on his back like a woman and raising his legs, and then the exquisite agony of the big penis forcing its way roughly into his anus. He had whimpered like a woman and then yelled as his orgasms overtook him and his semen squirted up on their bellies that were pressed tightly together.

"Look," he said aloud, releasing his erect penis from his bikini. "See what you do to me? The moment I see you. Three times last night I had to relieve myself."

She laughed. "Didn't anyone ever tell you that was bad for you? You could stunt your growth doing it so much."

He didn't laugh. "When are you going to spend a whole night with me? Just one time so that we could make love without my feeling that you always have one eye on the clock, so that we can fully take our pleasure of each other."

She laughed again. "You're too greedy. You forget that I am a married woman with responsibilities. I must be home every night so that I see my children when I wake up in the morning."

"What would be so terrible if you did not?" He pouted.

"Then I would be remiss in the one duty that my husband demands of me," she said. "And that I would not do."

"Your husband does not care. Otherwise he would have come to see you and the children at least once during these past three months," he said.

Her voice went cold. "What my husband does or does not do is none of your business."

He sensed instantly he had gone too far. "But I love you. I am going crazy for wanting you."

She nodded slowly, relaxing. "Then keep things in their proper perspective," she said. "And if you're going to keep playing with your cock, you'd better turn the boat back out to sea before we crash on the beach."

"If I do, will you suck me?"

"No," she said sharply. "I'm more in the mood for a cold glass of white wine."

She was high. Papagayo was packed. The strobe lights were like a stop-motion camera on her eyes, the heavy pounding of the rock group tortured the ears. She took another sip of white wine and looked down the table. There were fourteen people, all shouting at one another to be heard over the din in the discotheque.

Jacques was talking to the English woman on his right. She was an actress who had just finished a picture with Peter Sellers, and had been with a group of people who had come down from Paris for the weekend. Jordana had begun collecting them on the beach that afternoon. She'd completed the group at L'Escale, where they'd had cocktails and dinner. About midnight they had gone to the discotheque.

The reason for gathering the people was that she had been annoyed with Jacques. He seemed to take too much for granted. In some ways he was like a woman, only in his case he seemed to think that the world revolved around his cock. She was beginning to be bored with him, but apart from an occasional visiting male there was nothing really dependable around. It was the boredom that had led her to smoke a joint. Usually she never smoked in public. But when the English woman had offered her a toke in the ladies room, she had stayed until they finished the cigarettes between them.

After that, she didn't mind the evening at all. It seemed that she had never laughed so much in her life. Everyone was excruciatingly bright and witty. Now she wanted to dance but everyone was too busy talking.

She got out of her chair and went to the dance floor alone. Pushing her way into the crowd she began to dance. She gave herself to the music, happy that she was in the south of France where no one thought it strange that a woman or a man wanted to dance alone. She closed her eyes.

When she opened them, the tall good-looking black man was dancing in front of her. He caught her eye but they didn't speak. She had noticed him earlier that day on the beach; later at cocktail time he had been at the bar in L'Escale; now he was here. She had seen him sitting at a table not far from her own.

He moved fantastically well, his body fluid under the shirt, which was open to his waist and tied in a knot just over the seemingly glued-on black jeans. She began to move with him.

After a moment she spoke. "You're American, aren't you?"

His voice was Southern. "How did you know?"

"You don't dance like a Frenchman—they jerk up and down—the English hop and dip."

He laughed. "I never thought of that."

"Where are you from?"

"Cracker country," he said, "Georgia."

"I've never been there," she said.

"You're not missing anything," he replied. "I like it better here. We could never do this back there."

"Still?" she asked.

"Still," he said. "They never change."

She was silent.

"Je m'appelle Gerard," he said.

She was surprised. His French was Parisian without a trace of accent. "Your French is good."

"It should be," he said. "My folks sent me over here to school when I was eight. I went back when my father was killed—I was sixteen then but I couldn't take it. I headed right back to Paris the minute I got enough bread together."

She knew what French school cost and they weren't cheap. His family had to have money. "What did your father do?"

His voice was even. "He was a pimp. But he had a finger in every pie. But he was black and the honkies didn't like that, so they cut him up in an alley an' blamed it on a passing nigger. Then they hung the nigger an' everything was cool."

"I'm sorry."

He shrugged. "My father said that was the way they would do it someday. He had no complaints. He had a good life."

The music crashed to a stop and the group came down from the stage as the record player came on with a slow number. "Nice talking to you," she said, starting back to the table.

His hand on her arm stopped her. "You don't have to go back there."

She didn't speak.

"You look like a fast-track lady and there's nothin' but mudders back there," he said.

"What've you got in mind?" she asked.

"Action. That's something I got from my father. I'm a fast-track man. Why don't you meet me outside?"

Again she didn't speak.

"I saw the way you looked," he said. "You gotta be turned off on that crowd over there." He smiled suddenly. "You ever make it with a black man before?"

"No," she answered. She never had.

"I'm better than they say they are," he said.

She glanced at the table. Jacques was still busy talking to the English woman. He probably didn't even notice that she had left the table. She turned back to Gerard. "Okay," she said. "But we'll only have about an hour. I have to leave then."

"An hour's enough," he laughed. "In one hour I'll have you on a trip to the moon and back."

Chapter Two

When she came out he was on the quai opposite the discotheque, watching the last of the sidewalk artists pack up their wares for the night. He turned when he heard the sound of her high-stacked shoes on the sidewalk. "Any trouble getting out?" he asked.

"No," she answered. "I told them I was going to the ladies'."

He grinned. "Mind walking? My place is just up the street past Le Gorille."

"It's the only way to fly," she said, falling into step beside him.

Despite the hour there were still crowds walking back and forth. They were engaged in their principal form of amusement, looking at each other and the beautiful yachts tied up right alongside the street. For many, it was the only thing they could afford to do, after paying the exorbitant seasonal prices for their rooms and food. The French had no mercy for tourists of any nationality, even their own.

They turned up the street past Le Gorille with its smell of fried eggs and pommes frites and began to climb the narrow sidewalk. Halfway up the block he stopped in front of the door of one of the old houses which had a boutique on the ground floor. He opened it with a heavy old-fashioned iron key and pressed the button just inside to turn on the hall lights. "We're two flights up."

She nodded and followed him up the old wooden staircase. His apartment was at the head of the second flight. This door had a more modern lock. He opened and held it for her.

She stepped inside. The room was dark. The door closed behind her and at the same time she heard the click of the light switch. The room filled with soft red light from two lamps, one on either side of the bed against the far wall. She looked at the room curiously.

The furniture was cheap and worn, the kind with which the French supply the summer vacationer. In the corner of the room was a sink and under it was a bidet on a swivel. The W.C. was behind a narrow door that looked like a closet. There was no tub, shower or kitchen, only a hot plate on the top of a bureau, next to an armoire.

He caught her look. "It's not much," he said, "but it's home."

She laughed. "I've seen worse. You're lucky the toilet's not in the hall."

He went over to the bureau and opened a drawer. He took out a joint and lit it. The sweet acrid smell of the marijuana reached her nostrils as he held it toward her. "I don't have anything to drink."

"That's okay," she said, taking a toke from the reefer. "This is good grass."

He smiled. "A friend of mine just in from Istanbul dropped it off. He also laid some righteous good coke on me. Ever use it?"

"Sometimes," she said, passing the joint back to him. She looked at him as she dragged on it. She put down her beach bag and moved toward him. She felt him. She felt the buzzing in her head and the wetness between her legs. It was really good grass if one toke could do that. She pulled at the knot of his shirt. "Are we going to talk or fuck?" she asked. "I only have an hour."

Deliberately, he placed the joint in an ashtray and then pushed the see-through blouse down from her shoulders exposing her naked breasts. He cupped one in each hand, squeezing the nipples between a thumb and forefinger until the pain suddenly flashed through her. "White bitch," he said, smiling.

Her smile was as taunting as his own. "Nigger!"

His hands pressed her to her knees in front of him, "You better learn to beg a little if you want some cock in your hot little pussy."

She had the shirt untied, now she pulled the zipper on his jeans. He wore nothing underneath and his phallus leapt free as she pulled the pants down around his knees. She put a hand on his shaft and pulled it toward her mouth.

His hand held her face away from him. "Beg!" he said sharply.

She looked up at him. "Please," she whispered.

He smiled and relaxed his hands, letting her take him in her mouth while he reached into the open bureau drawer and took out a small vial filled with coke. The tiny spoon was attached to the cap with a small bead chain. Expertly, he took a spoonful and snorted it up each nostril. Then he looked down at her. "Your turn," he said.

"I'm happy," she said, kissing him and licking at his testicles. "I don't need any."

He pulled at her hair, snapping her head back. "White bitch!" He lifted her to her feet and filled a spoon and held it under a nostril. "You do as I say. Snort!"

She sniffed and the powder lifted from the spoon into her nose. Almost in the same second he had the filled spoon under the other nostril. This time she snorted without his saying a word. She felt the faint numbness in her nose almost immediately, then the powder exploded in her genitals. "God!" she exclaimed. "That's wild. I came just sniffing it."

He laughed. "You ain't seen nothin' yet, baby. I'm goin' to show you some tricks that my pappy taught me with that stuff."

A moment later they were naked on the bed and she was laughing. She had never felt so good. He took another spoonful and rubbed it on his gums, making her do the same. Then he licked her nipples until they were wet from his tongue and sprinkled a little of the white powder on them and began to work them over with his mouth and fingers.

She had never felt them grow so large and hard. After a few moments, she thought they were going to burst with the agonizing pleasure. She began to moan and writhe. "Fuck me," she said. "Fuck me!"

"Not yet," he laughed. "We only beginning." He jackknifed her legs and sprinkled the coke over her clitoris, then put his head between her legs.

After a moment she was screaming as she never had screamed before. Each orgasm seemed to take her higher than she had ever been. She reached down for his phallus and finding it pulled herself around so that she was able to take him into her mouth. Greedily she sucked at him. She wanted to swallow him alive, to choke herself to death on that giant beautiful tool.

Suddenly he held her away. She stared up at him, almost unable to breathe. He was on his knees between her legs, his phallus reaching out over her. He took the vial and sprinkled the powder until the glistening wet head looked as if it were coated with sugar. Then he held her legs wide apart as he eased into her slowly.

She felt her lungs congest. He felt so large. She was afraid for a moment she could not take him. Then he was all the way inside her and for a moment was still. She felt the tingling reach up inside her belly. Slowly he began to move, gently at first, with long smooth strokes, then picking up the tempo until he was slamming into her like a trip hammer.

Somewhere in the distance she could hear herself screaming as orgasm after orgasm ripped her apart. She had never come like this before. Never. She, who had always thought that this kind of sexual excitement was only something that people talked or read about. A kind of game they played on themselves to hide their feelings. And if it were true, she felt that it was something beyond her capacity to feel. For her, sex was her triumph over the male; any satisfaction in it for her was purely accidental. But this was different. Now she was being used, she was being pleasured, she was giving, she was taking, she was being completed.

Finally she could take it no more. "Stop," she cried. "Please stop!"

His body came to rest against her; he was still hard inside her. She looked up at him. In the dim red light the fine patina of sweat covering his face and chest glowed copper. His teeth shone white as he smiled. "You all right, white lady?"

She nodded her head slowly. "Did you come?"

"No," he said. "That's the only thing my pappy didn't tell me. Use enough to make a lady happy an' that's just enough to keep you from makin' it."

She stared at him for a long moment, then, suddenly and unaccountably she began to cry.

He watched her for a moment, then without speaking, got out of the bed and walked over to the sink. Bending over he swung the bidet out into the room and turned on the water. He straightened up and looked at her. "You have to let it run for a few minutes if you want to get hot water," he explained.

He opened the small cabinet over the sink and took out a towel and a washcloth which he hung over the connecting pipes. With a finger he tested the water. "It's all ready for you," he said.

She looked at him without speaking.

"You did say you only had an hour, didn't you?" he asked.

She nodded, sitting up. "I don't know if I can walk."

He smiled. "You'll be okay, once you get movin'."

She got out of bed. He was right. After the first step, the strength came back into her limbs. She squatted over the bidet and took the soap and washcloth from his outstretched hand. She washed herself quickly. The lukewarm water was refreshing. She picked up the towel and dried herself, then began to dress while he washed himself. "I'm sorry you didn't make it," she said.

"That's okay," he said. "I promised you a trip to the moon and I wanted you to have it."

"I had it all right," she said. "I'll never forget it."

He was hesitant. "Maybe we could do it again sometime?"

"Maybe," she said. Dressed, she reached for her beach bag and took out some money. She ripped off a few large bills and held them out toward him. "I hope you don't mind."

He took the money. "I could use it. But you don't have to."

"I didn't give you much else," she said.

"You gave me a lot, lady," he said. "You left all your friends to come with me. That's something."

Something in his tone of voice caught her. "Do you know me?"

He shook his head. "No."

"Then why did you ask me?"

"I saw you on the beach," he said. "After that man sent Jacques out to meet you."

"You know Jacques?" she asked.

"Yes," he said. "I spent last night with him."

She was silent for a moment. "Is Jacques . . ."

He nodded. "He'd rather be a girl."

"And you?"

"I like to fuck," he said. "I don't give a damn as long as there's a hole to stick it in."

"Do you know the man who spoke to Jacques?"

"I never saw him before. He had dark hair and spoke French with an Arabic accent. I heard him say that Jacques had to get something by tonight because you were leaving for California tomorrow and that Jacques shouldn't worry because he had fixed it so that the San Marco wouldn't be able to take you back to Cannes."

Suddenly it all came together in her head. Youssef was the only one who knew that she was leaving tomorrow. He had come down from Paris to handle the flight arrangements for her on Baydr's instructions.

A long time ago she had heard there had once been a connection between Youssef and Princess Mara. And Mara had pushed Jacques on to her. What she didn't understand was what possible benefit Youssef could get from it. Unless—unless he meant to use it against her with Baydr.

An unfamiliar feeling of fear came over her. Youssef had never really liked her but that didn't seem to be enough of an explanation for something like this. She just didn't know. All she did know was that she had better get back to the villa tonight.

But that was a problem. There were no taxis in St. Tropez after midnight. And she had given Guy, her chauffeur, the night off so she could not call him.

She looked at Gerard. "Do you have a car?"

"No."

"Damn!" A worried look crossed her face.

"I have a bike,' he said. "I'll take you back if you'll ride behind me."

"You're lovely,' she said, smiling suddenly. She threw her arms around him in a sudden burst of relief and kissed his cheek. "It should be great fun."

He put her arms down, suddenly embarrassed. "Don't be too sure, lady. Just see if you think so after I get you there."

Chapter Three

It was about two hours after they had taken off from Paris. The cabin attendants were busy preparing to serve lunch. Jordana looked back at Youssef. "I think I'd like to get some sleep now."

Youssef unfastened his seat belt and rose to his feet. "I'll have them prepare your seats right away." He glanced at Diana, Jordana's secretary. She was dozing in the window seat next to his, her unfinished drink resting on the tray in front of her.

He made his way to the chief steward, who was standing near the galley. "Madam Al Fay would like to rest."

"But we are about to serve déjeuner," the steward protested.

"She is not hungry."

"Oui, monsieur," the steward said quickly. He left the galley and went back through the curtains that separated first class from economy.

Youssef turned and looked at Jordana. Her eyes were completely hidden by the large dark glasses but there wasn't a line on her face to indicate that she had not slept the night before. She was looking at the Air France magazine on her lap, sipping from a glass of white wine.

He suppressed a yawn. He was exhausted. He had been awake since four that morning when Jacques had called him from St. Tropez to tell him that she had disappeared.

The San Marco was still in the port and there was no trace of her anywhere in the village. Jacques had been to every restaurant and discotheque that was still open. Youssef had put down the telephone still fuming.

There was nothing he could do but wait until he went to the villa in the morning to take her to the airport. He could not get back to sleep. All the money he had given Jacques, all the plans he had made, were for naught. Even telling the mechanic at the Citroën garage to take the SM away from Jacques that morning had given him no satisfaction.

Jordana had been at breakfast when he arrived at the villa at nine o'clock. She said nothing about the evening, nor did she mention anything about how she had returned home. Casually, he had found out from one of the security guards at the villa that she had arrived by taxi from Cannes at about five that morning.

In the limousine on the way to the airport he had explained the arrangements for the flight. They had the last four seats in the first-class section. Two were for her. He and her secretary would occupy the seats directly behind. He had also reserved the first three seats in the economy section so that when she wanted to rest she could lie down there. Special handling had also been arranged for her luggage. It would be placed in the cabin so that she would not have to wait for it in Los Angeles. There would be a special U.S. Customs agent waiting for them on arrival so that they could transfer quickly to the helicopter which would take them to Rancho del Sol. E.T.A. for A.F. 003 was 4 p.m. Los Angeles time; dinner at Rancho del Sol was set for 8 p.m. If everything went according to schedule she would have ample time to dress.

The steward came back to him. "It is ready for madame."

"Thank you," Youssef said. He walked back to the seat: "It's okay," he told her.

She nodded and rose to her feet. She opened her purse and took out a small vial and shook two pills into her hand. She swallowed them quickly with a sip of wine. "That's to make sure that I sleep."

"Of course."

"Please see that I'm awakened at least an hour and a half before we land."

"I'll take care of that," he answered. "Have a good rest."

She stared at him for a moment. "Thank you."

He watched her disappear through the curtains and sank back into his seat. Beside him, Diana stirred but did not open her eyes. He looked at his watch and glanced out the window. There were still eleven hours left. This time he did not suppress his yawn. He closed his eyes, hoping that he could get some rest.

Air France had done a good job. Temporary curtains, like those used for the second flight crew on these extra long nonstop flights had been rigged around her seats. The window blinds were drawn and it was dark as she stretched out and pulled the blanket over her.

She lay there quietly waiting for the sleeping pills to take effect. She began to feel the aching protest of her body as the exhaustion seeped through her. She could still feel the pounding of the motorcycle against the road as they raced through the early dawn toward Cannes. She had made Gerard drop her at the railroad station in the center of town. There were always taxis there.

She had offered him more money but he had refused. "You've given me enough," he said.

"Thank you," she said.

He put the bike into gear. "Look me up when you come back to St. Tro."

"I will. And thank you again."

He took the crash helmet he had loaned her and strapped it onto the back seat. "Goodbye."

"Goodbye." He gunned the engine and took off. She watched him turn the corner toward the sea, then walked over to the first taxi on line and got in.

It had been daylight and a few minutes after five o'clock when she entered her bedroom at the villa. Her suitcases, neatly packed and still open in case there was anything she wanted to put in at the last moment, were against the wall. A note from her secretary was propped against the lamp on the night table. She picked it up. It was terse, in Diana's usual style:

Departure Villa—9 A.M.

Departure Nice—Paris—10 A.M.

Departure Paris—L.A.—12 N.

E.T.A. Los Angeles—4 P.M. Pacific Coast Time.

She looked at the clock again. If she wanted to have breakfast with the boys at seven there was no point in going to bed now. She would be better off trying to sleep on the plane.

She went into the bathroom, opened the medicine cabinet and took out a vial of tablets. She popped a Dexamyl into her mouth and swallowed it with a drink of water. It would keep her going at least until the plane took off from Paris.

Slowly she began to undress. When she was naked, she looked at herself in the full-length mirror that was built into the wall of her dressing room. There were faint bruises on her breasts where Gerard had squeezed them, but they could not be seen in dim light, and in the daytime a little body makeup would cover them. Her belly was just flat enough and there was no extra flesh on her hips or thighs. She placed her hands on her pubis and gently parting the soft blond hair, examined herself critically. Her vagina felt heavy and swollen and seemed slightly red and irritated. A faint tingling went through her as she thought about the way the black had taken her. She had never dreamed that she could come as many times as she had. She turned back to the medicine cabinet and took out a packet of Massengill. A douche wouldn't hurt and at least it would be soothing. As she mixed the solution another thought flashed through her mind.

What if the black had a venereal disease? There was always a possibility. Especially since she knew he was bi. Somewhere she had read that homosexuals had the highest rate of venereal infections. Again she opened the medicine cabinet. This time she swallowed two penicillin tablets. She put the vial in her handbag so that she would not forget to keep taking them for the next few days.

The Dexamyl was beginning to take effect and when she finished her douche she went right into the shower. Hot and cold, hot and cold, hot and cold, three times, as she had learned to do it from Baydr. When she stepped out of the shower she felt as refreshed as if she had slept all night.

She sat down at her dressing table and slowly began to put on her make-up. Afterward she dressed and went downstairs to the breakfast room to join the boys.

They were surprised to see her. Usually she did not have breakfast with them. Instead they would come to her room after she had awakened, which was generally just before her lunch.

"Where are you going, Mommy?" Muhammad asked.

"I'm going to meet Daddy in California."

His face brightened. "Are we going too?"

"No darling. It's just a quick trip. I will be back in a few days."

He was visibly disappointed. "Will Daddy be coming back with you?"

"I don't know," she said. It was the truth. She didn't know. Baydr had only asked her to join him. He had said nothing about his future plans.

"I hope he does come," Samir said.

"I hope so too," she said.

"I want him to hear how well we speak Arabic," the little one said.

"Will you tell him, Mommy?" Muhammad asked.

"I will tell him. Daddy will be very proud of you."

Both children smiled. "Also tell him that we miss him," Muhammad said.

"I will."

Samir looked up at her. "Why doesn't Daddy come home like other daddies? My friends' daddies come home every night. Doesn't he like us?"

"Daddy loves you both. But Daddy is very busy and has to work very hard. He wants to come home to see you but he can't."

"I wish he could come home like other daddies," Samir said.

"What are you doing today?" Jordana asked to change the subject.

Muhammad's face brightened. "Nanny's taking us on a picnic."

"That should be fun."

"It's all right," he said. "But it's more fun when Daddy takes us water-skiing."

She looked at her sons. There was something about their serious faces and large dark eyes that reached into her heart. In many ways they were miniatures of their father, and sometimes she felt that there was so very little that she could do for them. Boys needed to model themselves after their father. She wondered if Baydr knew that. Sometimes she wondered if Baydr cared about anything but his business.

The nanny came into the room. "Time for your riding lesson, boys," she said in her dry Scottish voice. "The teacher is here."

They jumped from their chairs and ran, whooping to the door. "Just a moment boys," the nanny said. "Haven't you forgotten something?"

The two boys looked at each other, then, shamefacedly, trooped back to their mother. They held their cheeks up to be kissed.

"I have an idea," Samir said, looking up at her.

She looked at the little one, a smile coming to her face. She knew what was coming. "Yes?"

"When you come back, you surprise us with a present," he said seriously. "Don't you think that's a good idea?"

"It's a good idea. What kind of a present do you have in mind?"

He leaned over and whispered into his brother's ear. Muhammad nodded. "You know those baseball caps that Daddy wears when he's on the boat?" he asked.

She nodded.

"Can you get us some like those?" he asked.

"I'll try."

"Thank you, Mommy," they chorused. She kissed them again and they ran off without a backward glance. She sat at the table for a moment, then rose and went back to her room. At nine o'clock, when Youssef arrived with the limousine, she was waiting for him.

The drone of the jets and the sleeping pills began to take effect. She closed her eyes and thought about Youssef. What had he been trying to do? Was he acting on his own or at Baydr's instructions? It was odd that Baydr had been away for almost three months. That was longer than they had ever been separated before. And it wasn't just another woman. She understood him better than that. She had known about Baydr and his women long before they had got married. Just as he had known about her passing affairs.

Neither of them knew or wanted to know the details. No, this was something else. Deeper and more important. But she would never know what it was unless he told her.

Though he had been Westernized in many ways and she had become a Muslim, they were still separated by a thousand years of different philosophies. Because although the Prophet had granted women more rights than they had ever had until that time, He still had not granted them full equality. In truth all their rights were subject to man's pleasure.

That was one thing that was clear in their relationship. She knew it and he knew it. There was nothing she had that he could not take away from her if he so desired, even her children.

A chill ran through her. Then she dismissed the thought. No, he would never do that. He still needed her in many ways. Like now, when he wanted her to appear beside him in the Western world so that they would not think him so much a stranger.

This was Jordana's last thought before she fell asleep.

Chapter Four

The noon sun filtered through the trees into the loggia outside the Polo Lounge of the Beverly Hills Hotel, tracing delicate lines on the pink tablecloths. Baydr sat in the shadows of one of the booths, sheltered from the sun. Carriage and the two Japanese were opposite him. He watched them as they finished their lunch.

Meticulously their knives and forks were placed lengthwise across their plates in the European manner to signify that they were finished with the course.

"Coffee?" he asked.

They nodded. He signaled the waiter and ordered four coffees. He offered them cigarettes, which they refused. Baydr lit one and sat there looking at them.

The elder Japanese said something in his own language to his associate. The younger man leaned across the table. "Mr. Hokkaido asks if you have had time to consider our proposition."

Baydr addressed himself to the young man even though he knew that Hokkaido understood every word.

"I have thought about it."

"And?" The young man could not restrain his eagerness.

Baydr saw the flash of disapproval cross the old man's face and quickly disappear.

"It won't work," he said "The arrangements are entirely too one-sided."

"I don't understand," the young man said. "We are prepared to build the ten tankers at the price you offered. All we ask is that you use our banks to finance."

"I don't think you understand," Baydr said quietly. "You are talking about making a sale and I am interested in forming a total consortium. I can see no point in our competing with one another to purchase certain properties. All we succeed in doing is driving up the price we ultimately pay. Take the Rancho del Sol deal, for example. One of your groups just bought it."

"It was another group, not ours," the young man said quickly. "But I didn't know you were interested in it."

"I was not," Baydr said. "But there is another big development in that area that we are interested in and so is your group. The end result is that the asking price has almost doubled and which ever one of us gets it has lost before we begin."

"You are negotiating through your bank in La Jolla?" the young man asked.

The young man turned to Hokkaido and spoke quickly in Japanese. Hokkaido listened attentively, nodding, then replied. The young man turned back to Baydr. "Mr. Hokkaido expresses his regrets that we find ourselves in competition for that property but says that negotiations began before we were ourselves in contact with each other."

"I regret it also. That was why I came to you. To find a rapprochement. Neither of us needs the other's money. Each of us has more than enough of his own. But if we work together perhaps we can be helpful to one another on other matters. That is why I spoke to you about building tankers for us."

"But even that you make difficult," the young man said. "We will build the ten tankers you want but where will we find ten tankers to deliver to you immediately? There are none on the market."

"I know that, but your shipping line has over one hundred. It would be a simple matter for you to transfer them to our company, one in which we could each own fifty percent. In that manner, you are really not losing the benefit of them."

"We're losing fifty percent of the income they produce," the young man said. "And we see nothing to replace that."

"Fifty percent of the income from the additional tankers you are building will more than take care of that," Baydr said. "And fifty percent of your foreign investment supplied by me will certainly be looked on with favor by your government."

"We have been having no trouble getting our foreign investments approved," the young man said.

"World conditions change," Baydr said smoothly. "A recession in the Western world could alter your favorable balance of payments."

"There is nothing like that on the horizon at this time," the young man said.

"One never knows. A change in the world's supply of energy could bring its technocracy to a screeching halt. Then you would be faced with two problems. One, a shortage of customers; two, an inability to maintain your own rate of productivity."

Again the young man addressed himself to Hokkaido. The older man nodded slowly as he listened. Then he turned to Baydr and spoke in English. "If we agree to your proposition, would you use the tankers to bring oil to Japan?"

Baydr nodded.

"Exclusively?"

Again Baydr nodded.

"How much oil would you be able to guarantee?" Hokkaido asked.

"That would depend entirely on what my government would allow. I think under the right circumstances a satisfactory agreement could be reached."

"Would you be able to secure a most-favored nation clause?"

"I could do that."

Hokkaido was silent for a moment. His next words were very clear and precise. "To recap, Mr. Al Fay, in effect you are saying that if we give you five ships now at half price and build five more ships for you with our own money, you will then be good enough to use those ships to bring to our country the oil we buy from you."

Baydr did not answer. His face was impassive.

The Japanese smiled suddenly. "Now I know why you are called the Pirate. You are indeed samurai. But I will still have to discuss the entire matter with my associates in Japan."

"Of course."

"Would you be able to come to Tokyo if we should desire to go ahead?"

"Yes."

The Japanese got to their feet. Baydr rose also. Mr. Hokkaido bowed and held out his hand. "Thank you for a most enjoyable and informative lunch, Mr. Al Fay." Baydr shook his head. "Thank you for your time and patience."

Carriage signaled for the check as the Japanese walked away. "I don't know what they're complaining about," he said with a laugh. "We're paying for the lunch." He signed the check and added, "Michael Vincent is waiting in the bungalow for us."

"Okay," Baydr asked. "What time is Jordana's plane arriving?"

"E.T.A. is four o'clock," Dick answered. "I checked just before lunch. It's running about fifteen minutes late. We should leave the hotel no later than three-thirty."

They walked into the dark Polo Lounge and out again into the sunlight to take the path which led to their bungalows. Their footsteps echoed on the pink cement walk.

"Did you check with Rancho del Sol?" Baydr asked.

Carriage nodded. "Everything's ready. We've taken a private house for you near the main building, overlooking the golf course. The bank people have all been booked into the club itself. Dinner will be in a private room with cocktails first. That will give all of us a chance to get to know each other."

"Any cancellations?"

"No. They'll all be there. They're as curious about you as you are about them."

Baydr laughed. "I wonder what they would think if I showed up in a traditional costume?"

Carriage laughed with him. "They'd probably shit. I've already heard talk that they suspect you of being a simple savage. That's a very snobbish group down there. All W.A.S.P. No Jews, no Catholics, no foreigners."

"They should love Jordana then," Baydr said. It was true. She was a born and bred California girl and they didn't come any W.A.S.P.ier.

"They will," Carriage answered.

"Still, it's not going to be easy. I have noticed a lack of enthusiasm in their pursuit of new business and we have dropped some important accounts since we've taken over the bank."

"According to their reports, they blame it on the Jewish-controlled Los Angeles banks."

"That's too easy an excuse to satisfy me. I always get suspicious when they tell me something they think I will accept. They bungled the Star Ranch offer and let the Japanese maneuver us into a bid situation."

"They said the Japanese were working through the L.A. banks."

"Not good enough. They were there on the ground floor. We should have had it all wrapped up before L.A. even heard about it. Now it's had time to get all the way to Tokyo and back."

They were at the bungalow. Carriage opened the door and they went into the cottage. The cool, dark air-conditioned room felt good after the white heat of the sun.

Vincent got to his feet, the inevitable glass of whiskey on the cocktail table before him. "Baydr, it's good to see you again."

"It's always good to see you again, my friend." They shook hands and Baydr walked around the small table to the couch and sat down. "How is the script coming?"

"That's what I wanted to see you about. At first, I thought it would be easy. You know. Like my films about Moses and Jesus, there would always be some miracles to fall back on for visual excitement. The parting of the Red Sea for the Israelites, the Resurrection. But it's not like that at all. Your Prophet has no miracles going for him. He was just a man."

Baydr laughed. "That's true. Just like a man. Like all of us. No more and no less. Does that disappoint you?"

"Cinematically, yes," Vincent answered.

"It would seem to me that should make the message of the Prophet even more convincing and dramatic. That a man, just like any of us, should bring the revelations of Allah to his fellow men. What about his persecution by the pagan Arabs and the taunts of the Jews and Christians, and his banishment and flight from Medina? And what about his battle to return to Mecca? Surely, there should be enough drama in that for several films."

"For the Muslim world perhaps, but I doubt very much that the Western world would take to the idea of their being the villains of the piece. And you did say that you wanted this film to be shown all over the world, didn't you?"

"Yes."

"There's our problem," Vincent answered. He picked up the whiskey and drained his glass. "We're going to have to solve that before we begin on the script."

Baydr was silent. The truth in the Koran was self evident—why, then, was there always this problem? The unbelievers didn't even want to listen. If, only once, they would open their minds and hearts to the Prophet's message the light would come to them. He looked thoughtfully at the director. "If I remember your version, the film on Christ had him crucified by the Romans, not the Jews, is that right?"

Vincent nodded.

"Was that not contrary to fact?" Baydr asked. "In reality did the Jews themselves not condemn Christ to the cross?"

"There are different opinions," Vincent said. "Because Christ Himself was a Jew and betrayed by one of His own apostles, Judas, who also was a Jew, and because He was hated by the rabbis of the Orthodox temples for threatening their power and authority, many believe that the Jews pushed the Romans into crucifying Him."

"But the pagan Romans were made the villains of the film, were they not?"

"Yes."

"Then we have the answer," Baydr said. "We will build our film around the Prophet's conflict with the Quraish, which led to his flight to Medina. The Prophet's wars in reality were not with the Jews, who already had accepted the principle of one God, but with the three great Arab tribes who worshipped many gods. It was they who drove him away from Mecca, not the Jews."

Vincent stared at him. "I remember reading it but I never thought of it in that light. Somehow I felt that the Arabs had always been with him."

"Not in the beginning," Baydr said. "The Quraish tribe consisted of pagan Arabs who worshipped many gods and it was to them rather than the Jews and Christians that Muhammad first directed his teachings of the true Allah. It was they whom he first called 'unbelievers'."

"I'll try that approach," Vincent said. He refilled his glass and looked across the table at Baydr. "Are you sure you would not be interested in writing the script with me?"

Baydr laughed. "I'm a businessman, not a writer, I'll leave that to you."

"But you know the story better than anyone I have met."

"Read the Koran again. Maybe then you will see what I see." He got to his feet. "Youssef will be arriving later this afternoon and we'll all get together after the weekend. Now if you'll excuse me, I'm going out to the airport to meet my wife."

Vincent got to his feet. "I won't hold you up then. But I am glad that we could talk. I think you've set me on the right track. I'll get right to work on the new approach."

They shook hands and Vincent left the bungalow. Baydr turned to Carriage. "What do you think?" he asked.

"If I may say so, chief, I think you ought to pay him off and forget the whole thing. The only thing you can guarantee yourself in a film like that is losses."

"The Koran teaches that man can benefit in many ways by his actions, to seek not only the profit but the good."

"I hope you're right, but I would still be very cautious before you go ahead with the film."

"You're a strange young man. Don't you ever think of anything but dollars and cents?"

Carriage met his gaze. "Not when I'm working. I don't imagine you hired me for my social graces."

"I guess not," he said. "But there are some things more important than money."

"That's not my decision to make," Dick said. "Not when it's your money." He began to put some papers into his attache case. "My job is to be sure that you are aware of all the risks. The rest is up to you."

"And you think the film is risky?"

"Very."

Baydr thought for a moment. "I'll keep that in mind before we proceed. We'll go into it again when the script is completed and budgeted."

"Yes, sir."

Baydr walked to his bedroom door. "Thank you, Dick," he said quietly. "I don't want you ever to feel that I don't appreciate what you're trying to do for me."

Dick flushed. It wasn't often that Baydr complimented him. "You don't have to thank me, chief."

Baydr smiled. "I'll grab a quick shower and I'll be ready to go in a few minutes. Have the car brought around in front of the bungalow."

"Will do, chief." Carriage was on the telephone before Baydr closed the bedroom door.

Chapter Five

As usual, the plane from Paris was an hour late. Silently Baydr cursed the airlines. They were all alike. They never gave accurate arrival information until it was too late to do anything but sit at the airport and wait for the plane to come down.

The telephone rang in the small V.I.P. room and the hostess picked it up. She listened for a moment, then turned to them. "Double-o-three is touching down right now. It should be at the gate in a few minutes."

Baydr got to his feet. She rose from her desk and walked toward them. "Mr. Hansen will meet you at the gate and expedite Mrs. Al Fay through the formalities."

"Thank you," Baydr said.

There was a crowd around the arrival area. Mr. Hansen, a heavy-set man in an Air France uniform, came to meet them. Quickly, he ushered them downstairs through the restricted customs area. A uniformed immigration officer joined them and they went into the entrance room, just as Jordana came from the plane.

He nodded to himself in approval. Jordana had great instincts. The casual tie-dyed jeans and see-through clothing she affected in the south of France were nowhere in evidence. Instead, she was the fashionably dressed stylish young Californian wife. The Dior suit with its modestly cut skirt, the slouch hat and lightly applied makeup were exactly right in the society they were about to enter. He moved forward to greet her.

She held her cheek for his kiss. "You look lovely," he said.

"Thank you," she smiled.

"The flight comfortable?"

"I slept all the way. They fixed up a special bunk for me."

"Good. We have a kind of difficult schedule in front of us."

Youssef, slightly rumpled in his dark suit, appeared behind her with her secretary. Baydr shook hands with them, as the Air France representative collected their passports for clearance. He led Jordana away from the crowd of people so they could talk privately.

"I'm sorry I could not get back this summer," he said.

"We were too. The boys especially. They gave me a message for you."

"Yes?"

"They wanted to tell you that they are doing very well in their Arabic. That you would not have to be ashamed of them."

"Are they?" he asked.

"I think so. They insist on speaking nothing but Arabic to all the help whether they are understood or not."

He smiled, pleased. "I'm glad." His eyes met her own. "And you? What have you been doing with yourself?"

"Nothing much, the usual thing."

"You look very well."

She did not answer.

"Were there many parties this year?"

"There are always parties."

"Anything exciting?"

"Not particularly." She looked at him. "You've lost weight. You look thin."

"I'll have to eat more," he said. "It would never do if I were to go back to the Middle East looking like this. They might think I was falling on hard times."

She smiled. She knew what he was talking about. The Arabs still judged a man's success by his girth. A portly man was always more highly regarded than a thin one. "Eat bread and potatoes," she said. "And more lamb."

He laughed aloud. She knew how Western his taste was. He disliked starchy and fatty foods, preferring to eat beefsteaks. "I'll remember that."

Hansen came over to them. "Everything's okay," he said. "We have a car waiting on the field to take you over to the helipad."

"We can go then," Baydr said. He gestured to Youssef, who came toward them. "Vincent's at the Beverly Hills Hotel," Baydr told him. "You spend the weekend with him and try to find out exactly where we're at. I'll be in touch with you on Monday."

Youssef tried to conceal his disappointment. He hated to be left out of anything that might be important. "Do you think there's a problem with Vincent?"

"I don't know, but it would seem to me that in three months he should have at least made a start."

"Leave it to me, chief," Youssef said confidently. "I'll build a fire under him."

"It will take about a half-hour to get down there," the helicopter pilot said as they lifted off.

"What's the dress for tonight?" Jordana asked. "How much time will we have?"

Baydr looked at his watch. "Cocktails are at eight, dinner at nine. Black tie."

Jordana looked at him. She knew how he hated evening dress. "You're going all out."

"That's right," he said. "I want to make a good impression. I have a feeling they resent me for taking over the bank."

"I'm sure they'll get over it once they meet you."

"I hope so," Baydr said seriously. "But I don't know. They're very clannish down there."

"They will. I know that crowd very well. Expatriate Pasadena. But they're no different from anyone else. They go with the money."

The giant bouquet of red roses presented to Jordana by the president of the bank, Joseph E. Hutchinson III, and his wife, Dolly, when they arrived proved that she was at least partly right.

There was a soft knock at the door, and the muffled sound of Jabir's voice announcing, "It is fifteen minutes past seven, master."

"Thank you," Baydr called back. He rose from the small table at which he had been reading the latest bank reports. He would have time for another shower before he changed into his dinner jacket. Quickly, he took off his shirt and trousers and, naked, he started for the bathroom which separated his bedroom from Jordana's.

He opened the door, just as she rose, glistening, from the scented bath. He stood for a moment, staring. "I'm sorry"—the apology sprang to his lips without thought—"I didn't know you were still in here."

She returned his look. "It's all right," she said, a faint tinge of irony in her voice. "There's no need to apologize."

He was silent.

She reached for a bath towel and began to wrap it around her. He put out a hand to stop her. She looked at him questioningly.

"I'd almost forgotten how beautiful you are," he said.

Slowly, he took the towel from her hand. He let it fall to the floor. His fingers traced a line from her cheek, across the flushed, rising nipple, past the tiny indentation of her navel to the soft swelling of her mound. "Just beautiful," he whispered.

She didn't move.

"Look at me!" he said, a sudden insistence in his voice.

She looked up into his face. There was a gentle sorrow in his eyes. "Jordana."

"Yes?"

"Jordana, what has happened to us that we have become strangers?"

Unexpectedly her eyes began to fill with tears. "I don't know," she whispered.

He took her into his arms and pressed her head against his shoulder. "There are so many things that are wrong," he said. "I would not know where to begin to correct them."

She wanted to talk to him but she could not find the words. They came from different worlds. In his world the woman was nothing, the man was everything. If she said to him that she had the same needs he did, the same sexual and social drives, he would regard it as a threat to his male supremacy. And he would think that she was not being a proper wife. Still, these needs were what had brought them together in the beginning.

She pressed her face against his cheek, weeping silently.

He stroked her hair gently. "I've missed you," he said. He put a hand under her chin and raised her eyes. "There is no one else like you for me."

"Then why do you stay away? Why the others?" she thought to herself.

He answered almost as if he were reading her mind. "They mean nothing," he said. "They are only to pass the time."

She still did not speak.

"Is it like that with you?" he asked.

She stared up into his eyes. He knew. He had always known. And yet he had never once spoken about it. She nodded.

His lips tightened for a moment. Then he sighed. "A man begins his own heaven or hell right here on this earth. As I have begun my own."

"You're not angry with me?" she whispered.

"Have I the right?" he asked. "Judgment is for the time we stand before Allah and our book is read. My own sins are enough for me to bear. And you are not one of us, so even the rules that might be applied could not hold true. There is but one request that I make of you."

"What is that?" she asked.

"Let it not be with a Jew," he said. "To all others I will be as blind as you."

Her eyes fell. "Must there be others?"

"I cannot answer that for you," he said. "I am a man."

There was nothing she could say.

He raised her head again and kissed her. "I love you, Jordana," he said.

She felt his warmth flowing into her as she clung to him. His strength hardened against her belly. Her hand dropped to encircle him. He was hard and moist in her fingers. "Baydr," she cried, "Baydr."

He stared into her eyes for a long moment, then lifting her under her arms, he raised her into the air before him. Automatically, her legs widened to encircle his waist, then slowly he lowered her onto him. She gasped as she felt him penetrate her. It seemed as if he were thrusting a burning steel rod into her heart. Still standing, still holding her, he began to move slowly inside her.

The heat began to run through her and she could not contain herself. Clinging to him like a monkey she began to move spastically on him as orgasm after orgasm began to shake her. The thoughts were racing crazily through her head. It was not right. This was not what she should have. This was not the punishment she sought.

She opened her eyes and stared wildly into his face. "Hurt me," she said.

"What?"

"Hurt me. Please. Like you did the last time. I deserve no better."

He stood very still for a moment, then slowly, he lowered her to the ground and took her arms from around him. His voice was suddenly cold. "You'd better dress," he said, "or we'll be late for the party."

He turned abruptly and went back into his room. After a moment, she began to shiver. She reached for the towel, cursing to herself. She could do nothing right.

Chapter Six

The heat from the white glaring sun seemed to bounce off the jagged rocks and the sands of the desert that stretched in front of them. An occasional wild scrub leaned brown and weary in the warm wind. The chatter of the machine gun somewhere ahead of them fell silent.

Leila lay motionless in the small foxhole. She felt the sweat gathering in her armpits, between her breasts and between her legs. Carefully, she rolled over on her back. She heaved a sigh of relief. The ache in her breasts from pressing so hard into the ground began to ease. She squinted up into the sky and wondered how long she should lie here. The Syrian mercenary in charge of their training had told her not to move until the rest of the platoon caught up to her. She glanced sidewise at her heavy man's chronograph. They should have been here at least ten minutes ago.

Stoically she forced herself to wait. Maybe it was only a training exercise but those were real bullets they were using and already one woman had been killed and three others wounded. After the last exercise the grim joke throughout the camp had been the question as to who would get the most credit for wiping out the Fedayeen—themselves or the Israelis?

She wanted a cigarette but did not move. A shadow of smoke in the clear air would be an invitation to draw fire. A rustling sound came from behind the foxhole.

Silently, she rolled over on her belly and turned to face it, pulling the rifle toward her at the same time. She inched toward the top of the foxhole and began to raise her head over the edge.

A heavy hand came down on her, jamming the steel helmet and liner over her ears. Through the pain, she heard the mercenary's gruff voice. "Stupid cunt! You were told to keep your head down. I could have picked you off from a hundred yards away."

He tumbled into the foxhole beside her, breathing heavily. He was a squat, heavy-set man, short of breath and patience. "What's going on up there?" he asked.

"How the hell should I know?" she retorted angrily. "You told me to keep my head down."

"But you were supposed to be the advance scout."

"You tell me how I'm supposed to do both," she said, sarcastically, "find out what's happening without raising my head out of the foxhole."

He was silent. Without a word, he took out a package of cigarettes and held one out to her. She took it and he lit the cigarettes for both of them.

"I thought we weren't supposed to smoke," she said.

"Their mother's cunt," he said. "I'm getting tired of playing these stupid games."

"When is the platoon coming up?"

"Not until dark. We decided it wouldn't be safe for them to move until then."

"Then why did you come up here?"

He looked at her, his dark eyes moody. "Somebody had to let you know of the change in plan."

She stared back at him. He could have sent one of the others; he didn't have to come up himself. But she knew why he did. By now she must be the only one of the women in the platoon he had not had.

She wasn't too concerned. She could handle him if she had to. Or wanted to. In many ways everything had been made too easy. All the traditional taboos of the Muslims had disappeared. In the fight for freedom, the women were told that it was their duty to give solace and comfort to their men. In the new, free society, there would be no one to point a finger against them. It was just another way the women could help win the battle.

He pulled the canteen from his belt and unscrewed the cap. He tilted his head back and let the water trickle slowly into his throat, then handed it to her. She poured a drop onto her fingers and delicately wiped her face. "By Allah, it is hot," he said.

She nodded, giving him back the canteen. "You're lucky," she said. "I've been out here two hours already. You have less than that until dark."

She rolled over on her back once again and pulled the helmet visor down so that her eyes were shaded from the sun. She could at least try to make herself comfortable while she waited. After a few moments she became aware of his gaze. Through narrowed eyelids, she could see him staring at her. She became very conscious of the dark blotches of sweat on her cotton uniform, under her arms, across her waist, and in the crotch of her trousers. It was almost as if she'd marked off her private areas.

"I'm going to try to rest," she said. "This heat's worn me out."

He didn't answer. She looked up at the sky. It was that peculiar shade of blue that always seemed to come toward the end of summer. Strange that it should be like that. Until now she had always associated it with the end of summer vacation and the return to school. A memory flashed through her mind. It had been a day like this, under the same blue sky, that her mother had told her that her father was going to get a divorce. Because of that American bitch. And because a miscarriage had left her barren, so that she could not give him a son.

Leila had been playing on the beach with her older sister that afternoon when suddenly Farida, their housekeeper, appeared. She seemed oddly agitated. "Come back to the house immediately," she said. "Your father has to leave and wants to say goodbye to you."

"All right," she had said. "We'll change out of our wet bathing suits."

"No," Farida said sharply. "There's not time for that. Your father is in a hurry."

She turned and began to waddle quickly back to the house. They fell into step behind her.

"I thought Daddy was planning to stay for a while," Amal said, "Why is he going?"

"I don't know, I am only a servant. It is not my place to ask."

The two girls exchanged glances. Farida made it her business to know everything. If she said she didn't know it was because she didn't want them to know.

She stopped in front of the side entrance to the house. "Wipe the sand from your feet," she commanded. "Your father is waiting in the front salon."

They wiped their feet quickly and ran through the house. Their father was waiting near the front door. Jabir was already taking his suitcases out to the car.

Baydr turned to them and smiled suddenly. But there was a curious dark sadness in his eyes. He dropped to one knee to embrace them as they came running up to him. "I'm so glad you came in time," he said. "I was afraid I would have to leave without saying goodbye to you."

"Where are you going, Daddy?" Leila asked.

"I have to go back to America on important business."

"I thought you were going to stay," Amal said.

"I can't."

"But you promised to take us water-skiing," Leila said.

"I'm sorry." His voice seemed to choke and suddenly his eyes were moist. He held them close to him. "You both be good girls now and listen to your mother."

There was something wrong. They could feel it but they did not know what it was. "When you come back, will you take us water-skiing?" Leila asked.

Her father didn't answer. Instead he held them very tightly. Abruptly he let them go and got to his feet. Leila looked up at him, thinking how handsome he was. None of the other fathers looked like him.

Jabir appeared in the doorway behind him. "It is getting late, master. We must hurry if we are to make the plane."

Baydr bent down and kissed them, first Amal, then Leila. "I'm depending on both you girls to take care of your mother and obey her."

Silently they nodded. He started for the door and they followed him. He was halfway down the steps toward the car when Leila called after him. "Will you be gone long, Daddy?"

He seemed to hesitate for a moment but he was in the car and the door closed without his giving an answer. They watched the car roll down the driveway and then went back into the house.

Farida was waiting for them. "Is Mother in her room?" Amal asked.

"Yes," Farida said. "But she's resting. She's not feeling well and asked that she not be disturbed."

"Will she come down for dinner?" Leila asked.

"I don't think so. Now you girls take your baths and wash all that sand off of you. Whether your mother comes to dinner or not, I want you both to be clean and fresh at the table."

It was not until later that night that they learned what was happening. Their mother's parents came over after dinner and when their grandmother saw them she burst into tears.

Anxiously she pulled them close to her heavy bosom. "My poor little orphans," she cried. "What will you do now?"

Grandfather Riad immediately grew angry. "Silence, woman!" he roared. "What are you trying to do? Frighten the children to death?"

Amal immediately began to cry. "My daddy's plane crashed!" she wailed.

"See?" Grandfather's voice was triumphant. "What did I tell you?" He pushed his wife aside and swept the oldest girl up into his arms. "Nothing happened to your daddy. He's fine."

"But Nana said we were orphans."

"You're not orphans," he said. "You still have your mother and your father. And us."

Leila stared up at her grandmother. The heavy eye makeup the old lady wore streaked her cheek. "Then why is Nana crying?"

The old man was uncomfortable. "She's upset because your daddy went away. That's why."

Leila shrugged. "That's nothing. Daddy is always going away. But it's all right. He comes back."

Grandfather Riad looked at her. He did not speak. Farida came into the salon. "Where is your mistress?" he asked.

"She is in her room," Farida replied. She looked at the children. "It is time to go to bed."

"That's right," Grandfather Riad said quickly. "Go to bed. We will see you in the morning."

"Will you take us to the beach?" Leila asked.

"Yes," her grandfather replied. "Now do as Farida said. Go to bed."

As they started up the stairs Leila heard her grandfather say, "Tell your mistress that we await her in the salon."

Farida's voice was disapproving. "The mistress is very upset. She will not come down."

Her grandfather's voice grew firm. "She will come down. You tell her that I said it was important."

Later, when they were in bed, they heard the loud sound of voices coming from downstairs. They crept out of their beds and opened the door. Her mother's voice was very shrill and angry.

"I have given him my life!" she wailed. "And this is the thanks I get for it. To be left for an American bitch with blond hair who has given him a bastard son!"

Their grandfather's voice was lower and calmer but they could still hear him. "He had no choice. It was the Prince's command."

"You defend him!" their mother said accusingly. "Against your own flesh and blood you defend the injustice. All you are concerned about is your bank and your money. As long as you have their deposits you do not care what happens to me!"

"And what is happening to you, woman?" Grandfather roared. "Is there anything you lack? You are left a millionaire. He did not take the children away from you as he could have done under the law. He gave you the property and the homes, here and in Beirut, and a special allowance for the girls. What more can you ask?"

"Is it my fault I could not give him a son?" Maryam cried. "Why is is always the woman who is to blame? Did I not bear him children, was I not a faithful wife, despite the fact that I knew he was carrying on with infidel whores all over the world. In the sight of Allah, which of us has lived a good life? Certainly it was I, not he."

"It is the will of Allah that a man must have a son," her father said. "And since you did not, it was not only his right but his duty to provide himself with an heir."

Maryam's voice was quieter now but it held a note of deadly intent. "It may be the will of Allah but he will pay for it someday. His daughters will know of his betrayal and he will be as nothing in their eyes. He will not see them again."

Then the voices dropped and they could hear no more from downstairs. Silently, the children closed the door and went back to their beds. It was all very strange and they did not really understand.

The next day when they were on the beach Leila suddenly looked up at her grandfather, who was sitting in a chair under an umbrella reading his newspaper. "If Daddy really wanted a son," she said, "why didn't he ask me? I would have been glad to be a boy."

Grandfather Riad put down the paper. "It's not as easy as that, child."

"Is it true what Mother said?" she asked. "Will we never see him again?"

He was silent for a long moment before he answered. "Your mother was angry. She'll get over it in time."

But she never did. And with the passing of the years, the girls gradually began to accept their mother's attitude toward their father. And since their father made no attempt to bridge the gap between them, they finally were convinced that she was right.

The air was growing cool as the sun began to drop and the summer blue faded into darkness. Leila rolled onto her side and looked at the Syrian. "How much more time?"

"About another half-hour," he said, smiling. "There's enough time for us." He reached for her.

She moved away from him quickly. "Don't."

He stared at her. "What is the matter with you? Are you a lesbian?"

"No," she said quietly.

"Then don't be so old-fashioned. Why do you think they're giving you girls those pills?"

She stared at him. Contempt crept into her voice. Men were all alike. "For my protection, not your convenience," she said.

He gave her what he thought was a winning smile. "Come on then," he said, reaching for her again. "Maybe I can teach you to enjoy it."

She moved quickly; her rifle prodded his belly. "I doubt it," she said quietly. "You may have taught me how to use this gun but I already know how to fuck."

He looked down at the rifle then up unto her face. A genuine laugh bubbled up in his throat. "I didn't doubt that for a minute," he said quickly. "I was only worried that you might get out of practice."

Chapter Seven

Tortuously, Leila squirmed across the hard, sandy surface of the rock until she reached the rows of barbed wire. She stopped, gasping for breath. After a moment, she turned and peered back through the pale moonlight. Soad, the big Egyptian woman, and Ayida, the Lebanese, were inching up behind her. "Where's Hamid?" she asked.

"How the hell do I know?" swore the Egyptian. "I thought he was up here in front of us."

"Jamila scraped her knee when she came across the rocks," Ayida said. "I saw him putting a bandage on it."

"That was an hour ago," Soad said sarcastically. "By now he's probably got her cunt in a sling."

"What are we going to do?" Leila asked. "We need wire cutters to get through this."

"I think Farida has a pair," Ayida said.

"Pass the word back," Leila said.

Quickly the message traveled down the line of women strung out behind her. A moment later, the wire cutters passed forward from hand to hand until they reached Leila.

Soad gave them to her. "Did you ever use these before?"

"No," Leila said. "Did you?"

Soad shook her head.

"It shouldn't be too difficult. I saw the way Hamid did it the last time."

She took the heavy wire cutters and inched up to the barbed wire fence, then rolled over on her back. She raised the cutters slowly over her head. The polished metal blades reflected the moonlight. It could only have lasted a fraction of a second but immediately the machine gun forward began to chatter, and the bullets whined over their heads.

"Damn," Leila exclaimed in disgust, trying to press her body into the ground. She didn't dare move her head to look back at the others. "Where are you?" she called.

"We're here," Soad said. "We're not moving."

"We have to move," Leila said. "They've got us spotted."

"You move. I'm not goin' anywhere until that gun stops."

"If we crawl we're safe—they're firing three feet over our head."

"They're Arabs," Soad said sarcastically. "And I've never known one that could shoot straight. I'm staying right here."

"I'm going. You can stay here all night if you want to."

Cautiously she rolled over on her stomach and began to crawl along the wire fence. After a few moments, she heard scratching noises behind her. She looked back. The other women were following.

Almost a half-hour later, she stopped. The machine gun was still firing but the bullets were no longer whistling over their heads. They had passed out of its range.

This time she took no chances. She smeared dirt over the blades of the cutters so that no light would be reflected. Again she rolled over on her back and reached up for the wire. It was harder than she thought it would be and the noise resounded in the stillness of the night but no one else seemed to hear. A few minutes later she had cut her way through the first row. She crawled through the opening and toward the next row. Two more and they would be in the clear.

Despite the chill, she was beginning to sweat. Anxiously she went to work on the second row. It was constructed of double strands and they took almost twenty minutes to cut through. The last row was made up of triple strands, and it was forty minutes more before she was finished.

She lay on her back, gasping for breath, her arms and shoulders aching with pain. After a moment, she looked down at Soad. "We stay down until we reach the white markers. That should be about two hundred meters farther on. After that we're in the clear."

"Okay," Soad answered.

"Remember to keep your heads down," Leila said.

She rolled back on to her belly and began to crawl forward. Two hundred meters seemed like a thousand miles on your belly.

Finally she could see the white markers sticking out of the ground a few meters in front of them. At the same time, she heard voices—men's voices.

Leila held out a hand, palm backwards so the woman would be silent. It would be a shame if they were spotted now. They all hugged themselves into the ground.

The voices came from her left. In the moonlight, she could see three soldiers. One of them was lighting a cigarette; the others were seated behind a machine gun. The match spun away from the soldier in a flaming arc, landing near Leila's face.

"Those whores are still out there," the soldier with the cigarette said.

One of the others stood up, swinging his arms to warm himself. "Hamid's going to find himself with a lot of frozen pussy on his hands."

The soldier with the cigarette laughed. "He can give some to me. I'll show how to thaw them out."

"Hamid gives away nothing," the seated one said. "He acts like a pasha with his harem."

A faint buzzer sounded. The soldier with the cigarette picked up a walkie-talkie. Leila could not hear what he said as he spoke into it but she could hear him addressing his companions after he put it down. "That was Post One. They had them spotted but they lost them. They think they might be coming in this direction."

"They're full of crap," one of the others said. "I can see half a mile in this moonlight. Nothing's out there."

"Just the same keep your eyes peeled. It wouldn't look good if a couple of girls made donkey's asses out of us."

Leila smiled grimly to herself. That was exactly what they were going to do. She reached back and tapped Soad on the shoulder. She mouthed the words silently. "Did you hear?"

Soad nodded, as did the women behind her. They had all heard.

Leila moved her hand in wide sweeping gestures. They understood. They would crawl in a wide circle that would bring them back to the machine gun emplacement from behind. Slowly, holding their breaths they began to move.

It took almost an hour and they were well behind the white markers and directly behind the machine gun when Leila gave the signal.

With a yell, the women sprang to their feet and charged. Cursing, the soldiers turned toward them, and found themselves staring into barrels of the rifles.

"You're our prisoners," Leila said.

The corporal smiled suddenly. "I guess so," he admitted.

Leila recognized him as the one with the cigarette. She couldn't keep the note of triumph out of her voice.

"Maybe you'll think differently about women soldiers now."

The corporal nodded. "Maybe."

"Now what do we do?" Soad asked.

"I don't know," Leila said. "I think we should call in and report their capture." She turned to the corporal. "Give me your walkie-talkie."

He held it out to her. He was still smiling. "May I make a suggestion?"

"If you like." Leila's voice was businesslike.

"We are your prisoners, aren't we?"

Leila nodded.

"Why don't you rape us before you report in? We promise not to complain."

The women began to snicker. Leila was angry. Arab men were the worst kind of male chauvinist pigs. She jammed down the call button on the walkie-talkie. But before she could get a reply, Hamid and Jamila came strolling up to them, as casually as if they had spent the afternoon in the park.

"Where in the hell were you?" she yelled at Hamid.

"Right behind you."

"Why didn't you help us?"

He shrugged. "What for? You were doing all right."

She looked at Jamila. The pudgy Palestinian had a relaxed look on her face and Leila knew why. She turned back to Hamid. "How did you get through the barbed wire?"

"Easily," he said, a broad smile coming to his lips. "We dug ourselves a little trench and fucked our way through it."

Leila held a straight face as long as she could then started to laugh. The Syrian mercenary had a strange sense of humor, but he was funny. She handed the walkie-talkie to him. "Here, call us in," she said. "Maybe you can get them to send a truck for us. I think we could all use a hot bath."

The steam rose over the tops of the barracks shower stalls. Above the splashing of the running water came the chatter of the women.

The stalls each had four jets and were designed for communal use, four women to a shower. Since there were only two stalls, there was always a line of women waiting for a shower to open up. Leila liked to wait until most of the others had finished their baths, so that she did not have to hurry to make way for the next one. She leaned against the window smoking a cigarette, listening to the chatter.

Almost three months had passed since she had come to the camp, and all during that time she had been drilled from morning until night. Whatever fat there had been on her body had long since disappeared. Now she was lean, her belly and flank muscles firm, her breasts like two apples. Her lustrous black hair, cut short for convenience when she arrived, now fell to her shoulders.

Every morning there had been two hours of calisthenics and drill before breakfast. After breakfast there had been manual training in which the women learned about guns—how to use them and how to take care of them. They also learned about grenades and the use of plastique, the techniques of preparing and concealing letter bombs and the practicality of transistorized timer-detonator devices. After-noons were spent in practising the techniques of manual combat, hand to hand and weapon to weapon. Later in the day, they were given political lectures. The ideo-logical indoctrination was important because each of them was considered a missionary for a new order in the Arab world.

Later the political lectures gave way to lessons in military tactics, paramilitary infiltration and sabotage, guerilla warfare and subversive diversion.

For the last month they had all been training in the field. Everything they had learned had been put to use. Gradually Leila could feel herself toughening. She thought of herself as a woman less and less. The purpose for which she trained possessed her and became a way of life. It was through her and others like her that a new world would come. For a moment she thought of her mother and her sister. They were in Beirut, still living in that old world—her sister with her petty family and social problems; her mother, still bitter and resentful over the way she had been tossed aside by her father but doing nothing constructive with her life. She closed her eyes for a moment, remembering that day in the south of France before she had come here. She thought of her father and his sons water-skiing on the bay in front of the Carlton. Her father hadn't changed since she had last seen him almost nine years before. He was till tall and handsome, filled with strength and vitality. If only he could understand, if only he knew how much he could do to help free the Arab from the imperialism of Israel and America. If he only knew the need, the suffering, the oppression of his brothers, he would not stand idly by and permit this to happen. But she was only wishfully dreaming. Of course he knew. He had to know.

It was just that he didn't care. Wealth was his by birth and his only concern was to increase it. He loved the luxury and the power that sprang to his beckoning finger. And the terrible truth was that he was not alone. The sheiks, the princes and kings, the bankers and men of wealth were all the same. Arab or not. They cared only for themselves. Whatever benefits filtered down from their efforts were only incidental to their own. There were still millions of peasants in every Arab land who lived on the fringes of starvation while their rulers drove in air-conditioned Cadillacs, flew in private jets, maintained palaces and homes all over the world and then talked pompously about freedom for their people.

Eventually it had to come. The war was not only against the foreigners—that was only the first step. The second step and probably the most difficult would be the war against their own oppressors — men like her father, men who took everything and shared nothing.

A shower stall was now vacant, and Leila threw her coarse large towel over the wall panel and stepped under the streaming shower. The heat of the water spread over her like a soothing balm. She could feel the tension in her muscles loosen. Slowly, languidly, she began to soap herself, the touch of her fingers on her skin giving her a sensual pleasure.

In that she was like her father. Again she saw him on the water skis, the muscles straining against the lead, his entire being enjoying the physical effort of skill and balance.

She lathered the soft pubic hair until the dark curls were covered with the white fluff. Then she thrust her hips forward and let the shower beat directly down on her. The tingling and the warmth ran through her. Softly, almost automatically, she stroked herself. Her orgasm and the vision of her father on skis with hips thrust forward came together, taking her by surprise. Before she could stop, another orgasm shook her body. She felt shock, then anger, then disgust at herself. She was sick to even allow such thoughts. Violently she turned off the hot water and held herself rigid under the icy stream until her flesh was blue with the cold. Then she stepped from the stall, wrapping the towel around her.

It was crazy. She had never had thoughts like that before. But it was in her blood. Her mother had said so many times. She was like her father. His body ruled him; his lusts and appetites were never to be satisfied. Her mother had told them stories about him and his women. He was not a man who could ever be satisfied with one good woman. Bad blood, her mother had said in warning.

She rubbed herself dry and then, tying the towel around her, went into the barracks.

Soad, whose bed was next to her, was almost dressed.

"What are you doing tonight?"

Leila reached for a robe. "Nothing. I thought I would just stay in bed and read."

Soad began to apply her lipstick. "I've got a date with Abdullah and a friend of his. Why don't you come along?"

"I don't really feel like it."

Soad looked at her. "Come on. It would do you good to get out."

Leila didn't answer. She remembered Soad on her first day here. She had come to be near her boyfriend and had told everyone how she couldn't wait to be with him. But when he didn't appear she hadn't been upset. She took her female liberation seriously. Women had equal rights in this army and by now she had fucked her way through the entire camp and made no bones about it. "Cairo was never like this," she'd say with a burst of raucous laughter.

"Tell you what," Soad said seriously. "If you come along I'll left you have Abdullah. He's the best cocksman in the camp. I'll settle for the friend."

Leila looked at her. "I don't think so."

"What are you saving it for?" Soad asked. "Even if you don't want it for yourself, it's part of your duty. Didn't the C.O. tell us that it was our responsibility to give solace and comfort to our men? I can't imagine a better way to combine duty and pleasure all at the same time."

Leila began to laugh. Soad had a one-track mind. "You're fantastic," she said. "But none of those men appeal to me."

"You'll never know until you try them," Soad said. "Men can surprise you. The greatest lovers look like nothing sometimes."

Leila shook her head.

A puzzled look came over Soad's face. "Are you a virgin?"

Leila smiled. "No."

"Then you're in love." It was a statement.

"No."

Soad gave up. "I don't understand you."

That was the truest thing Soad had ever said. But how could she make the woman understand that there were things more important to her than sex.

Chapter Eight

It was just ten minutes after reveille when the barracks door opened unexpectedly and Hamid shouted from the doorway. "Attention!"

There was a flurry of motion as the women fell into place, in front of their beds, in various stages of dress.

Hamid stepped back from the doorway and the C.O. entered. Her sharp dark eyes took in the entire barracks in one sweeping glance, then she walked into the center of the room. The fact that some of the women were half-naked seemed to make no difference to her.

She was silent for a long moment before she spoke. Her voice was clear and emotionless. "Today will be your last day. Your training has been completed. Our work has been done. This camp will be closed and each of us assigned to duties elsewhere."

She paused for a moment. The women did not stir, nor did they take their eyes from her face. "I am proud of you," she said. "All of you. There have been those who have looked upon us with disdain and skepticism. They have said that women, especially Arab women, could not make good soldiers, that they were fit only for cooking, cleaning and taking care of the children. We have proved them wrong. You are members of Al-Ikhwah. You are the equal of any man in our armies. You have completed the same training as the men have and you had done as well as any of them."

The women were still silent. The C.O. began again. "You will have exactly one hour to pack your personal belongings and be ready to leave. I will see each of you individually to give you your next assignment. This assignment is not, I repeat, is not to be discussed among you. It is your own, and highly secret. Any discussion of your individual assignment will be regarded as treason and will be punishable by death—for one poorly chosen confidence can cause death of many of our comrades."

She walked back to the door, then turned to face them. "An–nasr, I salute you. May Allah protect you." Her hand snapped up in a salute.

"An-nasr!" they shouted, returning her salute. "Idbah–al-adu."

The room filled with their voices, as the door closed behind her.

"Something big must be in the wind."

"This is a month earlier than we had been told."

"Something is wrong."

Leila didn't speak at all. She opened her locker and began to take out the clothing she had worn on her arrival. Silently she laid her uniforms and fatigues in a neat pile on the bed. Even the brassieres and panties, shoes, boots and stockings were placed into a neat stack.

She opened the small suitcase that she had brought with her. She took out the blue jeans she had bought in France just before she came and put them on. It was then that she realized how much her body had changed. The jeans, which had once hugged her were now big around the waist and in the seat. Even the shirt was loose, and she rolled the sleeves because they seemed to have grown longer. She tied the shirt across her waist and slipped into the soft sandals. She packed her comb, brush and cosmetics, then carefully checked the locker. It was empty. She snapped the suitcase shut.

She sat down on the bed and lit a cigarette. The other women were still debating what to take and what to leave. Soad looked across at her. "You're wearing your own clothes?"

Leila nodded. "The C.O. said personal belongings. These are the only things that are mine."

"What about the uniforms?" one of the others called.

"If they wanted us to take them they would have said so."

"I think Leila is right," Soad said. She turned toward her locker. "I think I won't mind getting into my own clothes for a change." A moment later she gasped in dismay. "Nothing fits. Everything's too big!"

Leila laughed. "It's not too bad." She put out her cigarette. "Think of all the fun you'll have getting new things."

As she walked out of the building, the sun was coming up over the mountain. The morning air was fresh and clean. She breathed deeply.

"Ready?" Hamid's voice came from behind her.

She turned. He was leaning against the building, the ever-present cigarette dangling from his lips. "Ready as I'll ever be," she said.

He looked at her steadily. "You're not like the others, you know that."

She didn't answer.

"You didn't have to do this. You're rich. You could have everything you want." The mercenary's eyes were appraising.

"Could I? How do you know what I want?"

"You don't believe all this empty talk, do you?" He laughed. "I've been through three wars. Each time it has been the same thing. The slogans, the shouting, the threats, the promises of vengeance. Then when the bullets begin to fly it's all over. They turn and run. Only the politicians go on forever."

"Maybe someday it will be different," she said.

He fished another cigarette from his pocket and lit it from the butt of the other. "What do you think will happen if we take Palestine back?"

"The people will be free," she said.

"Free for what? Free to starve like the rest of us? With all the money coming into the Arab countries now, the people are still starving."

"That will have to be changed too."

"Hussein, the oil sheiks, even your father and his Prince, do you think they would willingly share what they have with the masses? At least now they have to do something. But if we win and there is no pressure on them, what then? Who is there to make them share? No, they will only grow richer."

"It will be up to the people to change them."

Hamid laughed bitterly. "I'm sorry to see this job finished. It was a good one. Now I'll have to find another."

"What do you mean?" she asked. "Don't they have another assignment for you?"

"Assignment?" he laughed. "I'm a professional. I got paid. One thousand Lebanese pounds a month for this job. I don't know any place where I can make that kind of money."

"For one-fifty a month I can get my ass worked off," he said. "I prefer the Brotherhood. It pays better. They always seem to have lots of money to throw around."

"Don't you believe in what we're doing?" she asked.

"Sure I do," he said. "I just don't believe in our leaders. There are too many of them, each busy lining his own pockets while trying to become the top dog."

"They can't all be like that."

He smiled at her. "You're young yet. You'll learn."

"What happened?" she asked. "Why the sudden change in plans?"

He shrugged his shoulders. "I don't know. The orders came last night and the C.O. seemed to be as surprised as any of us. She was up all night getting things ready."

"She's an extraordinary woman, isn't she?"

Hamid nodded. "Maybe if she were a man, I would have more faith in our leaders." He looked at her quizzically. "You know you owe me something."

"I do?" she asked, puzzled. "What?"

He gestured at the barracks behind them. "There are fourteen girls in that platoon. You're the only one I haven't fucked."

She laughed. "I'm sorry."

"You should be," he said half-seriously. "Thirteen is an unlucky number. Something bad is going to happen."

"I don't think so." She smiled. "Look at it this way: You have something to look forward to."

He grinned. "I'll strike a bargain. If we ever meet again—no matter where—we'll do it."

She held out her hand. "Agreed."

They shook hands. He looked into her eyes. "You know, you're not a bad soldier for a girl."

"Thank you." she said.

He glanced at his watch. "Do you think they're ready?"

"They should be," she said. None of them had very much to take.

He threw his cigarette down and turned and opened the barracks door. "Okay, girls," he shouted in his field voice. "On the double!"

It was almost two hours before they were ushered into the C.O.'s headquarters. While they waited the camp was being dismantled before their eyes. Men and trucks were moving everyting—beds, clothing, weapons—out of the building. Already the camp was beginning to look like a ghost town. And with doors and windows open, the desert sand was swirling in, anxious to reclaim its own.

The women stood outside headquarters watching truck after loaded truck pull away. The headquarters building itself was the last to be dismantled. Furniture was being moved out as they were ushered in.

Following alphabetical order, Leila was the first to be called. She closed the door behind her, and stepped forward to the C.O.'s desk and saluted smartly. "Al Fay reporting." Somehow it didn't seem as proper in blue jeans as it had in uniform.

The C.O. returned her salute wearily. "At ease, An-nasr," she said. She looked down at the sheet of paper before her. "Al Fay, is that your name?"

"Yes, ma'am." For the first time Leila thought of her as a woman. The C.O. was tired.

"You are to return to your mother's home in Beirut," she said. "You will be contacted there and directed to your next assignment."

"Is that all, ma'am? Nothing else?"

"That is all at this time. But don't worry, you'll hear from us."

"But how will I know? Isn't there a code name or some way that I will be sure of—"

The C.O. interrupted. "When the call comes, you will know," she said. "For now, your assignment is to go home and wait. You will not involve yourself or go near any political groups no matter how sympathetic they are to our cause. You will keep your own counsel and remain in the normal social confines of your family. Do you understand that?"

"Yes, ma'am."

The C.O. looked at her for a moment. She seemed about to say more but then she stopped. "Good luck," she said. "Dismissed."

Leila saluted, executed a smart about-face and left the room. She walked through the outer office. The other women looked at her with curiosity, but she didn't speak.

There was a truck parked outside. Hamid gestured toward it. "Your limousine awaits."

Leila nodded, silently climbed in the back and sat down on one of the rows of benches. It took less than a half-hour before the truck was filled.

They were peculiarly silent. Suddenly there were all strangers, bound by their orders, afraid that they might unwittingly reveal something.

It was Soad who broke the tension. "You know," she said in her coarse Egyptian voice, "I'm really going to miss this place. it wasn't so bad and I got some of the best fucking I ever had."

With that, they all laughed and began to talk at once. There were so many things they had to remember and joke about—the accidents, the mistakes, even the hardships. A half-hour passed and still the truck hadn't moved.

"What are we waiting for?" one of the women called to Hamid.

"The C.O.," he replied. "She'll be out in a minute."

He was right. A moment later she appeared in the doorway behind him. The women fell silent as they stared at her.

It was the first time any of them had ever seen her out of uniform. She was wearing an ill-fitting French tailored wool suit. The jacket was too short, the skirt too long. The seams of her stockings were crooked and she walked uncomfortably on the high-heeled shoes she wore to give her height. Somehow the commanding presence she had in uniform had disappeared. Even her face looked pudgy and uncertain.

If she were a little heavier, Leila thought, she would look no different than my mother. Or any of the women in my family.

Hamid opened the door and she got into the truck beside the driver. He ran around to the back and climbed in with the women. "Okay," he called to the driver.

The last of the furniture was being removed as they drove onto the road and fell into line behind the other trucks. A moment later the last truck came up behind them and blew its horn as a signal. Up front the first truck began to move and soon they were all rolling down the road toward the coast.

They had their last glimpse of the camp as they turned the curve around the mountain on the southern end. It was as empty and deserted as yesterday. Again the women were silent. There were no more jokes. They were all preoccupied with their own thoughts.

They had been on the road for less than an hour when they heard the sounds of explosions coming from behind them in the area of the camp. A moment later they heard the whine of the aircraft and just as suddenly the planes were upon them. Up ahead a truck burst into flames.

Hamid stood up in the back of the truck. "Israeli fighters!" he shouted to the driver. "Get off the road!"

But in the roar and the noise the driver didn't hear him. Instead he put on a burst of speed and crashed into the truck ahead. At the same time another jet made a pass low over the convoy.

More bullets whistled through the air. Another truck was struck and blew up. The women were screaming and trying to get off the back of the trucks.

"Over the sides!" Hamid yelled. "Take cover in the ditches!"

Leila moved automatically. She hit the ground, rolled over and scrambled toward the side of the road, diving head-first into a drainage ditch.

Another jet roared down on them. This time she could see the flaming trails left by its rockets. More trucks seemed to explode in clouds of smoke.

"Why aren't we shooting back at them?" she heard someone shouting.

"With what?" someone else shouted back. "All the guns have been stowed on the trucks!"

Another woman jumped into the ditch beside her. Leila heard her sobbing. She didn't raise her head to look. Another plane was making a pass.

This time a missile hit the truck she had been on. It exploded in a thousand fragments and anguished screams filled the air. The debris that fell around her contained scraps of metal and also parts of human bodies.

She burrowed further into the ditch, trying to bury herself in the fetid earth. Somehow she had to escape death at the hands of the flying monsters.

Again the planes roared by, the shrieking whistles of their jets trailing behind them as the missiles tore once more into the convoy. Then they were gone as suddenly as they had come, climbing high into the sky and turning to the west, the sunlight glancing off the blue painted stars on their sides.

For a moment there was silence, then the sound of pain began to rise in the air. Moans and screams and cries for help. Slowly Leila raised her head from the ditch.

On the road a few people began to move. She turned to look at the woman who had jumped into the ditch beside her. It was Soad.

"Soad," she whispered. "Are you all right?"

Slowly the Egyptian turned toward her. "I think I'm hurt," she said, in an oddly soft voice.

"Let me help you," Leila said, moving towards her.

"Thanks," Soad whispered. She tried to raise her head then slipped gently back to the ground. A rush of blood bubbled up through her mouth and nose, staining the ground beneath her, and then her eyes went wide and staring.

Leila looked at her. It was the first time she had ever seen anyone die, but she did not have to be told that Soad was dead. Leila felt a cold chill. She forced herself to look away and got to her feet.

She stumbled out of the ditch. The ground was covered with debris. In front of her was a severed hand. The diamond ring on one of the fingers sparkled in the light of the sun. She kicked it away and walked toward the truck.

There was nothing left but twisted wood and iron and around it were strewn broken and mangled bodies. She stared at it dully then walked around to the front. The C.O.'s body lay half over the driver, half out of the open door. Her skirt was twisted obscenely over her pudgy thighs.

Out of the corner of her eye, Leila saw a movement. A soldier had found the hand and was pulling the diamond ring from its finger. When he had the ring, he threw the hand away, carefully examined the diamond, then put it in his pocket. He looked up as he became aware of her stare.

She didn't speak.

He smiled sheepishly. "The dead need nothing," he said. Then he walked behind the truck.

The nausea rose in her throat and she bent double with pain as she retched and spewed her vomit onto the road. She felt herself growing faint and was beginning to fall when a strong arm came around her shoulders.

"Easy," Hamid said. "Easy."

She was empty now but weak and trembling. She turned toward him and buried her face against his shoulders. "Why?" she cried. "Why did they have to do this to us? We never did anything to them."

"It's war," Hamid said.

She looked up into his face. There was blood across his cheek. "They knew the raid was coming, that's why they were moving us out."

Hamid didn't answer.

"It was stupid then," she said angrily. "Keeping all those trucks together on the road. Giving them a target like that."

Hamid looked at her without expression.

"Is this what we trained for? To be slaughtered like sheep?"

"It won't be like that when we listen to the radio tonight," he said. "My guess is that we heroically shot down at least six Israeli jets."

"What are you talking about?" she asked, bewildered. "Are you crazy? We never fired a shot."

He spoke in a quiet voice. "That's right. But there are one hundred million Arabs who were not here to see that."

"The Jews. They are animals. We were defenseless and still they came."

"Yesterday we won a great victory, according to the radio," he said. "In Tel Aviv a school bus was blown up, killing thirty children. I guess this was their way of showing they didn't like it."

"The Brotherhood is right," she said. "The only way to stop them is to exterminate them."

He looked at her silently for a moment, then he reached into his pocket and took out a cigarette and lit it. He exhaled the smoke through his nose. "Come, little one, let's leave this. There is nothing here for us to do and we have a long walk ahead of us."

"We could stay and help bury them."

He pointed behind them. She turned and saw men searching through the debris. "Right now, they are busy looking for whatever they can find. Later they will fight among themselves to keep what they find. After that there will be only you to fight about. You are the only woman left."

She stared at him speechlessly.

"I don't think your desire to give solace and comfort to our comrades extends to twenty or thirty men at the same time."

"How do you know they won't come after us?"

He bent swiftly and picked something up from the ground at his feet. For the first time she saw that he was carrying an automatic rifle, then she saw the gun stuck into his belt.

"You expected this?"

He shrugged his shoulders. "I told you I was a professional. I had these under my bench and grabbed them before I jumped from the truck. Besides, I had a feeling. Didn't I also tell you that thirteen was an unlucky number?"

Chapter Nine

Badyr watched Jordana across the room. He felt satisfied. He had made the right decision. Jordana was just the balance he had needed. Now she was bidding goodnight to the Hutchinsons. She had made an impression on the wives and there was no doubt that it had made a difference in his relationships with the bank's officers. Now they were a team.

Of course his new profit-sharing proposal had been a great help. Fifteen percent of the profits to be distributed among the employees on a stock dividend basis had not hurt at all. There was one thing all people had in common—greed.

Joe Hutchinson came over to him. "I'm glad we were able to get together," he said in his hearty California voice. "It's sure good to know that the man you're working with has the same ideas that you have."

"I feel good too, my friend," Baydr said.

"The girls hit it off pretty good too," Hutchinson said, looking back at his wife. "Your little lady invited Dolly to visit her in the south of France next summer."

"Good," Baydr smiled. "You come too. We can have some fun."

The Californian winked his eye and grinned. "I heard about them French babes," he said. "Is it true they all go around topless on the beaches?"

"On some of them."

"I'll be there, you can bet on that. I never got as far as Europe during the war. I caught some flak in North Africa and the only girls I ever saw were gook whores.

And no self-respecting man would touch them. Either they were full of clap or else they had a nigger up an alley to run a knife into you."

Apparently Hutchinson didn't realize he was talking about Arab countries. In his mind there could be no association between the natives of North Africa and the man who stood before him. "The war was a bad time," Baydr said.

"Was your family in it?"

"Not really. Our country is small and I guess no one thought it important enough to fight over." He didn't mention that Prince Feiyad had entered into an agreement stipulating that if Germany won they would have been placed in charge of all the oil development in the Middle East.

"What do you think?" Hutchinson asked. "Will there be another war in the Middle East?"

Baydr looked him in the eye. "Your guess is as good as mine."

"Well, if anything does happen," Hutchinson said. "I hope you give 'em hell. It's about time somebody put those Jews in their place."

"We don't have many Jewish customers, do we?" Baydr asked.

"No, sir," the banker said enthusiastically. "We just don't encourage them, that's why."

"Do you think that's why we blew the Rancho del Sol development?" Baydr asked. "Because some of the developers were Jewish?"

"That has to be the reason," Hutchinson said quickly. "They wanted to do business with the Jewish banks in Los Angeles."

"I was curious. Somebody told me that we were underbid. L.A. gave them the money at prime and we wanted a point and a half over."

"The Jews did that deliberately to undercut us," Hutchinson said.

"Next time you cut right back. I want our bank to be competitive. It's the only way to attract the big deals."

"Even if they're Jews."

Baydr's voice was flat. "Don't get confused. What we're talking about is dollars. United States dollars. That deal could have made us two million in three years at prime. If we undercut it by a half point, it would still be a million and a half. That's the kind of money I don't like to pass up."

"But the Jews would have underbid us anyway."

"Maybe," Baydr said. "But we just might remember that from now on we'll be an equal-opportunity lender."

"Okay," Hutchinson said. "You're the boss."

"By the way," Baydr said. "Is that last figure you quoted me on Leisure City still firm?"

"Twelve million dollars, yes. The Japs have forced it up."

"Put a hold on it at that figure."

"But wait a minute. We haven't that kind of money available," Hutchinson protested.

"I said put a hold on it, not buy it. I think we may have a partner by the end of the week."

"The hold will cost us ten percent, a million, two hundred thousand. If the partner doesn't show up we lost it. And there go our profits for the year. The examiners won't like that."

"I'll take the chance. If worst comes to worst, I'll put up the money myself." If everything worked out right, neither he nor the bank would have to put up a penny. The Japanese would put up six million and the other six would come from the Middle Eastern group which the bank in New York could finance and he would have it three ways. The bank would collect interest on the money and an equity, he could collect an equity for his share in the Japanese consortium, and he also had an equity in the Middle Eastern group. Money, it seemed, had a strange power to feed on itself and grow.

Finally the Hutchinsons were gone. Jordana came back into the room. She sank into a chair exhausted. "Jesus," she said. "I don't believe it."

He smiled. "What don't you believe?"

"That there are still people in the world like that. I thought they were all gone by now. I remember them from when I was a child."

"You'll find people don't really change."

"I think they do. You've changed. I've changed."

He met her eyes. "That's not necessarily for the good, is it?"

"It depends on how you feel. I don't think I could ever go back to that kind of life. No more than you can go back home and stay there."

He was silent. In a way she was right. There was no way he could ever go back and live as his father lived. There was too much going on in the world.

"I could use a smoke," she said, looking up at him. "Does Jabir have any of that private hash of his?"

"I'm sure he has," Baydr said, clapping his hands.

Jabir appeared from the adjacent room. "Yes, master?"

Baydr spoke rapidly in Arabic. A moment later Jabir was back with a silver cigarette case. He opened it and held it out to Jordana. The cigarettes were beautifully rolled, complete with cork tips. Carefully she took one. He then turned and extended it toward Baydr who also took one. Jabir placed the cigarette case on the coffee table in front of Jordana and struck a match. He held the flame at the right distance so that only the tip touched the cigarette and none of the heat came through. He lit Baydr's cigarette in exactly the same manner.

"Thank you," Jordana said.

Jabir salaamed, making the gesture of obeisance. "I am honored, mistress." He left the room quietly.

Jordana sucked the smoke deep into her lungs. She felt its tranquil effects. "This is beautiful," she said. "No one seems to get it the way Jabir does."

"It is grown by his own family on their own little farm, not far from where my father was born. The Arabs call it the stuff of which dreams are made."

"They're right." She laughed suddenly. "You know, I think I'm high already. I'm not tired anymore."

"Neither am I." Baydr said down in the chair opposite her, put his cigarette into an ashtray and leaning forward took her hand. "What would you like to do?"

She looked into his face. Suddenly her eyes filled with tears. "I would like to go back," she said, "back to the time we first met and begin all over again."

He was silent for a moment, then he spoke. "So would I," he said gently. "But we can't."

She stared at him, the tears running down her cheeks. Then she hid her face in her hands. "Baydr, Baydr," she cried. "What has happened to us? What went wrong? We were so in love then."

He drew her head to his chest and stared somberly into space. His voice was a low rumble in her ears. "I don't know," he said quietly, remembering how beautiful she had been the first time he saw her.

He remembered the cold and the white blinding light reflected from the snow and the white buildings surrounding the inaugural stands. It was January 1961. The greatest country in the world was inaugurating its new President, a young man by the name of John F. Kennedy.

Six months ago no one in the Middle East had even known the young man's name. Then, suddenly, he was the candidate of the Democratic party and there was a telegram from the Prince on his desk. "What is Kennedy's policy on the Middle East?"

His reply had been terse. "Pro Israel. Not much else known."

The telephone call he had received the next day was equally terse. The Prince himself had called. "Find a way to contribute one million dollars to the Nixon campaign," the Prince had said.

"It will not be easy," he had replied. "The United States has peculiar rules about campaign contributions."

The Prince chuckled slyly. "Politicians are the same everywhere. I am sure you will find a way. Mr. Nixon and Mr. Eisenhower were very good to us when the British and French tried to take over the Suez in fifty-six. We should at least show we are grateful."

"I'll work it out," Baydr replied. "But I would like to suggest that we also make a token contribution to the Kennedy campaign, just in case."

"Why?" the Prince asked. "Do you think he has a chance?"

"Not according to the polls, but this is America. One never knows."

"I will leave it in your hands," the Prince said. "I'm beginning to think you're more American than Arab."

Baydr laughed. "The Americans don't think so."

"How are your wife and daughters?" the Prince asked.

"They're fine," he answered. "I spoke to them last night. They're in Beirut."

"You had better make a visit home," the Prince said. "I am still waiting for that heir you promised me. I would like to see him before too long. I am not growing any younger."

"Allah will preserve you," Baydr said. "You will live forever."

"In paradise I hope." The Prince's whispery laugh echoed in the telephone. "But not on this earth."

Baydr had put down the telephone thoughtfully. The Prince never said anything casually. He wondered if he had heard that Maryam could not bear any more children after the birth of the last girl. But if he had heard he would not have asked about an heir.

He would have insisted that Baydr get a divorce and marry another. Barrenness was a valid reason for divorce under Muslim law. But Baydr was reluctant. It was not that he was in love with Maryam. There never had been that between them and the longer they were married the less they seemed to have in common. She was too provincial; she really disliked Europe and America. She was only truly happy when she was in her own environment, Baydr thought. She was much too an Arab. And the thought of having to marry another Arab woman just didn't appeal to him.

Maybe the Prince had been right. Maybe he was too American. For he definitely preferred Western women to his own. There was a life about them, a style, a look, a freedom that Arab women didn't have.

Baydr found a way to make the contributions. Both of them. They had many friends among the businessmen in both parties. The token contribution had paid off and the Prince had received a special invitation from the inaugural committee. The Prince declined on the grounds of poor health and appointed Baydr to be his special representative at the inauguration.

Baydr was in the section reserved for the representatives of foreign countries, fairly close to the inaugural platform itself. He was uncomfortable in the freezing cold, despite the thermal underwear under his formal swallow-tailed suit, pearl gray vest and trousers. The top hat, pressed down on his head to prevent it from being blown off by the gusts of wind didn't help very much in keeping his head warm.

He looked around. Some of the other diplomats and their wives were better prepared than he was. They were older and probably had been through this before. He could see them nipping from small silver flasks and there were more than a few thermos bottles in evidence.

He glanced at his watch. It was almost a quarter past twelve. They were running late. The ceremony was due to start at noon. He reached into his pocket for the dark glasses. His eyes were weary with squinting against the sun and snow, but he changed his mind. None of the others were wearing them. There was a flurry on the stands. He looked up as the applause began. The President-elect was coming onto the platform.

There was something young and very vulnerable about him as he walked forward with firm strides, the wind ruffling his hair. The cold seemed not to bother him. He alone of all on the platform wore no hat or coat.

A moment later a priest came forward and delivered the invocation. His voice was singsong and monotonous like all priests' voices no matter what their faith, but the young President stood quietly, hands clasped, his head respectfully inclined. Allah would not have insisted on so long a prayer in such cold weather, Baydr thought.

When the priest had finished, another man was led forward. He was old and white-haired and his face seemed carved out of the same granite as the building behind him. Baydr heard the whispers around him. The man was Robert Frost, one of American's great poets.

The old man began to speak, his breath smoky in the winter air. Baydr could not distinguish the words. A moment later he stopped. There seemed to be a problem.

Another man stepped forward and held a hat over the lectern. Apparently the sun had blinded the old man so that he could not read what was on the sheet in front of him. Another whisper ran through the stand. The man who held his hat was Lyndon Johnson, the future Vice-President. The old man said something, the Vice-President-elect stepped back and the old man began to recite a poem from memory. His voice rang through the public address system but Baydr had stopped listening. He had noticed a girl on the platform about three rows behind the President.

She seemed tall but he could not really tell. The platform was tiered so that all could see and be seen. She was bare-headed with long, straight blond hair, framing a golden tanned face. Her bright blue eyes were set above high cheekbones that fell into planed lines to an almost square chin. Her lips parted as she listened to the poet, revealing white even teeth. When the poet finished, she smiled and laughed and clapped her hands enthusiastically. For some reason Baydr thought, she's a California girl.

Then the President was being sworn in. The ceremony itself only seemed to take a moment after which he turned to the lectern to begin his speech. Baydr listened carefully.

There was one line that made him wonder if the President had read the Koran. It could have been taken from the Holy Book. "Civility is not a sign of weakness, and sincerity is always subject to proof."

When the President had finished speaking, Baydr looked for the girl but she had already gone. He tried to find her in the crowds that were moving away from the platform but she was nowhere to be see.

Still her face kept appearing before his eyes all through that afternoon as he rested in his suite in the hotel. He watched several replays of the inauguration ceremony on television, hoping to catch another glimpse of her, but the angle of the camera was always wrong.

There was only one other chance. Spread across Baydr's desk were invitations to four inauguration balls, each of which promised an appearance by the President. She would have to be at one of them, he thought. But which one? That was the question.

The answer was simple. He would go to all of them. If the President could do it, so could he.

Chapter Ten

Baydr allowed himself no more than an hour at each ball. One was very much like another, crowded and noisy, the floor covered with people, drunk and sober, dancing, talking or just walking about aimlessly. The one thing they had in common was that they were all Democrats, glad to be back in the sun after eight years in the dark. After a while Baydr began to wonder if there were any Republicans left in the country.

He arrived at the first ball just after the President had left for the second. Carefully, his eyes swept the room. He never realized before just how many blondes there were in Washington, but none of them was the one he sought. He went to the bar and ordered a glass of champagne.

A man came up to him and grabbed him by the arm. "Did you see him?" he asked excitedly.

"Who?" Baydr asked.

"The President, that's who," the man answered in an aggrieved voice. "Who else would I be asking about?"

Baydr smiled. "I saw him."

"Great, wasn't he?" The man smiled and walked off without waiting for an answer.

Baydr put his drink down and decided to go on to the next ball. It was a good thing it wasn't far because the streets were still icy. Again the President had come and gone by the time he arrived. Baydr screened the room and when he saw that the girl wasn't there, he didn't even stay for a drink.

He got to the third ball in the middle of a dance. People were crowded around the periphery of the floor, trying to peer through the crowds of dancers.

Baydr pushed his way through. He tapped a man on the shoulder. "What's happening?"

"The President's dancing with some girl out there," the man said without turning around.

On the far side of the floor the flashbulbs were popping. Baydr made his way toward them. As he passed he heard a woman speak in disapproving tones, "Why doesn't he dance with Jackie?"

He heard her husband's disgusted reply: "He has to do those things, Mary. It's politics."

"Then why does it always have to be a pretty girl?" the wife retorted. "I don't see him dancing with any of us who worked so hard on his campaigns."

Baydr was at the edge of the floor. The photographers and cameramen were climbing over each other to get pictures of the President. For a moment, he was pinned against a post, then he managed to slip past them.

There was a small clear space around the President and his partner. The other dancers didn't really move; they just shuffled in a semicircle, staring at the President. Baydr stared too. The President was dancing with his girl.

He had a sick feeling of disappointment. From the way they were laughing and talking, they seemed to know each other fairly well. His hopes of finding someone they both knew to introduce them were dashed. One couldn't very well ask the President of the United States to introduce one to a girl. Besides, he too had heard some of the stories about the President. It seemed he was quite a man with the ladies.

As he watched, the music ended and they started from the floor. Immediately, they were surrounded by throngs of people. Photographers were taking some more pictures. Then the President turned to the girl. Smiling, he said something to her. She nodded and the President turned and started away. The crowd followed him and a moment later the girl was standing almost alone.

He took a deep breath and went up to her. "Miss?"

She was even more beautiful up close than she had been from a distance. "Yes?" she asked politely. Her voice was low and slightly Western in intonation.

"How did it feel to dance with the President of the United States?"

"That's a strange question."

"What's your name?"

"Are you a reporter?"

"No," he answered. "Do you know the President well?"

"You ask a lot of questions for a man who says he's not a reporter."

He smiled. "I guess I do. But I can't think of any other way to keep you from walking away."

For the first time she looked directly at him. "I can," she said. "Why don't you ask me to dance?"

Chapter Eleven

Her name was Jordana Mason and she had been born and raised in San Francisco. So he'd been right about one thing. She was a California girl. Her father and mother had been divorced when she was a child. Both parents had since remarried but relations were good between them, and Jordana was in close touch with her father even though she lived with her mother. She was nineteen years old, a junior at Berkeley and one of the organizers of the Students for Kennedy movement, which was the reason she'd been invited to the inaugural.

She had caught the candidate's eye at a rally in San Francisco. His press people had made a big thing of getting photographs of him with the students and he had promised her that if he won she would receive an invitation.

She was not naïve enough to believe that he would remember the promise. She was sure that there were more important things on his mind. So she was surprised when the invitation arrived in the mail one morning.

Excitedly, she called her mother. "Isn't it wonderful?"

Her mother was cool. The whole family was solidly Republican. "I hope they have provided a chaperone," her mother said.

"Mother," Jordana said. "This is 1960, not 1900. I'm a grown girl. I can take care of myself."

"I'm not sure you can, dear," her mother said smoothly. "But have they arranged for a good place for you to stay? And who is paying for your air fare?"

"I'm supposed to take care of all that myself. The invitation is only for the inauguration. And it says I'm to have a place on the same stand with the President."

"I still don't like it," her mother sniffed. "I think you'd better discuss this with your father."

She called her father at his office in the Civic Center. He was no more enthusiastic, but he did understand how much it meant to her. He cautioned her about Kennedy's reputation even though he knew that she could take care of herself. Besides, now that the man was President, he was sure that he would change his ways. He agreed to buy her ticket but he wanted her to check again with her mother to see if she knew some friends with whom she could stay. The hotels in Washington were notorious dens of iniquity, filled with all kinds of Southern and black politicians and foreigners who were trying to promote something. In the end they found out that all their friends were Republicans and that Jordana would be better off staying in a hotel than letting one of them know that one of their own family had gone over to the other side.

All this Baydr learned during the first dance. After the number was over, he led her in search of an empty table where they could sit and talk. They found one in a small room off the main ballroom. The waiters were scurrying about frantically trying to fill the orders that came at them from all directions.

Baydr solved the problem simply. He caught the eye of the maître d' by waving a hand in which he concealed a ten-dollar bill. A moment later a bottle of Dom Pérignon appeared at their table.

"That's expensive," Jordana said. "Are you sure you can afford it?"

"I think so," Baydr said noncommittally. He raised his glass. "To the most beautiful girl in Washington."

She laughed. "How would you know? You haven't see all of them."

"I've seen enough."

She sipped the wine. "This is delicious. They say California champagnes are as good as the French but they're not like this."

"California champagnes aren't bad."

"I'll bet you never drank any," she accused.

He laughed. "I went to Harvard, then spent a few years at Stanford."

"What do you do?"

"I'm a businessman."

She looked at him doubtfully. "You seem kind of young for that."

"Age doesn't matter much in these times," he said. "Kennedy is only forty-three and he's President."

"You're not forty-three," she said. "How old are you?"

"Old enough," he said, refilling their glasses. "When do you plan to go back?"

"Tomorrow morning."

"Don't go. Now that I've gone to so much trouble to find you, you can't vanish so quickly."

She laughed. "I have to be in school on Monday." A puzzled look crossed her face. "What do you mean you went to so much trouble to find me?"

"I saw you this afternoon at the inauguration ceremony. I couldn't get you out of my mind so I decided to attend every one of the balls until I found you. I was sure you would be at one of them."

"Honestly?"

He nodded without speaking.

She looked down at her glass. "I have to go back."

"But not tomorrow," he said. "There's the whole weekend before you have to be back."

"It's freezing here. I've never been so cold in my life. I haven't got clothes for this weather."

"We can take care of that. We can leave for Acapulco tonight. It's warm there."

"Is there a plane leaving this late?" she asked.

"There are always planes."

"That's crazy," she said, smiling. "Besides, how can I be sure that I'll make a connection to San Francisco. You know those Mexican airlines."

"I'll guarantee it," he said confidently. "What do you say?"

She looked at him skeptically. "I don't know. I'm not sure."

"Of what?"

"Why are you doing this. You don't even know me."

"It's the one way of getting to know you better."

She met his eyes. "What are you getting out of it?"

He returned her gaze evenly, "The pleasure of your company."

"That's all? Nothing else?"

"Isn't that enough? He laughed. "I'm not a sex maniac if that's what you're thinking. You have absolutely nothing to worry about."

"But I don't even know your name."

"We can fix that." He took a card from his wallet and gave it to her.

She looked down at it. "Baydr Al Fay. MEDIA 70 Wall Street, New York," she read aloud. "MEDIA— what does that stand for?"

"That's the name of my company," he said. "Middle Eastern Development and Investment Associates."

"You're not American?"

"No. Did you think I was?"

"I thought you were Jewish," she said.

"Why?"

"I don't know. The way you look I guess."

"Many people make the same mistake," he said easily. "I'm an Arab."

She fell silent. Again she looked at the card.

"Is there anything wrong?" he asked quickly.

"No. I was just thinking, that's all." She looked up at him. "I've never done anything like this before."

"There's always a first time for everything."

"Can I think about it and let you know in the morning?"

"Of course you can, but it would really be a shame to miss a whole day in the sunshine."

She hesitated again. "Do you really mean it? There are no strings attached?"

"Absolutely no strings."

She raised the glass of champagne to her lips and emptied it. "My room's upstairs in this hotel. I'll go upstairs and pack. I can be ready in fifteen minutes."

"Good," he said, signalling for the check. "That will give me time to make a few phone calls and arrange for the flight. We can pick up my things on the way to the airport."

It had begun to snow again as the limousine slowly made its way to the airport. Jabir sat silently on the seat next to the chauffeur, smoking a cigarette.

"I hope we won't be late for the flight," she said.

"We won't," Baydr said.

"Do you think the weather might keep us from taking off?"

"I've taken off in much worse."

The airport was practically deserted as they walked through. Jabir and the chauffeur were behind them with the luggage. "I don't see any passengers," she said as they walked toward the departure gate. "Are you sure there's a plane?"

"There's a plane." He smiled.

It wasn't until there were on the ramp, climbing up the steps into the Lear Jet, that she realised they were boarding a private plane. She paused on the top step and looked at him.

He nodded reassuringly.

The steward was waiting just inside the door. "Good evening, madam. Good evening, Mr. Al Fay." He turned to Jordana. "Let me show you to your seat, if I may."

He led Jordana to a comfortable reclining chair and took her coat. He then leaned across and fastened her seat belt. "Are you comfortable, madame?"

"Very, thank you."

"Thank you, madame," he said and walked away.

Baydr sat down next to her and fastened his seat belt. A moment later the steward was back with a bottle of Dom Pérignon and two glasses. At a nod from Baydr, he filled the two glasses and went forward again.

Baydr raised his glass. "Welcome aboard *The Star of the East*."

"You didn't tell me it would be your own plane," she said.

"You didn't ask me. You only asked if I were sure there would be a flight."

She sipped at the champagne. "This is good. You know a girl could get hooked on stuff like this."

"I can think of worse," Baydr smiled.

The plane began to move out toward the strip. She reached for his hand automatically. "I always get nervous at take-off."

He smiled, holding her hand gently. "There's nothing to worry about. I have two very good pilots aboard."

She glanced out the window into the falling snow. "But they can't see very much."

"They don't have to," he said. "It's all worked by radar and instruments."

There was a surge of jets; a moment later they were airborne. When they were above the snow and clouds high in the star-filled night, she turned and saw that her hand was still in his. She looked at him. "You're a strange man," she said softly. "Do you do things like this often?"

"No," he said. "This is the first time for me too."

She was silent for a moment while she took another sip of her champagne. "Why me?" she asked.

His eyes were as blue as the night sky. "I think I fell in love with you the moment I first saw you."

The steward came back, refilled their glasses and disappeared. She sipped at the wine, then suddenly laughed. She saw the puzzled look on his face. "I just had the funniest thought," she said.

"Tell me."

"In the movies I've seen, the sheik comes riding in from the desert, sweeps the girl up on his white charger and gallops off into the night. In a way isn't that what you're doing?"

"I should hope so," he smiled. "You see, I intend to marry you."

Chapter Twelve

They were to be together for three years before they were married. And that was only after the birth of their first son, Muhammad.

During those three years they were inseparable. Wherever he went in the world, she went with him. Except when he returned to the Middle East. There she would not go.

"Not until we are married," she said. "I will not be treated as a concubine."

"We can be married," he said. "Under Muslim law I am allowed four wives."

"Fine," she said sarcastically. "Marry three other Arab girls."

"That's not the point, Jordana," he said. "I don't want to marry anyone else. I want to marry you."

"Then get a divorce."

"No."

"Why not?" she asked. "You don't love her. You never see her. And divorce is simple for a Muslim, isn't it? You said so yourself."

"We were married by the Prince's command. I would need his permission to divorce and he would not give it so that I could marry an unbeliever."

"Baydr, I love you," she said. "And I want to be your wife. But your only wife. Do you understand that? That's the way I was brought up. One wife at a time."

He smiled. "It's not that important really. It's just the way you look at it."

"Okay, then," she said with finality. "That's the way I look at it. I won't change."

He didn't answer. Actually he was not that anxious to get married again. Not that there were other women. There had been very few since he had been with her. And then only on those rare occasions when they happened to be apart. When they were together he never felt the need for another woman.

At first her parents had been aghast at her actions. It was not until Baydr placed substantial brokerage accounts with her stepfather that they began to come around. After that, they would sometimes have dinner with her parents when they were in San Francisco. But the dinners were always private, family affairs. No one wanted to explain that Jordana was living in sin, especially with an Arab.

Baydr bought a villa in the south of France and they spent as much time there during the summers as they could. Jordana studied and became proficient in French. She loved the Riviera. It was gay and bubbly and everyone was there for a good time. People cared nothing about your private life. Only that you had the money to enjoy it.

During the winter, they lived in New York and vacationed in Acapulco, where he bought the house in which they had spent their first weekend together. Occasionally they would go skiing but since he disliked the cold, she couldn't persuade him to go very often. Every three months Baydr returned home for two weeks. While he was away, Jordana would visit her family in San Francisco. But always when the two weeks were up, she would be there to meet him in New York or London or Paris or Geneva or wherever he had to be on business.

Only one time when he came into the apartment in New York, she was not waiting to greet him. "Have you heard from the madame?" he asked the butler, who took his hat and coat at the door.

"No, sir," the butler answered. "As far as I know, madame is still in San Francisco."

He waited all day for her to arrive and finally, after dinner that night he called her mother's house in San Francisco. Jordana answered the telephone.

"Darling, I was beginning to worry," he said. "When are you coming home?"

Her voice was tired. "I'm not."

"What do you mean, you're not?" The shock crept into his voice.

"Just what I said. I'm twenty-one and I have to do something with my life. I'm not coming back."

"But I love you."

"It's not enough," she said. "I'm tired of living in limbo. I think two years of that is enough for any girl. It's time I grew up."

"Is there someone else?"

"No. You know better than that. There has been no one else since you."

"Then what is it?"

"Would you believe that I'm just tired of the way we're living? Tired of playing at being Mrs. Al Fay when I'm not." She began to cry.

"Jordana."

"Don't try to talk me out of it, Baydr. I'm not like the Arab women you know. I just can't accept it. I have a mind of my own."

"I won't try to talk you out of it. I just want you to think it over."

"I have thought it over, Baydr. I'm not coming back."

He felt anger rising within him. "Then don't expect me to come running after you," he said. "I did that once."

"Goodbye, Baydr."

The telephone went dead in his hand. He looked at it, then slammed it down angrily. For a few minutes he stared into space, then picked up the telephone and called again.

This time it was her mother who answered. "May I speak with Jordana, please?" he asked.

"She ran up to her room," her mother said. "I'll call her."

Baydr held on until her mother came back on the telephone. "She said she doesn't want to speak to you."

"Mrs. Mason. I don't understand what's happening. What's the matter with her?"

"It's quite normal, Baydr," she said calmly. "Pregnant girls are usually quite excitable."

"Pregnant?" he shouted. "She's pregnant?"

"Of course," Mrs. Mason said. "Didn't she tell you?"

Seven months later, he stood at the side of her hospital bed. His son lay in her arms.

"He looks exactly like you," she said shyly. "The same blue eyes."

He remembered what his father had once told him. "All newborn children have blue eyes," he said. "We'll name him Muhammad."

"John," she said. "After my grandfather."

"Muhammad," he repeated. "After the Prophet." He looked down at her. "Now will you marry me?"

She met his gaze. "Will you get a divorce first?"

"I cannot have an unbeliever as my only wife," he said. "Will you take the faith?"

"Yes," she said.

He picked up the child and held it close to him. The baby began to cry. He looked down at Jordana with a proud father's smile. "Our son will be a prince," he said.

The old Prince looked up as Baydr came into his room. He gestured with his hand and the young boy who had been sitting at his feet rose and left the room. "How are you, my son?" the old man asked.

"I bring you news of an heir to the throne, your highness," he said. "I have a son. With your permission I shall name him Muhammad."

The old man looked at him shrewdly. "The child of an infidel concubine cannot pretend to a throne of the Prophet."

"I will marry this woman," Baydr said.

"Will she accept the faith?"

"She already has," Baydr replied. "And already she knows the Holy Koran better than I."

"You have my permission then to marry this woman."

"I request a further boon of your highness."

"What is that?"

"It is not seemly that the heir to the throne is issue from a second wife in the house. I ask your permission to divorce first."

"There must be grounds," the Prince said. "It is forbidden by the Koran to divorce because of vanity or whim."

"There are grounds," Baydr replied. "My first wife has been barren since the birth of her last child."

"I had heard such talk. Is it true?"

"Yes, your highness."

The Prince sighed. "Permission is then granted. But the settlement must be just and conform to the Holy Writings."

"It will be more than just."

"When you have married this woman, I would like you to bring her and your son to see me."

"It shall be as you wish, your highness."

"All is the will of Allah," the old man said. "When your son reaches the age of ten years he will be named my heir." He leaned and Baydr kissed his hand and rose. "Go then in peace, my son."

At their marriage Jordana pleased and surprised him and his parents by speaking to them in Arabic. Unknown to him, she had hired tutors and had taken a crash course so that now she spoke the language well but with a delightful soft American accent that made it sound almost musical. Baydr remembered how fascinated his mother and sisters had been by her hair, now they touched it, almost caressingly, remarking upon its softness and its spun-gold color. He remembered too how proud his father had been when he held his first grandson in his arms. "My little prince," Samir said softly.

After the marriage ceremony, they made the pilgrimage to Mecca, not by camel across the desert as his father and mother had done, but by Lear Jet which made the trip in hours instead of days. Together, they stood in the calm quiet of the square, dressed in white flowing robes, as were the other pilgrims and when the call to prayer came, each prostrated themselves on the ground before the Kaaba, the Holy House of Allah.

Afterward in the plane on their way to visit the Prince, he turned to her, speaking in Arabic. "Now you are truly Muslim."

"I have been from the moment we first met," she said. "I just didn't know it."

He had taken her hand, "I love you, my wife."

In the Arab tradition she raised his hand to her lips and kissed it. "And I love you, my master."

"If your son is to be my heir," the old Prince had said, "you will make your home near mine, so that I may see him grow and prosper."

Baydr had seen the startled look in Jordana's eyes above the traditional veil she wore for public meetings. He shook his head so that she would not speak.

"You will live in a house," the Prince continued, "within the palace walls so that you may be guarded from evil."

"But my work, your highness," Baydr protested. "It keeps me away most of the time."

The Prince smiled. "In that case you will arrange to come home more often. It is not good for a man to be separated from his family for too long."

That night in their own chambers, Jordana spoke to him. "He can't mean it," she said. "There is nothing for me to do here. I'll go crazy."

"It won't be for long. We have to humor him for a little while, then I will tell him I need you to help me in my work and he will understand."

"I won't do it!" she exclaimed. "I'm not an Arab woman who can be ordered about like a slave!"

His voice grew cold. It was a side of Baydr she had never seen before. "You are a Muslim wife," he said, "and you will do as you are told!"

Perhaps it was then that things began to change between them. Baydr was true to his word. But it was six months before he could convince the Prince that they would have to make their home elsewhere. By that time the damage had been done. For both of them.

An invisible barrier had grown between them and their love and no matter how they tried, they could not break it down.

Chapter Thirteen

Jordana could not sleep. Her eyes wide, she stared into the darkness, listening to his soft deep breathing on the far side of the king-size bed. Nothing had changed. Not even Jabir's stuff of dreams could bring them together now.

Before they were married, their sex had been warm and filled with lovely tender moments, despite the fact that there were certain acts of love he would not permit. He would kiss her breasts and belly but he would not engage in oral sex with her. Many times she had tried to lead him to it and although he delighted when she took him in her mouth, he would never allow her to assume the superior position so that she could control their movements. Without putting it in words, he had let her know that the things she wanted him to do were beneath his dignity as a man. A man should never be subservient to a woman in any way.

Still none of this had mattered. He had been a good lover. But she noticed a change soon after they were married. Sex became almost perfunctory. He entered her without preparation and was quickly finished. At first, she had blamed it on the pressure of his work. The Prince was making greater and greater demands upon him. His business was expanding into all the countries of the Western world and his organization was increasingly complex. Gradually Baydr gathered a staff of young men who, like himself, were of Middle Eastern extraction and versed in the ways of the West. These staff members were stationed in the countries with which they were most familiar, and it was their job to keep a day-to-day watch on his investments. But Baydr himself traveled from one to the other to make the final decisions and coordinate the various endeavors into a profitable whole.

To meet the pressures on his time, the Lear Jet had given way to a Mystère Twenty, then to a Super Caravelle and finally to a Boeing 707 Intercontinental. Now he could cover the long distances without having to make a stop, but even so, his travel kept them more and more apart. There was always some other place he had to be, some other emergency that only he could resolve. Their summers in France fell by the wayside, and more often than not the giant yacht they had bought for their mutual enjoyment lay idle in the harbor.

Soon after the birth of Samir, their second son, their love-making seemed to disappear altogether. And one night, when in her despair she reached for him, he took her hand and placed it on the cover between them. His voice was cold. "It is unseemly for a wife to make advances."

Stung by the rejection, she started to cry, then she became angry. She turned on the light, sat up in bed and reached for a cigarette. Carefully she lit it and took a deep puff, trying to compose herself. "What is it, Baydr? Don't I do anything for you anymore?"

He didn't answer.

"Is there someone else?"

He opened his eyes and looked at her steadily. "No."

"Then what is it?"

He was silent for a moment, then got out of the bed. "I am tired," he said. "I wish to sleep."

She looked up into his face. "And I want to fuck," she said bluntly. "Is there anything wrong with that?"

"It is enough that you are acting like a whore," he said. "You do not have to speak like one."

"You should know," she said bitingly. "You spend enough time with them."

His face darkened with anger. "What I do is none of your concern."

"I am your wife, and you have not been with me in months. What do you mean that is not my concern?"

"It is a wife's duty to bow to her husband's will."

"Marrying you did not make me a second-class citizen," she snapped. "I have rights and feelings too."

"You have forgotten what is written," he said. "You are my wife, my possession, and you are only entitled to those rights and feelings which I allow you."

She stared at him. "Then I ask you for a divorce. I won't live like this."

"I reject your request," he said. "You will live as I order you to."

"This isn't the Middle Ages," she said. "Neither are we in the Middle East, where you can lock me in a harem. Tomorrow I will leave for home and file for divorce."

His eyes were ice cold. "If you do," he said quietly, "you will never see your children again. You know I have that power."

The hurt and shock leaped into her voice. "You couldn't do a thing like that!"

"I can and I will," he said flatly.

The tears flooded her eyes and she could not speak.

He stared down at her for a moment, and when he spoke it was without any sympathy. "There will be no divorce. There is too much at stake. I will not have my son's accession to the throne despoiled by scandal. Not after I made so great a sacrifice to obtain it for him."

She looked at him incredulously. "What sacrifices have you made?"

"I swallowed my pride and asked permission to marry an infidel despite all the counsel I received against such an act. But I wanted the throne for my son. It had been promised."

"But I took the faith, didn't I?" she cried.

"With your lips but not with your heart. If you accepted it truly you would know your position and not question my acts."

She covered her face with her hands in despair. "Oh God!" she cried.

"What God do you call on?" he asked in a cruel voice. "Yours or mine?"

She lowered her hands and looked at him. "There is no God but Allah."

"Say the rest of it."

She was silent for a moment, then her eyes fell. "And Muhammad is His prophet," she whispered.

He took a deep breath and started for the door. "Remember that."

"Baydr." Her voice held him. "What do you want me to do?"

He looked at her steadily. "I grant you freedom to do whatever you wish as long as we remain married, but there are two restrictions. The first is discretion. You will do nothing to bring disgrace upon our house. To the world our marriage must appear as it always has been."

"And the second?"

"You will avoid Jews. That I will not tolerate."

She was silent for a moment, then she nodded. "It will be as you wish."

He went into the other room, leaving the door open behind him. A moment later he was back, a yellow metal box in his fingers. He shut the door behind him and walked to the edge of the bed and looked down at her. He opened the box and placed it on the night table beside the bed. She saw the ampules in their yellow netting. "You know I don't like amyl nitrate."

"I don't care what you like or what you do not," he said harshly. "You act and speak like a whore — you will be treated as one."

He unbuttoned his pajama top and took it off, then pulled the cord of the pants. They fell on the floor and he stepped free of them. "Take off your night dress," he commanded.

She did not move.

Quickly he reached down and, grasping the front of it, tore it from her. Her breasts leapt free and he cupped one in his hand. "Is this what you want?" he asked.

She did not answer.

He increased the pressure. The pain made her gasp involuntarily. She looked into his eyes for a moment, then her gaze fell to his hand. He was holding his rapidly hardening phallus toward her. "Is that what you want?"

"Baydr!" she cried.

He thrust himself into her mouth. She choked and coughed. His voice was derisive. "That is not what you want, infidel whore?" He held her face away from him and looked into her eyes. "Perhaps you will like this better."

Quickly he pushed her flat on the bed and thrust three fingers deep into her. It was swift and unexpected and the tearing brought a moan of pain to her lips. Rapidly he began to move his fingers in and out while with his free hand he took an ampule from the box.

She felt the explosion in her brain as he broke the capsule under her nose. Her heart felt as if it would burst in her chest and in spite of herself she began to feel the throes of orgasm begin to rack her body.

Abruptly he withdrew his fingers and turned her belly down on the bed. "On your hands and knees like the infidel bitch that you are!" he commanded.

She could not move.

His open palm slashed across her buttocks. She screamed. Again and again his hand cracked across her flesh. She began to writhe and moan. It was crazy, she thought. I can't take this. But she was beginning to enjoy the heat spreading through her loins.

"Like a dog, woman!" he commanded.

"Yes, yes," she moaned, pushing herself back on her knees, holding her buttocks high in the air. Her breasts hung toward the bed as she leaned on her elbows. She felt him positioning himself behind her and turned to look at him.

"Don't look at me, infidel bitch!" he shouted, roughly pulling her hair so that her face turned away from him.

The trembling she felt inside rapidly spread throughout her body, even her knees were shaking. Once she had seen a mare trembling, waiting to be mounted by a stallion. She knew now exactly how the animal had felt. Then she remembered the stallion with its giant red shaft springing from him and ripping into the mare and how the mare had gone to her knees with the fierceness of the onslaught.

He pulled her head back by her hair so that her neck was stretched taut and exploded another capsule under her nose. Again the orgasms began.

She heard him break another capsule but this time it was not for her but for him. Then she felt the hardness of him tear into her and the fierce slamming thrust of his body against her buttocks.

She screamed once with the pain and the violence of her orgasm as he began to thrust into her. Then, like the mare, she went down under the impact.

Afterward she lay very still on her side of the bed, the pain and trembling slowly leaving her body. He, too, was silent. He made no gesture. There was no communication between them.

After a moment, he spoke. His voice was calm as if nothing had passed between them. "Now, woman, do you understand your position?"

She felt the tears come to her eyes. "Yes," she whispered in a low voice.

And that was how it had been ever since. It was no longer an act of love, not even an act of cruelty. Purely and simply it was an assertion of his power over her.

It was later that summer that she took her first lover. After that it was easy. But with very few of them did she achieve satisfaction. Still there was something she did get. Whether it was true or not, whether they felt it or not, whether she paid them or not, they all made love to her.

And that was something Baydr never did.

Chapter Fourteen

The buzzing of the electric razor woke her. Jordana rolled over in the bed. Through the open door leading to the bathroom she could see him standing in front of the mirror, a towel wrapped around his flat waist. The look of concentration on his face was familiar. Shaving seemed to absorb him completely.

She sat up in the bed and reached for a cigarette. It had been a strange weekend. Strange, because there had been moments when they had seemed to be approaching the closeness they once had. But each time it happened, one or the other would draw away or do something to destroy the feeling.

Twice that weekend they had made love. The first time she had ruined it by her request for pain. "Hurt me," she had said and, as she said it, felt him turn off.

The second time had been the night before, after they had smoked Jabir's cigarette. This time she was ready. The hashish had relaxed her and she felt slow and easy. She wanted only to make love beautifully and simply. She wanted him to be as she had been when they first met.

But it wasn't like that at all. He had taken her roughly, thrusting himself into her. Three times, he went in and out of her; the fourth time he emptied himself.

Taken by surprise at his quickness, she had stared up into his face. It was impassive, as if nothing were happening to him. She could see neither joy nor pleasure.

A moment later he left her and was on his side of the bed, asleep. She lad lain for a long time without sleeping and had thought about that first time when he had taken her without love and made her feel as if she were nothing but a receptacle for his own use and convenience. He had made it clear then that it was the way it would be and it had been like that until this weekend.

After the first failure, she had hoped that there would be another, better time together. But it was not to be. Whatever he had sought from her at the beginning of that weekend was over. And she wondered if she would ever get another chance.

He came out of the bathroom, wet from the shower, and looked down at her. "We're leaving for Los Angeles this morning," he said in a casual voice. "What are your plans after that?"

He was acting as if they were strangers. "So nice to see you," she said. "Look forward to seeing you again."

A puzzled look crossed his face. "What did you say?"

"Nothing. I haven't made any plans."

"Are you going back to France?"

"What about you?" she asked. "It wouldn't be a bad idea if you saw the children. You've been gone all summer and they miss you."

"I can't," he said flatly. "There's just too much to do right now. Besides, I plan to spend some time with them in Beirut this fall. I will be there at least six weeks."

"A few days would mean a lot to them."

His voice grew edgy. "I said I can't spare the time." He crossed to the dresser and took out a shirt. "I may have to leave for Japan immediately."

"I've never been to Japan. I hear it's fascinating."

He was buttoning his shirt. "Tokyo's a madhouse," he said noncommittally. "Traffic is awful and everything is so crowded that you can't breathe."

She gave up. He didn't want her with him. He had no use for her there. "I think I may stay in L.A. a few days. I'll see some friends and then maybe go up to San Francisco to visit my family."

He slipped into his trousers. "That's not a bad idea. But arrange to be back in France by the beginning of next week. I don't want the boys to be left alone too long."

"I'll arrange that," she said. With four servants, two bodyguards and the nanny, the children weren't exactly alone.

The telephone rang and he picked it up. He listened for a moment, then nodded, pleased. "Good, Dick," he said. "Call the plane and tell them we'll leave as soon as I get to the L.A. airport."

He put down the telephone. "I'm leaving for Tokyo right away," he said. "You can use my bungalow at the hotel if you like."

"That would be nice."

"Youssef is there in the hotel meeting with Vincent. If there's anything you need, you can call on him."

"Thank you."

He slipped into his shoes and walked to the door. "How long do you think it will take you to get ready to leave here?"

"Not long."

He nodded and left the room. For a moment, she sat without moving. Then she ground out the cigarette and got out of bed. She stood in front of the mirror, let her gown drop to the floor and looked at her naked body.

Physically, she was still the same. Perhaps her breasts had become slightly fuller since the birth of the children but they were firm and her body had the muscle tone of her youth. She should have been pleased. But she wasn't. The abundance of wealth and the comforts it brought were just not enough. There had to be more to life than standing by and waiting to be used.

The telephone in Youssef's bedroom began to ring. He didn't move, hoping it would stop. He was exhausted. The young American man he had met in After Dark last night had worn him out. He had been insatiable. Finally, when he could scarcely move, Youssef had given him fifty dollars and sent him away.

The man had looked at the fifty-dollar bill, then back at him. "Do you want me to call you?"

"I won't be here. I'm leaving in the morning."

"I'd like to see you again."

Youssef knew exactly what he wanted to see. Another fifty-dollar bill. "I'll let you know when I get back to town."

"I don't have a telephone, but you can leave a message for me with the bartender."

"Okay," Youssef said.

The man left and Youssef sank into the sleep of the dead. Now the damned telephone would not stop ringing. If Baydr were still in town, he would have leapt for the phone, but Baydr had left for Japan last night.

The phone in the bedroom stopped ringing, but started up in the living room. Youssef pulled one of the pillows over his head and tried to get back to sleep, but a moment later the bedroom phone began again.

Cursing, Youssef reached for it. "Hello," he growled hoarsely.

The words were spoken in French but with a heavy Arabic accent. "Monsieur Ziad?"

Automatically Youssef answered in Arabic. "Yes."

The voice switched to their native language. "We have not met in person but we have spoken over the telephone. And we were at the same party aboard the Al Fay yacht, the night of Madam Al Fay's birthday. "My name is Ali Yasfir."

"Ahlan wa Sahlan," Youssef said, now wide awake. He knew of Ali Yasfir.

"Ahlan fik," Yasfir replied formally.

"How may I serve you?" Youssef asked politely.

"If you can arrange the time, I would like to meet with you on matters of important mutual interest."

"Where are you?"

"Here in Los Angeles. Perhaps we might take lunch together?"

"It can be arranged. Where would you like to meet?"

"Anywhere. At your convenience."

"One o'clock. In the Polo lounge, here in the hotel."

He put down the telephone. He knew the results of Baydr's last meeting with Yasfir. He was also sure that Yasfir knew that he knew. Still, something big had to be under way for Yasfir to contact him. Yasfir usually went right to the top.

He reached for the telephone again. "Good morning, Mr. Ziad," the operator said cheerfully.

"Would you ring Mr. Vincent's room for me." There was no way he could have two lunches at the same time. Vincent would have to be put off.

In accordance with Arab custom, Ali Yasfir did not come to the point of the meeting until their coffee had been placed before them. "I understand your importing company is beginning to bring many things from abroad into the United States."

Youssef nodded. "That is true. It is amazing to discover how many things that we can have manufactured in the Middle East that Americans will buy."

"I also understand that it is your responsibility to discover the small factories in the Middle East whose products you think can be marketed in America?"

Youssef nodded.

"I, too, represent certain manufacturers who are desirous of expediting shipment of their products to the United States. At the moment we deal with European exporters and we are having many problems with them."

Youssef was silent. He knew of the problems. Too many shipments had been intercepted by the Federal Bureau of Narcotics. There were rumors in the Middle East that certain important people were very disappointed in Yasfir's performance. "I had understood that you were moving a great portion of your operation to South America," he said.

"That is true" — Yasfir nodded — "but that is part of our expansion program. The demand for our other products is as great as ever."

"I wish I could be of service to you," Youssef said smoothly. "But Mr. Al Fay has already formed our policy and I doubt whether he would change his mind on my advice."

"I'm sure that Mr. Al Fay does not concern himself with the details of each item that you import. I'm sure that is left in your more than capable hands."

That was true. Baydr did not have to know. Thousands of dollar's worth of small items were shipped, and without his knowing what they were.

"A most lucrative arrangement would be made for you if we find a way to work together." Ali Yasfir smiled. "You know the prices our merchandise brings. Sometimes as much as a million dollars for a shipment that takes no more space than a crate of dolls from Egypt. You could enjoy a bonus of ten percent merely for your good offices. There would be no risk involved."

Youssef looked at him. It was a lot of money. Reluctantly, he shook his head. He hated to let it pass. But despite what Yasfir said, it was too risky. Sooner or later, there would be a leak. And then, it would all be over. "I'm sorry," he said. "At this time we do not have the facilities. Our operation is just beginning. Perhaps, later, when we are bigger and better equipped."

Ali Yasfir nodded. He was satisfied. Sooner or later, Youssef would agree. It was simply a question of raising the stakes until it reached the point where he couldn't resist. "You think about it. We will talk again when you return to Paris."

"Yes," Youssef said. "Perhaps by then the situation will change."

Ali Yasfir raised his coffee cup. "Mr. Al Faiy is on his way to Japan?"

Youssef nodded. He had never realized that they kept such a close watch on Baydr's movements.

"His negotiation with the Japanese is very enterprising," Ali Yasfir said.

"I know very little about it," Youssef said quickly.

Yasfir smiled. "Even more important than the little business we discussed would be an association with him. He is very highly regarded by us."

"By everyone," Youssef added.

"Still, we feel that he could be more influential in our cause," Yasfir said. "If he were to become more assertive, perhaps it would have a greater influence on those who, like him, hold more conservative views."

Youssef didn't speak. Yasfir was right. This was a great deal more important than the transhipment of narcotics.

"If you could find a way to influence him to support our cause," Yasfir said, "you would spend the rest of your days in luxury and Allah would shower His blessings on you for the help given to His oppressed people."

"Mr. Al Fay is not a man who is easily influenced."

"He is human," Yasfir answered. "A way will be found. Sooner or later."

Youssef signaled for the check and signed it. On their way out of the Polo Lounge, they ran into Jordana.

"I thought Mr. Vincent was joining you for lunch," she said, "and I just was going to stop by and tell him that I would be happy to attend the party tonight."

"I will tell him," Youssef said. "Perhaps we can go together."

She noticed Ali Yasfir standing nearby. He bowed. "Madame Al Fay," he said. "So nice to see you again."

Youssef saw the puzzled look on her face. "You remember Mr. Yasir," he said quickly. "He was at your birthday party on the boat."

"Of course," she said. "How are you, Mr. Yasfir?"

He bowed again. "I am fine, and you are even more beautiful than I remembered. But I must apologize. I am already late for an appointment."

She watched him hurry down the lobby then turned back to Youssef. "I hope Baydr does not have any business with that man," she said.

Youssef was surprised. It was the first time he had ever heard her say anything about Baydr's business associates. "I don't think so," he answered. Then his curiosity overcame him. "What makes you say that?"

A veil seemed to drop over her eyes. "I don't know," she answered. "Maybe it's woman's intuition. But I sense something dangerous in him.

Chapter Fifteen

Jordana glanced around the large darkened living room and reached for her glass of wine. The other guests sat on couches and chairs around the room, staring in absorption at the big motion picture screen at the far end. It was not the fun kind of Hollywood party she had expected. It had all been rather solemn and dull.

She looked toward the back of the room where the host sat by himself at the bar, his back to the screen. It seemed that the moment the picture had begun he had lost all interest in his guests. Maybe that was what was called the star's privilege.

Rick Sullivan had been a film star for many years in what was called the big picture, the kind of spectacle that had been made by C.B. DeMille and more recently by Michael Vincent but was no longer in vogue. Actually Sullivan had played the lead in Michael's film about Moses and that was the reason for this dinner. The word had gone out in Hollywood that Michael was about to make another big score and Sullivan thought it would not be a bad idea to remind the director that he was still around.

Not that he needed the money. Or the work. For the past five years, he had had one of the most successful series on television. But television was not the same as motion pictures.

He did not like large parties so he had kept his guest list to about sixteen. Of course, his agent and his publicity man were there, as well as one of Hollywood's leading columnists. Other guests were mutual friends of Vincent and himself, several actors and actresses who were not important enough to threaten his status as the star of the evening.

Sullivan turned from the bar and saw the look of complete boredom on Jordana's face as she watched the screen. She had not been at all what he had expected.

For some reason, he had expected an older woman. Perhaps it was because he assumed that a man with as much money as her husband was reputed to have should be further along in years. He glanced across the room looking for the man called Ziad who had come with them. He was sitting next to Vincent on the large couch. At first he'd thought the man might be the woman's lover but then he dismissed that idea. The man was clearly a homosexual. He had to be a watchdog.

Dinner had been pleasant, the conversation self-serving and filled with mutual flattery. Everybody loved everybody — typical Hollywood table talk. At the end of the meal he announced that he had obtained a print of Michael Vincent's great film and was about to screen it for them. Michael was pleased and the guests seemed happy as they went into the living room to take their places in front of the screen.

Rick picked up his drink, walked over to Jordana and sat down in the chair next to her. He looked up at the screen, then almost immediately turned away. It was one of the early scenes where the young Moses first confronted the Pharaoh. It had been almost twenty years since the film had been made and he hated to look at pictures of himself as a young man. They made him too aware of his age.

He saw her watching him and smiled ruefully. "I don't like to watch myself. I think it's the height of vanity or something."

"I can imagine that might be a problem," she said politely.

"You don't seem too interested in the picture either."

"I've already seen it," she answered frankly. "It wasn't my thing at that time either."

He laughed. "What kind of pictures do you like?"

She thought for a moment. "Modern pictures. You know, the kind of pictures they make today."

"You don't mean the X-rated pictures?"

"I've never seen an X picture."

He looked at her for a moment. "Would you like to see one?"

She met his gaze. "I suppose so. But I can't imagine going into one of those sleazy theaters."

"You don't have to do that. I can arrange a screening for you."

"That might be interesting. When do you think you might be able to do it?"

"How about right now?" he asked. He saw the puzzled expression on her face as she glanced quickly around the room. "In another room, of course."

"But what about the others?" she asked.

"They won't miss us. This picture runs another two and a half hours. We'll be back before then."

No one even looked up as they left the room. She followed him into the hallway and then to his suite. He closed the door behind him. He gestured casually. "I hope you don't mind watching it in my bedroom?"

"Not at all," she said. "But I don't see a screen."

He laughed, pressing a button on the wall. There was a whir of machinery and a platform dropped from the ceiling over the foot of the bed. On the platform was a giant television set, angled downward. "I've had the films transferred to videotape," he said. "The only handicap is that you have to watch from the bed."

"The bed doesn't look that uncomfortable."

"I'll have to put a tape on the machine," he said. "I'll be back in a moment."

"Okay."

He started for the door, then stopped and gestured toward the night table. "The silver box has cigarettes of the finest Columbian grass; the pink glass bottle with the gold spoons around it holds the best coke in town."

"Lovely," she smiled. "Then may I ask you to bring back a bottle of cold white wine. Dope always dehydrates me."

When he came back, she was lying naked on the bed, holding a joint carefully between her fingers. The film was already in progress.

Quickly, he stripped and sat down on the bed beside her. He reached for the coke bottle and a spoon. "How about a hit?" he asked. "This stuff will blow your mind."

"Sounds good."

He took a heavy snort up each nostril, then held the spoon for her. He could see her eyes brighten as the dope hit her. "How is it?" he asked.

"Couldn't be better." She reached for him. "You are a big man."

"I used to think so, until I saw that little man up there on the screen. He's really big."

She giggled. "I don't believe it. He's got to be a freak." She stared at the screen fascinated. "Oh, no!" she exclaimed. "That girl can't take it all in her mouth. It has to be a trick."

"It's no trick," he said. "Since this picture has come out, she's made a fortune teaching Beverly Hills ladies how to do it. It's all in the way you relax your throat, she says."

She leaned over, her tongue delicately licking at him. "I'll be happy if I can take half of yours."

He laughed aloud and she looked up at him questioningly. "You know, when I first met you, I thought you were a very straight lady."

"I am a very straight lady." She smiled demurely. "I've never watched a fuck movie before." Then she went down on him.

"Beautiful," he said, watching her as he reached down the side of the bed to press the invisible button that would start the videotape recorder. He didn't tell her that the only pictures he liked to watch of himself were those taken in this bed by a hidden camera. "Just beautiful."

After a while Youssef grew tired. It seemed the movie would never come to an end. Idly he glanced around the room. Suddenly the picture was forgotten. Jordana was gone. And so was the host. He was angry with himself. He had not seen them leave.

He rose from his seat. Vincent looked at him. "I have to go to the bathroom," he explained in a whisper. He tiptoed silently from the room and stood in the corridor.

It was a large house. They could be in any one of a half-dozen rooms. He tried the study, the dining room, the breakfast room, the patio, but they were nowhere to be found.

Annoyed, he went into the bathroom and washed his face and hands with cold water. He was stupid. He should have known she would be off with him. He was a big man, attractive, and, most of all, a movie star. He was nothing like the gigolos she found on the Riviera.

He came out of the bathroom and walked down the hall toward the living room. It was then that he noticed the whir of machinery coming from behind the closed door. He paused, thinking it might be the air-conditioning unit. The Americans had a way of installing that kind of equipment in closets. But then he heard the faint hum of what sounded like voices coming from a speaker. He reached for the knob. The door wouldn't open. It was locked.

He looked around quickly to make sure the corridor was empty. Youssef had learned many tricks, including the use of plastic credit cards.

A moment later the closet door was open and Youssef was staring in surprise at the small monitor of a videotape recorder. The sound volume was depressed but the picture was in color and bright as day. Jordana was naked, on her back, her face contorted in the throes of orgasm. She seemed to be staring directly up into the camera as her legs gripped tightly around the waist of the man who was bucking like a bronco rider. The faint echo of her gasp whined in the speaker as the man began to spend himself inside her. Then slowly he rolled over on his side and came out of her, damp and already softening. He turned toward Jordana and smiled, his hand dropping to the side of the bed. Youssef had just enough time to recognize the face of their host before the screen went blank.

He was frozen for a moment, then moved quickly. He knew the machine. Baydr had the same system installed on the boat, but only the playback units, not the recorder. Youssef depressed the key which released the videotape cartridge and took it from the machine. Placing it under his jacket, he stepped back into the corridor. He closed the door and heard the lock click.

He walked down the hall to the foyer. A servant rose from a seat near the front door and he opened it as Youssef approached.

"Is the gentleman leaving?" he asked.

"No. I just thought I could use a moment of fresh air."

"Very good, sir," the servant said, closing the door behind him.

Youssef walked to his car. The chauffeur came out of the front seat. "Is my attache case still in the trunk?" Youssef asked.

"Yes, sir." The chauffeur went to the back of the car and opened the trunk. He took out the case and gave it to Youssef. Quickly, Youssef placed the video cassette inside and locked it. He gave it to the chauffeur. "Remind me to take it when we go back to the hotel tonight."

"Yes, sir."

Youssef watched the man replace it in the trunk, then went back into the house. He could feel his heart pounding. This was even more than he had planned, more than he had hoped for. Now it was simply a matter of deciding when it could best be used.

He slipped back into the seat beside Vincent and looked up at the screen. Vincent turned to him and whispered, "Rick made a fantastic Moses, don't you think?"

"Yes," Youssef answered. "How did you know he'd be so good in the part?"

Vincent turned to him with a smile. "I couldn't go wrong," he said. "Sullivan changed his name from Solomon when he went into pictures. How could a Solomon be bad at playing Moses?"

Youssef stared at the closeup of Moses that filled the entire screen. Of course. He wondered why he had not seen it before. The man had the face of a Jew.

There was a sound at the back of the room. Jordana and Rick were back. From the corner of his eye he watched them cross to the bar and sit there. He saw Rick glance over his shoulder at the screen and say something to her. She laughed and picked up the fresh glass of wine the barman had placed before her.

Youssef felt a rush of hatred. "Laugh, you bitch!" he thought savagely. "That's it. Laugh, you Jew-fucking bitch!"

He knew now exactly what he was going to do with the tapes. Baydr would be eternally grateful to him for protecting his name by keeping from the world the knowledge that his wife had betrayed him with a Jew.

Chapter Sixteen

Leila looked across the room at her mother. "I told you, Mother, many times. Hamid is just a friend, that's all. I am not serious about him. I do not intend to marry him. He's just a friend."

Maryam sighed heavily. "I don't know what's wrong with you. He's just an ordinary Syrian, not even from a good family. I can't imagine what you see in him."

Leila lit a cigarette. "I have to talk to someone."

"There are many nice boys you can talk to. My father said the industrialist Fawaz spoke to him. His son is of the marrying age and they are interested in you."

"Who?" Leila asked sarcastically. "Fawaz or his son?"

"Don't be disrespectful. Grandfather means nothing but the best for you."

"Like he did for you?" Leila asked pointedly.

"It wasn't his fault," Maryam said defensively. "None of us knew then what your father was like. We did everything correctly. No one can point a finger at us."

"I don't see anyone pointing a finger at my father either," Leila said. "Apparently nobody cares what you do as long as you have enough money."

Maryam shook her head in exasperation. "It's just as I've always said, you take after your father more than you do me. You only see things the way you want to see them. I should never have allowed you to go away to school in Switzerland. The only thing they taught you was how to talk back to your mother. Your sister doesn't act like that."

"My sister is stupid!" Leila snapped. "All she cares about is her home and her children and her problems with servants."

"That's all a woman has to care about," Maryam said. "What else is there?"

Leila gestured toward the window. "There's a whole world out there, Mother. Can't you see it? For too many years we've been oppressed, our people have been ridiculed and enslaved. Our brothers cry under the yoke of the Jews in Palestine. And you ask what else there is."

"Those are the problems that men must solve," Maryam said. "We should attend to our own affairs."

"There's no use," Leila said in disgust. She walked to the door. "I'm going out."

"Where are you going? To meet that Hamid again?"

"No. Just out. That's all."

"What's the hurry then? It's almost dinnertime."

"I'm not hungry. Don't wait for me."

Maryam watched the door close behind her. A few minutes later she heard the car start up in front of the house. She got out of her chair and walked to the window just in time to see the small Mercedes convertible turn into the street.

Leila was like her father. There was no one who could talk to her. She thought about the day last month when she had shown up at the front door with her friend the Syrian, Hamid. They were so ragged and dirty that at first the servant, who was new to the house, would not let them in. Finally, reluctantly, she had called her mistress.

Maryam was shocked at the way her daughter looked. Her skin was dark and leathery as if she had spent days in the desert sun, and there wasn't a curve on her body. She was as thin and straight as a boy.

"What happened?" she cried.

"Nothing, Mother," Leila replied calmly.

"But, look at you, you're in rags. You look as if you hadn't had a bath in months."

"I'm all right, Mother," Leila said stubbornly.

"Where did you come from? I thought you were still in school."

"We hitched our way home," Leila answered.

"What for? All you had to do was telephone. We would have bought you a ticket."

"If I had wanted a ticket I would have called. I wanted to do it this way."

For the first time, Maryam noticed Hamid, standing outside the threshold. She looked at him, then at her daughter.

"This is my friend Hamid," Leila said. "He's Syrian."

Hamid took a step forward. He touched his finger to his forehead, "Tasharrafna."

"Hasalli sharaf," she replied automatically. She did not add the other customary words of welcome.

"I met Hamid on the road," Leila said. "He's on his way home to Damascus."

Maryam said nothing.

"He was very nice to me," Leila said. "If it weren't for him, I might have had some trouble."

Maryam turned back to the Syrian. "Enter," she said. "And make yourself welcome in our house."

He bowed again. "Thank you, madame, but I have some friends I can stay with."

She did not demur. He seemed coarse and common. But then so did most Syrians.

"I am glad you are home," he said to Leila. "Now I must be going."

Leila held out her hand to him. "You will get in touch with me before you leave Beirut?"

He nodded, and they shook hands. Despite their formality, Maryam sensed the familiarity between them. "I will call you," he said.

But that had been almost a month ago and still he had not left Beirut. What he was doing, she did not know. But she did know that he and Leila met almost every day at the Phoenicia Hotel. She had been told that by friends who had seen them sitting in the coffee shop drinking Coca-Colas.

She parked the car in the street and went into the coffee shop through the outside entrance. She did not like to walk through the ornate lobby with its crowds of packaged American and European tourists. He was sitting alone at his usual table in the corner near a window. The inevitable Coca-Cola with its slice of lemon was in front of him. He looked up as she sat down opposite him. Without a word, the waitress brought her a Coca-Cola.

He waited until the waitress had gone. "I'm leaving tomorrow," he said.

She looked at him. His face was expressionless. "Home?" she asked.

"Might as well," he said. "There's nothing going on here and I had a letter from my cousin. I can get a sergeant's job in the army with time and bonuses. They're recruiting veterans with experience."

"I don't understand it," she said. "I haven't heard a word from them and it's almost a month now. Maybe they think I was killed with all the others."

"They know you're here. I told them when I went in to collect my last pay."

"Then why don't they call me? I'm going crazy waiting around here. My mother never stops nagging me."

"They have other things on their mind. There was a story going around that Al-Ikhwah wanted your father to handle their foreign investments."

"I know. He turned them down. That happened before I left France." She sipped her drink through the straw. "They're crazy. My father won't lift a finger to help anyone but himself."

"They're going back to him again. They seem to think he's important."

"I wish them luck. There's only one way they'll ever get him to help them. At the point of a gun."

"What makes you say that?"

"I know my father. He still thinks that money will cure everything."

"Anyway I'm leaving tomorrow. That army job is better than nothing."

"Maybe I should go down and talk to them. I didn't get all that training to sit here in my mother's house."

"Don't do that," he said quickly. "Your orders were to wait until you were contacted."

She looked at him. "Do you have to go?"

"I have to do something. My money's almost gone."

"I have money."

"No."

She was silent for a moment, staring down at her drink, then she looked up at him. "I was hoping we would be sent on a mission together."

"I'm not the type," he said. "They would rather have the students for missions. People pay less attention to them."

"You're not that old. You could still pass for a student," she said quickly.

"Maybe," he laughed. "In the dark."

"If you go back in the Syrian army, they'll never let you get out."

"Maybe I won't want to. The way we're building up and the way Egypt is preparing, the chances are something is going to happen. And if there is a war, I can make officer."

"Is that what you want?"

"No."

"What do you want then?"

"Just to make a lot of money," he smiled, "like your father."

"Stop talking about him!" she snapped, suddenly angry. "That's all I hear everywhere I go. My father this, my father that. Even my mother never stops talking about him."

"Did you see the paper today?" he asked.

"No."

"You should have. Maybe then you would know why they talk about your father."

"What did he do?"

"He just closed the biggest oil tanker deal ever made with Japan. He bought ten ships and they're building twenty more for him. All supertankers. It will be the largest Arab-owned shipping line in the world."

"Allah be praised," she said sarcastically. "How much richer does that make him?"

"At least he's doing something. There's no reason for the Greeks and all the others to monopolize the shipping from our ports."

"How does that help the Palestinians?" she asked.

He was silent.

"I'm sorry," she said quickly "I didn't mean to quarrel with you. I'm just getting edgy sitting around."

"That's all right."

She looked at him. "Would you like me to go back to your room with you?"

"Okay," he said, then he smiled. "But is it all right with you if we go to a movie first? The only pictures in Damascus are at least ten years old."

Baydr felt the warm sake buzzing in his head as he put down his cup. Almost as soon as it touched the table, the geisha sitting on her knees just behind him filled the tiny cup. Baydr looked at it. He wasn't used to drinking. A glass of champagne occasionally but no more. And though he had only had three of the tiny cups he felt them.

"Enough," he said, starting to get up. He felt slightly dizzy as he rose. The geisha was there to help him as soon as he put out his hand. He smiled at her. "Sleep," he said.

She looked at him blankly.

"Sleep," he repeated. He placed the palms of his hand together and held them at the side of his face, closing his eyes.

"Hai! Hai! Sleep."

He nodded.

Still holding one arm under his elbow, she reached out and slid back the screen separating the rooms. She led him into the bedroom and closed the panel behind her. The bed was very low to the floor and he almost fell backward as he sat down on it. He thought that was very funny and began to laugh. She laughed with him.

"I almost fell."

"Hai, hai," she said, reaching behind him and pulling open the sash that held his robe. Gently she slipped it from his shoulders and he rolled back onto the bed as she pulled it from him.

"Tired," he mumbled into the pillow. He rolled onto his stomach, face down. As if from a great distance, he heard the gentle rush of her kimona. He smelled the faint perfume of the talcum powder settling on his skin like a soft cloud.

Her hands felt like gentle feathers as they softly stroked his back, her fingers tracing his spine from his neck to his coccyx. A moment later, she began kneading his flesh with slightly warmed oil. He sighed in contentment.

Her hands went down his back, cupping and stroking his buttocks, then he felt her slowly part them and gently place a probing finger inside him. She found his prostrate and massaged it in a circular motion.

Almost asleep, he felt himself growing hard and began to move to his side. Gently but firmly, she held him so that he could not move. Her other hand, moist with the warm oil, began to stroke his throbbing phallus.

He tried to move with her but couldn't. Then he became aware that there was not one but two geishas in the room. The second woman came around the other side of the bed and knelt before him. Now there were four hands instead of two. There was no part of him that was not being touched, stroked, caressed all at the same time.

The pressure on his prostate and testicles, the increasing rapidity of the moving hand on his penis became too much. He felt himself begin to contract into a knot, the agony became almost unbearable. A groan escaped him. He opened his eyes.

The tiny Japanese woman still clad in her kimona smiled sweetly at him. Then she opened her mouth to gently encircle his glans. The explosion came and for a moment he felt close to death as the semen flooded forth like a gusher. Explosion followed explosion until he was completely drained and all that was left was a mildly pleasant emptiness.

He was still watching the tiny geisha as she rose to her feet and moved silently away. He felt other hands draw the soft sheets around him. He closed his eyes and fell into dreamless sleep.

When he awakened it seemed as if he had slept only for a few minutes. But it was broad daylight and Jabir was standing over his bed.

"I'm sorry to disturb you, master," he said, "but this cable just arrived and Mr. Carriage said it was most important."

He sat up slowly and took the yellow sheet. The message was simple, and one that only he and the Prince could understand.

THE DATE HAS BEEN SET FOR THE INVESTITURE OF YOUR SON AS MY HEIR. PLEASE RETURN AT ONCE TO COMPLETE ALL ARRANGEMENTS.

(signed) FEIYAD, PRINCE

He was wide awake now. He knew that had nothing to do with his son. A long time ago they had agreed on the meaning of this message.

War. War with Israel. The time to avenge themselves for the defeat of 1967 was close at hand. Or so they thought. A feeling of sadness came over him.

It was too soon. Much too soon. Perhaps they would win a minor victory at first, but the Israelis were too experienced for them. If the war ran more than a week it would mean another defeat for the Arabs.

Even the Prince agreed with him about that. But there was much to be done. If the world thought they were united perhaps more than a minor victory could be won. Not on the battlefield where men died, but in the banks and boardrooms where they lived.

ANOTHER PLACE: OCTOBER 1973

The dusty dung-colored Volkswagen, its paint pocked by years of desert sand and wind, coughed and sputtered to a stop a few yards short of the parking lot gate. The sentries watched curiously as the old man in equally dusty Bedouin robes climbed out and walked around behind the car. He raised the trunk lid, exposing the engine, and stared at it dolefully.

One of the sentries walked over. "What is the trouble, old man?"

"I wish I knew. Even a camel needs water sometimes. But this creature — I tell you there is something ungodly about a creature that never needs water. If it were a camel I would know what to do."

The young soldier laughed. "What would you do if it were a camel?"

"I would give it some water. Then, if that didn't work, I would kick it in the ass."

"Why don't you try that?" the soldier suggested.

"I already did. It doesn't work. Nothing works."

Leaving the old man staring at the engine, the soldier looked into the car. The interior was as decrepit as the exterior. The upholstery was in ribbons, and the gauges were encrusted with a layer of dust. The soldier reached in and wiped the dirt from the gas gauge, then he straightened up and turned to the old man. "You're out of gas."

"I don't understand that. It never happened before."

"It's happened now," the soldier said with a faintly condescending air.

The old man shrugged. "Oh, well, I'm glad it was nothing serious. I was afraid the poor thing had died." He started for the gate. "Push it over to the side," he called back over his shoulder. "I'll send someone out to fill the tank."

"Wait a minute, old man!" The sentry ran in front of him. "You can't go in there without a pass. That's a top-level security area."

"I have a pass," the old man said, holding out his hand. The sun reflected from the plastic card like a mirror.

The soldier took the card, looked at it and snapped to rigid attention. "I beg your pardon, general," he said, saluting.

Ben Ezra returned his salute. "It's all right, soldier. At ease."

The young man relaxed. "Do you know the way, sir?" he asked respectfully.

"I know the way," Ben Ezra smiled. He held out his hand. "May I have the pass back?"

"Yes, sir," the sentry said quickly. "And don't worry about your car, sir. We'll take care of it."

The general smiled. "Thank you." He turned and started off, his Bedouin robes flowing gently with his stride.

"Who was that?" the other sentry asked curiously.

The first soldier's voice was hushed and respectful. "General Ben Ezra."

"The Lion of the Desert?" There was a note of surprise in the other soldier's voice. He turned to look after the old man. "I thought he was dead."

"Well, he's not," the first soldier said. "Come on. Give me a hand with the general's car."

There were only five men seated around the table in the conference room. The three Americans who had attended the earlier meeting, Ben Ezra and General Eshnev.

"I'm sorry for the small turnout, gentlemen," Eshnev apologized. "But all the others are at the front."

"No need to apologize," Weygrin said. "We understand." He smiled. "Incidentally, congratulations. You're boys did a good job of boxing in the Egyptian Third Army."

Eshnev nodded grimly. "Your anticipating. We're not that sure yet."

"You've got them," the American colonel said confidently.

"We still need help," Eshnev said. "Lots of help. We paid too high a price letting them get the jump on us."

"Who ever would have thought they would launch the attack on Yom Kippur?" Harris of the state department asked, trying to be consoling.

Ben Ezra's voice was matter of fact. "I did. I thought I made that very clear at our last meeting."

"It was a wild guess," Harris said defensively.

"Everything's guesswork," Ben Ezra said quietly. "But even if it hadn't been, you people weren't going to do anything about it, were you?"

Harris didn't answer.

"Tell me," the old general's voice was confidential. "Did you report back to your chief?"

Harris nodded. "Of course."

Ben Ezra looked at him. He shook his head sadly. "All this tragedy could have been prevented."

"I don't see how," Harris said.

"We should have done what we did the last time. The war would have been over now."

"And world opinion would have been against you," Harris said.

"A lot of good world opinion is doing us now," Ben Ezra retorted. "I don't see any armies coming in to help us."

"It's all after the fact," Eshnev said quickly. "That's not the purpose of this meeting, general. We're here to listen to your evaluation of the present situation."

"So that you can ignore it as you did the last time," Ben Ezra said sarcastically. He saw the expression of hurt in Eshenev's eyes and was instantly contrite. "I'm sorry, my friend," he said in a gentler voice. "I forget that your frustrations must be even greater than mine."

Eshnev didn't answer.

Ben Ezra looked across the table at the Americans. "It is lonely when you grow old," he said.

No one at the table spoke.

"Would you gentlemen be kind enough to answer a question for me?" he asked. "Tell me, why are you at this meeting? It must be as obvious to you as it is to me that nothing will come of it, nothing will be changed, nothing will be done."

"That's not true, General Ben Ezra," Colonel Weygrin said quickly. "We have the highest respect for your opinions and ideas."

Ben Ezra smiled. "And I for yours. If only I could understand them. I still can't make up my mind whether you love us or hate us."

Again Eshnev tried to bring the meeting back on track. "You received the Al Fay file?"

"Yes," Ben Ezra nodded.

"What conclusions do you draw from it?"

"If the Arabs were smart they would disband their armies, find three more like him and conquer the world without firing a shot."

"How could that be done?" Harris asked.

Ben Ezra permitted himself a smile. "Simply enough. They would buy the world." No one laughed.

"The war is already lost, you know that," the old man said.

"What do you mean?" Weygrin asked. "It's not over yet. The Israelis are on the move into Egypt and Syria. Sadat is already talking peace. He knows when he's licked."

"He knows when he's won," Ben Ezra said dryly. "What he wanted to do was to restore Arab pride. He's done that. The Arab soldiers have fought bravely. Their honor has been restored. That was what he set out to do." He reached into his robe and took out a sheet of paper. "We might still win this war but it depends on how much time you will allow us."

"I don't quite understand," Harris said.

"We need two more weeks," Ben Ezra said. "Egypt is no longer important. We must bypass Cairo, occupy Libya on one side and take Syria. If we do that, we break the back of the threatened oil blockade; if we do not, then it's just a question of time and we will be isolated."

"What have we got to do with giving you time?" Harris asked. "Russia is already putting on the pressure for a cease-fire."

Ben Ezra looked at him. "You can't be that stupid." He shook his head sadly. "Where was Russia when the Arabs were winning? Trying to protect us with a ceasefire demand? No. They were silent until the tide of battle had turned. Now they want a cease-fire to protect their gains. The Arabs have come up with a better weapon than they ever dreamed of — an oil embargo. That can stop the Western world faster than an atom bomb.

"If we control the oil of Libya and the Syrian pipelines, the embargo would fall apart. We could supply the whole world if we had to. Iran is already firmly in the Western camp. Jordan would jump in quickly and there would be no threat.

"But if we do not, the whole world economy may come tumbling down around our ears. The Arabs will split the world. France will immediately try to leap into the breach and break the European entente. Japan will be forced to go along because they get eighty percent of their oil from the Arabs. And bit by bit, the Arabs will turn the countries of the world away from us. And I would not blame them, because their own survival is as important to them as ours is to us."

"If you pushed the war into Syria and Libya, Russia might intervene," Harris said.

"I doubt it," Ben Ezra said. "They are as fearful as you are of a confrontation."

"That's your opinion," Harris said coldly.

"True," the old man said. "Still, if your Mr. Kissinger would slow down just a little, we could accomplish it."

Harris looked at Eshnev. "Fortunately this is not your government's policy."

Eshnev nodded reluctantly. "It is not."

Harris turned back to Ben Ezra. "It is Mr. Kissinger's hope to have an effective cease-fire agreement in two days."

"My congratulations to Mr. Kissinger." Ben Ezra's voice was sarcastic. "He may yet prove himself the Neville Chamberlain of the seventies."

"I think this discussion is beyond the scope of our meeting," Harris said stiffly, "and should be dealt with on a higher level. What we are most interested in now is what we can do about Al Fay."

Ben Ezra looked at him. "I don't think there is anything we can do about him except to pray that he continues to resist the pressures from the left and holds as close as he can to the middle course. He certainly isn't interested in turning his wealth and power over to the masses, any more than any of the other rich sheiks. But they are all walking a narrow line. How long they can maintain it is anyone's guess." He turned to Eshnev. "Have you had any further information about him since the war began?"

"Very little," Eshnev replied. "Communication has been difficult. Al Fay was called home just before the conflict began and has remained there ever since. We know that he is going to head up the unified investment committee for all the oil-producing countries but that the actual oil negotiations are to be conducted by a joint committee of the foreign ministers of those countries. They are being very cautious about separating the exportation of oil as a political tool and the use of the money they receive from its sale. Internally, they are de-emphasizing the profit line. The new line is 'Oil for justice'."

"Do you think he will have any influence over the oil policies?" Harris asked.

"Very little at first," Eshnev said. "Perhaps more later when they realize that slowing down or collapsing the world economy will only result in losses of their own investments. I think Al Fay and his Prince Feiyad recognize that and that is the reason he took over that committee rather than playing a more political role. By virtue of being nonpolitical he will be in a good position to negotiate freely with both sides."

"Where is his family?" Ben Ezra asked.

"His wife and sons are still in Beirut," Eshnev answered. "Also his ex-wife and daughter."

"The one that was in the Swiss school?" the old man asked curiously.

"Yes," Eshnev answered.

"Not anymore." For the first time the C.I.A. agent spoke. "The younger daughter,

Leila, left three days ago on a flight to Rome. There was another girl and a young man with her."

Eshnev was surprised. "How did you happen to find out?"

"The young man," Smith answered. "We've had him under surveillance for a long time. He was mixed up in the drug traffic in Vietnam and lately moved over to the Middle East." He reached for a cigarette. "He used to be associated with the Mafia but recently went to work for Ali Yasfir."

"What's the connection with the Al Fay girl?" the old man asked.

"We're checking into it," Smith said. "I have some information already. She left school last spring for guerilla training. For some reason, after she got out she spent the entire summer at home. Then this man contacted her and in less than a week they took off."

"Does our intelligence have this information?" Eshnev asked.

"Yes. I passed it on to them the same day I got it."

"Are they still in Rome?" Eshnev asked.

"I don't know," Smith answered. "They split up at the airport. The girls got in one taxi and the man in another. My man could only follow one cab. He stuck with the man."

"Is the man still in Rome?" Eshnev asked.

"Yes. In the morgue. He was killed two hours after he arrived. The police think it was a gang killing. It probably was. The Mafia doesn't like losing one of its soldiers to the competition."

"We should locate the girl," the old man said.

"I'll have our people get on it," Eshnev replied. He got to his feet. "I guess that does it, gentlemen. Unless you have anything further to discuss?"

The Americans looked at one another. The meeting was over. They rose and shook hands. Colonel Weygrin and Harris were very formal with the old man but Smith was different.

He wrinkled up his face as he stared up at Ben Ezra. "You know, general," he said in his nasal Midwestern voice, "you're absolutely right. I wish more of our people would listen to you."

"Thank you, Mr. Smith. I wish they would too."

"You have my card," the C.I.A. man said. "Give me a call if there's anything I can do for you."

"Thank you again," Ben Ezra said.

The Americans left the room and the two Israelis looked at one another. "What do you think Isaiah?" Eshnev asked.

The old man shrugged. "Do you speak Yiddish, Lev?"

"No," Eshnev answered. "I'm sabra. I never learned it."

"They have a saying," the old man said. "I think it originated many years ago in Poland or Russia during one of the pogroms. 'Schver tzu sahn a Yid'."

"What does that mean?" Eshnev asked.

The old man smiled, but there was no humor in it. "It's tough to be a Jew," he said.

BOOK THREE

THE END OF AUTUMN 1973

Chapter One

Dick Carriage knocked softly on the door of Baydr's bedroom. Baydr's voice came through the door, slightly muffled. "Come in."

Dick opened the door and blinked for a moment. The drapes were drawn wide and the room was flooded with the Swiss morning sun. Baydr was seated at the small desk with his back to the window. His face was shadowed by the light coming from behind him. He looked up at Carriage. "Yes?"

"The French are here, chief."

Baydr looked at his watch. "They're up early."

Carriage smiled. "They're taking no chances. They don't want anyone to get to you before they do."

Baydr laughed. "That's the nice thing about the French. You can always depend on them not to honor any allegiances except to themselves."

"What shall I tell them?"

"Tell them to wait." He held some papers out to Carriage. "What do you know about this?"

Carriage took the report and looked down at it. The block letters printed across the top read: ARABDOLLS LTD. Inside the folder was a series of shipping tickets and billing invoices. Each bill was stamped paid. He looked back at Baydr. "No more than you do, except that they pay their bills promptly."

Baydr took back the folder. "That's just it. It's out of character. Do you know any Lebanese who pays his bills promptly?"

"I don't understand. They're good customers. What have we got to complain about?"

"Another thing," Baydr said. "They're paying premium for express delivery. What the hell is so important about dolls that they should pay premium for shipment? That's out of character too. The Lebanese wouldn't be willing to pay premium for anything even if their lives depended on it."

"Christmas is coming. Maybe they want the dolls in the stores before then."

"Could be if they were shipping now. But they began in September." Baydr gave the file to Carriage. "Get me a rundown on that company."

"Will do, chief." He went to the door. "Anything else?"

Baydr shook his head. "Give the French some coffee. I'll be out in a few minutes."

When the door closed behind Carriage, Baydr rose, opened the French doors behind his desk and went out onto the terrace. The clear morning air held the first promise of the coming Swiss winter. Baydr breathed deeply, taking it into his lungs.

In the distance the mountains loomed clear and blue-green, snow already gracing the peaks. Baydr looked down at the city, which was just coming awake. There was a feeling of excitement in the streets.

Geneva. It was all here. The money, the power, the diplomacy, the trading. This was where the war would be won, not on the battlefields of the Middle East. The banks and trading halls of this strange old Swiss city gave the illusion of being above strife and struggle, but they were willing to take profit from every changing wind no matter what direction it came from.

Baydr went back into his room and looked around. The suite in the hotel was leased on an annual basis and it had served its purpose for his occasional visits. But now, he wondered. For the next year he would have to spend a great deal more time here. It would not be big enough, important enough, for the entertaining he was supposed to do.

The more he thought about it the more sense it began to make. A permanent base here would not be wasted. Besides, the winter season in Switzerland was always good. Between St. Moritz and Gstaad the whole world would be there. And he had no doubt that Jordana would love it, the parties, the social scene, the winter sports.

He made a note to call her later and tell her of his decision. Also to have Carriage let the real estate broker know he was in the market for a home in Geneva and a villa in Gstaad. He was sure he would find something quickly. Money had a way of getting things done.

He walked over to the mirror and looked at himself. In his white shirt and dark slacks he looked more European than Arab. He went to the closet. A moment later he came out with his robes in his hand. Quickly, he slipped into the dark brown mishlah and black-banded, white headcloth that fell to his shoulders. Again he looked into the mirror. This time he nodded in satisfaction. Now he looked like an Arab. He smiled to himself as he went to the door. There were advantages in going native. Especially when it came to dealing with the French, who thought themselves superior to everyone on the face of the earth.

"We are a small country, Monsieur Duchamps," Baydr said in French, "completely landlocked with no access to the sea except through the kindness of our neighbors, so you can very well understand our problem. Water. We have oil but no water. I have heard my prince say many times that he would gladly exchange his surfeit of oil wells for wells pumping water. With water our country would bloom."

Duchamps glanced at his associate and nodded understandingly. "Monsieur Al Fay, France has always been among the first nations in the world to understand the difficulties of the Middle Eastern nations and their desire for self-determination and freedom. We have publicly deplored the exploitation of your resources and have indicated our support of your case, often to the detriment of our relations with the great powers and against public sentiment. Do you not remember that during the previous conflict in sixty-seven we refused Israel shipment of fifty fighter jet Mirage aircraft?"

"I remember." He did not add that he recalled that France not only refused Israel the shipment but also refused to return to Israel the hundred million dollars they had collected for the aircraft. Still he could not resist a dig. "Ever since you so generously gave Algeria its freedom, you have been in the forefront of those recognizing the great principle of Arab self-determination."

A momentary look of discomfort flashed across the Frenchman's face, then disappeared. "France stands ready now to fill any orders of material to the Arab countries. Our factories are in full operation, building planes, autos, tanks, almost anything the Arab world needs to demonstrate its ability to defend itself."

Baydr smiled politely. "I am pleased. I will certainly relay this message to the proper committee. As you know, I am not in military procurement. I have absolutely nothing to do with that. I am in the industrial development area. If you have a machine that will manufacture water I would be most interested."

"There are plants that can manufacture water but unfortunately they require water to start with."

Baydr allowed himself to appear naïve. "Yes?"

"Nuclear desalination plants. They are expensive but they work. Unfortunately your country is land-locked."

"True, but we have agreements with our neighbors — Syria, Iraq, Jordan, Saudi Arabia — to develop water-manufacturing resources for our mutual benefit."

"Do you represent those countries also?" the Frenchman asked.

"For the first time the Arab world is united in this area. Together we will develop our industrial and agricultural potential. We have, for example, reached a new agreement with Fiat of Italy to manufacture a version of their car. The manufacturing plants will be spread among our various countries so that the workers of each will benefit."

"Very commendable," the Frenchman said stiffly.

"Of course, it will cost us slightly more to make these cars ourselves rather than import them. But since we are not interested in profit as much as in the idea of becoming self-sufficient, we feel it is very worthwhile. We are also negotiating in other fields such as household appliances and television. It is amazing how much one can do when one is willing to work."

"How much more do you estimate it will cost to make rather than buy these things?" Duchamps asked.

Baydr shrugged. "Fifty percent, one hundred percent. What does it matter? We have the money to pay for it. We can afford it."

The Frenchman was silent for a moment. When he spoke he was not quite as sure of himself as he had been earlier. "We also are interested in aiding your industrial program. I am sure that we can find many projects that would be mutually beneficial. Our manufacturing industry stands second to none in the world."

"I am glad to hear that. What is of special interest to me is your plans for nuclear desalination of water. This is certainly an area that deserves intensive study and one in which we can most certainly work together."

"That is, perhaps, the most expensive project of all," Duchamps said quickly.

"As I said, money is not important. In my small country alone, the revenues from oil exceed one million dollars a day. When you multiply that by the rest of the Arab world the sum becomes astronomical."

"France is not poor. We have all the dollars we need. More than enough in fact."

"I am aware of that, but there are other mediums of exchange and while I am not in charge of policy my recommendations will be looked on favorably when determinations are made."

The Frenchman looked at him steadily. They both knew what Baydr was saying. The bargaining power was oil, not for money, but for cooperation. "Monsieur Al Fay," he said. "I cannot tell you how pleased I am that we have found an area in which we can cooperate. You can be sure that I will be back to you shortly with several very concrete proposals."

Baydr got to his feet. "I shall look forward to your return with great expectations." The Frenchman also rose. Baydr bowed formally, making the conventional Arab gesture of farewell. "Go with peace."

Carriage came back into the room the moment the Frenchman had gone. "They're beginning to back up out there," he said. "It's a minor version of the U.N. — Germans, Italians, Rumanians, Norwegians."

"It didn't take long for the word to get around, did it?"

Carriage shook his head. They had just arrived the day before. "They're like dogs around a bitch in heat."

Baydr laughed. "Better call the bank and see if they can lend us a couple of secretaries. Then set up an appointment schedule. We'll have to see them all."

"Why? There are very few that will have anything for us."

"I know that, but it doesn't matter. Right now they are all in shock over the embargo. They still don't believe it. When it sinks in, they will be panicky and angry. One of our jobs is to keep as many friends as we can."

"Right, chief." Carriage started for the door.

Baydr stopped him. "Dick, get Mrs. Al Fay on the phone for me. She's in Beirut at my father's house."

"Will do." The door closed behind him and a moment later the telephone rang. The Swiss telephone service prided itself on its efficiency. Jordana was on the line.

"How are the children?" he asked.

Jordana's voice was dull. "Fine."

"Are they enjoying school?"

"I don't know whether they like it or not but they're going."

"Are you very busy?"

A moment's silence. "You've got to be kidding," she said. "I'm in Beirut. There is absolutely nothing for me to do here."

"Then maybe you won't mind coming up here and helping me out. I've decided to get a house here in Geneva and a villa in Gstaad and I'll be too busy to attend to it."

"Baydr, do you mean it?"

"Why shouldn't I mean it? It looks like we'll be spending a great deal of time here in the near future. Will you come?"

She laughed. "I'll be on the next plane."

"Good." He smiled into the telephone. "Let us know the flight and I'll have Jabir pick you up at the airport."

Dick came back into the room as soon as he had put down the telephone. There was a strange look on his face. "There's a girl outside to see you."

Suddenly Baydr was annoyed. "You ought to know better than that, Dick," he said sharply. "I have too much to do to bother with girls today. Send her away."

"I did that once already, sir," Dick said. "But she came back a few minutes later with Jabir. He said you would want to see her."

Baydr found that curious. Usually Jabir never concerned himself with the women. "Who is she?"

"I don't know, sir. Neither she nor Jabir would give me her name. They said they wanted to surprise you."

Baydr thought for a moment. It had to be something important. Jabir wasn't given to playing games. "Okay, I'll see her," he said. "But only for a moment. And tell Jabir that I'm doing this only as a favor to him and that I don't want it repeated."

"Yes, sir."

Baydr walked over to the sideboard and filled a cup with coffee. Holding it in his hand he walked back toward his desk. He heard the door open behind him and turned toward it.

A young woman stood in the doorway almost shyly. Baydr looked at her. There was something vaguely familiar about her. She was beautiful, her face almost heart-shaped, with dark blue eyes and shining black hair that fell past her shoulders. She was dressed in the shirt and blue jeans that most of the young people wore these days, but from what he could see, her figure was good. He noticed the uncertain hint of fear creep into her dark blue eyes. Suddenly it all came together.

"Leila!" he exclaimed.

A tremulous smile broke through the fear. "Hello, father," she said softly.

He crossed the room and took her in his arms.

Chapter Two

"I'm almost nineteen, Father, and it's not happening for me in school," she said. "Too many important things are going on out there and I want to be a part of it."

He smiled. There was so much about her that reminded him of himself. The same impatience, the same curiosity and desire to participate. "Exactly what is it you want to do?"

She was vague. "I don't know. All I know is what I don't want to do. I don't want to be like my sister. I don't want marriage and a family to be the only goals in my life. There must be something I can do."

"Have you talked to your mother about this?"

"You know Mother. She doesn't understand. She thinks I should do exactly what I said I don't want to do. Grandfather even has somebody picked out for me to marry."

Baydr was amused. "Your grandfather hasn't changed. I suppose it's a rich man from a very good family?"

"Of course." She laughed. "Grandfather. Riad has always been very good at that."

Baydr laughed. "I should know that, but seriously, there are many things you could do. Like teaching. We need all the teachers we can get."

"You mean the accepted ladylike professions." She could not keep the slight note of scorn from her voice. "I don't want that either. I just don't want to do the things that women have been permitted to do for generations. I want to be involved in something real, something that moves us forward. In my way I want to do what you've been doing by helping to bring us into today's world and making the world accept us on our own terms."

"It's not as easy as that. Do you know how many people in this world still have the idea that we are primitive people?"

"I know," she said quickly. "And that's what I want to change. Now that we have won the war, we have a chance to make the world recognize that we are as good as they are."

"Do you believe we won the war?" Baydr asked curiously.

"I know we did. If we hadn't been forced into a cease-fire, we could have destroyed the Israeli armies once and for all. They were moving right into the traps set for them in both Syria and Egypt."

Baydr looked at her. There was so much she did not know. This was the standard line fed to the people by the pan-Arab propagandists. It was a source of continual amazement to him that the majority of Arabs believed it. That Israel had cut off Eygpt's Third Army and in a few days more could have occupied both Cairo and Damascus never seemed to enter their minds. "I still don't know what you can do," he said.

"I have an idea."

"What?"

"I could work for you." She looked into his eyes.

She was so intent that he did not smile. "Doing what?" he asked gently.

"I could be your assistant," she said seriously. "Mother always said that I should have been a boy. That I was exactly like you."

"I'm afraid not," he said kindly. "My assistants all have had special training for their positions. Much of the work is highly technical and specialized."

"I don't mean right away," she said quickly. "I could start as a clerk or maybe a secretary until I learned enough."

"Can you take shorthand and type?" he asked.

"I can type a little."

He was silent, then he shook his head. "I'm afraid not. Even for those jobs we need someone who has been trained."

"I could be a receptionist. I'd be willing to start anywhere."

"You're my daughter. How do you think that would look?"

"No one would have to know. We could keep it a secret."

"No. It wouldn't work. There are no secrets in this business."

She was crestfallen. "I won't go back to that school," she said stubbornly. "I hate it."

"You don't have to. I have another idea."

She looked up at him hopefully.

"If you are serious about what you say, I could arrange for you to go to a university in the States where you can major in business administration. In a few years you would know enough to fit in some place in the organization."

"That would take years," she said impatiently. "What about now? By the time I finish school everything will have been done."

He laughed. "I don't think so. There's more than enough to last both our lifetimes."

"Can't I go to school right here?" she asked. "That way I can work after school and learn at the same time."

"It's not the same. All they could teach you is stenography, typing and maybe some simple accounting."

"It would be a start, then if I found that I was good at it, I could go to school in the States."

"Let me think about it."

"There's nothing to think about," she said positively. "I heard your man calling the bank for secretaries. While you're waiting for them, I could answer telephones and act as your receptionist. I'm very good on the telephone. Really."

He began to laugh. "You're a very determined young lady."

She met his eyes. "You just don't know how much."

"I'm beginning to get the idea." He chuckled, then the smile left his face. "You know I'll have to talk to your mother about this."

"Why? You never talked to her about me before."

"Is that what she said?"

"Yes." Her eyes fell for a moment, then she looked up at him. "Why didn't you ever want to see us after you left."

Baydr met her gaze. "Is that what your mother told you?"

She nodded.

Baydr was silent. There was no point in telling her of the many requests he made to see her or have her visit him only to have Maryam refuse by saying that she wanted nothing more to do with him. Leila knew only that he had left them and that was the way it should remain. He took a deep breath and then let the air slowly out. "Well, it's not true," he said quietly.

She didn't speak.

He sensed her doubt. "But it doesn't matter now," he said gently. "You are here and I am seeing you."

She nodded, still silent.

"Tell me," he said awkwardly. "How is your sister?"

"Fine. She's married. I don't see much of her or her husband. We don't have much in common. They're very social. And, oh yes, Amal thinks she might be pregnant."

He smiled. "You mean I'm about to become a grandfather?"

"It's possible."

He let out a slow whistle.

"That's very American," she said quickly.

"What is?"

"That whistle. What does it mean?"

He laughed. "I have a lot of adjustments to make. First I have to realize that I'm the father of a nineteen-year-old, now suddenly, I'm a grandfather."

Leila laughed. "Don't count on it. Amal thinks she's pregnant every month. This might be like all the others."

"You know, you have two brothers."

"I know. Muhammad and Samir."

"You know their names?"

"It's not exactly a secret. The newspapers always have stories about you. And pictures."

"They're good boys. You would like them."

"I want to meet them."

"You will. Soon." He got to his feet. "Where are you staying?"

"With a girl friend," she said. "Her family lives in Geneva."

"Swiss?"

"Yes."

"Would you rather stay there or would you like to move in here with me?"

"Whatever you would like," she said, her eyes falling away from him.

"Get your things together then," he said. "Can you be back here in time for dinner?"

She raised her head. Her eyes were smiling. "I think so."

"Okay, get going then. I have work to do."

She rose from the chair and threw her arms around him. "Thank you, Father."

He kissed the top of her head lightly. "Don't thank me. After all, I am your father, aren't I?"

She stood in the doorway of the coffeehouse and scanned the tables. The restaurant was almost empty, just a few office workers dallying over their morning coffee before going to work. She looked at her watch. Eleven o'clock. They should be here any minute now. She went to a table and sat down.

A waiter appeared instantly. "Oui, mademoiselle?"

"Coca avec citron."

He brought the drink and went away. She lit a cigarette, then sipped at her drink. It was sweet. Not as sweet as the Coca-Cola in Lebanon but sweeter than the French, although it was served French style. One small stingy piece of ice floated on the top, not quite enough to cool the drink unless you sipped the liquid past it.

Two young men and a young woman appeared in the doorway. They were dressed much like she was in jeans, shirt and jacket. She waved to them and they came to her table and sat down. Again the waiter appeared. A moment later he brought their coffees and went away.

They looked at her expectantly. She looked back without speaking. Finally, she put down her cigarette and held up her two fingers in a V sign.

The others broke into a smile. "It went all right?" the woman asked in hesitant English.

"Perfectly."

"He didn't ask any questions?"

"Only the usual fatherly questions," she answered. Then she broke into a grin. "You know I'll have to talk to your mother about this," she imitated.

An expression of concern crossed the woman's face. "What if he does?"

"He won't," she said confidently. "I know my mother. She hasn't spoken to him in ten years and she's not going to now."

"Are you going to work for him?" one of the young men asked.

"Part-time. He thinks I should go to business school first to learn some skills. Then I can go to work full-time."

"Are you going to go?" the woman asked.

"Of course. If I didn't he might get suspicious. Besides, it will only be for a little while."

"What's he like?" the woman asked.

Leila looked at her as if seeing her for the first time. "My father, you mean?"

"Who else would I be talking about?" the woman retorted. "Is he anything like those stories we've read about him? You know, a playboy the ladies can't resist and all that?"

Leila's eyes grew thoughtful. "I suppose so," she said hesitantly. "But I don't see him like that at all."

"How do you see him?"

Leila's voice grew bitter. "I look at him and I see all the things we're fighting against. The money, the power, the ego. The kind of person who is concerned only for himself. He couldn't care less about the struggle of our people. He thinks only about the profit he can make from it."

"Do you really believe that?"

"If I didn't believe it," Leila answered in a hard flat voice. "I wouldn't be here doing what I agreed to do."

Chapter Three

The first thought that flashed through Leila's mind as Jordana came into the room was how beautiful she was. Tall, honey-colored blond hair, tanned California glow, slim body and long lovely legs. She was everything an Arab woman could never be. For a moment she understood why her father had done what he did.

Then the old bitterness and animosity bubbled up and she had all she could do to keep it from her eyes as Jordana came toward her.

"This is Leila," Baydr said proudly.

Jordana's eyes were clear and direct, her smile genuine and warm. She held out her hand. "I'm so glad to meet you at last. Your father used to speak often about you."

Leila took her hand. Jordana's grip was as warm as her greeting. "I'm pleased to meet you too," she said awkwardly.

"Baydr, your father, tells me you are planning to stay."

"If I'm not in the way."

"You won't be," Jordana assured her. "And I'm delighted. Now, maybe, I'll have someone to talk to when he's away. He travels quite a bit."

"I know," Leila said. She looked at her father. "I'm sorry. I'm a little tired. Is it all right if I skip dinner and go right to bed?"

Baydr cast a quick glance at Jordana then back at Leila. "Of course."

"And you won't mind, will you?" she asked Jordana. "Besides, you two must have many things to talk about."

"I don't mind," Jordana answered.

"Good night then."

"Good night."

When the door had closed behind her, Baydr turned to Jordana. "What do you think?" he asked.

"I think she doesn't like me."

"How can you say that?" The surprise echoed in his voice. "She doesn't even know you."

"Your daughter is jealous."

"You're being foolish," he said, annoyance creeping into his voice. "What has she to be jealous of? I asked her to stay, didn't I?"

Jordana looked at him. There were some things men would never understand. But she remembered how possessive she had been about her father and how she had felt when she had seen him with his new wife for the first time. "It doesn't really matter," she said. "I'm glad for you."

He didn't answer.

"She's a very pretty girl," she said.

"Yes."

"What made her decide to leave school so suddenly?"

"She said she felt life was passing her by," he answered. Then he chuckled. "At nineteen."

"That's not so funny," she said. "I can understand that."

"You can?" He was surprised. "Then maybe you can explain to me why after all those years she suddenly wanted to see me?"

"Why shouldn't she? You are her father. Girls have a very special thing for their fathers."

He was silent for a moment. "I should call her mother and tell her."

"I have a feeling you won't have to. That her mother already knows."

"What makes you think that?"

"Your father told me that she had spent almost the whole summer with her mother and that she just left Beirut a few weeks ago. Her mother must have known where she was going."

He stared at her. That was strange. Leila had led him to believe that she had come from school. She had said nothing about being at home. He wondered why she didn't tell him, but decided to say nothing to Jordana. "I think I'll call my father," he said. "I'll let him talk to her mother."

Jordana smiled. In some ways he was very transparent. He did not want to talk to his former wife. "The boys asked if they could come to visit when we get a house. They've never had a chance to play in the snow."

Baydr laughed. "You tell them that they can come up here the very first day the snow begins to fall."

Dick Carriage leaned back in his chair and took off his reading glasses. He took a tissue from the box on his desk and turning his chair away from the bright tensor lamp, slowly began to wipe the lenses. Large white lazy flakes floated past the window.

They had been in Switzerland almost a month before the snow began to fall and Baydr, true to his word, had had his sons flown in the same day. Now they were in Gstaad for the weekend. He had remained in Geneva to clean up the pile of paperwork. Baydr had called that morning in very good humor. The boys were really enjoying themselves.

Carriage smiled to himself. Fathers were pretty much alike no matter what their background. Baydr felt much the same as he did about his own sons. He swung back to the desk and looked at the photographs of his wife and sons. The picture, taken in his garden in California, suddenly made him feel very much alone. They were a long way from the snow in Switzerland.

He heard the click of the front door latch outside the study that he and Baydr used as an office when they were in the big house in Geneva. He looked at his watch. It was a little after two o'clock in the morning. He heard the sound of hard-soled shoes on the marble floors of the entrance foyer. They had an unmistakably feminine rhythm. It had to be Leila. She was the only member of the family who had not gone to Gstaad. She had said something about special classes at school on Saturday but she hadn't gone. Instead she had stayed in her room until after lunch, then she had gone out and had not returned until just now.

There was something strange about her, he thought. Despite the outward pleasantness and apparent willingness to cooperate, he sensed a certain withdrawal, a restraint in her calculating eyes. Occasionally he would catch a glimpse of her resentment, especially toward Jordana, although she obviously tried to keep it concealed.

The footsteps reached the staircase and began to ascend, then they came to a stop. A moment later the knob of the study door moved tentatively. "Come in," he called.

The door swung open and Leila stood there, dressed in her inevitable blue jeans. Sometimes he wondered if she owned any other clothes.

"I don't mean to disturb you. I saw the light coming from under the door."

"It's okay. You're not bothering me. I was just taking a break anyway."

She came into the room and he could see the flakes of snow melting in her hair and on her clothes. "You haven't stopped since my father left yesterday morning."

He smiled. "It's the only chance I have to catch up on the paperwork. When he's around I don't have much time for it."

"Don't you ever take time off?"

"Sure. When we were in California a few months ago, I had a whole week with my family."

"But since then," she persisted. "You don't even take time for yourself on weekends."

"What for?" he asked. "There's nothing I want to do."

"You could go out to dinner. Go to a movie."

"I'd rather work. I don't like doing those things alone."

"You don't have to be alone. There are lots of girls in Geneva looking for dates."

He laughed. "There are lots of girls everywhere. But, you forget, I'm a married man."

"My father is a married man and that doesn't stop him," she said.

He looked at her sharply, wondering how much she knew. "There are certain things your father has to do," he said quickly. "That's his business."

"Is it? I've heard lots of stories about him."

He was silent.

"I've heard stories about Jordana too." Her eyes were challenging. "Is that business also?"

He met her gaze coolly. "There are always people who are quick to gossip. Most of them don't know what they are talking about. I've learned that the most important contribution I can make toward your father's business is to mind my own."

She laughed. "I can see why my father trusts you so much. You are loyal to him."

"He's my employer," he said stiffly. "I respect him a great deal."

"But do you like him?" she asked pointedly.

His answer was prompt and direct. "Yes."

"Even if he doesn't give you any days off?"

"That's my option," he said evenly. "If I choose not to take them, it's my own affair."

She walked around the corner of his desk and glanced down at the pile of papers. "Money buys a lot of things, doesn't it?" It was a statement not a question. "You're as much a slave to the system as anyone."

"The only better way I know to make a living," he answered in Arabic, "is to have a rich father."

He saw the quick anger flash in her eyes and knew he'd hit a nerve. "I don't have—" Then she caught herself and stopped abruptly.

"You don't have — what?" he asked softly.

The anger was quickly replaced by self-control. She smiled. "Nothing. Where did you learn to speak Arabic so well?"

"At home."

She was surprised. "I thought you were American."

"I am," he smiled. "But my parents came from Jordan. Their name was Khureiji. My father changed it to Carriage before I was born when he opened his first restaurant. He thought it would be easier for Americans to say Carriage House than Khureiji House."

"Are they still alive?"

"No."

"Didn't they ever want to go home?"

"Yes."

"Maybe it's just as well they didn't," she said quickly. "Not as long as the Jews were on their doorstep."

He looked at her without speaking. The real tragedy was that they had gone back. Perhaps if they hadn't they would still be alive today.

She took his silence for agreement. "It won't always be like that. Soon we will get rid of the Jews. We almost did this time, but we were betrayed."

"By whom?"

"Some of our own people. People who thought only of their own pockets, their own power. If they hadn't stopped us, we would have driven the Jews into the sea."

"I still don't know who these people are."

"You'll find out," she said, suddenly secretive. "Soon enough." She smiled and changed the subject. "Would you like me to make some coffee?"

"That's very kind of you. But I don't want to put you to any trouble."

"It's no trouble at all. Besides, I'd like a cup myself. American or Turkish?"

"Turkish," he said, though he much preferred American.

"Good," she said, starting for the door. "I'll be right back."

He stared at the door after she had gone. She was strange. If only he could discover what she was really thinking. Idly he picked up the next folder from the pile of papers. It was the report Baydr had asked him to get on Arabdolls Ltd. His vision blurred and he put it back on the desk. He was more tired than he had realized. It could wait until after he had coffee.

It was almost a quarter of an hour before she came back with the coffee. When he saw her, his mouth almost fell open in surprise. She did have other clothes. Instead of the perennial blue jeans, she was wearing a white caftan with gold piping which led down the front and followed the lines of the buttons that joined the two sides of the garment. Flashes of her golden, tanned body, visible through the spaces in the caftan revealed that she wore nothing beneath it.

She placed the silver coffee tray on a small table in front of the couch. The white steam rose in curlicues as she slowly poured the coffee into the small cups. She looked up at him. "You can come out from behind that desk for the coffee," she said. "I promise not to tell my father."

He smiled and got to his feet. "Something tells me you wouldn't anyway."

"Right."

He sat down on the couch beside her. She picked up a cup and handed it to him. "Taste it."

Obediently, he sipped at it. The sweetness almost gagged him. He took his coffee without sugar.

"Sweet enough?"

"Perfect," he said with a straight face.

She smiled, pleased. "I love my coffee extra sweet."

"It's very good."

She sipped at her coffee. "Do you smoke?" she asked.

"I have cigarettes on the desk," he said, beginning to rise.

Her hand stopped him. "I don't mean that kind."

"Oh," he said, looking at her. "Sometimes. But not when I'm working."

She opened the small silver box which was on the tray next to the coffee pot. "Don't you think you've worked enough for tonight?"

He looked down at the neatly rolled joints.

"Jabir gave me these," she said. "He's got the best hashish in the world. He rolls them especially for my father."

"I know," he said.

She took a cigarette and struck a match. The flame glowed for a moment as the sulfur burned off, then she held it to the cigarette. After she had taken a few puffs, she held it out to him.

He looked at it, without moving.

"Come on," she urged. "Relax. Loosen up a little. The work will still be there in the morning."

"Oh, okay," he said. He took the cigarette from her hand and dragged on it. After a few tokes he gave it back to her. "It is good," he said.

"That's better," she said, dragging on the joint again. She smiled. "You know, for the first time you're beginning to look human."

He took the cigarette from her and puffed on it. He began to feel a buzzing in his head. "How do I usually look?"

She leaned back against the couch. "Very serious usually. Very businesslike all the time. No expression. You very rarely smile. You know what I mean."

"I didn't realize that."

"Most people aren't aware of how they look." She looked at him. "You know you'd be kind of handsome without those glasses." She reached out and took them from his face. "Go look in the mirror and see for yourself."

"I don't have to. I know what I look like. I shave myself every morning."

She began to laugh. "That's very funny."

He smiled. "Is it?"

She nodded. "You know you're not too bad for an American. I usually don't like Americans. But you seem different. Maybe it's because your parents were Arabs."

He didn't speak.

She stared at him silently for a moment, then leaned forward and suddenly and kissed him on the mouth. He was caught by surprise and held very still.

She drew back and looked into his eyes. "What's the matter? Don't you like it?"

"That's not it," he said awkwardly. "After all, I am a married man."

"I know that, but your wife is at the other end of the world."

"Is that supposed to make a difference?"

"Does it?" she asked looking at him.

He didn't answer. Instead he took another drag on the cigarette. The buzzing suddenly left his head, leaving it extraordinarily clear. He felt as if all his senses had been sharpened. He was no longer tired. "What is it exactly that you want from me?"

She met his eyes. "I want to learn everything about my father's business. And you can help teach me."

"I would do that without you having to sleep with me." He didn't tell her that Baydr had instructed him to encourage her interest in the business.

Her eyes were steady. "But I want to sleep with you."

He reached for her but she held out a hand, stopping him. "Wait just a minute."

He watched her get to her feet and cross to his desk and turn off the light. It seemed almost as if she were floating. She went around the room slowly turning off all the lights except one lamp in the far corner. Then she came back to the couch and, standing in front of him, slowly undid the buttons down the front of her caftan and let it fall to the floor around her.

He held out his arms toward her and she came down into them. He pressed his mouth to her lips almost roughly.

"Take it easy," she whispered. "You still have your clothes on." She began to undo the buttons on his shirt. "Relax. Let me undress you."

Later, when she was moaning beneath him, when he was marvelling at the firm strength in her young rounded body, when he felt the power of her clutching loins drawing him onto her like a vacuum, he heard her begin to whimper almost inaudibly.

He forced his mind to clear so that he could listen to her words. They were the same word over and over as she was caught in the throes of a strange physical and mental orgasm.

"Daddy! Daddy! Daddy!"

Chapter Four

Despite the late November chill and rain that covered Paris like a gloomy gray wrapping, Youssef felt good as he walked up Avenue George V, turning past Fouquet's into his offices on the Champs-Elysées. He entered the narrow French elevator, closed the gate and pressed the button for the top floor. Slowly the iron cage climbed toward the roof.

He smiled to himself, thinking about his new little friend, a Greek boy, slim and young, with dark black ringlets around his face and enormous dark eyes. The boy was in love with him. He was sure of that. It had to be the real thing. When he had offered him money, the boy had been hurt, his eyes filled with tears. He apologized quickly and kissed away the tears. The boy had smiled radiantly when he promised to see him the following evening.

The iron cage creaked to a stop at his floor. He left the elevator, closing the gate carefully behind him so that it could respond to another summons. In true French style the office door was wooden with the company name stenciled in black lettering on the large pane of opaque glass: MEDIA (FRANCE) S.A.

His secretary, who also served as the receptionist, looked up as he came in the door and smiled, "Bonjour, Monsieur Ziad."

"Bonjour, Marguerite," he answered, walking past her into his office. He closed the door behind him, took off his raincoat and went to the window. Despite the rain the Champs-Elysées was crowded. Already tourists were buying tickets for tonight's performance at the Lido on the other side of the boulevard and the stores were filled with customers.

The door opened behind him and, without turning around, he held out his raincoat. "Anything new?" he asked, as a woman took the coat from him.

"There was a telex from Genève on the machine when I arrived this morning," she answered.

"Where is it?"

"In the folder on your desk. I put it on top of the other papers."

He opened the folder, picked up a yellow telex sheet and read it quickly.

ZIAD CANCEL FILM PROJECTILE AND SETTLE VINCENT CONTRACT IMMEDIATELY
STOP. ALSO REFUSE FURTHER SHIPMENTS ON A/C ARABDOLLS UNTIL FURTHER
NOTICE. WE HAVE COMPANY UNDER INVESTIGATION STOP. INFORM ME OF
TERMS VINCENT SETTLEMENT SOONEST. STOP. REGARDS. ALFAYMED.

He felt a clutch of pain in his bowels. He sank into his chair, and the sweat broke
out on his forehead. Thoughts raced through his brain. Something has gone wrong.
Somehow he had been discovered. He felt the nausea in the back of his throat and
barely made it to the bathroom.

After he had thrown up, he felt better. He took a glass of water from the carafe
on his desk and sipped it slowly as he re-read the telex. His stomach began to settle
down. Maybe it wasn't at all what he had first thought. It had been his own guilt
and fear that had choked him. Baydr could have had a thousand valid business
reasons for his decisions other than the ones he feared.

He had to remain calm so that he could think, and determine the true reasons
for Baydr's actions. Then he would know what to do. He lit a cigarette and turned
the telex face down on the desk. Right now, he had to execute the orders he had
received. He picked up the telephone. "Locate Michael Vincent for me," he said to
his secretary.

"Oui, Monsieur Ziad," Marguerite answered. "Do you wish to speak with him?"

"Not just yet," he replied. "First I want to speak with Monsieur Yasfir. You will
have to locate him also."

He put down the telephone and started trying to get his thoughts in order. He
had received four hundred thousand dollars on Vincent's account already but
he had only disbursed half of that amount to him. He wondered if he could make
a deal to close at that figure. They would then be out only for what they had
already paid. Baydr could not help but be impressed by that. He began to feel
better. Maybe things were not as bad as they had seemed.

The telephone on his desk buzzed. It was his secretary. "I have Monsieur Yasfir
on the telephone for you."

"Where is he?"

"In Genève."

He punched the button and spoke in Arabic so that if anyone overheard they
would not understand. "I have received instructions to stop shipments for Arabdolls.
Do you have any idea why?"

Yasfir's voice was calm. "No. Did they give a reason?"

"Not really. All they said was that they had the company under investigation."
Yasfir was silent.

"I will have to cable our office in Beirut," Youssef said.

"No." Yasfir's voice was cold. "We have shipments scheduled twice each week
until Christmas. This is the most important season of the year for us."

"I can't help it," Youssef explained. "If I do not comply it will mean my job."

"Then you have a problem, my friend. If those shipments are not made my
associates could lose more than twenty million dollars. And that is something they
would not care to do."

"I can't help it," Youssef repeated. "I don't like to lose my commission either. But I must keep my job."

"You are missing the point," Yasfir said. "To be unemployed and alive, or to be employed—and dead."

Abruptly the connection was broken. The French operator came on quickly. "Avez - vous terminé, monsieur?"

Youssef stared at the telephone a moment. "Oui," he answered quickly. Again he felt the pain in his bowel, and the sweat came out on his forehead. He placed his head in his hands. He had to think. He had to find a way to make Baydr change his mind.

The telephone buzzed again. He picked it up. His secretary's voice was annoyingly cheerful. It was amazing how the French considered each successfully completed long-distance call a personal victory. "Monsieur Vincent has just left London for Paris," she said. "He is expected at the George V at one o'clock."

"Leave word that I must see him for lunch. It is most important."

He put down the telephone and picked it up again almost immediately. "Bring me two aspirin," he said. "And then get Monsieur Carriage in Genève."

The aspirin didn't help much. And now the circuits to Geneva were busy. Youssef looked at his watch. It was after eleven o'clock. Ordinarily he was not a drinking man but this time he could make an exception.

He got to his feet and left his office. "I will return in a few moments," he said to his secretary.

Marguerite was puzzled. "Are you all right?" she asked in a concerned voice.

"I'm fine," he snapped. He went out into the hallway and got into the iron cage, which slowly took him down to the ground floor. He walked out of the doorway of his office building and turned left into Fouquet's.

He walked up to the bar. The bartender came forward immediately. "Bonjour, Monsieur Ziad. What is your pleasure?"

"What do you have to settle a nervous stomach?"

The bartender looked at him. "Alka-Seltzer. I find that very effective."

"No." Youssef was abrupt. "Something stronger than that."

"Fernet-Branca, monsieur," the bartender said quickly. "It is an old remedy but still the best."

"I will have that. Make it a double."

"A double, monsieur?" The bartender looked at him strangely.

"Yes. And be quick about it." Youssef was annoyed. Why did everything have to be so difficult?

"Oui, monsieur." The bartender turned and took down a bottle. A moment later the dark brown liquor was in an old-fashioned glass in front of Youssef. "Je pense que c'est trop, monsieur," he said. "Va doucement."

Youssef looked at him with contempt. The French always insisted that you had to do things their way. He picked up the glass and threw the drink back. For a moment, he stood paralyzed as the horrible-tasting liquor burned its way down his throat. Then clapping his hand over his mouth, he turned and ran up the staircase to the washroom.

Michael Vincent was relaxed as he opened the door for Youssef. He smiled and held out his hand. "I have good news," he said warmly. "I've completed the first draft of the screenplay."

Youssef looked at him without enthusiasm. "We have problems we must discuss, my friend."

Vincent was instantly wary. He knew that "problems" in the lexicon of the film business was a word of doom. But he also knew better than to respond directly. "There are no problems that cannot be solved."

Youssef looked at the American. For the first time since he had met him, the man seemed completely sober. Why did it have to be at this time? He always felt better dealing with Vincent when he was partly drunk. "I have taken the liberty of reserving a table downstairs for lunch," he said.

Vincent smiled. "Excellent. I'm starved. I haven't had any breakfast."

"What would you like to drink?" Youssef asked after they had been seated at their table.

Vincent shook his head. "Never drink on an empty stomach."

Youssef turned to the captain. "We will see the menu then."

"We have an excellent poached salmon, Monsieur Ziad," the captain suggested.

Youssef didn't care what he ate. "That sounds fine." He looked at the American. "How about you?"

"Sounds good to me too."

Youssef cursed to himself. The man was entirely too pleasant. He had hoped he would take a drink. "A bottle of Montrachet," he said to the captain. Perhaps a good white wine would help.

The captain bowed and went away. For a moment the two men were silent. Vincent spoke first. "You mentioned problems."

"Yes," Youssef replied seriously. He looked at Vincent and decided to use a direct approach, however foreign it was to his own nature. "I have just received instructions this morning to cancel the project."

There was no expression on Vincent's face. Then a small sigh escaped his lips. "I thought something like that might happen. It was going too well to be true."

"You're not surprised?"

The director shook his head. "No. Not since I read in the Hollywood trades a few weeks ago that another company was ready to begin filming a story of the Prophet in Morocco next spring."

Youssef felt an immediate sense of relief. So that was the reason for the telex. At least it was not because they suspected his arrangement. "Yes," he said, keeping his face impassive.

"Don't look so glum," Vincent said. "If you'd been around the film business as long as I have, you would have seen worse."

"Even so," Youssef said, "there is still an unpleasant matter for us to deal with. I have been asked to work out a settlement of your contract."

Vincent was alert. "There is nothing to settle. My contract is firm. I receive a million dollars regardless of whether the film is made."

"I don't think so. As I understand it, half your fee is to be paid only during the filming. If we do not begin production that would mean payment would not be made. Also the million dollars includes two hundred thousand for expenses contingent on performance. If that is halted we do not have to pay that sum either."

"I read the contract differently. I think I can enforce the payment of the whole amount."

"How?" Youssef asked flatly. "If you read the contract, you will find that the laws of Lebanon govern the agreement and any questions regarding it are to be settled in Lebanese courts. Do you think that you, a foreigner, would have a chance against Al Fay? You would get nothing. In fact you would probably not even find an attorney who would take your case against us."

Vincent was silent. That was the one clause in the contract he had not liked. It was also the one clause in the contract they had been firm about. Now he knew why.

Youssef felt more secure now. "Friends have no place in a court of law," he said. "It would be much more agreeable to work out a settlement between us. The world is small. You never can tell when we may be of help to one another in the future."

"What do you suggest?"

"You have already received two hundred thousand. Payment of another one hundred thousand completes our obligation for the screenplay. I suggest that we stop at that."

Vincent was silent.

"And I will waive my commission," Youssef said quickly. "I think that's only fair since the project did not go through. That way, all the money would be yours."

"What about my expenses?" he asked. "One hundred thousand of that was supposed to be paid during the writing of the screenplay."

Youssef thought for a moment. What the American said was true. In addition, he already had the money with which to pay him so there would be no problem. As far as Baydr knew the money had already been dispersed. Still he could not suppress his natural greed. "If we pay the expenses then I will insist on my commissions."

Vincent did the arithmetic in his head. Three hundred thousand dollars net or four thousand less twenty per cent. The difference was only twenty thousand dollars but it was better than nothing. He laughed suddenly. "Agreed," he said. "With one condition."

"What is that?" Youssef asked cautiously.

"That you use every effort to get me on the other picture."

Youssef smiled in relief. "We would do that anyway," he said.

The wine steward arrived, opened the bottle with a flourish and poured a taste for Youssef's approval. "Trés bon," Youssef said, gesturing to the steward to fill Vincent's glass.

Vincent held up his hand. "I've changed my mind," he said. "Bring me a double Scotch on the rocks."

Chapter Five

Ali Yasfir walked into the cafe across the street from the President Wilson Hotel in Geneva. He looked at his watch. It was almost six o'clock and the cafe was crowded with office people having a drink before they left the city for their homes in the outskirts. He found a quiet table in the back of the restaurant against the wall, ordered a coffee and prepared to wait. She had told him she didn't think she could get away much before six o'clock. He opened his copy of the Paris *Herald Tribune*.

The newspaper was filled with stories of the panic in the United States over the oil embargo. At first the country had been in a state of shock. People could not believe that it was really happening to them. But then they had settled in and begun to maneuver to increase their supplies. He smiled to himself. There was not very much they could do. By winter they would really feel the pinch. By spring, when they realized it would take five years for them to redevelop their own sources of oil which they had allowed to lapse because of the cheapness of import, they would be on their knees begging for mercy.

That is, if the Arabs were able to maintain their unity. Already chinks were beginning to develop in the armor. There were rumors that oil tankers bound for America were still slipping through the Gulf of Oman not only from Iran but also from United Arab Emirates, Kuwait and even Saudi Arabia. He never doubted for a moment that the rumors were true. All of those countries were tied to America not only by sentiment but by cold hard money. Their investment in the American economy was so great that they dared not tamper with it too much for fear that it would lead to chaos and the loss of all their investments. The fact that their self-interest stood in the way of complete freedom for the Arab world meant nothing to the select few who ruled those countries. They only used the crisis to enhance their own power and wealth. These were men like Al Fay — perhaps the worst of all — who would have to be purged before the Arabs could assume their rightful place in the sun. What they gave to the movement was a mere pittance when measured against their own benefit.

The Prophet had said, "Look to the day of Judgment." But they were not ready to wait that long. Already plans had been made to turn the power of these men against themselves. Soon it would begin and in time they would feel the wrath of a people betrayed.

Ali Yasfir was on his second cup of coffee when the young woman came in and stood before him. He gestured to the chair across the table without speaking.

She sat down and the waiter appeared. "Coca-Cola avec citron," she said. When the waiter had gone, she looked at him. "I'm sorry I'm late, but it was difficult for me to get away on such short notice."

"I would not disturb you if it were not important."

"I understand that." The waiter came with her drink and went away again. "What is happening?" she asked.

"Many things," he said heavily. "Perhaps the worst is that the embargo is in danger of being bypassed."

She sipped at her drink without speaking, her eyes fixed on his face.

"The United States is bringing a great deal of pressure to bear on men like your father. They threaten confiscation of their investment in the States."

"I haven't seen anything like that. And I am in the office every day. I read almost every piece of paper that comes through."

"They are not that stupid. There are some things that would never be committed to paper. But the threats are still there. And your father is responding to them."

"How? My father has nothing to do with the allocation of oil."

"But his influence in the council is great. Sooner or later they will listen to him and others like him."

She lit a cigarette and inhaled deeply. "Things are never really what they seem, are they?"

Ali Yasfir nodded. "We may have to take action sooner than we had thought."

She let the smoke drift slowly from her mouth.

"You have not changed your mind?" he asked quickly. "You are still of the same beliefs?"

"I have not changed my mind. How can I? I still remember the atrocity perpetrated on us by the Israeli planes. I can still see the dead bodies and faces of my friends. I have seen the unprovoked cruelty of the Israelis. I will not change my mind until they are all dead."

He relaxed slightly. "I was afraid your American lover might have changed your beliefs."

She met his eyes steadily. "He is not my lover," she said coldly. "I use him so that I can have access to what is going on in my father's business."

"Then you know about the order to stop the shipments from Arabdolls?"

"Yes."

"Do you know why?"

"I'm not sure but I think they suspect that Ziad has been taking money from them on the side. They are investigating now to find out if that is true."

"It's too late for that now. I have made arrangements for you and the children to return to Beirut the day after tomorrow. You will remain there in our home in seclusion. You are not to leave the house, you are not to see anyone, you are not to correspond or talk to anyone by telephone except immediate members of our family and servants until January, when Muhammad is officially invested as prince and heir to the throne."

"And after that?"

"The day after the investure you will be permitted to return home to America to visit your parents. You will remain there quietly until you receive the papers of our divorce."

"What about the children?"

His eyes were as dark as blue ice. "You will never see them again."

The pain in her heart choked off her breath. "What if I refuse?" she managed to ask.

There was an implacability about him that she had never seen before. "You have no choice. Under the laws of Islam the punishment for an adultress is death by stoning. Would you have your children see that?"

"You wouldn't!" she exclaimed, horrified.

His eyes were unwavering. "I would."

Suddenly she knew the truth. "Youssef! You killed him!"

His voice was contemptuous. "Youssef killed himself," he said, gesturing at the videotape player. "With this."

She was beaten. No longer able to control her tears, no longer able to look at him, she sank to her knees, covering her face with her hands. Her body was racked by sobs.

He stood there impassively, looking down at her; only a pulse beating in his temple gave any sign of his own effort at self-control.

After a while the tears stopped and she looked up at him. Her eyes swollen, her face drawn with pain. "What will I do?" she whispered in a hoarse hollow voice almost to herself. "What will my life be without them?"

He didn't answer.

Slowly she rose to her feet and began to walk toward the door. Halfway she turned back. "Baydr," she said, the pleading clear in her eyes and her voice.

The cold implacability was still in his voice. "Don't waste your time, woman, begging my forgiveness. Instead, go and thank Allah for His mercy."

Their eyes met for a brief moment, then her eyes fell. There was no more fight left in her. Slowly she walked from the room.

He locked the door behind her and went back to the desk. He stood looking down at the videotape player for a long time, then he reached down and pressed the start button once more. Almost at the same moment, he pressed the other button marked ERASE.

The tape raced through the machine at ten times normal playing speed. Forty minutes of tape went through in only four minutes. There was a click and he pressed the stop. A moment later he pressed the start button again. This time the tape moved at playing speed. But the screen remained blank and empty.

The tape had been wiped clean.

Baydr pressed the stop button. Machines made everything so simple.

If only there were a button that one could press to wipe the ribbon of life clean so that one could begin again.

Chapter Ten

When she boarded the plane, Jordana was surprised to find Leila there with two young men. The young men, dressed in ill-fitting dark suits with bulging pockets customarily worn by Middle Eastern office workers abroad, got to their feet politely.

"I didn't know you were coming with us," Jordana said.

There was a strange challenging tone in Leila's voice. She spoke in Arabic. "Do you mind?"

Jordana was puzzled. Leila had always spoken to her in English or French. But perhaps it was because her friends were not as proficient in these languages as she.

She dismissed the thought and answered in Arabic. "Not at all. I am glad to have you with us. I was just surprised. Your father hadn't mentioned it."

"He might have forgotten," Leila said.

He didn't forget, Jordana thought. She hadn't seen him since the morning when he told her she would have to leave. Later in the day he had returned to Geneva and had only stopped by at the house to say goodbye to the boys. "He has many things on his mind," she said, still in Arabic. She turned politely to the two young men.

Leila got the hint and introduced then. "Madame Al Fay, my father's second wife. This is Fouad Aziz and Ramadan Sidki. They are joining me for a weekend at home."

"Ahlan," Jordan said.

"Ahlan fiki," they replied awkwardly, bowing jerkily as if it were not customary for them.

Just then the two children, their Scottish nanny, Anne, and her personal maid, Magda, came up the ramp into the plane. The boys broke into happy cries when they saw their sister. "Leila! Leila!" they exclaimed, running to her.

She was almost cool to them, though when they had first met, she had made a big fuss over them and spent the better part of two days playing with them before they left for Gstaad.

Jordana thought she did not want to bother with them because of her friends. "Take your seats, children," she said. "And remember to fasten your seat belts. We'll be taking off in a few minutes."

"Can we sit next to Leila," Samir asked. "Can we?"

She looked at Leila. "If your sister wouldn't mind?"

"I don't mind," Leila said. Again Jordana noticed a grudging tone in her voice.

"All right, but you must behave yourselves."

"Mother," Muhammad asked, "why are you speaking Arabic?"

Jordana smiled. "I think it's because your sister's friends may not be as conversant in English as we are. That's the polite thing to do if people don't understand what you are saying."

"We speak English, ma'am," the young man called Ramadan said in a clear British accent.

"So you do," she said. She looked at Leila, whose face was impassive. "I apologize for my misunderstanding then."

Raoul, the steward, came back into the cabin, "Captain Hyatt would like to know if you are ready for take off, madame?"

"We will be as soon as everyone is in their places," she said, moving to the rear seat near the round table that Baydr usually occupied.

There was a flurry of activity as the boys were strapped in and the others took their seats, Raoul and the stewardess, a pretty American named Margaret, made a swift round of the cabin checking the seat belts. He nodded to Jordana, then went forward. A moment later the big plane moved down the runway.

Once they were in the air and the seat belt sign was off, Jordana got out of her seat. She gestured to Raoul, who came forward. "Would you please prepare the bed in Mr. Al Fay's cabin. I think I would like to lie down and rest."

"Yes, madame." He signaled swiftly, dispatching the stewardess to perform the function.

The boys were crawling all over Leila, who seemed nervous and barely able to tolerate them. "Don't bother your sister," Jordana said sharply. "Maybe she's tired."

Obediently the boys returned to their seats.

"I'm not feeling too well," Jordana explained. "I thought I might lie down for a bit."

Leila nodded without speaking. She watched Jordana make her way to the rear and enter the stateroom. She really could not understand what her father saw in her. In broad daylight, she was not as pretty as she had first thought. Without makeup, her face was drawn, there were dark circles under her eyes and her hair was stringy and not quite as blond as it had seemed. Just as well the woman had gone to sleep. It might make things easier.

She looked across the aisle at Fouad and Ramadan. Fouad glanced at his wristwatch, then back at her. "Another half-hour," he said.

She nodded and leaned back against the headrest. She closed her eyes. Another half-hour was not too long to wait after all the time she had spent preparing for it.

It seemed to Jordana as if she had just closed her eyes when in her sleep she heard a child crying. She stirred restlessly, hoping the sound would stop. But it didn't and gradually it penetrated that it was one of her children crying. She sat up in the bed abruptly, listening.

It was Samir. But it was not his usual cry or whimper. There was a peculiar note in it. A note of fear.

Quickly she rose from the bed and straightened her dress. Then she opened the door and went out into the cabin and down the narrow corridor to the forward lounge. At the entrance she stopped, suddenly transfixed. Her mind could not take in what she saw. It has to be a nightmare, she thought wildly. It has to be.

Huddled in the area just behind the galley in the small space that Carriage used as an office when he was on board were the children, their nanny, her maid and the cabin crew, Raoul and Margaret. Raoul had one hand on the bulkhead to support himself and blood was streaming down his face from a cut on his cheekbone. In front of them stood Leila and her two friends.

But it was a Leila she had never seen before. In her hand she held a heavy automatic, from the belt of her blue jeans hung two hand grenades. The two men were even more heavily armed. In addition to the grenades hanging from their belts, each carried an automatic rapid-fire rifle.

Samir was the first to see her. "Mommy! Mommy!" he cried breaking loose from his nanny's grasp and running toward her.

Leila made a grab for him but he was too quick. Jordana bent forward and the child leaped into her arms. The tears were running down his cheeks. "They hit Raoul and he's bleeding!" he cried.

"It's all right, it's all right," she said soothingly, holding him tightly.

Leila gestured with her gun. "Get up there with the others."

Jordana stared at her. "Have you gone mad?" she said angrily.

"You heard me," Leila said. "Get up there with the others."

Instead Jordana turned on her heel and started back down the corridor to the cabin. Leila moved so swiftly that Jordana did not know she was behind her until the sudden thrust of the gun against her back sent her sprawling in the narrow corridor, knocking the child from her arms.

Immediately, the child began to cry again. He sprang at his sister, flailing his little fists. "Don't you hit my mommy, you bad girl, you!"

Indifferently, Leila sent him sprawling with a slap across the cheeks. The child fell in a huddle against his mother and she put her arm around him.

At the far end of the cabin, Muhammad began to cry. He pulled loose from the nanny and ran to her, kneeling on the floor beside her. Jordana put her other arm around him.

"These children are your brothers," she said, ignoring the screaming pain in the small of her back as she tried to sit up. She looked up at Leila. "You will answer to God for your sins."

"Slut!" Leila's lips drew back in a snarl. "They are not my brothers. They are the children of an American whore!"

"It is written in the Koran that brothers and sisters are united by their father," Jordan said.

"Don't quote the Holy Book to me, bitch!" Leila snapped. "True brothers and sisters are united, not those you managed to convince my father were his own. I've heard all about that from my mother."

"You are still committing a crime against your father," Jordana said.

Leila laughed. "My father has betrayed any allegiance I may have felt for him. He has betrayed his own people and become an accomplice and tool of the Jews and the imperialists."

Oddly enough, Jordana thought, she felt no fear for herself, only for the children. "It will be all right," she whispered to them. "Don't cry any more."

"On your feet!" Leila snapped.

Wincing with pain, Jordana struggled upright. Leila gestured with her gun for them to go forward. Painfully, holding Samir in one arm and leading Muhammad by the hand, she moved through the cabin.

"Give the children to their nurse," Leila commanded.

Jordana looked at her.

"Do what I say! Quickly! Or they will be the next to be hurt!" Leila made a savage gesture.

Silently, Jordana gave the boys over to the nanny. They looked up at her with frightened eyes. She patted them reassuringly. "Don't be frightened. It will be okay."

She almost screamed with pain as she felt the prod of a gun in the small of her back. When she turned, she saw the strange look of pleasure in Leila's eyes. She tightened her lips. She would not give her the pleasure of hearing her moan.

"You go forward to the flight deck with Ramadan," Leila said.

The young man made her walk in front of him. As she opened the door to the cockpit, he shoved her violently. She stumbled forward to her knees and he sprang into the narrow space behind her.

Captain Hyatt, the co-pilot, Bob, and the flight engineer, George, turned around in surprise. George reached overhead for a wrench.

Moving with unexpected speed, Ramadan hit him in the side of the face with the butt of the rifle, knocking him back into his seat. Blood began spurting from his broken nose. "Don't any of you try anything foolish," he said in his clipped British accent, "or you'll kill everyone on this plane."

Andy Hyatt looked up at him, then over at his flight engineer. "Are you okay, George?"

George nodded, holding a handkerchief to his nose. Jordana got to her feet. "Where's the first aid kit?"

"In the cabinet over George's seat," Bob answered.

She took down the metal box and opened it. Quickly she stripped the wrapping from several packages of gauze bandages and gave them to George. She looked down at the captain. "Raoul has a bad cut on his cheek." She started back into the cabin.

"Wait a minute!" Ramadan blocked her path. "You're not through here yet." He turned to the captain. "There are three of us aboard and we're all armed with automatic weapons and grenades. That puts us in charge of this plane, do you understand that?"

Hyatt's voice was puzzled. "Three of you?"

"Leila is one of them," Jordana said.

"Leila?" Hyatt let out a long slow whistle. "Well, I'll be damned. This has got to beat it all. To be hijacked by your boss's own daughter."

"Now that you understand, you will follow my orders exactly as I give them to you," Ramadan said.

Hyatt glanced at Jordana. She nodded. He looked up at the young man. "Yes," he answered.

"First, you will inform Beirut that there has been a change of flight plan; you will request clearance from Lebanon to Damascus."

Hyatt made some notes on the scratch pad beside him. "Got it."

"When we get into Syria, tell them there's been another change in plans and get clearance over Iraq to Teheran."

Hyatt looked at him. "I didn't take on enough fuel to get us to Teheran."

"Don't worry," Ramadan said confidently. "We're not going there."

"Where are we going then?" the captain asked.

Ramadan took a piece of paper from his jacket pocket. He handed it to the pilot. "That's where we're going."

The captain glanced at it then back at him. "You're crazy," he said. "There's no place to put a plane this size down there. It's nothing but mountains."

"There is a place," Ramadan said. "I'll show it to you when we get there."

"Is there equipment for an instrument landing?" Hyatt asked.

"No," Ramadan answered. He gave a short nervous laugh. "But you have the reputation for being one of the best pilots around. Surely Al Fay would have nothing but the best. You shouldn't have any trouble making a visual approach and landing."

"I hope you're right," Hyatt muttered. He reached for the radio switch. "I'd better get on to Beirut."

"Just a minute!" Ramadan pulled the extra set of ear phones from the flight engineer's desk and held one of them to his ear while keeping a finger on the trigger of the rifle in the crook of his other arm. "Now you can call. And, remember, no words of a hijacking or I'll kill you right in your seat. We don't want anyone to know about this. Just yet."

Hyatt looked at him grimly and nodded.

"Now can I go back to help Raoul?" Jordana asked.

"Of course." Ramadan seemed more relaxed. "And while you're about it, you can tell them that I have everything under control up here."

Chapter Eleven

Baydr came into Dick's office about four o'clock in the afternoon. He had been at the bank for lunch and gone to several meetings later. He glanced around the office. "Where's Leila?"

Dick looked up at him in surprise. "She went to Beirut this morning."

"Beirut?"

Dick saw the blank expression on his face. "I thought you knew. She left with Jordana and the children. She told me it was okay with you if she and two friends made the trip. She wanted to go home for the weekend."

"I must be getting old. Strange, but I don't remember a thing about it."

He went into his office, closing the door behind him. Dick stared after him, a vague apprehension beginning to build inside him. It wasn't like Baydr to forget anything. The telephone rang; he picked it up. He listened for a moment then pressed down the hold button and went into Baydr's office.

Baydr looked up from behind his desk. "Yes?"

Dick kept his voice level. "I have our man at the Beirut airport on the line. He's been there since one o'clock and the plane hasn't arrived yet."

Baydr picked up the phone, then covered the mouthpiece with one hand. "What time was it due there?"

"About one-thirty."

Baydr's face paled slightly. He removed his hand from the mouthpiece. "This is Al Fay," he said. "Call the air controller and find out if they have word on the plane. I'll hold on."

He looked up at Dick, covering the mouthpiece again, "I hope nothing's happened."

"Don't worry," Dick said reassuringly. "Andy's too good a pilot to let anything go wrong."

A voice came back on the line. Baydr listened for a moment then seemed to relax slightly. "Okay, thank you very much."

He put down the phone. There was a puzzled look on his face. "I don't understand it. Air control in Beirut said the pilot requested clearance for Damascus."

Dick didn't say anything.

"Get on the phone to Damascus and find out if they're on the ground there."

"Right away, chief." Dick went back into his office and picked up the telephone. It took him twenty minutes to connect with air traffic control in Damascus. He listened for a moment then nodded, placed another call and went back into Baydr's office.

"Are they down there?" Baydr asked.

Dick shook his head. "No. They told me they cleared the plane for Teheran via Baghdad."

Baydr exploded. "Hyatt's gone out of his mind! He'll hear from me about this." Then he calmed down. "Put calls in to those airports and see what you can find out."

"I've already done that," Dick said.

"Good. Let me know as soon as you get word." He leaned back in his chair and watched the door close behind Dick. There was only one possible reason for the change in flight plans. Jordana. She was trying to get the children away from him. He felt anger at his own stupidity, He never should have been so confident that she would do his bidding. Not after what had happened.

A half-hour later Carriage returned. His face was grim. "They didn't land at Teheran, and Baghdad reports that there was no radar track of their crossing Iraqi territory. I checked back with Damascus and they report no signs of trouble or any word from the plane since it flew over them at about two o'clock this afternoon."

"The plane couldn't have vanished just like that without leaving a trace." Baydr was silent for a moment. "I think we'd better call for a search."

"Before we do that I have a man outside I think you should talk to," Dick said.

"Tell him to come back," Baydr snapped. "I have more important things on my mind right now than business!"

"I think what he has to say could have a bearing on where the plane might be." Baydr stared at him. "Show him in."

Dick opened the door. "Would you please come in, Mr. Dupree?" A medium-size man in a nondescript gray suit came through the door. Dick walked with him to the desk. "Mr. Dupree, Mr. Al Fay."

Dupree bowed. "Honoured, monsieur."

Baydr nodded but did not speak. He looked questioningly at Dick. "What has he got to do with the plane?"

"Maybe nothing," Dick said quickly. "But first perhaps I'd better explain."

Baydr nodded.

Dick cleared his throat. It was evident that he was uncomfortable. "Mr. Dupree is a private investigator. We have used him several times before on confidential matters and he has proved himself to be completely trustworthy. Early this week because of certain remarks that Leila made I took it upon myself to have him place her under surveillance."

Baydr's voice was cold. "Why?"

Dick met his gaze. "Because the day after we stopped the Arab doll shipment she asked me to let them continue. When I refused because it was against your orders, she said that the Riad and Mafrad families were old friends and that her grandfather Riad would be very embarrassed by it. She also said that I could have the shipments continued and that you would never have to know about them." He took a deep breath. "When I found out from you that they were not friends I decided to learn what I could about her."

Baydr turned to the private detective. "What have you found out?"

Mr. Dupree took some papers from his inside jacket pocket and unfolded them. He placed one copy on the desk before Baydr, gave one to Dick and held the other in his own hand. "Typewritten on that sheet of paper are the names of every person your daughter came into contact with this week, together with the times and places of their meetings."

Baydr looked down at the paper. One name stood out above all the others: Ali Yasfir. Leila had met with him five times this week, twice yesterday. Several other names were repeated, but they were not familiar to him. He looked up at the private detective.

"I'm afraid your daughter has been keeping dangerous company, monsieur," the detective said. "Almost all the names on that list are known Arab terrorists or partisans and, as such, are kept under close surveillance by the Swiss police. They are young and a man called Yasfir appears to be their greatest financial supporter.

"So the Swiss police gave a sigh of relief when Fouad Aziz and Ramadan Sidki, the two who were considered most dangerous because they were both experts in the use of bombs and weapons, boarded the plane with your daughter and left the country. You may be sure that they will never be granted a re-entry visa."

Baydr studied the paper for a moment. "Is there anything else?"

"Only this, monsieur," Dupree answered. "I took the liberty of calling the school your daughter used to attend in Montreux. I hoped to get some information on several of the girls she had been seeing. But they couldn't give me anything except that they had not seen your daughter since early last May, when she left school in the company of a gentleman named Mr. Yasfir who represented himself as an associate of yours. The school was told that they were going to join you at the Cannes film festival. She never returned."

Baydr looked at Dick, then turned back to the private detective. "Thank you very much, Mr. Dupree. You've been most helpful."

The detective sighed. "The children nowadays." He opened his hands in a typically Gallic gesture. "I have a teenage daughter myself. One never knows what they're up to." He bowed. "If there's anything further I can do for you, Monsieur Al Fay, please do not hesitate to call on me." He bowed to Dick and left the office.

Dick turned to Baydr. "I don't like what I'm thinking, do you?"

"No." Baydr let out a deep breath. "But at least now we know the plane is safe even if we don't know where it is."

"It's a big plane. They can't hide one that size for long."

"Maybe." Baydr's voice was noncommital.

"What do we do now?"

"Wait."

"Wait?" There was surprise in Dick's voice.

"Yes." Baydr looked up at him. "We were wondering what Ali Yasfir's next move would be. Now we know. Soon he will be in touch with us to tell us what he wants."

They stood at the edge of the small forest and looked back at the silver 707. Nine men were scrambling over the plane putting the camouflage netting in place so that it would be concealed from aerial view. Another plane would have to fly over it at less than twenty feet to spot it.

Jordana turned to Hyatt who was standing near her, his eyes fixed on the plane. "You put her down beautifully, captain. Thank you."

"It was a little hairy there for a moment. I thought we were going to run into those trees at the end of the runway." He turned back to the plane. "Why do you think they built a runway as big as this up here? From the looks of it, it's at least three years since it's been used."

"I wouldn't know, captain," she said.

The man called Fouad came up to them. "Okay. Move out." His English bore an American accent. He gestured with his gun toward the forest.

Jordana walked over to the children, who were standing between their nanny and her maid, Magda. The boys were watching the camouflaging of the plane with great interest. She took their hands and waited.

In front of them stood two soldiers in rough, poorly fitted battle uniforms. There were no markings on them to indicate what army, if any, they belonged to. At a signal from Fouad, they began to lead the way. Several other soldiers came up and walked beside them; others fell in behind. All had their rifles pointing at them.

Jordana walked silently with the children. Leila and Ramadan were nowhere to be seen. They had been the first off the plane and a few minutes after landing they had disappeared.

The forest grew thicker and the branches of the trees and the bushes caught and tore at their clothing. Jordana tried to protect the children but within ten minutes there were scratches all over their arms and faces. She called to the nanny. "Anne, if you, Magda, Margaret and I walk in front with the children close behind us, they won't get as many scratches."

The nanny nodded and the other girls came up to join them, forming a semicircle with the children in the middle.

A few minutes later they came out of the forest onto a narrow dirt road. Two jeeps were parked there, each with a driver.

"Into the cars," Fouad said. "The ladies with the children in the first car, the men in the second."

A moment later the cars started up to the road. It was narrow and bumpy and filled with potholes, a winding road that seemed to lead in and out of the forest but climbed continuously up the side of the mountain. After about ten minutes, the air began to feel cooler.

Jordana looked up at the sky. It was growing dark. Evening had come. She turned to the boys, wishing she had thought to bring their coats. But they had been left aboard the plane along with everything else.

Five minutes later they came out of the forest into a clearing. At the edge of the clearing was a group of dilapidated wooden buildings. The buildings were surrounded by a low wall on the top of which were mounted heavy machine guns at intervals. Each gun was attended by two soldiers. And there were searchlights on each corner.

Jordana looked up at the soldiers as they drove into the camp and they returned her gaze with open interest. A few called ribald comments after them but they could not be heard over the noise of the rattling jeep engines.

The jeeps pulled to a stop in front of the largest of the buildings. The driver gestured for them to get out.

Two men came out of the building and stood watching them. Ramadan, now dressed in uniform, was one of them. But Jordana had to look twice before she recognized the other. It was the uniform that fooled her. The second soldier was Leila.

Leila came toward her. Somehow, in the uniform, she seemed larger and coarser. All the prettiness that Jordana had seen in her was erased by the hardness of her manner. "You will occupy one cabin with the children and the other women," she said. "The men another. Dinner will be brought to you in one hour. After you have eaten, the lights will be extinguished for the night. No smoking will be permitted after dark. From the sky, the light from a cigarette can sometimes be seen for miles. Any infraction of our rules will be severely punished. Do you understand that?"

"You won't get away with it," Jordana said. "When your father learns about this there will be no place left on earth or in heaven for you to hide."

Leila stared at her with contempt. "My father will do as he is told — that is, if he ever wants to see any of you alive again."

Chapter Twelve

It was the next morning before they heard from him. His voice crackled over the wire. "We have important matters to discuss," he said. "Much too important for the telephone. I think a meeting between us would be of mutual benefit."

Baydr's voice was cool. "It might."

"Where would it be convenient for you?" Yasfir asked.

"I'm in my office."

"I don't think that would be a very good idea. With all due respect to you, there are too many opportunities to be overheard."

"We would be alone."

"Only Allah knows how many bugs lie hidden in the walls of buildings," Yasfir said.

"Where do you suggest?"

"A mutually agreeable place, perhaps a bench in the park across the street from your hotel?"

"When will you be there?"

"I can be there in fifteen minutes."

"I will be there." Baydr put down the telephone. He pressed the buzzer on his desk. Dick came into the office.

"He wants me to meet him in the park across the street from the hotel. Do you think our electronics man can pick up our conversation with a telescopic microphone from here?"

"I don't know. We can try."

"Get him up here then. We only have fifteen minutes."

The man was in the office in less than ten. Baydr took him to the window and pointed to the park across the street. "Can you get us from here?"

"Maybe," the man answered. "It depends on a lot of things. Street noises. Movement. It would help if you were to remain in one place."

"I don't know," Baydr answered. "A great deal will depend on the other man."

"I'll set up. We'll see what happens."

The man worked swiftly. He was checking out his amplifiers when Dick stuck his head in the door. "It's almost time."

Reluctantly Baydr got ready to leave. He would have preferred to wait a few minutes more to find out whether the electronic eavesdropper would work but he was afraid to be late. He walked through the outer office to the door. Jabir rose to follow him.

Baydr gestured. "Wait here," he said.

Jabir returned to his seat. As soon as the door had closed behind Baydr, Dick beckoned him. "Your master will be in the park across the street," he said. "Follow him but keep your distance and do not allow him to see you. I fear for him."

Jabir nodded and without speaking left the office. When he came out of the entrance to the hotel, Baydr was already crossing the street. Jabir stationed himself near the corner, where he could keep his eyes on him.

Baydr crossed the street and entered the small park. An old woman was sitting on the first bench, wrapped against the cold autumn winds, feeding the pigeons. Baydr sat down on the far end of the bench away from the old woman. He looked up and down the path. There was no one there — not even office workers taking a shortcut on their way to work. He reached for a cigarette.

Fifteen minutes later he was on his fourth cigarette and beginning to wonder whether Yasfir had led him on a wild goose chase when abruptly the old woman got up and left the bench. His eyes followed her curiously as she walked to the curb outside the park and got into a taxi. Odd that a woman dressed as shabbily as she should be able to afford a taxi. Then the thought struck him. He looked at the corner of the bench where she had been sitting. There, under the bag of peanuts she had left behind, was a sheet of ordinary white paper. His eyes scanned the typewritten message.

My apologies for not meeting but urgent business has taken me from the country. Besides our meeting would serve no effective purpose for our requests are simple and can be transmitted on this sheet of paper. I am pleased to inform you that your wife and children have arrived safely at their destination and are all well. Tomorrow morning you will receive a tape of your wife's voice reassuring you of this fact. In order to guarantee our continued interest in their well-being you will comply with the following requests:

1. Deposit $100,000 U.S. each morning before 12 noon to the account No. AX1015 at the Banque d'Assurance in Geneva. This is to reimburse us for the care given your family while they are our guests.

2. Allow the shipments previously rescinded to continue as planned. The next shipments will take place four days from now to be followed by a shipment every other day until the end of the year.

3. You will have prepared and signed by yourself, in blank, an effective instrument of transfer in the amount of a 50 per cent equity in your company. This together with a payment of $10,000,000 U.S. WILL be turned over to the account at the bank listed above not later than 5 Jan. 1974.

In the event that all of the above conditions are met promptly, your wife and sons will be returned to you before 10 Jan. in time for the investiture of your eldest son as prince. Any breach of the confidentiality of this agreement, any failure to meet with the terms exactly as specified could lead to the death of one or all members of your family. As further indication of our good will and in order to assure you of their continued well-being, you will receive each day at your office in Geneva a tape of your wife's voice in which she will read a headline from the previous day's Paris *Herald Tribune* and give you some personal word regardingtheir general condition. Of course, your aid in the war against our common enemies is expected.

IDBAH AL-ADU!

It was signed BROTHERHOOD OF PALESTINIAN FREEDOM FIGHTERS.

Slowly Baydr got to his feet and started back to his office in the hotel. Dick was waiting for him as he came in the door.

"What happened? We didn't see anyone there and we couldn't pick up anything."

"No one came," Baydr said. "Only this." He gave the paper to Dick, who followed him into his office.

He went behind the desk and sank heavily into his chair. Dick continued to read the paper while the electronics expert quickly gathered his equipment and left.

"They're crazy," Dick said when he had finished. "There's no way you can comply with this."

Baydr nodded in weary agreement. There was no way he could satisfy the third and last request. He didn't own fifty percent of the companies in his name. At best, he averaged a twenty percent equity. "I know that and you know that," he said in a tired voice. "But they don't know that. And how do you negotiate with someone who won't talk to you? Someone you can't find?"

"We'll have to find him. There must be a way."

"We'll find him all right, but what worries me is what will happen to the children and Jordana when we do."

"Then what can we do?" Dick asked.

"First we'll make arrangements to make that deposit every day and let the shipments go through as they requested. That will buy us time."

"Those shipments can cause the death of hundreds of people in the States. I wouldn't want this on my conscience."

"Neither do I. We will have to find a way to stop the shipments on the other side."

"How do you plan to do that?"

"I have a friend in New York, Paul Gitlin. He is an attorney, a man of great moral fortitude and with a strong sense of justice. I am sure that he will understand my position and respect our confidence. He will find a way to stop the shipments there and protect us at the same time."

"And then?"

"We must use our time to find out where they are keeping my family and get them out." He rose from the chair and walked to the window. "Arrange the bank deposits and place the call to New York," he said without turning around.

"Yes, sir," Dick said, starting from the office.

"And, Dick!"

Dick turned back.

Baydr was facing him. There were lines on his face that Dick had never seen before. "Call Uni-Jet and charter a plane for me. I will pick up my father in Beirut and we will go together to see the Prince. Perhaps he will be able to help us."

The old Prince finished reading the sheet of paper, then took off his glasses with palsied fingers. His wrinkled hawklike face under the ghutra looked at Baydr and his father sympathetically. "I know of this organization," he said. "They are a splinter group expelled from Al Fatah because of their nihilistic aims."

"I had heard that, your highness," Baydr said. "I thought that with your sponsorship we could gather enough support to force them into the open."

"And then what would you do?" the Prince asked.

"Destroy them!" Baydr said savagely. "They are thieves, blackmailers and murderers. They demean and bring dishonour to the cause they pretend to serve."

"Everything you say is true, my son. But there is nothing we can do."

"Why not?" Baydr demanded. He had all he could do to contain his anger. "It is your heir, the heir to your throne, whose life they endanger."

The old man's eyes were weak and rheumy, but his words were clear and distinct. "He is not yet my heir. And he will not be until I appoint him."

"Then you offer no help?" Baydr asked.

"I cannot — officially," the Prince replied. "And neither can the heads of any other states you might go to. This organization that calls itself the Brotherhood has garnered great support among certain elements. Even Al Fatah finds that it must leave them alone." He picked up the sheet of paper and held it toward Baydr.

Baydr took it silently.

"Unofficially, if you can locate where these fiends are holding your family, you can call on me for as many men and as much money as it takes to free them."

Baydr rose to his feet with a heavy heart. "I thank you for your boons, your highness," he said properly. But he knew it was of no use. Without official help they would never be found.

The old Prince sighed as he held out his hand. "If I were a younger man," he said, "I would be at your side in your search. Go with God, my son. I shall pray to Allah for the safety of your loved ones."

Outside the great palace, in the blinding sun, Dick waited in the air-conditioned limousine. He saw them walking toward the car. "What did he say?" he asked.

"There's nothing he can do," Baydr's father answered.

Baydr stared out the window as the car began to roll down the road. "It's hopeless," he said in a dull voice. "There's nothing anyone can do. There's no one willing to help me."

Dick was silent for a long moment. So much was at stake, so many years. All the work, all the effort that had gone into getting him here would go down the drain. But there were some things that were more important than work. Like the lives of innocent children. He thought of his own two and how he would feel if they were in the same position. That was what finally decided it.

He turned on the jump seat so that he could face Baydr. "I know of some that would help you," he said.

"Who?"

Dick's voice was quiet. "The Israelis."

Baydr's laugh was bitter. "Why should they want to help me? I was born their enemy."

Samir looked at his son. "Men are not born enemies. That is something they learn."

"What difference does it make?" Baydr retorted sarcastically. He turned back to Dick. "Why should they help me?" he asked again.

Dick's eyes went straight into his. "Because I'll ask them to," he said quietly.

Baydr was silent for a moment. Then a small weary sigh escaped his lips. "You work for them?"

Dick nodded. "Yes."

"You're not Israeli," Baydr said. "Why?"

"My parents went back to Jordan to live," Dick said. "One day a man named Ali Yasfir came to visit them and asked them to allow his organization to use their small village as a base. After a few months, during which three girls were raped and many were abused, the villagers demanded that they leave. What the Fedayeen gave them in answer was death. Ali Yasfir personally led his men on a systematic house-by-house extermination of the village. Only a small boy and two girls managed to escape. They told us the true story while the Fedayeen loudly proclaimed the latest Israeli atrocity. The two girls personally saw Ali Yasfir slaughter my mother and father."

"And so now that you have betrayed me," Baydr said bitterly, "you think that you should help me."

Dick met his look honestly. "Not for that reason. But because we both believe that the Arabs and Israelis can live and work together in peace. It is men like Ali Yasfir who kill this possibility. They are our enemies. They are the ones who must be destroyed."

Chapter Thirteen

Baydr looked at the two men in the doorway. If anything, they looked even more Arab than either his father or himself. The old man was tall. His headcloth almost hid his face except for the large hawklike nose, and his dusty faded jellaba trailed to the floor. The young man was dark and swarthy, with a heavy Syrian moustache over his lips. He wore faded tan khaki shirt and trousers.

Baydr and his father rose as General Eshnev led them to him. "Dr. Al Fay, Mr. Al Fay — General Ben Ezra."

The general stared at Samir for a moment, then smiled. "It has been a long time, my friend."

Samir's face suddenly went pale. He felt himself trembling inside. From the corner of his eyes he looked at Baydr hoping that his nervousness would not be noticed. Baydr was looking at the general.

"And this is your son," the general said. "Allah has been good to you. He is a fine man."

Samir's nervousness left him. "It is good to see you again, general."

Baydr looked at his father. "You know each other?"

His father nodded. "Our paths crossed one time in the desert. Many years ago."

General Eshnev spoke quickly. "I must repeat our official position, gentlemen, so that we may all understand it clearly. A very delicate cease-fire exists at the moment so that we dare not condone any official action which might involve entering enemy territory. Such an action could destroy the sincere efforts that are being made to maintain the peace that Israel so profoundly desires."

He paused for a moment. "But there is nothing that we can do about the actions of private citizens as long as we are not aware of what they are doing. Have I made myself clear?"

The others nodded.

"Good," he said. "General Ben Ezra is, of course, a private citizen. He has been retired from the Israeli army for many years. And so is the young man with him. A former first sergeant in the Syrian army, he was taken prisoner on the Golan Heights and at the general's request was released in his custody. He goes by the name of Hamid."

The Syrian bowed respectfully. "I am honored."

"The honor is ours," Baydr and his father replied.

"And now, gentlemen, I must leave you," General Eshnev said. "Unfortunately I have duties that take me elsewhere."

When the door closed behind him, they sat down at the small round table. From beneath his jellaba, Ben Ezra produced several rolls of maps. He spread them open on the table. "One week ago, after your arrival in Tel Aviv, I was told of your problem. On my own I undertook to examine the feasibility of a rescue plan. But first I knew we had to locate the camp in which the prisoners were held. In order to do that, I asked that Hamid be released in my custody. Many years ago, when we were both very young, Hamid's grandfather and I soldiered together in the British army and in the family tradition, Hamid grew up as a professional soldier. I knew that before the war Hamid's last job was as an instructor in a particular camp where the Brotherhood was training a women's corps similar to that of Al Fatah. It failed."

He looked at Baydr, then continued in the same even tone. "Your daughter, Leila, spent three months in that camp. Hamid reports to me that she was a good soldier, much more serious than most in her application to duty, and much more idealistic in her politics. After her stint at the camp, Hamid accompanied her to Beirut, where he remained until he decided to return to Syria for military duty since there were no longer any opportunities for mercenaries among the Fedayeen."

Baydr looked at Hamid. "Then you knew my daughter?"

"Yes, sir."

"Did she ever talk about me?"

"No, sir."

"What did she talk about?"

"Freeing Palestine mostly," Hamid answered. "It was her feeling that it was not only the Jews who held back the liberation but also the wealthy, elite Arabs who wanted to perpetuate their power over the land and its peoples."

"Do you think she included me in that group?"

Hamid hesitated, then nodded. "Yes, sir, I believe she did."

Baydr turned back to Ben Ezra. "I'm sorry, general, I'm still trying to understand what happened."

The general nodded. He looked down at the map and pointed to a spot. "We think we have located the one camp where they might be. You say your plane was a 707?"

Baydr nodded. "Yes."

"Then I'm sure we have it," he said, a faint note of triumph entering his voice. "There is an old camp, built by the Syrians and abandoned more than ten years ago. It is located just north of the Jordanian border, west of your own country. At the time it was built, they had planned to use it as a base for giant bombers but since they could not purchase the planes, the entire project was given up. But the airstrip is still there and there have been rumors in the countryside that the camp has been occupied by the Brotherhood. There is one major difficulty however: the airstrip is in the mountains on a plateau seven hundred meters up and the camp itself is one hundred and fifty meters high. There are only two ways to penetrate. We could go in by air, but the sound of planes would give them too much warning and they would have the captives executed before we could get to them. The other way is to go on foot. To avoid detection we would have to set down at least fifty miles from the camp, concealing ourselves by day and traveling by night through terrible terrain. We would have two nights of forced march and attack on the third night. My estimate based on the size of the camp is that they may have as many as one hundred men there. So even if we are successful in freeing the captives, we still have the problem of getting them to safety before we are pursued."

He looked up at them. "That's my speech. Any questions?"

"How do we know that we're going to the right camp? Or that they will be there when we get there?" Baydr asked.

The general's voice was flat. "We don't. But that's the chance we take. Right now it's the only possibility we have. Unless you know of another place where a 707 can land."

"I don't know of any other."

"Then it is you who must make the decision to go or not to go."

Baydr looked at his father for a moment, then he turned back to the general. "I say we go."

The general smiled. "Well said. Since this is an unofficial action we will need to recruit volunteers. I say fifteen, not more than twenty men. Any more than that would be unwieldy and make us too visible. They will be paid, very high wages of course, for such dangerous work."

"I will pay whatever they ask."

"Good. I know ten men I can be sure of."

"I would like to volunteer," Hamid said. "I have been at that camp once. I know the layout."

"Accepted," the general said grimly. "Even though you may have already been drafted."

"My prince promised me as many men as I needed," Baydr said.

"Are they good?"

"His personal guards are all mountain warriors from the Yemen."

"They'll do," the general said. The Yemeni mountain men were considered the most savage fighters in all Islam. "We will need equipment, guns, grenades, portable rocket launchers, food, water and other supplies as well as planes to get us to our starting point. It will be expensive."

"You will have them."

"And one more thing. We will need a helicopter to get us out. We will time its arrival at the airstrip with our attack."

"That too," Baydr said.

The general nodded.

"How long will it take to get ready?" Baydr asked.

"Three days if you can get your men here by then."

"They'll be here," Baydr answered. He turned to his father. "Would you be kind enough to see the Prince and ask him for the assistance he promised? I would like to remain here with the general and see that everything is in readiness."

Samir nodded. "I will do that."

"Thank you, Father."

Samir looked at him. "They are my grandchildren also." He turned to Ben Ezra. "My heartfelt gratitude, my friend," he said. "Once again, it seems, Allah has sent you to me in my time of need."

"Do not thank me, my friend," Ben Ezra said in Arabic. "It would seem to me that we are both blessed."

Chapter Fourteen

"Mommy, when will Father come for us?"

Jordana looked down at Samir's little face peering up at her over the edge of the blanket that was tucked under his chin. She glanced at Muhammad in the other cot. He was already asleep, his eyes tightly shut, his face pressed against the hard pillow. She turned back to Samir. "Soon, my darling, soon," she whispered reassuringly.

"I wish he would come tomorrow," Samir said. "I don't like it here. The people are not nice."

"Daddy will come soon. Close your eyes and go to sleep."

"Good night, Mommy."

She bent and kissed his forehead. "Good night, darling." She straightened up and walked back into the other room of the small two-room cabin in which they were living. A small oil lamp glowed in the center of the little table where they took their meals. The three other women were sitting around the table, staring into the lamp. There was nothing for them to do, nothing to read. Even conversation had run dry. After two weeks there was nothing left to talk about, and they hadn't had much in common to begin with.

"The children are asleep," she said, just to hear the sound of a voice.

"Bless the little darlings," Anne, the nanny, answered. Then she fell silent again. The others did not even raise their heads.

"My God!" Jordana exclaimed. "Look at us. We're as tatty a bunch of females as ever existed."

This time they did look up. "We have to make up our minds," she said forcefully. "Tomorrow we'll have to do something about ourselves. Surely there has to be a needle and thread somewhere in this damned camp."

"If there is," Margaret, the stewardess, replied, "they probably won't let us have it. We have all the clothes we need on the plane but they won't send anyone down to get them for us."

"We'll have to insist."

"It wouldn't do any good," Margaret said. She looked up at Jordana. "I don't understand why Mr. Al Fay won't pay the ransom and get us out of here."

Jordana looked at her. "How do we know that he hasn't? And that they are not holding out for even more?"

"It doesn't make sense to me," Margaret said. She covered her face with her hands and began to cry. "It's terrible here. They won't let us out except to go to the toilet, and then the guard stands in front of the open door watching. They won't let us talk to the men. We don't even know how they are. They may be dead for all we know."

"They're okay," Jordana said. "I saw a man bringing them their food trays the other day."

Abruptly the stewardess stopped crying. "I'm sorry, Mrs. Al Fay. I didn't mean to let it out on you. I guess it's just got to be too much for me, that's all."

Jordana nodded sympathetically. "I think it's just too much for all of us. The real hell is not knowing what is going on. They know that and that is why they keep us the way they do."

She walked over to the boarded window and peeked through a tiny crack between the boards. She could see nothing except the darkness of the night. She went back to the table and sat down in the vacant chair. A moment later, she, too, was staring into the glowing lamp.

She lost all track of time. She didn't know whether it was a half-hour, an hour or two hours later when the cabin door was abruptly thrown open. She, like the others, stared at the two soldiers in the doorway in surprise.

One of the soldiers pointed to her. "You," he said harshly in Arabic. "You come with us."

"Me?" she asked stunned. It was the first time this had happened. Even the daily tape recordings were made in the cabin. She would be handed a small clipping from the *Herald Tribune* carrying the date and a headline and nothing else. She would read it into the microphone and then add a few words about herself and the children. Then the microphone and recorder would be taken away. She could only guess that the tapes were being used to assure Baydr that they were alive and well.

"Yes, you!" he repeated.

The others looked at her fearfully. "Don't worry," she said quickly. "Maybe the information we have been waiting for has come. I'll be back soon and tell you all about it."

She rose from the chair and went out the door. The soldiers fell in beside her and silently walked her to the command cabin. They opened the door for her and, after closing it behind her, remained outside.

She stood, her eyes blinking at the unaccustomed brightness of the light. There were no little oil lamps here. Somewhere behind the building a generator hummed. Electricity. In the background a radio was playing Arabic music.

Leila and Ramadan were sitting at a table with a third man she didn't recognize until he rose and turned to greet her.

"Madame Al Fay." He bowed.

She stared at him. "Mr. Yasfir!"

He smiled. "I see you remember my name. I am honored."

She didn't answer.

"I trust that you are comfortable," he said smoothly. "I regret that we cannot reciprocate the lavishness of your hospitality, but we do the best we can."

"Mr. Yasfir," she said coldly. "Why don't you just skip the bullshit and get to the point!"

Yasfir's eyes hardened. "I had almost forgotten you were American." He reached behind him and picked up a sheet of paper from the desk. "You will read the statement into a tape recorder."

"And if I refuse?"

"It would be most unfortunate. You see, the message you are to read into the tape recorder is our last effort to save your life and the lives of your children."

She looked from him to Leila. Leila's face was devoid of expression. A Coca-Cola bottle stood half-empty on the table before her. She turned back to Yasfir. "I'll do it."

"Over here." He led her to the far corner of the room, where the tape recorder had been set up on a table between two chairs. He picked up the mike and gave it to her. "Speak slowly and distinctly," he said. "It is important that every word on this tape be understood." He pressed the start button. "Now."

She looked down at the paper and began to read it aloud.

"Baydr, this message is being read by me because it is a final warning and they want me as well as you to know it. It has just been learned that every shipment made under their agreement with you has been confiscated by the United States. It is believed that you are responsible for those losses and you

are hereby assessed $10,000,000 additional to be paid into the account agreed
upon not later than the Monday following the receipt of this tape. Your
failure to do so and any further confiscation of shipments will constitute a
breach of the agreement and will result in an immediate application of the
extreme penalty. Only you can now prevent the execution of your family."

She paused and stared at him in horror.

He gestured to her to read on.

"It has also been learned that you have applied to your Prince and various
other Arab sources for assistance. We trust that you are convinced by now
that the Arab world is with us. We advise you to cease wasting your time
searching for help you will not get."

He snatched the microphone from her hand and spoke into it. "This is our final
message. There will be no further warnings. Only action." He pressed the stop
button.

"You can't mean that," she said.

He smiled at her. "Of course not," he replied. "But your husband is a very
difficult man as you must know. He must be convinced of our threat." He got to
his feet. "You must be exhausted." he said. "May I offer you a drink?"

She sat numbly without answering. Suddenly it had all become too much for her
to understand. It was more than just a kidnapping; there were political implications
that had not occurred to her before. It seemed to her that there was no way in
God's creation that Baydr could live up to all the demands being made upon him.

She was going to die. She knew that now. And in a strange way it no longer
mattered. Even if she lived there would be nothing in life. She herself had destroyed
any chance she might have had for Baydr's love.

Then a chill ran through her. The children. They had done nothing to bring this
upon themselves. They should not be made to pay for the sins of their parents.

She got to her feet. "I think I will have that drink now," she said. "Do you have
any wine by any chance?"

"Yes." He turned. "Leila, bring the bottle of wine."

Leila stared at him, then slowly got to her feet. Reluctantly she went into the
next room and came back with the wine. She placed it on the table and began to
return to her seat.

"Two glasses, Leila," he said.

She walked to a cupboard and came back with two ordinary tumblers. She placed
them beside the wine and sat down. "We have no opener," she said.

"It doesn't matter," Yasfir said. He picked up the bottle and crossed to a washbasin in the corner of the room. Sharply he rapped the corked neck of the bottle
against the porcelain. The neck broke cleanly away. He had been so expert that
only a few drops of the wine had been lost. He came back, smiling, and filled the
two glasses. Picking them up, he turned to Jordana and held one toward her.

She stared in fascination at the redness of the wine in the glass. She didn't move.
The color reminded her of blood. Her blood. Her children's blood.

"Take it," he said harshly.

His voice broke through the paralysis that had gripped her. "No!" she suddenly screamed, striking the glass from his hand. "No!"

The glass flew against his chest, staining his suit and shirt with the red wine. He looked down at himself, then back at her, a violent anger leaping into his eyes. "Bitch!" he cried, hitting her in the face.

She fell to the floor. Strange that she felt no pain, only a dull shock. The room seemed to be reeling about her. Then she saw his face bending over her and his hand. She closed her eyes as the pain began to explode in her face, first on one cheek, then the other.

Then the explosions ended and she felt hands tearing at her clothing. She heard the ripping of the cloth as he pulled at the front of her dress. She opened her eyes. Suddenly the room had filled with soldiers.

Yasfir stood over her, his face flushed with exertion; next to him was Leila, a strange kind of joy in her eyes. Slowly she turned her head. The two soldiers who had brought her here were looking down at her and next to them were the two guards who had been outside the cabin. Behind them there were other soldiers she had never seen before. But all the faces seemed the same, all were wearing the same fiercely sensuous expression. Only Ramadan had not moved. He remained in his chair, an expression of disdain on his face.

Suddenly she became aware of her nakedness. She moved her hands, trying to cover herself from their searching eyes.

Leila laughed again. "The slut hides what she once was so proud to display." She dropped to one knee and grabbed Jordana's wrists, forcing them away from her body, spread-eagling her on the floor. She looked up at the soldiers. "Who will be the first man to avail himself of my father's whore?"

"Your father's wife!" Jordana screamed, struggling against Leila's grip. "We were married according to the Koran in the eyes of Allah!"

There was a sudden silence in the room, a subtle change had come over the soldiers. Awkwardly, uncomfortably, they looked at each other, then slowly, they began to shuffle to the door.

"Are you cowards?" Leila screamed after them. "Afraid to match your manhood against this whore?"

The soldiers did not look back. One by one, they filed from the cabin. Only Yasfir remained, looking down at them. Then he too turned away and went back to the table and sat down. He lifted the glass of wine to his lips with trembling fingers and drained it in a single swallow.

Abruptly, Leila let go of her wrists and rose to her feet. She glanced at the two men seated at the table, then went to the far corner of the room. She sank into the chair next to the tape recorder and sat silently, not looking at them.

For the first time Ramadan moved. He knelt beside Jordana and slipped a supporting arm under her shoulder. Gently, he raised her to her feet.

Vainly, she tried to cover herself with her torn dress. He guided her toward the door and took a soldier's coat that was hanging on the wall and wrapped it around her. He opened the door and called to the soldiers outside. "Escort Madame Al Fay back to her cabin."

"Thank you," she whispered.

He didn't answer.

"There is no hope for us?" she asked.

Though he did not speak, a subtle change in the expression of his eyes gave her the answer.

She looked up into his face. "I don't care what you do with me. But my children. Please don't let them die."

"I am nothing but a soldier who must obey the orders he is given," he said, not without sympathy. "But I will do what I can."

She looked into his eyes, then nodded and turned away. She felt weak and stumbled slightly. One of the soldiers put an arm under her elbow to support her. Oddly enough, she felt her strength returning as she walked toward their cabin.

There was some hope. Maybe not much. But some.

Chapter Fifteen

Hamid lowered his night glasses. From his position in the trees just outside the camp, he had been able to determine which cabin held the women. The men had to be in the cabin next to them. Carefully, soundlessly, he slipped down the trunk of the tree.

Ben Ezra looked at him. "Well?"

"I have located the cabins which contain the prisoners. They are in the center of the camp. We must pass all the other cabins to reach them. The first cabin holds the men; the second, the women. Each cabin has two guards stationed in front and two behind. The command cabin is the large one just beyond the entrance. At the moment, there are three jeeps parked in front of it."

"How many men do you estimate they have?"

Hamid calculated swiftly. Twelve machine guns mounted on the walls, two men to a gun always on duty. If each man covered for twelve hours, that alone would account for forty-eight men. Eight guards for the prisoners' cabins. Plus the others he had seen. "Ninety, one hundred maybe."

Ben Ezra nodded thoughtfully. He had at the most eighteen men he could use in the assault. He had had to leave two behind to secure the airstrip which they had taken less than one hour ago. There had been seven Brotherhood soldiers there. Now they were all dead. The Yemenis had requested permission to take the airstrip and he had given it. Too late he had remembered that the Yemenis might take no prisoners.

He had wanted Baydr and Carriage to remain at the airstrip but Baydr insisted on coming with him, so he'd had to assign two of his own volunteers, men that he could sorely spare. He looked at his watch. It was ten o'clock. At four o'clock in the morning, the large helicopter that Baydr had secured would be waiting for them at the airstrip. Dr. Al Fay with a complete medical team would be on it. Everything had to be timed to the split second so that they would reach the airstrip before a pursuit force could be mounted.

The attack had to begin at two o'clock. They had to be on their way down to the airstrip not later than three. One hour was barely enough time to allow for the journey on foot, especially when they didn't know the condition of the eight captives. He hoped they would be strong enough to make it without help. If any of them had to be carried, he might not have the men to spare.

He checked his watch again. Four hours to zero. He looked at Hamid. "Do you think you can get inside and plant the plastiques?"

"I can try."

"The first things I want knocked out are those four giant searchlights. Then the jeeps."

Hamid nodded.

"I want all the timers set for two hundred hours."

"It will be done," Hamid answered.

"Will you need help?"

"I could use one man," Hamid said politely.

Ben Ezra turned and looked back at the soldiers. They were professionals, all of them highly trained. There was really none that he could spare; he had work for each of them. His eyes fell on Jabir. The man was not young but he had an air of quiet competence. He caught his eye and gestured to him.

"Hamid needs one man to help with the plastiques," Ben Ezra said. "Will you volunteer?"

Jabir glanced back at Baydr. "I will be honoured. If you will guard my master in my absence."

Ben Ezra nodded. "I will guard him as my own." Later the thought of what he had said would come back to him. He was his own.

He called the Israeli corporal in charge of that group. "Set the rocket launchers and aim them at the walls below the machine guns. After that the target will be the command cabin."

The Israeli saluted and went away.

He motioned to the Yemeni captain. "I have selected your soldiers to lead the assault. At the first detonation of the plastiques, you will pick off as many of the men on the machine guns as you can. Then, without waiting for results, you will follow me through the gate and deploy your men around the soldiers' cabins while we seek out the captives."

The captain saluted. "We are grateful for the honor you have given us. We shall fulfill our duty unto death."

Ben Ezra returned the salute. "I thank you, captain."

He turned and looked back at the walls of the camp. They gleamed ghostly white in the faint moonlight. He turned back. Already the men were scattering, taking up their positions, preparing for the attack. He walked slowly back to Baydr and Carriage and sank down on his haunches beside them.

"How is it going?" Baydr asked.

Ben Ezra looked at his son. How strange, he thought. There is so much we might have been to one another. And yet, the ways of the Lord were beyond human understanding. After so many years to be brought together in an alien world, to reach across the borders of hatred, to answer in each other a common need.

The old man seemed lost in thought. "How is it going?" Baydr repeated.

Ben Ezra's eyes cleared. He nodded his head slowly. "It goes," he said. "From this moment on we are in the hands of God."

"What time do we attack?"

"At two hundred hours." His voice grew stern. "And I don't want you to get in our way. You are not a soldier and I don't want you getting yourself killed. You wait out here until I send for you."

"It's my family in there," Baydr said.

"You will do them no good if you are dead."

Baydr leaned back against the tree trunk. The general was a remarkable old man. In two nights of long and arduous march over the worst terrain Baydr had ever seen, the general had moved as agilely and rapidly as any of them. Not once had Baydr seen him weary. What was it the Israelis called him? The Lion of the Desert? It was a name truly given.

Ben Ezra turned to the Israeli corporal. "Fifteen minutes to zero hour. Pass the word."

The soldier immediately ran off. The general looked worried. "Hamid and Jabir have not yet returned."

Baydr got to his feet. He looked toward the camp. All was quiet.

There was a rustle from the trees to one side. A moment later, Hamid and Jabir appeared.

"What took you so long?" the general asked angrily.

"We had to work around the guards," Hamid said. "They're crawling around the place like flies. I think my estimate may have been low. There are maybe a hundred and fifty men in there."

"It changes nothing," Ben Ezra said. "You stay close to me when we go in. As soon as the rockets are gone, the Israelis are coming in to help us with the captives."

"Yes, sir." Hamid looked around. Baydr was out of earshot. "I saw his daughter. She was in the command cabin. There were two men with her. I recognized one of them as Ali Yasfir. I didn't know the other."

Ben Ezra made a face. Like it or not, she was his grandchild. "Pass the word not to harm the girl if possible," he said.

"Yes, sir." Hamid ran off and disappeared among the trees.

Ten minutes to zero. Ben Ezra reached under his jellaba and unfastened his sword belt. Swiftly he buckled it outside his flowing robe. Reaching across his waist, he drew the scimitar from its scabbard. The gracefully curved steel glinted in the light from the moon. Ben Ezra felt himself grow young once more. The sword without which he had never gone into battle was at his side. All was right with the world.

Leila took a fresh bottle of Coca-Cola and brought it back to the table. "When are you going back?" she asked Ali Yasfir.

"In the morning."

"I wish I were going with you. I'm going crazy up here. There's nothing to do."

"The only girl with one hundred and forty men and you're bored?"

"You know what I mean," Leila said angrily.

"Soon it will be over. Then you can come back to Beirut."

"What happens to them when its over?"

He shrugged his shoulders.

"Do we have to? Even if my father gives us everything we've asked for?"

"There are too many of them. They could always identify us."

"But the children, do they have to die also?"

"What's come over you? I thought you hated them. They stole your heritage."

"Not the children. Jordana and my father, yes. But not the children."

"Children can identify us also."

She sat silently for a moment, then got to her feet. "I think I'll go outside for some air," she said.

After the door had closed behind her, Yasfir turned to Ramadan. "If I don't get back in time you have your orders."

"Yes," Ramadan replied.

"She must go first," Yasfir said. "She, more than any of the others can get us hanged. She knows too much about us."

The night air was cool and it felt good against her face. Leila walked slowly in the direction of her own cabin. So much had happened that she hadn't anticipated. There was none of the glamour and excitement that she had envisioned. Mostly it was just boredom. Boredom and empty days and nights.

And there was none of the feeling of participating in the cause of freedom. She had long given up trying to connect what was taking place here with the struggle to free the Palestinians. All the soldiers were mercenaries. And very well paid, too. Not one of them seemed to care about the cause. Only about their monthly pay. It was not at all what the boys and girls in school had talked about. Here, freedom was just another word.

She remembered that Hamid had once tried to explain that to her. But she had refused to understand it then. It seemed so long ago. Yet it had only been six months. Why was it that she had felt so young then and so old now?

She paused at the entrance to her cabin and looked out at the camp. It was quiet. Something disturbed her but she didn't know what it was. Her eyes caught a glimpse of motion on the wall. One of the machine gunners had straightened up to stretch. Against the pale moonlight she could see his hands reach toward the sky. Then, suddenly, he pitched forward head first into the camp. A moment later there was the crack of rifle shot. Even as she froze in surprise, the skies seemed to open up and the fires of hell to pour down on them.

The thought flashed crazily through her mind even as she began to run. Now she knew what had disturbed her. The quiet. It had been much too quiet.

Chapter Sixteen

The children came awake screaming with terror. The tiny cabin reverberated with the concussions coming from the explosions that seemed to be taking place all around them. Jordana leaped from her cot, ran to them and held them close to her.

She heard one of the women in the other room screaming but she could not tell who it was. Through the cracks in the boarded-up windows she could see flashes of red and orange lights. The whole cabin seemed to shudder convulsively as another explosion tore the night.

Oddly enough she wasn't frightened. For the first time since her hijacking she felt secure.

"What's happening, Mommy?" Muhammad asked, between tears.

"Daddy's come for us, darling. Don't be frightened."

"Where is he?" Samir asked. "I want to see him."

"You will," she said soothingly. "In just a few minutes now."

Anne, the nanny, appeared in the doorway. "Are you all right, madame?" she called.

"We're fine," Jordana shouted back over the noise. "And you?"

"Magda's got a splinter of wood in her arm but otherwise we're all right." She paused as another violent concussion rocked the cabin. "Do you need any help with the children?"

"No, we're fine," Jordana said. She remembered something from a war movie she had once seen. "Tell the girls to lie down on the floor with their hands over their heads. They'll be safer that way."

"Yes, madame," Anne answered, her Scottish imperturbability unruffled. She disappeared from the doorway.

"On the floor, boys," Jordana said, pulling them down with her. They stretched out, one on either side, and she placed her arms over them, sheltering their heads under her shoulders.

The noise from the explosions was diminishing. Now more and more she heard the sounds of rifle fire mixed with the noises of men running about and shouting. She held the children very tightly and waited.

Leila ran through the camp, which was filled with men running back and forth in confusion. The attack seemed to be coming from all sides.

Only one man seemed to have a purpose. She saw Ramadan, his rifle in his hand, running toward the women's cabin.

Suddenly she remembered the automatic in her belt and pulled it out. The cold steel weight was comforting in her hand. Now she did not feel as alone and unprotected. "Ramadan!" she yelled after him.

He didn't hear her and kept going, disappearing from sight around the corner of the women's cabin. Without knowing why, she ran after him.

The door of the cabin was open when she got there. She ran inside and suddenly stopped in shock. Huddled against the wall of the back room, the women had gathered in a group around Jordana and the boys. Ramadan, standing in the narrow doorway between the rooms, his back to her, was bringing his automatic rifle to firing position.

"Leila!" Jordana screamed. "They're your brothers!"

Ramadan wheeled, the rifle turned toward Leila.

It wasn't until Leila saw the cold absence of expression on Ramadan's face that she realised the truth. She meant no more to Al Ikhwah than her brothers. They had recognized the ties of blood even if she hadn't. To them, she was only a tool, to be used and discarded when their need of her no longer existed.

She held the heavy automatic in front of her with both hands. By reflex, her fingers tightened on the trigger. It wasn't until the clip had emptied itself and Ramadan had pitched violently onto the floor that she realized she had pulled the trigger.

Looking across his body, she saw Jordana quickly turn the faces of the boys away from the sight of the blood welling from Ramadan's body.

Suddenly Leila felt a strong pair of arms seize her from behind, pinning her own arms against her body. Violently she struggled to free herself.

"Leila! Stop it!" a familiar voice snapped in her ear.

She twisted her head to see who it was. "Hamid!" she exclaimed in surprise. "Where did you come from?"

"Time for that later." He pulled her backward through the doorway. Loosening his grip but holding on to one arm, he dragged her after him behind the cabins through an opening that had been blasted in the camp wall.

When they got to the edge of the forest, he pushed her down flat against the earth. She raised her head to look at him. "What are you doing here?"

He pushed her head down again. "Don't you remember the first thing I taught you?" he said harshly. "Keep your head down!"

"You didn't answer my question," she said, her voice muffled.

"I came to get you."

"Why, Hamid, why?"

"Because I didn't want you to get yourself killed, that's why," he said huskily. "You always were a lousy soldier."

"Hamid, you love me," she said, a note of wonder coming into her voice.

He didn't answer.

"Why didn't you ever say anything?"

He turned to look at her. "What right have I to love a girl like you?"

Ben Ezra strode about, directing his soldiers, his scimitar flashing over his head. He glanced around fiercely. The resistance seemed to be slowing down. He looked around for Hamid, but he was nowhere to be seen. Aloud he cursed him. He hated soldiers who became too involved in the battle to remember their orders. He had told him to stay near him.

He signaled the Israeli corporal. "Gather your men!" A moment later he caught Jabir's eye. "Fetch your master," he shouted. "We're bringing out the captives!"

There was a burst of gunfire on the other side of the camp. He saw several of the Yemenis run toward it. He nodded to himself grimly. He had made the right choice. They were magnificent fighting men.

Baydr was the first to enter the cabin. He felt his heart leap as he saw his sons. He dropped to one knee to bring them in his arms as they ran to him, screaming, "Daddy! Daddy!"

He kissed one, then the other and felt the salt of his own tears on his lips.

"We weren't frightened, honest, Father," Muhammad said. "We knew you would come for us."

"Yes," Samir piped up. "Mommy told us that every day."

He looked up at her. His vision was blurred with tears. Slowly he rose to his feet.

Jordana didn't move; her eyes were fixed upon him.

Silently, he held out his hand to her.

Slowly, almost tentatively, she took it.

He looked into her eyes for a long moment. His voice was husky. "We almost didn't make it."

She smiled tremulously. "I never for a moment doubted."

"Can you forgive me?" he asked.

"That's easy. I love you," she said. "But can you forgive me?"

He grinned. Suddenly he was the Baydr she had first known and loved. "Easy," he said. "I love you too."

"Move out," the Israeli corporal yelled from the door behind them. "We haven't got all night!"

Ben Ezra was standing near the camp entrance. "Anyone else?" the general asked.

"That's all of us," the corporal answered.

He turned to the Yemeni captain. "Rear guard posted?"

"Yes, sir," the captain replied. "Four men with automatic rifles ought to keep them occupied for a while. We're not to wait for them. They'll backtrack and we'll pick them up at our original landing place in a few days."

Ben Ezra nodded. That was good soldiering. "How many casualties?"

"One dead, a few superficial wounds — that's all."

Ben Ezra turned to the Israeli.

"Two dead."

"We were lucky," the general said grimly. "We caught them with their pants down!" He looked out on the road. The captives were in the midst of a joyous reunion. The men of the flight crew were in good shape and so were the women. They huddled together in a tight group, all trying to talk at once. "Better get them started," Ben Ezra said. 'It won't take our friends very long to figure out how few of us there are and then they'll be coming after us."

The Israeli started off. Ben Ezra called him back. "Did you see the Syrian?"

The soldier shook his head. "I haven't seen him since we first went in after the rockets were fired. He was in front of me and then he just disappeared."

Ben Ezra was puzzled. It didn't make sense. Unless the man had been killed and was lying undiscovered somewhere. But no, that wasn't possible. The Syrian was just too good a soldier. He would turn up sooner or later. Ben Ezra turned and started down the road after them. He looked at his watch. Just three o'clock. Right on schedule.

Now, if the helicopter made it on time, they would be having breakfast at the Prince's palace in the morning.

Chapter Seventeen

Dick Carriage moved slowly through the camp. Through the open gate, he could see the others going down the road on their way to the airstrip. But he wasn't ready to leave yet. There was still some unfinished business for him to attend to.

The sporadic sound of rifle fire came from the various corners of the camp. The Yemenis were doing their job. Slowly, carefully, he opened one cabin door after another and still there was no sign of him.

Yet the man had to be there. He couldn't have got out before the attack. No one could have left the camp without being seen. Besides, he had heard Hamid report to the general that he had seen him fifteen minutes before the attack had begun. The man hadn't even time to run into the forest the way the command cabin was located. They were all around it.

He turned to look back at the command cabin. In front of it were three burned-out smashed jeeps. Thoughtfully he turned and walked back to it. He had already gone through the cabin once but maybe there was something he had overlooked.

Cautiously he approached the door again. His automatic in his hand, he stood to one side and pushed it wide. He waited for a moment. There was no sound from inside.

He went through the doorway. The first room was a shambles. Rockets had torn gaping holes in the sides of the cabin. Papers and furniture were scattered around the room as if a tornado had struck.

He went through into the other room. Slowly he looked around. It was imposs-ible. There was just no place for the man to hide. He started back outside, then stopped.

He felt the hairs on the back of his neck begin to rise. The man was here. His instinct told him. It didn't matter that he couldn't find him. The man was here.

He turned and slowly looked around the cabin again. Nothing. He stood very still for a moment and then went over to the bench beside the wash basin where he had noticed several oil lamps.

Breaking them open, he quickly scattered the oil around the room. Then he took a chair and put it in the outer doorway and sat down in it, facing the room. He took a book of matches from his pocket, struck one, held it to the other matches until the book erupted in flame and then threw it into the room.

The fire raced rapidly across the floor, then climbing the walls. Smoke began to fill the room and still he sat. The heat grew intense but he did not move.

Suddenly there was a faint sound from inside. He tried to peer through the smoke but saw nothing. Again the sound came, a creaking sound, as if a door were opening on rusted hinges. But he could see through to the other room and there were no other doors.

Then something on the floor moved. He got to his feet. Part of the wooden floor seemed to be shifting. He moved toward it on catlike feet.

He stopped at the side of the floorboard. Now he took out a handkerchief and held it over his nose and mouth to protect himself against the smoke. Suddenly, the floorboard was flung to one side and a man sat up, coughing.

The Israeli agent nodded to himself in satisfaction. This was the man he had come back for, this was the man he had come to get. It was never the idealist who had to be feared, only the man who corrupted the ideal. This man was the corrupter. Slowly, deliberately, before the man even realized that he was there, Dick emptied the clip of his automatic into him.

Then he turned and without even a backward look walked out of the cabin toward the road, leaving the dead Ali Yasfir lying in his fiery coffin.

He was a quarter of a mile down the road when he came upon them. He had just walked around a curve as they emerged from the forest. They stopped, staring at one another.

"Leila!" he said.

Hamid turned to her. He saw the strange look on her face. He remained silent.

"Dick," she said in a strained voice. "I—"

The sound of a rifle shot interrupted her. A look of intense surprise suddenly appeared on Dick's face. Then a strangle bubble of blood appeared in the corner of his mouth and he slipped slowly to the road.

Hamid reacted immediately. Throwing Leila to the ground, he flung himself on his belly, facing the direction from which the shot had come. A moment later, he saw the man between the trees. Carefully, he lined the sights of his automatic rifle between the two trees where the man would pass. He waited until the man was dead center, then he squeezed the trigger. The automatic rifle almost cut the man in half.

He turned back to Leila. "Come on," he said harshly. "Let's get out of here!"

Dick moaned.

"We can't leave him here," Leila said. "He'll die!"

"He'll die anyway," Hamid said callously. "Let's go."

"No. You'll have to help me to get him to the others."

"Are you crazy? Do you know what will happen to you if you go back? If they don't hang you, you'll spend the rest of your life in jail!"

"I don't care," she said stubbornly. "Are you going to help me or not?"

Hamid looked at her and shook his head. He gave her the rifle. "Here, carry this." He bent over, picked up Dick and slung him over his shoulder. "Let's go. There'll be others behind that one in just a few minutes."

Ben Ezra checked his watch. It was almost four o'clock. "Where's that damned helicopter?"

No sooner were the words out of his mouth than the sound of the plane came from the distance. He peered into the sky. But now that the moon was gone, he could see nothing but the blackness of the night.

Ten minutes later, the sound came from overhead. A moment afterward it passed the crest of the mountain and disappeared.

A crackling of rifle fire came from the direction of the road through the forest. The Israeli corporal came running up. "They're coming down the road after us!"

"Keep them busy. The helicopter should be down any minute."

But the gunfire grew more intense and still the helicopter did not come down. Occasionally the sound of its engines could be heard, but then it would vanish again.

The Israeli corporal returned. "We better make it quick, general," he said. "They're coming down with some real heavy stuff now."

"Get back there!" Ben Ezra snapped. He peered up at the sky. "You know what I think? I think that damn fool up there is lost and can't find us in the dark."

"Maybe if we light a fire," Baydr suggested. "It would serve as a beacon for him."

"Good idea," the general said. "But we've got nothing to make a big enough fire with. It would take us an hour to gather enough branches and they wouldn't burn anyway. Everything's too damp from the night moisture."

"I've got something that will burn."

"What?"

Baydr gestured to the 707 under the camouflage. "That would make a hell of a fire."

"You wouldn't?" Ben Ezra's voice was questioning.

The sounds of the fighting grew closer. "I came to get my family out of this and that's what I'm going to do!"

He turned to Captain Hyatt. "Andy, how would you go about setting it on fire?" The pilot looked at him.

"I'm not joking, Andy," Baydr snapped. "Our lives depend on it!"

"Open the wing tanks and fire some incendiaries into it," Hyatt said.

"Open them," Baydr ordered.

Andy and his copilot ran to the plane. They climbed up into the cabin. A moment later they reappeared with a fuel tank wrench. One ran to either side of the plane. In less than two minutes they were back.

"We're ready now," Andy said. "But you better move everybody down to the far end of the strip just in case she blows up."

Ben Ezra bellowed his orders. It took almost five minutes to get them all to the other end of the field. "Get down everybody," he said, giving the signal to the riflemen.

The automatic rifles set up a screaming chatter. A moment afterward there was a strange hiss, then a groan as the giant plane blew. A geyser of flame climbed a hundred feet into the air.

"If they don't see that, they're blind," Hyatt said sadly.

Baydr saw the look on his face. "Don't feel bad. It's only money. If we get out of here, I'll get you another one."

Hyatt smiled half-heartedly. "I'll keep my fingers crossed, chief."

Baydr's eyes were grim as he scanned the sky. Behind them the sound of gunfire came closer. He moved toward Jordana. "You all right?"

She nodded, the boys clinging to her. They all searched the sky.

"I think I hear it!" Muhammad yelled.

They listened. The faint sound of the rotors came toward them, growing louder with each passing moment. Two minutes later it was overheard, reflected in the glare of the burning plane. Slowly it began to descend.

The flashes of gunfire were almost at the side of the air strip now as the soldiers fell back according to plan.

The helicopter touched down. The first man off the plane was Baydr's father. The two boys ran to him. "Grandfather!"

He scooped them up in his arms as Baydr and Jordana came toward him. Everybody began to converge on the helicopter. The boarding was swift, just a few men still in the field holding off the guerillas.

Baydr stood at the foot of the ramp, next to Ben Ezra. "Everybody on board?" the general asked.

"Yes," Baydr answered.

Ben Ezra cupped his hand around his mouth. "Bring them in, corporal!" he yelled in stentorian voice that could be heard all over the field.

Another fuel tank blew on the 707, bathing the entire field in daylight glow. Baydr could see the soldiers backing in from the edge of the field, their guns firing into the forest.

A moment later they were almost at the foot of the ramp. The first of them turned and started up the stairs. Ben Ezra swatted him on the behind with his sword in an approving gesture.

The yellow light from the burning plane reached the edge of the forest. Baydr, watching, thought he heard someone calling him. Then suddenly he saw her, running from the forest. Behind her was a man carrying a body across his shoulders.

Automatically a soldier swung his rifle toward her. Baydr struck at the gun so that the barrel pointed at the sky. "Hold it!" he yelled.

"Daddy! Daddy!" Leila cried.

Baydr ran toward her. "Leila! This way!" he shouted.

She turned, making a straight line for him, and ran into his arms. A soldier came dashing up to him. "We've got to get out of here, sir!"

Baydr gestured toward Hamid. "Help him," he said to the soldier.

He turned and with one arm around his daughter went up the steps into the plane. Hamid and the soldier, carrying Dick between them, were right behind them. Ben Ezra came up the ramp and stood in the open door.

Already Hamid and the soldier had placed Dick on a cot, and Dr. Al Fay and the medical team had hooked up the plasma and glucose. "Take it up!" Ben Ezra yelled.

As the big rotors began to turn sluggishly overhead, Hamid went back to the general. Behind the general, Hamid could see the guerillas running onto the field. "I wouldn't stand there if I were you, general," he said respectfully.

"Where the hell were you all night?" Ben Ezra shouted angrily as the helicopter began to lift heavily.

"I was merely obeying your orders, sir," the Syrian said with a straight face. He gestured toward Leila, who was kneeling beside Dick. "I was making sure that no harm would come to her."

"You were ordered to stay at my si—!" The anger faded from the old man's voice and was replaced by a note of surprise. "Oh, my God!" he exclaimed. The scimitar fell from his suddenly nerveless hand. He took a tentative step toward the Syrian, then began to fall.

Hamid caught him in outstretched arms. He felt the old man's blood gushing through the soft Bedouin robes. Hamid lurched and almost fell as the helicopter seemed to leap into the air. "The General's been shot!" he yelled.

Baydr and his father were at his side almost before the word had left his mouth. Gently, they moved Ben Ezra to a cot. Dr. Al Fay rolled him on his side, quickly cutting away the robe.

"Do not bother, my friend," the general whispered. "Save your time for the young man there."

"The young man will be all right!" Samir said almost angrily.

"So will I," Ben Ezra said softly. "Now that I have seen my son, I am not afraid to die. You have done well, my friend. You have raised a man."

Samir felt the tears blur his eyes. He knelt down and placed his lips close to the old man's ear. "For too long I have allowed him to live a lie. It is time for him to learn the truth."

A faint smile came to the dying soldier's lips. "What is the truth? You are his father. That is all he needs to know."

"You are his father, not I!' Samir whispered vehemently. "He must learn that it was your God who brought him into this world!"

Ben Ezra looked up with rapidly glazing eyes. His gaze turned to Baydr, then back to the doctor. His voice was faint as he summoned all his strength into his last breath. He was dead the moment the words had left his lips.

"There is but one God . . ."

"It is very important to us that those shipments continue. It is our main source of American dollars. Do you think you have enough influence with your American friend to get those orders rescinded?"

"I don't know," she said doubtfully. "He was instructed by my father to stop those shipments." She looked at him. "What if I spoke directly to my father?"

"No. Your father knows nothing about those shipments. If he did, he would surely halt them. He refused us before."

"I don't know what I can do then."

"Perhaps you can persuade the American to report to your father that there is no problem with the shipments, that Ziad is not getting any money from them."

"Is that true?"

"Of course not," he said testily. "Don't be so naïve. How do you think we could get a swine like him to cooperate with us except by bribery? You could tell your friend that you just learned that Arabdolls is owned by friends of yours and you would not like to see them upset."

"Do you think he would believe that?"

"Who can tell? You should know better than anyone how much power you have over him."

A faint smile came to her lips. "He might do it. We have been together at least four times a day while my father has been in Gstaad. He is like a madman. He never lets me alone."

"If that is true, then you should have no difficulty with him."

"But what if he refuses?"

"You can threaten to go to your father and tell him of your affair." He saw the shocked expression on her face and added quickly, "But that is only a last resort. For now you will do no more than ask him. We will meet again at the same time tomorrow evening and you will let me know his answer."

"Is there anything else?"

"Not now."

"How long must I remain here?" she asked. "I did not spend all that time in a training camp to be a secretary. When will I get an opportunity to do something real?"

"You are doing something very important for us right now. But perhaps the other thing will come sooner than you think."

Carriage looked up at the clock after the special messenger from the consul's office had left. Seven o'clock. He opened his desk drawer and took out the matching key that would open the pouch. It had to be something very important to have been sent by sealed diplomatic pouch on the last plane of the day from Beirut.

Inside was a single folder with one sheet of paper. Typewritten across the folder in bold red letters were the words CONFIDENTIAL REPORT — ARABDOLLS.

He opened the folder and began to read quickly. The contents were brief and to the point. Arabdolls was a front for the drug syndicate. Among its listed owners were an American Mafioso, a French Coriscan who was a known operator of heroin refineries and two Lebanese, one a man who had wide contacts among the poppy growers in both Lebanon and Turkey, the other a banker who represented various Fedayeen groups in many of their financial transactions.

Now the premium paid for the shipments began to make sense. They had found a legitimate shipper to bring the drugs into the United States for them because MEDIA not only provided the carrier, but as a licensed U.S. Customs broker they also cleared the shipments for them and delivered direct to the consignee in New York. Although the New York consignee was a well-known American wholesale toy importer, he didn't doubt that they had made adequate arrangements for the handling of the shipments in the States.

Carriage picked up a telephone and placed a call to the managing director of the MEDIA shipping office in Beirut. There was one thing more he had to find out.

The director came on the line sputtering from the honor of a personal call from Mr. Al Fay's executive assistant. It was the first time he had spoken to anyone further up in the hierarchy than Youssef. He was most cooperative.

No, he personally knew nothing about Arabdolls, only that they were very polite and that their invoices were paid promptly. He wished that all his clients were that timely but alas, you know how they are.

Dick sympathized with him saying that Mr. Al Fay was quite aware of his problems and very understanding. Then he inquired how they got the account — which of their agents had solicited it.

The director was apologetic. Unfortunately, none of his men had been alert enough to get the account. He had to give full credit to Mr. Ziad, who had made all the arrangements in Paris. All they had to do was service the account. And they were taking special care to see that the client had the very best service. Good accounts such as these were hard to come by.

Dick thanked him and put down the telephone. He wondered how much Youssef knew about the contents of the shipments. It was hard for him to believe that Yousef would dare proceed against Baydr's policy. Especially after the Ali Yasfir incident in Cannes last summer, he was well aware that Baydr had refused to act as a front for the illegal activities of the Fedayeen no matter how worthy they claimed their motivations were.

Still, there was only one way that the deal could have been made. Someone had to have reached Youssef. He wondered how well Youssef knew Ali Yasfir. He tried to recall if he had seen them together in Cannes but all he could remember was that he had asked Youssef to relay to Yasfir Baydr's invitation for the party on the yacht.

He had just locked the folder in the safe when Leila returned. He looked up at her, thinking as he did so that he would call Baydr first thing in the morning.

"What's wrong?" Leila asked quickly. "You look very serious."

"Too much on my mind, I guess." He forced a smile. "How were your friends?"

She returned his smile. "Silly girls. They were okay at school but now I think I've outgrown them. All they can talk about is boys."

He laughed. "That seems normal to me."

"That's all they think about too."

"And what do you think about?"

She came over to his desk and bent over him so that her face was almost touching his. "Fucking you," she said.

Chapter Six

Baydr came on the telephone, sounding cheerful. "Good morning, Dick."

"Morning, chief. How is it up there?"

"Just beautiful. And the boys love it. You ought to see them on skis. They're naturals."

"Good," Dick said. "I've got some business to talk about. Is the scrambler attached?"

"No," Baydr answered. "Call me back in ten minutes on the other line. I'll have it hooked up by then."

Dick put down his telephone and checked to make sure his own scrambler was tied into the line. He flipped the switch and the red light came on. It was working. He turned it off. The scrambler had been especially made for them so that anyone who might even accidentally come on their line would hear nothing but a series of unintelligible sounds.

He thought back to last night. The affair of Arabdolls was becoming stranger by the minute. Now there was a new ramification. Out of left field Leila had shown an unexpected interest in it.

She had led up to the subject obliquely, in true Arabic fashion. They were lying naked on his bed, smoking a joint, after making love. He felt himself drifting hazily. "I wonder if we'll be able to meet like this when my father comes back," she said.

"We'll find a way."

"You won't have time. When he's around you never have a moment to yourself." He didn't answer.

"Sometimes I think you're even more of a slave than Jabir."

"It's not as bad as that."

"It's bad enough," she said, her eyes seeming to fill with tears.

"Hey, cut that out," he said, reaching for her.

She moved her head down to his chest. "I'm sorry," she whispered. "I'm just beginning to get used to you, just beginning to discover how wonderful you are."

"You're pretty wonderful yourself."

"I have a confession to make."

"No confessions."

But she went on. "You're the first real man I've ever been with. All the others were just boys. I never felt anything with them like I feel with you."

He didn't answer.

"Is it like that with you? Do you feel the same thing with your wife that you feel with me?"

He thought of his wife and sons, who were six thousands miles away, and felt a twinge of conscience. "That's not fair," he remonstrated.

"I'm sorry, that was stupid of me. I won't ask you again." She reached up and took the joint from his fingers. "Give me a toke."

He watched her inhale the sweet fragrance. After a few drags she gave the cigarette back to him. He took it and placed it in an ashtray. Then he turned her on her back and went down on her.

She moaned softly, her hands holding his face tightly against her. "By the life of Allah, how I love it!" She raised his face so that she could look at him. "Do you know you are the first man who ever ate me?"

He shook his head.

"None of the boys I went with ever did that. But they were all Arabs," she said. "Arab boys are lousy lovers. All they think about is their own pleasure. Tell me, do all Americans do that?"

"I really don't know."

"Do you like me to eat you?"

He nodded.

"Let me then," she said, pushing him over. She took his erect phallus in her two hands and covered his glans with her lips. After a moment she raised her head and looked up at him. "You have a beautiful cock, do you know that? Thick and lovely. It's very American."

He laughed aloud.

"Don't laugh, I mean it," she said seriously. "All the Arab boys I knew had long skinny ones."

He didn't tell her that might have been because the boys were young and had not reached their growth. "Is it only Arab boys that you knew?" he asked.

"No, once I had a French boy. But it was dark and he was so quick I never really had a chance to see it." She looked down at him. "You know I'll miss it."

Then, unexpectedly, she laughed. "I just had a crazy idea. I saw an ad in a magazine where they sold life-size inflatable dolls. Do you think I might have one made of you? That way I could keep you in my room and if you could not be there in person I would just blow it up and there you'd be."

"That is crazy." He laughed.

"I bet I could get my friends at Arabdolls to make one," she said.

The warning bell in his head rang loud and clear. "I wouldn't think they were into that sort of thing," he said.

"They might do it for me. Essam Mafrad's father owns the company and he is a close friend of my mother's father."

Mafrad was the Lebanese banker who represented Al Ikhwah, and it was more than likely that her grandfather knew him. The Lebanese banking community was a tightly knit one. But he dismissed the possibility of mere coincidence after her next question.

Sitting up in bed, as if the thought had just come to her, she asked, "Isn't that the company my father doesn't want to handle the shipments for?"

He nodded.

"He can't do that. They're our very good friends. They would be very upset."

"Then tell your father. I'm sure if he knew that he would reconsider."

"I can't do that. You know my father. He doesn't like anyone to tell him what to do."

He was silent.

"You could do something about it. You could okay the shipments."

"Then what about your father? If he found out he would have my ass."

"He would never have to know. Just don't show him the reports. He has so much on his mind, he would never think of it."

"I couldn't do that."

"Why not? You would really be doing him a favor. Our families have been friends for years and you would be saving him a great deal of embarrassment."

"It's not my place. I haven't the authority."

"Then do it for me. And if Father finds out, you can tell him that I asked you to do it. I'm only trying to avoid trouble between the families."

"I'm sorry," he said firmly.

Suddenly she was angry. She got out of the bed and stood over him. "You act as if I'm just a silly girl!" she stormed. "I'm all right as something to fuck but as far as anything else goes, forget it!"

"Hey, wait a minute," he said in a conciliatory voice. "I don't think anything of the sort. I have a great deal of respect for your opinion. I don't doubt that you're right, but you're asking me to do something I haven't the authority to do. But I will do something. Tomorrow I will tell your father what you told me and I'm sure he will approve the shipments."

"I don't need your favors!" she snapped. "I don't want you to tell him anything, do you understand that? Anything!"

"I won't then, if that's what you want."

"That's what I want. If I have anything to tell him, I will tell him myself!"

"Okay, okay," he said.

She snatched her robe from the chair and walked to the door, then turned back to face him. "You're all afraid of my father, but I'm not. And someday all of you will find that out!"

For a long time, he had sat in bed smoking cigarette after cigarette. It had to be more than coincidence. Even if the Riad and Mafrad families were good friends, the whole thing coming from her at this particular time was just a little too pat.

He wondered whether he should tell Baydr about it, but decided against it. It would only expose their relationship and that would be the end of his job. As liberal as Baydr might be about many things, he was still her father.

Maybe by morning she would have calmed down. In the meantime he made up his mind to do one thing.

Despite the late hour, he reached for the private telephone on his night table, pressing down the anti-eavesdropping button so that no one in the house could listen in on an extension. He dialed the number of a private investigator the company had used several times.

When he put down the telephone after talking with the man, he felt better. From now on, whenever Leila left the house she would be under surveillance. By the end of the week he would have a good idea of who she was seeing and every friend she had in Geneva. Maybe when all was put together he might be able to make some sense out of her actions.

He had gone to the office before eight o'clock, when he knew there would be no one else around and he could reach Baydr at breakfast. Now it was almost time to call Baydr back. He would have the scrambler connected. He dialed the number.

Baydr answered, "Dick?"

"Yes."

"Turn your switch on."

He heard the buzz in his line and pressed down the scrambler button. Abruptly the buzz disappeared. "Okay now?"

"Perfect," Baydr said. "What is it?"

'Arabdolls." He was succinct. "They're a front. I'm afraid we've been running dope for them." Quickly he reviewed everything he had learned.

Baydr was silent for a moment. "How did we get into this?" he asked. "Was the deal made in Beirut?"

"No, in Paris. I was informed that the contract came from Youssef himself."

"I was afraid of that. I had heard that he'd been meeting Ali Yasfir. But I didn't think that Youssef would have the nerve to do anything like that on his own. The money had to be very big to move him."

Carriage was surprised. "You knew of the contacts between them?"

"Yes, but I thought it was just Youssef's way of keeping in touch. Apparently I was wrong. I accepted all his little side deals. Those were more or less customary. But this is something else."

"What should we do about it?"

"There's not much we can do. We can't open it up because it could turn into a Pandora's box for us. One word and we lose our U.S. Customs brokerage as well as our shipping franchises. We'll have to handle it internally. The first thing to do is to get Youssef up here. We have to find out how deeply we're actually involved."

"Will you come here to meet him?" Dick asked.

"No. Geneva is filled with inquisitive eyes. Better ask him to come to Gstaad to see me."

'Okay. Would you like me to come also?"

"I think you'd better remain down there. The less people he sees around the better."

Another thought ran through Dick's mind. "I've picked up some talk that Mafrad and Riad are very close. Do you think your former father-in-law might be involved with them?"

"Impossible!" Baydr's reaction was convincing. "Riad is an old-fashioned conservative. He wouldn't go near a hustler like Mafrad if he were coated in gold."

"I just thought you should know," Dick said. Again he thought of Leila. The words were almost on his lips when he reconsidered. It would keep until the end of the week, when he would know more. After he had put down the telephone, he sat for some moments lost in thought. If there was no connection between the families, why had she made such an important point of saying that there was? None of it made any real sense, at least not yet.

The door opened and his secretary came in. She paused in surprise. "Mr. Carriage," she said in her English-sounding Swiss accent. "You're in early."

"Yes. I had some important calls to make."

"Would you like some coffee?"

"Please. And bring in your book. I want to send a telex to Ziad in Paris."

When she returned with her book, he changed his mind and decided to place a call instead. He could be more casual about Baydr's summons on the telephone than in a cold telex. He was sipping his coffee when Youssef answered his phone.

"The chief asked me to call you and ask you to come up to Gstaad to see him if you're free," he said.

A note of worry crept into Youssef's voice. "Is it anything special?"

Dick laughed. "I don't think so. Between us I think he's getting a little bored playing the family man. Maybe he's looking for an excuse to get out of there."

Dick could sense his relief. "I've got just the excuse. Vincent agreed to let us out of the contract without our paying him anything more than we have already paid him. I can say that the chief has to come down to sign the papers."

"He'd like that," Carriage said.

Feeling that confidentiality had been established, Youssef let a note of camaraderie come into his voice. "What's the chief's interest in Arabdolls all about?"

Dick kept his voice on the same level. "I really couldn't say. He didn't tell me. But you know him as well as I do. He's interested in any new business that has the smell of money about it. Maybe he wants in."

"From what I've heard, it's just a small operation. I don't think it's big enough for him."

"If it should come up while you're there," Dick said, still casual, "you could tell him."

"That's an idea." Dick could almost hear the wheels turning in the man's head.

"I have a few things to clean up down here. Tell the chief I'll be up there sometime this evening."

"I'll tell him," Dick said and put down the telephone.

His secretary came into the office with another pot of coffee. "Miss. Al Fay is outside," she said, as she placed the tray on his desk. "She asks if you would have a moment for her this morning?"

"Ask her to come in," Dick said. Leila must have something on her mind, he thought as he poured his coffee. Usually she never came to the office in the morning.

Somehow she looked more like a young girl this morning than he had ever remembered. She stood hesitantly in front of his desk. "I hope I'm not disturbing anything," she said in a small voice. "I won't take too much of your time."

"That's all right. Would you like some coffee?"

"No, thanks. I came in especially to tell you that I was sorry about last night."

"Forget it. I already have."

"No, I mean it," she said insistently. "I behaved like a spoiled child. I had no right to ask you things like that. I don't want it to change anything between us."

"It won't."

"Honestly?"

"Honestly," he answered.

He saw her look of relief and the strange hint of triumph hiding in her eyes. "Can I come to your room tonight?" she asked, still in the small voice.

"I would be very unhappy if you didn't."

"I promised some friends I would have dinner with them tonight, I'll get through it as quickly as I can and come home."

"I'll be waiting."

She came around the desk, took his hand and held it to her breast. "I don't know whether I can wait until tonight," she said.

The telephone rang. He took his hand from her breast and reached for it. "I'm afraid, young lady," he said with mock severity, "we'll both have to." He picked up the telephone. "Hold on just a moment," he said. Then he covered the mouth-piece with his hand and looked up at her. "You see, I have work to do."

She kissed him swiftly on the lips and started for the door. Halfway there, she stopped as if struck by an afterthought. "By the way, you're not going to mention anything to my father, are you?"

"No," he answered, his hand still covering the mouth-piece.

She nodded, smiling. "Good." She blew him a kiss. "Until tonight."

He kept the smile on his face until the door had closed behind her, but a troubled look came over his face as he took his hand from the mouthpiece.

Deep in the marrow of his bones he knew that something was wrong. Very wrong.

Chapter Seven

Baydr picked up the telephone. Youssef's voice was cheerful. "I'm down at the hotel in town and I brought something very special from Paris with me," he said. "Would you like to come and have some dinner?"

"I don't think I can."

"Chief, you know me. When I say this is something special, it's something special. She's got a body you can't believe and she's crazy, completely crazy. There isn't anything you can think of that she doesn't love to do."

"Put her on ice. It will just have to be another time. We have some people in for dinner tonight."

"Maybe in the morning then."

"That's out too. I have some meetings here in the house tomorrow morning."

"Then when will you want to see me?" Youssef asked. "Lunch tomorrow?"

"The whole day is locked up. It will have to be tonight."

"Tonight?" A note of concern crept into Youssef's voice.

"Yes. My dinner guests should be gone by midnight. Supposing you get up here around half-past."

"Sure you wouldn't want to come down here?" Youssef suggested. "The girl will be very disappointed. I told her what a great guy you were."

"Buy her a little something in the jewelry shop in the hotel and give it to her with my compliments and tell her that I am as disappointed as she is."

"Okay, chief. I'll see you tonight then. Twelve-thirty, right?"

"Right," Baydr said and put down the phone. He was still sitting in the semidarkness of the library when Jordana came into the room.

"The boys are going to bed," she said. "They asked if you would come up and say good night to them."

"Of course," he said, getting to his feet. He started past her when her hand on his arm stopped him.

"Is there anything wrong?" she asked, looking up into his face.

"What makes you ask?"

"You look troubled. Who was it on the phone?"

"Youssef. He's coming up to see me after our guests leave."

"Oh."

"He's coming alone. We have some important business to discuss."

She was silent.

"You don't like him, do you?"

"I never liked him," she answered. "You know that. He's like so many of the men I see around you. They gather like predatory vultures hoping to pounce on the leavings. Meanwhile they suck up to you as if you were some kind of god. There's another one I met, twice, once on the boat and once in California after you had gone. Ali Yasfir. He's like that."

"I didn't know he was in California," Baydr said.

"He was. I saw him going into the Polo Lounge just as I was leaving. He was going to meet Youssef. I wouldn't dare turn my back on either of them."

He stared at her. Strange that she should group the two of them together. She was more aware than he had thought.

"You better go up," she said. "The boys are waiting and there won't be much time left to dress before our guests arrive."

"Okay."

"Baydr!"

He turned back again.

"Thank you."

"For what?"

"I've never seen the boys so happy. Do you know you've spent more time with them these past two weeks than you have in the past three years? They like having a father around. I do too."

"I liked it too."

"I hope we can have more of it." She placed her hand on his arm. "It hasn't been like this for a long time."

He didn't move.

"Do you think we will?" she asked.

'We'll see. There's always so much to do."

Her hand fell from his arm. She kept her face carefully expressionless. "Better hurry," she said, turning away from him. "I have to check out some last-minute dinner arrangements."

He watched her cross the room to the other door leading to the grand salon. It was not until she had gone that he went out into the hall and up the staircase to the boys' room.

They were sitting up in their beds waiting for him. He spoke in Arabic. "Did you have fun today?"

They answered in the same language, almost in chorus. "Yes, Father."

"Mother said you wanted to see me."

The children looked at each other. "You ask him," Muhammad said.

"No," answered Samir. "You ask him. You're the oldest."

Baydr laughed. "One of you had better ask because I have to go and get dressed."

"Ask him," Samir urged his brother.

Muhammad looked at his father. His eyes were wide and serious. "We like it here, Father."

"I'm glad," Baydr said.

Muhammad looked at his younger brother for support. "I like it too," Samir said in his thin voice. He looked over at his brother in the other bed. "Now you can ask him."

Muhammad took a deep breath. "We'd like to live here, Father, with you."

"But what about Beirut?"

"We don't like it, Father," Muhammad said quickly. "There's nothing to do there. There's no snow or anything."

"But what about school?"

"Our Arabic is much better now, Father," Samir said quickly. "Couldn't you — we thought — " his voice trailed off. He looked frantically at Muhammad.

"We mean," Muhammad picked up, "Couldn't you bring the school up here to us? That way we could have the snow and still go to school."

Baydr laughed. "It's not that easy."

"Why?" Samir asked.

"You just can't pick up a whole school and move it. What would the rest of the students do? They'd have no school to go to."

"We could bring them along," Muhammad said. "I bet they'd like it better here too."

"Nanny says you can do anything you want to," Samir said.

Baydr smiled. "Well, she's wrong. There are some things even I can't do. That happens to be one of them."

He saw the looks of disappointment on their faces. "But I tell you what I will do," he added.

"What is that?" Muhammad asked.

"You have another school holiday in about two months," he said. "I'll bring you back here then."

"But the snow might be all gone," Samir said.

"It will still be here. I promise you that." He knelt over and kissed each one in turn. "Now go to sleep. I'll talk to the ski instructor. Maybe he'll let us try the north slope tomorrow."

"Where the big boys ski?" Muhammad asked excitedly.

"Yes, but you'll have to promise to be extra careful."

"We will, Father," they both said at once.

"Good night, then."

"Good night, Father," they replied.

He started for the door. "Father," Muhammad called after him.

"Yes?"

"We forgot to thank you. Thank you, Father."

He stood very still for a moment. "Allah keep you, my sons. Sleep well."

Jordana was waiting in the hall when he came out of their bedroom. "Are they asleep?"

He smiled. "I've just tucked them in. Did you know what they were going to ask me?"

"No. They wouldn't tell me, only that it was important."

He started down the corridor to their suite. She walked beside him. "They said they wanted to live here. They didn't want to go back to Beirut."

She didn't speak.

"They even wanted me to move the school up here with all the pupils." He laughed. "You never know what wild ideas children will come up with."

"It's not that wild," she said. "Not when you know what they're really asking."

"And what is that?"

Her eyes looked into his. "They love you," she said. "You're their father and nothing can take your place. They want to live with you."

"Didn't you ever explain to them that I have many things to do? Surely they can be made to understand that."

"It's not as easy as you think," she answered. "How can you explain to a child that the sun in the heavens from which all life comes is something you can't have every day?"

Chapter Eight

Despite the cold, Youssef's face was covered with a fine mist of perspiration as he carried the heavy suitcase up the steps to the villa. Jabir opened the door, "Ahlan," he said.

"Ahlan fiki," Youssef replied as he crossed the threshold and put down the valise. He straightened up. "Will you hold this for me until I leave?" he asked.

"It will be my pleasure, sir," Jabir replied. "The master awaits you in the library. If you will please follow me."

Youssef slipped out of his coat and gave it to Jabir, then followed him through the large entrance hall to a pair of heavy wooden doors. Jabir knocked softly.

"Come in," Baydr called.

Jabir opened the door and held it for Youssef, then closed it softly behind him. Youssef looked around the library. It was a large old-fashioned room with floor-to-ceiling book shelves. Baydr was seated behind a desk, his back to the tall French doors that led to the garden behind him. A beautiful shaded lamp on Baydr's desk cast the only light in the room and left his face in the shadows. He did not get up as Youssef walked towards him.

"The villa is beautiful," Youssef said. "But then, I expected nothing less."

"It's comfortable."

"You should have warned me about the drive up here," Youssef smiled. "Parts of the road were covered with sheets of ice. Especially on the curves near the edge of the mountain."

"I didn't think of it," Baydr said politely. "I forgot that the road sometimes freezes at night. I should have sent one of the chauffeurs down for you."

"No matter. I made it all right." He sank into the chair opposite the desk. "Too bad you couldn't make it down to the hotel tonight. The girl was very disappointed."

"The bauble didn't help ease her pain?"

"I bought her a gold Piaget. It helped."

Baydr looked at him. He wasn't very imaginative. But then what else was there to buy for a girl in Switzerland except a watch? He saw the shine of perspiration on Youssef's face. "Would you care for coffee? Or a cold drink, champagne perhaps?"

"Is there anything else?" Youssef laughed, a little too readily.

Baydr tugged the bell cord behind him. Jabir opened the door. "A bottle of champagne for Mr. Ziad."

"Did Dick tell you of the settlement I made with Michael Vincent?" Youssef asked when Jabir had gone to get the wine.

"Yes. How did you get him to let us off so easily?"

"It wasn't that easy. But I finally made him understand that it would do him no good to take us to court. That we would tie him up for years and eventually it would cost him everything he had already received in legal fees. Then I promised him we would try to get him on the other picture and if we had anything in the future we would certainly come back to him."

"That was very well done," Baydr said.

Jabir came back into the room with a bottle of Dom Pérignon in an ice bucket and two glasses on a silver tray.

"I'm glad you're pleased," Youssef said, watching Jabir open the bottle expertly and fill the two glasses. The servant left the room again and Youssef picked up a glass. He looked at Baydr. "Aren't you having any?"

Baydr shook his head. "I have to be up early. I promised the boys I would go skiing with them in the morning."

"Cheers then," Youssef said. He emptied his glass in one thirsty swallow and refilled it. "I didn't realize I was so thirsty."

Youssef sipped the second glass of wine more slowly. He leaned back in his chair, feeling a little more at ease. Baydr's next words put an end to that.

"Tell me about Arabdolls," he said.

Youssef felt the sweat break out again on his forehead. "What is there to tell? They're good clients. Other than that I know very little about them."

Baydr looked at him steadily. "That's not like you. Usually you know everything about the people we do business with. That's always been one of our cardinal rules."

"They're not a very big client. I saw no reason to look into them. The shipments were small but they paid very well."

"Premium," Baydr said. "Wasn't that enough to make you curious?"

"No, I had other more important deals on my mind."

"Didn't you think it was unusual that they contacted you in Paris instead of our office in Beirut? Certainly that would have seemed normal for a business that size."

"I thought it was just a coincidence," Youssef said quickly. "I met this American in the bar at the George V and he told me of the problems he had arranging for the import of dolls into the United States and I told him to contact our office in Beirut. That we might be able to help him."

"According to the Beirut office they acted on a shipping contract sent by you. They never contacted anyone at the company."

Youssef felt the perspiration under his arms. "That could be possible. I might have left instructions with my secretary to follow through. As I said, I didn't think it important enough for me to concern myself."

"You're lying," Baydr said quietly.

Youssef was stunned. "What? What?" he stammered as if he hadn't understood.

"I said, 'You're lying'," Baydr repeated. "We know everything about that company now. You've placed us in a position of running drugs in the United States. Because of that we are liable to lose everything we have worked for all these years. Now I want you to tell me the truth."

Baydr watched him reach for a cigarette and light it with trembling fingers. "Tell me," he said softly, "how much did Ali Yasfir give you to make those shipments?"

Youssef fell apart before his eyes. Now his voice was trembling as well as his fingers. "He made me do it, master," he cried. "He forced me into it. I only did it to protect you."

"Protect me?" Baydr's voice was cold.

"He had pictures, master. He threatened to expose them to the world."

"Who would give credence to pictures of me? Especially from a source like that? Why didn't you come to me at once?"

"I didn't want to hurt you, master. They were pictures of your wife." Youssef's eyes were filled with real tears.

"You have them with you?"

"Yes, master." Youssef's voice was hushed. "They are in a valise I left in the entrance hall. I was hoping it would not come to this."

"Get it," Baydr said calmly.

Youssef almost ran from the room and came back a moment later carrying the suitcase. Baydr watched him silently as he opened the suitcase and removed the portable video cassette player and a small-screen American television set. Quickly he connected the two machines. He looked around the room for an electrical outlet. There was one at the side of the desk. He plugged the wire into it, then placed the cassette in the player.

He hesitated, looking down at Baydr. "I still feel you should not subject yourself to this, master."

Baydr's voice was almost savage. "Turn it on!"

Youssef pressed the button and the screen filled with bright empty light. There was a faint hum from the unwinding tape. A moment later the first blurred images appeared in color. Youssef made an adjustment and the pictures were suddenly in sharp focus.

Jordana and a man were lying on their backs in bed, apparently filmed from a camera overhead. They were both naked and passing a cigarette between them while obviously watching something happening off camera. Abruptly the screen went blank for a moment, and resumed with the sound of their voices issuing from the speaker. Jordana was going down on the man. "Just beautiful," the man said, looking down at her.

Baydr did not say a word until the cassette had finished and the screen gone blank. Then he reached across the desk, and turned it off. His face was inscrutable. "I've seen the man before. Who is he?"

"An American actor," Youssef answered. "Rick Sullivan. His real name is Israel Solomon."

"A Jew?"

Youssef nodded. "That was another reason I did not want to have the pictures exposed."

There was still no expression on Baydr's face. "When did this take place?"

"At a party at the actor's home in California after you left for Tokyo."

"Was Yasfir at this party?"

"No."

"Were you?"

"Yes. I accompanied Michael Vincent and your wife to the party. But I left early with a headache."

"How did Yasfir get this tape?"

"I don't know. He didn't tell me."

"Are there other copies?"

Youssef took a deep breath. If Baydr believed his next statement, he might still save himself. "He said he had others which he would distribute if anything happened to stop the shipments."

"Why did he leave this with you?"

Youssef hesitated. "I don't know."

"He didn't suggest to you that if there were any problems you were to show the tape to me?"

"No, master, you must believe me," Youssef said sincerely. "Only the thought that you believed I betrayed you forced me to reveal this to you." He fell to his knees before Baydr, then seized and kissed his hand. "By my father's life, I would rather die than betray you." He began to weep.

Baydr looked down at him silently for a moment. When he spoke, his voice was harsh. "Compose yourself, man. Do not weep like a woman."

Youssef got to his feet, the tears falling on his cheeks. "I must have the words of forgiveness from your lips, oh master," he cried.

"I forgive you," Baydr said heavily. He got to his feet, gesturing to a door. "There is a bathroom. Bathe your face. It would not do to have you appear thus before the servants."

"Thank you, master!" Youssef said fervently, seizing Baydr's hand again and kissing it. "The light once more comes back into my life now that the burden has been lifted from my soul."

Baydr watched him go into the bathroom and close the door behind him. He didn't believe a word the man had said. He had condemned himself with his own words. No one but Youssef himself could have obtained that tape. There was no way Yasfir could have got it if he was not at that party. Silently, he moved across the room and opened the door.

Jabir was seated on a bench across the corridor. He rose to his feet when he saw Baydr. Baydr crossed the hall to meet him.

"Yes, master?"

Baydr's voice was calm. "That piece of camel dung has brought grave dishonor to our name."

Jabir's eyes turned cold, the skin tightening across his cheekbones. He did not speak.

"A mile down the road there is a curve around the mountain where the cliff drops off almost two hundred meters. It is too bad that his car must skid off the icy road."

Jabir nodded. His voice was a deep growl in his throat. "It will be a tragedy, master."

Baydr went back into the library. A moment later he heard the sounds of an automobile engine coming through the closed window. He turned and looked out between the drapes in time to see Jabir's Land Rover disappear down the driveway. He went back to his desk and sat down wearily.

A moment later, Youssef returned from the bathroom. He looked more like himself. Even the tone of his voice reflected the return of his confidence. "What shall we do about this, chief?"

"I must have time to think before I can make any decision. There is nothing more we can accomplish tonight."

"I guess not," Youssef said hesitatingly.

"We might as well try to get some rest. You'd better go back to the hotel."

Youssef looked at the video cassette player. "Would you like me to guard that for you?"

"No leave that with me," Baydr got to his feet. "I will let you out. The servants have all gone to bed."

It wasn't until the powerful Land Rover, its headlights blackened out, came at him from his blind side, pushing his tiny rented Opel inexorably toward the precipice, that Youssef looked back frantically to see Jabir hunched grimly over the steering wheel and remembered the one thing he never should have forgotten. The thought came to him at exactly the same moment that his car snapped the frail wires that served as a guard rail at the edge of the cliff and went hurtling into the air. He never heard the scream of fear that leaped from his throat as he plunged toward oblivion, but the thought burned in his brain.

Jabir never went to sleep while Baydr was awake.

Chapter Nine

Baydr was seated alone in the breakfast alcove overlooking the garden, reading the Paris *Herald Tribune* and sipping coffee when the snobbish English butler came into the room. The man cleared his throat, and Baydr looked up.

There was a disapproving tone in the butler's precise voice. "There are some gentlemen from the police asking to see your excellency."

Baydr looked at him. No matter how many times he had explained to the butler that he did not hold a rank which entitled him to be addressed as "excellency", the man refused to address him in any other manner. His last employer had been the pretender to the throne of Spain and "excellency" was about as far down as he would descend from "highness".

"Show them into the library," Baydr said. "I will join them in a moment."

"Yes, your excellency." The butler left the room, his straight back and squared shoulders somehow carrying a hint of disapproval.

Slowly Baydr folded the newspaper and placed it neatly on the table. He took a last sip of coffee, then rose and went into the library.

There were two policemen, one in uniform, one in plain clothes.

The plainclothesman bowed. He spoke in English. "Mr. Al Fay?"

Baydr nodded.

The policeman bowed again. "Permit me to introduce ourselves. I am Inspector Froelich and this is my associate, Sergeant Werner."

"What can I do for you gentlemen?"

"First I must apologize to you for intruding upon your breakfast but I am afraid I bring some rather unpleasant news. Are you acquainted with a Mr. Youssef Ziad?"

"Yes. He is the managing director of my Paris bureau. We had a meeting here last night. Why do you ask about him? Is he in some sort of trouble?"

"No, Mr. Al Fay, he is no trouble at all. He is dead," the inspector said.

"Dead?" Baydr pretended shock. "What happened?"

"Apparently he lost control of his car and went off the road. The car fell almost two hundred metres."

Baydr stared at him for a moment, then walked around behind the desk and sat down. His face was grim. "Excuse me, gentlemen," he said. "But this is quite a shock. Mr. Ziad was an old and valued associate."

"We understand, sir," the plainclothesman said politely. "We have a few routine questions but we will try to be as brief as possible." He took a small notebook from his pocket and opened it. "You mentioned that you met Mr. Ziad last night. At what time did he arrive here?"

"About half past twelve."

"Was there any particular reason for his arrival at that late hour?"

"There were important business matters to discuss. And unfortunately my wife and I had guests for dinner which precluded our meeting earlier."

"And approximately what time did he leave?"

"About two o'clock, I imagine."

"Did Mr. Ziad have anything to drink while he was here?"

"Nothing much."

"Could you be more specific?"

"We had a bottle of Dom Pérignon. He drank almost all of it. But that shouldn't have bothered him. Mr. Ziad drank it constantly. It was his favorite wine."

"He had good taste," the inspector said. He looked at the uniformed sergeant. A subliminal signal passed between them. The inspector closed his book and turned back to Baydr. "I guess that completes our questions, Mr. Al Fay," he said, satisfaction in his voice. "Thank you for your cooperation."

Baydr rose. "I will have to make arrangements for the funeral. His body will have to be flown home. Where is he now?"

"At the police morgue." This was the first time the sergeant had spoken. "What there is left of him."

"That bad?"

The inspector shook his head sadly. "We have gathered what remains we could find. Identification was made from his wallet and passport. The car itself is in a thousand pieces. It is too bad that people don't realize what a difference even the smallest amount of alcohol can make on an icy road at night."

Baydr sat for a moment after the policemen had left, then reached for the telephone and called Dick in Geneva.

"Call me back on the scrambler," Baydr said when Dick answered. A moment later the other telephone rang and he picked it up. The buzz cleared almost as soon as he held the receiver to his ear. "Dick?"

"Yes."

Baydr kept his voice expressionless. "The police just left. Youssef ran his car off the road last night and was killed."

"My God! What happened?"

"The road was icy and the police think he had a little too much to drink. He was quite upset when he left here and he did finish almost a whole bottle of champagne."

Dick was silent for a moment. "Did you learn anything from him about Arabdolls?"

"He claimed that he was coerced into it by Ali Yasfir."

"Then we were right. Did he admit that he was paid for it?"

"No. He swore that he received no money from them."

"I don't believe that," Dick said.

"It doesn't matter now, does it? He's dead, and it's over."

"Is it?" Dick replied. "We don't know what Yasfir will do now." ˙

"There's very little he can do. He knows that he can't coerce us."

"I hope so. But you never can tell with a son of a bitch like that. You don't know what he'll come up with next."

"We'll deal with him when it comes," Baydr said calmly. "Right now, we have some unfinished business. I may send you down to the Paris office next week to take over until we can find a replacement for him."

"Right."

"Meanwhile see to it that his family and the Paris office are notified of the accident. Also make arrangements with a mortician to collect the remains from the police morgue in Gstaad and ship them to his home."

"I'll take care of it."

"Alert the crew to have the plane ready for a flight to Beirut on Friday. Jordana and the boys will be going home."

"Isn't that a week earlier than planned, chief?"

Baydr's voice grew edgy. "Just do it. I think they'll be better off at home." He almost slammed down the receiver and sat there staring at the videotape player.

Abruptly he crossed the room and locked the doors. Then, taking the key from his pocket, he unlocked the center drawer of the desk and took out the cassette. He inserted it into the machine and pressed the start button.

The screen went white for a moment, then the picture and the sound came on. He sat there almost immobilized as the tape unreeled before him. It was all there, just as it had been with him. The beauty of her body, the langurous sensuous movements, the words, the tiny animal-like cries rising to screaming orgiastic crescendos. It was all there, but this time it was not for him. It was for another man. A Jew.

The screen went black just as the knot in his stomach exploded into blazing pain. Angrily he slammed his fist down on the stop button, almost smashing the machine. Then he held his hands in front of him and looked at his trembling fingers.

Abruptly he closed them into fists and beat them against the desk. Over and over he pounded them in unison to his muttered words — "Damn you! Damn you! Damn you!" — until his hands were painful and swollen.

He stared again at his hands, then at the machine. "Jordana!" he cried as if she were inside the machine. "Is it for this I have made myself into a murderer?"

The screen did not answer him. It was blank. He put his face down on the desk and wept, as he had not done since he was a boy. A prayer he had not uttered since childhood came to his lips:

In the name of Allah, the Beneficent, the Merciful.
I seek refuge in the Lord of men,
The King of men,
The God of men,

From the evil of the whispering of the slinking devil,
Who whispers into the hearts of men.

The comfort of the prayer flowed through him. The tears stopped and he felt the hurt and pain leave him. Too easily one forgot the wisdom of Allah, the wisdom revealed by the Prophet. And much too easily, one forgot that the laws of Allah, revealed by the Prophet, were given to men to live by.

For too long had he tried to live by the laws of the unbelievers but they were not for him. Now he would live as he was intended. By the one true law. The laws of Allah.

Jordana came into the library. The shock was still in her voice. "I just heard about Youssef," she said. "I can't believe it."

"He was dung," he said coldly. "But now he stands before the throne of judgement and must answer himself for his own sins. And even Allah, the most merciful, will not find forgiveness for him. Most certainly he will see the fires of hell for all eternity."

"But he was your friend." She could not understand the change in him. "He has served you, for many years."

"He served only himself. He was no man's friend but his own."

She was bewildered. "What happened between the two of you? What did he do?"

His face was an impenetrable mask, his eyes hooded. "He betrayed me, as did you."

She stared at him. "Now I really don't know what you're talking about."

He looked at her almost as if he did not see her. "You don't?"

She shook her head silently.

"Then I will show you." He crossed the room and locked the library door. He went back to the desk and pressed the button on the videotape player. "Come here."

She stood behind the desk next to him and looked down at the small screen. It was white and shining for a moment then the picture came on. She half-cried, her breath catching in her throat in shocked disbelief. "No!" she cried aloud.

"Yes," he said quietly.

"I won't watch!" she said, starting to leave.

His hand gripped her arm tightly, so tightly that she felt a pain shoot up into her shoulder. "You will stay, woman, and watch."

She closed her eyes and turned her head away. His fingers gripped her chin like claws of steel, forcing her face back to the screen. "You will watch," he said coldly. "All of it. All of your shame. As I had to."

Silently she stood there as the tap he unwound. It seemed to last forever. She felt the sickness in her. It was crazy. All of it. There had been a camera on them all the time and there was only one way it could have been done. Sullivan had to have controlled it himself.

Then it came back to her. That time he left the room, just before they began. He was starting the machine. And his insistence at always staying in the upper portion of the giant bed. The camera must have been fixed to cover that area. He had to be sick, sicker than anyone knew.

Suddenly, it was over. The screen went black and Baydr turned off the player. She turned to look at him.

His face was expressionless. "I had asked discretion of you. You were not discreet. I had specifically told you to avoid Jews. The man is a Jew."

"He is not!" she flashed. "He is an actor named Rick Sullivan."

"I know his name. His real name is Israel Solomon."

"I didn't know."

He didn't answer. It was obvious that he didn't believe her.

Suddenly she remembered. Youssef had been at that party. "Did Youssef bring you that tape?"

"Yes."

"That was more than three months ago. Why did he wait so long to give it to you?"

He didn't answer.

"He had to be guilty of something," she guessed shrewdly. "And he thought by using this he could clear himself."

'He said he was coerced by someone who brought him this tape. And unless he did their bidding they would expose you."

"I don't believe that! He was the only one there who would have an interest in getting it. He had to be lying!"

Again he didn't answer. Everything she said only confirmed his own belief.

'Are there other copies?"

"I hope not, for my sons sake as well as your own. I would not like them to learn that their mother committed adultery with a Jew."

For the first time the pain he felt crept into his voice. "Do you know what you have done, woman? If this were to become public, Muhammad could never be adopted heir to the throne. When we are at war with Israel, how can any Arab accept as his ruler and spiritual leader one whose mother has committed adultery with a Jew. Even his own legitimacy would become subject to question. By your action you could not only lose your own son the heritage to which he was born but cause the loss of everything my father and I have struggled for all our lives."

"I'm sorry, Baydr," she said. "But we have grown so far apart that I thought nothing between us mattered anymore. I knew of your women. I even accepted them. Now I see I did not even have the right to accept the options you granted me. Perhaps if I were an Arab woman I would have known that. But I am not. And I could never live the life of pretense that they do, seeing but not seeing, believing the words that belied the deeds."